Thomas Mann

DOCTOR FAUSTUS

Thomas Mann was born in Germany in 1875. He was awarded the Nobel Prize for Literature in 1929, and left Germany for good in 1933 Among his major novels are *Buddenbrooks* (1901), *The Magic Mountain* (1924), the tetralogy *Joseph and His Brothers* (1933, 1934, 1936, 1943), and *Doctor Faustus* (1948). He is equally well known for his short stories and essays. Thomas Mann died in 1955.

VINTAGE

INTERNATIONAL

Books by Thomas Mann,

AVAILABLE FROM VINTAGE

Death in Venice
Buddenbrooks
The Magic Mountain
Doctor Faustus
Confessions of Felix Krull, Confidence Man
The Transposed Heads

DOCTOR FAUSTUS

Thomas Mann

DOCTOR FAUSTUS

The Life of the German Composer
ADRIAN LEVERKÜHN
as Told by a Friend

Translated from the German by H. T. LOWE-PORTER

Lo giorno se n'andava e l'aere bruno
toglieva gli animai che sono in terra
dalle fatiche loro, ed io sol uno
m'apparecchiava a sostener la guerra
sì del cammino e sì della pietate,
che ritrarrà la mente que non erra.
O Muse, o alto ingegno, or m'aiutate,
o mente che scrivesti ciò ch'io vidi,
qui si parrà la tua nobilitate.

Dante: *Inferno*, Canto II

Vintage International • *Vintage Books*
A Division of Random House, Inc. • *New York*

FIRST VINTAGE INTERNATIONAL EDITION, APRIL 1992

Copyright © 1948 by Alfred A. Knopf, Inc.

All rights reserved under International and Pan-American
Copyright Conventions. Published in the United States by
Vintage Books, a division of Random House, Inc., New York, and
simultaneously in Canada by Random House of Canada Limited,
Toronto. Originally published in Germany by Bermann-Fischer
Verlag A. B., Stockholm. Copyright 1947 by Thomas Mann.
First published in hardcover in the United States by
Alfred A. Knopf, Inc., in 1948.

Library of Congress Cataloging-in-Publication Data
Mann, Thomas, 1875–1955.
[Doktor Faustus. English]
Doctor Faustus : the life of the German composer, Adrian
Leverkühn, as told by a friend/ Thomas Mann ; translated from the
German by H. T. Lowe-Porter. —1st Vintage International ed.
p.   cm.
Translation of: Doktor Faustus.
ISBN 0-679-73905-X (pbk.)
I. Lowe-Porter, H. T. (Helen Tracy), 1876–1963.   II. Title.
PT2625.A44D63   1992
833'.912—dc20   91-58079
CIP

Manufactured in the United States of America
10 9 8 7 6 5 4 3 2 1

TRANSLATOR'S NOTE

"Les traductions sont comme les femmes: lorsqu'elles sont belles, elles ne sont pas fidèles, et lorsqu'elles sont fidèles, elles ne sont pas belles." From a more familiar source we are instructed that "to have honesty coupled to beauty is to have honey a sauce to sugar." And on the highest authority of all we know that the price of a virtuous woman, with no mention of other charm, is above rubies. All things considered, what remains to hope is only that the English version of *Doctor Faustus* here presented may at least not conjure up the picture of a femme ni belle ni fidèle.

It is to be feared. The author himself has feared it. I venture to quote on this point, lifting it from its context in the Epilogue, some words of the narrator, who here surely speaks for the author himself: "In actual fact I have sometimes pondered ways and means of sending these pages to America, in order that they might first be laid before the public in an English translation. . . . True, there comes the thought of the essentially foreign impression my book must make in that cultural climate; and coupled with it the dismaying prospect that its translation into English must turn out, at least in some all too radically German parts, to be an impossibility."

Grievous difficulties do indeed confront anyone essaying the role of copyist to this vast canvas, this cathedral of a book, this woven tapestry of symbolism. Translations deal with words; and in two fields at least the situation is unsatisfactory (I do not include in the list the extended musical discussion and critique, since music, and talk about it, uses an exact and international language). But dialect cannot be translated, it can only be got round by a sort of trickery which is usually unconvincing. Again, there are chapters resorting to an archaic style and spelling. The English-speaking world boasts no Luther in the history of its language; and the vocabulary of Wycliffe, Tindale, Thomas More can scarcely evoke for us the emotions of the literate German in so far as these are summoned up by the very words themselves which Luther used. On the other hand this archaic style is employed only in a few chapters, as a device to suggest an element that is indicated by other means as well. And the final difficulty is hardly a linguistic one, but rather a matter of the "cultural climate" of which the author speaks: that knotted and combined association, symbolism, biography, and autobiography which might make even German readers be glad of a key to unlock its uttermost treasure.

So, after all, these difficulties are seen to be a matter of degree. Against them, far outweighing them, is the fact that this *monstrum aller Romane* is addressed not only to Germans, not only to Europeans, but equally to ourselves. All that our world has lived through in this past quarter-century has forced us to enter this climate and to recognize that these are our proper stresses. Readers of *Faustus* will and must be involved, with shudders, in all three strands of the book: the German scene from within and its broader, its universal origins; the depiction of an art not German alone but vital to our whole civilization; music as one instance of the arts and the state in which the arts find themselves today; and, finally, the invocation of the dæmonic. It is necessary for us to read *Faustus*, even in a version which cannot lay claim to being beautiful, though in every intent it is deeply faithful.

The translator wishes to express warm and heartfelt thanks to the scholars who have been so helpful in certain chapters: especially to Dr. Mosco Carner, conductor and musicologist, adviser to the Musical Staff of the B.B.C.; and Mr. Graham Orton, of the University of Durham, England, who has been indefatigably resourceful and suggestive in the mediæval portions. Other scholars in various fields, notably Professor R. D. Welch, head of the Music Department of Princeton University, and Mrs. Welch, have helped the translator with comments and suggestions in ways too numerous to specify in detail. That they have done so is a tribute to the author of *Faustus*.

DOCTOR FAUSTUS

CHAPTER I

I WISH to state quite definitely that it is by no means out of any wish to bring my own personality into the foreground that I preface with a few words about myself and my own affairs this report on the life of the departed Adrian Leverkühn. What I here set down is the first and assuredly very premature biography of that beloved fellow creature and musician of genius, so afflicted by fate, lifted up so high, only to be so frightfully cast down. I intrude myself, of course, only in order that the reader — I might better say the future reader, for at this moment there exists not the smallest prospect that my manuscript will ever see the light unless, by some miracle, it were to leave our beleaguered European fortress and bring to those without some breath of the secrets of our prison-house — to resume: only because I consider that future readers will wish to know who and what the author is do I preface these disclosures with a few notes about myself. Indeed, my mind misgives me that I shall only be awakening the reader's doubt whether he is in the right hands: whether, I mean, my whole existence does not disqualify me for a task dictated by my heart rather than by any true competence for the work.

I read over the above lines and cannot help remarking in myself a certain discomfort, a physical oppression only too indicative of the state of mind in which I sit down today in my little study, mine these many years, at Freising on the Isar, on the 27th of May 1943, three years after Leverkühn's death (three years, that is, after he passed from deep night into the deepest night of all), to make a beginning at describing the life of my unhappy friend now resting — oh, may it be so! — now resting in God. My words, I say, betray a state of mind in anguished conflict between a palpitating impulse to communicate and a profound distrust of my own adequacy. I am by nature wholly moderate, of a temper, I may say, both healthy and humane, addressed to reason and harmony; a scholar and *conjuratus* of the "Latin host," not lacking all contact with the arts (I play the viola d'amore) but a son of the Muses in that academic sense which by preference regards it-

self as descended from the German humanists of the time of the
"Poets."

Heir of a Reuchlin, a Crotus of Dornheim, of Mutianus and
Eoban of Hesse, the dæmonic, little as I presume to deny its influence upon human life, I have at all times found utterly foreign
to my nature. Instinctively I have rejected it from my picture of
the cosmos and never felt the slightest inclination rashly to open
the door to the powers of darkness: arrogantly to challenge, or if
they of themselves ventured from their side, even to hold out my
little finger to them. To this attitude I have made my sacrifices,
not only ideally but also to my practical disadvantage: I unhesi-
tatingly resigned my beloved teaching profession, and that before
the time when it became evident that it could not be reconciled
with the spirit and claims of our historical development. In this
respect I am content with myself. But my self-satisfaction or, if
you prefer, my ethical narrow-mindedness can only strengthen
my doubt whether I may feel myself truly called to my present
task.

Indeed, I had scarcely set my pen in motion when there escaped
it a word which privately gave me a certain embarrassment. I
mean the word "genius": I spoke of the musical genius of my departed friend. Now this word "genius," although extreme in degree, certainly in kind has a noble, harmonious, and humane ring.
The likes of me, however far from claiming for my own person
a place in this lofty realm, or ever pretending to have been blest
with the *divinis influxibus ex alto*, can see no reasonable ground
for shrinking, no reason for not dealing with it in clear-eyed confidence. So it seems. And yet it cannot be denied (and has never
been) that the dæmonic and irrational have a disquieting share in
this radiant sphere. We shudder as we realize that a connection
subsists between it and the nether world, and that the reassuring
epitheta which I sought to apply: "sane, noble, harmonious, humane," do not for that reason quite fit, even when — I force myself, however painfully, to make this distinction — even when they
are applied to a pure and genuine, God-given, or shall I say God-
inflicted genius, and not to an acquired kind, the sinful and morbid corruption of natural gifts, the issue of a horrible bargain. . . .

Here I break off, chagrined by a sense of my artistic shortcomings and lack of self-control. Adrian himself could hardly — let
us say in a symphony — have let such a theme appear so prematurely. At the most he would have allowed it to suggest itself
afar off, in some subtly disguised, almost imperceptible way. Yet
to the reader the words which escaped me may seem but a dark,

distrustable suggestion, and to me alone like a rushing in where angels fear to tread. For a man like me it is very hard, it affects him almost like wanton folly, to assume the attitude of a creative artist to a subject which is dear to him as life and burns him to express; I know not how to treat it with the artist's easy mastery. Hence my too hasty entry into the distinction between pure and impure genius, a distinction the existence of which I recognize, only to ask myself at once whether it has a right to exist at all. Experience has forced me to ponder this problem so anxiously, so urgently, that at times, frightful to say, it has seemed to me that I should be driven beyond my proper and becoming level of thought, and myself experience an "impure" heightening of my natural gifts.

Again I break off, in the realization that I came to speak of genius, and the fact that it is in any case dæmonically influenced, only to air my doubt whether I possess the necessary affinity for my task. Against my conscientious scruples may the truth avail, which I always have to bring into the field against them, that it was vouchsafed me to spend many years of my life in close familiarity with a man of genius, the hero of these pages; to have known him since childhood, to have witnessed his growth and his destiny and shared in the modest role of adjuvant to his creative activity. The libretto from Shakespeare's comedy *Love's Labour's Lost*, Leverkühn's exuberant youthful composition, was my work; I also had something to do with the preparation of the texts for the grotesque opera suite *Gesta Romanorum* and the oratorio *The Revelation of St. John the Divine*. And perhaps there was this, that, and the other besides. But also I am in possession of papers, priceless sketches, which in days when he was still in health, or if that is saying too much, then in comparatively and legally sound ones, the deceased made over to me, to me and to no other; on these I mean to base my account, yes, I intend to select and include some of them direct. But first and last — and this justification was always the most valid, if not before men, then before God — I loved him, with tenderness and terror, with compassion and devoted admiration, and but little questioned whether he in the least returned my feeling.

That he never did — ah, no! In the note assigning his sketches and journals there is expressed a friendly, objective, I might almost say a gracious confidence, certainly honourable to me, a belief in my conscientiousness, loyalty, and scrupulous care. But love? Whom had this man loved? Once a woman, perhaps. A child, at the last, it may be. A charming trifler and winner of

hearts, whom then, probably just because he inclined to him, he
sent away — to his death. To whom had he opened his heart,
whomever had he admitted into his life? With Adrian that did
not happen. Human devotion he accepted, I would swear often
unconsciously. His indifference was so great that he was hardly
ever aware what went on about him, what company he was in.
The fact that he very seldom addressed by name the person he
spoke with makes me conjecture that he did not know the name,
though the man had every reason to suppose he did. I might compare his absentness to an abyss, into which one's feeling towards
him dropped soundless and without a trace. All about him was
coldness — and how do I feel, using this word, which he himself,
in an uncanny connection, once also set down? Life and experience can give to single syllables an accent utterly divorcing them
from their common meaning and lending them an aura of horror,
which nobody understands who has not learned them in that
awful context.

CHAPTER II

My name is Serenus Zeitblom, Ph.D. I deplore the extraordinary delay in introducing myself, but the literary nature of my material has prevented me from coming to the point until now. My age is sixty, for I was born A.D. 1883, the eldest of four brothers and sisters, at Kaisersaschern on the Saale, in the district of Merseburg. In the same town it was that Leverkühn too spent his school-days; thus I can postpone a more detailed description until I come to them. Since altogether my personal life was very much interwoven with that of the Meister, it will be well to speak of them both together, to avoid the error of getting ahead of my story — which, when the heart is full, tends to be the case.

Only so much must be set down for the nonce, that it was in the modest rank of a semi-professional middle class that I came into the world. My father, Wohlgemut Zeitblom, was an apothecary, though the first in the town, for the other pharmacy in Kaisersaschern never enjoyed the same public confidence as the Zeitblom shop of the "Blessed Messengers" and had at all times a hard struggle against it. Our family belonged to the small Catholic community of the town, the majority of its population of course being of the Lutheran confession. In particular my mother was a pious daughter of the Church, punctually fulfilling her religious duties, whereas my father, probably from lack of time, was laxer in them, without in the least denying his solidarity, which indeed had also its political bearing, with the community of his faith. It was remarkable that besides our priest, Eccl. Councillor Zwilling, the rabbi of the place, Dr. Carlebach by name, used also to visit us in our home above the shop and laboratory, and that, in Protestant houses, would not have been easy. The man of the Roman Church made the better appearance. But I have retained the impression, based principally, I suppose, upon things my father said, that the little long-bearded, cap-wearing Talmudist far surpassed his colleague of another faith in learning and religious penetration. It may be the result of this youthful experience, but also because of the keen-scented receptivity of Jewish circles for

Leverkühn's work; but I have never, precisely in the Jewish problem and the way it has been dealt with, been able to agree fully
with our Führer and his paladins; and this fact was not without
influence on my resignation from the teaching staff here. Certainly specimens of the race have also crossed my path — I need
only think of the private scholar Breisacher in Munich, on whose
dismayingly unsympathetic character I propose in the proper
place to cast some light.

As for my Catholic origin, it did of course mould and influence
my inner man. Yet that lifelong impress never resulted in any
conflict with my humanistic attitude in general, my love of the
"liberal arts" as one used to call them. Between these two elements of my personality there reigned an unbroken harmony,
such as is easily preserved if like me one has grown up within the
frame of "old-world" surroundings whose memories and monuments reach back into pre-schismatic times, back into a world of
unity in Christ. True, Kaisersaschern lies in the midst of the native home of the Reformation, in the heart of Lutherland. It is the
region of cities with the names of Eisleben, Wittenberg, Quedlin-
burg, likewise Grimma, Wolfenbüttel and Eisenach — all, again,
rich with meaning for the inner life of the Lutheran Leverkühn
and linked with the direction his studies originally took, the theological one. But I like to compare the Reformation to a bridge,
which leads not only from scholastic times to our world of free
thought, but also and equally back into the Middle Ages, or perhaps even further, as a Christian-Catholic tradition of a serene
love of culture, untouched by churchly schism. For my part I
feel very truly at home in that golden sphere where one called
the Holy Virgin *Jovis alma parens*.

But to continue with the most indispensable facts in my *vita:*
my parents allowed me to attend our gymnasium, the same school
where, two forms below me, Adrian was taught. Founded in the
second half of the fifteenth century, it had until very recently
borne the name of "School of the Brethren of the Common Life,"
finally changed out of embarrassment at the too historical and for
the modern ear slightly comic sound of this name. They now
called themselves after the neighbouring Church of St. Boniface.
When I left school, at the beginning of the present century, I
turned without hesitation to the study of the classic tongues, in
which the schoolboy had already shown a certain proficiency. I
applied myself to them at the universities of Giessen, Jena, Leipzig and from 1904 to 1906 at Halle, at the same time — and that
not by chance — as Leverkühn also studied there.

Here, as so often, I cannot help dwelling on the inward, the almost mysterious connection of the old philological interest with a lively and loving sense of the beauty and dignity of reason in the human being. The bond is expressed in the fact that we give to the study of the ancient tongues the name of the *humaniora;* the mental co-ordination of language and the passion for the humanities is crowned by the idea of education, and thus the election of a profession as the shaper of youth follows almost of itself out of having chosen philology as a study. The man of the sciences and practical affairs can of course be a teacher too; but never in the same sense or to the same extent as his fellow of the *bonæ literæ.* And that other, perhaps more intense, but strangely inarticulate language, that of tones — if one may so designate music — does not seem to me to be included in the pedagogic-humanistic sphere, although I well know that in Greek education and altogether in the public life of the *polis* it played an ancillary role. Rather, it seems to me, in all its supposedly logical and moral austerity, to belong to a world of the spirit for whose absolute reliability in the things of reason and human dignity I would not just care to put my hand in the fire. That I am even so heartily affected to it is one of those contradictions which, for better or worse, are inseparable from human nature.

This is a marginal note. And yet not so marginal; since it is very pertinent to my theme, indeed only too much so, to inquire whether a clear and certain line can be drawn between the noble pedagogic world of the mind and that world of the spirit which one approaches only at one's peril. What sphere of human endeavour, even the most unalloyed, the most dignified and benevolent, would be entirely inaccessible to the influence of the powers of the underworld, yes, one must add, quite independent of the need of fruitful contact with them? This thought, not unbecoming even in a man whose personal nature lies remote from everything dæmonic, has remained to me from certain moments of that year and a half spent by me in visiting Italy and Greece, my good parents having made the journey possible after I had passed my state examinations. When from the Acropolis I looked down upon the Sacred Way on which the initiates marched, adorned with the saffron band, with the name of Iacchus on their lips; again, when I stood at the place of initiation itself, in the district of Eubulus at the edge of the Plutonian cleft overhung by rocks, I experienced by divination the rich feeling of life which expresses itself in the initiate veneration of Olympic Greece for the deities of the depths; often, later on, I explained to my pupils that culture is in very truth the pious and regulating, I might say propitiatory entrance of the dark and uncanny into the service of the gods.

Returned from this journey, the twenty-five-year-old man found a position in the high school of his native town, where he had received his own education. There, for some years, I assumed by modest stages the teaching in Latin, Greek, and also history, until, that is, the twelfth year of the present century, at which time I entered the service of the Bavarian Department of Education and moved to Freising. I took up my abode there as professor in the gymnasium and also as docent in the theological seminary, in the two fields, and for more than two decades enjoyed a satisfying activity.

Quite early, soon after my appointment at Kaisersaschern, I married: need for regularity and desire for a proper establishment in life led me to the step. Helene, born Oelhafen, my excellent wife, who still accompanies my declining years, was the daughter of an older colleague at Zwickau in Saxony. At the risk of making the reader smile I will confess that the Christian name of the budding girl, Helene, those beloved syllables, played not the least considerable role in my choice. Such a name means a consecration, to its pure enchantment one cannot fail to respond, even though the outward appearance of the bearer correspond to its lofty claims only to a modest middle-class extent and even that but for a time, since the charms of youth are fleeting. And our daughter, who long since married a good man, manager at the Regensburg branch of the Bavarian Securities and Exchange Bank, we also called Helene. Besides her my dear wife presented me with two sons, so that I have enjoyed the due to humanity of the joys and sorrows of paternity, if within moderate limits. None of my children ever possessed a childhood loveliness even approaching that of little Nepomuk Schneidewein, Adrian's nephew and later idol — I myself would be the last to say so. Today my two sons serve their Führer, the one in civil life, the other with the armed forces; as my position of aloofness vis-à-vis the authorities of the Fatherland has made me somewhat isolated, the relations of these two young men with the quiet paternal home must be called anything but intimate.

CHAPTER III

THE Leverkühns came of a stock of superior hand-workers and small farmers, which flourished partly in the Schmalkalden region and partly in the province of Saxony, along the Saale. Adrian's own family had been settled for several generations at Buchel, a farm belonging to the village community of Oberweiler, near Weissenfels, whence one was fetched by wagon after a three quarters-hour journey by train from Kaisersaschern. Buchel was a property of a size corresponding to the ownership of a team and cattle; it was a good fifty acres of meadow and ploughed land, with communal rights to the adjoining mixed woodland and a very comfortable wood and frame dwelling-house on a stone foundation. With the lofts and stalls it formed an open square in the centre of which stood a never-to-be-forgotten ancient linden tree of a mighty growth. It had a circular green bench round it and in June it was covered with gloriously fragrant blossoms. The beautiful tree may have been a little in the way of the traffic in the courtyard: I have heard that each heir in turn in his young years, on practical grounds, always maintained against his father's veto that it ought to be cut down; only one day, having succeeded to the property, to protect it in the same way from his own son.

Very often must the linden tree have shaded the infant slumbers and childhood play of little Adrian, who was born, in the blossom-time of 1885, in the upper storey of the Buchel house, the second son of the Leverkühn pair, Jonathan and Elsbeth. His brother, George, now long since the master of Buchel, was five years his senior. A sister, Ursel, followed after an equal interval. My parents belonged to the circle of friends and acquaintances of the Leverkühns in Kaisersaschern and the two families had long been on particularly cordial terms. Thus we spent many a Sunday afternoon in the good time of year at the farm, where the town-dwellers gratefully partook of the good cheer of the country-side with which Frau Leverkühn regaled them: the grainy dark bread with fresh butter, the golden honey in the comb, the

delicious strawberries in cream, the curds in blue bowls sprinkled
with black bread-crumbs and sugar. In Adrian's early childhood
— he was called Adri then — his grandparents sat with us still,
though now retired, the business being entirely in the hands of
the younger generation. The old man, while most respectfully
listened to, took part only at the evening meal and argued with
his toothless mouth. Of these earlier owners, who died at about
this time, I have little memory. So much the more clearly stands
before my eyes the picture of their children Jonathan and Elsbeth
Leverkühn, although it too has seen its changes and in the course
of my boyhood, my schoolboy, and my student years glided
over, with that imperceptible effectiveness time knows so well,
from the youthful phase into one marked by the passiveness of
age.

Jonathan Leverkühn was a man of the best German type, such
as one seldom sees now in our towns and cities, certainly not
among those who today, often with blatant exaggeration, represent our German manhood. He had a cast of features stamped as
it were in an earlier age, stored up in the country and come down
from the time before the Thirty Years' War. That idea came into
my head when as a growing lad I looked at him with eyes already
half-way trained for seeing. Unkempt ash-blond hair fell on a
domed brow strongly marked in two distinct parts, with prominent veins on the temples; hung unfashionably long and thick in
his neck and round the small, well-shaped ears, to mingle with the
curling blond beard that covered the chin and the hollow under
the lip. This lower lip came out rather strong and full under the
short, slightly drooping moustache, with a smile which made a
most charming harmony with the blue eyes, a little severe, but
a little smiling too, their gaze half absent and half shy. The bridge
of the nose was thin and finely hooked, the unbearded part of the
cheeks under the cheekbones shadowed and even rather gaunt.
He wore his sinewy throat uncovered and had no love for "city
clothes," which did not suit his looks, particularly not his hands,
those powerful, browned and parched, rather freckled hands, one
of which grasped the crook of his stick when he went into the village to town meeting.

A physician might have ascribed the veiled effort in his gaze, a
certain sensitiveness at the temples, to migraine; and Jonathan did
in fact suffer from headaches, though moderately, not oftener
than once a month and almost without hindrance to his work. He
loved his pipe, a half-length porcelain one with a lid, whose odour
of pipe tobacco, peculiar to itself and far pleasanter than the stale

smoke of cigar or cigarette, pervaded the atmosphere of the lower rooms. He loved too as a night-cap a good mug of Merseburg beer. On winter evenings, when the land of his fathers lay under snow, you saw him reading, preferably in a bulky family Bible, bound in pressed pigskin and closed with leather clasps; it had been printed about 1700 under the ducal licence in Brunswick, and included not only the "*Geist-reichen*" prefaces and marginal comments of Dr. Martin Luther but also all sorts of summaries, *locos parallelos*, and historical-moralizing verses by a Herr David von Schweinitz explaining each chapter. There was a legend about this volume; or rather the definite information about it was handed down, that it had been the property of that Princess of Brunswick-Wolfenbüttel who married the son of Peter the Great. Afterwards they gave out that she had died, and her funeral took place, but actually she escaped to Martinique and there married a Frenchman. How often did Adrian, with his keen sense of the ridiculous, laugh with me later over this tale, which his father, lifting his head from his book, would relate with his mild, penetrating look and then, obviously unperturbed by the slightly scandalous provenance of the sacred text, return to the versified commentaries of Herr von Schweinitz or the "Wisdom of Solomon to the Tyrants."

But alongside the religious cast his reading took another direction, which in certain times would have been characterized as wanting to "speculate the elements." In other words, to a limited extent and with limited means, he carried on studies in natural science, biology, even perhaps in chemistry and physics, helped out occasionally by my father with material from our laboratory. But I have chosen that antiquated and not irreproachable description for such practices because a tinge of mysticism was perceptible in them, which would once have been suspect as a leaning to the black arts. But I will add, too, that I have never misunderstood this distrust felt by a religious and spiritual-minded epoch for the rising passion to investigate the mysteries of nature. Godly fear must see in it a libertine traffic with forbidden things, despite the obvious contradiction involved in regarding the Creation, God, Nature and Life as a morally depraved field. Nature itself is too full of obscure phenomena not altogether remote from magic — equivocal moods, weird, half-hidden associations pointing to the unknown — for a disciplined piety not to see therein a rash overstepping of ordained limits.

When Adrian's father opened certain books with illustrations in colour of exotic lepidoptera and sea creatures, we looked at them, his sons and I, Frau Leverkühn as well, over the back of his leather-cushioned chair with the ear-rests; and he pointed with his forefinger at the freaks and fascinations there displayed in all the colours of the spectrum, from dark to light, mustered and modelled with the highest technical skill: genus Papilio and genus Morpho, tropical insects which enjoyed a brief existence in fantastically exaggerated beauty, some of them regarded by the natives as evil spirits bringing malaria. The most splendid colour they displayed, a dreamlike lovely azure, was, so Jonathan instructed us, no true colour at all, but produced by fine little furrows and other surface configurations of the scales on their wings, a miniature construction resulting from artificial refraction of the light rays and exclusion of most of them so that only the purest blue light reached the eyes.

"Just think," I can still hear Frau Leverkühn say, "so it is all a cheat?"

"Do you call the blue sky a cheat?" answered her husband looking up backwards at her. "You cannot tell me the pigment it comes from."

I seem as I write to be standing with Frau Elsbeth, George, and Adrian behind their father's chair, following his finger across the pictured pages. Clearwings were there depicted which had no scales on their wings, so that they seemed delicately glassy and only shot through with a net of dark veins. One such butterfly, in transparent nudity, loving the duskiness of heavy leafage, was called *Hetæra esmeralda*. Hetæra had on her wings only a dark spot of violet and rose; one could see nothing else of her, and when she flew she was like a petal blown by the wind. Then there was the leaf butterfly, whose wings on top are a triple chord of colour, while underneath with insane exactitude they resemble a leaf, not only in shape and veining but in the minute reproduction of small imperfections, imitation drops of water, little warts and fungus growths and more of the like. When this clever creature alights among the leaves and folds its wings, it disappears by adaptation so entirely that the hungriest enemy cannot make it out.

Not without success did Jonathan seek to communicate to us his delight in this protective imitation that went so far as to copy blemishes. "How has the creature done it?" he would ask. "How does Nature do it through the creature? For one cannot ascribe the trick to its own observation and calculation. Yes, yes, Nature knows her leaf precisely: knows not only its perfection but also its small usual blunders and blemishes; mischievously or benevolently she repeats its outward appearance in another sphere, on

the under side of this her butterfly, to baffle others of her creatures. But why is it just this one that profits by the cunning? And
if it is actually on purpose that when resting it looks just like a
leaf, what is the advantage, looked at from the point of view of
its hungry pursuers, the lizards, birds, and spiders, for which
surely it is meant for food? Yet when it so wills, however keen
their sight they cannot make it out. I am asking that in order that
you may not ask me."

This butterfly, then, protected itself by becoming invisible. But
one only needed to look further on in the book to find others
which attained the same end by being strikingly, far-reachingly
visible. Not only were they exceptionally large but also coloured
and patterned with unusual gorgeousness; and Father Leverkühn
told us that in this apparently challenging garb they flew about in
perfect security. You could not call them cheeky, there was something almost pathetic about them; for they never hid, yet never
an animal — not ape or bird or lizard — turned its head to look at
them. Why? Because they were revolting. And because they advertised the fact by their striking beauty and the sluggishness of
their flight. Their secretions were so foul to taste and smell that
if ever any creature mistakenly thought one of them would do
him good he soon spat it out with every sign of disgust. But all
nature knows they are inedible, so they are safe — tragically safe.
We at least, behind Jonathan's chair, asked ourselves whether this
security had not something disgraceful about it, rather than being a cause for rejoicing. And what was the consequence? That
other kinds of butterfly tricked themselves out in the same forbidding splendour and flew with the same heavy flight, untouchable although perfectly edible.

I was infected by Adrian's mirth over this information; he
laughed till he shook his sides, and tears squeezed out of his eyes,
and I had to laugh too, right heartily. But Father Leverkühn
hushed us; he wished all these matters to be regarded with reverence, the same awe and sense of mystery with which he looked
at the unreadable writing on the shells of certain mussels, taking
his great square reading-glass to help him and letting us try too.
Certainly the look of these creatures, the sea-snails and salt-water
mussels, was equally remarkable, at least when one looked at their
pictures under Jonathan's guidance. All these windings and vaultings, executed in splendid perfection, with a sense of form as bold
as it was delicate, these rosy openings, these iridescent faience
splendours — all these were the work of their own jellylike proprietors. At least on the theory that Nature makes itself, and leav

ing the Creator out. The conception of Him as an inspired crafts-
man and ambitious artist of the original pottery works is so
fantastic that the temptation lies close to hand — nowhere closer
— to introduce an intermediate deity, the Demiurge. Well, as I was
saying, the fact that these priceless habitations were the work of
the very mollusc which they sheltered was the most astonishing
thing about them.

"As you grew," said Jonathan to us, "and you can easily prove
it by feeling your elbows and ribs, you formed in your insides a
solid structure, a skeleton which gives your flesh and muscles sta-
bility, and which you carry round inside you — unless it be more
correct to say it carries you around. Here it is just the other way:
these creatures have put their solid structure outside, not as frame-
work but as house, and that it is an outside and not an inside must
be the very reason for its beauty."

We boys, Adrian and I, looked at each other, half-smiling, half
taken aback at such remarks from his father as this about the
vanity of appearances.

Sometimes it was even malignant, this outward beauty: certain
conical snails, charmingly asymmetric specimens bathed in a
veined pale rose or white-spotted honey brown, had a notoriously
poisonous sting. Altogether, according to the master of Buchel, a
certain ill fame, a fantastic ambiguity, attached to this whole extraordinary field. A strange ambivalance of opinion had always
betrayed itself in the very various uses to which the finest specimens were put. In the Middle Ages they had belonged to the
standing inventory of the witches' kitchen and alchemist's vault:
they were considered the proper vessels for poisons and love po-
tions. On the other hand, and at the same time, they had served
as shrines and reliquaries and even for the Eucharist. What a con-
frontation was there! — poison and beauty, poison and magic,
even magic and ritual. If we did not think of all that ourselves,
yet Jonathan's comments gave us a vague sense of it.

As for the hieroglyphs which so puzzled him, these were on a
middle-sized shell, a mussel from New Caledonia: slightly red-
dish-brown characters on a white ground. They looked as though
they were made with a brush, and round the rim became purely
ornamental strokes; but on the larger part of the curved surface
their careful complexity had the most distinct look of explanatory remarks. In my recollection they showed strong resemblance
to ancient Oriental writings, for instance the old Aramaic *ductus*.
My father had actually brought archæological works from the
not ill-provided town library of Kaisersaschern to give his friend

the opportunity for comparison and study. There had been, of course, no result, or only such confusion and absurdity as came to nothing. With a certain melancholy Jonathan admitted it when he showed us the riddling reproduction. "It has turned out to be impossible," he said, "to get at the meaning of these marks. Unfortunately, my dears, such is the case. They refuse themselves to our understanding, and will, painfully enough, continue to do so. But when I say refuse, that is merely the negative of reveal — and that Nature painted these ciphers, to which we lack the key, merely for ornament on the shell of her creature, nobody can persuade me. Ornament and meaning always run alongside each other; the old writings too served for both ornament and communication. Nobody can tell me that there is nothing communicated here. That it is an inaccessible communication, to plunge into this contradiction, is also a pleasure."

Did he think, if it were really a case of secret writing, that Nature must command a language born and organized out of her own self? For what man-invented one should she choose, to express herself in? But even as a boy I clearly understood that Nature, outside of the human race, is fundamentally illiterate — that in my eyes is precisely what makes her uncanny.

Yes, Father Leverkühn was a dreamer and speculator, and I have already said that his taste for research — if one can speak of research instead of mere dreamy contemplation — always leaned in a certain direction — namely, the mystical or an intuitive half-mystical, into which, as it seems to me, human thinking in pursuit of Nature is almost of necessity led. But the enterprise of experimenting on Nature, of teasing her into manifestations, "tempting" her, in the sense of laying bare her workings by experiment; that all this had quite close relations with witchcraft, yes, belonged in that realm and was itself a work of the "Tempter," such was the conviction of earlier epochs. It was a decent conviction, if you were to ask me. I should like to know with what eyes one would have looked on the man from Wittenberg who, as we heard from Jonathan, a hundred and some years before had invented the experiment of visible music, which we were sometimes permitted to see. To the small amount of physical apparatus which Adrian's father had at his command belonged a round glass plate, resting only on a peg in the centre and revolving freely. On this glass plate the miracle took place. It was strewn with fine sand, and Jonathan, by means of an old cello bow which he drew up and down the edge from top to bottom made it vibrate, and according to its motion the excited sand grouped and arranged itself in astonishingly precise and varied figures and arabesques. This visible acoustic, wherein the simple and the mysterious, law and miracle, so charmingly mingled, pleased us lads exceedingly; we often asked to see it, and not least to give the experimenter pleasure.

A similar pleasure he found in ice crystals; and on winter days when the little peasant windows of the farmhouse were frosted, he would be absorbed in their structure for half an hour, looking at them both with the naked eye and with his magnifying glass. I should like to say that all that would have been good and belonging to the regular order of things if only the phenomena had kept to a symmetrical pattern, as they ought, strictly regular and mathematical. But that they did not. Impudently, deceptively, they imitated the vegetable kingdom: most prettily of all, fern fronds, grasses, the calyxes and corollas of flowers. To the utmost of their icy ability they dabbled in the organic; and that Jonathan could never get over, nor cease his more or less disapproving but also admiring shakes of the head. Did, he inquired, these phantasmagorias prefigure the forms of the vegetable world, or did they imitate them? Neither one nor the other, he answered himself; they were parallel phenomena. Creatively dreaming Nature dreamed here and there the same dream: if there could be a thought of imitation, then surely it was reciprocal. Should one put down the actual children of the field as the pattern because they possessed organic actuality, while the snow crystals were mere show? But their appearance was the result of no smaller complexity of the action of matter than was that of the plants. If I understood my host aright, then what occupied him was the essential unity of animate and so-called inanimate nature, it was the thought that we sin against the latter when we draw too hard and fast a line between the two fields, since in reality it is pervious and there is no elementary capacity which is reserved entirely to the living creature and which the biologist could not also study on an inanimate subject.

We learned how bewilderingly the two kingdoms mimic each other, when Father Leverkühn showed us the "devouring drop," more than once giving it its meal before our eyes. A drop of any kind, paraffin, volatile oil — I no longer feel sure what it was, it may have been chloroform — a drop, I say, is not animal, not even of the most primitive type, not even an amœba; one does not suppose that it feels appetite, seizes nourishment, keeps what suits it, rejects what does not. But just this was what our drop did. It hung by itself in a glass of water, wherein Jonathan had submerged it, probably with a dropper. What he did was as follows: he took a tiny glass stick, just a glass thread, which he had coated with shellac, between the prongs of a little pair of pincers and brought it close to the drop. That was all he did; the rest the drop did itself. It threw up on its surface a little protuberance, something like a mount of conception, through which it took the stick into itself, lengthwise. At the same time it got longer, became pear-shaped in order to get its prey all in, so that it should not stick out beyond, and began, I give you my word for it, gradually growing round again, first by taking on an egg-shape, to eat off the shellac and distribute it in its body. This done, and returned to its round shape, it moved the stick, licked clean, crosswise to its own surface and ejected it into the water.

I cannot say that I enjoyed seeing this, but I confess that I was fascinated, and Adrian probably was too, though he was always sorely tempted to laugh at such displays and suppressed his laughter only out of respect for his father's gravity. The devouring drop might conceivably strike one as funny. But no one, certainly not myself, could have laughed at certain other phenomena, "natural," yet incredible and uncanny, displayed by Father Leverkühn. He had succeeded in making a most singular culture; I shall never forget the sight. The vessel of crystallization was three-quarters full of slightly muddy water — that is, dilute water-glass — and from the sandy bottom there strove upwards a grotesque little landscape of variously coloured growths: a confused vegetation of blue, green, and brown shoots which reminded one of algæ, mushrooms, attached polyps, also moss, then mussels, fruit pods, little trees or twigs from trees, here and there of limbs. It was the most remarkable sight I ever saw, and remarkable not so much for its appearance, strange and amazing though that was, as on account of its profoundly melancholy nature. For when Father Leverkühn asked us what we thought of it and we timidly answered him that they might be plants: "No," he replied, "they are not, they only act that way. But do not think the less of them. Precisely because they do, because they try to as hard as they can, they are worthy of all respect."

It turned out that these growths were entirely unorganic in their origin; they existed by virtue of chemicals from the apothecary's shop, the "Blessed Messengers." Before pouring the water-glass, Jonathan had sprinkled the sand at the bottom with various crystals; if I mistake not potassium chromate and sulphate of copper. From this sowing, as the result of a physical process called "osmotic pressure," there sprang the pathetic crop for which their producer at once and urgently claimed our sympathy. He showed us that these pathetic imitations of life were light-seeking, heliotropic, as science calls it. He exposed the aquarium to the sunlight, shading three sides against it, and behold, toward that one pane through which the light fell, thither straightway slanted the whole equivocal kith and kin: mushrooms, phallic polyp-stalks, little trees, algæ, half-formed limbs. Indeed, they so yearned after warmth and joy that they actually clung to the pane and stuck fast there.

"And even so they are dead," said Jonathan, and tears came in his eyes, while Adrian, as of course I saw, was shaken with suppressed laughter.

For my part, I must leave it to the reader's judgment whether that sort of thing is matter for laughter or tears. But one thing I will say: such weirdnesses are exclusively Nature's own affair, and particularly of nature arrogantly tempted by man. In the highminded realms of the *humaniora* one is safe from such impish phenomena.

CHAPTER IV

SINCE the foregoing section has swollen out of all conscience, I
shall do well to begin a new one, for it is my purpose now to do
honour to the image of the mistress of Buchel, Adrian's dear
mother. Gratitude for a happy childhood, in which the good
things she gave us to eat played no small part, may add lustre to
my picture of her. But truly in all my life I have never seen a
more attractive woman than Elsbeth Leverkühn. The reverence
with which I speak of her simple, intellectually altogether unassuming person flows from my conviction that the genius of the
son owed very much to his mother's vigour and bloom.

Jonathan Leverkühn's fine old-German head was always a joy
to my eyes; but they rested with no less delight on his wife's figure, so altogether pleasant it was, so individual and well propor-
tioned. She was born near Apolda, and her type was that brunette
one which is sometimes found among us, even in regions where
there is no definite ground to suspect Roman blood. The darkness
of her colouring, the black hair, the black eyes with their quiet,
friendly gaze, might have made me take her for an Italian were
it not for a certain sturdiness in the facial structure. It was a
rather short oval, this face, with somewhat pointed chin, a not
very regular nose, slightly flat and a little tilted, and a tranquil
mouth, neither voluptuous nor severe. The hair half covered the
ears, and as I grew up it was slowly silvering; it was drawn
tightly back, as smooth as glass, and the parting above the brow
laid bare the whiteness of the skin beneath. Even so, not always,
and so probably unintentionally, some loose strands hung charmingly down in front of the ears. The braid, in our childhood still
a massive one, was twined peasant-fashion round the back of the
head and on feast-days it might be wound with a gay embroidered
ribbon.

City clothes were as little to her liking as to her husband's: the
ladylike did not suit her. On the other hand, the costume of the
region, in which we knew her, became her to a marvel: the heavy
home-made skirt and a sort of trimmed bodice with a square

opening leaving bare the rather short, sturdy neck and the upper part of the breast, where hung a simple gold ornament. The capable brown hands with the wedding ring on the right one were neither coarse nor fastidiously cared for; they had, I would say, something so humanly right and responsible about them that one enjoyed the sight of them, as well as the shapely feet, which stepped out firmly, neither too large nor too small, in the easy, low-heeled shoes and the green or grey woollen stockings which spanned the neat ankles. All this was pleasant indeed. But the finest thing about her was her voice, in register a warm mezzo-soprano, and in speaking, though with a slight Thuringian inflexion, quite extraordinarily winning. I do not say flattering, because the word seems to imply intention. The vocal charm was due to an inherently musical temperament, which, however, remained latent, for Elsbeth never troubled about music, never so to speak "professed" it. She might quite casually strum a few chords on the old guitar that decorated the living-room wall; she might hum this or that snatch of song. But she never committed herself, never actually sang, although I would wager that there was excellent raw material there.

In any case, I have never heard anyone speak more beautifully, though what she said was always of the simplest and most matter-of-fact. And this native, instinctive taste, this harmony, was from the first hour Adrian's lullaby. To me that means something, it helps to explain the incredible ear which is revealed in his work — even though the objection lies to hand that his brother George enjoyed the same advantage without any influence upon his later life. George looked more like his father too, while Adrian physically resembled the mother — though again there is a discrepancy, for it was Adrian, not George, who inherited the tendency to migraine. But the general habit of my deceased friend, and even many particular traits: the brunette skin, the shape of eye, mouth, and chin, all that came from the mother's side. The likeness was plain as long as he was smooth-shaven, before he grew the heavy beard. That was only in his latter years; it altered his looks very much. The pitch-black of the mother's eyes had mingled with the father's azure blue to a shadowy blue-grey-green iris with little metallic sprinkles and a rust-coloured ring round the pupils. To me it was a moral certainty that the contrast between the eyes of the two parents, the blending of hers into his, was what formed his taste in this respect or rather made it waver. For never, all his life long, could he decide which, the black or the blue, he liked

better. Yet always it was the extreme that drew him: the very
blue, or else the pitch-black gleam between the lashes.

Frau Elsbeth's influence on the hands at Buchel — not very numerous save at harvest-time, and then the neighbours came in to
help — was of the very best; if I am right, her authority among
them was greater than her husband's. I can still see the figures of
some of them; for instance, that of Thomas, the ostler, who used
to fetch us from Weissenfels and bring us back: a one-eyed, extraordinarily long and bony man, with a slight hump, on which
he used to let little Adrian ride; it was, the Meister often told me
later, a most practical and comfortable seat. And I recall the cow-
girl Hanne, whose bosoms flapped as she walked and whose bare
feet were always caked with dung. She and the boy Adrian had a
close friendship, on grounds still to be gone into in detail. Then
there was the dairywoman Frau Luder, a widow in a cap. Her
face was set in an expression of exaggerated dignity, probably
due to her renown as a mistress of the art of making liqueurs and
caraway cheese. It was she, if not Elsbeth herself, who took us to
the cow-stalls, where the milkmaid crouched on her stool, and
under her fingers there ran into our glasses the lukewarm foam-
ing milk, smelling of the good and useful animal that gave it.

All this detail, these memories of our country world of childhood in its simple setting of wood and meadow, pond and hill —
I would not dwell upon them but that just they formed the early
surroundings of Adrian up to his tenth year. This was his parental home, his native heath, the scene where he and I so often came
together. It was the time in which our *du* was rooted, the time
when he too must have called me by my Christian name. I hear
it no more, but it is unthinkable that at six or eight years he
should not have called me Serenus or simply Seren just as I called
him Adri. The date cannot be fixed, but it must certainly have
been in our early school-days that he ceased to bestow it on me
and used only my last name instead, though it would have seemed
to me impossibly harsh to do the same. Thus it was — though I
would not have it look as though I wanted to complain. Yet it
seemed to me worth mention that I called him Adrian; he on the
other hand, when he did not altogether avoid all address, called
me Zeitblom. — Let us not dwell on the odd circumstance, which
became second nature to me, but drop it and return to Buchel.

His friend, and mine too, was the yard dog, Suso. The bearer of
this singular name was a rather mangy setter. When one brought
her her food she used to grin across her whole face, but she was

by no means good-natured to strangers, and led the unnatural
life of a dog chained all day to its kennel and only let free to
roam the court at night. Together Adrian and I looked into the
filthy huddle in the pigsty and recalled the old wives' tales we
had heard about these muddy sucklings with the furtive white-
eyelashed little blue eyes and the fat bodies so like in colour to
human flesh: how these animals did sometimes actually devour
small children. We forced our vocal chords to imitate the throaty
grunt of their language and watched the rosy snouts of the litter
at the dugs of the sow. Together we laughed at the hens behind
the wire of the chicken-house: they accompanied their fatuous
activities by a dignified gabbling, breaking out only now and then
into hysterical squawks. We visited the beehives behind the
house, but kept our distance, knowing already the throbbing pain
caused by these busy creatures when one of them blundered
against your nose and defended itself with its sting.

I remember the kitchen garden and the currant bushes whose
laden stems we drew through our lips; the meadow sorrel we nib-
bled; certain wild-flowers from whose throats we sucked the drop
of fine nectar; the acorns we chewed, lying on our backs in the
wood; the purple, sun-warmed blackberries we ate from the way-
side bushes to quench our childish thirst with their sharp juice.
We were children — ah, it is not on my own account but on his
that I am moved as I look back, at the thought of his fate, and
how from that vale of innocence he was to mount up to inhospitable, yes, awful heights. It was the life of an artist; and because
it was given to me, a simple man, to see it all so close by, all the
feelings of my soul for human lot and fate were concentrated
about this unique specimen of humanity. Thanks to my friendship
with Adrian, it stands to me for the pattern of how destiny shapes
the soul, for the classic, amazing instance of that which we call
becoming, development, evolution — and actually it may be just
that. For though the artist may all his life remain closer, not to
say truer, to his childhood than the man trained for practical
life, although one may say that he, unlike the latter, abides in the
dreamy, purely human and playful childlike state, yet his path out
of his simple, unaffected beginnings to the undivined later stages
of his course is endlessly farther, wilder, more shattering to
watch than that of the ordinary citizen. With the latter, too, the
thought that he was once a child is not nearly so full of tears.

I beg the reader to put down entirely to my own account the
feelings here expressed and not ascribe them to Leverkühn. I am
an old-fashioned man who has stuck by certain romantic notions

dear to me, one of which is the highly subjectivizing contrast I feel between the nature of the artist and that of the ordinary man. Adrian — if he had found it worth the trouble — would have coldly contradicted such a view. He had extremely neutral views about art and artists; he reacted so witheringly to the "romantic tripe" which the world in its folly had been pleased to utter on the subject that he even disliked the words "art" and "artist," as he showed in his face when he heard them. It was the same with the word "inspiration." It had to be avoided in his company and "imagination" used, if necessary, instead. He hated the word, he jeered at it — and when I think of that hatred and those jeers, I cannot help lifting my hand from the blotter over my page, to cover my eyes. For his hatred and mockery were too tormented to be a merely objective reaction to the intellectual movements of the time. Though they were objective too; I recall that once, even as a student, he said to me that the nineteenth century must have been an uncommonly pleasant epoch, since it had never been harder for humanity to tear itself away from the opinions and habits of the previous period than it was for the generation now living.

I referred above to the pond which lay only ten minutes away from the house, surrounded by pasture. It was called the Cow Trough, probably because of its oblong shape and because the cows came there to drink. The water, why I do not know, was unusually cold, so that we could only bathe in it in the afternoon when the sun had stood on it a long time. As for the hill, it was a favourite walk of half an hour: a height called, certainly from old days and most inappropriately, Mount Zion. In the winter it was good for coasting, but I was seldom there. In summer, with the community bench beneath the oak trees crowning its summit, it was an airy site with a good view, and I often enjoyed it with the Leverkühn family before supper on Sunday afternoons.

And now I feel constrained to comment as follows: the house and its surroundings in which Adrian later as a mature man settled down when he took up permanent quarters with the Schweigestills at Pfeiffering near Waldshut in Oberbayern — indeed, the whole setting — were a most extraordinary likeness and reproduction of his childhood home; in other words, the scene of his later days bore a curious resemblance to that of his early ones. Not only did the environs of Pfeiffering (or Pfeffering, for the spelling varies) have a hill with a community bench, though it was not called Mount Zion, but the Rohmbühel; not only was there a pond, at somewhat the same distance from the house as the Cow Trough, here called the Klammer pond, the water of which was strikingly cold. No, for even the house, the courtyard, and the family itself were all very like the Buchel setting. In the yard was a tree, also rather in the way and preserved for sentimental reasons — not a lime tree, but an elm. True, characteristic differences existed between the structure of the Schweigestill house and that of Adrian's parents, for the former was an old cloister, with thick walls, deep-vaulted casements, and rather dank passages. But the odour of pipe tobacco pervaded the air of the lower rooms as it did at Buchel; and the owner and his wife, Herr and Frau Schweigestill, were a father and a mother too; that is, they were a long-faced, rather laconic, quiet, and contemplative farmer and his no longer young wife, who had certainly put on flesh but was well-proportioned, lively, energetic, and capable, with hair smoothed tightly back and shapely hands and feet. They had a grown son and heir, Gereon (not George), a young man very progressive in agricultural matters, always thinking about new machinery, and a later-born daughter named Clementine. The yard dog in Pfeiffering could laugh, even though he was not called Suso, but Kaschperl — at least originally. For the boarder had his own ideas about this "originally" and I was a witness of the process by which under his influence the name Kaschperl became slowly a memory and the dog himself answered better to Suso. There was no second son, which rather strengthened the case than otherwise, for who would this second son have been?

I never spoke to Adrian about this whole singular and very obvious parallel. I did not do so in the beginning, and later I no longer wanted to. I never cared for the phenomenon. This choice of a place to live, reproducing the earliest one, this burying oneself in one's earliest, outlived childhood, or at least in the outer circumstances of the same — it might indicate attachment, but in any case it is psychologically disturbing. In Leverkühn it was the more so since I never observed that his ties with the parental home were particularly close or emotional, and he severed them early without observable pain. Was that artificial "return" simply a whim? I cannot think so. Instead it reminds me of a man of my acquaintance who, though outwardly robust and even bearded, was so highly strung that when he was ill — and he inclined to illnesses — he wished to be treated only by a child-specialist. Moreover the doctor to whom he went was so small in person that a practice for grown people would obviously not have been suitable and he could only have become a physician for children. I ought to say at once that I am aware of digressing in telling this anecdote about the man with the child-specialist, in so far as neither of them will appear in this narrative. If that is an error, and while without doubt it was an error to yield to the temptation to bring in Pfeiffering and the Schweigestills before their time, I would implore the reader to attribute such irregularities to the excitement which has possessed me since I began this biography, and to tell the truth not only as I write. I have been working now for several days on these pages; but though I try to keep my sentences balanced and find fitting expression for my thoughts, the reader must not imagine that I do not feel myself in a state of permanent excitement, which even expresses itself in a shakiness in my handwriting, usually so firm. I even believe, not only that those who read me will in the long run understand this nervous perturbation, but also that they themselves will in time not be strange to it.

I forgot to mention that there was in the Schweigestill courtyard, Adrian's later home, and certainly not surprisingly, a stable-girl, with bosoms that shook as she ran and bare feet caked with dung; she looked as much like Hanne of Buchel as one stable-girl does look like another, and in the reproduction was named Waltpurgis. Here, however, I am not speaking of her but of her prototype Hanne, with whom little Adrian stood on a friendly footing because she loved to sing and used to do little exercises with us children. Oddly enough, though Elsbeth Leverkühn, with her lovely voice, refrained, in a sort of chaste reserve, from song, this creature smelling of her animals made free with it, and sang to us lustily, of evenings on the bench under the linden tree. She had a strident voice, but a good ear; and she sang all sorts of popular tunes, songs of the army and the street; they were mostly either gruesome or mawkish and we soon made tunes and words our own. When we sang with her, she accompanied us in thirds, and from there went down to the lower fifth and lower sixth and left us in the treble, while she ostentatiously and predominantly sang the second. And probably to fix our attention and make us properly value the harmonic enjoyment, she used to stretch her mouth and laugh just like Suso the dog when we brought her her food.

By we I mean Adrian, myself, and George, who was already thirteen when his brother and I were eight and ten years old. Little sister Ursel was too small to take part in these exercises, and moreover, of us four probably one was superfluous in the kind of vocal music to which Hanne elevated our lusty shoutings. She taught us, that is, to sing rounds — of course, the ones that children know best: *O, wie wohl ist mir am Abend, Es tönen die Lieder,* and the one about the cuckoo and the ass; and those twilight hours in which we enjoyed them remain in my memory — or rather the memory of them later took on a heightened significance because it was they, so far as I know, that first brought my friend into contact with a "music" somewhat more artistically organized than that of mere unison songs.

Here was a succession of interweaving voices and imitative entries, to which one was roused by a poke in the ribs from the stable-girl Hanne when the song was already in progress; when the tune had got to a certain point but was not yet at the end. The melodic components presented themselves in different layers, but no jangle or confusion ensued, for the imitation of the first phrase by the second singer fitted itself very pleasantly point for point to the conti. uation sung by the first. But if this first part — in the case of the piece *O, wie wohl ist mir am Abend* — had reached the repeated "*Glocken läuten*" and begun the illustrative "Ding-dang-dong," it now formed the bass not only to "*Wenn zur Ruh*'," which the second voice was just then singing, but also to the beginning "*O, wie wohl*," with which, consequent on a fresh nudge in the ribs, the third singer entered, only to be relieved, when he had reached the second stage of the melody, by the first starting again at the beginning, having surrendered to the second as the fundamental bass the descriptive "Ding-dang-dong" — and so on. The fourth singer inevitably coincided with one of the others, but he tried to enliven the doubling by roaring an octave below, or else he began before the first voice, so to speak before the dawn with the fundamental bell-figure and indefatigably and cheerfully carried on with it or the fa, la, la that gaily plays round the earlier stages of the melody during the whole duration of the song.

In this way we were always separate from each other in time, but the melodic presence of each kept together pleasantly with that of the others and what we produced made a graceful web, a body of sound such as unison singing did not; a texture in whose polyphony we delighted without inquiring after its nature and cause. Even the eight- or nine-year-old Adrian probably did not notice. Or did the short laugh, more mocking than surprised, which he gave when the last "Ding-dong" faded on the air and which I came later to know so well — did it mean that he saw through the device of these little songs, which quite simply consists in that the beginning of the melody subsequently forms the second voice and that the third can serve both as bass? None of us was aware that here, led by a stable-girl, we were moving on a plane of musical culture already relatively very high, in a realm of imitative polyphony, which the fifteenth century had had to discover in order to give us pleasure. But when I think back at Adrian's laugh, I find in retrospect that it did have in it something of knowledge and mocking initiate sense. He kept it as he grew up; I often heard it, sitting with him in theatre or concert-hall, when he was struck by some artful trick, some ingenious device within the musical structure, noticed only by the few; or by some fine psychological allusion in the dialogue of a drama. In the beginning it was unsuitable for his years, being just as a grown person would have laughed: a slight expulsion of air from nose and mouth, with a toss of the head at the same time, short, cool, yes, contemptuous, or at most as though he would say: "Good, that; droll, curious, amusing!" But his eyes were taking it in, their gaze was afar and strange, and their darkness, metal-sprinkled, had put on a deeper shade.

CHAPTER V

THE chapter just finished is also, for my taste, much too extended. It would seem only too advisable to inquire how the reader's patience is holding out. To myself, of course every word I write is of burning interest; but what care must I take not to see this as a guarantee of the sympathy of the detached reader! And certainly I must not forget that I am writing for posterity; not for the moment, nor for readers who as yet know nothing of Leverkühn and so cannot long to know more about him. What I do is to prepare these pages for a time when the conditions for public interest will be quite different, and certainly much more favourable; when curiosity about the details of so thrilling an existence, however well or ill presented, will be more eager and less fastidious.

That time will come. Our prison, so wide and yet so narrow, so suffocatingly full of foul air, will some day open. I mean when the war now raging will have found, one way or the other, its end — and how I shudder at this "one way or the other," both for myself and for the awful impasse into which fate has crowded the German soul! For I have in mind only one of the two alternatives: only with this one do I reckon, counting upon it against my conscience as a German citizen. The never-ending public instruction has impressed on us in all its horrors the crushing consequences of a German defeat; we cannot help fearing it more than anything else in the world. And yet there is something else — some of us fear it at moments which seem to us criminal, but others quite frankly and steadily — something we fear more than German defeat, and that is German victory. I scarcely dare ask myself to which of these groups I belong. Perhaps to still a third, in which one yearns indeed, steadily and consciously, for defeat, yet also with perpetual torments of conscience. My wishes and hopes must oppose the triumph of German arms, because in it the work of my friend would be buried, a ban would rest upon it for perhaps a hundred years, it would be forgotten, would miss its own age and only in a later one receive historic honour. That is the special motivation of my criminal attitude; I share it with a scattered number of men who can easily be counted on the fingers of my two hands. But my mental state is only a variant of that which, aside from cases of ordinary self-interest or extraordinary stupidity, has become the destiny of a whole people; and this destiny I am inclined to consider in the light of a unique and peculiar tragedy, even while I realize that it has been before now laid on other nations, for the sake of their own and the general future, to wish for the downfall of their state. But considering the decency of the German character, its confidingness, its need for loyalty and devotion, I would fain believe than in our case the dilemma will come to a unique conclusion as well; and I cannot but cherish a deep and strong resentment against the men who have reduced so good a people to a state of mind which I believe bears far harder on it than it would on any other, estranging it beyond healing from itself. I have only to imagine that my own sons, through some unlucky chance, became acquainted with the contents of these pages and in Spartan denial of every gentler feeling denounced me to the secret police — to be able to measure, yes, actually with a sort of patriotic pride, the abysmal nature of this conflict.

I am entirely aware that with the above paragraph I have again regrettably overweighted this chapter, which I had quite intended to keep short. I would not even suppress my suspicion, held on psychological grounds, that I actually seek digressions and circumlocutions, or at least welcome with alacrity any occasion for such, because I am afraid of what is coming. I lay before the reader a testimony to my good faith in that I give space to the theory that I make difficulties because I secretly shrink from the task which, urged by love and duty, I have undertaken. But nothing, not even my own weakness, shall prevent me from continuing to perform it — and I herewith resume my narrative, with the remark that it was by our singing of rounds with the stable-girl that, so far as I know, Adrian was first brought into contact with the sphere of music. Of course I know that as he grew older he went with his parents to Sunday service in the village church at Oberweiler, where a young music student from Weissenfels used to prelude on the little organ and accompany the singing of the congregation, even attending its departure with timid improvisations. But I was almost never with them, since we usually went to Buchel only after morning church and I can but say that I never heard from Adrian a word to indicate that his young mind was any way moved by the offerings of that youthful adept; or — that being scarcely likely — that the phenomenon of music itself had ever struck him. So far as I can see, even at that time and for years afterwards he gave it no attention and kept concealed from himself that he had anything to do with the world of sound. I see in that a mental reserve; but a physiological explanation is also possible, for actually it was at about his fourteenth year, at the time of beginning puberty, and so at the end of the period of childhood, in the house of his uncle at Kaisersaschern, that he began of his own motion to experiment on the piano. And it was at this time that the inherited migraine began to give him bad days.

His brother George's future was conditioned by his position as heir, and he had always felt in complete harmony with it. What should become of the second son was for the parents an open question, which must be decided according to the tastes and capacities he might show; and it was remarkable how early the idea was fixed in his family's head and in all of ours that Adrian was to be a scholar. What sort of scholar remained long in doubt; but the whole bearing of the lad, his way of expressing himself, his clear definition, even his look, his facial expression, never left a doubt, in the mind of my father for instance, that this scion of the Leverkühn stock was called to "something higher"; that he would be the first scholar of his line.

The decisive confirmation of this idea came from the ease, one might say the superior facility, with which Adrian absorbed the instruction of the elementary school. He received it in the paternal home, for Jonathan Leverkühn did not send his children to the village school, and the chief factor in this decision was, I believe, not so much social ambition as the earnest wish to give them a more careful education than they could get from instruction in common with the cottage children of Oberweiler. The schoolmaster, a still young and sensitive man, who never ceased to be afraid of the dog Suso, came over to Buchel afternoons when he had finished his official duties, in winter fetched by Thomas in the sleigh. By the time he took young Adrian in hand he had already given the thirteen-year-old George all the necessary foundation for his further training as agronomist. But now he, schoolmaster Michelson, was the very first to declare, loudly and with a certain vehemence, that the boy must "in God's name," go to high school and the university, for such a learning head and lightning brain he, Michelson, had never seen, and it would be a thousand pities if one did not do everything to open to this young scholar the way to the heights of knowledge. Thus or something like it, certainly rather like a seminarist, did he express himself, speaking indeed of *ingenium*, of course in part to show off with the word, which sounded droll enough applied to such childish achievements. Yet obviously it came from an awed and astonished heart.

I was never present at these lesson-hours and know only by hearsay about them; but I can easily imagine that the behaviour of my young Adrian must sometimes have been a little hard on a preceptor himself young, and accustomed to drive his learning with whip and spurs into dull and puzzled or rebellious heads. "If you know it all already," I once heard him say to the boy, "then I can go home." Of course it was not true that the pupil "knew it all already." But his manner did suggest the thought, simply because here was a case of that swift, strangely sovereign and anticipatory grasp and assimilation, as sure as easy, which soon dried up the master's praise, for he felt that such a head meant a danger to the modesty of the heart and betrayed it easily to arrogance. From the alphabet to syntax and grammar, from the progression of numbers and the first rules to the rule of three and simple sums in proportion, from the memorizing of little poems (and there was no memorizing, the verses were straightway and with the utmost precision grasped and possessed) to the written setting down of his own train of thought on themes out of the geography — it was always the same: Adrian gave it his ear, then turned round with an air that seemed to say: "Yes, good, so much is clear, all right, go on!" To the pedagogic temperament there is something revolting about that. Certainly the young schoolmaster was tempted again and again to cry: "What is the matter with you? Take some pains!" But why, when obviously there was no need to take pains?

As I said, I was never present at the lessons; but I am compelled to conclude that my friend received the scientific data purveyed by Herr Michelson fundamentally with the same mien, so hard to characterize, with which under the lime tree he had accepted the fact that if a horizontal melody of nine bars is divided into three sections of three bars each, they will still produce a harmonically fitting texture. His teacher knew some Latin; he instructed Adrian in it and then announced that the lad — he was now ten years old — was ready if not for the fifth, then certainly for the fourth form. His work was done.

Thus Adrian left his parents' house at Easter 1895 and came to town to attend our Boniface gymnasium, the school of the Brethren of the Common Life. His uncle, Nikolaus Leverkühn, his father's brother, a respected citizen of Kaisersaschern, declared himself ready to receive the lad into his house.

CHAPTER VI

AND as for Kaisersaschern, my native town on the Saale, the stranger should be informed that it lies somewhat south of Halle, towards Thuringia. I had almost said it *lay*, for long absence has made it slip from me into the past. Yet its towers rise as ever on the same spot, and I would not know whether its architectural profile has suffered so far from the assaults of the air war. In view of its historic charm that would be in the highest degree regrettable. I can add this quite calmly, since I share with no small part of our population, even those hardest hit and homeless, the feeling that we are only getting what we gave, and even if we must suffer more frightfully than we have sinned, we shall only hear in our ears that he who sows the wind must reap the whirlwind.

Neither Halle itself, the industrial town, nor Leipzig, the city of Bach the cantor of St. Thomas, nor Weimar, nor even Dessau nor Magdeburg is far distant; but Kaisersaschern is a junction, and with its twenty-seven thousand inhabitants entirely self-sufficient; feeling itself like every German town a centre of culture, with its own historical dignity and importance. It is supported by several industries: factories and mills for the production of machinery, leather goods, fabrics, arms, chemicals, and so on. Its museum, besides a roomful of crude instruments of torture, contains a very estimable library of twenty-five thousand volumes and five thousand manuscripts, among the latter two books of magic charms in alliterative verse; they are considered by some scholars to be older than those in Merseburg. The charms are perfectly harmless: nothing worse than a little rain-conjuring, in the dialect of Fulda. The town was a bishopric in the tenth century, and again from the beginning of the twelfth to the fourteenth. It has a castle, and a cathedral church where you may see the tomb of Kaiser Otto III, son of Adelheid and husband of Theophano, who called himself Emperor of the Romans, also Saxonicus; the latter not because he wanted to be a Saxon but in the sense on which Scipio called himself Africanus, because he had conquered the Saxons. He was driven out of his beloved Rome and died in misery in the year 1002; his remains were brought to Germany and buried in the cathedral in Kaisersaschern — not at all what he would have relished himself, for he was a prize specimen of German self-contempt and had been all his life ashamed of being German.

As for the town — which I refer to by choice in the past tense, since after all I am speaking of the Kaisersaschern of our youth — there is this to be said of it, that in atmosphere as well as in outward appearance it had kept a distinctly mediæval air. The old churches, the faithfully preserved dwelling-houses and warehouses, buildings with exposed and jutting upper storey; the round towers in the wall, with their peaked roofs; the tree-studded squares with cobblestones; the Town Hall of mixed Gothic and Renaissance architecture, with a bell-tower on the high roof, loggias underneath, and two other pointed towers forming bays and continuing the façade down to the ground — all these gave a sense of continuity with the past. More, even, the place seemed to wear on its brow that famous formula of time-lessness, the scholastic *nunc stans*. Its individual character, which was the same as three hundred, nine hundred years ago, asserted itself against the stream of time passing over it, constantly making changes in many things, while others, decisive for the picture, were preserved out of piety; that is to say, out of a pious defiance of time and also out of pride in them, for the sake of their value and their memories.

This much of the scene itself. But something still hung on the air from the spiritual constitution of the men of the last decades of the fifteenth century: a morbid excitement, a metaphysical epidemic latent since the last years of the Middle Ages. This was a practical, rational modern town. — Yet no, it was not modern, it was old; and age is past as presentness, a past merely overlaid with presentness. Rash it may be to say so, but here one could imagine strange things: as for instance a movement for a children's crusade might break out; a St. Vitus's dance; some wandering lunatic with communistic visions, preaching a bonfire of the vanities; miracles of the Cross, fantastic and mystical folk-movements — things like these, one felt, might easily come to pass. Of course they did not — how should they? The police, acting in agreement with the times and the regulations, would not have allowed them. And yet what all in our time have the police not allowed — again in agreement with the times, which might readily, by degrees, allow just such things to happen again now? Our time itself tends, secretly — or rather anything but secretly; indeed, quite consciously, with a strangely complacent conscious-

ness, which makes one doubt the genuineness and simplicity of
life itself and which may perhaps evoke an entirely false, unblest
historicity — it tends, I say, to return to those earlier epochs; it
enthusiastically re-enacts symbolic deeds of sinister significance,
deeds that strike in the face the spirit of the modern age, such, for
instance, as the burning of the books and other things of which I
prefer not to speak.

The stamp of old-world, underground neurosis which I have
been describing, the mark and psychological temper of such a
town, betrays itself in Kaisersaschern by the many "originals,"
eccentrics, and harmlessly half-mad folk who live within its walls
and, like the old buildings, belong to the picture. The pendant to
them is formed by the children, the "young 'uns," who pursue the
poor creatures, mock them, and then in superstitious panic run
away. A certain sort of "old woman" used always in certain
epochs without more ado to be suspected of witchcraft, simply
because she looked "queer," though her appearance may well
have been, in the first place, nothing but the result of the suspicion
against her, which then gradually justified itself till it resembled
the popular fancy: small, grey, bent, with a spiteful face, rheumy
eyes, hooked nose, thin lips, a threatening crook. Probably she
owned cats, an owl, a talking bird. Kaisersaschern harboured
more than one such specimen; the most popular, most teased and
feared was Cellar-Lise, so called because she lived in a basement in
Little Brassfounder's Alley — an old woman whose figure had so
assimilated itself to popular prejudice that even the most unaffected could feel an archaic shudder at meeting her, especially
when the children were after her and she was putting them to
flight by spitting curses. Of course, quite definitely there was
nothing wrong with her at all.

Here let me be bold enough to express an opinion born of the
experiences of our own time. To a friend of enlightenment the
word and conception "the folk" has always something anachronistic and alarming about it; he knows that you need only tell a
crowd they are "the folk" to stir them up to all sorts of reactionary evil. What all has not happened before our eyes — or just not
quite before our eyes — in the name of "the folk," though it could
never have happened in the name of God or humanity or the law!
But it is the fact that actually the folk remain the folk, at least in
a certain stratum of its being, the archaic; and people from Little
Brassfounder's Alley and round about, people who voted the Social-Democratic ticket at the polls, are at the same time capable
of seeing something dæmonic in the poverty of a little old woman

who cannot afford a lodging above-ground. They will clutch
their children to them when she approaches, to save them from
the evil eye. And if such an old soul should have to burn again
today, by no means an impossible prospect, were even a few
things different, "the folk" would stand and gape behind the barriers erected by the Mayor, but they would probably not rebel.
— I speak of the folk; but this old, folkish layer survives in us all,
and to speak as I really think, I do not consider religion the most
adequate means of keeping it under lock and key. For that, literature alone avails, humanistic science, the ideal of the free and
beautiful human being.

To return to those oddities of Kaisersaschern: there was a man
of indefinite age who, if suddenly called to on the street, had a
compulsion to execute a sort of twitching dance with his legs
drawn up. His face was both ugly and sad, but as though he were
begging pardon, he would smile at the urchins bawling at his
heels. Then there was a woman named Mathilde Spiegel, dressed
in the fashion of a bygone time: she wore a train trimmed with
ruffles, and a *fladus* — a ridiculous corruption of the French *flûte
douce*, originally meaning flattery, but here used for a curious
coiffure with curls and ornaments. She wore rouge too, but was
not immoral, being far too witless; she merely rambled through
the streets with her nose in the air, accompanied by pug dogs
with satin saddle-cloths. — A small rentier was another such freak;
he had a bulbous purple nose, and a big seal ring on his forefinger. His real name was Schnalle, but he was called Tootle-oo,
because he had a habit of adding this senseless chirrup to everything he said. He liked to go to the railway station, and when
a freight train pulled out would lift his finger and warn the man
sitting on the roof of the last car: "Don't fall off, don't fall off,
tootle-oo!"

It may be that these grotesque memories are unworthy of in-
clusion here — I am inclined to believe it. Yet all these figures
were, in a way, public institutions, uncommonly characteristic of
the psychological picture of my native town, Adrian's setting till
he went to the university, for nine years of his young life. I spent
them at his side, for though by age I was two forms beyond him,
we kept together, apart from our respective class-mates, during
the recesses in the walled courtyard, and also met each other in
the afternoons, in our little studies: either he came over to the
shop or I went to him in the house of his uncle at Parochialstrasse 15, where the mezzanine storey was occupied by the well-
known Leverkühn musical-instruments firm.

CHAPTER VII

It was a quiet spot, removed from the business section of Kaisers-aschern, the Market Street, or Gritsellers' Row: a tiny street without a pavement, near the Cathedral; Nikolaus Leverkühn's house stood out as the most imposing one in it. It had three storeys, not counting the lofts of the separate roof, which was built out in bays; and in the sixteenth century it had been the dwelling-house of an ancestor of the present owner. It had five windows in the first storey above the entrance door and only four, with blinds, in the second, where, instead of in the first, the family living-rooms lay. Outside, the foundation storey was un-whitewashed and unadorned; only above it did the ornamental woodwork begin. Even the stairs widened only after the beginning of the mezzanine, which lay rather high above the stone entry, so that visitors and buyers — many of these came from abroad, from Halle and even Leipzig — had not too easy a climb to the goal of their hopes, the instrument warehouse. But as I mean to show forthwith, it was certainly worth a steep climb.

Nikolaus, a widower — his wife died young — had up to Adrian's coming lived alone in the house with an old-established house-keeper, Frau Butze, a maid, and a young Italian from Brescia, named Luca Cimabue (he did actually bear the family name of the thirteenth-century painter of Madonnas), who was his assist-ant and pupil at the trade of violin-making; for Uncle Leverkühn also made violins. He was a man with untidy ash-coloured hair hanging loose about his beardless, sympathetically moulded face; prominent cheekbones, a hooked, rather drooping nose, a large, expressive mouth, and brown eyes with good heartedness and concern as well as shrewdness in their gaze. At home one always saw him in a wrinkled fustian smock closed to the throat. I think it pleased the childless man to receive a young kinsman in his far too spacious house. Also I have heard that he let his brother in Buchel pay the school fees, but took nothing himself for board and lodging. Altogether he treated Adrian, on whom he kept an indefinitely expectant eye, like his own son, and greatly enjoyed

having this family addition to his table, which for so long had
had round it only the above-mentioned Frau Butze and, in patriarchal fashion, Luca, his apprentice.

That this young Italian, a friendly youth speaking a pleasantly
broken German, had found his way to Kaisersaschern and to
Adrian's uncle, when he surely must have had opportunity at
home to improve himself in his trade, was perhaps surprising, but
indicated the extent of Nikolaus Leverkühn's business connections, not only with German centres of instrument-making, like
Mainz, Braunschweig, Leipzig, Barmen, but also with foreign
firms in London, Lyons, Bologna, even New York. He drew his
symphonic merchandise from all quarters and had a reputation for
a stock-in-trade not only first-class as to quality but also gratify-
ingly complete and not easily obtainable elsewhere. Thus there
only needed to be anywhere in the kingdom a Bach festival in
prospect, for whose performance in classic style an oboe d'amore
was needed, the deeper oboe long since disappeared from the orchestra, for the old house in Parochialstrasse to receive a visit
from a client, a musician who wanted to play safe and could try
out the elegiac instrument on the spot.

The warerooms in the mezzanine often resounded with such re-
hearsals, the voices running through the octaves in the most varied
colours. The whole place afforded a splendid, I might say a culturally enchanting and alluring sight, stimulating the aural imagination till it effervesced. Excepting the piano, which Adrian's
foster-father gave over to that special industry, everything was
here spread out: all that sounds and sings, that twangs and crashes,
hums and rumbles and roars — even the keyboard instruments, in
the form of the celesta, the lovely *Glockenklavier*, were always
represented. There hung behind glass, or lay bedded in recepta-
cles which like mummy cases were made in the shape of their
occupants, the charming violins, varnished some yellower and
some browner, their slender bows with silver wire round the nut
fixed into the lid of the case; Italian ones, the pure, beautiful
shapes of which would tell the connoisseur that they came from
Cremona; also Tirolese, Dutch, Saxon, Mittenwald fiddles, and
some from Leverkühn's own workshop. The melodious cello,
which owes its perfect form to Antonio Stradivari, was there in
rows; likewise its predecessor, the six-stringed viola da gamba, in
older works still honoured next to it; the viola and that other
cousin of the fiddle, the viola alta, were always to be found, as
well as my own viola d'amore, on whose seven strings I have all

my life enjoyed performing. My instrument came from the Parochialstrasse, a present from my parents at my confirmation.

There were several specimens of the violone, the giant fiddle,
the unwieldy double-bass, capable of majestic recitative, whose
pizzicato is more sonorous than the stroke of the kettle-drum, and
whose harmonics are a veiled magic of almost unbelievable quality. And there was also more than one of its opposite number
among the wood-wind instruments, the contra-bassoon, sixteen-
foot likewise — in other words, sounding an octave lower than the
notes indicate — mightily strengthening the basses, built in twice
the dimensions of its smaller brother the humorous bassoon, to
which I give that name because it is a bass instrument without
proper bass strength, oddly weak in sound, bleating, burlesque.
How pretty it was, though, with its curved mouthpiece, shining
in the decoration of its keys and levers! What a charming sight
altogether, this host of shawms in their highly developed stage of
technical perfection, challenging the passion of the virtuoso in all
of their forms: as bucolic oboe, as *cor Anglais* well versed in
tragic ways; the many-keyed clarinet, which can sound so ghostly
in the deep chalumeau register but higher up can gleam in silvery
blossoming harmony, as basset horn and bass clarinet.

All of these, in their velvet beds, offered themselves in Uncle
Leverkühn's stock; also the transverse flute, in various systems and
varied execution, made of beechwood, granadilla, or ebony, with
ivory head-pieces, or else entirely of silver; next their shrill relative
the piccolo, which in the orchestral tutti piercingly holds the treble,
dancing in the music of the will-o'-the-wisp and the fire-magic.
And now the shimmering chorus of the brasses, from the trim
trumpet, visible symbol of the clear call, the sprightly song, the
melting cantilena, through that darling of the romantics, the vo-
luted valve-horn, the slender and powerful trombone, and the
cornet-à-pistons, to the weighty bass tuba. Rare museum pieces
such as a pair of beautifully curved bronze lurer turned right and
left, like steer-horns, were also to be found in Leverkühn's warehouse. But in a boy's eyes, as I see it again in retrospect, most gay
and glorious of all was the comprehensive display of percussion instruments — just because the things that one had found under the
Christmas tree, the toys and dream-possessions of childhood, now
turned up in this dignified grown-up display. The side drum, how
different it looked here from the ephemeral painted thing of
wood, parchment, and twine we thumped on as six-year-olds! It
was not meant to hang round your neck. The lower membrane

was stretched with gut strings; it was screwed fast for orchestral use, in conveniently slanting position, on a metal trivet, and the wooden sticks, also much nicer than ours, stuck invitingly into rings at the sides. There was the glockenspiel; we had had a childhood version of it, on which we practised *Kommt ein Vogel geflogen*. Here, in an elegant locked case, lying in pairs on cross-bars and free to swing, were the metal plates, so meticulously tuned, with the delicate little steel hammers belonging to them and kept in the lined lid of the case. The xylophone, which seems made to conjure up a vision of a dance of skeletons — here it was with its numerous wooden bars, arranged in the chromatic scale. There was the giant studded cylinder of the bass drum, with a felt-covered stick to beat it; and the copper kettle-drum, sixteen of which Berlioz still included in his orchestra. He did not know the pedal drum as represented here, which the drummer can with his hand easily adapt to a change of key. How well I remember the pranks we practised on it, Adrian and I — no, it was probably only I — making the sticks roll on the membrane while the good Luca tuned it up and down, so that a thudding and thumping in the strangest glissando ensued. And then there were the extraordinary cymbals, which only the Turks and the Chinese know how to make, because they have preserved the secret of hammering molten bronze. The performer, after clashing them, holds up their inner sides in triumph towards the audience. The reverberating gong, the tambourine beloved of the gypsies, the triangle with its open end, sounding brightly under the steel stick; the cymbals of today, the hollow castanets clacking in the hand. Consider all this splendid feast of sound, with the golden, gorgeous structure of the Érard pedal harp towering above it — and how easy it is to feel the fascination that Uncle's warehouse had for us, this silent paradise, which yet in hundreds of forms heralded sweetest harmony!

For us? No, I shall do better to speak only of myself, my own enchantment, my own pleasure — I scarcely dare to include my friend when I speak of those feelings. Perhaps he wanted to play the son of the house, to whom the warerooms were commonplace everyday; perhaps the coolness native to him in general might thus express itself; for he maintained an almost shoulder-shrugging indifference to all these splendours, replying to my admiring exclamations with his short laugh and a "Yes, very nice" or "Funny stuff" or "What all don't people think of!" or "More fun to sell this than groceries." Sometimes — I repeat that it was at my wish, not his — we would descend from his attic, which gave a pleasant view over the roofs of the town, the castle pond, the old water-

tower, and invade the show-rooms. They were not forbidden to
us; but young Cimabue came too, partly, I suspect, to keep guard,
but also to play cicerone in his pleasant way. From him we learned
the history of the trumpet: how once it had to be put together
out of several metal tubes with a ball connection, before we
learned the art of bending brass tubes without splitting them, by
first filling them with pitch and resin, then with lead, which was
melted again in the fire. And then he could explain the assertion
of the cognoscenti that it made no difference what material,
whether wood or metal, an instrument was made of, it sounded
according to its family shape and proportions. A flute might be
made of wood or ivory, a trumpet of brass or silver, it made no
difference. But his master, he said, Adrian's *zio*, disputed that. He
knew the importance of the material, the sort of wood and var-
nish used, and engaged to be able to tell by listening to a flute
what it was made of. He, Luca, would do the same. Then with
his small, shapely Italian hands he would show us the mechanism
of the flute, which in the last one hundred and fifty years, since
the famous virtuoso Quantz, saw such great changes and developments: the mechanism of Boehm's cylindrical flute, more powerful than the old conical, which sounds sweeter. He showed us
the system of fingering on the clarinet and the seven-holed bassoon with its twelve closed and four open keys, whose sound
blends so readily with that of the horns; instructed us about the
compass of the instruments, the way to play them and more such
matters.

There can now be no doubt that Adrian, whether he was aware
of it or not, followed these demonstrations with at least as much
attention as I — and with more profit than it was given me to draw
from them. But he betrayed nothing, not a gesture indicated that
all this concerned or ever would concern him. He let me ask Luca
the questions, yes, he moved away, looked at something else than
the thing under discussion, and left me alone with the assistant.
I will not say that he was shamming, and I do not forget that at
that time music had hardly any reality to us other than that of
the purely material objects in Nikolaus Leverkühn's storerooms.
We were indeed brought into cursory contact with chamber music, for every week or so there was a performance in Adrian's
uncle's house, but only occasionally in my presence and by no
means always in his. The players were our Cathedral organist,
Herr Wendell Kretschmar, a stutterer, who was later to become
Adrian's teacher, and the singing-master from the Boniface gymnasium; Adrian's uncle played with them, quartets by Haydn and

Mozart, he himself playing first violin, Luca Cimabue second, Herr Kretschmar cello, and the singing-master the viola. These were masculine evenings, with the beer-glass on the floor beside the chair, a cigar in the mouth, and frequent bursts of talk, strange, dry interruptions in the middle of the language of music; tapping of the bow and counting back of the bars when the players got out, which was almost always the fault of the singing-master. A real concert, a symphony orchestra, we had never heard, and whoever likes may find therein an explanation of Adrian's obvious indifference to the world of instruments. At any rate he seemed to think it must be sufficient, and so considered it himself. What I mean is he hid himself behind it, hid himself from music: very long, with instinctive persistence, he hid himself from his destiny.

Anyhow, nobody for a long time thought of connecting young Adrian in any way with music. The idea that he was destined to be a scholar was fixed in their minds and continually strengthened by his brilliant performance in school, his rank in his form, which began slightly to waver only in the upper forms, say from the fifth on, when he was fifteen. This was on account of the migraine, which from then on hindered him in the little preparation he had to do. Even so he easily mastered the demands made on him — though the word "mastered" is not well chosen, for it cost him nothing to satisfy them. And if his excellence as a pupil did not earn for him the affection of his masters, for it did not, as I often observed — one saw instead a certain irritation, a desire to trap him — it was not so much that they found him conceited, though they did. They did not, however, think him proud of his achievements; the trouble was, he was not proud enough, just therein lay his arrogance. He obviously looked down on all this that was so easy for him: that is, the subject-matter of the lessons, the various branches of study, the purveying of which made up the dignity and the livelihood of the masters. It was only too natural that they should not enjoy seeing these things so competently and carelessly dismissed.

For my own part I had much more cordial relations with them — no wonder, since I was soon to join their number and had even seriously announced my intention. I too might call myself a good pupil; but I was and might call myself so only because my reverent love for my chosen field, especially the ancient tongues and the classic poets and writers, summoned and stimulated what powers I had, while he on every occasion made it clear — to me he made no secret of it and I fear it was not one to the masters

either — how indifferent and so to speak unimportant to him the
whole of his education was. This often distressed me, not on account of his career, which thanks to his facility was not endangered, but because I asked myself what was not indifferent and
unimportant to him. I did not see the "main thing," and really it
was not there to see. In those years school life is life itself, it
stands for all that life is, school interests bound the horizon that
every life needs in order to develop values, through which, however relative they are, the character and the capacities are sustained. They can, however, do that, humanly speaking, only if the
relativeness remains unrecognized. Belief in absolute values, illusory as it always is, seems to me a condition of life. But my
friend's gifts measured themselves against values the relative character of which seemed to lie open to him, without any visible possibility of any other relation which would have detracted from
them as values. Bad pupils there are in plenty. But Adrian presented the singular phenomenon of a bad pupil as the head of the
form. I say that it distressed me, but how impressive, how fascinating, I found it too! How it strengthened my devotion to him,
mingling with it — can one understand why? — something like
pain, like hopelessness!

I will make one exception to this uniform ironic contempt
which he presented to what the school offered him and the claims
it made upon him. That was his apparent interest in a discipline
in which I myself did not shine — mathematics. My own weakness in this field, which was only tolerably made good by joyful
application in philology, made me realize that excellence in performance is naturally conditioned by sympathy with the subject
and thus it was a real boon to me to see this condition — at least
here — fulfilled by my friend too. *Mathesis*, as applied logic, which
yet confines itself to pure and lofty abstractions, holds a peculiar
middle position between the humanistic and the practical sciences,
and from the explanations which Adrian gave me of the pleasure
he took in it, it appeared that he found this middle position at
once higher, dominating, universal, or, as he expressed it, "the
true." It was a genuine pleasure to hear him describe anything as
"the true," it was an anchor, a hold, not quite in vain did one inquire about "the main thing." "You are a lout," he said, "not to
like it. To look at the relations between things must be the best
thing, after all. Order is everything. Romans xiii: 'For there is no
power but of God: the powers that be are ordained of God.' "
He reddened, and I looked at him large-eyed. It turned out that
he was religious.

With him everything had first to "turn out," one had to take
him by surprise, catch him in the act, get behind the words; then
he would go red, and one would have liked to kick oneself for not
having seen it before. He went further than necessary in his algebra, played with the logarithmic tables for sheer amusement,
sat over equations of the second class before he had been asked to
identify unknown quantities raised to a higher power. I caught
him at all that by mere chance, and even then he spoke mockingly
of them before he made the above admissions. Another discovery,
not to say unmasking, had preceded this: I have already mentioned his self-taught and secret exploration of the keyboard, the
chord, the compass of tonality, the cycle of fifths, and how he,
without knowledge of notes or fingering, used this harmonic basis
to practise all sorts of modulations and to build up melodic pictures rhythmically undefined. When I discovered all this, he was
in his fifteenth year. I had sought him in vain one afternoon in
his room, and found him before a little harmonium which stood
rather unregarded in the corridor of the family rooms. For a moment I had listened, standing at the door, but not quite liking this
I went forward and asked him what he was doing. He let the bellows rest, took his hands from the manuals, blushed and laughed.
"Idleness," he said, "is the mother of all vice. I was bored. When
I am bored I sometimes poke about down here. The old treadle-
box stands here pretty forlorn; but for all its simpleness it has the
meat of the matter in it. Look, it is curious — that is, of course,
there is nothing curious about it, but when you make it out the
first time for yourself it is curious how it all hangs together and
leads round in a circle."

And he played a chord: all black keys, F sharp, A sharp, C
sharp, added an E, and so unmasked the chord, which had looked
like F-sharp major, as belonging to B major, as its dominant.
"Such a chord," he said, "has of itself no tonality. Everything is
relation, and the relation forms the circle." The A, which, forcing
the resolution into G sharp, leads over from B major to E major,
led him on, and so via the keys of A, D, and G he came to C major and to the flat keys, as he demonstrated to me that on each
one of the twelve notes of the chromatic scale one could build a
fresh major or minor scale.

"But all that is an old story," he said. "That struck me a long
time ago. Now look how you can improve on it!" And he began
to show me modulations between more distant keys, by using the
so-called relation of the third, the Neapolitan sixth.

Not that he would have known how to name these things; but he repeated:

"Relationship is everything. And if you want to give it a more precise name, it is ambiguity." To illustrate the meaning of the word, he played me chord-progressions belonging to no definite key; demonstrated for me how such a progression fluctuates between C major and G major, if one leaves out the F, that in G major turns into F sharp; how it keeps the ear uncertain as to whether that progression is to be understood as belonging to C major or F major if one avoids the B, which in F major is flattened to B flat.

"You know what I find?" he asked. "That music turns the equivocal into a system. Take this or that note. You can understand it so or respectively so. You can think of it as sharpened or flattened, and you can, if you are clever, take advantage of the double sense as much as you like." In short, in principle he showed himself aware of enharmonic changes and not unaware of certain tricks by which one can by-pass keys and use the enharmonic change for modulations.

Why was I more than surprised, namely moved and a little startled? His cheeks were hot, as they never were in school, not even over his algebra. I did indeed ask him to improvise for me a little, but felt something like relief when he put me off with a "Nonsense, nonsense!" What sort of relief was that? It might have taught me how proud I was of his general indifference, and how clearly I felt that in his "It is curious," indifference became a mask. I divined a budding passion — a passion of Adrian's! Should I have been glad? Instead, I felt at once ashamed and anxious.

I knew now that he, when he thought himself alone, worked on his music; indeed, in the exposed position of the old instrument that could not long remain a secret. One evening his foster-father said to him:

"Well, nephew, from what I heard today you were not practising for the first time."

"What do you mean, Uncle Niko?"

"Don't be so innocent! You were making music."

"What an expression!"

"It has had to serve for worse. How you got from F major to A major, that was pretty clever. Does it amuse you?"

"Oh, Uncle!"

"Well, of course. I'll tell you something: We'll put the old box up in your room, nobody sees it down here anyhow. Then you'll have it at hand, to use when you feel like it."

"You're frightfully good, Uncle, but surely it is not worth the trouble."

"It's so little trouble that even so the pleasure might be greater. And anyhow, nephew, you ought to have piano lessons."

"Do you think so, Uncle Niko? I don't know, it sounds like a girls' high school."

"Might be higher and still not quite girls'! If you go to Kretschmar, it will be something like. He won't skin us alive, because of our old friendship, and you will get a foundation for your castles in the air. I'll speak to him."

Adrian repeated this conversation to me literally, in the school court. From now on he had lessons twice a week from Wendell Kretschmar.

CHAPTER VIII

WENDELL KRETSCHMAR, at that time still young, at most in the second half of his twenties, was born in the state of Pennsylvania of German-American parentage. He had got his musical education in his country of origin; but he was early drawn back to the old world whence his grandparents had once migrated, and where his own roots lay and those of his art. In the course of his wanderings, the stages and sojourns of which seldom lasted more than a year or so, he had become our organist in Kaisersaschern. It was only an episode, preceded by others (he had worked as conductor in small state theatres in the Reich and Switzerland) and followed certainly by others still. He had even appeared as composer and produced an opera, *The Statue*, which was well received and played on many stages.

Unpretentious in appearance, a short, thickset, bullet-headed man with a little clipped moustache and brown eyes prone to laughter, with now a musing and now a pouncing look, he might have meant a real boon to the cultural life of Kaisersaschern if there had been any such life to begin with. His organ-playing was expert and excellent, but you could count on the fingers of one hand the number of those in the community able to appreciate it. Even so, a considerable number of people were attracted by his free afternoon concerts, in which he regaled us with organ music by Michael Pretorius, Froberger, Buxtehude, and of course Sebastian Bach, also all sorts of curious genre compositions from the time between Handel's and Haydn's highest periods. Adrian and I attended the concerts regularly. A complete failure, on the other hand, at least to all appearance, were the lectures which he held indefatigably throughout a whole season in the hall of the Society of Activities for the Common Weal, accompanied by illustrations on the piano and demonstrations on a blackboard. They were a failure in the first place because our population had on principle no use for lectures; and secondly because his themes were not popular but rather capricious and out of the ordinary; and in the third place because his stutter made listening to them a nerve-

racking occupation, sometimes bringing your heart into your
mouth, sometimes tempting you to laughter, and altogether calculated to distract your attention from the intellectual treat in
anxious expectation of the next convulsion.

His stutter was of a particularly typical and developed kind —
tragic, because he was a man gifted with great and urgent riches
of thought, passionately addicted to giving out information. And
his little bark would move upon the waters by stretches swift and
dancing, with a suspicious ease that might make one forget and
scout his affliction. But inevitably, from time to time, while constantly and only too justifiably awaited, came the moment of disaster; and there he stood with red, swollen face on the rack;
whether stuck on a sibilant, which he weathered with wide-
stretched mouth, making the noise of an engine giving off steam;
or wrestling with a labial, his cheeks puffed out, his lips launched
into a crackling quick-fire of short, soundless explosions; or
finally, when with his breathing in helpless disorder, his mouth
like a funnel, he would gasp for breath like a fish out of water;
laughing with tears in his eyes, for it is a fact that he himself
seemed to treat the thing as a joke. Not everybody could take
that consoling view; the public was really not to be blamed if it
avoided the lectures with that degree of unanimity that in fact several times not more than half a dozen hearers occupied the seats:
my parents, Adrian's uncle, young Cimabue, the two of us, and a
few pupils from the girls' high school, who did not fail to giggle
when the speaker stuttered.

Kretschmar would have been ready to defray out of his own
pocket such expenses for hall and lighting as were not covered
by the ticket money. But my father and Nikolaus Leverkühn had
arranged in committee to have the society make up the deficit, or
rather relinquish the charge for the hall, on the plea that the lectures were important for culture and served the common good.
That was a friendly gesture; the effect on the common weal was
doubtful, since the community did not attend them, in part, as I
said, because of the all too specialized character of the subjects
treated. Wendell Kretschmar honoured the principle, which we
repeatedly heard from his lips, first formed by the English tongue,
that to arouse interest was not a question of the interest of others,
but of our own; it could only be done, but then infallibly was, if
one was fundamentally interested in a thing oneself, so that when
one talked about it one could hardly help drawing others in, in-
fecting them with it, and so creating an interest up to then not

present or dreamed of. And that was worth a great deal more than catering to one already existent.

It was a pity that our public gave him almost no opportunity to prove his theory. With us few, sitting at his feet in the yawning emptiness of the old hall with the numbered chairs, he proved it conclusively, for he held us charmed by things of which we should never have thought they could so capture our attention; even his frightful impediment did in the end only affect us as a stimulating and compelling expression of the zeal he felt. Often did we all nod at him consolingly when the calamity came to pass, and one or the other of the gentlemen would utter a soothing "There, there!" or "It's all right," or "Never mind!" Then the spasm would relax in a merry, apologetic smile and things would run on again in almost uncanny fluency, for a while.

What did he talk about? Well, the man was capable of spending a whole hour on the question: Why did Beethoven not write a third movement to the Piano Sonata Opus 111? It is without doubt a matter worth discussing. But think of it in the light of the posters outside the hall of Activities for the Common Weal, or inserted in the Kaisersaschern *Railway Journal*, and ask yourself the amount of public interest it could arouse. People positively did not want to know why Op. 111 has only two movements. We who were present at the explanation had indeed an uncommonly enriching evening, and this although the sonata under discussion was to that date entirely unknown to us. Still it was precisely through these lectures that we got to know it, and as a matter of fact very much in detail; for Kretschmar played it to us on the inferior cottage piano that was all he could command, a grand piano not being granted him. He played it capitally despite the rumbling noise the instrument made; analysing its intellectual content with great impressiveness as he went, describing the circumstances under which it — and two others — were written and expatiating with caustic wit upon the master's own explanation of the reason why he had not done a third movement corresponding to the first. Beethoven, it seems, had calmly answered this question, put by his famulus, by saying that he had not had time and therefore had somewhat extended the second movement. No time! And he had said it "calmly," to boot. The contempt for the questioner which lay in such an answer had obviously not been noticed, but it was justified contempt. And now the speaker described Beethoven's condition in the year 1820, when his hearing, attacked by a resistless ailment, was in progressive decay, and it had already become clear that he could no longer conduct his own works. Kretschmar told us about the rumours that the famous author was quite written out, his productive powers exhausted, himself incapable of larger enterprises, and busying himself like the old Haydn with writing down Scottish songs. Such reports had continually gained ground, because for several years no work of importance bearing his name had come on the market. But in the late autumn, returning to Vienna from Mödling, where he had spent the summer, the master had sat down and written these three compositions for the piano without, so to speak, once looking up from the notes, all in one burst, and gave notice of them to his patron, the Count of Brunswick, to reassure him as to his mental condition. And then Kretschmar talked about the Sonata in C minor, which indeed it was not easy to see as a well-rounded and intellectually digested work, and which had given his contemporary critics, and his friends as well, a hard æsthetic nut to crack. These friends and admirers, Kretschmar said, simply could not follow the man they revered beyond the height to which at the time of his maturity he had brought the symphony, the piano sonata, and the classical string quartet. In the works of the last period they stood with heavy hearts before a process of dissolution or alienation, of a mounting into an air no longer familiar or safe to meddle with; even before a *plus ultra*, wherein they had been able to see nothing else than a degeneration of tendencies previously present, an excess of introspection and speculation, an extravagance of minutiæ and scientific musicality — applied sometimes to such simple material as the arietta theme of the monstrous movement of variations which forms the second part of this sonata. The theme of this movement goes through a hundred vicissitudes, a hundred worlds of rhythmic contrasts, at length outgrows itself, and is finally lost in giddy heights that one might call other-worldly or abstract. And in just that very way Beethoven's art had overgrown itself, risen out of the habitable regions of tradition, even before the startled gaze of human eyes, into spheres of the entirely and utterly and nothing-but personal — an ego painfully isolated in the absolute, isolated too from sense by the loss of his hearing; lonely prince of a realm of spirits, from whom now only a chilling breath issued to terrify his most willing contemporaries, standing as they did aghast at these communications of which only at moments, only by exception, they could understand anything at all.

So far, so good, said Kretschmar. And yet again, good or right only conditionally and incompletely. For one would usually connect with the conception of the merely personal, ideas of limitless subjectivity and of radical harmonic will to expression, in contrast to polyphonic objectivity (Kretschmar was concerned to have us impress upon our minds this distinction between harmonic subjectivity and polyphonic objectivity) and this equation, this contrast, here as altogether in the masterly late works, would simply not apply. As a matter of fact, Beethoven had been far more "subjective," not to say far more "personal," in his middle period than in his last, had been far more bent on taking all the flourishes, formulas, and conventions, of which music is certainly full, and consuming them in the personal expression, melting them into the subjective dynamic. The relation of the later Beethoven to the conventional, say in the last five piano sonatas, is, despite all the uniqueness and even uncanniness of the formal language, quite different, much more complaisant and easy going. Untouched, untransformed by the subjective, convention often appeared in the late works, in a baldness, one might say exhaustiveness, an abandonment of self, with an effect more majestic and awful than any reckless plunge into the personal. In these forms, said the speaker, the subjective and the coventional assumed a new relationship, conditioned by death.

At this word Kretschmar stuttered violently; sticking fast at the first sound and executing a sort of machine-gun fire with his tongue on the roof of his mouth, with jaw and chin both quivering, before they settled on the vowel which told us what he meant. But when we had guessed it, it seemed hardly proper to take it out of his mouth and shout it to him, as we sometimes did, in jovial helpfulness. He had to say it himself and he did. Where greatness and death come together, he declared, there arises an objectivity tending to the conventional, which in its majesty leaves the most domineering subjectivity far behind, because therein the merely personal — which had after all been the surmounting of a tradition already brought to its peak — once more outgrew itself, in that it entered into the mythical, the collectively great and supernatural.

He did not ask if we understood that, nor did we ask ourselves. When he gave it as his view that the main point was to hear it, we fully agreed. It was in the light of what he had said, he went on, that the work he was speaking of in particular, Sonata Op. 111, was to be regarded. And then he sat down at the cottage piano and played us the whole composition out of his head, the first and the incredible second movement, shouting his comments into the midst of his playing and in order to make us conscious of the treatment demonstrating here and there in his enthusiasm by singing as well; altogether it made a spectacle partly entrancing, partly funny; and repeatedly greeted with merriment by his little audience. For as he had a very powerful attack and exaggerated the *forte*, he had to shriek extra loud to make what he said half-way intelligible and to sing with all the strength of his lungs to emphasize vocally what he played. With his lips he imitated what the hands played. "Tum-tum, tum-tum, tum-tr-r!" he went, as he played the grim and startling first notes of the first movement; he sang in a high falsetto the passages of melodic loveliness by which the ravaged and tempestuous skies of the composition are at intervals brightened as though by faint glimpses of light. At last he laid his hands in his lap, was quiet a moment, and then said: "Here it comes!" and began the variations movement, the "*adagio molto semplice e cantabile.*"

The arietta theme, destined to vicissitudes for which in its idyllic innocence it would seem not to be born, is presented at once, and announced in sixteen bars, reducible to a motif which appears at the end of its first half, like a brief soul-cry — only three notes, a quaver, a semiquaver, and a dotted crotchet to be scanned as, say: "heav-en's blue, lov-ers' pain, fare-thee well, on a-time, mead-ow-land" — and that is all. What now happens to this mild utterance, rhythmically, harmonically, contrapuntally, to this pensive, subdued formulation, with what its master blesses and to what condemns it, into what black nights and dazzling flashes, crystal spheres wherein coldness and heat, repose and ecstasy are one and the same, he flings it down and lifts it up, all that one may well call vast, strange, extravagantly magnificent, without thereby giving it a name, because it is quite truly nameless; and with labouring hands Kretschmar played us all those enormous transformations, singing at the same time with the greatest violence: "Dim-dada!" and mingling his singing with shouts. "These chains of trills!" he yelled. "These flourishes and cadenzas! Do you hear the conventions that are left in? Here — the language — is no longer — purified of the flourishes — but the flourishes — of the appearance — of their subjective — domination — the appearance — of art is thrown off — at last — art always throws off the appearance of art. Dim-dada! Do listen, how here — the melody is dragged down by the centrifugal weight of chords! It becomes static, monotonous — twice D, three times D, one after the other — the chords do it — dim-dada! Now notice what happens here — "

It was extraordinarily difficult to listen to his shouts and to the highly complicated music both at once. We all tried. We strained, leaning forward, hands between knees, looking by turn at his hands and his mouth. The characteristic of the movement of course is the wide gap between bass and treble, between the right and the left hand, and a moment comes, an utterly extreme situation, when the poor little motif seems to hover alone and forsaken above a giddy yawning abyss — a procedure of awe-inspiring unearthliness, to which then succeeds a distressful making-of-itself-small, a start of fear as it were, that such a thing could happen. Much else happens before the end. But when it ends and while it ends, something comes, after so much rage, persistence, obstinacy, extravagance: something entirely unexpected and touching in its mildness and goodness. With the motif passed through many vicissitudes, which takes leave and so doing becomes itself entirely leave-taking, a parting wave and call, with this D G G occurs a slight change, it experiences a small melodic expansion. After an introductory C, it puts a C sharp before the D, so that it no longer scans "heav-en's blue," "mead-owland," but "O-thou heaven's blue," "Green-est meadowland," "Fare-thee well for aye," and this added C sharp is the most moving, consolatory, pathetically reconciling thing in the world. It is like having one's hair or cheek stroked, lovingly, understandingly, like a deep and silent farewell look. It blesses the object, the frightfully harried formulation, with overpowering humanity, lies in parting so gently on the hearer's heart in eternal farewell that the eyes run over. "Now for-get the pain," it says. "Great was — God in us." "'Twas all — but a dream," "Friendly — be to me." Then it breaks off. Quick, hard triplets hasten to a conclusion with which any other piece might have ended.

Kretschmar did not return from the piano to his desk. He sat on his revolving stool with his face turned towards us, in the same position as ours, bent over, hands between his knees, and in a few words brought to an end his lecture on why Beethoven had not written a third movement to Op. 111. We had only needed, he said, to hear the piece to answer the question ourselves. A third movement? A new approach? A return after this parting — impossible! It had happened that the sonata had come, in the second, enormous movement, to an end, an end without any return. And when he said "the sonata," he meant not only this one in C minor, but the sonata in general, as a species, as traditional art-form; it itself was here at an end, brought to its end, it had fulfilled its destiny, reached its goal, beyond which there was no going, it cancelled and resolved itself, it took leave — the gesture of farewell of the D G G motif, consoled by the C sharp, was a leave-taking in this sense too, great as the whole piece itself, the fare-well of the sonata form.

With this Kretschmar went away, accompanied by thin but prolonged applause, and we went too, not a little reflective, weighed down by all these novelties. Most of us, as usual, as we put on our coats and hats and walked out, hummed bemusedly to ourselves the impression of the evening, the theme-generating motif of the second movement, in its original and its leave-taking form, and for a long time we heard it like an echo from the re-moter streets into which the audience dispersed, the quiet night streets of the little town: "Fare — thee well," "fare thee well for aye," "Great was God in us."

That was not the last time we heard the stutterer on Beethoven. He spoke again soon, this time on "Beethoven and the Fugue." This lecture too I remember quite clearly, and see the announce-ment before me, perfectly aware that it, as little as the other, was likely to produce in the hall of the "Common Weal" any crowd so large as to endanger life and limb. But our little group got from this evening too the most positive pleasure and profit. Al-ways, we were told, the opponents and rivals of the bold inno-vator asserted that Beethoven could not write a fugue. "That he just cannot," they said, and probably they knew what they were talking about, for this respectable art-form stood at the time in high honour, and no composer found favour in the high court of music or satisfied the commands of the potentates and great gen-tlemen who issued them if he did not stand his man in the perfec-tion of the fugue. Prince Esterházy was an especial friend of this master art, but in the Mass in C which Beethoven wrote for him, the composer, after unsuccessful attempts, had not arrived at a fugue; even socially considered, that was a discourtesy, but artis-tically it had been an unpardonable lack, and the oratorio *Christ on the Mount of Olives* altogether lacked any fugue form, al-though it would have been most proper there. Such a feeble effort as the fugue in the third quartet of Op. 59 was not calculated to counteract the view that the great man was a bad contrapuntist — in which the opinion of the authoritative musical world could only have been strengthened by the passages in fugue form in the funeral march in the *"Eroica"* and the Allegretto of the A major Symphony. And now the closing movement of the Cello Sonata in D, Op. 102, superscribed "Allegro fugato"! The outcry, the fist-shaking, had been great, Kretschmar told us. Unclear to the point of unenjoyableness, that was what they taxed the whole with being; but at least for twenty bars long, they said, there reigned such scandalous confusion — principally in consequence of too strongly coloured modulations — that after it one could close the case for the incapacity of this man to write in the "strict style."

I interrupt myself in my reproduction to remark that the lecturer was talking about matters and things in the world of art, situations that had never come within our horizon and only appeared now on its margin in shadowy wise through the always compromised medium of his speech. We were unable to check up on it except through his own explanatory performances on the cottage piano, and we listened to it all with the dimly excited fantasy of children hearing a fairy-story they do not understand, while their tender minds are none the less in a strange, dreamy, intuitive way enriched and advantaged. Fugue, counterpoint, "Eroica," "confusion in consequence of too strongly coloured modulations," "strict style" — all that was just magic spells to us, but we heard it as greedily, as large-eyed, as children always hear what they do not understand or what is even entirely unsuitable — indeed, with far more pleasure than the familiar, fitting, and adequate can give them. Is it believable that this is the most intensive, splendid, perhaps the very most productive way of learning: the anticipatory way, learning that spans wide stretches of ignorance? As a pedagogue I suppose I should not speak in its behalf; but I do know that it profits youth extraordinarily. And I believe that the stretches jumped over fill in of themselves in time.

Beethoven, then, so we heard, was reputed not to be able to write a fugue; and now the question was how far this malicious criticism was true. Obviously he had taken pains to refute it. Several times he had written fugues into his later piano music, and indeed in three voices: in the "Hammerklavier" Sonata as well as the one in A major. Once he had added: "with some liberties" ("mit einigen Freiheiten"), in token that the rules he had offended against were well known to him. Why he ignored them, whether arbitrarily or because he had not managed it, remained a vexed question. And then had come the great fugue overture, Op. 124, and the majestic fugues in the Gloria and the Credo in evidence at last that in the struggle with this angel the great wrestler had conquered, even though thereafter he halted on his thigh.

Kretschmar told us a frightful story, impressing upon our minds an unforgettable and awful picture of the sacred trials of this struggle and the person of the afflicted artist. It was in high sum-

mer of the year 1819, at the time when Beethoven was working
on the *Missa solemnis* in the Haffner house at Mödling, in despair
because each movement turned out much longer than he had anticipated, so that the date of completion, March of the following
year, in which the installation of the Archduke Rudolf as Bishop
of Olmütz was to take place, could not possibly be kept to. It
was then that two friends and professional colleagues visited him
one afternoon and found an alarming state of things. That same
morning the master's two maids had made off, for the night before, at about one o'clock, there had been a furious quarrel, rousing the whole house from slumber. The master had wrought late
into the night, on the Credo, the Credo with the fugue, without
a thought of the meal that stood waiting on the hearth; while the
maids, yielding to nature, had at last fallen asleep. When the master, between twelve and one, demanded something to eat, he
found the maids asleep, the food burnt and dried up. He had burst
into the most violent rage, sparing the nightly rest of the house
the less because he himself could not hear the noise he made.
"Could you not watch one hour with me?" he kept thundering.
But it had been five or six hours, and the outraged maidservants
had fled at dawn, leaving such an ill-tempered master to himself,
so that he had had no midday meal either — nothing at all since
the middle-day before. Instead he worked in his room on the
Credo, the Credo with the fugue — the young ones heard him
through the closed door. The deaf man sang, he yelled and
stamped above the Credo — it was so moving and terrifying that
the blood froze in their veins as they listened. But as in their
great concern they were about to retreat, the door was jerked
open and Beethoven stood there — in what guise? The very most
frightful! With clothing dishevelled, his features so distorted as
to strike terror to the beholders; the eyes dazed, absent, listening,
all at once; he had stared at them, they got the impression that he
had come out of a life-and-death struggle with all the opposing
hosts of counterpoint. He had stammered something unintelligi-
ble, and then burst out complaining and scolding at the fine kind
of housekeeping he had, and how everybody had run away and
left him to starve. They had tried to pacify him, one of them
helped him to put his clothing to rights, the other ran to the inn
to get him some solid food. . . . Only three years later was the
Mass finished.

Thus Kretschmar, on "Beethoven and the Fugue"; and certainly it gave us matter for talk on the way home — ground too
for being silent together and for vague and silent reflection upon

the new, the far, and the great, which sometimes glibly running on, sometimes appallingly impeded, had penetrated into our souls. I say into ours, but it is of course only Adrian's that I have in mind. What I heard, what I took in, is quite irrelevant.

What principally impressed him, as I heard while we were walking home, and also next day in the school courtyard, was Kretschmar's distinction between cult epochs and cultural epochs, and his remark that the secularization of art, its separation from divine service, bore only a superficial and episodic character. The pupil of the upper school appeared to be struck by the thought, which the lecturer had not expressed at all but had kindled in him, that the separation of art from the liturgical whole, its liberation and elevation into the individual and culturally self-purposive, had laden it with an irrelevant solemnity, an absolute seriousness, a pathos of suffering, which was imaged in Beethoven's frightful apparition in the doorway, and which did not need to be its abiding destiny, its permanent intellectual constitution. Hearken to the youth! Still almost without any real or practical experience in the field of art, he speculated in the void and in precocious language on the probably imminent retreat from its present role to a more modest, happier one in the service of a higher union, which did not need to be, as it once was, the Church. What it would be he could not say. But that the cultural idea was a historically transitory phenomenon, that it could lose itself again in another one, that the future did not inevitably belong to it, this thought he had certainly singled out from Kretschmar's lecture.

"But the alternative," I threw in, "to culture is barbarism."

"Permit me," said he. "After all, barbarism is the opposite of culture only within the order of thought which it gives us. Outside of it the opposite may be something quite different or no opposite at all."

I imitated Luca Cimabue, saying: "Santa Maria!" and crossing myself. He gave his short laugh. Another time he asserted:

"For a cultural epoch, there seems to me to be a spot too much talk about culture in ours, don't you think? I'd like to know whether epochs that possessed culture knew the word at all, or used it. Naïveté, unconsciousness, taken-for-grantedness, seems to me to be the first criterion of the constitution to which we give this name. What we are losing is just this naïveté, and this lack, if one may so speak of it, protects us from many a colourful barbarism which altogether perfectly agreed with culture, even with very high culture. I mean: our stage is that of civilization — a very praiseworthy state no doubt, but also neither was there any doubt that we should have to become very much more barbaric to be capable of culture again. Technique and comfort — in that state one talks about culture but one has not got it. Will you prevent me from seeing in the homophone-melodic constitution of our music a condition of musical civilization — in contrast to the old contrapuntal polyphone culture?"

In such talk, with which he teased and irritated me, there was much that was merely imitative. But he had a way of adapting what he picked up and giving it a personal character which took from his adaptations anything that might sound ridiculous, if not everything boyish and derivative. He commented a good deal too — or we commented in lively exchange — on a lecture of Kretschmar's called "Music and the Eye" — likewise an offering which deserved a larger audience. As the title indicates, our lecturer spoke of his art in so far as — or rather, also as — it appeals to the sense of sight, which, so he developed his theme, it does in that one puts it down, through the notation, the tonal writing which — since the days of the old neumes, those arrangements of strokes and points, which had more or less indicated the flow of sound — had been practised with growing care and pains. His demonstration became very diverting, and likewise flattering, since it assumed in us a certain apprentice and brush-washer intimacy with music. Many a turn of phrase in musician's jargon came not from the acoustic but the visual, the note-picture: for instance, one speaks of *occhiali* because the broken drum-basses, half-notes that are coupled by a stroke through their necks, look like a pair of spectacles; or as one calls "cobbler's patches" (*rosalia*) certain cheap sequences one after another in stages at like intervals (he wrote examples for us on the blackboard). He spoke of the mere appearance of musical notation, and assured us that a knowledgeable person could get from one look at the notation a decisive impression of the spirit and value of a composition. Thus it had once happened to him that a colleague, visiting his room where an uninspired work submitted to him by a dilettante was spread out on the desk, had shouted: "Well, for heaven's sake, what sort of tripe is that you've got there?" On the other hand he sketched for us the enchanting pleasure which even the visual picture of a score by Mozart afforded to the practised eye; the clarity of the texture, the beautiful disposition of the instrumental groups, the ingenious and varied writing of the melodic line. A deaf man, he cried, quite ignorant of sound, could not but delight in these gracious visions. "To hear with eyes belongs to love's fine wit," he quoted from a Shakespeare sonnet, and asserted that in all time composers had secretly nested in their writings things that were meant more for the reading eye than for the ear. When, for instance, the Dutch masters of polyphony in their endless devices for the crossing of parts had so arranged them contrapuntally that one part had been like another when read backwards; that could not be perceived by the way they actually sounded, and he would wager that very few people would have detected the trick by ear, for it was intended rather for the eye of the guild. Thus Orlandus Lassus in the *Marriage at Cana* used six voices to represent the six water-jugs, which could be better perceived by seeing the music than by hearing it; and in the St. John Passion by Joachim von Burck "one of the servants," who gave Jesus a slap in the face, has only one note, but on the "*zween*" (two) in the next phrase, "with him two others," there are two.

He produced several such Pythagorean jests, intended more for the eye than the ear, which music had now and again been pleased to make and came out roundly with the statement that in the last analysis he ascribed to the art a certain inborn lack of the sensuous, yes an anti-sensuality, a sacret tendency to asceticism. Music was actually the most intellectual of all the arts, as was evident from the fact that in it, as in no other, form and content are interwoven and absolutely one and the same. We say of course that music "addresses itself to the ear"; but it does so only in a qualified way, only in so far, namely, as the hearing, like the other senses, is the deputy, the instrument, and the receiver of the mind. Perhaps, said Kretschmar, it was music's deepest wish not to be heard at all, nor even seen, nor yet felt; but only — if that were possible — in some Beyond, the other side of sense and sentiment, to be perceived and contemplated as pure mind, pure spirit. But bound as she was to the world of sense, music must ever strive after the strongest, yes, the most seductive sensuous realization: she is a Kundry, who wills not what she does and flings soft arms of lust round the neck of the fool. Her most powerful realization for the senses she finds in orchestral music, where through the ear she seems to affect all the senses with her opiate wand and to mingle the pleasures of the realm of sound with those of colour and scent. Here, rightly, she was the penitent in the garb of the seductress. But there was an instrument — that is to say, a musical means of realization — through which music, while becoming audible to the sense of hearing, did so in a half-unsensuous, an almost abstract way, audible, that is, in a way peculiarly suited to its intellectual nature. He meant the piano, an instrument that is not an instrument at all in the sense of the others, since all specialization is foreign to it. It can, indeed, like them, be used in a solo performance and as a medium of virtuosity; but that is the exceptional case and speaking very precisely a misuse. The piano, properly speaking, is the direct and sovereign representative of music itself in its intellectuality, and for that reason one must learn it. But piano lessons should not be — or not essentially and not first and last — lessons in a special ability, but lessons in m-m —

"Music!" cried a voice from the tiny audience, for the speaker could simply not get the word out, often as he had used it before, but kept on mumbling the m.

"Yes, of course," said he, released and relieved. Took a swallow of water and went his way.

But perhaps I may be pardoned for letting him appear once more. For I am concerned with a fourth lecture which he gave us, and I would have left out one of the others if necessary, rather than this, since no other — not to speak of myself — made such a deep impression on Adrian.

I cannot recollect its exact title. It was "The Elemental in Music" or "Music and the Elemental" or "The Elements of Music" or something like that. In any case the elemental, the primitive, the primeval beginning, played the chief role in it, as well as the idea that among all the arts it was precisely music that — whatever the richly complicated and finely developed and marvellous structure she had developed into in the course of the centuries — had never got rid of a religious attitude towards her own beginnings; a pious proneness to call them up in solemn invocation — in short, to celebrate her elements. She thus celebrates, he said, her cosmic aptitude for allegory; for those elements were, as it were, the first and simplest materials of the world, a parallelism of which a philosophizing artist of a day not long gone by — it was Wagner again of whom he spoke — had shrewdly, perhaps with somewhat too mechanical, too ingenious cleverness, made use, in that in his cosmogonic myth of the *Ring* he made the basic elements of music one with those of the world. To him the beginning of all things had its music: the music of the beginning was that, and also the beginning of music, the E-flat major triad of the flowing depths of the Rhine, the seven primitive chords, out of which, as though out of blocks of Cyclopean masonry, primeval stone, the "Götterburg" arose. Surpassingly brilliant, in the grand style, he presented the mythology of music at the same time with that of the world; in that he bound the music to the things and made them express themselves in music, he created an apparatus of sen-

suous simultaneity — most magnificent and heavy with meaning,
if a bit too clever after all, in comparison with certain revelations
of the elemental in the art of the pure musicians, Beethoven and
Bach; for example, in the prelude to the cello suite of the latter —
also an E-flat major piece, built up in primitive triads. And he
spoke of Anton Bruckner, who loved to refresh himself at the organ or piano by the simple succession of triads. "Is there anything
more heartfelt, more glorious," he would cry, "than such a progression of mere triads? Is it not like a purifying bath for the
mind?" This saying too, Kretschmar thought, was a piece of evidence worth thinking about, for the tendency of music to plunge
back into the elemental and admire herself in her primitive beginnings.

Yes, the lecturer cried, it lay in the very nature of this singular
art that it was at any moment capable of beginning at the beginning, of discovering itself afresh out of nothing, bare of all knowledge of its past cultural history, and of creating anew. It would
then run through the same primitive stages as in its historical beginnings and could on one short course, apart from the main mas-
sif of its development, alone and unheeded by the world, reach
most extraordinary and singular heights. And now he told us a
story which in the most fantastic and suggestive way fitted into
the frame of his present theme.

At about the middle of the eighteenth century there had flourished in his native home in Pennsylvania a German community of
pious folk belonging to the Baptist sect. Their leading and spiritually most respected members lived celibate lives and had therefore been honoured with the name of Solitary Brethren and Sisters; but the majority of them reconciled with the married state
an exemplarily pure and godly manner of life, strictly regulated,
hard-working and dietetically sound, full of sacrifice and self-
discipline. Their settlements had been two: one called Ephrata, in
Lancaster County, the other in Franklin County, called Snowhill; and they had all looked up reverently to their head shepherd
and spiritual father, the founder of the sect, a man named Beissel,
in whose character fervent devotion to God mingled with the
qualities of leadership, and fanatic religiosity with a lively and
blunt-spoken energy.

Johann Conrad Beissel had been born of very poor parents at
Eberbach in the Palatinate and early orphaned. He had learned
the baker's trade and as a roving journeyman had made connections with Pietists and devotees of the Baptist confession, which
had awakened in him slumbering inclinations towards an explicit

service of the truth and a freely arising conviction of God. All this had brought him dangerously near to a sphere regarded in his country as heretical, and the thirty-year-old man decided to flee from the intolerance of the Old World and emigrate to America. There, in various places, in Germantown and Conestoga, he worked for a while as a weaver. Then a fresh impulse of religious devotion came over him and he had followed his inward voice, leading as a hermit in the wilderness an entirely solitary and meagre life, fixed only upon God. But as it will happen that flight from mankind sometimes only involves the more with humanity the man who flees, so Beissel had soon seen himself surrounded by a troop of admiring followers and imitators of his way of life, and instead of being free of the world, he had unexpectedly become, in the turning of a hand, the head of a community, which quickly developed into an independent sect, the Seventh-Day Anabaptists. He commanded them the more absolutely in that, so far as he knew, he had never sought the leadership, but was rather called to it against his intention and desire.

Beissel had never enjoyed any education worth mentioning; but in his awakened state he had mastered by himself the skills of reading and writing, and as his mind surged like the sea, tumultuous with mystical feelings and ideas, the result was that he filled his office chiefly as writer and poet and fed the souls of his flock: a stream of didactic prose and religious songs poured from his pen to the edification of the brethren in their silent hours and to the enrichment of their services. His style was high-flown and cryptic, laden with metaphor, obscure Scriptural allusions, and a sort of erotic symbolism. A tract on the Sabbath, *Mystyrion Anomalias*, and a collection of ninety-nine *Mystical and Very Secret Sayings* were the beginning. A series of hymns followed on, which were to be sung to well-known European choral melodies, and appeared in print under such titles as *Songs for God's Love and Praise, Jacob's Place of Struggle and Elevation, Zionist Hill of Incense*. It was these little collections that a few years later, enlarged and improved, became the official song-book of the Seventh-Day Baptists of Ephrata, with the sweetly mournful title "Song of the Lonely and Forsaken Turtle Dove, the Christian Church." Printed and reprinted, further enriched by the emulative members of the sect, single and married, men and even more women, the standard work changed its title and also appeared once as *Miracle Play in Paradise*. It finally contained not less than seven hundred and seventy hymns, among them some with an enormous number of stanzas.

The songs were meant to be sung, but they lacked music. They were new texts to old tunes and were so used for years by the community. But now a new inspiration visited Johann Conrad Beissel. The spirit commanded him to take to himself in addition to the role of poet and prophet that of composer.

There had been a young man staying at Ephrata, a young adept of the art of music, who held a singing-class; Beissel loved to attend and listen to the instruction. He must thus have made the discovery that music afforded possibilities for the extension and realization of the kingdom of the spirit, in a way of which young Herr Ludwig never dreamed. The extraordinary man's resolve was swiftly formed. No longer of the youngest, already far on in the fifties, he applied himself to work out a musical theory of his own, suited to his special requirements. He put the singing-teacher aside and took things firmly in his own hands — with such success that before long he had made music the most important element in the religious life of the community.

Most of the chorals, which had come over from Europe, seemed to him much too forced, complicated, and artificial to serve for his flock. He wanted to do something new and better and to inaugurate a music better answering to the simplicity of their souls and enabling them by practice to bring it to their own simple perfection. An ingenious and practical theory of melody was swiftly and boldly resolved on. He decreed that there should be "masters" and "servants" in every scale. Having decided to regard the common chord as the melodic centre of any given key, he called "masters" the notes belonging to this chord, and the rest of the scale "servants." And those syllables of a text upon which the accent lay had always to be presented by a "master," the unaccented by a "servant."

As for the harmony, he made use of a summary procedure. He made chord-tables for all possible keys, with the help of which anybody could write out his tunes comfortably enough, in four or five parts; and thus he caused a perfect rage for composition in the community. Soon there was no longer a single Seventh-Day Baptist, whether male or female, who, thus assisted, had not imitated the master and composed music.

Rhythm was now the part of theory which remained to be dealt with by this redoubtable man. He accomplished it with consummate success. He painstakingly followed with the music the cadence of the words, simply by providing the accented syllables with longer notes, and giving the unaccented shorter ones. To establish a fixed relation between the values of the notes did not

ı; and just for that reason he preserved considerable
: his metre. Like practically all the music of his time
:n in recurrent metres of like length — that is to say,
: he either did not know this or did not trouble about
it. ɪʜᴦ .g..ɔrance or unconcern, however, was above all else to
his advantage; for the free, fluctuating rhythm made some of his
compositions, particularly his setting of prose, extraordinarily
effective.

This man cultivated the field of music, once he had entered it,
with the same persistence with which he had pursued all of his
other aims. He put together his thoughts on theory and published
them as a preface to the book of the *Turtle Dove*. In uninter-
rupted application he provided with musical settings all the poems
in the *Mount of Incense*, some of them with two or three, and set
to music all the hymns he had himself ever written, as well as a
great many by his pupils. Not satisfied with that, he wrote a number of more extended chorals, with texts taken direct from the
Bible. It seemed as though he was about to set to music according to his own receipt the whole of the Scriptures; certainly he
was the man to conceive such a plan. If it did not come to that, it
was only because he had to devote a large part of his time to the
performance of what he had done, the training in execution and
instruction in singing — and in this field he now achieved the simply extraordinary.

The music of Ephrata, Kretschmar told us, was too unusual,
too amazing and arbitrary, to be taken over by the world outside,
and hence it had sunk into practical oblivion when the sect of the
German Seventh-Day Baptists ceased to flourish. But a faint legend
had persisted down the years, sufficient in fact to make known
how utterly peculiar and moving it had been. The tones coming
from the choir had resembled delicate instrumental music and
evoked an impression of heavenly mildness and piety in the hearer.
The whole had been sung falsetto, and the singers had scarcely
opened their mouths or moved their lips — with wonderful acoustic effect. The sound, that is, had thus been thrown up to the
rather low ceiling of the hall, and it had seemed as though the
notes, unlike any familiar to man, and in any case unlike any
known church music, floated down thence and hovered angeli-
cally above the heads of the assemblage.

His own father, Kretschmar said, had often heard these sounds
as a young man, and in his old age, when he talked to his family
about it, his eyes had always filled with tears. He had spent a summer near Snowhill and on a Friday evening, the beginning of the

Sabbath, had once ridden over as an onlooker at the house of worship of those pious folk. After that he had gone again and again: every Friday, as the sun set, driven by a resistless urge, he had saddled his horse and ridden the three miles to listen. It had been quite indescribable, not to be compared with anything in this world. He had, so the elder Kretschmar had said, sat in English, French, and Italian opera houses; that had been music for the ear, but Beissel's rang deep down into the soul and was nothing more nor less than a foretaste of heaven.

"A great art," so our reporter said in closing, "which, as it were aloof from time and time's great course, could develop a little private history of this kind, and by forgotten side-paths lead to such exceptional beatitudes."

I recall as though it were yesterday how I went home with Adrian after this lecture. Although we did not talk much, we were unwilling to separate; and from his uncle's house, whither I accompanied him, he went back with me to the shop, and then I back with him to Parochialstrasse. Though of course we often did that. We both made merry over the man Beissel, this backwoods dictator with his droll thirst for action, and agreed that his music reform reminded us very much of the passage in Terence: "to behave stupidly with reason." But Adrian's attitude to the curious phenomenon differed from mine in what was after all so distinctive a way that it soon occupied me more than the subject itself. I mean that even while he mocked he set store by preserving the right to appreciate: set store by the right, not to say the privilege of keeping a distance, which includes in itself the possibility of good-natured acceptance, of conditioned agreement, half-admiration, along with the mockery and laughter. Quite generally this claim to ironic remoteness, to an objectivity which surely is paying less honour to the thing than to the freedom of the person, has always seemed to me a sign of uncommon arrogance. In so young a person as Adrian then was, the presumption of this attitude, it must be admitted, is disquieting; it was calculated to cause one concern for the health of his soul. Of course it is also very impressive to a companion with a simpler mental constitution, and since I loved him, I loved his arrogance as well — perhaps I loved him for its sake. Yes, that is how it was: this arrogance was the chief motive of the fearful love which all my life I cherished for him in my heart.

"Leave me alone," said he, as with our hands in our overcoat pockets we went to and fro between our two dwellings, in the wintry mist that wrapped the gas-lamps, "leave me in peace with my old codger, I can do with him. At least he had a sense of order, and even a silly order is better than none at all."

"Surely," I answered him, "you won't defend such a ridiculous and dogmatic arrangement, such childish rationalism as this invention of masters and servants. Imagine how these Beissel hymns must have sounded, in which every accented syllable had to have one note of the chord fall on it!"

"In any case not sentimental," he responded, "rather rigidly conforming to the law, and that I approve. You can console yourself that there was plenty of play for the fancy you put high above the law, in the free use of the servant notes."

He had to laugh at the word, bent over as he walked, and laughed down upon the wet pavement.

"Funny, it's very funny," he said. "But one thing you will admit. Law, every law, has a chilling effect, and music has so much warmth anyhow, stable warmth, cow warmth, I'd like to say, that she can stand all sorts of regulated cooling off—she has even asked for it."

"There may be some truth in that," I admitted. "But our Beissel isn't after all any very striking example of it. You forget that his rhythm, quite unregulated and abandoned to feeling, at least balanced the rigidity of his melody. And then he invented a singing style for himself—up to the ceiling and then floating down in a seraphic falsetto—it must have been simply ravishing and certainly gave back to music all the bovine warmth that it had previously taken away through the pedantic cooling off."

"Ascetic, Kretschmar would say," he answered, "the ascetic cooling off. In that Father Beissel was very genuine. Music always does penance in advance for her retreat into the sensual. The old Dutchmen made her do the rummest sort of tricks, to the glory of God; and it went harder and harder on her from all one hears, with no sense appeal, excogitated by pure calculation. But then they had these penitential practices sung, delivered over to the sounding breath of the human voice, which is certainly the most stable-warm imaginable thing in the world of sound. . . ."

"You think so?"

"Why not? No unorganic instrumental sound can be compared with it. Abstract it may be, the human voice — the abstract human being, if you like. But that is a kind of abstraction more like that of the naked body — it is after all more a pudendum." I was silent, confounded. My thoughts took me far back in our, in his past.

"There you have it," said he, "your music." I was annoyed at the way he put it, it sounded like shoving music off on me, as though it were more my affair than his. "There you have the whole thing, she was always like that. Her strictness, or whatever you like to call the moralism of her form, must stand for an excuse for the ravishments of her actual sounds."

For a moment I felt myself the older, more mature.

"A gift of life like music," I responded, "not to say a gift of God, one ought not to explain by mocking antinomies, which only bear witness to the fullness of her nature. One must love her."

"Do you consider love the strongest emotion?" he asked.

"Do you know a stronger?"

"Yes, interest."

"By which you presumably mean a love from which the animal warmth has been withdrawn."

"Let us agree on the definition!" he laughed. "Good night!"

We had got back to the Leverkühn house, and he opened his door.

CHAPTER IX

I WILL not look back, I will take care not to count the pages I have covered between the last Roman numeral and this one I have just written down. The evil — in any case quite unanticipated — has come to pass and it would be useless to expend myself in excuses or self-accusations. The question whether I might and should have avoided it by giving a chapter to each one of Kretschmar's lectures I must answer in the negative. Each separate division of a work needs a certain body, a definite volume sufficient to add to the significance of the whole, and this weight, this volume of significance, pertains to the lectures only collectively (in so far as I have reported them) and not to the single ones.

But why do I ascribe such significance to them? Why have I seen myself induced to reproduce them in such detail? I give the reason, not for the first time. It is simply this: that Adrian heard these things then, they challenged his intelligence, made their deposit in the vessel of his feelings, and gave matter to feed or to stimulate his fancy. And for the fancy, food and stimulant are one and the same. The reader must perforce be made a witness of the process; since no biography, no depiction of the growth and development of an intellectual life, could properly be written without taking its subject back to the pupil stage, to the period of his beginnings in life and art, when he listened, learned, divined, gazed and ranged now afar, now close at hand. As for music in particular, what I want and strive to do is to make the reader see it as Adrian did; to bring him in touch with music, precisely as it happened to my departed friend. And to that end everything his teacher said seems to me not only not a negligible means but even an indispensable one.

And so, half jestingly, I would address those who in that last monstrous chapter have been guilty of some skipping: I would remind them of how Laurence Sterne once dealt with an imaginary listener who betrayed that she had not always been paying attention. The author sent her back to an earlier chapter to fill in the gaps in her knowledge. After having informed herself, the lady rejoins the group of listeners and is given a hearty welcome.

The passage came to my mind because Adrian as a top-form student, at a time when I had already left for the University of Giessen, studied English outside the school courses, and after all outside the humanistic curriculum, under the influence of Wendell Kretschmar. He read Sterne with great pleasure. Even more enthusiastically he read Shakespeare, of whom the organist was a close student and passionate admirer. Shakespeare and Beethoven together formed in Kretschmar's intellectual heaven a twin constellation outshining all else, and he dearly loved calling his pupil's attention to remarkable similarities and correspondences in the creative principles and methods of the two giants — an instance of the stutterer's far-reaching influence on my friend's education, quite aside from the piano lessons. As a music-teacher, of course, he had to give Adrian the childish beginnings; but on the other hand, and in strange contrast, he gave him at the same time and almost in passing his earliest contact with greatness. He opened to him the ample page of world literature; whetting his appetite by small foretastes, he lured him into the broad expanses of the Russian, English, and French novel; stimulated him to read the lyrical poems of Shelley and Keats, Hölderlin and Novalis; gave him Manzoni and Goethe, Schopenhauer and Meister Eckehart. Through Adrian's letters, as well as by word of mouth when I came home in the holidays, I shared in these conquests, and I will not deny that sometimes, despite my knowledge of his facility, I was concerned for his strength. After all, these acquirements were premature, they must have burdened his young system, in addition to the preparations for his finals. About the latter, indeed, he spoke contemptuously. He often looked pale, and that not only on days when the hereditary migraine laid him low. Obviously he had too little sleep, for his reading was done in the night hours. I did not refrain from confessing my concern to Kretschmar and asking him if he did not see in Adrian, as I did, a nature that in the intellectual field should rather be held back than urged forwards. But the musician, although so much older than I, proved to be a thoroughgoing partisan of impatient youth avid of knowledge, unsparing of his strength. Indeed, the man showed in general a certain ideal harshness and indifference to the body and its "health," which he considered a right philistine, not to say cowardly value.

"Yes, my dear friend," said he (I omit the hitches which detracted from his impressiveness), "if it is healthiness you are after

— well, with mind and art it has not got much to do, it even in a sort of way opposes them, and anyhow they have never troubled much about each other. To play the family doctor who warns against premature reading because it was always premature to him all his life — I'm no good for that. And besides, I find nothing more tactless and barbarous than nailing a gifted youth down to his 'immaturity' and telling him in every other word: 'That is nothing for you yet.' Let him judge for himself! Let him see how he comes on! That the time will be long to him till he can crawl out of the shell of this sleepy old place is only too easy to understand."

So there I had it — and Kaisersaschern too. I was vexed, for the standards of the family doctor were certainly not mine either. And besides that, I saw not only that Kretschmar was not content to be a piano-teacher and trainer in a special technique, but that music itself, the goal of his teaching, if it were pursued one-sidedly and without connection with other fields of form, thought, and culture, seemed to him a stunting specialization, humanly speaking. As a matter of fact, from all that I heard from Adrian, the lesson-hours in Kretschmar's mediæval quarters in the Cathedral were a good half of the time taken up with talks on philosophy and poetry. Despite that, so long as I was still in school with him, I could follow his progress literally from day to day. His self-won familiarity with keyboard and keys accelerated of course the first steps. He practised conscientiously, but a lesson-book, so far as I know, was not used; instead Kretschmar simply let him play set chorals and — however strange they sounded on the piano — four-part psalms by Palestrina consisting of pure chords with some harmonic tensions and cadenzas; then somewhat later little preludes and fuguettes of Bach, two-part inventions also by him, the Sonata Facile of Mozart, one-movement sonatas by Scarlatti. Kretschmar did not hesitate to write little pieces himself, marches and dances, partly for playing solo, partly as duets in which the musical burden lay in the second part, while the first, for the pupil, was kept quite simple so that he had the satisfaction of sharing in the performance of a production which as a whole moved on a higher plane of technical competence than his own.

All in all it was a little like the education of a young prince. I remember that I used the word teasingly in talk with my friend; remember too how he turned away with the odd short laugh peculiar to him, as though he would have pretended not to hear. No doubt he was grateful to his teacher for a kind of instruction

taking cognizance of the pupil's general mental development,
which did not belong at the childish stage of his present and
rather tardy musical beginnings. Kretschmar was not unwilling,
in fact he rather preferred, to have this youth, plainly vibrating
with ability, hurry on ahead in music too and concern himself
with matters that a more pedantic mentor would have forbidden
as time-wasting. For Adrian scarcely knew the notes when he began to write and experiment with chords on paper. The mania he
then developed of thinking out musical problems, which he solved
like chess problems, might make one fear lest he thought this con-
triving and mastering of technical difficulties was already composition. He spent hours in linking up, in the smallest possible
space, chords that together contained all the notes of the chromatic scale, without their being chromatically side-slipped and
without producing harshnesses in their progression. Or he amused
himself by writing very sharp dissonances and finding all possible
resolutions for them, which, however, just because the chord contained so many discordant notes, had nothing to do with each
other, so that that acid chord, like a magic formula, created relations between the remotest chords and keys.

One day the beginner in the theory of harmony brought to
Kretschmar, to the latter's amusement, the discovery he had himself made of double counterpoint. That is, he gave to his teacher
to read two parts running simultaneously, each of which could
form the upper or the lower part and thus were interchangeable.
"If you have got the triple counterpoint," said Kretschmar, "keep
it to yourself. I don't want to hear about your rashness."

He kept much to himself, sharing his speculations with me only
in moments of relaxation, and then especially his absorption in
the problem of unity, interchangeability, identity of horizontal
and vertical writing. He soon possessed what was in my eyes an
uncanny knack of inventing melodic lines which could be set
against each other simultaneously, and whose notes telescoped into
complex harmonies — and, on the other hand, he invented chords
consisting of note-clusters that were to be projected into the
melodic horizontal.

In the schoolyard, between a Greek and a trigonometry class,
leaning on the ledge of the glazed brick wall, he would talk to me
about these magic diversions of his idle time: of the transformation of the horizontal interval into the chord, which occupied
him as nothing else did; that is, of the horizontal into the vertical,
the successive into the simultaneous. Simultaneity, he asserted, was
here the primary element; for the note, with its more immediate

and more distant harmonics, was a chord in itself, and the scale only the analytical unfolding of the chord into the horizontal row.

"But with the real chord, consisting of several notes, it is after all something different. A chord is meant to be followed up by another, and so soon as you do it, carry it over into another, each one of its component notes becomes a voice-part. I find that in a chordal combination of notes one should never see anything but the result of the movement of voices and do honour to the part as implied in the single chord-note — but not honour the chord as such, rather despise it as subjective and arbitrary, so long as it cannot prove itself to be the result of part-writing. The chord is no harmonic narcotic but polyphony in itself, and the notes that form it are parts. But I assert they are that the more, and the polyphonic character of the chords is the more pronounced, the more dissonant it is. The degree of dissonance is the measure of its polyphonic value. The more discordant a chord is, the more notes it contains contrasting and conflicting with each other, the more polyphonic it is, and the more markedly every single note bears the stamp of the part already in the simultaneous sound-combination."

I looked at him for some time, nodding my head with half-humorous fatalism.

"Pretty good! You're a wonder!" said I, finally.

"You mean that for me?" he said, turning away as he so often did. "But I am talking about music, not about myself — some little difference."

He insisted upon this distinction, speaking of music always as a strange power, a phenomenon amazing but not touching him personally, talking about it with critical detachment and a certain condescension; but he talked about it, and had more to say, because in these years, the last I spent with him at school, and my first semesters as university student, his knowledge of the world's musical literature rapidly broadened, so that soon, indeed, the difference between what he knew and what he could do lent to the distinction he emphasized a sort of strikingness. For while as pianist he was practising such things as Schumann's *Kinderscenen* and the two little sonatas of Beethoven, Opus 45, and as a music pupil dutifully harmonizing choral themes so that the theme came to lie in the centre of the chord; he was at the same time, and with an excessive, even headlong acceleration of pace, gaining a comprehensive view, incoherent indeed, but with extensive detail, of preclassic, classic, romantic, late-romantic, and modern production, all this of course through Kretschmar, who was himself too much in love with everything — just everything — made of notes not to burn to introduce to a pupil who knew how to listen as Adrian did this world of shapes and figures, inexhaustibly rich in styles, national characteristics, traditional values, and charms of personality, historic and individual variations of the ideal beauty.

I need scarcely say that opportunities to listen to music were, for a citizen of Kaisersaschern, extraordinarily few. Aside from the evenings of chamber music at Nikolaus Leverkühn's and the organ concerts in the Cathedral we had almost no opportunity at all, for seldom indeed would a touring virtuoso or an orchestra with its conductor from some other city penetrate into our little town. Now Kretschmar had flung himself into the breach, and with his vivid recitals had fed, if only temporarily and by suggestion, a partly unconscious, partly unconfessed yearning of my young friend for culture. Indeed, the stream was so copious that I might almost speak of a cataract of musical experience flooding his youthful receptivity. After that came years of disavowal and dissimulation, when he had far less music than at the time I speak of, although the circumstances were much more favourable.

It began, very naturally, with the teacher demonstrating for him the structure of the sonata in works by Clementi, Mozart, and Haydn. But before long he went on to the orchestra sonata, the symphony, and performed (in the piano-abstraction) to the watching listener sitting with drawn brows and parted lips the various chronological and personal variations of this richest manifestation of creative musical art, speaking most variedly to senses and mind. He played instrumental works by Brahms and Bruckner, Schubert, Robert Schumann; then by the later and the latest, Tchaikovsky, Borodin, and Rimsky-Korsakov; by Anton Dvořák, Berlioz, César Franck, and Chabrier, constantly challenging his pupil's power of imagination with loud explanations, to give orchestral body and soul to the insubstantial piano version: "Cello cantilena! You must think of that as drawn out. Bassoon solo! And the flutes give the flourishes to it! Drum-roll! There are the trombones! Here the violins come in! Follow it on the score! I have to leave out the little fanfare with the trumpets, I have only two hands!"

He did what he could with those two hands, often adding his voice, which crowed and cracked, but never badly; no, it was all even ravishing, by reason of its fervid musicality and enthusiastic rightness of expression.

Dashing from one thing to another, or linking them together, he heaped them up — first because he had endless things in his head, and one thing led on to the next; but in particular because it was his passion to make comparisons and discover relations, display influences, lay bare the interwoven connections of culture. It pleased him to sharpen his young pupil's sense; hours on hours he spent showing him how French had influenced Russians, Italians Germans, Germans French. He showed him what Gounod had from Schumann, what César Franck from Liszt, how Debussy based on Mussorgsky and where D'Indy and Chabrier wagnerized. To show how sheer contemporaneity set up mutual relations between such different natures as Tchaikovsky and Brahms, that too belonged to these lesson-hours. He played him bits from the works of the one that might well be by the other. In Brahms, whom he put very high, he demonstrated the reference to the archaic, to old church modes, and how this ascetic element in him became the means of achieving a sombre richness and gloomy grandeur. He told his pupil to note how, in this kind of romanticism, with a noticeable reference to Bach, the polyphonic principle seriously confronted the harmonic colour and made it retreat. But true independence of parts, true polyphony, that was not; and had already not been with Bach, in whom one does indeed find the contrapuntal devices peculiar to the vocal polyphony of an older period, but who by blood had been a harmonist and nothing else — already as the man to use the tempered scale, this premise for all the later art of modulation, and his harmonic counterpoint had at bottom no more to do with the old vocal polyphony than Handel's harmonic alfresco style.

It was precisely such remarks as these for which Adrian's ear was so peculiarly keen. In conversations with me he went into it.

"Bach's problem," he said, "was this: how is one to write pregnant polyphony in a harmonic style? With the moderns the question presents itself somewhat differently. Rather it is: how is one to write a harmonic style that has the appearance of polyphony? Remarkable, it looks like bad conscience — the bad conscience of homophonic music in face of polyphony."

It goes without saying that by so much listening he was led to the enthusiastic reading of scores, partly from his teacher's, partly from the town library. I often found him at such studies and at written instrumentation. For information about the compass of the individual orchestral instruments (instruction which the instrument-dealer's foster-son hardly needed) also flowed into the lessons, and Kretschmar had begun giving him to orchestrate short classical pieces, single piano movements from Schubert and Beethoven, also the piano accompaniments of songs: studies whose weaknesses and slips he then pointed out and corrected. This was the beginning of Adrian's acquaintance with the glorious period of the German lied, which after fairly jejune beginnings bursts out wonderfully in Schubert, to celebrate its incomparable national triumphs with Schumann, Robert Franz, Brahms, Hugo Wolf, and Mahler. A glorious conjunction! I was happy to be present and share all this. A jewel and miracle like Schumann's *Mondnacht*, with the lovely, delicate seconds in the accompaniment! Other Eichendorff compositions of the same master, like that piece invoking all the romantic perils and threats to the soul, which ends with the uncannily moral warning: "*Hüte dich, sei wach und munter!*" a masterly invention like Mendelssohn's *Auf Flügeln des Gesanges*, the inspiration of a musician whom Adrian used to extol very highly to me, calling him the most gifted of all in his use of different metres — ah, what fruitful topics for discussion! In Brahms as a song-writer my friend valued above all else the peculiarly new and austere style in the *Four Serious Songs* written for Bible texts, especially the religious beauty of "*O Tod, wie bitter bist Du!*" But Schubert's always twilit genius, death-touched, he liked above all to seek where he lifts to the loftiest expression a certain only half-defined but inescapable destiny of solitude, as in the grandly self-tormenting "*Ich komme vom Gebirge her*" from the Smith of Lübeck and that "*Was vermeid' ich denn die Wege, wo die andern Wandrer gehn?*" from the *Winterreise*, with the perfectly heart-breaking stanza beginning:

> *Hab' ja doch nichts begangen*
> *Dass ich Menschen sollte scheu'n.*

These words, and the following:

> *Welch ein törichtes Verlangen*
> *Treibt mich in die Wüstenei'n?*

I have heard him speak to himself, indicating the musical phrasing, and to my unforgettable amazement I saw the tears spring to his eyes.

Of course his instrumental writing suffered from a lack of experience through actual hearing and Kretschmar set himself to remedy the defect. In the Michaelmas and Christmas holidays they went (with Uncle Niko's permission) to operas and concerts in near-by cities: Merseburg, Erfurt, even Weimar, in order that he might realize in actual sound what he had received in the abstract and seen at most on paper. Thus he could take in the childlike solemnity and esoteric mystery of *The Magic Flute*, the for-

midable charm of *Figaro*, the dæmony of the low clarinets in
Weber's glorious transmuted operetta *Der Freischütz;* similar figures of painful and sombre solitude like those of *Hans Heiling*
and *The Flying Dutchman;* finally the lofty humanity and broth-
erhood of *Fidelio*, with the great Overture in C, played before
the final scene. This last, of course, was the most impressive, the
most absorbing, of all that his young receptive mind came in contact with. For days after that evening he kept the score of No. 3
by him and read it constantly.

"My friend," said he, "probably they haven't been waiting for
me to say so; but that is a perfect piece of music. Classicism —
yes, it isn't sophisticated at all, but it is great. I don't say: *for* it is
great, because there is such a thing as sophisticated greatness; but
this is at bottom much more intimate. Tell me, what do you think
about greatness? I find there is something uncomfortable about
facing it eye to eye, it is a test of courage — can one really look
it in the eye? You can't stand it, you give way. Let me tell you,
I incline more and more to the admission that there is something
very odd indeed about this music of yours. A manifestation of the
highest energy — not at all abstract, but without an object, energy
in a void, in pure ether — where else in the universe does such a
thing appear? We Germans have taken over from philosophy the
expression 'in itself,' we use it every day without much idea of
the metaphysical. But here you have it, such music is energy itself, yet not as idea, rather in its actuality. I call your attention
to the fact that that is almost the definition of God. *Imitatio Dei*
— I am surprised that it is not forbidden. Perhaps it is. Anyhow
that is a very nice point — in more than one sense of the word.
Look: the most powerful, most varied, most dramatic succession
of events and activities, but only in time, consisting only of time
articulated, filled up, organized — and all at once almost thrust
into the concrete exigencies of the plot by the repeated trumpet-
signals from without. All that is most elegantly and grandly conceived, kept witty and rather objective, even in the high spots —
neither scintillating nor all too splendid, nor even very exciting in
colour, only just masterly beyond words. How all that is brought
in and transformed and put before you, how one theme is led up
to and another left behind, taken apart; yet in the process something new is getting ready, so that there is no empty or feeble
passage; how flexibly the rhythm changes, a climax approaches,
takes in tributaries from all sides, swells like a rising torrent, bursts
out in roaring triumph, triumph itself, triumph 'in and for itself'
— I do not like to call it beautiful, the word 'beauty' has always

been half offensive to me, it has such a silly face, and people feel wanton and corrupt when they say it. But it is good, good in the extreme, it could not be better, perhaps it ought not to be better. . . ."

Thus Adrian. It was a way of talking that in its mixture of intellectual self-criticism and slight feverishness affected me as indescribably moving. Moving because he felt the feverishness in it and found it offensive, was unpleasantly aware of the tremble in his still boyishly thin voice and turned away, flushing.

A great advance in musical knowledge and enthusiastic participation took place at that time in his life, only to get no further for years — at least to all appearance.

CHAPTER X

DURING his last year at school, in the highest form, Leverkühn in addition to everything else began the study of Hebrew, which was not obligatory and which I did not pursue. Thus he betrayed the direction of his plans for a profession: it "turned out" (I purposely repeat the expression I used to describe the moment when by a chance word he betrayed his religious inner life), it turned out that he intended to study theology. The approach of the final examinations demanded a decision, the election of a faculty, and he declared his choice: declared it in answer to his uncle, who raised his brows and said "Bravo!" — declared it of his own accord to his parents at Buchel, who received the news even better pleased; and had already told me earlier, confessing at the same time that he did not envisage his choice as preparation for taking a parish and assuming a cure of souls, but as an academic career.

That should have been a kind of reassurance to me; indeed, it was that, for it went against me to imagine him as a candidate for the office of preacher or pastor, or even as councillor of the consistory or other high office. If only he had been a Catholic, as we were! His easily imaginable progress up the stages of the hierarchy, to a prince of the Church, would have seemed to me a happier, more fitting prospect. But the very resolve was itself something of a shock and I think I changed colour when he told me. Why? I could hardly have said what he should else have chosen. Actually, to me there was nothing good enough for him; that is, the civilian, empirical side of any calling did not seem to me worthy of him, and I should have looked round in vain for another in the practical, professional performance of which I could properly imagine him. The ambition I cherished on his account was absolute. And yet a shudder went through me when I divined — divined very clearly — that he had made his choice out of arrogance.

We had on occasion agreed, of course, or more correctly we had both espoused the general view, that philosophy was the queen of the sciences. Among them, we had affirmed, she took a

place like that of the organ among instruments: she afforded a
survey; she combined them intellectually, she ordered and refined
the issues of all the fields of research into a universal picture, an
overriding and decisive synthesis comprehending the meaning of
life, a scrutinizing determination of man's place in the cosmos. My
consideration of my friend's future, my thoughts about a "profession" for him, had always led me to similar conclusions. The
many-sidedness of his activities, while they made me anxious for
his health, his thirst for experience, accompanied as it was by a
critical attitude, justified such dreams. The most universal field,
the life of a masterly polyhistor and philosopher seemed to me
just right for him — and further my powers of imagination had not
brought me. Now I was to learn that he on his side had privately
gone much further. Without giving a sign — for he expressed his
decision in very quiet, unassuming words — he had outbid and put
to shame the ambitions of his friend for him.

But there is, if you like, a discipline in which Queen Philosophy
becomes the servant, the ancillary science, academically speaking
a subsidiary branch of another; and that other is theology. Where
love of wisdom lifts itself to contemplation of the highest essence,
the source of being, the study of God and the things of God,
there, one might say, is the peak of scientific dignity, the highest
and noblest sphere of knowledge, the apex of all thinking; to the
inspired intellect its most exalted goal is here set. The most exalted because here the profane sciences, for instance my own,
philology, as well as history and the rest, become a mere tool for
the service of knowledge of the divine — and again, the goal to be
pursued in the profoundest humility, because in the words of the
Scriptures it is "higher than all reason" and the human spirit
thereby enters into a more pious, trusting bond than that which
any other of the learned professions lays upon him.

This went through my mind when Adrian told me of his decision. If he had made it out of an instinct of spiritual self-discipline,
out of the wish to hedge in by a religious profession that cool and
ubiquitous intellect of his, which grasped everything so easily and
was so spoilt by its own superiority — then I should have agreed.
It would not only have tranquillized my indefinite concern, always present, albeit silently; and moreover it would have touched
me deeply, for the *sacrificium intellectus*, which of necessity contemplation and knowledge of the other world carries with it,
must be esteemed the more highly, the more powerful the intellect that makes it. But I did not at bottom believe in my friend's
humility. I believed in his pride, of which for my part I was proud

too, and could not really doubt that it was the source of his decision. Hence the mixture of joy and concern, the grounds of the
shudder that went through me.

He saw my conflict and seemed to ascribe it to a third person,
his music-teacher.

"You mean, of course, Kretschmar will be disappointed," he
said. "Naturally, I know he would have liked me to give myself
to Polyhymnia. Strange, people always want you to follow the
same path they do. One can't please everybody. But I'll remind
him that through liturgy and her history music plays very
strongly into the theological; more practically and artistically, indeed, than into the mathematical and physical, or into acoustics."

In announcing his purpose of saying as much to Kretschmar, he
was really, as I well knew, saying it to me; and when I was alone
I thought of it again and again. Certainly, in relation to theology
and the service of God, music — of course like all the arts, and
also the secular sciences, but music in particular — took on an ancillary, auxiliary character. The thought was associated in my
mind with certain discussions which we had had on the destiny of
art, on the one hand very conducive, but on the other sadly hampering; we referred to her emancipation from cult, her cultural
secularization. It was all quite clear to me: his choice had been
influenced by his personal desire and his professional prospects,
the wish to reduce music again to the position that once, in times
he considered happier, she had held in the union of cults. Like the
profane disciplines, so likewise music: he would see them all beneath the sphere to which he would dedicate himself as adept.
And I got a strange vision, a sort of allegory of his point of view:
it was like a baroque painting, an enormous altarpiece, whereon
all the arts and sciences in humble and votive posture paid their
devotions to theology enthroned.

Adrian laughed loudly at my vision when I told him about it.
He was in high spirits at that time, much inclined to jest — and
quite understandably. The moment of taking flight, when freedom
dawns, when the school gate shuts behind us, the shell breaks, the
chrysalis bursts, the world lies open — is it not the happiest, or the
most exciting, certainly the most expectant in all our lives?
Through his musical excursions with Wendell Kretschmar to the
larger near-by cities, Adrian had tasted the outer world a few
times; now Kaisersaschern, the place of witches and strangelings,
of the instrument warehouse and the imperial tomb in the Cathedral, would finally loose its hold on him, and only on visits would
he walk its streets, smiling like one aware of other spheres.

Was that true? Had Kaisersaschern ever released him? Did he
not take her with him wherever he went and was he not conditioned by her whenever he thought to decide? What is freedom?
Only the neutral is free. The characteristic is never free, it is
stamped, determined, bound. Was it not "Kaisersaschern" that
spoke in my friend's decision to study theology? Adrian Leverkühn and Kaisersaschern: obviously the two together yielded theology. I asked myself further what else I had expected. He devoted himself later to musical composition. But if it was very
bold music he wrote, was it after all "free" music, world music?
That it was not. It was the music of one who never escaped; it
was, into its most mysterious, inspired, bizarre convolution, in
every hollow breath and echo it gave out, characteristic music,
music of Kaisersaschern.

He was, I said, in high spirits at that time — and why not? Dispensed from oral examination on the basis of the maturity of his
written work, he had taken leave of his teachers, with thanks for
all they had done; while on their side respect for the profession
he had chosen repressed the private annoyance they had always
felt at his condescending facility. Even so, the worthy director of
the School of the Brethren of the Common Life, a Pomeranian
named Dr. Stoientin, who had been Adrian's master in Greek,
Middle High German, and Hebrew, did not fail at their private
leave-taking to utter a word of warning.

"*Vale*," he said, "and God be with you, Leverkühn. — The parting blessing comes from my heart, and whether you are of that
opinion or not, it seems to me you may need it. You are a person
richly gifted and you know it — as why should you not? You
know too that He above, from whom all comes, gave you your
gifts, for to Him you now offer them. You are right: natural merits are God's merits in us, not our own. It is His foe who, fallen
through pride himself, would teach us to forget. He is evil to entertain, a roaring lion who goes about seeking whom he may
devour. You are among those who have reason to be on guard
against his wiles. It is a compliment I am paying you, or rather to
what you are from God. Be it in humility, my friend, not in defiance or with boasting; and be ever mindful that self-satisfaction
is like a falling away and unthankfulness against the Giver of all
mercies!"

Thus our honest schoolmaster, under whom later I served as
teacher in the gymnasium. Adrian reported it smiling, on one of
the many walks we took through field and forest, in that Easter-
tide at Buchel. For he spent several weeks of freedom there after

leaving school, and his good parents invited me to bear him company. Well I remember the talks we had as we strolled, about Stoientin's warning, especially about the expression "native merit" which he had used in his farewell. Adrian pointed out that he took it from Goethe, who enjoyed using it, and also "inborn merits," seeking in the paradoxical combination to divorce from the word "merit" its moral character, and, conversely, to exalt the natural and inborn to a position of extra-moral, aristocratic desert. That was why he was against the claims of modesty which were always put forward by those disadvantaged by nature, and declared that "Only good-for-nothings are modest." But Director Stoientin had used Goethe's words more in Schiller's sense, to whom everything had depended on freedom, and who therefore distinguished in a moral sense between talent and personal merit, sharply differentiating merit and fortune, which Goethe considered to be inextricably interwoven. The director followed Schiller, when he called nature God and native talent the merit of God in us, which we were to wear in humility.

"The Germans," said the new undergraduate, a grass blade in his mouth, "have a two-track mind and an inexcusable habit of combination; they always want one thing and the other, they want to have it both ways. They are capable of turning out great personalities with antithetic principles of thought and life. But then they muddle them, using the coinage of the one in the sense of the other; mixing everything all up and thinking they can put freedom and aristocracy, idealism and natural childlikeness under one hat. But that probably does not do."

"But they have both in themselves," I retorted; "otherwise they could not have exhibited both of them. A rich nation."

"A confused nation," he persisted, "and bewildering for the others."

But on the whole we philosophized thus but little, in these leisurely country weeks. Generally speaking, he was more inclined to laughter and pranks than to metaphysical conversation. His sense of the comic, his fondness for it, his proneness to laughter, yes, to laughing till he cried, I have already spoken of, and I have given but a false picture of him if the reader has not seen this kind of abandon as an element in his nature. Of humour I would not speak; the word sounds for my ear too moderate, too good-natured to fit him. His love of laughter was more like an escape, a resolution, slightly orgiastic in its nature, of life's manifold sternness; a product of extraordinary gifts, but to me never quite likable or healthy. Looking back upon the school life now ending, he gave this sense of the comic free rein, recalling droll types among pupils and teachers, or describing his last cultural expedition and some small-town opera performance, whose improvisations could not fail to be a source of mirth, though without detriment to the seriousness of the work performed. Thus a paunchy, knock-kneed King Heinrich in *Lohengrin* was the butt of much laughter; Adrian was like to split over the round black mouth-hole in a beard like a woolly rug, out of which there poured his thundering bass. That was but one instance, perhaps too concrete, of the occasions he found for his paroxysms. Oftener there was no occasion at all, it was the purest silliness, and I confess that I always had certain difficulties in seconding him. I do not love laughter so much, and when he abandoned himself to it I was always compelled to think of a story which I knew only from him. It was from St. Augustine's *De civitate Dei* and was to the effect that Ham, son of Noah and father of Zoroaster the magian, had been the only man who laughed when he was born — which could only have happened by the help of the Devil. It came inevitably to my mind whenever the occasion arose; but probably it was only an accompaniment to other inhibitions I had; for instance, I realize that the look that I inwardly directed upon him was too serious, not free enough from anxious suspense, for me to follow him whole-heartedly in his abandon. And perhaps my own nature has a certain stiffness and dryness that makes me inapt.

Later he found in Rüdiger Schildknapp, a writer and Anglophile whose acquaintance he made in Leipzig, a far better partner in such moods — wherefore I have always been a little jealous of the man.

CHAPTER XI

At Halle theological and philological educational traditions are interwoven in many ways; and first of all in the historical figure of August Hermann Francke, patron saint of the town, so to speak: that pietistic pedagogue who at the end of the seventeenth century — in other words, soon after the foundation of the university — formed in Halle the famous Francke Foundation of schools and orphanages, and in his own person and by its influence united the religious interest with the humanistic and linguistic. And then the Castein Bible Institute, first authority for the revision of Luther's language work, it too establishes a link between religion and textual criticism. Also there was active in Halle at that time an outstanding Latinist, Heinrich Osiander, at whose feet I ardently desired to sit; and more than that, as I heard from Adrian, the course in Church history given by Professor Hans Kegel, D.D., included an extraordinary amount of material for a student of profane history, which I wished to avail myself of, as I intended to elect history as my subsidiary course.

Thus there was good intellectual justification when, after studying for two semesters in Jena and Giessen, I decided to draw my further nourishment from the breast of Alma Mater Hallensis. And my imagination saw an advantage in the fact that it was identical with the University of Wittenberg, the two having been united when they were reopened after the Napoleonic Wars. Leverkühn had matriculated there a half-year before I joined him, and of course I do not deny that his presence had played a weighty, yes, a decisive part in my choice. Shortly after his arrival, and obviously out of some feeling of loneliness and forsakenness, he had even proposed to me to join him; and though some months would have to pass before I answered his call, I was at once ready, yes, probably would not have needed the invitation. My own wish to be near him, to see how he went on, what progress he made and how his talents unfolded in the air of academic freedom, this wish to live in daily intercourse with him, to watch over him, to have an eye on him from near by, would very likely have been enough of itself to take me to him. And there were besides, as I said, sufficing intellectual grounds.

Of course in these pages I can only picture in a foreshortened form, just as I did with his school-days, the two years of our youth that I spent at Halle with my friend; the course of them interrupted, indeed, by holidays in Kaisersaschern and at his father's farm. Were they happy years? Yes, they were, in the sense that they were the core of a period when with my senses at their freshest I was freely seeing, searching, and gathering in. Happy too in that I spent them at the side of a childhood companion to whom I clung, yes, whose life-problem, his being and becoming, at bottom interested me more than my own. For my own was simple, I did not need to spend much thought on it, only to ensure by faithful work the postulates for its prescribed solution. His was higher and in a sense more puzzling, a problem upon which the concern about my own progress always left me much time and mental energy to dwell. If I hesitate to describe those years by the epithet "happy" — always a questionable word — it is because by association with him I was drawn much more effectively into his sphere of studies than he into mine, and the theological air did not suit me. It was not canny, it choked me; besides, it put me in an inward dilemma. The intellectual atmosphere there had been for centuries full of religious controversy, of those ecclesiastical brawls which have always been so detrimental to the humanistic impulse to culture. In Halle I felt a little like one of my scientific forebears, Crotus Rubeanus, who in 1530 was canon at Halle, and whom Luther called nothing else than "the Epicurean Crotus" or "Dr. Kröte, lickspittle of the Cardinal at Mainz." He even said "the Divel's sow, the Pope," and was in every way an intolerable boor, although a great man. I have always sympathized with the embarrassment that the Reformation caused to spirits like Crotus, because they saw in it an invasion of subjective arbitrariness into the objective statutes and ordinances of the Church. Crotus had the scholar's love of peace; he gladly leaned to reasonable compromise, was not against the restitution of the Communion cup — and was indeed put after that in a painfully awkward position, through the detestable harshness with which his superior, Archbishop Albrecht, punished the enjoyment of the Communion at Halle in both kinds.

So goes it with tolerance, with love of culture and peace, between the fires of fanaticism. — It was Halle that had the first Lutheran superintendent: Justus Jonas, who went thither in 1541 and was one of those who, like Melanchthon and Hutten, to the distress of Erasmus, had gone over from the humanistic camp to the reformers. But still worse in the eyes of the sage of Rotterdam was the hatred that Luther and his partisans brought down upon classical learning — Luther had personally little enough of it — as the source of the spiritual turmoil. But what went on then in the bosom of the Universal Church, the revolt of subjective wilfullness, that is, against the objective bond, was to repeat itself a hundred and some years later, inside Protestantism itself, as a revolution of pious feelings and inner heavenly joy against a petrified orthodoxy from which not even a beggar would any longer want to accept a piece of bread: as pietism, that is, which at the foundation of the University of Halle manned the whole theological faculty. It too, whose citadel the town now long remained, was, as formerly Lutheranism, a renewal of the Church, a reform and reanimation of the dying religion, already fallen into general indifference. And people like me may well ask themselves whether these recurrent rescues of a hope already declining to the grave are from a cultural point of view to be welcomed; whether the reformers are not rather to be regarded as backsliding types and bringers of evil. Beyond a doubt, endless blood-letting and the most horrible self-laceration would have been spared the human race if Martin Luther had not restored the Church.

I should be sorry, after what I have said, to be taken for an utterly irreligious man. That I am not, for I go with Schleiermacher, another Halle theologian, who defined religion as "feeling and taste for the Infinite" and called it "a pertinent fact," present in the human being. In other words, the science of religion has to do not with philosophical theses, but with an inward and given psychological fact. And that reminds me of the ontological evidence for the existence of God, which has always been my favourite, and which from the subjective idea of a Highest Being derives His objective existence. But Kant has shown in the most forthright words that such a thesis cannot support itself before the bar of reason. Science, however, cannot get along without reason; and to want to make a science out of a sense of the infinite and the eternal mysteries is to compel two spheres fundamentally foreign to each other to come together in a way that is in my eyes most unhappy and productive only of embarrassment. Surely a religious sense, which I protest is in no way lacking in me, is something other than positive and formally professed religion. Would it not have been better to hand over that "fact" of human feeling for the infinite to the sense of piety, the fine arts, free contemplation, yes, even to exact research, which as cosmology, astronomy, theoretical physics, can serve this feeling with entirely religious devotion to the mystery of creation — instead of singling it out as the science of the spirit and developing on it structures of dogma, whose orthodox believers will then shed blood for a copula? Pietism, by virtue of its overemotional nature, would indeed make a sharp division between piety and science, and assert that no movement, no change in the scientific picture, can have any influence on faith. But that was a delusion, for theology has at all times willy-nilly let itself be determined by the scientific currents of the epoch, has always wanted to be a child of its time, although the time (in greater or less degree) made that difficult for it and drove it into an anachronistic corner. Is there another discipline at whose mere name we feel ourselves in such a degree set back into the past, into the sixteenth, the twelfth century? There is here no possibility of adaptation, of concession to scientific critique. What these display is a hybrid half-and-half of science and belief in revelation, which lies on the way to self-surrender. Orthodoxy itself committed the blunder of letting reason into the field of religion, in that she sought to prove the positions of faith by the test of reason. Under the pressure of the Enlightenment, theology had almost nothing to do but defend herself against the intolerable contradictions which were pointed out to her: and only in order to get round them she embraced so much of the anti-revelation spirit that it amounted to an abandonment of faith. That was the time of the "reasonable worship of God," of a generation of theologians in whose name Wolff declared at Halle: "Everything must be proved by reason, as on the philosophers' stone": a generation which pronounced that everything in the Bible which did not serve "moral betterment" was out of date, and gave out that the history and teaching of the Church were in its eyes only a comedy of errors. Since this went a little too far, there arose an accommodation theology, which sought to uphold a conservative middle ground between orthodoxy and a liberalism already by virtue of its reasonableness inclined to demoralization. But the two ideas "preserving" and "abandoning" have since then conditioned the life of "the science of religion" — ideas both of which have something provisional about them, for theology therewith prolonged its life. In its conservative form, holding to revelation and the traditional exegesis, it sought to save what was to be saved of the elements of Bible religion; on the other hand it liberally accepted the historico-critical methods of the profane science of history and abandoned to scientific criticism its own most important contents: the belief in miracles, considerable portions of Christology, the bodily resurrection of Jesus, and what not besides. But what sort of science is that, which stands in such a forced and precarious relation to reason, constantly threatened with destruction by the very compromises that she makes with it? In my view "liberal theology" is a *contradictio in adjecto*," a contradiction in terms. A proponent of culture, ready to adapt itself to the ideals of bourgeois society, as it is, it degrades the religious to a function of the human; the ecstatic and paradoxical elements so essential to the religious genius it waters down to an ethical progressiveness. But the religious cannot be satisfied in the merely ethical, and so it comes about that scientific thought and theological thought proper part company again. The scientific superiority of liberal theology, it is now said, is indeed incontestable, but its theological position is weak, for its moralism and humanism lack insight into the dæmonic character of human existence. Cultured indeed it is, but shallow; of the true understanding of human nature and the tragic nature of life the conservative tradition has at bottom preserved far more; for that very reason it has a profounder, more significant relation to culture than has progressive bourgeois ideology.

Here one sees clearly the infiltration of theological thinking by irrational currents of philosophy, in whose realm, indeed, the non-theoretic, the vital, the will or instinct, in short the dæmonic, have long since become the chief theme of theory. At the same time one observes a revival of the study of Catholic mediæval philosophy, a turning to Neo-Thomism and Neo-Scholasticism. On these lines theology, grown sickly with liberalism, can take on deeper and stronger, yes, more glowing hues; it can once more do justice to the ancient æsthetic conceptions which are involuntarily associated with its name. But the civilized human spirit, whether one call it bourgeois or merely leave it at civilized, cannot get rid of a feeling of the uncanny. For theology, confronted with that spirit of the philosophy of life which is irrationalism, is in danger, by its very nature, of becoming dæmonology.

I say all this only in order to explain the discomfort caused in me at times by my stay in Halle and my participation in Adrian's studies, the lectures that I followed as a guest hearer in order to hear what he heard. I found in him no understanding for my uneasiness. He liked to talk over with me the theological problems touched on in the lectures and debated in the seminar; but he avoided any discussion that would have gone to the root of the matter and have dealt with the problematic position of theology

among the sciences, and thus he evaded precisely the point which
to my easily aroused anxiety was more pressing than all the rest.
And so it was in the lectures as well: and so it went in association with his fellow-students, the members of the Christian Students' Union Winfried, which he had joined on external grounds
and whose guest I sometimes was. Of that perhaps more later.
Here I will only say that some of these young people were the
pale-complexioned "candidate" type, some robust as peasants,
some also distinguished figures who obviously came from good
academic circles. But they were all theologians, and conducted
themselves as such with a decent and godly cheerfulness. How
one can be a theologian, how in the spiritual climate of the present day one comes on the idea of choosing this calling, unless,
indeed, it were simply by the operation of family tradition, they
did not say, and for my part it would have been tactless and prying to cross-examine them. A forthright question on the subject
could at most have been in place and had any chance of results
in the course of a students' evening jollification, when tongues
and brains were loosened and livened by drink. But of course the
members of Winfried were superior; they condemned not only
duelling but also "boozing," and so they were always sober —
that is, they were inaccessible to questions they might not like to
answer. They knew that State and Church needed ghostly offi-
cers, and they were preparing themselves for that career. Theology was to them something given — and something historically
given it certainly is.

I had to put up with it too, when Adrian took it in the same
way, although it pained me that regardless of our friendship,
rooted in early days as it was, he no more permitted the question
than did his comrades. That shows how little he let one approach
him; what fixed bounds he set to intimacy. But did I not say that
I had found his choice of a profession significant and characteristic? Have I not explained it with the word "Kaisersaschern"?
Often I called the thought to my aid when the problem of Adrian's field of study plagued me. I said to myself that both of us had
shown ourselves true children of that corner of German antiquity
where we had been brought up, I as humanist and he as theologian. And when I looked round in our new circle I found that our
theatre had indeed broadened but not essentially changed.

CHAPTER XII

HALLE was, if not a metropolis, at least a large city, with more than two hundred thousand inhabitants. Yet despite all the modern volume of its traffic, it did not, at least in the heart of the town, where we both lived, belie its lofty antiquity. My "shop," as we students said, was in the Hansastrasse, a narrow lane behind the Church of St. Moritz, which might well have run its anachronistic course in Kaisersaschern. Adrian had found an alcoved room in a gabled dwelling-house in the Market Square, renting from the elderly widow of an official during the two years of his stay. He had a view of the square, the mediæval City Hall, the Gothic Marienkirche, whose domed towers were connected by a sort of Bridge of Sighs; the separate "Red Tower," a very remarkable structure, also in Gothic style; the statue of Roland and the bronze statue of Handel. The room was not much more than adequate, with some slight indication of middle-class amenity in the shape of a red plush cover on the square table in front of the sofa, where his books lay and he drank his breakfast coffee. He had supplemented the arrangements with a rented cottage piano always strewn with sheets of music, some written by himself. On the wall above the piano was an arithmetical diagram fastened with drawing-pins, something he had found in a second-hand shop: a so-called magic square, such as appears also in Dürer's *Melancolia*, along with the hour-glass, the circle, the scale, the polyhedron, and other symbols. Here as there, the figure was divided into sixteen Arabic-numbered fields, in such a way that number one was in the right-hand lower corner, sixteen in the upper left; and the magic, or the oddity, simply consisted in the fact that the sum of these numerals, however you added them, straight down, crosswise, or diagonally, always came to thirty-four. What the principle was upon which this magic uniformity rested I never made out, but by virtue of the prominent place Adrian had given it over the piano, it always attracted the eye, and I believe I never visited his room without giving a quick

glance, slanting up or straight down and testing once more the
invariable, incredible result.

Between my quarters and Adrian's there was a going to and fro
as once between the Blessed Messengers and his uncle's house: evenings after theatre, concert, or a meeting of the Winfried Verein,
also in the mornings when one of us fetched the other to the university and before we set out we compared out notebooks. Philosophy, the regular course for the first examination in theology,
was the point at which our two programs coincided, and both of
us had put ourselves down with Kolonat Nonnenmacher, then one
of the luminaries of the University of Halle. With great brilliance
and élan he discussed the pre-Socratic, the Ionian natural philosophers, Anaximander, and more extendedly Pythagoras, in the
course of which discussion a good deal of Aristotle came in, since
it is almost entirely through the Stagirite that we learn of the
Pythagorean theory of the universe. We listened, we wrote down;
from time to time we looked up into the mildly smiling face of
the white-maned professor, as we heard this early cosmological
conception of a stern and pious spirit, who elevated his fundamental passion, mathematics, abstract proportion, number, to the
principle of the origin and existence of the world; who, standing
opposite All-Nature as an initiate, a dedicated one, first addressed
her with a great gesture as "Cosmos," as order and harmony, as
the interval-system of the spheres, sounding beyond the range of
the senses. Number, and the relation of numbers, as constituting
an all-embracing concept of being and moral value: it was highly
impressive, how the beautiful, the exact, the moral, here solemnly
flowed together to comprise the idea of authority which animated
the Pythagorean order, the esoteric school of religious renewal of
life, of silent obedience and strict subjection under the "*Autós
épha.*" I must chide myself for being tactless, because involuntarily I glanced at Adrian at such words, to read his look. Or
rather it became tactless simply because of the discomfort, the
red, averted face, with which he met my gaze. He did not love
personal glances, he altogether refused to entertain them or respond to them, and it is hard to understand why I, aware though
I was of this peculiarity, could not always resist looking at him.
By so doing I threw away the possibility of talking objectively
afterwards, without embarrassment, on topics to which my wordless look had given a personal reference.

So much the better when I had resisted such temptation and
practised the discretion he exacted. How well, for instance, we
talked, going home after Nonnenmacher's class, about that im-

mortal thinker, influential down the millennia, to whose mediation
and sense of history we owe our knowledge of the Pythagorean
conception of the world! Aristotle's doctrine of matter and form
enchanted us; matter as the potential, possible, that presses
towards form in order to realize itself; form as the moving un-
moved, that is mind and soul, the soul of the existing that urges
it to self-realization, self-completion in the phenomenon; thus of
the entelechy, which, a part of eternity, penetrates and animates
the body, manifests itself shapingly in the organic and guides its
motive-power, knows its goal, watches over its destiny. Nonnenmacher had spoken beautifully and impressively about these
intuitions, and Adrian appeared extraordinarily impressed thereby. "When," he said, "theology declares that the soul is from
God, that is philosophically right, for as the principle which
shapes the single manifestations, it is a part of the pure form of
all being, comes from the eternally self-contemplating contemplation which we call God. . . . I believe I understand what
Aristotle meant by the word 'entelechy.' It is the angel of the individual, the genius of his life, in whose all-knowing guidance it
gladly confides. What we call prayer is really the statement of
this confidence, a notice-giving or invocation. But prayer it is correctly called, because it is at bottom God whom we thus address."

I could only think: May thine own angel prove himself faithful
and wise!

How I enjoyed hearing this course of lectures at Adrian's side!
But the theological ones, which I — though not regularly — attended on his account, were for me a more doubtful pleasure; and
I went to them only in order not to be cut off from what occupied
him. In the curriculum of a theology student in the first years the
emphasis is on history and exegesis, history of the Church and of
dogma, Assyriology and a variety of special subjects. The middle
years belong to systematics; that is to say, to the philosophy of
religion, ethics, and apologetics. At the end come the practical
disciplines, the science of preaching, catechesis, the care of souls,
Church law, and the science of Church government. But academic freedom leaves much room for personal preference, and
Adrian made use of it to throw over the regular order, devoting
himself from the first to systematics, out of general intellectual
interest, of course, which in this field comes most to account; but
also because its professor, Ehrenfried Kumpf, was the "meatiest"
lecturer in the whole university and had altogether the largest attendance from students of all years, not only theological ones. I
said indeed that we both heard Church history from Kegel, but

those were comparatively dull hours, and the tedious Kegel could
by no means vie with Kumpf.

The latter was very much what the students called a "powerful personality"; even I could not forgo a certain admiration for
his temperament, though I did not like him in the least and have
never been able to believe that Adrian was not at times unpleasantly impressed by his crude heartiness, though he did not make
fun of him openly. Powerful he certainly was, in his physical
person; a big, full-bodied, massive man with hands like cushions,
a thundering voice, and an underlip that protruded slightly from
much talking and tended to spit and sputter. It is true that Kumpf
usually read his lecture from a printed textbook, his own production; but his glory was the so-called "extra punches" which he
interpolated, delivered with his fists thrust into his vertical trouser-
pockets past the flung-back frock coat, as he stumped up and
down on his platform. Thanks to their spontaneity, bluntness,
coarse and hearty good humour, and picturesquely archaic style,
they were uncommonly popular with the students. It was his way
— to quote him — to say a thing "in good round terms, no mealy-
mouthing" or "in good old German, without mincing matters."
Instead of "gradually" he said "by a little and a little"; instead of
"I hope" he said "I hope and trow"; he never spoke of the Bible
otherwise than as Godes Boke. He said "There's foul work" instead of "There's something wrong." Of somebody who, in his
view, was involved in scientific error, he said "He's in the wrong
pew"; of a vicious man: "he spends his life like the beasts of the
field." He loved expressions like: "He that will eat the kernel
must crack the nut"; or "It pricketh betimes that will be a sharp
thorn." Mediæval oaths like "Gogs wownds," by "Goggys bodye,"
even "by the guts of Goliath" came easily to his lips and — especially the last — were received by the students with lusty
tramplings.

Theologically speaking, Kumpf was a representative of that
middle-of-the-road conservatism with critical and liberal traits
to which I have referred. As a student he was, as he told us in his
peripatetic extempores, dead set on classical literature and philosophy, and boasted of having known by heart all of Schiller's and
Goethe's "weightier" works. But then something had come over
him, connected with the revival movement of the middle of the
previous century, and the Pauline gospel of sin and justification
made him turn away from æsthetic humanism. One must be a
born theologian to estimate properly such spiritual destinies and
Damascus experiences. Kumpf had convinced himself that our

thinking too is a broken reed and needs justification, and precisely
this was the basis of his liberalism, for it led him to see in dog-
matism an intellectual form of phariseeism. Thus he had arrived
at criticism of dogma by a route opposite to that of Descartes, to
whom, on the contrary, the self-certainty of the consciousness,
the *cogitare*, seemed more legitimate than all scholastic authority.
Here we have the difference between theological and philosophical sanctions. Kumpf had found his in a blithe and hearty trust
in God, and reproduced it before us hearers "in good old German
words." He was not only anti-pharisaic, anti-dogmatic, but also
anti-metaphysical, with a position addressed entirely to ethics and
theoretic knowledge, a proponent of the morally based ideal of
personality and mightily opposed to the pietistic divorce of world
and religion; secularly religious, indeed, and ready for healthy enjoyment, an affirmer of culture, especially of German culture, for
on every occasion he showed himself to be a nationalist of the
Luther stamp, out of whole cloth. He could say of a man nothing
worse than that he thought and taught like a "flatulent furriner."
Red as a turkey-cock with rage, he might add: "And may the Divel
shit on him, Amen!" — which again was greeted with loud stamp-
ings of applause.

His liberalism, that is, was not based on humanistic distrust of
dogma, but on religious doubt of the reliability of our thinking.
It did not prevent him from believing stoutly in revelation, nor
indeed from being on a very familiar footing with the Devil, if
also, of course, the reverse of a cordial one. I cannot and would not
inquire how far he believed in the personal existence of the Great
Adversary. I only say to myself that wherever theology is, and
certainly in so "meaty" a personality as Ehrenfried Kumpf, there
too the devil belongs to the picture and asserts his complementary
reality to that of God. It is easy to say that a modern theologian
takes him "symbolically." In my view theology cannot be modern — one may reckon that to its advantage, of course — and as
for symbolism, I cannot see why one should take hell more symbolically than heaven. The people have certainly never done so.
Always the crass, obscenely comic figure of the "divel" has been
nearer to them than the Eternal Majesty; and Kumpf, in his way,
was a man of the people. When he spoke with relish of the "everlasting fire and brimstone" and of "hell's bottomless pit," that
picturesque form, while slightly comic, at least carried more conviction than ordinary words would have done. One did not at all
get the impression that he was speaking symbolically, but rather
that this was "good plain German, with nothing mealy-mouthed

about it." It was the same with Satan himself. I did say that Kumpf, as a scholar and man of science, made concessions to criticism in the matter of literal faith in the Bible, and at least by fits and starts "abandoned" much, with a great air of intellectual respectability. But at bottom he saw the Arch-Deceiver, the Wicked Fiend capitally at work on the reason itself and seldom referred to him without adding: *"Si Diabolus non esset mendax et homicida!"* He appeared reluctant to name him straight out, preferring to say "Divel" or "Debble"; sometimes "the great old Serpent," or, with literary relish, "Timothy Tempter." But just this half-jesting, half-shrinking avoidance had something of a grim and reluctant recognition about it. And he had at command still other pithy and forgotten epithets, some homely and some classic, such as: Old Blackie, Abaddon, Belial, also Master Dicis-et-non-facis, Black Kaspar, the old Serpent and the Father of Lies. They did, in a half-humorous way, express his highly personal and intimate animosity to the Great Adversary.

After Adrian and I had paid our formal call, we were now and again invited by Kumpf to his house, and took supper with him, his wife, and their two daughters, who had glaringly red cheeks and hair first wet and then so tightly plaited that it stuck straight out from their heads. One of them said grace while the rest of us bowed our heads discreetly over our plates. Then the master of the house, expatiating the while on God and the world, the Church, the university, politics, and even art and the theatre, in unmistakable imitation of Luther's *Table Talk*, laced powerfully into the meat and drink, as an example to us and in token that he had nothing against the healthy and cultured enjoyment of the good things of this world. He repeatedly urged us to fall to, not to despise the good gifts of God, the leg of mutton, the elder-blossom Moselle. After the sweet, to our horror, he took a guitar from the wall, pushed away from the table, flung one leg across the other, and sang in his booming voice, to the twanging of the strings: "To Wander is the Miller's Joy," "Lutzow's Wild Reckless Ride," "The Lorelei," *"Gaudeamus Igitur,"* "Wine, Women, and Song." Yes, it had to come, and it came. He shouted it out, and before our faces he took his plump wife round the waist. Then with his fat forefinger he pointed to a dark corner where the rays of the shaded lamp over the supper-table did not fall — "Look"! he cried. "There he stands in the corner, the mocking-bird, the make-bate, the malcontent, the sad, bad guest, and cannot stand it to see us merry in God with feasting and song. But he shall not harm us, the arch-villain, with his sly fiery arrows! *Apage!*" he thundered, seized a roll and flung it into the dark corner. After this he took his instrument again and sang: "He who the world will joyous rove."

All this was pretty awful, and I take it Adrian must have thought so too, though his pride prevented him from exposing his teacher. However, when we went home after that fight with the Devil, he had such a fit of laughter in the street that it only gradually subsided with the diversion of his thoughts.

CHAPTER XIII

But I must devote a few words to another figure among our teachers; the equivocal nature of this man intrigued me, so that I remember him better than all the rest. He was Privat-docent Eberhard Schleppfuss, who for two semesters at this time lectured at Halle among the *venia legendi* and then disappeared from the scene, I know not whither. Schleppfuss was a creature of hardly average height, puny in figure, wrapped in a black cape or mantle instead of an overcoat, which closed at the throat with a little metal chain. With it he wore a sort of soft hat with the brim turned up at the sides, rather like a Jesuit's. When we students greeted him on the street he would take it off with a very sweeping bow and say: "Your humble servant!" It seemed to me that he really did drag one foot, but people disputed it; I could not always be sure of it when I saw him walk, and would rather ascribe my impression to a subconscious association with his name. It was not in any case so far-fetched, considering the nature of his two-hour lectures. I do not remember precisely how they were listed. In matter certainly they were a little vague, they might have been called lectures on the psychology of religion — and very probably were. The material was "exclusive" in its nature, not important for examinations, and only a handful of intellectual and more or less revolutionary-minded students, ten or twelve, attended it. I wondered, indeed, that there were no more, for Schleppfuss's offering was interesting enough to arouse a more extended curiosity. But the occasion went to prove that even the piquant forfeits its popularity when accompanied by demands on the intellect.

I have already said that theology by its very nature tends and under given circumstances always will tend to become dæmonology. Schleppfuss was a good instance of the thing I mean, of a very advanced and intellectual kind, for his dæmonic conception of God and the universe was illuminated by psychology and thus made acceptable, yes, even attractive, to the modern scientific mind. His delivery contributed to the effect, for it was entirely calculated to impress the young. It was impromptu, well expressed, without effort or break, smooth as though prepared for the press, with faintly ironical turns of phrase; and he spoke not from the platform but somewhere at one side, half-sitting on the balustrade, the ends of his fingers interlaced in his lap, with the thumbs spread out, and his parted little beard moving up and down. Between it and the twisted moustaches one saw his pointed teeth like tiny splinters. Professor Kumpf's good out-and-out ways with the Devil were child's play compared to the psychological actuality with which Schleppfuss invested the Destroyer, that personified falling-away from God. For he received, if I may so express myself, dialectically speaking, the blasphemous and offensive into the divine and hell into the empyrean; declared the vicious to be a necessary and inseparable concomitant of the holy, and the holy a constant satanic temptation, an almost irresistible challenge to violation.

He demonstrated this by instances from the Christian Middle Ages, the classical period of religious rule over the life and spirit of man, and in particular from its ultimate century; thus from a time of complete harmony between ecclesiastical judge and delinquent, between inquisitor and witch on the fact of the betrayal of God, of the alliance with the Devil, the frightful partnership with demons. The provocation to vice proceeding from the sacrosanct was the essential thing about it, it was the thing itself, betrayed for instance in the characterization by apostates of the Virgin as "the fat woman," or by extraordinarily vulgar interpolations, abominable filthinesses, which the Devil made them mutter to themselves at the celebration of the Mass. Dr. Schleppfuss, with his fingers interlaced, repeated them word for word; I refrain from doing so myself, on grounds of good taste, but am not reproaching him for paying scientific exactitude its due. It was odd, all the same, to see the students conscientiously writing that sort of thing down in their notebooks. According to Schleppfuss all this — evil, the Evil One himself — was a necessary emanation and inevitable accompaniment of the Holy Existence of God, so that vice did not consist in itself but got its satisfaction from the defilement of virtue, without which it would have been rootless; in other words, it consisted in the enjoyment of freedom, the possibility of sinning, which was inherent in the act of creation itself.

Herein was expressed a certain logical incompleteness of the All-powerfulness and All-goodness of God; for what He had not been able to do was to produce in the creature, in that which He had liberated out of Himself and which was now outside Him, the incapacity for sin. That would have meant denying to the created being the free will to turn away from God — which would have been an incomplete creation, yes, positively not a creation at all, but a surrender on the part of God. God's logical dilemma had consisted in this: that He had been incapable of giving the creature, the human being and the angel, both independent choice, in other words free will, and at the same time the gift of not being able to sin. Piety and virtue, then, consisted in making a good use, that is to say no use at all, of the freedom which God had to grant the creature as such — and that, indeed, if you listened to Schleppfuss, was a little as though this non-use of freedom meant a certain existential weakening, a diminution of the intensity of being, in the creature outside of God.

Freedom. How extraordinary the word sounded, in Schleppfuss's mouth! Yes, certainly it had a religious emphasis, he spoke as a theologian, and he spoke by no means with contempt. On the contrary, he pointed out the high degree of significance which must be ascribed by God to this idea, when He had preferred to expose men and angels to sin rather than withhold freedom from them. Good, then freedom was the opposite of inborn sinlessness, freedom meant the choice of keeping faith with God, or having traffic with demons and being able to mutter beastlinesses at the Mass. That was a definition suggested by the psychology of religion. But freedom has before now played a role, perhaps of less intellectual significance and yet not lacking in seriousness, in the life of the peoples of the earth and in historical conflicts. It does so at this moment — as I write down this description of a life — in the war now raging, and as I in my retreat like to believe, not least in the souls and thoughts of our German people, upon whom, under the domination of the most audacious licence, is dawning perhaps for the first time in their lives a notion of the importance of freedom. Well, we had not got so far by then. The question of freedom was, or seemed, in our student days, not a burning one, and Dr. Schleppfuss might give to the word the meaning that suited the frame of his lecture and leave any other meanings on one side. If only I had had the impression that he did leave them on one side; that absorbed in his psychology of religion he was not mindful of them! But he was mindful of them; I could not shake off the conviction. And his theological definition of freedom was an apologia and a polemic against the "more modern," that is to say more insipid, more ordinary ideas, which his hearers might associate with them. See, he seemed to say, we have the word too, it is at our service, don't think that it only occurs in your dictionaries and that your idea of it is the only one dictated

by reason. Freedom is a very great thing, the condition of creation, that which prevented God making us proof against falling
away from Him. Freedom is the freedom to sin, and piety consists
in making no use of it out of love for God, who had to give it.

Thus he developed his theme: somewhat tendentiously, somewhat maliciously, if I do not deceive myself. In short, it irritated
me. I don't like it when a person wants the whole show; takes the
word out of his opponent's mouth, turns it round, and confuses
ideas with it. That is done today with the utmost audacity; it is
the main ground of my retirement. Certain people should not
speak of freedom, reason, humanity; on grounds of scrupulosity,
they should leave such words alone. But precisely about humanity did Schleppfuss speak, just that — of course in the sense of the
"classic centuries of belief" on whose spiritual constitution he
based his psychological discussion. Clearly it was important to
him to make it understood that humanity was no invention of the
free spirit, that not to it alone did this idea belong, for that it had
always existed. For example, the activities of the Inquisition were
animated by the most touching humanity. A woman, he related,
had been taken, in that "classic" time, tried and reduced to ashes,
who for full six years had had knowledge of an incubus, at the
very side of her sleeping husband, three times a week, preferably
on holy days. She had promised the Devil that after seven years
she would belong to him body and soul. But she had been lucky:
for just before the end of the term God in his loving-kindness
made her fall into the hands of the Inquisition, and even under a
slight degree of the question she had made a full and touchingly
penitent confession, so that in all probability she obtained pardon
from God. Willingly indeed did she go to her death, with the express declaration that even if she were freed she would prefer the
stake, in order to escape from the power of the demon, so repugnant had her life become to her through her subjection to her
filthy sin. But what beautiful unanimity of culture spoke in this
harmonious accord between the judge and the delinquent and
what warm humanity in the satisfaction at snatching through fire
this soul from the Devil at the very last minute and securing for
it the pardon of God!

Schleppfuss drew our attention to this picture, he summoned us
to observe not only what else humanity could be but also what it
actually was. It would have been to no purpose to bring in another word from the vocabulary of the free-thinker and to speak
of hopeless superstition. Schleppfuss knew how to use this word
too, in the name of the "classic" centuries, to whom it was far

from unknown. That woman with the incubus had surrendered to senseless superstition and to nothing else. For she had fallen away from God, fallen away from faith, and that was superstition. Superstition did not mean belief in demons and incubi, it meant having to do with them for harm, inviting the pestilence and expecting from them what is only to be expected from God. Superstition meant credulity, easy belief in the suggestions and instigations of the enemy of the human race; the conception covered all the chants, invocations, and conjuring formulæ, all the letting oneself in with the black arts, the vices and crimes, the *flagellum hæreticorum fascinariorum*, the *illusiones dæmonum*. Thus might one define the word "superstition," thus it had been defined, and after all it was interesting to see how man can use words and what he can get out of them.

Of course the dialectic association of evil with goodness and holiness played an important role in the theodicy, the vindication of God in view of the existence of evil, which occupied much space in Schleppfuss's course. Evil contributed to the wholeness of the universe, without it the universe would not have been complete; therefore God permitted it, for He was consummate and must therefore will the consummate — not in the sense of the consummately good but in the sense of All-sidedness and reciprocal enlargement of life. Evil was far more evil if good existed; good was far more good if evil existed; yes, perhaps — one might disagree about this — evil would not be evil at all if not for the good, good not good at all if not for evil. St. Augustine, at least, had gone so far as to say that the function of the bad was to make the good stand out more strongly; that it pleased the more and was the more lovely, the more it was compared with the bad. At this point indeed Thomism had intervened, with a warning that it was dangerous to believe that God wanted evil to happen. God neither wanted that nor did He want evil not to happen; rather He permitted, without willing or not-willing, the rule of evil, and that was advantageous to the completeness of the whole. But it was aberration to assert that God permitted evil on account of the good; for nothing was to be considered good except it corresponded to the idea "good" in itself, and not by accident. Anyhow, said Schleppfuss, the problem of the absolute good and beautiful came up here, the good and beautiful without reference to the evil and ugly — the problem of quality without comparison. Where comparison falls away, he said, the measure falls away too, and one cannot speak of heavy or light, of large or small. The good and beautiful would then be divested of all but being, unqualitied, which would be very like not-being, and perhaps not preferable to it.

We wrote that down in our notebooks, that we might go home more or less cheered. The real vindication of God, in view of the pains of creation, so we added, to Schleppfuss's dictation, consisted in His power to bring good out of evil. This characteristic certainly demanded, to the glory of God, practical use, and it could not reveal itself if God had not made over the creature to sin. In that case the universe would be deprived of that good which God knew how to create out of sin, suffering, and vice, and the angels would have had less occasion for songs of praise. Now indeed arose, the other way round, as history continually teaches, out of good much evil, so that God, to prevent it, had also to prevent the good, and altogether might not let the world alone. Yet this would have contradicted His existence as creator; and therefore He had to create the world as it is — namely, saturated with evil — that is to say, to leave it open in part to dæmonic influences.

It never became quite clear whether these were actually Schleppfuss's own dogmas which he delivered to us, or whether he was simply concerned with familiarizing us with the psychology of the classic centuries of faith. Certainly he would not have been a theologian without showing himself sympathetic with such a psychology. But the reason I wondered why more young men were not attracted to his lectures was this: that whenever the subject was the power of demons over human life, sex always played a prominent role. How could it have been otherwise? The dæmonic character of this sphere was a chief appurtenance of the "classical psychology," for there it formed the favourite arena of the demons, the given point of attack for God's adversary, the enemy and corrupter. For God had conceded him greater magic power over the venereal act than over any other human activity; not only on account of the outward indecency of the commission of this act, but above all because the depravity of the first father passed over as original sin to the whole human race. The act of procreation, characterized by æsthetic disgustingness, was the expression and the vehicle of original sin — what wonder that the Devil had been left an especially free hand in it? Not for nothing had the angel said to Tobias: "Over them who are given to lewdness the demon wins power." For the power of the demons lay in the loins of man, and these were meant, where the Evangelist said: "When a strong man armed watcheth his palace, his goods remain in peace." That was of course to be interpreted sexually;

such a meaning was always to be deduced from enigmatic sayings, and keen-eared piety always heard it in them.

But it was astonishing how lax the angelic watch had always been in the case of God's saints, at least so far as "peace" came in question. The book of the Holy Fathers was full of accounts to the effect that even while defying all fleshly lust, they have been tempted by the lust after women, past the bounds of belief. "There was given to me a thorn in the flesh, the messenger of Satan, to buffet me." That was an admission, made to the Corinthians, and though the writer possibly meant something else by it, the falling sickness or the like, in any case the godly interpreted it in their own way and were probably right after all, for their instinct very likely did not err when it darkly referred to the demon of sex in connection with the temptations that assailed the mind. The temptation that one withstood was indeed no sin; it was merely a proof of virtue. And yet the line between temptation and sin was hard to draw, for was not temptation already the raging of sin in the blood, and in the very state of fleshly desire did there not lie much concession to evil? Here again the dialectical unity of good and evil came out, for holiness was unthinkable without temptation, it measured itself against the frightfulness of the temptation, against a man's sin-potential.

But from whom came the temptation? Who was to be cursed on its account? It was easy to say that it came from the Devil. He was its source, but the curse had to do with its object. The object, the *instrumentum* of the Tempter, was woman. She was also, and by that token, indeed, the instrument of holiness, since holiness did not exist without raging lust for sin. But the thanks she got had a bitter taste. Rather the remarkable and profoundly significant thing was that though the human being, both male and female, was endowed with sex, and although the localization of the dæmonic in the loins fitted the man better than the woman, yet the whole curse of fleshliness, of slavery to sex, was laid upon the woman. There was even a saying: "A beautiful woman is like a gold ring in the nose of the sow." How much of that sort of thing, in past ages, has not been said and felt most profoundly about woman! It had to do with the concupiscence of the flesh in general; but was equated with that of the female, so that the fleshliness of the man was put down to her account as well. Hence the words: "I found the woman bitterer than death, and even a good woman is subject to the covetousness of the flesh."

One might have asked: and the good man too? And the holy man quite especially so? Yes, but that was the influence of the woman, who represented the collective concupiscence of the world. Sex was her domain, and how should she not, who was called *femina*, which came half from *fidus* and half from *minus* — that is, of lesser faith — why should she not be on evil and familiar footing with the obscene spirits who populated this field, and quite particularly suspect of intercourse with them, of witchcraft? There was the instance of that married woman who next to her trusting, slumbering spouse had carried on with an incubus, and that for years on end. Of course there were not only incubi but also succubi, and in fact an abandoned youth of the classical period lived with an idol, whose diabolic jealousy he was in the end to experience. For after some years, and more on practical grounds than out of real inclination, he had married a respectable woman, but had been prevented from consummating his marriage because the idol had always come and lain down between them. Then the wife in justifiable wrath had left him, and for the rest of his life he had seen himself confined to the unaccommodating idol.

Even more telling, Schleppfuss thought, for the psychological situation, was the restriction imposed upon a youth of that same period: it had come upon him by no fault of his own, through female witchcraft, and tragic indeed had been the means of his release. As a comment upon the studies I pursued in common with Adrian I will briefly recount the tale, on which Privat-docent Schleppfuss dwelt with considerable wit and relish.

At Merseburg near Constance, toward the end of the fifteenth century, there lived an honest young fellow, Heinz Klöpfgeissel by name and cooper by calling, quite sound and well-built. He loved and was loved by a maiden named Bärbel, only daughter of a widowed sexton, and wished to marry her, but the young couple's desire met with her father's opposition, for Klöpfgeissel was poor, and the sexton insisted on a considerable setting-up in life, and that he should be a master in his trade before he gave him his daughter. But the desires of the young people had proved stronger than their patience and the couple had prematurely become a pair. And every night, when the sexton went to ring the bell, Klöpfgeissel slipped in to his Bärbel and their embraces made each find the other the most glorious thing on earth.

Thus things stood when one day the cooper and some lively companions went to Constance to a church dedication and they had a good day and were a bit beyond themselves, so they decided to go to some women. It was not to Klöpfgeissel's mind, he did not want to go with them. But the others jeered at him for an

old maid and egged him on with taunts against his honour and
hints that all was not right with him; and as he could not stand
that, and had drunk just as much beer as the others besides, he let
himself be talked round, said: "Ho-ho, I know better than that,"
and went up with the others into the stews.

But now it came about that he suffered such frightful chagrin
that he did not know what sort of face to put on. For against all
expectation things went wrong with him with the slut, a Hungarian woman it was, he could give no account of himself at all,
he was just not there, and his fury was unbounded, his fright as
well. For the creature not only laughed at him, but shook her
head and gave it as her view that there must be something wrong,
it certainly had a bad smell, when a fine lusty chap like him all
of a sudden was just not up to it, he must be possessed, somebody
must have given him something — and so on. He paid her a goodly
sum so that she would say nothing, and went home greatly cast
down.

As soon as he could, though not without misgiving, he made a
rendezvous with his Bärbel, and while the sexton was ringing his
bell they had a perfect hour together. He found his manly honour
restored and should have been well content. For aside from the
one and only he cared for no one, and why should he care about
himself save only for her? But he had been uneasy in his mind
ever since that one failure; it gnawed at him, he felt he must make
another test: just once and never again, play false to his dearest
and best. So he sought secretly for a chance to test himself — himself and her too, for he could cherish no misgiving about himself
that did not end in slight, even tender, yet anxious suspicion of
her upon whom his soul hung.

Now, it so fell out that he had to tighten the hoops of two
casks in the wine-cellar of the inn landlord, a sickly pot-belly, and
the man's wife, a comely wench, still pretty fresh, went down
with him to watch him work. She patted his arm, put hers beside
it to compare, and so demeaned herself that it would have been
impossible to repulse her, save that his flesh, in all the willingness
of his spirit, was entirely unable, and he had to say he was not in
the humour, and he was in a hurry, and her husband would be
coming downstairs, and then to take to his heels, hearing her
scornful laughter behind him and owing her a debt which no
stout fellow should ever refuse to pay.

He was deeply injured and bewildered about himself, but about
himself not only; for the suspicion that even after the first mis-
hap had lodged in his mind now entirely filled him, and he had no

more doubt that he was indeed "possessed." And so, because the
healing of a poor soul and the honour of his flesh as well were at
stake, he went to the priest and told him everything in his ear
through the little grating: how he was bewitched, how he was
unable, how he was prevented with everybody but one, and how
about all that and had the Church any maternal advice to give
against such injury.

Now, at that time and in that locality the pestilence of witchcraft, accompanied by much wantonness, sin, and vice instigated
by the enemy of the human race, and abhorrent to the Divine
Majesty, had been gravely widespread, and stern watchfulness had
been made the duty of all shepherds of souls. The priest, all too
familiar with this kind of mischief, and men being tampered with
in their best strength, went to the higher authorities with Klöpfgeissel's confession. The sexton's daughter was arrested and examined, and confessed, truly and sincerely, that in the anguish of her
heart over the faithfulness of the young man, lest he be filched
from her before he was hers before God and man, she had procured from an old bath-woman a specific, a salve, said to be made
of the fat of an infant dead unbaptized, with which she had
anointed her Heinz on the back while embracing him, tracing a
certain figure thereon, only in order to bind him to herself. Next
the bathing-woman was interrogated, who denied it stoutly. She
had to be brought before the civil authorities for the application
of methods of questioning which did not become the Church; and
under some pressure the expected came to light. The old woman
had in fact a compact with the Devil, who appeared to her in the
guise of a monk with goat's feet and persuaded her to deny with
frightful curses the Godhead and the Christian faith, in return for
which he gave her directions for making not only that love unction but also other shameful panaceas, among them a fat, smeared
with which a piece of wood would instantly rise with the sor-
cerer into the air. The ceremonies by which the Evil One had
sealed his pact with the old crone came out bit by bit under repeated pressure, and were hair-raising.

Everything now depended upon the question: how far was the
salvation of the deceived one involved by her receiving and using
the unholy preparation? Unhappily for the sexton's daughter the
old woman deposed that the Dragon had laid upon her to make
many converts. For every human being she brought to him by
betraying it to the use of his gifts, he would make her somewhat
more secure against the everlasting flames; so that after assiduous
marshalling of converts she would be armed with an asbestos

buckler against the flames of hell. — This was Bärbel's undoing.
The need to save her soul from eternal damnation, to tear her from
the Devil's claws by yielding her body to the flames, was perfectly apparent. And since on account of the increasing ravages
of corruption an example was bitterly needed, the two witches,
the old one and the young, were burned at the stake, one beside
the other on the open square. Heinz Klöpfgeissel, the bewitched
one, stood in the throng of spectators with his head bared, murmuring prayers. The shrieks of his beloved, choked by smoke and
unrecognizable with hoarseness, seemed to him like the voice of
the Demon, croaking as against his will he issued from her. From
that hour the vile inhibition was lifted from him, for no sooner
was his love reduced to ashes than he recovered the sinfully alienated free use of his manhood.

I have never forgotten this revolting tale, so characteristic of
the tone of Schleppfuss's course, nor have I ever been able to be
quite cool about it. Among us, between Adrian and me, as well
as in discussions in Winfried it was much talked about; but neither in him, who was always taciturn about his teachers and what
they said, nor in his theological fellow-students did I succeed in
rousing the amount of indignation which would have satisfied my
own anger at the anecdote, especially against Klöpfgeissel. Even
today in my thoughts I address him breathing vengeance and call
him a prize ass in every sense of the word. Why did the donkey
have to tell? Why had he to test himself on other women when
he had the one he loved, loved obviously so much that it made
him cold and "impotent" with others? What does "impotent"
mean in this connection, when with the one he loved he had all
the potency of love? Love is certainly a kind of noble selective-
ness of sexuality, and if it is natural that sexual activity should decline in the absence of love, yet it is nothing less than unnatural
if it does so in the presence and face of love. In any case, Bärbel
had fixed and "restricted" her Heinz — not by means of any devil's
hocus-pocus but by the charm she had for him and the will by
which she held him as by a spell against other temptations. That
this protection in its strength and influence on the youth's nature
was psychologically reinforced by the magic salve and the girl's
belief in it, I am prepared to accept, though it does seem to me
simpler and more correct to look at the matter from his side and
to make the selective feeling given by his love responsible for the
inhibition over which he was so stupidly upset. But this point of
view too includes the recognition of a certain natural wonder-
working of the spiritual, its power to affect and modify the or-

ganic and corporeal in a decisive way — and this so to speak magic side of the thing it was, of course, that Schleppfuss purposely emphasized in his comments on the Klöpfgeissel case.

He did it in a quasi-humanistic sense, in order to magnify the lofty idea which those supposedly sinister centuries had had of the choice constitution of the human body. They had considered it nobler than all other earthly combinations of matter, and in its power of variation through the spiritual had seen the expression of its aristocracy, its high rank in the hierarchy of bodies. It got cold or hot through fear or anger, thin with affliction; blossomed in joy; a mere feeling of disgust could produce a physiological reaction like that of bad food, the mere sight of a dish of strawberries could make the skin of an allergic person break out; yes, sickness and death could follow purely mental operations. But it was only a step — though a necessary one — from this insight into the power of the mind to alter its own and accompanying physical matter, to the conviction, supported by ample human experience, that mind, whether wilfully or not, was able, that is by magic, to alter another person's physical substance. In other words, the reality of magic, of dæmonic influence and bewitchment, was corroborated; and phenomena such as the evil eye, a complex of experience concentrated in the saga of the death-dealing eye of the basilisk, were rescued from the realm of so-called superstition. It would have been culpable inhumanity to deny that an impure soul could produce by a mere look, whether deliberate or not, physically harmful effects in others, for instance in little children, whose tender substance was especially susceptible to the poison of such an eye.

Thus Schleppfuss in his exclusive course — exclusive because it was both intellectual and questionable. Questionable: a capital word, I have always ascribed a high philological value to it. It challenges one both to go in to and to avoid; anyhow to a very cautious going-in; and it stands in the double light of the remarkable and the disreputable, either in a thing — or in a man.

In our bow to Schleppfuss when we met him in the street or in the corridors of the university we expressed all the respect with which the high intellectual plane of his lectures inspired us hour by hour; but he on his side took off his hat with a still deeper flourish than ours and said: "Your humble servant."

CHAPTER XIV

MYSTIC numbers are not much in my line; I had been concerned to see that they fascinated Adrian, whose interest in them had been for a long time clearly though silently in evidence. But I feel a certain involuntary approval of the fact that the number thirteen, so generally considered unlucky, stands at the head of the foregoing chapter. I am almost tempted to think that there is more than chance at work here. But seriously speaking, it was chance after all; for the reason that this whole complex of Halle University life, just as in the earlier case of the Kretschmar lectures, does form a natural unity, and it was only out of consideration for the reader, who justly expects divisions and caesuras and places where he can draw breath, that I divided into several chapters matter which in the author's real and candid opinion has no claim to such articulation. If I had the say, we should still be in Chapter XI, and only my tendency to compromise has got Dr. Schleppfuss his number XIII. I wish him joy of it; yes, I would willingly have given the unlucky numeral to the whole corpus of memories of our student years at Halle; for as I said before, the air of that town, the theological air, did not suit me, and my guest visits to Adrian's courses were a sacrifice which, with mixed feelings, I made to our friendship.

To ours? I might better say to mine; for he did not in the least lay stress on my keeping at his side when we went to hear Kumpf or Schleppfuss; or think that I might be neglecting my own program. I did it of my own free will, only out of the imperative desire to hear what he heard, know what he learned, *to "keep track" of him* — for that always seemed to me highly necessary, though at the same time futile. A peculiarly painful combination that: necessity and futility. I was clear in my own mind that this was a life which one might indeed watch over, but not change, not influence; and my urge to keep a constant eye on my friend, not to stir from his side, had about it something like a premonition of the fact that it would one day be my task to set down an account of the impressions that moulded his early life. Certainly so much is clear, that I did not go into the matters dealt with above just in order to explain why I was not particularly comfortable in Halle. My reason was the same as that which made me so explicit on the subject of Wendell Kretschmar's Kaisersaschern lectures: namely, because I do and must stress the importance of making the reader a witness of Adrian's experiences in the world of intellect and spirit.

On the same ground I invite him to accompany us young sons of the Muses on the excursions we made in company, in the better times of the year, from Halle. As Adrian's childhood intimate, and of course because, although not a theologian, I seemed to display a decided interest in the field of religious study, I was welcomed into the guest circle of the Christian Society Winfried and permitted to share in the excursions made by the group in order .to enjoy the beauty of God's green creation.

They took place more frequently than we shared them. For I need hardly say that Adrian was no very zealous participant and his membership was more a matter of form than of punctual performance of activities. Out of courtesy and to show his good will towards the organization, he had let himself be persuaded; but under various pretexts, mostly on account of his headaches, he stopped away this or that time from the gatherings which took the place of the student "beer evenings." Even after a year or more he had got so little upon the *"frère et cochon"* footing with the seventy members that he did not manage to call them all by their right names or address them "in the singular." But he was respected among them. The shouts that greeted him when, I must almost say on rare occasions, he appeared at a session in the smoke-filled private room in Mütze's tavern, did contain a little fun at the expense of his supposed misanthropy; but they expressed genuine pleasure as well. For the group esteemed the part he played in their theological and philosophical debates, to which, without leading them, he would often throw in a remark and give an interesting turn. They were particularly pleased with his musical gift, which was useful because he could accompany the customary glees better than the others who tried it, with more animation and a fuller tone. Also he would oblige the assembly with a solo, a toccata of Bach, a movement of Beethoven or Schumann, at the instance of the leader, Baworinski, a tall dark lean person, with drooping lids and mouth puckered as though to whistle. Sometimes Adrian would even sit down unasked in the society's room at the piano, whose dull flat tone was strongly reminiscent of the inadequate instrument on which Wendell Kretschmar had imparted his knowledge to us in the hall of the Common Weal, and lose himself in free, experimental play. This especially happened before the beginning of a sitting, whilst the company were gathering. He had a way, I shall never forget it, of coming in, casually greeting the company, and then, sometimes without taking off his hat and coat, his face drawn with concentration, going straight to the piano, as though that alone were his goal. With a strong attack, bringing out the transition notes, with lifted brows, he would try chords, preparations, and resolutions which he may have excogitated on the way. But this rushing at the piano as though for refuge: it looked as though the place and its occupants frightened him; as though he sought shelter — actually within himself — from a bewildering strangeness into which he had come.

Then if he went on playing, dwelling on a fixed idea, changing and loosely shaping it, some one of those standing round, perhaps little Probst, a typical student, blond, with half-long, oily hair, would ask:

"What is that?"

"Nothing," answered the player, with a short shake of the head, more like the gesture with which one shakes off a fly.

"How can it be nothing," the other answered back, "since you are playing it?"

"He is improvising," explained the tall Baworinski sensibly.

"Improvising!" cried Probst, honestly startled, and peered with his pale blue eyes at Adrian's forehead as though he expected it to be glowing with fever.

Everybody burst out laughing, Adrian as well, letting his closed hands rest on the keyboard and bowing his head over them.

"Oh, Probst, what an ass you are!" said Baworinski. "He is making up, can't you understand? He just thought of that this very minute."

"How can he think up so many notes right and left at once," Probst defended himself, "and how can he say 'It is nothing' of something he is actually playing? One surely cannot play what is not?"

"Oh, yes," said Baworinski mildly. "One can play what does not yet exist."

I can still hear a certain Deutschlin, Konrad Deutschlin, a robust fellow with hair hanging in strings on his forehead, adding: "And everything was once nothing, my good Probst, and then became something."

"I can assure you," said Adrian, "that it really was nothing, in every sense of the word."

He had been bent over with laughter, but now he lifted his head and you could see by his face that it was no easy matter: that he felt exposed. I recall that there now ensued a lengthy discussion on the creative element, led by Deutschlin and by no means uninteresting. The limitations were debated, which this conception had to tolerate, by virtue of culture, tradition, imitation, convention, pattern. Finally the human and creative element was theologically recognized, as a far, reflected splendour of divinely existent power; as an echo of the first almighty summons to being, and the productive inspiration as in any case coming from above.

Moreover, and quite in passing, it was pleasant to me that I too, admitted from the profane faculty, could contribute when asked to the entertainment with my viol d'amore. For music was important in this circle, if only in a certain way, rather vaguely and as it were on principle: it was thought of as an art coming from God, one had to have "relations" with it, romantic and devout, like one's relations with nature. Music, nature, and joyous worship, these were closely related and prescribed ideas in the Winfried. When I referred to "sons of the Muses," the phrase, which to some perhaps would seem hardly suitable for students of theology, none the less found its justification in this combination of feeling, in the free and relaxed spirit, the clear-eyed contemplation of the beautiful, which characterized these tours into the heart of nature, to which I now return.

Two or three times in the course of our four terms at Halle they were undertaken *in corpore*, and Baworinski summoned up all the seventy members of Winfried. Adrian and I never joined these mass enterprises. But single groups, more intimately connected, also made similar excursions and these we repeatedly joined, in company with a few of the better sort. There was our leader himself; the sturdy Deutschlin; then a certain Dungersheim, Carl von Teutleben, and some others, named respectively Hubmeyer, Matthaeus Arzt, and Schappeler. I recall their names and to some extent their faces; it were superfluous to describe them.

The neighbourhood of Halle is a sandy plain, admittedly without charm. But a train conveys you in a few hours up the Saale into lovely Thuringia, and there, mostly at Naumburg or Apolda (the region where Adrian's mother was born), we left the train and set out with rucksacks and capes, on shanks's mare, in all-day marches, eating in village inns or sometimes camping at the edge of a wood and spending the night in the hayloft of a peasant's yard, waking in the grey dawn to wash and refresh ourselves at the long trough of a running spring. Such an interim form of living, the entry of city folk, brain workers, into the primitive country-side and back to mother earth, with the knowledge, after all, that we must — or might — soon return to our usual and "natural" sphere of middle-class comfort: such voluntary screwing down and simplification has easily, almost necessarily something artificial, patronizing, dilettante about it; of this we were humorously aware, and knew too that it was the cause of the good-natured, teasing grin with which many a peasant measured us on our request for his hayloft. But the kindly permission we got was due to our youth; for youth, one may say, makes the only proper bridge between the bourgeois and the state of nature; it is a pre-bourgeois state from which all student romance derives, the truly romantic period of life. To this formula the ever intellectually lively Deutschlin reduced the subject when we discussed it in our loft before falling asleep, by the wan light of the stable lantern in the corner. We dealt with the matter of our present mode of existence; and Deutschlin protested that it was poor taste for youth to explain youth: a form of life that discusses and examines itself thereby dissolves as form, and only direct and unconscious being has true existence.

The statement was denied, Hubmeyer and Schappeler contradicted it and Teutleben too demurred. It might be still finer, they ironically said, if only age were to judge youth and youth could only be the subject of outside observation, as though it had no share of objective mind. But it had, when it concerned itself too, and must be allowed to speak as youth about youth. There was something that one called a feeling of life, which came near to being consciousness of self, and if it were true that thereby the form of life was abrogated, then there was no sense of life possible at all. Mere dull unconscious being, ichthyosaurus-being, was no good, and today one must consciously not be wanting, one must assert one's specific form of life with an articulate feeling of self. It had taken a long time for youth to be so recognized.

"But the recognition has come more from pedagogy, that is from the old," Adrian was heard to say, "rather than from youth itself. It found itself one day presented, by an era that also talks about the century of the child and has invented the emancipation of woman, all in all a very compliant era, with the attribute of an independent form of life; of course it eagerly agreed."

"No, Leverkühn," said Hubmeyer and Schappeler, and the others supported them. He was wrong, they said, at least for the most part. It had been the feeling of life in youth itself that by dint of becoming conscious had asserted itself against the world, whether or no the latter had not been quite undecided for recognition.

"Not in the least," said Adrian. "Not at all undecided. I suppose one only needed to say to the era: 'I have this and this sense of life,' and the era just made it a low bow. Youth knocked on an open door." Moreover there was nothing to say against it, provided youth and its time understood each other.

"Why are you so supercilious, Leverkühn? Don't you find it good that today youth gets its rights in bourgeois society and that the values peculiar to the period of development are recognized?"

"Oh, certainly," said Adrian. "But I started, you started — that is, we started — with the idea — "

He was interrupted by a burst of laughter. I think it was Matthaeus Arzt who said: "That was perfect, Leverkühn. You led up to a climax. First you leave us out altogether, then you leave yourself out, then you manage to say 'we,' but you obviously find it very difficult, you hard-boiled individualist!"

Adrian rejected the epithet. It was quite false, he said, he was no individualist, he entirely accepted the community.

"Theoretically, perhaps," answered Arzt, "and condescendingly, with Adrian Leverkühn excepted. He talks of youth condescendingly too, as though he were not young himself; as though he were incapable of including himself and fitting in; as far as humility goes he knows very little about it."

"But we were not talking about humility," Adrian parried, "rather, on the contrary, of a conscious sense of life." Deutschlin suggested that they should let Adrian finish what he had to say.

"That was all," said the latter. "We started with the idea that youth has closer relations with nature than the mature man in a bourgeois society — something like woman, to whom also has been ascribed, compared with man, a greater nearness to nature. But I cannot follow. I do not find that youth stands on a particularly intimate footing with nature. Rather its attitude towards her is shy and reserved, actually strange. The human being comes to terms with his own natural side only with the years and only slowly gets accommodated to it. It is precisely youth, I mean more highly developed youth, that is more likely to shrink or be scornful, to display hostility. What do we mean by nature? Woods, meadows, mountains, trees, lakes, beauty of scenery? For all that, in my opinion, youth has much less of an eye than has the older, more tranquil man. The young one is by no means so disposed to see and enjoy nature. His eye is directed inwards, mentally conditioned, disinclined to the senses, in my opinion."

"*Quod demonstramus*," said somebody, very likely Dungersheim — "we wanderers lying here in our straw, marching through
the forests of Thuringia to Eisenach and the Wartburg."

" 'In my opinion,' you always say," another voice interjected.
"You probably mean: 'in my experience.' "

"You were just reproaching me," retorted Adrian, "for speaking condescendingly about youth and not including myself. Now
all of a sudden you tell me I am making myself stand for it."

"Leverkühn," Deutschlin commented, "has his own thoughts
about youth; but obviously he too regards it as a specific form of
life, which must be respected as such; and that is the decisive factor. I only spoke against youth's discussion of itself in so far as
that disintegrates the immediacy of life. But as consciousness of
self it also strengthens life, and in this sense — I mean also to this
extent — I call it good. The idea of youth is a prescriptive right
and prerogative of our people, the German people; the others
scarcely know it; youth as consciousness of self is as good as unknown to them. They wonder at the conscious bearing of German youth, to which the elder sections of the population give
their assent, and even at their unbourgeois dress. Let them! German youth, precisely as youth, represents the spirit of the people
itself, the German spirit, which is young and filled with the future: unripe, if you like, but what does unripe mean? German
deeds were always done out of a certain mighty immaturity, and
not for nothing are we the people of the Reformation. That too
was a work of immaturity. Mature, that was the Florentine citizen of the Renaissance, who before he went to church said to
his wife: "Well, let us now make our bow to popular error!"
But Luther was unripe enough, enough of the people, of the
German people, to bring in the new, the purified faith. Where
would the world be if maturity were the last word? We shall in
our unripeness vouchsafe it still some renewal, some revolution."

After these words of Deutschlin we were silent for a while.
Obviously there in the darkness each young man turned over in
his mind the feelings of personal and national youthfulness, mingling as one. The phrase "mighty immaturity" had certainly a
flattering ring for the most.

"If I only knew," I can hear Adrian say, breaking the silence,
"how it is we are so unripe, so young as you say we are, I mean
as a people. After all, we have come as far as the others, and perhaps it is only our history, the fact that we were a bit late getting
together and building up a common consciousness, which deludes
us into a notion of our uncommon youthfulness."

"But it is probably something else," responded Deutschlin. "Youth in the ultimate sense has nothing to do with political history, nothing to do with history at all. It is a metaphysical endowment, an essential factor, a structure, a conditioning. Have you never heard of German Becoming, of German Wandering, of the endless migratings of the German soul? Even foreigners know our word '*Wanderlust*.' If you like, the German is the eternal student, the eternal searcher, among the peoples of the earth — "

"And his revolutions," Adrian interpolated, with his short laugh, "are the puppet-shows of world history."

"Very witty, Leverkühn. But yet I am surprised that your Protestantism allows you to be so witty. It is possible, if necessary, to take more seriously what I mean by youth. To be young means to be original, to have remained nearer to the sources of life; it means to be able to stand up and shake off the fetters of an outlived civilization, to dare — where others lack the courage — to plunge again into the elemental. Youthful courage, that is the spirit of dying and becoming, the knowledge of death and rebirth."

"Is that so German?" asked Adrian. "Rebirth was once called *renascimento* and went on in Italy. And 'back to nature,' that was first prescribed in French."

"The first was a cultural renewal," answered Deutschlin, "the second a sentimental pastoral play."

"Out of the pastoral play," persisted Adrian, "came the French Revolution, and Luther's Reformation was only an offshoot and ethical bypath of the Renaissance, its application to the field of religion."

"The field of religion, there you are. And religion is always something besides archæological revival and an unheaval in social criticism. Religiosity, that is perhaps youth itself, it is the directness, the courage and depth of the personal life, the will and the power, the natural and dæmonic side of being, as it has come into our consciousness again through Kierkegaard, to experience it in full vitality and to live through it."

"Do you consider the feeling for religion a distinctively German gift?" asked Adrian.

"In the sense I mean, as soulful youth, as spontaneity, as faith, and Düreresque knighthood between Death and Devil — certainly."

"And France, the land of cathedrals, whose head was the All-

Christian King, and which produced theologians like Bossuet and
Pascal?"

"That was long ago. For centuries France has been marked out
by history as the European power with the anti-Christian mission.
Of Germany the opposite is true, and that you would feel and
know, Leverkühn, if you were not Adrian Leverkühn — in other
words, too cool to be young, too clever to be religious. With
cleverness one may go a long way in the Church, but scarcely in
religion."

"Many thanks, Deutschlin," laughed Adrian. "In good old German words, as Ehrenfried Kumpf would say, you have given it to
me straight, without any mealy-mouthing. I have a feeling that I
shan't go very far in the Church either; but one thing is certain,
that I should not have become a theologian without her. I know
of course that it is the most talented among you, those who have
read Kierkegaard, who place truth, even ethical truth, entirely in
the subjective, and reject with horror everything that savours of
herd existence. But I cannot go with you in your radicalism —
which certainly will not long persist, as it is a student licence — I
cannot go with you in your separation, after Kierkegaard, of
Church and Christianity. I see in the Church, even as she is today,
secularized and reduced to the bourgeois, a citadel of order, an in-
stitution for objective disciplining, canalizing, banking-up of the
religious life, which without her would fall victim to subjectivist
demoralization, to a chaos of divine and dæmonic powers, to a
world of fantastic uncanniness, an ocean of dæmony. To separate
Church and religion means to give up separating the religious
from madness."

"Oh, come!" from several voices. But:

"He is right," Matthaeus Arzt declared roundly. The others
called him the Socialist, because the social was his passion. He was
a Christian Socialist and often quoted Goethe's saying that Christianity was a political revolution which, having failed, became a
moral one. Political, he said now, it must again become, that is to
say social: that was the true and only means for the disciplining
of the religious element, now in danger of a degeneration which
Leverkuhn had not so badly described. Religious socialism, religiosity linked with the social, that was it; for everything depended on finding the right link, and the theonomic sanction
must be united with the social, bound up with the God-given
task of social fulfilment. "Believe me," he said, "it all depends on
the development of a responsible industrial population, an inter-

national nation of industry, which some day can form a right and
genuine European economic society. In it all shaping impulses
will lie, they lie in the germ even now, not merely for the technical achievement of a new economic organization, not only to result in a thorough sanitation of the natural relations of life, but
also to found new political orders."

I repeat the ideas of these young people as they were uttered,
in their own terminology, a sort of learned lingo, quite unaware
how pompous they sounded, flinging about the stilted and pretentious phrases with artless virtuosity and self-satisfaction. "Natural relations of life," "theonomic sanctions," such were their pre-
ciosities. Certainly they could have put it all more simply, but
then it would not have been their scientific-theological jargon.
With gusto they propounded the "problem of being," talked
about "the sphere of the divine," "the political sphere," or "the
academic sphere"; about the "structural principle," "condition
of dialectic tension," "existential correspondences," and so on.
Deutschlin, with his hands clasped behind his head, now put the
"problem of being" in the sense of the genetic origin of Arzt's
economic society. That was nothing but economic common sense,
and nothing but this could ever be represented in the economic
society. "But we must be clear on this point, Matthaeus," said he,
"that the social ideal of an economic social organization comes
from autonomous thinking in its nature enlightening, in short
from a rationalism which is still by no means grasped by the
mighty forces either above or below the rational. You believe you
can develop a just order out of the pure insight and reason of
man, equating the just and the socially useful, and you think that
out of it new political forms will come. But the economic sphere
is quite different from the political, and from economic expedi-
ency to historically related political consciousness there is no direct transition. I don't see why you fail to recognize that. Political organization refers to the State, a kind and degree of control
not conditioned by usefulness; wherein other qualities are represented than those known to representatives of enterprises and sec-
retaries of unions; for instance, honour and dignity. For such
qualities, my dear chap, the inhabitants of the economic sphere
do not contribute the necessary existential correspondences."

"Ach, Deutschlin, what are you talking about?" said Arzt. "As
modern sociologists we very well know that the State too is conditioned by utilitarian functions. There is the administration of justice and the preservation of order. And then after all we live in
an economic age, the economic is simply the historical character

of this time, and honour and dignity do not help the State one jot, if it does not of itself have a grasp of the economic situation and know how to direct it."

Deutschlin admitted that. But he denied that useful functions were the *essential* objects and raisons d'être of the State. The legitimacy of the State resided, he said, in its elevation, its sovereignty, which thus existed independent of the valuations of individuals, because it — very much in contrast to the shufflings of the Contrat Social — was there *before* the individual. The supra-individual associations had, that is, just as much original existence as the individual human beings, and an economist, for just that reason, could understand nothing of the State, because he understood nothing of its transcendental foundation.

To which Teutleben added:

"I am of course not without sympathy for the socio-religious combination that Arzt is speaking for, it is anyhow better than none at all, and Matthaeus is only too right when he says that everything depends on finding the right combination. But to be right, to be at once political and religious, it must be of the people, and what I ask myself is: can a new nationality rise out of an economic society? Look at the Ruhr: there you have your assembly centres of men, yet no new national cells. Travel in the local train from Leuna to Halle. You will see workmen sitting together, who can talk very well about tariffs; but from their conversation it does not appear that they have drawn any national strength from their common activity. In economics the nakedly finite rules more and more."

"But the national is finite too," somebody else said, it was either Hubmeyer or Schappeler, I don't know which. "As theologians we must not admit that the folk is anything eternal. Capacity for enthusiasm is very fine and a need for faith very natural to youth; but it is a temptation too, and one must look very hard at the new groupings, which today, when liberalism is dying off, are everywhere being presented, to see whether they have genuine substance, and whether the thing creating the bond is itself something real or perhaps only the product of, let us say, structural romanticism, which creates for itself ideological connections in a nominalistic not to say fictionalistic way. I think, or rather I am afraid, that the deified national State and the State regarded as a utopia are just such nominalistic structures; and the recognition of them, let us say the recognition of Germany, has something not binding about it because it has nothing to do with personal substance and qualitative content. Nothing is asked about that, and when one says 'Germany' and declares that to be his connecting link, he does not need to validate it at all. He will be asked by nobody, not even by himself, how much Germanism he in fact and in a personal — that is, in a qualitative sense — represents and realizes; or how far he is in a position to serve the assertion of a German form of life in the world. It is that which I call nominalism, or rather the fetish of names, which in my opinion is the ideological worship of idols."

"Good, Hubmeyer," said Deutschlin. "All you say is quite right, and in any case I admit that your criticism has brought us closer to the problem. I disagreed with Matthaeus Arzt because the domination of the utilitarian principle in the economic field does not suit me; but I entirely agree with him that the theonomic sanction in itself, that is to say the religious in general, has something formalistic and unobjective about it. It needs some kind of down-to-earth, empirical content or application or confirmation, some practice in obedience to God. And so now Arzt has chosen socialism and Carl Teutleben nationalism. These are the two between which we have today to choose. I deny that there is an outbidding of ideologies, since today nobody is beguiled by the empty word 'freedom.' There are in fact just these two possibilities, of religious submission and religious realization: the social and the national. But as ill luck will have it, both of them have their drawbacks and dangers, and very serious ones. Hubmeyer has expressed himself very tellingly on a certain nominalistic hollowness and personal lack of substance so frequently evident in the acceptance of the national; and, generally speaking, one should add that it is futile to fling oneself into the arms of a reinvigorating objectivism if it means nothing for the actual shaping of one's personal life but is only valid for solemn occasions, among which indeed I count the intoxication of sacrificial death. To a genuine sacrifice two valuations and qualitative ingredients belong: that of the thing and that of the sacrifice. . . . But we have cases where the personal substance, let us say, was very rich in Germanness and quite involuntarily objectivated itself also as sacrifice; yet where acknowledgment of the folk-bond not only utterly failed, but there was even a permanent and violent negation of it, so that the tragic sacrifice consisted precisely in the conflict between being and confession. . . . So much for tonight about the national sanction. As for the social, the hitch is that when everything in the economic field is regulated in the best possible manner, the problem of the meaning and fulfilment of existence and a worthy conduct of life is left open, just as open as it is today. Some day

we shall have universal economic administration of the world, the
complete victory of collectivism. Good; the relative insecurity of
man due to the catastrophic social character of the capitalistic
system will have disappeared; that is, there will have vanished
from human life the last memory of risk and loss — and with it
the intellectual problem. One asks oneself why then continue to
live. . . ."

"Would you like to retain the capitalist system, Deutschlin,"
asked Arzt — "because it keeps alive the memory of the insecurity
of human life?"

"No, I would not, my dear Arzt," answered Deutschlin with
some heat. "Still, I may be allowed to indicate the tragic antinomies of which life is full."

"One doesn't need to have them pointed out," sighed Dungersheim. "It is certainly a desperate situation, and the religious man
asks himself whether the world really is the single work of a benevolent God and not rather a combined effort, I will not say
with whom."

"What I should like to know," remarked von Teutleben, "is
whether the young of other nations lie about like us, plaguing
themselves with problems and antinomies."

"Hardly," answered Deutschlin contemptuously. "They have
a much easier and more comfortable time intellectually."

"The Russian revolutionary youth," Arzt asserted, "should be
excepted. There, if I am not mistaken, there is a tireless discursive
argumentation and a cursed lot of dialectic tension."

"The Russians," said Deutschlin sententiously, "have profun-
dity but no form. And in the west they have form but no pro-
fundity. Only we Germans have both."

"Well, if that is not a nationalistic sanction!" laughed Hubmeyer.

"It is merely the sanction of an idea," Deutschlin asserted. "It
is the demand of which I speak. Our obligation is exceptional, certainly not the average, for that we have already attained. What is
and what ought to be — there is a bigger gulf between them with
us than with others, simply because the 'ought to be,' the standard, is so high."

"In all that," Dungersheim warned us, "we probably ought not
to consider the national, but rather to regard the complex of
problems as bound up with the existence of modern man. But it
is the case, that since the direct faith in being has been lost, which
in earlier times was the result of being fixed in a pre-existent universal order of things, I mean the ritually permeated regulations

which had a certain definite bearing on the revealed truth . . .
that since the decline of faith and the rise of modern society our
relations with men and things have become endlessly complicated
and refracted, there is nothing left but problems and uncertain-
ties, so that the design for truth threatens to end in resignation
and despair. The search rising from disintegration, for the beginnings of new forces of order, is general; though one may also
agree that it is particularly serious and urgent among us Germans,
and that the others do not suffer so from historical destiny, either
because they are stronger or because they are duller — "

"Duller," pronounced von Teutleben.

"That is what you say, Teutleben. But if we count to our honour as a nation our sharp awareness of the historical and psychological complex of problems, and identify with the German character the endeavour after new universal regulation, we are already
on the point of prescribing for ourselves a myth of doubtful
genuineness and not doubtful arrogance: namely, the national, with
its structural romanticism of the warrior type, which is nothing
but natural paganism with Christian trimmings and identifies
Christus as 'Lord of the heavenly hosts.' But that is a position de-
cisively threatened from the side of the demons. . . ."

"Well, and?" asked Deutschlin. "Dæmonic powers stand beside
the order-making qualities in any vital movement."

"Let us call things by their names," demanded Schappeler — or
it might have been Hubmeyer. "The dæmonic, the German word
for that is the instincts. And that is just it: today even, along with
the instincts, propaganda is made for claims to all sorts of sanctions, and that one too, I mean, it takes them in and trims up the
old idealism with the psychology of instinct, so that there arises
the dazzling impression of a thicker density of reality. But just on
that account the bid can be pure swindle."

At this point one can only say "and so on"; for it is time to put
an end to the reproduction of that conversation — or of such conversations. In reality it had no end, it went on deep into the night,
on and on, with "bipolar position" and "historically conscious
analysis," with "extra-temporal qualities," "ontological natural-
ism," "logical dialectic," and "practical dialectic": painstaking,
shoreless, learned, tailing off into nothing — that is, into slumber,
to which our leader Baworinski recommended us, for in the
morning — as it already almost was — we should be due for an
early start. That kind nature held sleep ready, to take up the conversation and rock it in forgetfulness, was a grateful circum-

stance, and Adrian, who had not spoken for a long time, gave it expression in a few words as we settled down.

"Yes, good night, lucky we can say it. Discussions should always be held just before going to bed, your rear protected by sleep. How painful, after an intellectual conversation, to have to go about with your mind so stirred up."

"That is just an escapist psychology," somebody grumbled — and then the first sounds of heavy breathing filled our loft with its announcement of relaxation and surrender to the vegetative state; of that a few hours sufficed to restore youth's elasticity. For next day along with physical activity and the enjoyment of natural beauty, they would continue the usual theological and philosophical debates with almost interminable mutual instruction, opposition, challenge, and reply. It was the month of June, and the air was filled with the heavy scent of jasmine and elder-blossom from the gorges of the wooded heights that cross the Thuringian basin. Priceless it was to wander for days through the countryside, here almost free from industry, the well-favoured, fruitful land, with its friendly villages, in clusters of latticed buildings. Then coming out of the farming region into that of mostly grazing land, to follow the storied, beech- and pine-covered ridge road, the "Rennsteig," which, with its view deep down into the Werra valley, stretches from the Frankenwald to Eisenach on the Horsel. It grew ever more beautiful, significant, romantic; and neither what Adrian had said about the reserve of youth in the face of nature, nor what about the desirability of being able to retire to slumber after intellectual discussion, seemed to have any cogency. Even to him it scarcely applied; for, except when his headaches made him silent, he contributed with animation to the daily talks; and if nature lured from him no very enthusiastic cries and he looked at it with a certain musing aloofness, I do not doubt that its pictures, rhythms, the melodies of its upper airs, penetrated deeper into his soul than into those of his companions. It has even happened that some passage of pure, free beauty standing out from the tense intellectuality of his work has later brought to my mind those days and the experiences we shared.

Yes, they were stirring hours, days, and weeks. The refreshment of the out-of-doors life, and the oxygen in the air, the landscape, and the historical impressions, thrilled these young folk and raised their spirits to a plane where thought moved lavishly in free experimental flight as it will at that time of life. In later, more arid hours of an after-university professional career, even an intellectual one, there would be scarcely any such occasion. Often I looked at them during their theological and philosophical debates and pictured to myself that to some among them their Winfried period might in later years seem the finest time of their lives. I watched them and I watched Adrian, with the clear perception that it would not be so with him. I, as a non-theologian, was a guest among them; he, though a theologian, was even more of one. Why? I felt, not without a pang, the foreordained gulf between his existence and that of these striving and high-purposed youths. It was the difference of the life-curve between good, yes, excellent average, which was destined to return from that roving, seeking student life to its bourgeois courses, and the other, invisibly singled out, who would never forsake the hard route of the mind, would tread it, who knew whither, and whose gaze, whose attitude, never quite resolved in the fraternal, whose inhibitions in his personal relations made me and probably others aware that he himself divined this difference.

By the beginning of his fourth semester I had indications that my friend was thinking of dropping his theological course, even before the first exams.

CHAPTER XV

ADRIAN's relations with Wendell Kretschmar had never been broken off or weakened. The young "studiosus" of the divine science saw the musical mentor of his school-days in every vacation, when he came to Kaisersaschern; visited him and consulted him in the organist's quarters in the Cathedral; met him at Uncle Leverkühn's house, and persuaded the parents to invite him once or twice to Buchel for the week-end, where they took extended walks and also got Jonathan Leverkühn to show the guest Chladni's sound-patterns and the devouring drop. Kretschmar stood very well with the host of Buchel, now getting on in years. His relations with Frau Elsbeth were more formal if by no means actually strained. Perhaps she was distressed by his stutter, which just for that reason got worse in her presence and in direct conversation with her. It was odd, after all. In Germany music enjoys that respect among the people which in France is given to literature; among us nobody is put off or embarrassed, uncomfortably impressed, or moved to disrespect or mockery by the fact that a man is a musician; so I am convinced that Elsbeth Leverkühn felt entire respect for Adrian's elder friend, who, moreover, practised his activity as a salaried man in the service of the Church. Yet during the two and a half days which I once spent with him and Adrian at Buchel, I observed in her bearing towards the organist a certain reserve and restraint, held in check but not quite done away by her native friendliness. And he, as I said, responded with a worsening of his impediment amounting a few times almost to a calamity. It is hard to say whether it was that he felt her unease and mistrust or whatever it was, or because on his own side, spontaneously, he had definite inhibitions amounting to shyness and embarrassment in her presence.

As for me, I felt sure that the peculiar tension between Kretschmar and Adrian's mother had reference to Adrian; I divined this because in the silent struggle that went on I stood in my own feeling between the two parties, inclining now to the one and now to the other. What Kretschmar wanted, what he talked about on those walks with Adrian, was clear to me, and privately my own wishes supported him. I thought he was right when, also in talk with me, he pleaded for the musical calling of his pupil, that he should become a composer, with determination, even with urgency. "He has," he said, "the composer's eye; he bends on music the look of the initiate, not of the vaguely enjoying outsider. His way of discovering thematic connections that the other kind of man does not see; of perceiving the articulation of a short extract in the form of question and answer; altogether of seeing from the inside how it is made, confirms me in my judgment. That he shows no productive impulse, does not yet write or naïvely embark upon youthful productions, is only to his credit; it is a question of his pride, which prevents him from producing epigonal music."

I could only agree with all that. But I could thoroughly understand as well the protective concern of the mother and often felt my solidarity with her, to the point of hostility to the other side. Never shall I forget a scene in the living-room at Buchel when we chanced to sit there together, the four of us: mother and son, Kretschmar and I. Elsbeth was in talk with the musician, who was puffing and blowing with his impediment; it was a mere chat, of which Adrian was certainly not the subject. She drew her son's head to her as he sat beside her, in the strangest way, putting her arm about him, not round his shoulders but round his head, her hand on his brow, and thus, with the gaze of her black eyes directed upon Kretschmar and her sweet voice speaking to him, she leaned Adrian's head upon her breast.

But to return: it was not alone these meetings that sustained the relation between master and pupil. There was also frequent correspondence, an exchange, I believe every two weeks, between Halle and Kaisersaschern, about which Adrian from time to time informed me and of which I even got to see some part. It seemed that Kretschmar was considering taking a piano and organ class in the Hase private conservatoire in Leipzig, which next to the famous State Music School in that city was rejoicing in a growing reputation, constantly increased during the next ten years, up to the death of the capital musician Clemens Hase (it no longer plays any role, even if it still exists). I learned this fact in Michaelmas 1904. At the beginning of the next year Wendell accordingly left Kaisersaschern to take over his new position, and from then on the correspondence went forward between Halle and Leipzig, to and fro: Kretschmar's sheets covered on one side with large, scratching, spluttering letters; Adrian's replies on rough yellow paper, in his regular, slightly old-fashioned, rather florid script, written, as one could see, with a round-hand pen. I saw a draft of one of them, very compactly written, like figures, full of fine additions and corrections — I had early become familiar with his way of writing and read it quite easily — and he also showed me Kretschmar's reply to it. He did this, obviously, in order that I need not be too much surprised by the step he purposed to take when he should have actually settled on it. For that he had not as yet, was hesitating very much, doubting and examining himself, as the letter makes clear; he obviously wanted to be advised by me — God knows whether in a sense to encourage or to warn.

There could not be and would not have been on my side any possibility of surprise, even if I had been faced with the fact without preparation. I knew what was on the way: whether it would actually come to pass was another question; but so much was clear to me too, that since Kretschmar's move to Leipzig, his chances of getting his way were considerably improved.

Adrian's letter showed a more than average capacity to look at himself critically, and as a confession its ironic humility touched me very much. To his one-time mentor, now aspiring to be that again and much more, he set forth the scruples that held him back from a decision to change his profession and fling himself into the arms of music. He half-way admitted that theology, as an empiric study, had disappointed him; the reasons of course being to seek not in that revered science, nor with his academic teachers, but in himself. That was already plain from the fact that he certainly could not say what other, better choice he could then have made. Sometimes, when he took counsel with himself on the possibilities of a shift, he had, during these years, considered choosing mathematics, in which, when he was at school, he had always found "good entertainment" (his very words). But with a sort of horror at himself he saw it coming, that if he made this discipline his own, bound himself over, identified himself with it, he would very soon be disillusioned, bored; get as sick and tired of it as though he "had ladled it in with a cooking-spoon" (this grotesque simile also I recall literally). "I cannot conceal from your respected self," he wrote (for he sometimes fell into old-fashioned phrases and spellings), "neither you nor myself, that with your *apprendista* it is a god-forsaken case. It is not just an everyday thing with me, I would not lain it thus; it addresses itself to your verye bowells of compassion more than makes your heart leap up for joy." He had, he said, received from God the gift of a "toward wit"; from childhood up and with less than common pain

had grasped everything offered in his education — too easily, "belike," for any of it to win his proper respect. Too easily for
blood and brains ever to have got properly warmed up for the
sake of a subject and by effort over it. "I fear," he wrote, "dear
and beloved friend and master, I am a lost soul, a black sheep; I
have no warmth. As the Gode Boke hath it, they shall be cursed
and spewed out of the mouth who are neither cold nor warm but
lukewarm. Lukewarm I should not call myself. I am cold out of
all question; but in my judgment of myself I would pray to dis-
sent from the taste of that Power whose it is to apportion blessing
and cursing."

He went on:

"Oddly enough, it was best at the grammar school, there I was
still pretty much in the right place, because in the upper forms
they deal out the gretest variety of thinges, one after the other,
changing the subject from one five-and-forty minutes to the next
— in other words there was still no profession. But even those five-
and-forty minutes were too long, they bored me — and boredom
is the coldest thing in the world. After fifteen minutes at most I
had all that the good man chammed over with the other boys for
thirty more. Reading the authors, I read on further; I had done so
at home, and if I mought not always give answer, 'twas but because I was already in the next lesson. Three quarters of an hour
of Anabasis was too much of one thing for my patience, in sign
thereof my mygryms came on" (he meant his headaches) "and
never did they procede from fatigue due to effort, but from
satiety, from cold boredom, and, dear master and friend, sith I
no longer am a young bachelor springing from branch to branch
but have married me with one plot and one profession, it has
truly gone hevyli indeed with me.

"In feith, ye will not believe that I hold myself too good for
any profession. On the contrary, I am pitiful of that I make mine
own, and ye may see in that an homage, a declaration of love for
music, a special position towards her, that in her case I should feel
quite too deeply pitiful.

"You will ask if it was not so with theology? But I submitted
thereunto; not so much, though there was somewhat of that too
therein, that I saw in it the highest of the sciences; but for that I
would fain humble myself, bow the knee, and be chastened, to
castigate my cold contumacy, in short out of *contritio*. I wanted
the sack of heyre, the spiked girdle beneath. I did what those did
in earlier times who knocked at the gate of the cloister of strict
observance. It has its absurd and comic sides, this professionally

cloistered life, but assaye to understand that a secret terror warned me not to forsake it, to put the Scriptures under the bench and scape into the art to which you introduced me, and about which I feel that for me to practise it were shrewidness and shame.

"Ye think me called to this art, and give me to understand that the 'step aside' to her were no long one. My Lutheranism agrees, for it sees in theology and music neighbouring spheres and close of kin; and besides, music has always seemed to me personally a magic marriage between theology and the so diverting mathematic. Item, she has much of the laboratory and the insistent activity of the alchemists and nigromancers of yore, which also stood in the sign of theology, but at the same time in that of emancipation and apostasy; it was apostasy, not from the feith, that was never possible, but *in* the feith; for apostasy is an act of feith and everything is and happens in God, most of all the falling from Him."

My quotations are very nearly literal, even where they are not quite so. I can rely very well on my memory, and besides I committed much of it to paper at once after reading the draft, and in particular this about apostasy.

He then excused himself for the digression, which scarcely was one, and went on to the practical question of what branch of musical activity he should envisage in case he yielded to Kretschmar's pressure. He pointed out that he was useless, from the start and admittedly, for solo virtuosity. "It pricketh betimes that will be a sharp thorn," he wrote, quoting Kumpf, and that he had come too late into contact with the instrument, or even with the idea, from which followed, of course, the clear conclusion that he lacked any instinctive urge in that direction. He had gone to the keyboard not out of desire to master it, but out of private curiosity about music itself; he was entirely lacking in the gypsy blood of the concert artist, who produced himself before the public through music, music being the occasion he took. To that went mental premises which he did not satisfy: desire for love-affairs with the crowd, for laurel wreaths and bowing and kowtowing to applause. He avoided the adjectives which would actually have made clear what he meant: he did not say that even if he had not come to it too late, he was too self-conscious, too proud, too difficult, too solitary, to be a virtuoso.

These same objections, he went on, stood in the way of a career as a conductor. As little as a keyboard juggler could he see himself as a baton-waving, frock-coated prima donna of the orchestra, an interpreting ambassador and gala-representative of music on earth. But now there did escape him a word that belonged in the same class with those which I just said would have fitted the case: he spoke of being unsocial; he called himself that, and meant no compliment. This quality, he judged, was the expression of a want of warmth, sympathy, love, and it was very much in question whether one could, lacking them, be a good artist, which after all and always means being a lover and beloved of the world. Now putting these two aside, the solo artist and the conductor, what was left? Forsooth, music herself, the promise and vow to her, the hermetic laboratory, the gold-kitchen: composition. "Wonderful! Ye will initiate me, friend Albertus Magnus, into the mysteries of theory and certes I feel, I know aforehand, as already I know a little from experience, I shalbe no backward adeptus. I shall grasp all the shifts and controls, and that easily, in truth because my mind goeth to meet them, the ground is prepared, it already nourishes some seed therein. I will refine on the *prima materia*, in that I add to it the *magisterium* and with spirit and fire drive the matter through many limbecs and retorts for the refining thereof. What a glorious mystery! I know none higher, deeper, better; none more thrilling, or occult; none whereto less persuasion were necessary to persuade.

"And yet, why does an inward voice warn me: '*O homo fuge*'? I cannot give answer unto the question very articulately. Only this much I can say: I fear to make promises to art, because I doubt whether my nature — quite aside from the question of a gift — is calculated to satisfy her; because I must disclaim the robust naïveté which, so far as I can see — among other things, and not least among them — pertaineth to the nature of the artist. In its place my lot is a quickly satisfied intelligence, whereof, I suppose, I may speak, because I call heaven and hell to witness that I am not vain of it; it is that, together with the accompanying proneness to fatigue and disgust (with headake), which is the ground of my fear and concern. It will, it ought to, decide me to refrain. Mark me, good master, young as I am I am wel enow seen therein to know, and should not be your pupil did I not, that it passeth far beyond the pattern, the canon, the tradition, beyond what one learns from others, the trick, the technique. Yet it is undeniable that there is a lot of all that in it, and I see it coming (for it lieth also in my nature, for good or ill, to look beyond) that I am embarrassed at the insipidness which is the supporting structure, the conditioning solid substance of even the work of genius, at the elements thereof which are training and common property, at use and wont in achieving the beautiful; I blush at all that, weary thereof, get head-ake therefrom, and that right early.

"How stupid, how pretentious it would be to ask: 'Do you understand that?' For how should you not? It goes like this, when it is beautiful: the cellos intone by themselves, a pensive, melancholy theme, which questions the folly of the world, the wherefore of all the struggle and striving, pursuing and plaguing — all highly expressive and decorously philosophical. The cellos enlarge upon this riddle awhile, head-shaking, deploring, and at a certain point in their remarks, a well-chosen point, the chorus of wind instruments enters with a deep full breath that makes your shoulders rise and fall, in a choral hymn, movingly solemn, richly harmonized, and produced with all the muted dignity and mildly restrained power of the brass. Thus the sonorous melody presses on up to nearly the height of a climax, which, in accordance with the law of economy it avoids at first, gives way, leaves open, sinks away, postpones, most beautifully lingers; then withdraws and gives place to another theme, a songlike, simple one, now jesting, now grave, now popular, apparently brisk and robust by nature but sly as you make them, and for someone with some subtle cleverness in the art of thematic analysis and transformation it proves itself amazingly pregnant and capable of utter refinement. For a while this little song is managed and deployed, cleverly and charmingly, it is taken apart, looked at in detail, varied, out of it a delightful figure in the middle register is led up into the most enchanting heights of fiddles and flutes, lulls itself there a little, and when it is at its most artful, then the mild brass has again the word with the previous choral hymn and comes into the foreground. The brass does not start from the beginning as it did the first time, but as though its melody had already been there for a while; and it continues, solemnly, to that climax from which it wisely refrained the first time, in order that the surging feeling, the Ah-h-effect, might be the greater: now it gloriously bestrides its theme, mounting unchecked, with weighty support from the passing notes on the tuba, and then, looking back, as it were, with dignified satisfaction on the finished achievement, sings itself decorously to the end.

"Dear friend, why do I have to laugh? Can a man employ the traditional or sanctify the trick with greater genius? Can one with shrewder sense achieve the beautiful? And I, abandoned wretch, I have to laugh, particularly at the grunting supporting notes of the bombardone, Bum, bum, bum, bang! I may have tears in my eyes at the same time, but the desire to laugh is irresistible — I have always had to laugh, most damnably, at the most mysterious and impressive phenomena. I fled from this exaggerated sense of the comic into theology, in the hope that it would give relief to the tickling — only to find there too a perfect legion of ludicrous absurdities. Why does almost everything seem to me like its own parody? Why must I think that almost all, no, all the methods and conventions of art today *are good for parody only?* — These are of course rhetorical questions, it was not that I still expected an answer to them. But such a despairing heart, such a damp squib as I am, you consider as 'gifted' for music and summon me to you and to its service, instead of rather leaving me humbly to tarry with God and theology?"

Thus Adrian's confession in avoidance. And Kretschmar's reply: that document I have not by me. It was not found among the papers Leverkühn left. He must have preserved it for a while and then in some moving to Munich, to Italy, to Pfeiffering, it must have got lost. But I retain it in my memory almost as precisely as Adrian's own, even though I made no notes on it. The stutterer stuck by his summons, his monitions and allurements. Not a word in Adrian's letter, he wrote, could have made him for a moment falter in his conviction that it was music for which fate destined the writer, after which he hankered as music after him, and against which, half cowardly, half capricious, he had hidden himself behind these half-true analyses of his character and constitution, as previously behind theology, his first and absurd choice. "Affectation, Ádri — and the increase in your headaches is the punishment for it." His sense of the ludicrous of which he boasted, or complained, would suit with art far better than with his present unnatural occupation, for art, on the contrary, could use it; could, in general, much better use the repellent characteristics he attributed to himself than he believed or made pretence that he believed it could. He, Kretschmar, would leave the question open, how far Adrian was accusing himself in order to excuse his corresponding accusations against art; for this painting art as a marriage with the mob, as kiss-throwing, gala-posturing, as a bellows to blow up the emotions, was a facile misconstruction and a wilful one too. What he was trying to do was to excuse himself on account of certain characteristics, while these, on the other hand, were the very ones art demanded. Art needed just his sort today — and the joke, the hypocritical, hide-and-seek joke, was that Adrian knew it perfectly well. The coolness, the "quickly satisfied intelligence," the eye for the stale and absurd, the early fatigue, the capacity for disgust — all that was perfectly calculated to make a profession of the talent bound up with it. Why? Because it belonged only in part to the private personality; for the rest it was of an extra-individual nature, the expression of a collective feeling for the historical exhaustion and vitiation of the means and appliances of art, the boredom with them and the search for new ways. "Art strides on," Kretschmar wrote, "and does so through the medium of the personality, which is the product and the tool of the time, and in which objective and subjective motives combine indistinguishably, each taking on the shape of the others. The vital need of art for revolutionary progress and the coming of the new addresses itself to whatever vehicle has the strongest subjective sense of the staleness, fatuity, and emptiness of the means still current. It avails itself of the apparently unvital, of that personal satiety and intellectual boredom, that disgust at seeing 'how it works'; that accursed itch to look at things in the light of their own parody; that sense of the ridiculous — I tell you that the will to life and to living, growing art puts on the mask of these faint-hearted personal qualities, to manifest itself therein, to objectivate, to fulfill itself. Is that too much metaphysics for you? But it is just precisely enough of it, precisely the truth, the truth which at bottom you know yourself. Make haste, Adrian, and decide. I am waiting. You are already twenty, and you have still a good many tricks of the trade to get used to, quite hard enough to stimulate you. It is better to get a headache from exercises in canons, fugues, and counterpoint than from confuting the Kantian confutation of the evidence for the existence of God. Enough of your theological spinsterhood!

> 'Virginity is well, yet must to motherhood;
> Unear'd she is a soil unfructified for good.' "

With this quotation from the "Cherubinic Wandersmann" the letter ended, and when I looked up from it I met Adrian's subtle smile.

"Not badly parried, don't you think?" he asked.

"By no means," said I.

"He knows what he wants," he went on, "and it is rather humiliating that I do not."

"I think you do too," I said. For indeed in his own letter I had not seen an actual refusal, nor indeed had I believed he wrote it out of affectation. That is certainly not the right word for the will to make harder for oneself a hard decision, by deepening it with self-distrust. I already saw with emotion that the decision would be made; and it had become the basis for the ensuing conversation about our immediate futures. In any case, our ways were parting. Despite serious short-sightedness I was declared fit for military service, and intended to put in my year at once; I was to do it in Naumburg with the regiment of the 3rd Field Artillery. Adrian, on whatever grounds — narrow-chestedness, or his habitual headaches — was indefinitely excused; and he planned to spend some weeks at Buchel, in order, as he said, to discuss with his parents his change of profession. It came out that he would put it to them as though it involved merely a change of university. In a way, that was how he put it to himself too. He would, so he would tell them, bring his music more into the foreground, and accordingly he was going to the city where the musical mentor of his school-days was working. What did not come out was that he was giving up theology. In fact, his actual intention was to enroll himself again at the university and attend lectures in philosophy in order to make his doctorate in that school.

At the beginning of the winter semester, in 1905, Leverkühn went to Leipzig.

CHAPTER XVI

It scarcely needs saying that our good-bye was outwardly cool and reserved. There was hardly even a pressure of the hand, an exchange of looks. Too often in our young days we had parted and met again for us to have kept the habit of shaking hands. He left Halle a day earlier than I; we had spent the previous evening together at the theatre, without any of the Winfried group. He was leaving next morning, and we said good-bye on the street, as we had hundreds of times before. I could not help marking my farewell by calling him by name — his first name, as was natural to me, but he did not follow suit. "So long!" he said, that was all; he had the phrase from Kretschmar, and used it half-mockingly, as a quotation, having in general a definite liking to quote, to make word-plays on something or someone. He added some jest about the soldier's life I was now to pursue, and we went our different ways.

He was right not to take the separation seriously. After at most a year, when my military service should be finished, we would come together, one place or another. Still, it was in a way a break, the end of one chapter, the beginning of another; and if he seemed not to be conscious of the fact, I was, with a certain pang, well aware of it. By going to him in Halle I had, so to speak, prolonged our school-days; we had lived there much as in Kaisersaschern. Even the time when I was a student and he still at school I cannot compare with the change now impending. Then I had left him behind in the familiar frame of the gymnasium and the paternal city and had continued to return thither. Only now, it seemed to me, did our lives become detached, only now were both of us beginning on our own two feet. Now there would be an end to what seemed to me so necessary, though so futile withal; I can but describe it in the words I used above: I should no longer know what he did or experienced, no more be able to be near him, to keep watch over him. I must leave his side just at the very moment when observation of his life, although it could certainly change nothing in it, seemed most highly desirable, I mean when he abandoned the scholarly career, "put the Bible under the bench," to use his own words, and flung himself into the arms of music.

It was a significant decision, one pregnant with fate. In a way it cancelled the more immediate past and linked up with moments of our common life lying far, far back, the memory of which I bore in my heart: the hour when I had found the lad experimenting with his uncle's harmonium, and still further back, our canon-singing with Hanne the stable-girl, under the linden tree. It made my heart lift up for joy, this decision of his — and at the same time contract with fear. I can only compare the feeling with the catch in the breath that a child feels in a swing as it flies aloft, the mingled exultation and terror. The rightness of the change, its inevitability, the correction of the false step, the misrepresentation theology had been: all that was clear to me, and I was proud that my friend no longer hesitated to acknowledge the truth. Persuasion, indeed, had been necessary to bring him to it; and extraordinary as were the results I expected from the change, and despite all my joyful agitation, I took comfort from being able to tell myself that I had had no part in the persuasions — or at most had supported them by a certain fatalistic attitude, and a few words such as "I think you know, yourself."

Here I will follow on with a letter I had from him two months after I entered the service at Naumburg. I read it with feelings such as might move a mother at a communication of that kind from her son — only that of course one withholds that sort of thing from one's mother, out of propriety. I had written to him some three weeks before, ignorant of his address, in care of Herr Wendell Kretschmar at the Hase conservatoire; had described my new, raw state and begged him, if ever so briefly, to tell me how he lived and fared in the great city, and about the program of his studies. I preface his reply only by saying that its antiquated style was of course intended as a parody of grotesque Halle experiences and the language idiosyncrasies of Ehrenfried Kumpf. At the same time it both hides and reveals his own personality and stylistic leanings and his employment of the parodic, in a highly characteristic and indicative way.

He wrote:

> *Leipzig, Friday after*
> *Purificationis 1905*
> *In the Peterstrasse, house the 27th*

Most honourable, most illustrious, learned, and well-beloved Magister and Ballisticus!

We thank you kindly for the courtesy of your communication and the highly diverting tidings touching your present arrangements, so full of discipline, dullness, and hardship as they be. Your tales of the whip-cracking and springing to order, the currycombing and spit-and-polish, have made us heartily to laugh: above all that one of the under-officer which even as he planes and polishes and breketh to harness, yet holdeth so much in estimation your high education and grete learning that in the canteen you must needs mark off for him all the metres according to feet and *moræ* because this kind of learning seemeth to him the high prick of intellectual aristocracy. In requital thereof we will an we hold out counter thee with some right folish facecies and horseplay which we fell into here that you too mayst have to wonder and to laugh thereat. Albeit first our friendly hert and good will, trusting and playing that thou maist almost joyfully bear the rod and in tract of time be so holpen therehy, till at the last in braid and buttons thou goest forth as a reserve sergeant major.

Here the word is: Trust God, honour the King, do no man any nuisance. On the Pleisse, the Parthe, and the Elster existence and pulse are manifestly other then on the Saale; for here many people be gathered togyder, more then seven hundred thousand; which from the outset bespeaketh a certain sympathy and tolerance; as the Lord hath already for Nineveh's sin a knowing and humorous eye when He says excusingly: "Such a great city, therein more than a hundred thousand men." Thus maist thou think how among seven hundred thousand forbearance is counselled when in the autumn fair-times whereof I as novice had even now a taste, more stream from all parts of Europe, and from Persia, Armenia, and other the Asiatic lands.

Not as though this Nineveh particularly doth like me, 'tis not the fairest city of my fatherland, Kaisersaschern is fairer; yet may easier be both fair and stately, sithence it needs but be olde and quiet and have no pulse. Is gorgeously builded, my Leipzig, of clear stone as out of a costly box of toy bricks. The common people's tongue is a devilishly lewd speech so that one shrinks before every booth before one bargains. It is even as though our mildly slumbering Thuringian were woke up to a seven-hundred-thousand-man impudence and smattered abhominably, jaw stuck out — horrible, dreadful, but, God keep us, certes meaning no harm, and mixed with self-mockery which they can graunt unto themselves on the ground of their world-pulse. *Centrum musicæ, centrum* of the printing trade and the book rag-fair, illustrious universitie, albeit scattered in respect to buildings, for the chief building is in Augustusplatz, the library hard by the Cloth Hall, and to the divers faculties long severall college buildings, as the

Red House on the Promenade to the philosophic, to the juristic
the *Collegium Beatæ Virginis*, in my Peterstrasse, where I found
forthwith fresh from the station, on the next way into the town,
fitting lodging and accommodation. Came early in the afternoon,
left my fardels at the station, got hither as directed, read the notice on the rain-pipe, rang, and was straightaway agreed with the
fat landlady with the fiendish brogue on the two rooms on the
ground floor. Still so early that I had on that same day looked
over almost the whole town in the first flush of arrival — this time
really with a guide, to wit the porter who fetched my portmanteo
from the station; hence at the last the farce and foolery of which
I spake and may still reherse.

The fat frau made no bones about the clavicymbal, they
are used to that here. Sha'n't be assaulting her ears too much for
I am chiefly working on theory, with books and pen and paper,
the harmoniam and the *punctum contra punctum*, quite off my
own bat, I mean under the supervision and general direction of
amicus Kretschmar, to whom every few days I take that I have
practised and wrought, for his criticism, good or bad. Good soul
was uncommon glad that I came, and embraced me for that I was
not minded to betray his hope. And he will hear not of my going
to the conservatoire, either the big one or the Hase, where he
teaches; it were, he says, no atmosphere for me, I must rather do
as Father Haydn did, who had no preceptor at all, but got himself the *Gradus ad Parnassum* of Fux and some music of the time,
in especial the Hamburg Bach, and therewith sturdily practised
his trade. Just between ourselves, the study of harmony makes
me for to yawn, but with counterpoint I wax quick and lusty,
cannot concoct enough merry frolics in this enchanted field, with
joyous passion soyle the never-ending problems and have already
put together on paper a whole stook of droll studies in canon
and fugue, even gotten some praise from the Master therefore.
That is creative work, requirith phantasy and invention; playing
dominoes with chords, without a theme is meseemeth neither flesh
nor fowl. Should not one learn all that about suspensions, passing-
notes, modulation, preparations and resolution, much better *in
praxi* from hearing, experiencing, and inventing oneself, then out
of a boke? But altogether, now, and *per aversionem* it is foolish-
ness, this unthinking division of counterpoint and harmony, sith
they interact so intimately that one cannot teach them sunderlye
but only in the whole, as music — in so far as it can be taught.

Wherefore I am industrious, *zelo virtutis*, yea almost over-
burdened and overwhelmed with matters, for I go to lectures at

the academie in hist. phil. by Lautensack and Encyclopedia of the
philosophical sciences as well as logic from the famous Bermeter.
Vale. Jam satis est. Herewith I commit you to the Lord, may He
preserve you and all clear souls. Your most obedient servant, as
they say in Halle. — I have made you much too curious about the
jocus and jape, and what is afoot betwixt me and Satan; not much
to it after all, except that porter led me astray on the evening of
the first day — a base churl like that, with a strap round his waist,
a red cap and a brass badge and a rain-cape, same vild lingo as
everybody else here. Bristly jaw; looked to me like unto our
Schleppfuss by reason of his little beard, more than slightly, even,
when I bethink, or is he waxen more like in my recollection?
Heavier and fatter, that were from the beer. Introduces himself
to me as a guide and proved it by his brass badge and his two or
three scrapes of French and English, diabolical pronunciation;
"peautiful puilding, antiquldé extrèment indéressant."

Item: we struck a bargain, and the churl shewed me everything, two whole hours, took me everywhere: to the Pauluskirche
with wondrously chamfered cloisters, the Thomaskirche on account of Johann Sebastian, and his grave in St. John's, where is
also the Reformation monument, and the new Cloth Hall. Lively
it was in the streets, for as I said whilere the autumn fair still happened to be, and all sorts of banners and hangings advertising furs
and other wares hung out at windows down the house-fronts,
there was great bustle and prease in all the narrow streets, particularly in the heart of the town, nigh the old Town Hall, where
the chap shewed me the palace, and Auerbach's inn and the still
standing tower of the Pleissenburg — where Luther held his dis-
putacyon with Eck. Great shoving and shouldering in the narrow
streets behind the Market, very old, with steep gabled roofs; connected by a criss-crosse labyrinth of covered courts and passages,
and adjoining warehouses and cellars. All this close packed with
wares and the hosts of people look at you with outlandish eyen
and speak in tongues you've never heard a syllable of afore. Right
exciting, and you felt the pulse of the world beating in your
own body.

By little and little it gat dark, lights came on, the streets
emptied, I was aweary and ahungered. I bade my guide draw to
an ende by shewing me an inn where I could eat. "A good one?"
he asks, and winks. "A good one," quoth I, "so it be not too
dear." Takes me to a house in a little back lane behind the main
street — brass railing to the steps up to the door — polished as
bright as the fellow's badge, and a lantern over the door, red as

the fellow's cap. I pay him, he wishes me "Good appetite!" and
shogs off. I ring, the door opens of itself, and in the hall is a
dressed-up madame coming towards me, with carmine cheeks, a
string of wax-coloured beads on her blubber, and greets me with
most seemly gest, fluting and flirting, ecstatic as though she had
been longing for me to come, ushers me through portières into a
glistering room, with panelled tapestries, crystal chandelier, candelabra with mirrors behind them; satin couches, and on them
sitting your nymphs and daughters of the wilderness, ribaudes,
laced muttons all, six or seven, morphos, clear-wings, esmeraldas,
et cetera, clad or unclad, in tulle, gauze, spangs, hair long and
floating, hair short with heart-breakers; paps bare, thick-poudered,
arms with bangles; they look at you with expectant eyes, glistering in the light of the chandelier.

Look at me, mark wel, not thee. A hothouse the fellow, the
small-beer-Schleppfuss, had brought me into. I stood, not showing what I was feeling, and there opposite me I see an open piano,
a friend, I rush up to it across the carpet and strike a chord or
twain, standing up, I wot still what it was, because the harmonic
problem was just in my mind, modulation from B major to C
major, the brightening semitone step, as in the hermit's prayer in
the finale of the *Freischütz*, at the entry of timpani, trumpets,
and oboes on the six-four chord on G. I wot it now, afterwards,
but then I wist not, I but fell upon it. A brown wench puts herself nigh me, in a little Spanish jacket, with a big gam, snub nose,
almond eyes, an Esmeralda, she brushed my cheek with her arm.
I turn round, push the bench away with my knee, and fling myself back through the lust-hell, across the carpets, past the mincing
madam, through the entry and down the steps without touching
the brass railing.

There you have the trifle, so it befell me, told at its length,
in payment for the roaring corporal to whom you teach the
artem metrificandi. Herewith amen — and pray for me. Only a
Gewandhaus concert heard up till now with Schumann's Third
as pièce de résistance. A critic of that time belauded the comprehensive world-view of this music, which sounds like very unobjective gabble — the classicists made themselves thoroughly merry
over it. But it did have some sense, for it defines the improvement
in their status which music and musicians owe to romanticism. It
emancipated her from the sphere of a small-town specialism and
piping and brought her into contact with the great world of the
mind, the general artistic and intellectual movement of the time —
we should not forget that. All that proceeds from the Beethoven

of the last period and his polyphony; and I find it extraordinarily significant that the opponents of the romantic movement, that is of an art which progresses from the solely musical into the universally intellectual sphere, were the same people who also opposed and deplored Beethoven's later development. Have you ever thought how differently, how much more suffering and significant the individualization of the voice appears in his greatest works than in the older music where it is treated with greater skill? There are judgments which make one laugh by the crass truthfulness of them, which are at the same time a judgment on the judge. Handel said of Gluck: "My cook understands more about counterpoint than he does" — I love this pronouncement of a fellow-musician!

Playing much Chopin, and reading about him. I love the angelic in his figure, which reminds me of Shelley: the peculiarly and very mysteriously veiled, unapproachable, withdrawing, unadventurous flavour of his being, that not wanting to know, that rejection of material experience, the sublime incest of his fantastically delicate and seductive art. How much speaks for the man the deep, intent friendship of Delacroix, who writes to him: J'espère vous voir ce soir, mais ce moment est capable de me faire devenir fou." Everything possible for the Wagner of painting! But there are quite a few things in Chopin which, not only harmonically but also in a general, psychological sense more than anticipate Wagner, indeed surpass him. Take the C-sharp minor Nocturne Op. 27, No. 2, and the duet that begins after the enharmonic change from C-sharp minor to D-flat major. That surpasses in despairing beauty of sound all the *Tristan* orgies — even in the intimate medium of the piano, though not as a grand battle of voluptuosity; without the bull-fight character of a theatrical mysticism robust in its corruption. Take above all his ironic relation to tonality, his teasing way with it, obscuring, ignoring, keeping it fluctuating, and mocking at accidentals. It goes far, divertingly and thrillingly far. . . .

With the exclamation: "*Ecce epistola!*" the letter ends. Added is: "Goes without saying you destroy this at once." The signature is an initial, that of the family name: the *L*, not the *A*.

CHAPTER XVII

THE explicit order to destroy this letter I did not obey — and who on that ground will condemn a friendship which can claim for itself the description "deeply intent" used therein of Delacroix's friendship for Chopin? I did not obey it, in the first instance because I felt the need to read again and again a piece of writing at first run through so quickly; to study it, not so much read as study, stylistically and psychologically. Then, with the passage of time, the moment to destroy it had passed too; I learned to regard it as a document of which the order to destroy was a part, so that by its documentary nature it cancelled itself out.

So much I was certain of from the start: it was not the letter as a whole that had given occasion to the direction at the end; but only a part of it, the so-called *facetie* and farce, the experience with the fatal porter. But again, that part was the whole letter, on account of that part it was written; not for my amusement — doubtless the writer had known that the "jape" would have nothing comic about it for me — but rather to shake off a painful impression, for which I, the friend of his childhood, was of course the only repository. All the rest was only trimmings, wrappings, pretext, putting off, and afterwards a covering-up again with talk, music-critical aperçus, as though nothing had happened. Upon the *anecdote* — to use a very objective word — everything focuses; it stands in the background from the beginning on, announces itself in the first lines and is postponed. Still untold, it plays into the jests about the great city Nineveh and the tolerant sceptical quotation from the Bible. It comes near being told at the place where for the first time there is mention of the porter; then it is dropped again. The letter is ostensibly finished before it is told — "*Jam satis est*" — and then, as though it had almost gone out of the writer's head, as though only Schleppfuss's quoted greeting brought it back, it is told "to finish off with," including the extraordinary reference back to his father's lectures on butterflies. Yet it is not allowed to form the end of the letter, rather some remarks about Schumann, the romantic movement, Chopin, are appended to it, obviously with the intention of detracting from its weight, and so causing it to be forgotten — or more correctly, probably, to make it, out of pride, look as though that were the idea; for I do not believe the intention existed that I, the reader, should overlook the core of the letter.

Very remarkable to me, even on the second reading, was the fact that the style, the travesty or personal adaptation of Kumpf's old-German, prevailed only until the adventure was recounted and then was dropped regardless, so that the closing pages are entirely uncoloured by it and show a perfectly modern style. Is it not as though the archaizing tone had served its purpose as soon as the tale of the false guide is on paper? As though it is given up afterwards, not so much because it is unsuitable for the final observations put in to divert the attention, as because from the date onwards it was only introduced in order to be able to *tell the story* in it, which by that means gets its proper atmosphere? And what atmosphere, then? I will characterize it, however little the designation I have in mind will seem applicable to a jest. It is the religious atmosphere. So much was clear to me: on account of its historical affinity with the religious, the language of the Reformation — or the flavour of it — had been chosen for a letter which was to bring me this story. Without it, how could the word have been written down that pressed to be written down: "Pray for me!" There could be no better example of the quotation as disguise, the parody as pretext. And just before it was another, which even at the first reading went through and through me, and which has just as little to do with humour, bearing as it does an undeniably mystical, thus religious stamp: the word "lust-hell."

Despite the coolness of the analysis to which I there and then subjected Adrian's letter, few readers will have been deceived about the real feelings with which I read and reread it. Analysis has necessarily the appearance of coolness, even when practised in a state of profound agitation. Agitated I was, I was even beside myself. My fury at the obscene prank of that small-beer Schleppfuss knew no bounds — yet it was an impersonal fury, no evidence at all of prudishness in myself. I was never prudish, and if that Leipzig procurer had played his trick on me I should have known how to put a good face on it. No, my present feelings had entirely to do with Adrian's nature and being; and for that, indeed, the word "prudish" would be perfectly silly and unsuitable. Vulgarity itself might here have been inspired with a sense of the need to spare and protect.

In my feelings the fact played no small part that he should have told me the adventure at all, told it weeks after it had happened, breaking through a reserve otherwise absolute and always respected by me. However strange it may seem, considering our long intimacy, we had never touched in any personal or intimate way on the subject of love, of sex, of the flesh. We had never come on it otherwise than through the medium of art and literature, with reference to the manifestations of passion in the intellectual sphere. At such times he spoke in an objectively knowledgeable way divorced from any personal element. Yet how could it have been absent in a being like him? That it was not there was evidence enough in his repetition of certain doctrines taken over from Kretschmar on the not contemptible role of the sensual in art, and not only in art; in some of his comments on Wagner, and in such spontaneous utterances as that about the nudity of the human voice and the intellectual compensation provided for it through highly complicated art-forms in the old vocal music. That sort of thing had nothing old-maidish about it; it showed a free, unforced contemplation of the world of fleshly desire. But again, it was not indicative of my nature but of his that every time at such turns in the conversation I felt something like a shock, a catch, a slight shrinking within me. It was, to express myself strongly, as though one heard an angel holding forth on sin. One could expect no flippancy or vulgarity, no banal bad jokes. And yet one would feel put off; acknowledging his intellectual right to speak, one would be tempted to beg: "Hush, my friend! Your lips are too pure, too stern for such matters."

In fact, Adrian's distaste for the coarse or lascivious was forbidding and forthright. I knew exactly the wry mouth, the contemptuous expression with which he recoiled when that sort of thing was even remotely approached. At Halle, in the Winfried circle, he was fairly safe: religious propriety, at least in word, spared him attacks upon his fine feeling. Women, wives, "the girls," affairs, were never the subject of conversation among the members. I do not know how these young theologians did in fact, each for himself, behave, whether or not they preserved themselves in chastity for Christian marriage. As for myself, I will confess that I had tasted of the apple, and at that time had relations for seven or eight months with a girl of the people, a cooper's daughter, a connection which was hard enough to keep from Adrian — though truly I scarcely believe that he noticed it — and which I severed without ill feeling at the end of that time as the creature's lack of education bored me and I had never anything to say for myself with her except just the one thing. I had gone into it not so much out of hot blood as impelled by curiosity, vanity, and the desire to translate into practice that frankness of the ancients about sexual matters which was part of my theoretic convictions.

But precisely this element of intellectual complacence to which I, it may be a little pedantically, pretended, was entirely lacking in Adrian's attitude. I will not speak of Christian inhibitions nor yet apply the shibboleth "Kaisersaschern," with its various implications, partly middle-class and conventional, yet coloured as well with a mediævally lively horror of sin. That would do the truth scant justice and not suffice either to call out the loving consideration with which his attitude inspired me, the anger I felt at any injury he might receive. One simply could not and would not picture Adrian in any situation of gallantry; that was due to the armour of purity, chastity, intellectual pride, cool irony, which he wore; it was sacred to me, sacred in a certain painful and secretly mortifying way. For painful and mortifying — except perhaps to the malicious soul — is the thought that purity is not given to this life in the flesh; that instinct does not spare the loftiest intellectual pride, nor can arrogance itself refuse its toll to nature. One may only hope that this derogation into the human, and thereby also into the beast, may by God's will fulfill itself in some form of beauty, forbearance, and spiritual elevation, in feelings veiled and purified by devotion.

Must I add that precisely in cases like my friend's there is the least hope of this? The beautifying, veiling, ennobling, I mean, is a work of the soul, in a court of appeal interceding, mediating, itself instinct with poetry; where spirit and desire interpenetrate and appease each other in a way not quite free from illusion; it is a stratum of life peculiarly informed with sentiment, in which, I confess, my own humanity feels at ease, but which is not for stronger tastes. Natures like Adrian's have not much "soul." It is a fact, in which a profoundly observant friendship has instructed me, that the proudest intellectuality stands in the most immediate relation of all to the animal, to naked instinct, is given over most shamelessly to it; hence the anxiety that a person like me must suffer through a nature like Adrian's — hence too my conviction that the accursed adventure of which he had written was in its essence frightfully symbolic.

I saw him standing at the door of that room in the house of joy; slowly comprehending, eyeing the waiting daughters of the wilderness. Once — I had the picture clearly before me — I had seen him pass through the alien atmosphere of Mütze's tavern in

Halle. So now I saw him move blindly to the piano and strike
chords — what chords he only afterwards knew himself. I saw the
snub-nosed girl beside him, Hetæra esmeralda: her powdered
bosoms in Spanish bodice — saw her brush his cheek with her arm.
Violently, across space and back in time, I yearned thither. I felt
the impulse to push the witch away from him with my knee as
he had pushed the music-stool aside to gain his freedom. For days
I felt the touch of her flesh on my own cheek and knew with
abhorrence and sheer terror that it had burned upon his ever
since. Again I beg that it be considered indicative not of me but
of him that I was quite unable to take the event on its lighter side.
There was no light side there. If I have even remotely succeeded
in giving the reader a picture of my friend's character, he must
feel with me the indescribably profaning, the mockingly debasing
and dangerous nature of this contact.

That up to then he had "touched" no woman was and is to
me an unassailable fact. Now the woman had touched him — and
he had fled. Nor is there in this flight any trace of the comic, let
me assure the reader, in case he incline to seek such in it. Comic,
at most, this avoidance was, in the bitter-tragic sense of futility.
In my eyes Adrian had not escaped, and only very briefly, certainly, did he feel that he had. His intellectual pride had suffered
the trauma of contact with soulless instinct. Adrian was to return
to the place whither the betrayer had led him.

CHAPTER XVIII

MAY not my readers ask whence comes the detail in my narrative, so precisely known to me, even though I could not have been always present, not always at the side of the departed hero of this biography? It is true that repeatedly, for extended periods, I lived apart from Adrian: during my year of military service, at the end of which I resumed my studies at the University of Leipzig and became familiar with his life and circle there. So also for the duration of my educational travels to the classic lands in the years 1908 and 1909. Our reunion on my return was brief, as he already cherished the purpose of leaving Leipzig and going to southern Germany. The longest period of separation followed thereupon: the years when after a short stay in Munich he was in Italy with his friend the Silesian Schildknapp. Meanwhile I first spent my probation time at the Boniface gymnasium in Kaisersaschern and then entered upon my teaching office there. Only in 1913, when Adrian had settled in Pfeiffering in Upper Bavaria and I had transferred to Freising, were we near each other; but then it was to have before my eyes, for seventeen years, with no — or as good as no — interruption, that life already long since marked by fate, that increasingly vehement activity, until the catastrophe of 1930.

He had long ceased to be a beginner in music, that curiously cabbalistic craft, at once playful and profound, artful and austere, when he placed himself again under the guidance, direction, supervision of Wendell Kretschmar in Leipzig. His rapid progress was winged by an intelligence grasping everything as it flew and distracted at most by anticipatory impatience in the field of what could be taught, in the technique of composition, form, and orchestration. It seemed that the two-year theological episode in Halle had not weakened his bond with music or been any actual interruption to his preoccupation with it. His letter had told me something about his eager and accumulating exercises in counterpoint. Kretschmar laid even greater stress on the technique of orchestration; even in Kaisersaschern he had made him orchestrate much piano music, movements from sonatas, string quartets;

which then, in long conversations, would be discussed, criticized, and corrected. He went so far as to ask him to orchestrate the piano reductions of single acts from operas unknown to Adrian, and the comparison of that which the pupil tried, who had heard and read Berlioz, Debussy, and the German and Austrian late romantics, with that which Grétry or Cherubini had actually done made master and pupil laugh. Kretschmar was at that time at work on his own composition, *The Statue*, and gave his pupil one or the other scene in *particell* for instrumentation and then showed him what he himself had done or intended. Here was occasion for abundant debates, in which of course the superior experience of the master held the field, but once at least, nevertheless, the intuition of the apprentice won a victory. For a chord combination that Kretschmar rejected at first sight as being doubtful and awkward finally seemed to him more characteristic than what he himself had in mind, and at the next meeting he declared that he would like to take over Adrian's idea.

The latter felt less proud than one would expect. Teacher and pupil were in their musical instincts and intuitions at bottom very far apart, since in art almost of necessity the aspiring student finds himself addressed to the technical guidance of a craftsmanship already become somewhat remote, owing to the difference of a generation. Then it is well at least if the master guesses and understands the hidden leanings of the youth; he may even be ironic on the score of them if he takes care not to stand in the way of their development. Thus Kretschmar lived in the natural, taken-for-granted conviction that music had found its definitely highest manifestation and effect in orchestral composition; and this Adrian no longer believed. To the boy of twenty, more than to his elders, the close link of the most highly developed instrumental technique with a harmonic conception was more than a historical view. With him it had grown to be something like a state of mind, in which past and future merged together; the cool gaze he directed upon the hypertrophy of the post-romantic monster orchestra, the need he felt for its reduction and return to the ancillary role that it had played at the time of the preharmonic, the polyphonic vocal music; his tendency in this direction and thus to oratorio, a species in which the creator of *The Revelation of St. John* and the *Lamentation of Dr. Faustus* would later achieve his highest and boldest flights — all this came out very early in word and deed.

His studies in orchestration under Kretschmar's guidance were not the less zealous on that account. For he agreed with his

teacher that one must have command over what has been achieved
even though one no longer finds it essential. He once said to me
that a composer who is sick of orchestral impressionism and therefore no longer learns instrumentation seemed to him like a dentist
who no longer learns how to treat the roots of teeth and goes
back to the barber technique because it has lately been discovered
that dead teeth give people rheumatism of the joints. This comparison, extraordinarily far-fetched yet so characteristic of the
intellectual atmosphere of the time, continued to be an oft-quoted
allusion between us, and the "dead tooth" preserved by skilful
embalming of the root became a symbol for certain very modern
ern refinements of the orchestral palette, including his own symphonic fantasy *Ocean Lights*. This piece he wrote in Leipzig, still
under Kretschmar's eye, after a holiday trip to the North Sea
with Rüdiger Schildknapp. Kretschmar later arranged a semi-
public performance of it. It is a piece of exquisite tone-painting,
which gives evidence of an astonishing feeling for entrancing
combinations of sound, at first hearing almost impossible for the
ear to unravel. The cultured public saw in the young composer
a highly gifted successor to the Debussy-Ravel line. That he was
not, and he scarcely included this demonstration of colouristic
and orchestral ability in the list of his actual productions; almost
as little, indeed, as the wrist loosening and calligraphic practice
with which he had once occupied himself under Kretschmar's
direction: the six- to eight-part choruses, the fugue with the three
themes for string quintet with piano accompaniment, the symphony, whose *particell* he brought him by bits and whose instrumentation he discussed with him; the Cello Sonata in A minor
with the very lovely slow movement, whose theme he would
later use in one of his Brentano songs. That sound-sparkling
Ocean Lights was in my eyes a very remarkable instance of how
an artist can give his best to a thing in which he privately no
longer believes, insisting on excelling in artistic devices which for
his consciousness are already at the point of being worn out. "It
is acquired root-treatment," he said to me. "I don't rise to strepto-
coccus disinfection." Every one of his remarks showed that he
considered the genre of "tone-painting," of "nature moods," to be
fundamentally out of date.

But to be frank, this disillusioned masterpiece of orchestral brilliance already bore within itself the traits of parody and intellectual mockery of art, which in Leverkühn's later work so often
emerged in a creative and uncanny way. Many found it chilling,
even repellent and revolting, and these were the better, if not the

best sort, who thus judged. All the superficial lot simply called it witty and amusing. In truth parody was here the proud expedient of a great gift threatened with sterility by a combination of scepticism, intellectual reserve, and a sense of the deadly extension of the kingdom of the banal. I trust I have put that aright. My uncertainty and my feeling of responsibility are alike great, when I seek to clothe in words thoughts that are not primarily my own, but have come to me only through my friendship with Adrian. Of a lack of naïveté I would not speak, for in the end naïveté lies at the bottom of being, all being, even the most conscious and complicated. The conflict — almost impossible to simplify — between the inhibitions and the productive urge of inborn genius, between chastity and passion, just that is the naïveté out of which such an artist nature lives, the soil for the difficult, characteristic growth of his work; and the unconscious effort to get for the "gift" the productive impulse, the necessary little ascendancy over the impediments of unbelief, arrogance, intellectual self-consciousness: this instinctive effort stirs and becomes decisive at the moment when the mechanical studies preliminary to the practice of an art begin to be combined with the first personal, while as yet entirely ephemeral and preparatory plastic efforts.

CHAPTER XIX

I SPEAK of this because, not without tremors, not without a contraction of my heart, I have now come to the fateful event which happened about a year after I received in Naumburg the letter I quoted from Adrian; somewhat more than a year, that is, after his arrival in Leipzig and that first sight of the city of which the letter tells. In other words, it was not long before — being released from the service — I went to him again and found him, while outwardly unchanged, yet in fact a marked man, pierced by the arrow of fate. In narrating this episode, I feel I should call Apollo and the Muses to my aid, to inspire me with the purest, most indulgent words: indulgent to the sensitive reader, indulgent to the memory of my departed friend, indulgent lastly to myself, to whom the telling is like a serious personal confession. But such an invocation betrays to me at once the contradiction between my own intellectual conditioning and the colouration of the story I have to tell, a colouration that comes from quite other strata of tradition, altogether foreign to the blitheness of classical culture. I began this record by expressing doubt whether I was the right man for the task. The arguments I had to adduce against such doubts I will not repeat. It must suffice that, supported on them, strengthened by them, I propose to remain true to my undertaking.

I said that Adrian returned to the place whither the impudent messenger had brought him. One sees now that it did not happen so soon. A whole year long the pride of the spirit asserted itself against the injury it had received, and it was always a sort of consolation to me to feel that his surrender to the naked instinct that had laid its spiteful finger on him had not lacked all and every human nobility or psychological veiling. For as such I regard every fixation of desire, however crude, on a definite and individual goal. I see it in the moment of choice, even though the will thereto be not "free" but impudently provoked by its object. A trace of purifying love can be attested so soon as the instinct wears the face of a human being, be it the most anonymous, the

most contemptible. And there is this to say, that Adrian went
back to that place on account of one particular person, of her
whose touch burned on his cheek, the "brown wench" with the
big mouth, in the little jacket, who had come up to him at the
piano and whom he called Esmeralda. It was she whom he sought
there — and did not find her.

The fixation, calamitous as it was, resulted in his leaving the
brothel after his second and voluntary visit the same man as after
the first, involuntary one; not, however, without having assured
himself of the place where she was now. It had the further result
that under a musical pretext he made rather a long journey to
reach her whom he desired. It happened that the first Austrian
performance of *Salome*, conducted by the composer himself, was
to take place in Graz, the capital of Styria, in May 1906. Some
months earlier Adrian and Kretschmar had gone to Dresden to
see its actual première; and he had told his teacher and the friends
whom he had meantime made in Leipzig that he wanted to be
present at this gala performance and hear again that successful
revolutionary work, whose æsthetic sphere did not at all attract
him, but which of course interested him in a musical and technical sense, particularly as the setting to music of a prose dialogue.
He travelled alone, and one cannot be sure whether he carried
out his ostensible purpose and went from Graz to Pressburg, possibly from Pressburg to Graz; or whether he simply pretended
the stay in Graz and confined himself to the visit to Pressburg (in
Hungarian, Pozsony). She whose mark he bore had been hidden
in a house there, having had to leave her former place for hospital
treatment. The hunted hunter found her out.

My hand trembles as I write; but in quiet, collected words I
will say what I know, always consoled to a certain extent by the
thought to which I gave utterance above, the idea of choice, the
thought that something obtained here like a bond of love, which
lent to the coming together of the precious youth and that unhappy creature a gleam of soul. Though of course this consolation is inseparable from the other thought, so much more dreadful, that love and poison here once and for ever became a frightful
unity of experience; the mythological unity embodied in the
arrow.

It does look as though in the poor thing's mind something answered the feeling which the youth brought to her. No doubt she
remembered that fleeting visit. Her approach, that caressing of
his cheek with her bare arm, might have been the humble and
tender expression of her receptivity for all that distinguished him

from the usual clientèle. And she learned from his own lips that
he had made the journey thither on her account. She thanked
him, even while she warned him against her body. I know it from
Adrian: she warned him — is not this something like a beneficent
distinction between the higher humanity of the creature and her
physical part, fallen to the gutter, sunk to a wretched object of
use? The unhappy one warned him who asked of her, warned
him away from "herself"; that meant an act of free elevation of
soul above her pitiable physical existence, an act of human dis-
association from it, an act of sympathy, an act — if the word be
permitted me — of love. And, gracious heaven, was it not also
love, or what was it, what madness, what deliberate, reckless
tempting of God, what compulsion to comprise the punishment
in the sin, finally what deep, deeply mysterious longing for dæmonic conception, for a deathly unchaining of chemical change
in his nature was at work, that having been warned he despised
the warning and insisted upon possession of this flesh?

Never without a religious shudder have I been able to think of
this embrace, in which the one staked his salvation, the other
found it. Purifying, justifying, sublimating, it must have blessed
the wretched one, that the other travelled from afar and refused
whatever the risk to give her up. It seems that she gave him all
the sweetness of her womanhood, to repay him for what he
risked. She might thus know that he never forgot her; but it is
no less true that it was for her own sake he, who never saw her
again, remembered; and her name — that which he gave her from
the beginning — whispers magically, unheard by anyone but me,
throughout his work. I may be taxed with vanity, but I cannot
refrain from speaking here of the discovery which he one day
silently confirmed. Leverkühn was not the first composer, and he
will not have been the last, who loved to put mysteries, magic formulas, and charms into his works. The fact displays the inborn
tendency of music to superstitious rites and observances, the symbolism of numbers and letters. Thus in my friend's musical fabric
a five- to six-note series, beginning with B and ending on E flat,
with a shifting F and A between, is found strikingly often, a
basic figure of peculiarly nostalgic character, which in differing
harmonic and rhythmic garb, is given now to this part now to that,
often in its inversion, as it were turned on its axis, so that while
the intervals remain the same, the sequence of the notes is altered.
It occurs at first in the probably most beautiful of the thirteen
Brentano songs composed in Leipzig, the heart-piercing lied: "*O
lieb Mädel, wie schlecht bist du,*" which is permeated with it; but

most particularly in the late work, where audacity and despair mingle in so unique a way, the *Weheklag of Dr. Faustus*, written in Pfeiffering, where the inclination shows even more strongly to use those intervals also in a simultaneous-harmonic combination.

The letters composing this note-cipher are: h, e, a, e, e-flat: hetæra esmeralda.*

*

*   *

Adrian returned to Leipzig and expressed himself as entertained and full of admiration for the powerful and striking opera he was supposed to have heard a second time and possibly really had. I can still hear him say about the author of it: "What a gifted good fellow! The revolutionary as a Sabbath-day child, pert and *conciliant.* How after great expense of affronts and dissonances everything turns into good nature, beer good nature, gets all buttered up, so to speak, appeasing the philistine and telling him no harm was meant. . . . But a hit, a palpable hit!" Five weeks after he had resumed his musical and philosophical studies a local affection decided him to consult a physician. The specialist, by name Dr. Erasmi — Adrian had chosen him from the street directory — was a powerful man, with a red face and a pointed black beard. It obviously made him puff to stoop and even in an upright posture he breathed in pants with his lips open. The habit indicated oppression, but it also looked like contemptuous indifference, as though the man would dismiss or intended to dismiss something by saying "Pooh, pooh!" He puffed like that during the whole examination, and then, in contradiction to his pooh-poohing, declared the necessity for a thorough and rather lengthy treatment, on which he at once embarked. On three successive days Adrian went to him. Then Erasmi arranged a break of three days. Adrian was to come back on the fourth. When the patient — who was not ailing, his general state of health being entirely unaffected — returned at four o'clock on the appointed day, something utterly unexpected and startling confronted him.

He had always had to ring at the door of the apartment, which was up three steep flights of stairs in a gloomy building in the old city, and wait for a maid to open. But this time he found both outer and inner doors open, that to the waiting-room, the consulting-room, and facing him a door into the living-room, the so-called "best room" with two windows. Yes, there the windows were wide open too, and all four curtains blew in and out in the

* The English *B* is represented in German by *H*.

draught. In the middle of the room lay Dr. Erasmi, with his beard
sticking up, his eyes fast shut, in a white shirt with cuffs, lying
on a tufted cushion in an open coffin on two trestles.

What was going on, why the dead man lay there so alone and
open to the wind, where the maid and Frau Dr. Erasmi were,
whether perhaps the people from the undertaking establishment
were waiting to screw on the lid, or were coming back at once —
at what singular moment the visitor had been brought to the spot,
was never made clear. When I came to Leipzig, Adrian could only
describe to me the bewilderment in which he, after staring for a
moment, had gone down the stairs again. He seems not to have
inquired further into the doctor's sudden death, seems not to have
been interested. He merely thought that the man's constant puffing
and blowing had always been a bad sign.

With secret repugnance, struggling against unreasoning horror,
I must now relate that Adrian's second choice also stood under
an unlucky star. He took two days to recover from the shock.
Then he again had recourse to the Leipzig directory, chose another name, and put himself in the care of a certain Dr. Zimbalist,
in one of the business streets off the Marktplatz. On the ground
floor was a restaurant, then a piano warehouse; the doctor's house
occupied part of the upper storey, a porcelain shield with his
name on it being downstairs in the lobby. The dermatologist's
two waiting-rooms, one reserved for female patients, were adorned
with growing plants, palms and house trees in pots. Medical books
and magazines lay about, for instance an illustrated history of
morals, in the room where Adrian for the first and the second
time awaited his treatment.

Dr. Zimbalist was a small man with horn spectacles, an oval
bald spot running from the brow to the back of the head between
two growths of reddish hair, and a moustache left growing only
immediately under the nostrils, as was then the fashion in the
upper classes and would later become the attribute of a world-
famous face. His speech was slovenly and he inclined to bad masculine jokes. But one had not the impression that he felt very
jolly. One side of his cheek was drawn up in a sort of tic, the
corner of the mouth as well, and the eye winked in sympathy;
the whole expression was crabbed and craven to a degree; he
looked no-good, he looked odious. Thus Adrian described him to
me and thus I see him.

Now this is what happened: Adrian had gone twice for treatment; he went a third time. As he mounted the stairs he met, between the first and second storeys, the physician coming down

between two sturdy men wearing stiff hats on the backs of their
heads. Dr. Zimbalist's eyes were cast down like those of a man
taking heed to his steps on the stairs. One of his wrists was linked
with the wrist of one of his companions by a bracelet and little
chain. Looking up and recognizing his patient, he twitched his
cheek sourly, nodded at him, and said: "Another time!" Adrian,
his back to the wall, disconcerted, faced the three and let them
pass; looked after them awhile as they descended and then followed them down. He saw them mount a waiting car and drive
off at a fast pace. Thus ended the continuation of Adrian's cure
by Dr. Zimbalist, after its earlier interruption. I must add that he
troubled himself as little about the circumstances of his second
bad shot as about the extraordinary atmosphere of his first one.
Why Zimbalist had been taken away, and at the very hour for
which an appointment had been made — he let that rest. But as
though frightened off, he never took up the cure again after that
and went to no other doctor. He did so the less in that the local
affection healed itself without further treatment and disappeared,
and as I can confirm and would sustain against any professional
doubts, there were no manifest secondary symptoms. Adrian suffered once, in Wendell Kretschmar's lodgings, where he had just
presented some studies in composition, a violent attack of giddi-
ness, which made him stagger and forced him to lie down. It
passed into a two days' migraine, which except for its severity
was not different from other earlier attacks of the same kind.
When I came back to Leipzig, once more a civilian, I found my
friend unchanged in his walks and ways.

CHAPTER XX

Or was he? If during our year of separation he had not become a different person, at least he was now more definitely that which he was, and this was enough to impress me, especially since I had probably a little forgotten what he had been. I have described the coolness of our parting in Halle. Our reunion, at the thought of which I had so rejoiced, was not lacking in the same quality, so that I, put off, both amused and dismayed, had to swallow my feelings and suppress whatever surged upwards into my consciousness. That he would fetch me from the station I had not expected. I had even not let him know the hour. I simply sought him out in his lodgings, before I had looked out any for myself. His landlady announced me, and I entered the room, calling him in a loud and joyful shout.

He sat at his desk, an old-fashioned one with a roll top and cabinet, writing down notes. "Hallo!" said he, not looking up. "Just a minute, we can talk." And went on for some minutes with his work, leaving it to me to remain standing or to make myself comfortable. The reader must not misinterpret this, any more than I did. It was evidence of old-established intimacy, a life in common which could not be in the least affected by a year's separation. It was simply as though we had parted the day before. Even so I was a little dashed, if at the same time amused, as the characteristic does amuse us. I had long since let myself down in one of the armless upholstered chairs flanking the book-table, when he screwed the top on his fountain-pen and approached me, without particularly looking me in the face.

"You've come just at the right time," he said, and sat down on the other side of the table. "The Schaff-Gosch quartet is playing Op. 132 tonight. You'll come along?"

I understood that he meant Beethoven's late work, the A-minor String Quartet.

"Since I'm here," I replied, "I'll come with you. It will be good to hear the Lydian movement, the 'Thanksgiving for Recovery'; I've not heard it for a long time."

"That beaker," he said, "I drain at every feast. My eyes run over." And he began to talk about the Church modes and the Ptolemaic or "natural" system, whose six different modes were reduced by the tempered, i.e. the false system to two, major and minor; and about superiority in modulation of the "pure" scale over the tempered one. This he called a compromise for home use, as also the tempered piano was a thing precisely for domestic consumption, a transient peace-pact, not a hundred and fifty years old, which had brought to pass all sorts of considerable things, oh, very considerable, but about which we should not imagine that everything was settled for eternity. He expressed great pleasure over the fact that it was an astronomer and mathematician named Ptolemy, a man from Upper Egypt, living in Alexandria, who had established the best of all known scales, the natural or right one. That proved again, he said, the relation between music and astronomy, as it had been shown already by Pythagoras' cosmic theory of harmony. Now and then he came back to the quartet and its third movement, referring to its strange character, its suggestion of a moon-landscape, and the enormous difficulty of performing it.

"At bottom," said he, "every one of the four players has to be a Paganini and would have to know not only his own part but the three others' as well, else it's no use. Thank God, one can depend on the Schaff-Gosch. Today it can be done, but it is only just playable, and in his time it was simply not. The ruthless indifference of one who has risen above it towards the sheer earthly difficulties of technique is to me the most colossally entertaining thing in life. 'What do I care about your damned fiddle?' he said to somebody who complained."

We laughed — and the odd thing was, simply that we had never even said how do you do.

"Besides," he said, "there is the fourth movement, the incomparable finale, with the short, marchlike introduction and that noble recitative of the first violin, with which as suitably as possible the theme is prepared. Only it is vexatious, if you don't want to call it gratifying, that in music, at least in this music, there are things for which one cannot scare up, out of the whole rich realm of language, do what you like, any properly characterizing epithet or combination of epithets. I have been tormenting myself over that these days: you cannot find any adequate term for the spirit, the attitude, the behaviour of this theme. For there is a lot of behaviour there. Tragic? Bold? Defiant, emphatic, full of élan, the height of nobility? None of them good. And 'glorious' is of course

only throwing in your hand. You finally land at the objective direction, the name: *Allegro appassionato*. That is the best after all."

I agreed. "Perhaps," I thought, "this evening we might think of
something else."

"You must see Kretschmar soon," it occurred to him to say.
"Where do you live?"

I told him I would go to a hotel for the night and look out
something suitable in the morning.

"I understand," he said, "your not asking me to find something.
One cannot leave it to anyone else. I have," he added, "told the
people in Café Central about you and your arrival. I must take
you there soon."

By the people he meant the group of young intellectuals whose
acquaintance he had made through Kretschmar. I was convinced
that his attitude towards them was very like what it had been towards the Winfried brethren in Halle, and when I said it was good
to hear that he had quickly found suitable contacts in Leipzig he
answered:

"Well, contacts. . . ."

Schildknapp, the poet and translator, he added, was the most
satisfactory. But even he had a way, out of a sort of not precisely
superior self-confidence, of always refusing, as soon as he saw
anyone wanted anything of him or needed or tried to claim him.
A man with a very strong — or perhaps on the other hand not so
strong — feeling of independence, he said. But sympathetic, entertaining, and besides so short of money that he himself had to
help out.

What he had wanted of Schildknapp, who as a translator lived
intimately with the English language and was altogether a warm
admirer of everything English, emerged as we continued to talk.
I learned that Adrian was looking for a theme for an opera and,
years before he seriously approached the task, had had *Love's
Labour's Lost* in mind. What he wanted of Schildknapp, who was
musically equipped as well, was the preparation of the libretto.
But the other, partly on account of his own work, and partly, I
surmise, because Adrian would hardly have been able to pay him
in advance, would not hear to it. Well, later I myself did my
friend this service. I like to think back to our first groping talk
about it, on this very evening. And I found my idea confirmed:
the tendency to marriage with the word, to vocal articulation,
more and more possessed him. He was practising almost exclusively the composition of lieder, short and long songs, even epic
fragments, taking his material from a Mediterranean anthology,

which in a fairly happy German version included Provençal and Catalan lyrics of the twelfth and thirteenth centuries, Italian poetry, the loftiest visions of the *Divina Commedia*, and some Spanish and Portuguese things. It was, at that musical time of day and at the young adept's age, almost inevitable that here and there the influence of Gustav Mahler should be perceptible. But then would come a tone, a mood, a glimpse, a something lone-wandering and unique: it stood strange and firm on its own feet; and in such things we recognize today the master of the grotesque *Vision of the Apocalypse*.

This was clearest in the songs of the series taken from the *Purgatorio* and the *Paradiso*, chosen with a shrewd sense of their affinity with music. Thus in the piece which especially took me, and Kretschmar too had called very good, where the poet in the light of the planet Venus sees the smaller lights — they are the spirits of the blessed — some more quickly, the others more slowly, "according to the kind of their regard of God" drawing their circles, and compares this to the sparks that one distinguishes in the flame, the *voices* that one distinguishes in the song "when the one twines round the other." I was surprised and enchanted at the reproduction of the sparks in the fire, of the entwining voices. And still I did not know whether I should give the preference to these fantasies on the light in light or to the introspective, more-thought-than-seen pieces — those where all is rejected questioning, wrestling with the unfathomable, where "doubt springs at the foot of truth" and even the cherub who looks into God's depths measures not the gulf of the everlasting resolve. Adrian had here chosen the frightfully stern sequence of verses which speak of the condemnation of innocence and ignorance, and incomprehensible justice is questioned which delivers over to hell the good and pure but not baptized, not reached by faith. He had persuaded himself to put the thundering response in tones which announce the powerlessness of the creaturely good before Good in itself: the latter, being itself the source of justice, cannot give way before anything that our human understanding is tempted to call unjust. This rejection of the human in favour of an unattainable absolute foreordination angered me. And altogether, though I acknowledge Dante's greatness as a poet, I always feel put off by his tendency to cruelty and scenes of martyrdom. I recall that I scolded Adrian for choosing this almost intolerable passage as his theme. It was then that I met a look from his eye which I had not seen before; it had made me question whether I was quite right in asserting that I found him unchanged after our

year's separation. This look was something new, and it remained
peculiar to him, even though one encountered it only from time
to time and indeed without especial occasion. Mute, veiled, musing, aloof to the point of offensiveness, full of a chilling melancholy, it ended in a smile with closed lips, not unfriendly, yet
mocking, and with that gesture of turning away, so habitual, so
long familiar to me.

The impression was painful and, intentional or not, it wounded.
But I quickly forgave him as we went on, and I heard the moving
musical diction given to the parable in the *Purgatorio* of the man
who carries a light on his back at night, which does not light him
but lights up the path of those coming after. The tears came in my
eyes. I was still happier over the altogether successful shaping of
the address, only nine lines long, of the poet to his allegorical song,
which speaks so darkly and difficultly, with no prospect of its
hidden sense being understood of the world. Thus, its creator
lays upon it, may it implore perception if not of its depth at least
of its beauty. "So look at least, how beautiful I am!" The way the
music strives upward out of the difficulties, the artful confusion,
the mingled distresses of its first part to the tender light of the
final cry and there is touchingly resolved — all that I straightway
found admirable and did not hide my delighted approbation.

"So much the better if it is good for something already," said
he. In later talks it became clear what he meant by "already." The
word had not to do with his youth; he meant that he regarded
the composition of the songs, however much devotion he gave to
the single task, on the whole only as practice for a complete work
in words and music which hovered before his mind's eye, the
text of which was to be the Shakespeare comedy. He went about
theoretically to glorify this bond with the word, which he would
put in practice. Music and speech, he insisted, belonged together,
they were at bottom one, language was music, music a language;
separate, one always appealed to the other, imitated the other, used
the other's tools, always the one gave itself to be understood as
substitute of the other. How music could be first of all word, be
thought and planned as word, he would demonstrate to me by the
fact that Beethoven had been seen composing in words. "What is
he writing there in his notebook?" it had been asked. "He is composing." "But he is writing words, not notes." Yes, that was a way
he had. He usually sketched in words the course of ideas in a composition, at most putting in a few notes here and there. — Adrian
dwelt upon this, it visibly charmed him. The creative thought, he
said, probably formed its own and unique intellectual category,

but the first draft hardly ever amounted to a picture, a statue in words — which spoke for the fact that music and speech belonged together. It was very natural that music should take fire at the word, that the word should burst forth out of music, as it did towards the end of the Ninth Symphony. Finally it was a fact that the whole development of music in Germany strove towards the word-tone drama of Wagner and therein found its goal.

"One goal," said I, referring to Brahms and to the absolute music in the "light on his back." He agreed to the qualification, the more easily because what he had vaguely in mind was as un-Wagnerian as possible, and most remote from nature-dæmony and the theatrical quality of the myth: a revival of opéra bouffe in a spirit of the most artificial mockery and parody of the artificial: something highly playful and highly precious; its aim the ridicule of affected asceticism and that euphuism which was the social fruit of classical studies. He spoke with enthusiasm of the theme, which gave opportunity to set the lout and "natural" alongside the comic sublime and make both ridiculous in each other. Archaic heroics, rodomontade, bombastic etiquette tower out of forgotten epochs in the person of Don Armado, whom Adrian rightly pronounced a consummate figure of opera. And he quoted verses to me in English, which obviously he had taken to his heart: the despair of the witty Biron at his perjured love of her who had two pitch-balls stuck in her face for eyes; his having to sigh and watch for "by heaven one that will do the deed, though Argus were her eunuch and her guard." Then the judgment upon this very Biron: "You shall this twelvemonth term from day to day Visit the speechless sick, and still converse With groaning wretches"; and his cry: "It cannot be: mirth cannot move a soul in agony!" He repeated the passage and declared that some day he would certainly compose it, also the incomparable talk in the fifth act about the folly of the wise, the helpless, blinded, humiliating misuse of wit to adorn the fool's cap of passion. Such utterance, he said, as that of the two lines:

> The blood of youth burns not with such excess
> As gravity's revolt to wantonness

flourishes only on the heights of poetic genius.

I rejoiced at this admiration, this love, even though the choice of matter was not quite to my taste. I have always been rather unhappy at any mockery of humanistic extravagances; it ends by making humanism itself a subject for mirth. Which did not prevent me from preparing the libretto for him when he was ready.

What I at once tried my best to dissuade him from was his strange and utterly impractical idea of composing the comedy in English, because he found that the only right, dignified, authentic thing; also because it seemed indicated, on account of the plays on words and the old English verse with doggerel rhyme. The very important objection, that a text in a foreign language would destroy every prospect of its appearance on a German stage, he did not consider, because he altogether declined to imagine a contemporary public for his exclusive, eccentric, fantastic dreams. It was a baroque idea, but rooted deep in his nature, combined as that was of haughty shyness, the old-German provincialism of Kaisersaschern, and an out-and-out cosmopolitanism. Not for nothing was he a son of the town where Otto III lay buried. His dislike of his own very Germanness (it was that, indeed, which drew him to the Anglicist and Anglomaniac Schildknapp) took the two disparate forms of a cocoonlike withdrawal from the world and an inward need of world-wideness. These it was made him insist on expecting a German concert audience to listen to songs in a foreign language — or, more realistically put, on preventing their hearing them. In fact, he produced during my Leipzig year compositions on poems by Verlaine and the beloved William Blake, which were not sung for decades. The Verlaine ones I heard later in Switzerland. One of them is the wonderful poem with the closing line: "*C'est l'heure exquise*"; another the equally enchanting "*Chanson d'Automne*"; a third the fantastically melancholy, preposterously melodious three-stanza poem that begins with the lines: "*Un grand sommeil noir Tombe sur ma vie.*" Then a couple of mad and dissolute pieces from the "*Fêtes galantes*": "*He! Bonsoir, la Lune!*" and above all the macabre proposal, answered with giggles: "*Mourons ensemble, voulez-vous?*" — As for Blake's extraordinary poesy, he set to music the stanzas about the rose, whose life was destroyed by the dark secret love of the worm which found its way into her crimson bed. Then the uncanny sixteen lines of "A Poison Tree," where the poet waters his wrath with his tears, suns it with smiles and soft deceitful wiles, so that an alluring apple ripens, with which the thievish friend poisons himself: to the hater's joy he lies dead in the morning beneath the tree. The evil simplicity of the verse was completely reproduced in the music. But I was even more profoundly impressed at the first hearing by a song to words by Blake, a dream of a chapel all of gold before which stand people weeping, mourning, worshipping, not daring to enter in. There rises the figure of a serpent who knows how by force and force and force to make an entry into the shrine; the slimy length of its body it drags along the costly floor and gains the altar, where it vomits its poison out on the bread and on the wine. "So," ends the poet, with desperate logic, therefore and thereupon, "I turned into a sty and laid me down among the swine." The dream anguish of the vision, the growing terror, the horror of pollution, finally the wild renunciation of a humanity dishonoured by the sight — all this was reproduced with astonishing power in Adrian's setting.

But these are later things, though all of them belong to Lever-kühn's Leipzig years. On that evening, then, after my arrival we heard the Schaff-Gosch concert together and next day visited Wendell Kretschmar, who spoke to me privately about Adrian's progress in a way that made me proud and glad. Nothing, he said, did he fear less, than ever to have to regret his summons to a musical career. A man so self-assured, so fastidious in matters of taste and "pleasing the public," would of course have difficulties, outwardly as well as inwardly; but that was quite right, in such a case, since only art could give body to a life which otherwise would bore itself to death with its own facility. — I enrolled myself with Lautensack and the famous Bermeter, glad that I need not hear any more theology for Adrian's sake; and allowed myself to be introduced to the circle at Café Central, a sort of bohemian club, which had pre-empted a smoky den in the tavern, where the members read the papers afternoons, played chess, and discussed cultural events. They were students from the conservatoires, painters, writers, young publishers, also beginning lawyers with an interest in the arts, a few actors, members of the Leipzig Kammerspiele, under strong literary influence — and so on. Rüdiger Schildknapp, the translator, considerably older than we were, at the beginning of the thirties, belonged, as I have said, to this group. As he was the only one with whom Adrian stood on terms of any intimacy, I too approached him, and spent many hours with them both together. That I had a critical eye on the man whom Adrian dignified with his friendship will, I fear, be evident in the present sketch of his personality, though I will endeavour, as I always have endeavoured, to do him justice.

Schildknapp was born in a middle-sized town in Silesia, the son of a post-office official whose position elevated him above the lower ranks without leading to the higher administrative posts reserved for men with university degrees. Such a position requires no certificate or juristic training; it is arrived at after a term of years of preliminary service by passing the examinations for secretary in chief. Such had been the career of the elder Schildknapp. He was a man of proper upbringing and good form, also socially ambitious; but the Prussian hierarchy either shut him out of the upper circles of the town or, if they did by exception admit him, gave him to taste humiliation there. Thus he quarrelled with his lot and was an aggrieved man, a grumbler, visiting his unsuccessful career on his own family's head. Rüdiger, his son, portrayed to us very vividly, filial respect giving way before a sense of the ridiculous, how the father's social embitterment had poisoned his own, his mother's and his brothers' and sisters' lives; the more because it expressed itself, in accordance with the man's refinement, not in gross unpleasantness but as a finer capacity for suffering, and an exaggerated self-pity. He might come to the table and bite violently on a cherry-stone in the fruit soup, breaking a crown on one of his teeth. "Yes, you see," he would say, his voice trembling, stretching out his hands, "that is how it is, that's what happens to me, that is the way I am, it is in myself, it has to be like this! I had looked forward to this meal, and felt some appetite; it is a warm day and the cold fruit dish had promised me some refreshment. Then this has to happen. Good, you can see that joy is not my portion. I give it up. I will go back to my room. I hope you will enjoy it," he would finish in a dying voice, and quit the table, well knowing that joy would certainly not be their portion either.

The reader can picture Adrian's mirth at the drolly dejected reproduction of scenes experienced with youthful intensity. Of course we had always to check our merriment and remember that this was the narrator's father we were dealing with. Rüdiger assured us that the elder's feeling of social inferiority had communicated itself to them all in greater or less degree: he himself had taken it with him, a sort of spiritual wound, from his parents' house. Apparently his irritation over it was one of the reasons why he would not give his father the satisfaction of wiping out the stain in the person of his son, for he had frustrated the elder's hope of seeing the younger a member of government. Rüdiger had finished at the gymnasium and gone to the university. But he had not even got so far as an assessorship, devoting himself to literature instead, and preferring to forfeit any assistance from home rather than to satisfy the father's obnoxious wishes. He wrote poems in free verse, critical essays and short stories in a neat prose style. But partly under economic pressure, partly also because his own production was not exactly copious, he devoted most of his time to translation, chiefly from his favourite language, English. He not only supplied several publishers with German versions of

English and American literary provender, but also got himself commissioned by a Munich publisher of de luxe editions and literary curiosities to translate English classics, Skelton's dramatic moralities, some pieces of Fletcher and Webster, certain didactic poems of Pope; and he was responsible for excellent German editions of Swift and Richardson. He supplied this sort of product with well-found prefaces, and contributed to his translations a great deal of conscientiousness, taste, and feeling for style, likewise a preoccupation with the exactness of the reproduction, matching phrase for phrase and falling more and more victim to the charms and penalties of translation. But his work was accompanied by a mental state which on another plane resembled his father's. He felt himself to be a born writer, and spoke bitterly of being driven by necessity to till another's field, wearing himself out on work which only distinguished him in a way he found insulting. He wanted to be a poet, in his own estimation he was one; that on account of his tiresome daily bread he had to sink to a middleman's position in literature put him in a critical and derogatory frame towards the contributions of others and was the subject of his daily plaint. "If only I had time," he used to say, "if I could work instead of drudging, I would show them!" Adrian was inclined to believe it, but I, perhaps judging too harshly, suspected that what he considered an obstacle was really a welcome pretext with which he deceived himself over his lack of a genuine and telling creative impulse.

With all this, one must not imagine him as morose or sullen; on the contrary he was very jolly, even rather feather-headed, gifted with a definitely Anglo-Saxon sense of humour and in character just that which the English call boyish. He was always immediately acquainted with all the sons of Albion who came to Leipzig as tourists, idlers, music-students; talked with them with complete elective adaptation of his speech to theirs, chattering nonsense thirteen to the dozen and imitating irresistibly their struggles in German, their accents, their all too correct mistakes in ordinary everyday exchange, their foreign weakness for the written language: as for instance *Besichtigen Sie jenes!* when all they meant was: *Sehen Sie das!* And he looked just like them. I have not yet mentioned his appearance: it was very good, and — apart from the clothes, shabby and always the same, to which his poverty condemned him — elegant and gentlemanly, and rather sporting. His features were striking, their aristocratic character marred only by a soft, loose-lipped mouth such as I have often noticed among Silesians. Tall, broad-shouldered, long-legged, narrow-hipped, he wore day in, day out the same checked breeches, the worse for wear, long woollen stockings, stout yellow shoes, a coarse linen shirt open at the throat, and over it a jacket of a colour already vague, with sleeves that were a little short. But his hands were very aristocratic, with long fingers and beautifully shaped, oval, rounded nails. The whole was so undeniably "portrait of a gentleman" that in his everyday clothes, in themselves an offense to society, he could frequent circles where evening dress was the rule. The women preferred him just as he was to his rivals in correct black and white, and at such receptions he might be seen surrounded by unaffectedly admiring femininity.

And yet! And again! His needy exterior, excused by the tiresome want of money, could not affect adversely his rank as cavalier and gentleman or prevent the native truth from showing through and counteracting it. But this very "truth" was itself in part a deception, and in this complicated sense Schildknapp was a fraud. He looked like an athlete, but his looks were misleading, for he practised no sport, except a little skiing with his English friends in winter in the Saxon Alps; and he was subject to a catarrh of the bladder, which in my opinion was not quite negligible. Despite his tanned face and broad shoulders his health was not always sound and as a younger man he had spit blood; in other words, tended to be tubercular. The women were not quite so lucky with him as he was with them, so far as I saw; at least not individually, for collectively they enjoyed his entire devotion. It was a roving, all-embracing devotion, it referred to the sex as such, and the possibilities for happiness presented to him by the entire world; for the single instance found him inactive, frugal, reserved. That he could have as many love-affairs as he chose seemed to satisfy him, it was as though he shrank from every connection with the actual because he saw therein a theft from the possible. The potential was his kingdom, its endless spaces his domain — therein and thus far he was really a poet. He had concluded from his name that his forebears had been giant attendants on knights and princes, and although he had never sat a horse, nor ever tried to do so, he felt himself a born horseman. He ascribed it to atavistic memory, a blood heritage, that he very often dreamed of riding; he was uncommonly convincing when he showed us how natural it was for him to hold the reins in the left hand and pat the horse's neck with the right. — The most common phrase in his mouth was "One ought to." It was the formula for a wistful reflection upon possibilities for the fulfilment of which the resolve was lacking. One ought to do — this and that, have this or that. One ought to write a novel about Leipzig society: one ought, if even as a dish-washer, to take a trip round the world; one ought to study physics, astronomy; one ought to acquire a little land and cultivate the soil in the sweat of one's brow. If we went into a grocery to have some coffee ground, he was capable of saying when we came out, with a contemplative head-shake: "One ought to keep a grocery."

I have referred to his feeling of independence. It had expressed itself early, in his rejection of government service and choice of a free-lance life. Yet he was on the other hand the servant of many gentlemen and had something of the parasite about him. And why should he not, with his narrow means, make use of his good exterior and social popularity? He got himself invited out a good deal, ate luncheon here and there in Leipzig houses, even in rich Jewish ones, though one might hear him drop anti-Semitic remarks. People who feel slighted, not treated according to their deserts, yet rejoice in an aristocratic physique, often seek satisfaction in racial self-assertion. The special thing in his case was that he did not like the Germans either, was saturated with their social and national sense of inferiority and expressed it by saying that he would just as soon or sooner stick with the Jews. On their side, the Jewish publishers' wives and bankers' ladies looked up to him with the profound admiration of their race for German master-blood and long legs and greatly enjoyed making him presents: the knitted stockings, belts, sweaters, and scarves which he wore were mostly gifts, and not always quite unprompted. When he went shopping with a lady he might point to something and say: "Well, I would not spend any money on that. At most I would take it for a gift." And took it for a gift, with the bearing of one who had certainly said he would not give money for it. For the rest, he asserted his independence to himself and others by the fundamental refusal to be obliging: when one needed him, he was definitely not to be had. If a place was vacant at dinner and he was asked to fill in, he unfailingly declined. If somebody wished to assure himself of an agreeable companion for a prescribed sojourn at a cure, Schildknapp's refusal was the more certain the clearer it was that the other set store by his company. It was thus he had rejected Adrian's proposal that he make the libretto for *Love's Labour's Lost*. Yet he was fond of Adrian, he was really attached to him, and Adrian did not take it ill that he refused. He was altogether very tolerant of Schildknapp's weaknesses, over which the man himself laughed; and much too grateful for his sympathetic talk, his stories about his father, his English whimsies, to have wished to bear him a grudge. I have never seen Adrian laugh so much, laugh even to tears, as when he and Rüdiger Schildknapp were together. A true humorist, the latter knew how to draw a momentarily overwhelming funniness from the most unlikely things. It is a fact that the chewing of a dry rusk fills the ears of the chewer with a deafening crunch, shutting him away from the outer world; and Schildknapp demonstrated at tea that a rusk-chewing company could not possibly understand each other and would have to confine themselves to "What did you say?" "Did you speak?" "Just a moment, please!" How Adrian would laugh when Schildknapp fell out with his own reflection in the mirror! He was vain, that is, not in a common way, but in poetic reference to the endless potential of happiness in the world, far outbidding his own power of resolution, for which he wished to keep himself young and handsome, he was aggrieved at the tendency of his face to be prematurely wrinkled and weather-beaten. And his mouth did have something old-man about it, together with the nose drooping straight down over it, which otherwise one was willing to call classic. One could readily see how Rüdiger would look when he was old, adding a wrinkled brow, lines from nose to mouth, and various crow's-feet. He would approach his features mistrustfully to the glass, pull a wry face, hold his chin with thumb and forefinger, stroke his cheek in disgust and then wave his face away with the other hand so expressively that we, Adrian and I, burst out in loud laughter.

What I have not yet mentioned is that his eyes were exactly the same colour as Adrian's. There was really a remarkable similarity: they showed just the same mixture of blue, grey, and green, and both had the same rust-coloured ring round the pupil. However strange it may sound, it always seemed to me, seemed so with a certain soothing conviction, that Adrian's laughter-loving friendship for Schildknapp had to do with this likeness in the colour of their eyes — which is equivalent to saying that it rested upon an indifference as profound as it was light-hearted. I scarcely need to add that they always addressed each other with their last names and *Sie*. If I did not know how to entertain Adrian as Schildknapp did, I did have our childhood tie, our *du*, to my advantage over the Silesian.

CHAPTER XXI

This morning, while my good Helene was preparing our morning drink and a brisk Upper Bavarian autumn day began to clear away the usual early mists, I read in my paper of the successful revival of our submarine warfare, to which inside twenty-four hours not less than twelve ships, among them two large passenger steamers, an English and a Brazilian, with five hundred passengers, have fallen victim. We owe this success to a new torpedo of fabulous properties which German technicians have succeeded in constructing, and I cannot repress a certain satisfaction over our ever alert spirit of invention, our national gift of not being swerved aside by however many set-backs. It stands wholly and entirely at the service of the regime which brought us into this war, laid the Continent literally at our feet and replaced the intellectual's dream of a European Germany with the upsetting, rather brittle reality, intolerable, so it seems to the rest of the world, of a German Europe. But my involuntary satisfaction gives way to the thought that such incidental triumphs as the new sinkings or the splendid commando feat of snatching the fallen dictator of Italy from his prison can only serve to arouse false hopes and lengthen out a war which in the view of any reasonable and sensible man can no longer be won. Such is also the opinion of the head of our Freising theological seminary, Monsignor Hinterpförtner; he has confessed it to me in so many words, in private conversation as we sat over our evening glasses — a man who has nothing in common with the passionate scholar about whom in the summer the Munich student uprising centred, so horribly quenched in blood. Monsignor Hinterpförtner's knowledge of the world permits him no illusion, not even that which clings to the distinction between losing the war and not winning it. For that only veils the truth that we have played *va banque* and that the failure of our hopes of world conquest amounts to a first-class national catastrophe.

I say all this to remind the reader of the historical conditions under which I am setting down Leverkühn's biography, and to point out how the excited state bound up with my subject constantly assimilates itself to that produced by the shattering events of the time. I do not speak of distraction; for — at least so it seems to me — events have not actually the power of distracting me from my task. Even so, and despite my personal security, I may say that the times are not precisely favourable to the steady pursuance of such a work as this. And, moreover, just during the Munich disorders and executions, I got an influenza with fever and chills, which for ten days confined me to my bed and necessarily affected for some time the physical and mental powers of a man now sixty years old. It is no wonder that spring and summer have passed into autumn, and autumn is now well advanced, since I committed to paper the first lines of this narrative. Meanwhile we have experienced the destruction of our noble cities from the air, a destruction that would cry to heaven if we who suffer were not ourselves laden with guilt. As it is, the cry is smothered in our throats; like King Claudius's prayer, it can "never to heaven go." There is outcry over these crimes against culture, crimes that we ourselves invoked; how strange it sounds in the mouths of those who trod the boards of history as the heralds and bringers of a world-rejuvenating barbarism, revelling in atrocity. Several times the shattering, headlong destruction has come breath-takingly near my retreat. The frightful bombardment of the city of Dürer and Willibald Pirkheimer was no remote event; and when the last judgment fell on Munich too, I sat pallid, shaking like the walls, the doors, and the windowpanes in my study — and with trembling hand wrote on at this story of a life. For my hand trembles in any case, on account of my subject; it cannot much matter to me that it trembles a little more due to terror from without.

We have lived through, with the sort of hope and pride which the unfolding of German might must rouse in us, the new offensive of our Wehrmacht against the Russian hordes defending their inhospitable but obviously dearly loved land. It was an offensive which after a few weeks passed over into a Russian one and since then has led to endless, unavoidable abandonment of territory — to speak only of territory. With profound consternation we read of the landing of American and Canadian troops on the southeast coast of Sicily, the fall of Syracuse, Catania, Messina, Taormina. We learned, with a mixture of terror and envy — pierced by the knowledge that we ourselves were not capable of it, in either a good or a bad sense — how a country whose mental state still permitted it to draw the foregone conclusion from a succession of scandalous defeats and losses relieved itself of its great man, in order somewhat later to submit to unconditional surrender. That is what the world demands of us too, but to consent to it our most desperate situation would still be much too holy and dear. Yes, we are an utterly different people; we deny and reject the foregone conclusion; we are a people of mightily tragic soul, and our love belongs to fate — to any fate, if only it be one, even destruction kindling heaven with the crimson flames of the death of the gods!

The advance of the Muscovites into our destined granary, the Ukraine, and the elastic retreat of our troops to the Dnieper line accompanied my work, or rather my work accompanied those events. Some days since, the untenability of this defence line too seems proved, although oùr Führer, hurrying up, ordered a mighty halt to the retreat, uttered his trenchant rebuke, the words "Stalingrad psychosis," and commanded that the line of the Dnieper be held at all costs. The price, any price, was paid, in vain; whither, how far, the red flood the papers speak of will still pour on is left to our powers of imagination — and these are already inclined to reckless excess. For it belongs in the realm of the fantastic, it offends against all order and expectation that Germany itself should become the theatre of one of Germany's wars. Twenty-five years ago at the very last moment we escaped that fate. But now our increasingly tragic and heroic psychology seems to prevent us from quitting a lost cause before the unthinkable becomes fact. Thank God, wide stretches still lie between our home soil and destruction rushing on from the east. We may be prepared to take some painful losses now on this front in order to defend in greater strength our European territory against the deadly enemies of the German order advancing from the west. The invasion of our beautiful Sicily by no means proved that it was possible for the foe to gain a footing on the Italian mainland. But unhappily it did turn out to be possible, while in Naples last week a communistic revolt broke out in support of the Allies which made that city appear no longer a place worthy of German troops. After conscientious destruction of the library, and leaving a time-bomb behind in the post-office, we made our exit with our heads high. And now there is talk of invasion tests in the Channel, supposed to be covered with ships, and the civilian takes unlawful leave to ask himself whether what happened in Italy and farther up the peninsula can happen, all the prescribed beliefs in the inviolability of Fortress Europa to the contrary, also in France or some other place.

Yes, Monsignor Hinterpförtner is right: we are lost. In other words, the war is lost; but that means more than a lost campaign, it means in very truth that *we* are lost: our character, our cause, our hope, our history. It is all up with Germany, it will be all up with her. She is marked down for collapse, economic, political, moral, spiritual, in short all-embracing, unparalleled, final collapse. I suppose I have not wished for it, this that threatens, for it is madness and despair. I suppose I have not wished for it, because my pity is too deep, my grief and sympathy are with this unhappy nation, when I think of the exaltation and blind ardour of its uprising, the breaking-out, the breaking-up, the breaking-down; the purifying and fresh start, the national new birth of ten years ago, that seemingly religious intoxication — which then betrayed itself to any intelligent person for what it was by its crudity, vulgarity, gangsterism, sadism, degradation, filthiness — ah, how unmistakably it bore within itself the seeds of this whole war! My heart contracts painfully at the thought of that enormous investment of faith, zeal, lofty historic emotion; all this we made, all this is now puffed away in a bankruptcy without compare. No, surely I did not want it, and yet — I have been driven to want it, I wish for it today and will welcome it, out of hatred for the outrageous contempt of reason, the vicious violation of the truth, the cheap, filthy backstairs mythology, the criminal degradation and confusion of standards; the abuse, corruption, and blackmail of all that was good, genuine, trusting, and trustworthy in our old Germany. For liars and lickspittles mixed us a poison draught and took away our senses. We drank — for we Germans perennially yearn for intoxication — and under its spell, through years of deluded high living, we committed a superfluity of shameful deeds, which must now be paid for. With what? I have already used the word, together with the word "despair" I wrote it. I will not repeat it: not twice could I control my horror or my trembling fingers to set it down again.

*

*   *

Asterisks too are a refreshment for the eye and mind of the reader. One does not always need the greater articulation of a Roman numeral, and I could scarcely give the character of a main section to the above excursus into a present outside of Adrian Leverkühn's life and work. No, asterisks will serve capitally to give proportion to my page; and below them I will round out this section with some further information about Adrian's Leipzig years, though I realize that as a chapter it makes an impression of heterogeneous elements — as though it were not enough that I did not succeed better with what came before. I have re-read it all: Adrian's dramatic wishes and plans, his earliest songs, the painful gaze that he had acquired during our separation; the intellectual fascinations of Shakespearian comedy, Leverkühn's emphasis on foreign songs and his own shy cosmopolitanism; then the bohemian Café Central club, winding up with the portrait of Rüdiger Schildknapp, given in perhaps unjustifiable detail. And I quite properly ask myself whether such uneven material can actually make up a single chapter. But let me remember that from the first I had to reproach myself for the absence of a controlled and regular structure in my work. My excuse is always the same: my subject is too close to me. What is lacking is distance, con-trast, mere differentiation between the material and the hand that shapes it. Have I not said more than once that the life I am treat-ing of was nearer to me, dearer, more moving than my own? And being so near, so moving, and so intimate, it is not mere "mate-rial" but a *person*, and that does not lend itself to artistic treat-ment. Far be it from me to deny the seriousness of art; but when it becomes serious, then one rejects art and is not capable of it. I can only repeat that paragraphs and asterisks are in this book merely a concession to the eyes of the reader, and that I, if I had my way, would write down the whole in one burst and one breath, without any division, yes, without paragraphing or inter-missions. I simply have not the courage to submit such an insen-sate text to the eyes of the reading public.

*

*   *

Having spent a year with Adrian in Leipzig, I know how he lived during the other three of his stay there; his manner of life being so regular and conservative that I found it rigid and some-times even depressing. Not for nothing, in that first letter, had he expressed his sympathy for Chopin's lack of adventurous spirit, his "not wanting to know." He too wanted to know nothing, see nothing, actually experience nothing, at least not in any obvious, exterior sense of the word. He was not out for change, new sense impressions, distraction, recreation. As for the last, he liked to make fun of people who are constantly having "a little change," constantly getting brown and strong — and nobody knew for what. "Relaxation," he said, "is for those to whom it does no good." He was not interested in travel for the sake of sightseeing or "culture." He scorned the delight of the eye, and sensitive as his hearing was, just so little had he ever felt urged to train his sight in the forms of plastic art. The distinction between eye-men and ear-men he considered indefeasibly valid and correct and counted himself definitely among the latter. As for me, I have never thought such a distinction could be followed through thick and thin, and in his case I never quite believed in the unwillingness and reluctance of the eye. To be sure, Goethe too says that music is something inborn and native, requiring no great nourishment from outside and no experience drawn from life. But after all there is the inner vision, the perception, which is something different and comprehends more than mere seeing. And more than that, it is profoundly contradictory that a man should have, as Leverkühn did, some feeling for the human eye, which after all speaks only to the eye, and yet refuse to perceive the outer world through that organ. I need only mention the names of Marie Godeau, Rudi Schwerdtfeger, and Nepomuk Schneidewein to bring home to myself Adrian's receptivity, yes, weakness, for the magic of the eye, the black and the blue. Of course I am quite clear that I am doing wrong to bombard the reader with unfamiliar names when the actual appearance of their owners in these pages is still far off; it is a barefaced blunder which may well make one question the freedom of the will. What, indeed, is free will? I am quite aware that I have put down under a compulsion these too empty, too early names.

Adrian's journey to Graz, which did not occur for the journey's sake, was one interruption in the even flow of his life. Another was the excursion with Schildknapp to the sea, the fruit of which one can claim to be that one-movement symphonic tone-poem. The third exception, related to the second, was a journey to Basel, which he made in company with his teacher Kretschmar to attend the performances of sacred music of the baroque period, which the Basel Chamber Choir gave in St. Martin's Church. Kretschmar was to play the organ. They gave Monteverdi's Magnificat, some organ studies by Frescobaldi, an oratorio by Carissimi, and a cantata by Buxtehude. This *"musica riservata"* made a strong impression on Adrian, as a music of emotion, which in a rebound from the constructivism of the Netherlanders treated the Bible word with astonishing human freedom, with a declamatory expressiveness, and clothed it in a boldly descriptive instrumental garb. The impression it made was very strong and lasting. He wrote and spoke much to me about this outburst of modernity in Monteverdi's musical devices; he spent much time in the Leipzig library, and practised Carissimi's *Jeph-*

tha and the *Psalms of David* by Schütz. Who could fail to recognize in the quasi-ecclesiastical music of his later years, the *Apocalypse* and the *Faustus*, the stylistic influence of this madrigalism?
Always dominant in him was a will to go to extremes of expression; together with the intellectual passion for austere order, the
linear style of the Netherlands composers. In other words, heat
and cold prevail alongside each other in his work; sometimes in
moments of the greatest genius they play into each other, the *es-
pressivo* takes hold of the strict counterpoint, the objective blushes
with feeling. One gets the impression of a glowing mould; this,
like nothing else, has brought home to me the idea of the dæmonic.

As for the connection between Adrian's first journey to Switzerland and the earlier one to Sylt, it had come about thus: that
little mountain land, culturally so active and unhampered, had
and has a Society of Musicians, a Tonkünstler Verein, which
holds regular orchestral practices, the so-called *lectures d'orchestre*. A jury of authorities, that is, permits young aspirants to present their compositions, which are then given a try-out by one of
the symphony orchestras of the country and its conductor, the
public being excluded and only professionals admitted. Thus the
young composer has an opportunity to hear his creation, to get
experience and have his imagination instructed by the reality of
sound. Such a try-out was held in Geneva at almost the same time
with the Basel concert, by the Orchestre de la Suisse Romande,
and Wendell Kretschmar had succeeded through his connections
in having Adrian's *Meerleuchten* — by exception the work of a
young German — put on the program. For Adrian it was a complete surprise: Kretschmar had amused himself by keeping him
in the dark. He still knew nothing when he went with his teacher
from Basel to Geneva for the trial performance, and there
sounded under Herr Ansermet's baton his "root treatment," that
piece of darkly sparkling impressionism which he himself did not
take seriously, had not taken seriously even when he wrote it. Of
course while it was being performed he sat on pins and needles.
To know himself being identified by the audience with an
achievement which he himself has got beyond and which for him
means only a trifling with something not taken in earnest: that
must be for the artist a grotesque torment. Thank God, signs of
applause or displeasure were forbidden at these performances.
Privately he received words of praise or blame, exception was
taken, shortcomings pointed out in French and German; he said
nothing, either way, and anyhow he agreed with no one. A week

or ten days he remained with Kretschmar in Geneva, Basel and
Zürich and came into brief contact with musical circles there.
They will not have had much joy of him, nor even known how
to take him, at least in so far as they set store by inoffensiveness,
expansiveness, friendly responsiveness. Individuals here and there
might have been touched by his shyness and understood the solitude that wrapped him, the difficulties of his life — indeed, I know
that such was the case and I find it illuminating. In my experience
there is in Switzerland much feeling for suffering, much understanding of it, which, more than in other places of advanced culture, for instance intellectual Paris, is bound up with the old civic
life of the towns. Here was a hidden point of contact. On the
other hand, the introverted Swiss mistrust of the Reich-German
met here a special case of German mistrust of the "world" —
strange as it may seem to apply the word "world" to the tight
little neighbouring country by way of contrasting it with the
broad and mighty German Reich with its immense cities. But the
comparison has indisputable justice on its side. Switzerland, neutral, many-tongued, affected by French influence, open to western airs, is actually, despite its small size, far more "world," far
more European territory than the political colossus on the north,
where the word "international" has long been a reproach, and a
smug provincialism has made the air spoilt and stuffy. I have
already spoken of Adrian's inner cosmopolitanism. But German
citizenship of the world was always something different from
worldliness; and my friend was just the soul to be made uneasy
by the "world," and feel himself outside of it. A few days earlier
than Kretschmar he returned to Leipzig, certainly a world-minded
city, yet one where the world is present more as a guest than at
home; that city where people talk so outlandishly — and where
first desire had touched his pride. That experience was profound,
it was shattering; he had not expected it from the world, and I
think it did much to estrange him from it. It is indeed quite false,
and nothing but German provincial conceitedness, to deny depth
to the world. But the depth is a world-depth; and it is a destiny,
like another, which one must accept as such, to be born to the
provincial — and thus so much the more uncanny — depth of
Germany.

Adrian kept without changing during the whole four and a half
years he spent in Leipzig his two-room quarters in Peterstrasse,
near the Collegium Beatæ Virginis, where he had again pinned the
magic square above his cottage piano. He attended lectures in
philosophy and the history of music; read and excerpted in the

library and brought Kretschmar his exercises to be criticized: piano pieces, a "concerto" for string orchestra, and a quartet for flute, clarinet, basset horn, and bassoon. I mention the pieces which were known to me and are still extant, though never published. What Kretschmar did was to point out weak places, recommend corrections of tempo, the enlivening of a stiffish rhythm, the better articulation of a theme. He pointed out to him a middle part that came to nothing, a bass that did not move. He put his finger on a transition that was only a makeshift, not organic, and compromising the natural flow of the composition. Actually, he only told him what the artistic sense of the pupil might have said itself, or what it had already told him. A teacher is the personified conscience of the pupil, confirming him in his doubt, explaining his dissatisfactions, stimulating his urge to improve. But a pupil like Adrian at bottom needed no mentor or corrector at all. He deliberately brought to Kretschmar unfinished things in order to be told what he knew already, then to laugh at the artistic sense, the connoisseurship, of his teacher, which entirely coincided with his own: the understanding which is the actual agent of the work-idea — not the idea of a particular work but the idea of the opus itself, the objective and harmonic creation complete, the manager of its unified organic nature; which sticks the cracks together, stops up the holes, brings out that "natural flow" — which was not there in the first place and so is not natural at all, but a product of art — in short, only in retrospect and indirectly does this manager produce the impression of the spontaneous and organic. In a work there is much seeming and sham, one could go further and say that as "a work" it is seeming in and for itself. Its ambition is to make one believe that it is not made, but born, like Pallas Athene in full fig and embossed armour from Jupiter's head. But that is a delusion. Never did a work come like that. It is work: art-work for appearance's sake — and now the question is whether at the present stage of our consciousness, our knowledge, our sense of truth, this little game is still permissible, still intellectually possible, still to be taken seriously; whether the work as such, the construction, self-sufficing, harmonically complete in itself, still stands in any legitimate relation to the complete insecurity, problematic conditions, and lack of harmony of our social situation; whether all seeming, even the most beautiful, even precisely the beautiful, has not today become a lie.

One asks, I say, or rather I learned to ask myself, through my intercourse with Adrian, whose sharp-sightedness, or if I may in-

vent a word, sharp-feelingness, in these matters was of extreme
incorruptibility. Insights fundamentally remote from my own native easy-goingness he expressed in talk as casual aperçus; and they
pained me, not because of wounded feeling but on his account;
they hurt, depressed, distressed me, because I saw in them dangerous aggravations of his nature, inhibitions hampering the development of his gifts. I have heard him say:

"The work of art? It is a fraud. It is something the burgher
wishes there still were. It is contrary to truth, contrary to serious
art. Genuine and serious is only the very short, the highly consistent musical moment. . . ."

How should that not have troubled me, when after all I knew
that he himself aspired to a "work," and was planning an opera!

Again, I have heard him say: "Pretence and play have the conscience of art against them today. Art would like to stop being
pretence and play, it would like to become knowledge."

But what ceases to conform to his definition, does that not
cease to exist altogether? And how will art live as knowledge? I
recalled what he had written from Halle to Kretschmar about
the extension of the kingdom of the banal. Kretschmar had not
allowed it to upset his belief in the calling of his pupil. But these
later criticisms, levelled against pretence and play, in other words
against form itself, seemed to indicate such an extension of the
kingdom of the banal, of the no longer permissible, that it threatened to swallow up art itself. With deep concern I asked myself
what strain and effort, intellectual tricks, by-ways, and ironies
would be necessary to save it, to reconquer it, and to arrive at a
work which as a travesty of innocence confessed to the state of
knowledge from which it was to be won!

My poor friend had been instructed one day, or rather one
night, from frightful lips, by an awful ally, in more detail on the
subject I here touch upon. The document is extant, I will report
on it in its proper place. It first illuminated and clarified the instinctive fears which Adrian's remarks aroused in me. But what I
called above the "travesty of innocence": how often, from early
on, did it strangely stand out in his work! That work contains, on
a developed musical plane, against a background of the most extreme tensions, "banalities" — of course not in a sentimental sense
nor in that of a buoyant complacency, but banalities rather in the
sense of a technical primitivism, specimens of naïveté or sham
naïveté which Meister Kretschmar, in so gifted a pupil, let pass
with a smile. He did so, certainly, because he understood them
not as first-degree naïvetés, if I may so express myself, but as

something the other side of the new and cheap: as audacities
dressed in the garment of the primitive. The thirteen Brentano
songs are also to be regarded in this light. To them, before I
leave the subject, I must certainly devote a few words; they often
affect one like at once a mockery and a glorification of the fundamental, a painfully reminiscent ironic treatment of tonality, of
the tempered system, of traditional music itself.

That Adrian in these Leipzig years so zealously devoted himself to the composition of lieder doubtless came about because he
regarded this lyric marrying of music with words as a preparation
for the dramatic composition he had in mind. Probably it was also connected with the scruples he felt on the score of the destiny,
the historic situation of art itself, of the autonomous work. He
misdoubted form, calling it pretence and play. Thus the small
and lyric form of the lied might stand to him as the most acceptable, most serious, and truest; it might seem to him soonest to
fulfil his theoretic demand for brevity and condensation. But it
is not only that several of these productions, as for instance the
"O lieb Mädel," with the letter symbol, further the Hymns, the
"Lustigen Musikanten," the "Huntsman to the Shepherds," and
others, are quite long. Yet Leverkühn wanted them all regarded
and treated together, as a whole, proceeding from one definite,
fundamental stylistic conception, the congenial contact with a
particular, amazingly lofty, and deeply dream-sunken poet soul.
He would never permit the performance of single pieces, but always only the full cycle, a stern reservation, which in his lifetime stood very much in the way of their performance in public,
especially since one of them, the "Jolly Musicians," is written for
a quintet of voices, mother, daughter, the two brothers, and the
boy who "early broke his leg"; that is, for alto, soprano, baritone,
tenor, and a child's voice; these, partly in ensemble, partly solo,
partly in duet (the two brothers) must perform No. 4 of the
cycle. It was the first one that Adrian orchestrated, or more correctly, he set it at once for a small orchestra of strings, wood-
wind, and percussion; for in the strange poem much is said of the
pipes and tambourine, the bells and cymbals, the jolly violin
trills, with which the fantastic, frightened little troupe, by night
"when us no human eye does see" draws into the magic spell of
its airs the lovers in their chamber, the drunken guests, the lonely
maiden. In mood and spirit the piece, like a spectral serenade,
the music at once lovely and tortured, are unique. And still I
hesitate to award it the palm among the thirteen, several of which

challenge music in a more inward sense and fulfil themselves
more deeply in it than this one which treats of music in words.

"Grossmutter Schlangenköchin" is another one of the songs,
this *Maria, wo bist du zur Stube gewesen?* This seven times
repeated "Oh woe, Frau Mother, what woe!" that with incredibly intuitive art actually calls up the unearthly thrills and shudders so familiar to us in the field of the German folk-song. For it
is really the case that this music, wise and true and over-shrewd,
here continually and painfully woos the folk-air. The wooing
remains unrealized, it is there and not there, sounds fleetingly,
echoes, fades into a style musically foreign to it, from which
after all it constantly seeks to escape. The artistic effect is striking: it appears like a cultural paradox, which by inversion of the
natural course of development, where the refined and intellectual
grow out of the elementary, the former here plays the role of
the original, out of which the simple continually strives to wrest
itself free.

> Wafteth the meaning pure of the stars
> Soft through the distance unto my ears —

that is the sound, almost lost in space, the cosmic ozone of
another poem, wherein spirits in golden barks traverse the heavenly sea and the ringing course of gleaming songs wreathes itself
down and wells up again:

> All is so gently and friendly combining,
> Hand seeketh hand in sympathy kind,
> Lights through the night wind trusting, consoling,
> All is in union for ever entwined.

Very rarely in all literature have word and music met and married as here. Here music turns its eye upon itself and looks at its
own being. These notes, that consoling and trusting offer each
other the hand; that weaving and winding of all things in likeness
and change — of such it is, and Adrian Leverkühn is its youthful
master.

Kretschmar, before he left Leipzig to become first Kapellmeister
in the Lübeck State Opera House, saw to the publication of the
Brentano songs. Schott in Mainz took them on commission; that
is, Adrian, with Kretschmar's and my help (we both shared in it)
guaranteed the cost of printing and remained the owner, in that
he assured the publishers of a share in the profits amounting to
twenty per cent of the net receipts. He strictly supervised the

piano reduction, demanded a rough, mat paper, quarto format, wide margins, and notes printed not too close together. And he insisted upon a note at the beginning to the effect that performances in clubs and concerts were only by the author's permission and only permitted for all thirteen pieces as a whole. This was taken offence at as pretentious and, together with the boldness of the music itself, put difficulties in the way of their becoming known. In 1922, not in Adrian's presence, but in mine, they were sung in the Tonhalle in Zürich, under the direction of the excellent Dr. Volkmar Andreae. The part in *"Die lustigen Musikanten"* of the boy who "early broke his leg" was sung by a boy unfortunately really crippled, using a crutch, little Jacob Nägli. He had a voice pure as a bell, that went straight to the heart.

In passing, the pretty original edition of Clemens Brentano's poems which Adrian used in his work had been a present from me; I brought the little volume for him from Naumburg to Leipzig. Of course the thirteen songs were quite his own choice, I had no smallest influence upon that. But I may say that almost song for song they followed my own wish and expectations. — I do not mean they were my personal choice, nor will the reader find them so. For what had I, really, what had my culture and ethics to do with these words and visions of a romantic poet, these dreams of a child-world and folk-world which yet are for ever floating off, not to say degenerating, into the supernatural and spectral? I can only answer that it was the music of the words themselves which led me to make the gift — music which lies in these verses, so lightly slumbering that the slightest touch of the gifted hand was enough to awake it.

CHAPTER XXII

WHEN Leverkühn left Leipzig, in September 1910, at a time when I had already begun to teach in the gymnasium at Kaisersaschern, he first went home to Buchel to attend his sister's wedding, which took place at that time and to which I and my parents were invited. Ursula, now twenty years old, was marrying the optician Johannes Schneidewein of Langensalza, an excellent man whose acquaintance she had made while visiting a friend in the charming little Salza town near Erfurt. Schneidewein, ten or twelve years older than his bride, was a Swiss by birth, of Bernese peasant stock. His trade, lens-grinding, he had learned at home, but he had somehow drifted into Germany and there opened a shop with eye-glasses and optical goods of all sorts, which he conducted with success. He had very good looks and had kept his Swiss manner of speech, pleasant to the ear, deliberate, formal, interspersed with survivals of old-German expressions oddly solemn to hear. Ursel Leverkühn had already begun to take them on. She too, though no beauty, was an attractive creature, resembling her father in looks, in manner more like her mother, brown-eyed, slim, and naturally friendly. The two made a pair on whom the eye rested with approval. In the years between 1911 and 1923 they had four children born to them: Rosa, Ezekiel, Raimund, and Nepomuk, pretty creatures all of them, and Nepomuk, the youngest, was an angel. But of that later, only quite at the end of my story.

The wedding party was not large: the Oberweiler clergyman, the schoolmaster, the justice of the peace, with their wives; from Kaisersaschern besides us Zeitbloms only Uncle Nikolaus; relatives of Frau Leverkühn from Apolda; a married pair, friend of the Leverkühns, with their daughter, from Weissenfels; brother George, the farmer, and the dairy manageress Frau Luder — that was all. Wendell Kretschmar sent a telegram with good wishes from Lübeck, which arrived during the midday meal at the house in Buchel. It was not an evening party. It had assembled betimes in the morning; after the ceremony in the village church we gathered round a capital meal in the dining-room of the bride's home, bright with copper cooking-vessels. Soon afterwards the newly wedded pair drove off with old Thomas to the station at Weissenfels, to begin the journey to Dresden; the wedding guests still sat awhile over Frau Luder's good fruit liqueurs.

Adrian and I took a walk that afternoon to the Cow Trough and up Mount Zion. We needed to talk over the text of *Love's Labour's Lost,* which I had undertaken and about which we had already had much discussion and correspondence. I had been able to send him from Athens and Syracuse the scenario and parts of the German versification, in which I based myself on Tieck and Hertzberg and occasionally, when condensation was necessary, added something of my own in as adequate a style as possible. I was determined at least to put before him a German version of the libretto, although he still stuck to his project of composing the opera in English.

He was visibly glad to get away from the wedding party and out of doors. The cloud over his eyes showed that he was suffering from headache. It had been odd, in church and at the table, to see the same sign in his father too. That this nervous complaint set in precisely on festal occasions, under the influence of emotion and excitement, is understandable. It was so with the elder man. In the son's case the psychical ground was rather that he had taken part only of necessity and with reluctance in this sacrificial feast of a maidenhead, in which, moreover, his own sister was concerned. At least he clothed his discomfort in words which recognized the simplicity, good taste, and informality of our affair, the absence of "customs and curtsyings" as he put it. He applauded the fact that it had all taken place in broad daylight, the wedding sermon had been short and simple, and at table there had been no offensive speeches — or rather, to avoid offence, no speeches at all. If the veil, the white shroud of virginity, the satin grave-shoes had been left out as well, it would have been still better. He spoke particularly of the favourable impression that Ursel's betrothed, now her husband, had made upon him.

"Good eyes," he said. "Good stock, a sound, clean, honest man. He could court her, look at her to desire her, covet her as a Christian wife, as we theologians say with justified pride at swindling the Devil out of the carnal concomitant and making a sacrament of it, the sacrament of Christian marriage. Very droll, really, this turning the natural and sinful into the sacrosanct just by putting in the word Christian — by which it is not fundamentally altered. But one has to admit that the domestication of sex, which is evil by nature, into Christian marriage was a clever makeshift."

"I do not like," I replied, "to have you make over the natural to evil. Humanism, old and new, considers that an aspersion on the sources of life."

"My dear chap, there is not much there to asperse."

"One ends," I said undeterred, "by denying the works of God; one becomes the advocate of nothing. Who believes in the Devil, already belongs to him."

He gave his short laugh.

"You never understand a joke. I spoke as a theologian and so necessarily like a theologian."

"Never mind," I said, laughing as well. "You usually take your jokes more seriously than your seriousness." We carried on this conversation on the community bench under the maple trees on Mount Zion, in the sunshine of the autumn afternoon. The fact was that at that time I myself was going courting, though the wedding and even the public engagement had to wait on my being confirmed in my position. I wanted to tell him about Helene and of my proposed step, but his remarks did not precisely encourage me.

"And they twain shall be one flesh," he began again: "Is it not a curious blessing? Pastor Schröder, thank God, spared himself the quotation. In the presence of the bridal pair it is rather painful to hear. But it is only too well meant, and precisely what I mean by domestication. Obviously the element of sin, of sensuality, of evil lust altogether, is conjured away out of marriage — for lust is certainly only in flesh of two different kinds, not in one, and that they are to be one flesh is accordingly soothing but nonsensical. On the other hand, one cannot wonder enough that one flesh has lust for another; it is a phenomenon — well, yes, the entirely exceptional phenomenon of love. Of course, love and sensuality are not to be separated. One best absolves love from the reproach of sensuality by identifying the love element in sensuality itself. The lust after strange flesh means a conquest of previously existing resistances, based on the strangeness of I and You, your own and the other person's. The flesh — to keep the Christian terminology — is normally inoffensive to itself only. With another's it will have nothing to do. Now, if all at once the strange flesh become the object of desire and lust, then the relation of the I and the You is altered in a way for which sensuality is only an empty word. No, one cannot get along without the concept of

love, even when ostensibly there is nothing spiritual in play.
Every sensual act means tenderness, it is a give and take of desire,
happiness through making happy, a manifestation of love. 'One
flesh' have lovers never been; and the prescription would drive
love along with lust out of marriage."

I was peculiarly upset and bewildered by his words and took
care not to look at him, though I was tempted. I wrote down
above how I always felt when he spoke of the things of the flesh.
But he had never come out of himself like this, and it seemed to
me that there was something explicit and unlike him about the
way he spoke, a kind of tactlessness too, against himself and also
against his auditor. It disturbed me, together with the idea that
he said it when his eyes were heavy with headache. Yet with the
sense of it I was entirely in sympathy.

"Well roared, lion!" I said, as lightly as possible. "That is what
I call standing up to it! No, you have nothing to do with the
Devil. You do know that you have spoken much more as a hu-
manist than as a theologian?"

"Let us say a psychologist," he responded. "A neutral position.
But they are, I think, the most truth-loving people."

"And how would it be," I proposed, "if we just once spoke
quite simply, personally and like ordinary citizens? I wanted to
tell you that I am about to — "

I told him what I was about to do, told him about Helene, how
I had met her and we had got to know each other. If, I said, it
would make his congratulations any warmer, he might be assured
that I dispensed him beforehand from any "customs and curtsyings" at my wedding feast.

He was greatly enlivened.

"Wonderful!" he cried. "My dearest fellow — wilt marry thyself! What a goodly idea! Such things always take one by surprise, though there is nothing surprising about them. Accept my
blessing! 'But, if thou marry, hang me by the neck, if horns that
year miscarry!' "

" 'Come, come, you talk greasily,' " I quoted out of the same
scene. "If you knew the girl and the spirit of our bond, then you
would know that there is no need to fear for my peace of mind,
but that on the contrary everything is directed towards the
foundation of love and tranquillity, a fixed and undisturbed happiness."

"I do not doubt it," said he, "and doubt not of its success."

A moment he seemed tempted to press my hand, but desisted.
There came a pause in the talk, then as we walked home it turned

to our all-important topic, the opera, and the scene in the fourth
act, with the text of which we had been joking, and which was
among those I definitely wanted to leave out. Its verbal skirmish
was really offensive, and dramatically it was not indispensable. In
any case there had to be cuts. A comedy should not last four hours
— that was and remains the principal objection to the *Meistersinger*. But Adrian seemed to have planned to use precisely the
"old sayings" of Rosaline and Boyet, the "Thou canst not hit it,
hit it, hit it," and so on for the contrapuntal passages of his overture, and altogether haggled over every episode, although he had
to laugh when I said that he reminded me of Kretschmar's Beissel and his naïve zeal to set half the world to music. Anyhow he
denied being embarrassed by the comparison. He still retained
some of the half-humorous respect he had felt when he first heard
about the wonderful novice and lawgiver of music. Absurdly
enough, he had never quite ceased to think of him, and lately had
thought of him oftener than ever.

"Remember," he said, "how I once defended his childish tyranny with the 'master' and 'servant' notes against your reproach
of silly rationalism. What instinctively pleased me was itself something instinctive, in naïve agreement with the spirit of music: the
wish, which showed itself in a comic way, to write something in
the nature of the 'strict style.' On another, less childish plane we
would need people like him, just as his flock had need of him
then: we need a system-master, a teacher of the objective and organization, with enough genius to unite the old-established, the
archaic, with the revolutionary. One ought to — "

He had to laugh.

"I'm talking like Schildknapp. One ought to. What all ought
one not to?"

"What you say," I threw in, "about the archaic-revolutionary
schoolmaster has something very German about it."

"I take it," he responded, "that you use the word not as a compliment, but in a descriptive and critical way, as you should.
However, it could mean something necessary to the time, something promising a remedy in an age of destroyed conventions and
the relaxing of all objective obligations — in short, of a freedom
that begins to lie like a mildew upon talent and to betray traces of
sterility."

I started at the word. Hard to say why, but in his mouth, altogether in connection with him, there was something dismaying
about it, something wherein anxiety mixed in an odd way with
reverence. It came from the fact that in his neighbourhood steril-

ity, threatened paralysis, arrest of productivity could be thought
of only as something positive and proud, only in connection with
pure and lofty intellectuality.

"It would be tragic," I said, "if unfruitfulness should ever be
the result of freedom. But there is always the hope of the release
of the productive powers, for the sake of which freedom is
achieved."

"True," he responded. "And she does for a while achieve what
she promised. But freedom is of course another word for subjectivity, and some fine day she does not hold out any longer, some
time or other she despairs of the possibility of being creative out
of herself and seeks shelter and security in the objective. Freedom always inclines to dialectic reversals. She realizes herself very
soon in constraint, fulfils herself in the subordination to law, rule,
coercion, system — but to fulfil herself therein does not mean she
therefore ceases to be freedom."

"In your opinion," I laughed: "So far as she knows. But actually she is no longer freedom, as little as dictatorship born out of
revolution is still freedom."

"Are you sure of it?" he asked. "But anyhow that is talking
politics. In art, at least, the subjective and the objective intertwine
to the point of being indistinguishable, one proceeds from the
other and takes the character of the other, the subjective precipi-
tates as objective and by genius is again awaked to spontaneity,
'dynamized,' as we say; it speaks all at once the language of the
subjective. The musical conventions today destroyed were not
always so objective, so objectively imposed. They were crystal-
lizations of living experiences and as such long performed an office
of vital importance: the task of organization. Organization is
everything. Without it there is nothing, least of all art. And it was
æsthetic subjectivity that took on the task, it undertook to organ-
ize the work out of itself, in freedom."

"You are thinking of Beethoven."

"Of him and of the technical principle through which a dominating subjectivity got hold of the musical organization; I mean
the development, or working out. The development itself had
been a small part of the sonata, a modest republic of subjective
illumination and dynamic. With Beethoven it becomes universal,
becomes the centre of the whole form, which, even where it is
supposed to remain conventional, is absorbed by the subjective
and is newly created in freedom. The form of variations, something archaic, a residuum, becomes a means by which to infuse
new life into form. The principle of development plus variation

technique extends over the whole sonata. It does that in Brahms, as thematic working-out, even more radically. Take him as an example of how subjectivity turns into objectivity. In him music abstains from all conventional flourishes, formulas, and residua and so to speak creates the unity of the work anew at every moment, out of freedom. But precisely on that account freedom becomes the principle of an all-round economy that leaves in music nothing casual, and develops the utmost diversity while adhering to the identical material. Where there is nothing unthematic left, nothing which could not show itself to derive from the same basic material, there one can no longer speak of a 'free style.' "

"And not of the 'strict style' in the old sense, either!"

"Old or new, I will tell you what I understand by 'strict style.' I mean the complete integration of all musical dimensions, their neutrality towards each other due to complete organization."

"Do you see a way to do that?"

"Do you know," he countered, "when I came nearest to the 'strict style'?"

I waited. He spoke so low as to be hard to hear, and between his teeth, as he used to when he had headache.

"Once in the Brentano cycle," he said, "in 'O lieb Mädel.' That song is entirely derived from a fundamental figure, a series of interchangeable intervals, the five notes B, E, A, E, E-flat, and the horizontal melody and the vertical harmony are determined and controlled by it, in so far as that is possible with a basic motif of so few notes. It is like a word, a key word, stamped on everything in the song, which it would like to determine entirely. But it is too short a word and in itself not flexible enough. The tonal space it affords is too limited. One would have to go on from here and make larger words out of the twelve letters, as it were, of the tempered semitone alphabet. Words of twelve letters, certain combinations and interrelations of the twelve semitones, series of notes from which a piece and all the movements of a work must strictly derive. Every note of the whole composition, both melody and harmony, would have to show its relation to this fixed fundamental series. Not one might recur until the other notes have sounded. Not one might appear which did not fulfil its function in the whole structure. There would no longer be a free note. That is what I would call 'strict composition.' "

"A striking thought," said I. "Rational organization through and through, one might indeed call it. You would gain an extraordinary unity and congruity, a sort of astronomical regularity and legality would be obtained thereby. But when I picture it to my-

self, it seems to me that the unchanged recurrence of such a succession of intervals, even when used in different parts of the texture, and in rhythmic variations, would result in a probably
unavoidable serious musical impoverishment and stagnation."

"Probably," he answered, with a smile which showed that he
had been prepared for this reservation. It was the smile that
brought out strongly his likeness to his mother, but with the familiar look of strain which it would show under pressure of the
migraine.

"And it is not so simple either. One must incorporate into the
system all possible techniques of variation, including those decried
as artificial; that is, the means which once helped the 'development' to win its hold over the sonata. I ask myself why I practised so long under Kretschmar the devices of the old counterpoint and covered so much paper with inversion fugues, crabs,
and inversions of crabs. Well now, all that should come in handy
for the ingenious modification of the twelve-note word. In addition to being a fundamental series it could find application in this
way, that every one of its intervals is replaced by its inversion.
Again, one could begin the figure with its last note and finish it
on its first, and then invert this figure as well. So then you have
four modes, each of which can be transposed to all the twelve
notes of the chromatic scale, so that forty-eight different versions
of the basic series may be used in a composition and whatever
other variational diversions may present themselves. A composition can also use two or more series as basic material, as in the
double and triple fugue. The decisive factor is that every note,
without exception, has significance and function according to
its place in the basic series or its derivatives. That would guarantee what I call the indifference to harmony and melody."

"A magic square," I said. "But do you hope to have people hear
all that?"

"Hear?" he countered. "Do you remember a certain lecture
given for the Society for the Common Weal from which it followed that in music one certainly need not hear everything? If by
'hearing' you understand the precise realization in detail of the
means by which the highest and strictest order is achieved, like
the order of the planets, a cosmic order and legality — no, that
way one would not hear it. But this order one will or would hear,
and the perception of it would afford an unknown æsthetic satisfaction."

"Very remarkable," said I. "The way you describe the thing, it
comes to a sort of composing before composition. The whole dis-

position and organization of the material would have to be ready when the actual work should begin, and all one asks is: which is the actual work? For this preparation of the material is done by variation, and the creative element in variation, which one might call the actual composition, would be transferred back to the material itself — together with the freedom of the composer. When he went to work, he would no longer be free."

"Bound by a self-imposed compulsion to order, hence free."

"Well, of course the dialectic of freedom is unfathomable. But he could scarcely be called a free inventor of his harmony. Would not the making of chords be left to chance and accident?"

"Say, rather, to the context. The polyphonic dignity of every chord-forming note would be guaranteed by the constellation. The historical events — the emancipation of dissonance from its resolution, its becoming 'absolute' as it appears already in some passages of the later Wagner — would warrant any combination of notes which can justify itself before the system."

"And if the constellation produced the banal: consonance, common-chord harmonics, the worn-out, the diminished seventh?"

"That would be a rejuvenation of the worn-out by the constellation."

"I see there a restorative element in your Utopia. It is very radical, but it relaxes the prohibition which after all already hung over consonance. The return to the ancient forms of variation is a similar sign."

"More interesting phenomena," he responded, "probably always have this double face of past and future, probably are always progressive and regressive in one. They display the equivocalness of life itself."

"Is that not a generalization?"

"Of what?"

"Of our domestic experiences as a nation?"

"Oh, let us not be indiscreet! Or flatter ourselves either. All I want to say is that our objections — if they are meant as objections — would not count against the fulfilment of the old, the ever repeated demand to take hold and make order, and to resolve the magic essence of music into human reason."

"You want to put me on my honour as a humanist," said I. "Human reason! And besides, excuse me; 'constellation' is your every other word. But surely it belongs more to astrology. The rationalism you call for has a good deal of superstition about it — of belief in the incomprehensibly and vaguely dæmonic, the kind of thing we have in games of chance, fortune-telling with cards, and shaking dice. Contrary to what you say, your system seems to me more calculated to dissolve human reason in magic."

He carried his closed hand to his brow.

"Reason and magic," said he, "may meet and become one in that which one calls wisdom, initiation; in belief in the stars, in numbers. . . ."

I did not go on, as I saw that he was in pain. And all that he had said seemed to me to bear the mark of suffering, to stand in its sign, however intellectually remarkable it may have been. He himself seemed not to care for more conversation; his idle humming and sighing betrayed the fact as we sauntered on. I felt, of course, vexed and inwardly shook my head, silently reflecting as I walked that a man's thoughts might be characterized by saying that he had a headache; but that did not make them less significant.

We spoke little on the rest of the way home. I recall that we paused by the Cow Trough, took a few steps away from the path and looked into it, with the reflection of the setting sun in our faces. The water was clear: one could see that the bottom was flat only near the edge; it fell off rapidly into darkness. The pond was known to be very deep in the middle.

"Cold," said Adrian, motioning with his head; "much too cold to bathe. — Cold," he repeated a moment later, this time with a definite shiver, and turned away.

My duties obliged me to go back that evening to Kaisersaschern. He himself delayed a few days longer his departure for Munich, where he had decided to settle. I see him pressing his father's hand in farewell — for the last time; he knew it not. I see his mother kiss him and, perhaps in the same way as she had done that time with Kretschmar in the living-room, lean his head on her shoulder. He was not to return to her, he never did. She came to him.

CHAPTER XXIII

"HE that would eat the kernel must crack the nut," he wrote to me, copying Kumpf, from the Bavarian capital a few weeks later. He meant that he had begun the composition of *Love's Labour's Lost,* and he urged me to send the rest of the text. He needed, he said, to be able to see it as a whole, and he wanted, for the sake of providing musical links and connections, to anticipate the setting of some later parts of the libretto.

He lived in the Rambergstrasse, near the Academy, as a lodger with the widow of a Senator from Bremen, named Rodde, who with her two daughters occupied a ground-floor flat in a still new house. The room they gave him, fronting the quiet street, to the right of the entrance door, appealed to him on account of its cleanliness and impersonally comfortable furnishings. He had soon fully made it his own with more intimate belongings, books and notes. There was indeed one rather pointless decoration, relic of some past enthusiasm, framed in nutwood, on the left-hand wall: Giacomo Meyerbeer at the piano, with inspired gaze attacking the keys, surrounded by the hovering forms of characters from his operas. However, the apotheosis did not too much displease the young maestro, and when he sat in the basket-chair at his work-table, a simple green-covered extension-table, he had his back to it. So he let it stay.

A little harmonium, which might remind him of early days, stood in his room and was of use to him. But as the Frau Senator kept mostly to the garden side of the house, in the rear, and the daughters were invisible in the mornings, the grand piano in the salon, a rather old but soft-toned Bechstein, was also at his service. This salon was furnished with upholstered fauteuils, bronze candelabra, little gilt "occasional chairs," a sofa-table with a brocade cover, and a richly framed, very much darkened oil painting of 1850, representing the Golden Horn with a view of Galata. All these things were easily recognized as the remnant of a once well-to-do bourgeois household. The salon was not seldom the scene of small social affairs, into which Adrian let himself be drawn, at first resisting, then as a habit, and finally, as circumstances brought it about, rather like a son of the house. It was the artist or half-artist world that gathered there, a house-broke Bohemia, so to speak: well-bred yet free-and-easy, and amusing enough to fulfil the expectations that had caused the Frau Senator to move from Bremen to the southern capital. Frau Senator Rodde's background was easy to imagine. Her bearing and looks were ladylike: she had dark eyes, neatly waved hair only a little grey, an ivory complexion, and pleasant, rather well-preserved features. Her long life had been spent as an honoured member of a patrician society, presiding over a household full of servants and responsibilities. After the death of her husband (whose solemn likeness, in the garb of office, also adorned the salon) her circumstances were greatly reduced, so that she was probably not able to maintain her position in her accustomed milieu. At the same time there were now released in her certain still keen desires of an unexhaustible and probably never satisfied love of life, in some humanly warmer sphere. She entertained, she explained, in the interest of her daughters, but yet largely, as was pretty clear, to enjoy herself and hold court. One amused her best with mild little salacities, not going too far, jokes about barmaids, models, artists, to which she responded with a high, affected, suggestive laugh from between her closed lips.

Obviously her daughters, Inez and Clarissa, did not care for this laugh; they exchanged cold and disapproving looks, which showed all the irritation of grown children at the unsatisfied humanity in their mother's nature. In the case of the younger, Clarissa, the uprooting out of her hereditary middle class had been conscious, deliberate, and pronounced. She was a tall blonde, with large features whitened by cosmetics, a full lower lip and under-developed chin; she was preparing for a dramatic career and studied with an elderly actor who played father parts at the Hof-theater. She wore her golden-yellow hair in bold and striking style, under hats like cart-wheels, and she loved eccentric feather boas. Her imposing figure could stand these things very well and absorb their extravagance into her personality. Her tendency to the macabre and bizarre made her interesting to the masculine world which paid her homage. She had a sulphur-coloured tom-cat named Isaac, whom she put in mourning for the deceased Pope by tying a black satin bow on his tail. The death's-head motif appeared repeatedly in her room; there was actually a pre-pared skeleton, in all his toothiness; and a bronze paperweight that bore the hollow-eyed symbol of mortality and "healing" lying on a folio bearing the name of Hippocrates. The book was hollow, the smooth bottom of it being screwed in with four tiny screws, which could be unscrewed with a fine instrument. Later, after Clarissa had taken her life with the poison from this box, Frau Senator Rodde gave me the object as a memento and I have it still.

A tragic deed was also the destiny of the elder sister, Inez. She represented — or shall I say: yet she represented? — the conservative element in the little family; being a living protest against its transplantation, against everything South German, the art-metropolis, Bohemia, her mother's evening parties. She turned her face obstinately back to the old, paternal, middle-class strictness and dignity. Still one got the impression that this conservatism was a defence mechanism against certain tensions and dangers in her own nature; though intellectually she ascribed some importance to these as well. She was more delicate in figure than Clarissa, with whom she got on very well, whereas she distinctly though unobtrusively turned away from her mother. Heavy ash-blond hair weighed down her head, so that she held it thrust out sidewise, with extended neck. Her mouth wore a pinched smile, her nose was rather beaked; the expression of her blue eyes, blurred by the drooping lids, was weakly, dull, suspicious; it was a look of knowledge and suffering, if not without some effort at roguishness. Her upbringing had been no more than highly correct: she had spent two years in an aristocratic girls' boarding-school in Karlsruhe, patronized by the court. She occupied herself with no art or science, but laid stress on acting as daughter of the house. She read much, wrote extraordinarily literary letters "back home" — to the past, her boarding-house mistress and earlier friends. Secretly she wrote verse. Her sister showed me one day a poem by her, called "The Miner." I still remember the first stanza:

> A miner I who in the dark shaft mines
> Of the soul, descending fearless from the light
> To where the golden ore of anguish shines
> With fugitive priceless glimmer through the night.

I have forgotten the rest, except the last line:

> And never more upwards to joy I yearn.

So much for the present about the daughters, with whom Adrian came into relations as housemates. They both looked up to him and influenced their mother to follow suit, although she found him not very "artistic." As for the guests of the house, some of them, including Adrian, or, as the hostess said, "our lodger, Herr Dr. Leverkühn," a larger or smaller group, might be invited to supper in the Rodde dining-room, which was furnished with an oak sideboard much too monumental and richly carved for the room. Others came in at nine o'clock or later, for music, tea and talk. There were Clarissa's male and female colleagues, one or the other ardent young man who rolled his r's, and girls with voices placed well forwards; a couple named Knöterich — the man, Konrad Knöterich, a native of Munich, looked like a primitive German, Sugambian or Ubian, he only lacked the bushy tuft on top. He had some vaguely artistic occupation, had probably been a painter, but now dabbled at making instruments, and played cello, wildly and inaccurately, snorting violently as he played. His wife, Natalia, also had something to do with painting; she was an exotic brunette with a trace of Spanish blood, wearing earrings and black ringlets dangling on her cheeks. Then there was a scholar, Dr. Kranich, a numismatic expert, and Keeper of the Cabinet of Coins: clear, decided, cheerful and sensible in conversation, though with a hoarse asthmatic voice. There were two friends, both painters belonging to the Secession group, Leo Zink and Baptist Spengler; one an Austrian from near Bozen, a jester by social technique, an insinuating clown, who in a gentle drawl ceaselessly made fun of himself and his exaggeratedly long nose. He was a faunish type, making the women laugh with the really very droll expression of his close-set eyes — always a good opening. The other, Spengler, from central Germany, with a flourishing blond moustache, was a sceptical man of the world, with some means, no great worker, hypochondriac, well-read, always smiling and blinking rapidly as he talked. Inez Rodde mistrusted him very much — why, she did not say, but to Adrian she called him disingenuous, a sneak. Adrian said that he found Spengler intelligent and agreeable to talk to. He responded much less to the advances of another guest, who really took pains to woo Adrian's reserve and shyness. This was Rudolf Schwerdtfeger, a gifted young violinist, member of the Zapfenstösser Orchestra, which next to the Hoftheater orchestra played a prominent role in the musical life of the town and in which he was one of the first violins. Born in Dresden, but in origin low-German, of medium height and neat build, and with a shock of flaxen hair, he had the polish, the pleasing versatility of the Saxon, and was in equal measure good-natured and desirous to please. He loved society and spent all his free time in at least one but oftener two or three evening parties, blissfully absorbed in flirtation with the other sex, young girls as well as more mature women. Leo Zink and he were on a cool, sometimes even ticklish footing; I have often noticed that charmers do not appreciate each other, a fact equally applicable to masculine and to feminine conquistadores. For my part I had nothing against Schwerdtfeger, I even liked him sincerely, and his early, tragic death, which had for me its own private and peculiar horror, shook me to my depths. How clearly I still see the figure of this young man: his boyish way of shrugging up one shoulder inside his coat and drawing down one corner of his mouth in a grimace. It was further his naïve habit to watch someone talking, very tense, as it were in a fury of concentration, his lips curled, his steel-blue eyes burrowing into the speaker's face, seeming to fix now on one eye and now on the other. What good qualities too did he not have quite aside from his talent, which one might almost reckon as one of his charms! Frankness, decency, open-mindedness, an artistic integrity, indifference to money and possessions — in short, a certain cleanness; all these looked out of his — I repeat it — beautiful steel-blue eyes and shone in a face full of youthful attractiveness if just slightly like a pug dog's. He often played with the Frau Senator, who was no indifferent pianist — and thus somewhat encroached upon Knöterich, who wanted to sweep his cello, whereas the company were looking forward to hearing Rudolf. His playing was neat and cultivated, his tone not large, but of beautiful sweetness and technically not a little brilliant. Seldom has one heard certain things of Vivaldi, Vieuxtemps and Spohr, the C-minor Sonata of Grieg, even the Kreutzer Sonata, and compositions by César Franck, more faultlessly played. With all this he was simple, untouched by letters, but concerned for the good opinion of prominent men of intellect — not only out of vanity, but because he seriously set store by intercourse with them and wanted to elevate and round himself out by its means. He at once had his eye on Adrian, paid court to him, practically neglecting the ladies; consulted his judgment, asked to be accompanied — Adrian at that time always refused — showed himself eager for musical and extra-musical conversation, and was put off by no reserve or rebuff. That may have been a sign of uncommon ingenuousness; but it displayed unselfconscious understanding and native culture as well. Once when Adrian, on account of a headache and utter distaste for society, had excused himself to the Frau Senator and remained in his room, Schwerdtfeger suddenly appeared, in his cut-away and black tie, to persuade him, ostensibly on behalf of several or all of the guests, to join them. They were so dull without him. . . . It was even embarrassing, on the whole, for Adrian was by no means a lively social asset. I do not know if he let himself be persuaded. Probably it was in order to win him over that Schwerdtfeger said he was voicing the wish of the company; yet my friend must have felt a certain pleasant surprise at such invincible attentiveness.

I have now rather fully introduced the personæ of the Rodde salon, mere figures at present, whose acquaintance, together with other members of Munich society I later made as a professor from Freising. Rüdiger Schildknapp joined the group quite soon; Adrian's example having instructed him that one should live in Munich instead of Leipzig, he pulled himself together to act upon the conviction. The publisher of his translations from English classics had his offices in Munich, a fact of practical importance for Rüdiger; besides that he had probably missed Adrian, whom he at once began to delight with his stories about his father and his *"Besichtigen Sie jenes!"* He had taken a room in the third storey of a house in Amalienstrasse, not far from his friend; and there he now sat at his table, by nature quite exceptionally in need of fresh air, the whole winter through with wide-open windows, wrapped in mantle and plaid, vaporizing cigarettes and wrestling, half full of hatred, half passionately absorbed in his problems, and striving after the exact German value for English words, phrases, and rhythms. At midday he ate with Adrian, in the Hoftheater restaurant or in one of the *Keller* in the centre of the city; but very soon, through Leipzig connections, he had entrée to private houses, and managed aside from evening invitations to have here and there a cover laid for him at the midday meal, perhaps after he had gone shopping with the housewife and intrigued her by a display of his lordly poverty. Such invitations came from his publisher, proprietor of the firm of Radbruch & Co. in the Fürstenstrasse; and from the Schlaginhaufens, an elderly well-to-do and childless pair, the husband of Suabian origin and a private scholar, the wife from a Munich family. They had a somewhat gloomy but splendid house in the Briennerstrasse, where their pillared salon was the meeting-place of a society of mingled aristocratic and artistic elements. Nothing better pleased the housewife, a von Plausig by birth, than to have both elements represented in the same person, as in the Generalintendant of the Royal Theatres, His Excellency von Riedesel, who was often a guest. Schildknapp also dined with the industrialist Bullinger, a rich paper-manufacturer, who occupied the *bel étage* in the block of flats built by himself in Wiedemayerstrasse on the river; with the family of a director of the Pschorrbräu joint-stock company; and in other houses.

At the Schlaginhaufens' Rüdiger had also introduced Adrian, who then, a monosyllabic stranger, met the titled stars of the artist world, the Wagner heroine Tanya Orlanda, Felix Mottl, ladies from the Bavarian court, the "descendant of Schiller," Herr von Gleichen-Russwurm, who wrote books on cultural history; also other writers who wrote nothing at all but made themselves socially interesting as specialists in the art of conversation, superficially and without tangible results. However, it was here that Adrian made the acquaintance of Jeanette Scheurl, a woman of peculiar charm and sincerity, a good ten years older than he, daughter of a deceased Bavarian government official. Her mother was a Parisian, a paralysed old lady, confined to her chair but full of mental energy, who had never given herself the trouble of learning German. She had no need to, since French was by good fortune generally the mode and hers so to speak ran on wheels, gaining her both living and position. Mme Scheurl lived near the Botanical Gardens with her three daughters, of whom Jeanette was the eldest; their quarters were small, the atmosphere entirely Parisian. In her little salon she gave extraordinarily popular musical teas, where the exemplary organs of the court singers male and female filled the little rooms to bursting, and the blue coaches from the court often stood in front of the house.

Jeanette was a writer of novels. Grown up between two languages, she wrote ladylike and original studies of society in a charmingly incorrect idiom peculiar to herself alone. They did not lack psychological or melodic charm and were definitely a literary achievement. She noticed Adrian at once, and took to him; he, in his turn, felt at home in her presence and conversation. She was aristocratically ugly and good form, with a face like a sheep, where the high-born and the low-born met, just as in her speech her French was mingled with Bavarian dialect. She was extraordinarily intelligent and at the same time enveloped in the naïvely inquiring innocence of the spinster no longer young. Her mind had something fluttering and quaintly confused about it, at which she herself laughed more heartily than anyone else — though by no means in the fashion of Leo Zink, who laughed at himself as a parlour trick, whereas she did the same out of sheer lightness of heart and sense of fun. She was very musical, a pianist, a Chopin enthusiast, a writer on Schubert; on friendly terms with more than one bearer of a great name in the contemporary world of music. Her first conversation with Adrian had been a gratifying

exchange upon the subject of Mozart's polyphony and his relation to Bach. He was and remained her attached friend for many
years.

But no one will suppose that the city he had chosen to live in
really took him to her bosom or ever made him her own. The
beauty of the grandiose village under the melting blue of the Al-
pine sky, with the mountain stream rushing and rippling through
it: that might please his eye; the self-indulgent comfort of its
ways, the suggestion it had of all-the-year-round carnival freedom, might make even his life easier. But its spirit — *sit venia
verbo!* — its atmosphere, a little mad and quite harmless; the decorative appeal to the senses, the holiday and artistic mood of this
self-satisfied Capua: all that was of course foreign to the soul of
a deep, stern nature like his. It was indeed the fitting and proper
target for that look of his I had so long observed: veiled and cold
and musingly remote, followed by the smile and averted face.

The Munich I speak of is the Munich of the late Regency, with
only four years between it and the war, whose issue was to turn
its pleasantness to morbidity and produce in it one sad and grotesque manifestation after another; this capital city of beautiful
vistas, where political problems confined themselves to a capricious opposition between a half-separatist folk-Catholicism and
the lively liberalism professed by the supporters of the Reich;
Munich, with its parade concerts in the Feldherrnhalle, its art
shops, its palaces of decorative crafts, its recurring exhibitions, its
Bauern-balls in carnival time, its seasonal "*Märzbräu*" carouses
and week-long monster fair on the "Oktoberwiese," where a stout
and lusty folkishness, now long since corrupted by modern mass
methods, celebrated its saturnalia; Munich, with its residuary
Wagnerism, its esoteric coteries performing their æsthetic devotions behind the Siegestor; its Bohemia, well bedded down in public approval and fundamentally easy-going. Adrian looked on at
all that, moved in it, tasted of it, during the nine months that he
spent at this time in Oberbayern — an autumn, a winter, and a
spring. At the artist festivals that he attended with Schildknapp in
the illusory twilight of artistically decorated ballrooms he met
members of the Rodde circle, the young actors, the Knöterichs,
Dr. Kranich, Zink and Spengler, the daughters of the house. He
sat at a table with Inez and Clarissa, Rüdiger, Spengler, and Kranich, perhaps Jeanette Scheurl. And Schwerdtfeger, in peasant
dress or in the Florentine quattrocento which set off his handsome legs and made him look like Botticelli's youth in the red
cap, would come up, dissolved in festival mirth, all intellectual

elevation quite forgot, and in order to be "nice" invite the Rodde girls to dance. "Nice" was his favourite word; he insisted on having everything happen "nicely" and on leaving out all that was not "nice." He had many obligations and pending flirtations in the room, but it would not have seemed "nice" to him to neglect entirely the ladies of the Rambergstrasse, with whom he was on a brotherly footing. This compulsion to be "nice" was so visible in his business-like approach that Clarissa said pertly:

"Good heavens, Rudolf, if you didn't put on the air of a knight rescuing a damsel in distress! I assure you we have danced enough, we do not need you at all."

"Need!" he replied, with pretended anger, in his rather guttural voice. "And the needs of my heart are not to count at all?"

"Not a brass farthing," said she. "Anyhow, I am too big for you."

But she would go off with him even so, proudly tilting her insufficient chin, with no hollow under the full lip. Or it was Inez he had asked, who with pinched lips and drooping head followed him to the dance. But he was "nice" not alone to the sisters. He kept guard over his forgetfulness. Suddenly, especially if someone had declined to dance, he might became serious and sit down at the table with Adrian and Baptist Spengler. The latter was always in a domino, and drinking red wine. Blinking, a dimple in his cheek above the thick moustaches, he would be citing the Goncourt diaries or the letters of Abbé Galiani, and Schwerdt-feger, positively furious with attention, would sit and bore his gaze into the speaker's face. Or he would talk with Adrian about the program of the next Zapfenstösser concert; or demand, as though there were no more pressing interest or obligations anywhere, that Adrian explain and enlarge upon something that he had lately said at the Roddes' about music, about the state of the opera, or the like. He would devote himself to Adrian, take his arm and stroll with him at the edge of the crowd, round the hall, addressing him with the carnival *du*, heedless that the other did not respond. Jeanette Scheurl told me later that when Adrian once returned to the table after such a stroll, Inez Rodde said to him:

"You shouldn't give him the pleasure. He wants everything."

"Perhaps Herr Leverkühn wants everything too," remarked Clarissa, supporting her chin on her hand.

Adrian shrugged his shoulders.

"What he wants," he responded, "is that I should write a violin concerto for him with which he can be heard in the provinces."

"Don't do it," Clarissa said again. "You wouldn't think of anything but prettinesses if you considered him while you were
doing it."

"You have too high an opinion of my flexibility," he retorted,
and had Baptist Spengler's bleating laugh on his side.

But enough of Adrian's participation in the Munich joy of life.
Trips into the environs, justly celebrated if somewhat spoiled by
mass resort, he had made with Schildknapp, mostly on the latter's
initiative. Even in the glittering winter they spent days in Ettal,
Oberammergau, Mittenwald; and when spring came, these excursions increased, to the famous lakes and the theatrical castles built
by the nation's madman. Often they went on bicycles (for Adrian
loved them as a means of independent travel) at random into the
greening country, lodging at night humbly or pretentiously, just
as it fell out. I am reminded of the fact because it was thus that
Adrian made acquaintance with the place that he later chose as
the permanent setting of his life: Pfeiffering near Waldshut and
the Schweigestill farm.

The little town of Waldshut, devoid of interest or charm, lies
on the Garmisch-Partenkirchen line, an hour from Munich. The
next station, only ten minutes farther on, is Pfeiffering or Pfeffering, where the through trains do not stop. They leave to one side
the onion-shaped dome of Pfeiffering church, rising out of a landscape which at this point is in no way remarkable. Adrian and
Rüdiger visited the place by mere chance. They did not even
spend the night at Schweigestill's, for both had to work next
morning and must take the train back from Waldshut to Munich.
They had eaten their midday meal in the little square at Waldshut, and as the time-table left them some hours to spare, they
rode along the tree-lined highway to Pfeiffering, pushed their
bicycles through the village, inquired of a child the name of the
near-by pond, and heard that it was called the Klammer; cast a
glance at the tree-crowned height, the Rohmbühel, and asked for
a glass of lemonade from a barefoot girl under the gate of the
manor-house, which was adorned with ecclesiastical arms. They
asked less from thirst than because the massive and characteristic
peasant baroque structure attracted their attention. The yard dog
on his chain bayed loudly, and the girl shouted at him: "Kaschperl, hush your noise!"

I do not know how far Adrian took notice at that time; or
whether it was only afterwards, gradually and from memory, that
he recognized certain correspondences, transposed, as it were, into
another but not far removed key. I incline to the belief that the

discovery at first remained unconscious and only later, perhaps as in a dream, came to him as a surprise. At least he did not utter a syllable to Schildknapp, nor did he ever mention to me the singular correspondence. Of course I may be mistaken. Pond and hill, the gigantic old tree in the courtyard — an elm, as a matter of fact — with its round green bench, and still other details might have attracted him at his first glance; it may be no dream was needed to open his eyes. That he said nothing is of course no proof at all.

It was Frau Else Schweigestill who advanced towards the travellers with dignified tread, met them at the gate, gave a friendly ear to their wants, and made lemonade in tall glasses with long spoons. She served it in the best room, left of the entry, a sort of peasant hall, with a vaulted ceiling, a huge table, window embrasures which showed the thickness of the walls, and the Winged Victory of Samothrace in plaster above the tall, gaily painted press. There was a dark brown piano as well. The room was not used by the family, Frau Schweigestill explained as she sat down with her guests. They sat of evenings in a smaller room diagonally opposite, near the house door. The building had much extra space; farther along on this side was another sightly room, the so-called Abbot's chamber, probably thus named because it had served as a study to the head of the Augustine Order of monks, who had once presided over the place. So it had formerly been a cloister; but for three generations Schweigestills had been settled here.

Adrian mentioned that he himself was country-bred, though he had lived now for some time in towns. He inquired how much land there was and learned that there was about forty acres of ploughed land and meadow, with a wood-lot as well. The low building with the chestnut trees on the vacant space opposite the courtyard also belonged to the property. Once it had been occupied by lay brothers, now it was nearly always empty and scarcely furnished enough to live in. Summer before last a Munich painter and his wife had rented it; he wanted to make landscapes of the neighbourhood, the Waldshut moors and so on, and had done some pretty views, though rather gloomy, being painted in a dull light. Three of them had been hung in the Glaspalast, she had seen them there herself, and Herr Director Stiglmayer of the Bavarian Exchange Bank had bought one. The gentlemen were painters themselves?

She very likely mentioned the tenants in order to raise the subject and find out with whom she had to deal. When she heard that no, they were a writer and a musician, she lifted her brows respectfully and said that was more unusual and interesting. Painters were thick as blackberries. The gentlemen had seemed serious people to her, whereas painters were mostly a loose lot, without much feeling for the serious things of life — she did not mean the practical side, earning money and that, no, when she said serious she meant the dark side of life, its hardships and troubles, but she did not mean to be unfair to artists: her lodgers, for instance, had been an exception to that kind of light-headed gentry, he being a quiet, reserved sort of man, rather low-spirited if anything — and his pictures had looked like that too, the atmosphere of the moors, and the lonely woods and meadows, yes, it was perhaps surprising that Director Stiglmayer should have bought one, the gloomiest of all, of course he was a financial man but maybe he had a streak of melancholy himself.

She sat with them, bolt upright, her brown hair, only touched with grey, drawn smoothly away from the parting, so that you saw the white skin; in her checked apron, an oval brooch at the opening of her frock, her well-shaped, capable little hands with the plain wedding ring folded together on the table.

She liked artists, she said. Her language, seasoned with dialect, with *halt* and *fei* and *gellen's ja*, was yet not coarse. Artists were people of understanding, she thought, and understanding was the best and most important thing in life, the way artists were so lively depended on that, she would say, at bottom, there was a lively and a serious kind of understanding, and it had never come out yet which one was better, maybe the best of all was still another one, a quiet kind of understandingness, anyhow artists, of course, had to live in the towns, because that was where the culture was, that they spent their time on, but actually they belonged more with peasant folk, who lived in the middle of nature and so nearer to understanding, much more than with townspeople, because these had had their understanding stunted, or else they had smothered it up for the sake of being regular and that came to the same thing, but she did not want to be unfair to the townsfolk either, there were always exceptions, maybe one didn't always know, and Director Stiglmayer, just to mention him again, when he bought the gloomy painting had shown he was a man of understanding, and not only artistic either.

Hereupon she offered her guests coffee and pound-cake; but Schildknapp and Adrian preferred to spend what time they had left looking at the house and grounds, if she would be so good as to show them.

"Willingly," said she; "only too bad my Maxl" (that was Herr Schweigestill) "is out on the farm with Gereon, that's our son, they wanted to try a new manure-spreader Gereon bought, so the gentlemen will have to make do with me."

They would not call that making-do, they answered, and went with her through the massively built old house. They looked at the house-place in front, where the prevailing odour of pipe tobacco was strongest; farther back was the Abbot's room, very pleasing, not very large, and rather earlier in style than the exterior architecture of the house, nearer 1600 than 1700; wainscoted, with carpetless wooden floor and stamped-leather hangings below the beamed ceiling. There were pictures of saints on the walls of the flat-arched window embrasures, and leaded windowpanes that had squares of painted glass let into them. There was a niche in the wall, with a copper water-kettle and basin, and a cupboard with wrought-iron bolts and locks. There was a corner bench with leather cushions, and a heavy oak table not far from the window, built like a chest, with deep drawers under the polished top and a sunken middle part where a carved reading-desk stood. Above it there hung down from the beamed ceiling a huge chandelier with the remains of wax candles still sticking in it, a piece of Renaissance decoration with horns, shovel-antlers, and other fantastic shapes sticking out irregularly on all sides.

The visitors praised the Abbot's room warmly. Schildknapp, with a reflective head-shake, even thought that one ought to settle down and live here; but Frau Schweigestill had her doubts whether it would not be too lonely for a writer, too far from life and culture. And she led her guests up the stairs to the upper storey, to show them a few of the numerous bedrooms, in a row on a whitewashed, musty corridor. They were furnished with bedsteads and chests in the style of the painted one below, and only a few were supplied with the towering feather beds in peasant style. "What a lot of rooms!" they exclaimed. Yes, they were mostly empty, replied the hostess. One or two might be occupied temporarily. For two years, until last autumn, a Baroness von Handschuchsheim had lived here and wandered about through the house. a lady of rank, whose ideas, as Frau Schweigestill expressed it, had not been able to fit in with those of the rest of the world so that she had sought refuge here from the conflict. She, Frau Else Schweigestill, had got on very well with her and liked to talk with her; had sometimes even succeeded in making her laugh at her own outlandish notions. But unfortunately it had

been impossible either to do away with these or to prevent them
from gaining ground; in the end the dear Baroness had had to be
placed in professional care.

Frau Schweigestill came to the end of this tale as they went
back down the stair again and out into the courtyard to have a
glimpse of the stables. Another time, she said, before that, one of
the many sleeping-rooms had been occupied by a Fräulein from
the best social circles who had here brought her child into the
world — talking with artists she could call things, though not people, by their right names — the girl's father was a judge of the
high court, up in Bayreuth, and had got himself an electric
automobile and that had been the beginning of all the trouble, for
he had hired a chauffeur too, to drive him to his office, and this
young man, not a bit out of the common run, only very smart in
his braided livery, had made the girl lose her head altogether, she
had got with child by him, and when that was plain to see there
had been outbreaks of rage and despair, hand-wringing and hair-
tearing, cursing, wailing, berating on the part of the parents, such
as one would not have dreamt possible, of understanding there
had been none, either of an artistic or a natural kind, nothing but
a crazy fear for their social reputation, like people in towns have,
and the girl had regularly writhed on the floor before her parents,
beseeching and sobbing while they shook their fists, and in the
end mother and daughter fainted at the very same minute, but the
high judge found his way here one day and talked with her, Frau
Schweigestill, a little man with a pointed grey beard and gold eye-
glasses, quite bowed with affliction and they had made up that the
girl be brought to bed here secretly, and afterwards, under the
pretext of anæmia, should stop on for a while. And when the high
official had turned to go, he had turned round again and with
tears behind his gold glasses had pressed her hand again with the
words: "Thank you, thank you, for your understanding and goodness," but he meant understanding for the bowed-down parents,
not for the girl.

She came, then, a poor thing, with her mouth always open and
her eyebrows up, and while she awaited her hour she confided a
good deal in Frau Schweigestill. She was entirely reasonable about
her own guilt and did not pretend that she had been seduced —
on the contrary, Carl, the chauffeur, had even said: "It's no good,
Fräulein, better not," but it had been stronger than she was, and
she had always been ready to pay with death, and would do, and
being ready for death, so it seemed to her, made up for the whole

thing, and she had been very brave when her time came, and her child, a girl, was brought into the world with the help of good Dr. Kürbis, the district physician, to whom it was all one how a child came, if everything was otherwise in order and no transverse positions, but the girl had remained very weak, despite good nursing and the country air, she had never stopped holding her mouth open and her eyebrows up, and her cheeks seemed hollower than ever and after a while her little high-up father came to fetch her away and at the sight of her, tears came in his eyes behind the gold eye-glasses. The infant was sent to the Grey Sisters in Bamberg, but the mother was from then on only a very grey sister herself, with a canary-bird and a tortoise which her parents gave her out of pity, and she had just withered away in her room in a consumption, which the seeds of had probably always been in her. Finally they sent her to Davos, but that seemed to have been the finishing touch, for she died there almost at once, just as she had wished and wanted it, and if she had been right in her idea that everything had been evened up by the readiness for death, then she was quits and had got what she was after.

They visited the stables, looked at the horses and the pigsties while their hostess was talking about the girl she had sheltered. They went to look at the chickens and the bees behind the house, and then the guests asked what they owed her and were told nothing at all. They thanked her for everything and rode back to Waldshut to take their train. That the day had not been wasted and that Pfeiffering was a remarkable spot, to that they both heartily agreed.

Adrian kept the picture in his mind; but for a long time it did not determine his decisions. He wanted to go away, but farther away than an hour's journey towards the mountains. Of the music of *Love's Labour's Lost* he had written the piano sketch of the expository scenes; but then he had got stuck, the parodistic artificiality of the style was hard to keep up, needing as it did a supply of whimsicality constantly fresh and sustained. He felt a desire for more distant air, for surroundings of greater unfamiliarity. Unrest possessed him. He was tired of the family pension in Rambergstrasse; its privacy had been an uncertain quantity, people could always intrude on it. "I am looking," he wrote to me, "I keep asking round about and hankering for news of a place buried from and untroubled by the world, where I could hold speech alone, with my life, my destiny. . . ." Strange, ominous words! Must not my hand tremble, must I not feel cold in the pit of my stomach, at thought of the meeting, the holding speech, the compact for which he, consciously or unconsciously, sought a theatre?

It was Italy on which he decided; whither he, at an unusual time for a tourist, the beginning of June and the summer, set off. He had persuaded Rüdiger Schildknapp to go with him.

CHAPTER XXIV

In the long vacation of 1912 and still from Kaisersaschern, I, with my young bride, visited Adrian and Schildknapp in the nest they had found in the Sabine Hills. It was the second summer the friends had spent there. They had wintered in Rome, and in May, as the heat strengthened, they had again sought the mountains and the same hospitable house where, in a sojourn lasting three months, they had learned to feel at home the year before.

The place was Palestrina, birthplace of the composer; ancient Præneste, and as Penestrino citadel of the Colonna princes, mentioned by Dante in the twenty-seventh canto of the *Inferno:* a picturesque hillside settlement, reached from the church below by a lane of shallow steps, overhung by houses and not even of the cleanest. A sort of little black pig ran about on the steps, and one of the pack-mules that passed up and down with its projecting load might push the unwary pedestrian to the wall. The street continued on above the village as a mountain road, past a Capuchin friary, up to the top of the hill and the acropolis, only surviving in a few ruins and the remnant of an ancient theatre. Helene and I climbed up several times to these dignified relics during our visit, whereas Adrian, who "did not want to see anything," had never in all those months got further than the shady garden of the Capuchin convent, his favourite spot.

The Manardi house, where Adrian and Rüdiger lodged, was probably the most imposing in the place, and although the family were six in number, they easily took us in as well. It was on the lane, a sober, solid edifice, almost like a palazzo or castello, which I judged to be from about the second third of the seventeenth century, with spare decorative mouldings under the flat, slightly profiled tiled roof; it had small windows and a door decorated in early baroque style, but boarded up, with the actual door-opening cut into the boarding and furnished with a tinkling little bell. Extensive quarters had been vacated for our friends on the ground floor, consisting chiefly of a two-windowed living-room as large as a salon, with stone floors like all the rest of the house. It was shaded, cool, a little dark, and very simply furnished, with wicker chairs and horsehair sofas, and in fact so large that two people could carry on their work there separated by considerable space, neither disturbing the other. Adjoining were the roomy bedchambers, also very sparsely furnished, a third one being opened for us.

The family dining-room and the much larger kitchen, in which friends from the village were entertained, lay in the upper storey. The kitchen had a vast and gloomy chimney, hung with fabulous ladles and carving-knives and -forks which might have belonged to an ogre; while the shelves were full of copper utensils, skillets, bowls, platters, tureens, and mortars. Here Signora Manardi reigned, called Nella by her family — I believe her name was Peronella. She was a stately Roman matron, with arched upper lip, not very dark, the good eyes and hair were only chestnut brown, with at most a faint silver network on the smooth head. Her figure was full and well-proportioned, the impression she made both capable and rustically simple, as one saw her small work-hardened hands, the double widow's ring on the right one, poised on the firm strong hips, bound by their stiff apron-strings.

She had but one daughter from her marriage, Amelia, a girl of thirteen or fourteen years, inclined to weak-headedness. Amelia had a habit, at table, of moving spoons or forks to and fro in front of her eyes and repeating with a questioning intonation some word that had stuck in her mind. A little time previously an aristocratic Russian family had lodged with the Manardis, whose head, a count or prince, had been a seer of ghosts and from time to time had given the family unquiet nights, by shooting at wandering spirits who visited him in his chamber. All this naturally enough made an impression on Amelia; it was the reason why she often and insistently questioned her spoons: "*Spiriti, spiriti?*" But she could remember lesser matters as well; for instance it had happened that a German tourist had once made the mistake of saying: "*La* melona," the word being feminine in German though masculine in Italian; and now the child would sit wagging her head, following with her forlorn look the movement of her spoons and murmuring "*La melona, la melona?*" Signora Peronella and her brothers paid no heed or did not hear; such things were an everyday matter to them and only if the guest seemed put off would they smile at him, less in excuse than almost tenderly, as though the child had done something winning.

Helene and I soon got used to Amelia's uncanny murmurs; as

for Adrian and Schildknapp, they were no longer conscious of them.

The housewife's brothers, of whom I spoke, were two, one older and one younger than herself: Ercolano Manardi, lawyer, mostly called *l'avvocato* for short, yet with some satisfaction too, he being the pride of the otherwise unlettered and rustic family, a man of sixty with bristling grey moustaches and a hoarse, complaining voice, which began with an effort like a donkey's bray; and Sor Alfonso, the younger, perhaps in the middle of his forties, intimately addressed by his family as Alfo, a farmer. Often, returning from our afternoon walk in the campagna, we saw him coming home from his fields on his little long-cars, his feet almost on the ground, under a sunshade, with blue glasses on his nose. The lawyer apparently no longer practised his profession, he only read the newspaper, read it indeed all the time; on hot days he permitted himself to do it sitting in his room in his drawers, with the door open. He drew down upon himself the disapproval of Sor Alfo, who found that the man of law — "*quest'* *uomo*" he called him in this connection — took too much upon himself. Loudly, behind his brother's back he censured this provocative licence and would not be talked round by his sister's soothing words, to the effect that the advocate was a full-blooded man, in danger of a heat stroke, which made light clothing a necessity to him. Then "*quest'uomo*" should at least keep the door shut, retorted Alfo, instead of exposing himself in so négligé a state to the eyes of his family and the *distinti forestieri*. A higher education did not justify such offensive slackness. It was clear that a certain animosity was being expressed by the contadino against the educated member of the family, under a well-chosen pretext indeed — although, or even because, Sor Alfo in the depths of his heart shared the family admiration for the lawyer, whom they considered the next thing to a statesman. But the politics of the brothers were in many matters far asunder, for the advocate was of a conservative and devout cast, Alfonso on the other hand a free-thinker, *libero pensatore*, and a critical mind, hostile to Church, monarchy, and government, which he painted as permeated with scandalous corruption. "*A capito, che sacco di birbaccione*" (did you understand what a pack of rascals they are?), he would close his indictment, much more articulately than the advocate, who after a few gasping protests would retire behind his newspaper.

A connection of the three, brother of Signora Nella's deceased husband, Dario Manardi, a mild, grey-bearded rustic, walking

with a stick, lived with his simple, ailing wife in the family
house. They did their own housekeeping while Signora Peronella
provided for us seven from her romantic kitchen — the brothers,
Amelia, the two permanent guests, and the visiting pair — with
an amplitude that bore no relation to the modest pension price.
She was inexhaustible. For when we had already enjoyed a powerful minestra, larks and polenta, scallopini in Marsala, a joint of
mutton or boar with compote, thereto much salad, cheese and
fruit, and our friends had lighted their government-monopoly
cigarettes to smoke with the black coffee, she might say as one
suggesting a captivating idea: "Signori, a little fish, perhaps?" A
purple country wine which the advocate drank like water, in
great gulps, croaking the while — a growth too fiery really to be
recommended as a table beverage twice daily, yet on the other
hand a pity to water it — served to quench our thirst. The padrona encouraged us with the words: "Drink, drink! *Fa sangue il
vino.*" But Alfonso upbraided her, saying it was a superstition.

The afternoons were spent in beautiful walks, during which
there were many hearty laughs at Rüdiger Schildknapp's Anglo-
Saxon jokes; down to the valley by roads lined with mulberry
bushes and out a stretch into the well-cultivated country with its
olive trees and vine garlands, its tilled fields divided into small
holdings separated by stone walls with almost monumental entrance gates. Shall I express how much — aside from the being
with Adrian again — I enjoyed the classic sky, where during the
weeks of our stay not one single cloud appeared; the antique
mood that lay over the land and now and then expressed itself
visibly, as for instance in the rim of a well, a picturesque shepherd, a goat's head suggestive of Pan? A smiling, slightly ironic
nod was Adrian's only response to the raptures of my humanistic
soul. Artists pay little heed to their surroundings so long as these
bear no direct relation to their own field of work; they see in
them no more than in indifferent frame, either more or less favourable to production. We looked towards the sunset as we returned to the little town, and another such splendour of the
evening sky I have not seen. A golden layer, thick and rich like
oil, bordered with crimson, was on the western horizon; the sight
was utterly extraordinary and so beautiful that it might well ex-
hilarate and expand the soul. So I confess I felt slightly put off
when Schildknapp, gesturing towards the marvellous spectacle,
shouted his "*Besichtigen Sie jenes!*" and Adrian burst out into the
grateful laughter which Rüdiger humour always drew from him.
For it seemed to me he seized the occasion to laugh at Helene's

and my emotion and even at the glory of nature's magnificence as well.

I have already mentioned the garden of the cloister above the town, to which our friends climbed every morning with their portfolios to work apart. They had asked permission of the monks to sit there and it had been benignly granted. We often accompanied them into the spice-scented shade of the not too well-tended plot surrounded by crumbling walls, where we would leave them to their devices and invisible to them both, who were themselves invisible to each other, isolated by bushes of oleander, laurel, and broom, spend the increasingly hot afternoon, Helene with her crochet-work, I with a book, but dwelling in my thoughts on the pleasurable excitement of the knowledge that Adrian was working on his opera close by.

On the badly out-of-tune square piano in the friends' living-room he played to us once during our stay — unfortunately only once — from the completed sections, mostly already scored for a specially chosen orchestra, of the "pleasant well-conceited comedy Love's Labour's Lost," as the piece was called in 1598. He played characteristic passages and a few complete scene sequences: the first act, including the scene outside Armado's house, and several later numbers which he had partly anticipated: in particular Biron's monologues, which he had had especially in mind from the first, the one in verse at the end of the third act, as well as the prose one in the fourth: "They have pitched a toil, I am toiling in a pitch — pitch that defiles"; which, while always preserving the atmosphere of the comic and grotesque, expresses musically still better than the first the deep and genuine despair of the young man over his surrender to the suspect black beauty, his raging abandonment of self-mockery: "By the Lord, this love is as mad as Ajax; it kills sheep; it kills me, I a sheep": this partly because the swift-moving, unjointed, ejaculatory prose, with its many plays on words, inspired the composer to invent musical accents of quite peculiar fantasticality; partly, also, because in music the repetition of the significant and already familiar, the suggestive or subtle invention, always makes the strongest and most speaking impression. And in the second monologue elements of the first are thus delightfully recalled to the mind. This was true above all for the embittered self-castigation of the heart because of its infatuation with the "whitely wanton with a velvet brow, with two pitch-balls stuck in her face for eyes," and again quite particularly for the musical picture of these beloved accursed eyes: a melisma darkly flashing out of the sound of combined cellos and flutes, half lyrically passionate and half burlesque, which in the prose, at the place "O, but her eye — by this light, but for her eye, I would not love her," recurs in a wildly carica- tured way, where the darkness of the eyes is intensified by the pitch, but the lightning flash of them is this time given to the pic- colo.

There can be no doubt that the strangely insistent and even unnecessary, dramatically little justified characterization of Rosa- line as a faithless, wanton, dangerous piece of female flesh — a description given to her only in Biron's speeches, whereas in the actual setting of the comedy she is no more than pert and witty — there can be no doubt that this characterization springs from a compulsion, heedless of artistic indiscrepancies, on the poet's part, an urge to bring in his own experiences and, whether it fits or not, to take poetic revenge for them. Rosaline, as the lover never tires of portraying her, is the dark lady of the second sonnet sequence, Elizabeth's maid of honour, Shakespeare's love, who betrayed him with the lovely youth. And the "part of my rhyme and here my melancholy" with which Biron appears on the stage for the prose monologue ("Well, she hath one o' my sonnets already") is one of those which Shakespeare addressed to this black and whitely beauty. And how does Rosaline come to apply to the sharp-tongued, merry Biron of the play such wisdom as:

> The blood of youth burns not with such excess
> As gravity's revolt to wantonness?

For he is young and not at all grave, and by no means the person who could give occasion to such a comment as that it is lamenta- ble when wise men turn fools and apply all their wit to give folly the appearance of worth. In the mouth of Rosaline and her friends Biron falls quite out of his role; he is no longer Biron, but Shakespeare in his unhappy affair with the dark lady; and Adrian, who had the sonnets, that profoundly extraordinary trio of poet, friend, and beloved, always by him in an English pocket edition, had been from the beginning at pains to assimilate the character of his Biron to this particular and favourite dialogue and to give him a music which, in suitable proportion to the burlesquing style of the whole, makes him "grave" and intellectually considerable, a genuine sacrifice to a shameful passion.

That was beautiful, and I praised it highly. And how much reason there was besides for praise and joyful amaze in what he played to us! One could say in earnest what the learned hair-split- ter Holofernes says of himself: "This is a gift that I have, simple,

simple: a foolish extravagant spirit, full of forms, figures, shapes, objects, ideas, apprehensions, motions, revolutions: these are begot in the ventricle of memory, nourished in the womb of pia mater, and delivered upon the mellowing of occasion." Wonderful! In a quite incidental, a ludicrous setting the poet there gives an incomparably full description of the artist essence, and involuntarily one referred it to the mind that was here at work to transfer Shakespeare's satirical youthful work into the sphere of music.

Shall I completely pass over the little hurt feeling, the sense of being slighted, which I felt on the score of the subject itself, the mockery of classical studies, which in the play appear as ascetic preciosity? Of the caricature of humanism not Adrian but Shakespeare was guilty, and from Shakespeare too come the ideas wrenched out of their order in which the conceptions "culture" and "barbarism" play such a singular role. That is intellectual monkishness, a learned overrefinement deeply contemptuous of life and nature both, which sees the barbaric precisely in life and nature, in directness, humanity, feeling. Biron himself, who puts in some good words for nature to the sworn *précieux* of the groves of academe, admits that he has "for barbarism spoke more than for that angel knowledge you can say." The angel knowledge is indeed made ridiculous, but again only through the ridiculous; for the "barbarism" into which the group falls back, the sonnet-drunk infatuation that is laid upon them as a punishment for their disastrous alliance, is caricature too, in brilliant style, love-persiflage; and only too well did Adrian's music see to it that in the end feeling came no better off than the arrogant forswearing of it. Music, so I felt, was by its very nature called to lead men out of the sphere of absurd artificiality into fresh air, into the world of nature and humanity. But it refrained. That which the noble Biron calls barbarism, that is to say the spontaneous and natural, celebrates here no triumph.

As art this music of my friend was admirable indeed. Contemptuous of a mass display, he had originally wanted to score for the classical Beethoven orchestra; and only for the sake of the bombastic and absurd figure of the Spaniard Armado had he introduced a second pair of horns, three trombones, and a bass tuba. But everything was in strict chamber-music style, a delicate airy filigree, a clever parody in notes, ingenious and humoristic, rich in subtle, high-spirited ideas. A music-lover who had tired of romantic democracy and popular moral harangues and demanded an art for art's sake, an ambitionless — or in the most exclusive sense ambi-

tious — art for artists and connoisseurs, must have been ravished
by this self-centred and completely cool esoteric; but which now,
as esoteric, in the spirit of the piece in every way mocked and
parodistically exaggerated itself, thus mixing into its ravishment
a grain of hopelessness, a drop of melancholy.

Yes, admiration and sadness mingled strangely as I contemplated this music. "How beautiful!" the heart said to itself — mine
at least said so — "and how sad!" The admiration was due to a
witty and melancholy work of art, an intellectual achievement
which deserved the name of heroic, something just barely possible, behaving like arrogant travesty. I know not how otherwise
to characterize it than by calling it a tense, sustained, neck-break-
ing game played by art at the edge of impossibility. It was just
this that made one sad. But admiration and sadness, admiration
and doubt, is that not almost the definition of love? It was with
a strained and painful love for him and what was his that I listened to Adrian's performance. I could not say much; Schildknapp, who always made a very good, receptive audience, expressed the right things much more glibly and intelligently than I.
Even afterwards, at dinner, I sat benumbed and absent at the
Manardi table, moved by feelings with which the music we had
heard so fully corresponded. "*Bevi, bevi!*" said the padrona. "*Fa
sangue il vino!*" And Amelia moved her spoons to and fro before
her face and murmured: "*Spiriti? Spiriti?*"

This evening was one of the last which we, my good wife and
I, spent with the two friends in their novel quarters. A few days
later, after a stay of three weeks, we had to leave and begin the
return journey to Germany. The others for months still, on into
the autumn, remained true to the idyllic uniformity of their existence between cloister garden, family table, campagna framed in
rich gold, and stone-floored study, where they spent the evenings
by lamplight. So it had been the whole of the summer before,
and their winter way of life in the town had not been essentially
different. They lived in via Torre Argentina, near the Teatro
Costanzi and the Pantheon, three flights up, with a landlady who
gave them breakfast and luncheon. In a near-by trattoria they
took their dinner at charge of a monthly sum. The role of the
cloister garden of Palestrina was played in Rome by the Villa
Doria Pamfili, where on warm spring and autumn days they pursued their labours beside a classically lovely fountain where from
time to time a roving and pasturing cow or horse came to drink.
Adrian seldom failed the afternoon municipal concerts in Piazza
Colonna. On occasion there was an evening of opera; as a rule

they spent it playing dominoes over a glass of hot orange punch, in a quiet corner of some café.

More extended society than this they had none — or as good as none. Their isolation was almost as complete in Rome as in the country. The German element they avoided entirely — Schildknapp invariably took to flight so soon as a sound of his mother tongue struck on his ear. He was quite capable of getting out of an omnibus or train when there were "Germans" in it. But their solitary way of life — solitary *à deux*, it is true — gave little opportunity to make even Italian friends. Twice during the winter they were invited by a lady of indefinite origins who patronized art and artists, Mme de Coniar, to whom Rüdiger Schildknapp had a Munich letter of introduction. In her home on the Corso, decorated with personally signed photographs in plush and silver frames, they met hordes of international artists, theatre people, painters, musicians, Polish, Hungarians, French, also Italians; but individual persons they soon lost sight of. Sometimes Schildknapp separated from Adrian to drink malmsey with young Britishers into whose arms his English predilection had driven him; to make excursions to Tivoli or the Trappist monastery at Quattro Fontane, to consume eucalyptus brandy and talk nonsense with them as a relief from the consuming difficulties of the art of translation.

In short, in town as in the isolation of the country village the two led a life remote from the world and mankind, entirely taken up by the cares of their work. At least one can so express it. And shall I say that the departure from the Manardi house, however unwillingly I now as always left Adrian's side, was accompanied with a certain private feeling of relief? To utter it is equivalent to the obligation of justifying the feeling, and that is hard to do without putting myself and others in a somewhat laughable light. The truth is: in a certain point, *in puncto puncti* as young people like to say, I formed in the company a somewhat comic exception and fell so to speak out of the frame; namely, in my quality and way of life as a benedict, which paid tribute to what we half excusingly, half glorifyingly called "nature." Nobody else in the castello-house on the terraced lane did so. Our excellent hostess, Signora Peronella, had been a widow for years, her daughter Amelia was a half-idiot child. The brothers Manardi, lawyer and peasant, seemed to be hardened bachelors, yes, one could imagine that neither of them had ever laid a finger on a woman. There was Cousin Dario, grey and mild, with a tiny, ailing little wife, a pair whose love could certainly be interpreted only in the caritas sense of the word. And finally there were Adrian and Rüdiger

Schildknapp, who spent month after month in this austere and peaceful circle that we had learned to know, living not otherwise than did the cloistered monks above. Would not that, for me, the ordinary man, have something mortifying and depressing about it?

Of Schildknapp's particular relation to the wide world of possibilities for happiness, and of his tendency to be sparing with them, as he was sparing with himself, I have spoken before. I saw in it the key to his way of life, it served me as explanation for the fact, otherwise hard for me to understand, that he succeeded in it. It was otherwise with Adrian, although I felt certain that this community of chastity was the basis of their friendship, or if the word is too strong, their life together. I suspect that I have not succeeded in hiding from the reader a certain jealousy of the Silesian's relations with Adrian; if so, he may also understand that it was this life in common, this bond of continence, with which after all my jealousy had to do.

If Schildknapp, let us say, lived as a roué of the potentialities, Adrian — I could not doubt it — since that journey to Graz or otherwise Pressburg, lived the life of a saint — as indeed he had done up to then. But now I trembled at the thought that his chastity since then, since that embrace, since his passing contagion and the loss of his physicians, sprang no longer from the ethos of purity but from the pathos of impurity.

There had always been in his nature something of *noli me tangere*. I knew that; his distaste for the too great physical nearness of people, his dislike of "getting in each other's steam," his avoidance of physical contact, were familiar to me. He was in the real sense of the word a man of disinclination, avoidance, reserve, aloofness. Physical cordialities seemed quite impossible to associate with his nature, even his handshake was infrequent and hastily performed. More plainly than ever this characteristic came out during my visit and to me, I cannot say why, it was as though the "Touch me not!" the "three paces off," had to some extent altered its meaning, as though it were not so much that an advance was discouraged as that an advance from the other side was shrunk from and avoided — and this, undoubtedly, was connected with his abstention from women.

Only a friendship as keen-eyed and penetrating as mine could feel or divine such a change of significance; and may God keep me from letting my pleasure in Adrian's company be affected thereby! What was going on in him could shatter me but never sever me from him. There are people with whom it is not easy to live; but to leave impossible.

CHAPTER XXV

THE document to which repeated reference has been made in these pages, Adrian's secret record, since his demise in my possession and guarded like a frightful and precious treasure, here it is, I offer it herewith. The biographical moment has come. And accordingly I myself must cease to speak, since in spirit I have turned my back on his deliberately chosen refuge, shared with the Silesian, where I had sought him out. In this twenty-fifth chapter the reader hears Adrian's voice direct.

But is it only his? This is a dialogue which lies before us. Another, quite other, quite frightfully other, is the principal speaker, and the writer, in his stone-floored living-room, only writes down what he heard from that other. A dialogue? Is it really a dialogue? I should be mad to believe it. And therefore I cannot believe that in the depths of his soul Adrian himself considered to be actual that which he saw and heard — either while he heard and saw it or afterwards, when he put it on paper; notwithstanding the cynicisms with which his interlocutor sought to convince him of his objective presence. But if he was not there, that visitor — and I shudder at the admission which lies in the very words, seeming even conditionally and as a possibility to entertain his actuality — then it is horrible to think that those cynicisms too, those jeerings and jugglings, came out of the afflicted one's own soul. . . .

It goes without saying that I have no idea of turning over Adrian's manuscript to the printer. With my own hand I will transcribe it word for word in my text from the music-paper covered with his script, which I characterized earlier in these memoirs: his small, old-fashioned, florid, very black round-hand, the writing of a scribe, a monk, one might say. He used his music notepaper obviously because no other was at hand at the moment, or because the little shop down in the Piazza St. Agapitus had no proper writing-paper. There are always two lines on the upper five-line system and two on the bass; the white spaces in between are covered throughout with two lines each.

Not with entire definiteness can the time of writing be made out, for the document bears no date. If my conviction is worth anything, it was certainly not written after our visit to the mountain village or during our stay there. Either it comes from earlier in the summer, of which we spent three weeks with the friends, or it dates from the summer before, the first they spent as guests of the Manardis. That at the time we were there the experience which is the basis of the manuscript lay already in the past; that Adrian at that time had already had the conversation which follows, amounts with me to a certainty; so does it that he wrote it down at once after the event, presumably the very next day.

So now I copy it down — and I fear that no distant explosions jarring my retreat will be needed to make my hand shake as I write and my letters to be ill-formed.

*

*   *

Whist, mum's the word. And certes I schal be mum, will hold my tunge, were it sheerly out of shame, to spare folkes feelings, for social considerations forsooth! Am firmly minded to keep fast hold on reason and decency, not giving way even up till the end. But seen Him I have, at last, at last! He was with me, here in this hall, He sought me out; unexpected, yet long expected. I held plenteous parley with Him, and now thereafter I am vexed but sith I am not certain whereat I did shake all the whole time: an 'twere at the cold, or at Him. Did I beguile myself, or He me, that it was cold, so I might quake and thereby certify myself that He was there, Himself in person? For verily no man but knows he is a fool which quaketh at his proper brain-maggot; for sooner is such welcome to him and he yieldeth without or shaking or quaking thereunto. Mayhap He did but delude me, making out by the brutish cold I was no fool and He no figment, since I a fool did quake before Him? He is a wily-pie.

Natheles I will be mum, will hold my tonge and mumchance hide all down here on my music-paper, whiles my old jester-fere *in eremo*, far away in the hall, travails and toils to turn the loved outlandish into the loathed mother tongue. He weens that I compose, and were he to see that I write words, would but deem Beethoven did so too.

All the whole day, poor wretch, I had lien in the dark with irksome mygrym, retching and spewing, as happeth with the severer seizures. But at eventide quite suddenly came unexpected betterment. I could keep down the soup the Mother brought me

("*Poveretto!*"); with good cheer drank a glass of *rosso* ("*Bevi, bevi!*") and on a sudden felt so staunch as to allow myself a cigarette. I could even have gone out, as had been arranged the day before. Dario M. wanted to take us down to his club and introduce us to the better sort of Prænestensians, show us reading-room, billiard-room, and about the place. We had no heart to offend the good soul, but it came down to Sch. going alone, I being forgiven due to my attack. From *pranzo* he stalked off with a sour countenance, down the street at Dario's side to the farmers and philistines, and I stopped by myself.

I sate alone here, by my lamp, nigh to the windows with shutters closed, before me the length of the hall, and read Kirkegaard on Mozart's *Don Juan*.

Then in a clap I am stricken by a cutting cold, even as though I sat in a winter-warm room and a window had blown open towards the frost. It came not from behind me, where the windows lie; it falls on me from in front. I start up from my boke and look abroad into the hall, belike Sch. is come back for I am no more alone. There is some bodye there in the mirk, sitting on the horse-hair sofa that stands almost in the myddes of the room, nigher the door, with the table and chairs, where we eat our breakfasts. Sitting in the sofa-corner with legs crossed; not Sch., but another, smaller than he, in no wise so imposing and not in truth a gentilman at all. But the cold keeps percing me.

"*Chi e costà?*" is what I shout with some catch in my throat, propping my hands on the chair-arms, in such wise that the book falls from my knees to the floore. Answers the quiet, slow voice of the other, a voice that sounds trained, with pleasing nasal resonance:

"Speak only German! Only good old German without feignedness or dissimulation. I understand it. It happens to be just precisely my favoured language. Whiles I understand only German. But fet thee a cloak, a hat and rug. Thou art cold. And quiver and quake thou wilt, even though not taking a cold."

"Who says *thou* to me?" I ask, chafing.

"I," he says. "I, by your leave. Oh, thou meanest because thou sayst to nobody thou, not even to thy jester gentilman, but only to the trusty play-fere, he who clepes thee by the first name but not thou him. No matter. There is already enough between us for us to say thou. Wel, then: wilt fet thyself some warm garment?"

I stare into the half-light, fix him angrily in mine eye. A man: rather spindling, not nearly so tall as Sch., smaller even then I.

A sports cap over one ear, on the other side reddish hair standing up from the temple; reddish lashes and pink eyes, a cheesy face, a drooping nose with wry tip. Over diagonal-striped tricot shirt a chequer jacket; sleeves too short, with sausage-fingers coming too far out; breeches indecently tight, worn-down yellow shoes. An ugly customer, a bully, a *strizzi*, a rough. And with an actor's voice and eloquence.

"Well?" he says again.

"First and foremost I fain would know," say I in quaking calm, "who is bold enough to force himself in to sit down here with me."

"First and foremost," he repeats. "First and foremost is not bad at all. But you are oversensitive to any visit you hold to be unexpected and undesired. I am no flattering claw-back come to fetch you into company, to woo you that you may join the musical circle; but to talk over our affairs. Wilt fetch thy things? It is ill talking with teeth chattering."

I sat a few seconds lenger, not taking my eyes off him. And the cutting cold, coming from him, rushes at me, so that I feel bare and bald before it in my light suit. So I go. Verily I stand up and pass through the next door to the left, where my bedchamber is (the other's being further down on the same side), take my winter cloke out of the presse that I wear in Rome on tramontana days and it had to come along as I wist not where I might leave it else; put my hat on too, take my rug and so furnished go back to my place.

There he still sits in his, just as I left him.

"Ye're still there," say I, turning up my coat-collar and wrapping my plaid about my knees — "even after I've gone and come back? I marvel at it. For I've a strong suspicion y'are not there at all."

"No?" he asks in his trained voice, with nasal resonance. "For why?"

I: "Because it is nothing likely that a man should seat himself here with me of an evening, speaking German and giving out cold, with pretence to discuss with me gear whereof I wot nor would wot naught. Miche more like is it I am waxing sicke and transferring to your form the chills and fever against the which I am wrapped, sneaped by frost, and in the beholding of you see but the source of it."

He (quietly and convincingly laughing, like an actor): "Tilly-vally, what learned gibberidge you talk! In good playne old German, 'tis fond and frantick. And so artificial! A clever artifice, an 'twere stolen from thine own opera! But we make no music here, at the moment. Moreover it is pure hypochondria. Don't imagine any infirmities! Have a little pride and don't lose grip of yourself! There's no sickness breaking out, after the slight attack you are in the best of youthful health. But I cry you mercy, I would not be tactless, for what is health? Thuswise, my goodly fere, your sickness does not break out. You have not a trace of fever and no occasion wherefore you should ever have any."

I: "Further, because with every third word ye utter you uncover your nothingness. You say nothing save things that are in me and come out of me but not out of you. You ape old Kumpf with turns of phrase yet look not as though you ever had been in academic or higher school or ever sat next to me on the scorner's bench. You talk of the needy gentilman and of him to whom I speak in the singular number, and even of such as have done so and reaped but little thank. And of my opera you speak too. Whence could you know all that?"

He (laughs again his practised laugh, shaking his head as at some priceless childishness): "Yea, whence? But see, I do know it. And you will conclude therefrom to your own discredit that you do not see aright? That were truly to set all logick upsodown, as one learns at the schools. 'Twere better to conclude, not that I am not here in the flesh, but that I, here in my person, am also he for whom you have taken me all the whole time."

I: "And for whom do I take you?"

He (politely reproachful): "Tut, tut! Do not lain it thus, as though you had not been long since expecting me! You wit aswel as I that our relation demands a dispicion. If I am — and that I ween you do now admit — then I can be but One. Or do you mean, what I hyght? But you can still recall all the scurrile nicknames from the schoole, from your first studies, when you had not put the Good Boke out of the door and under the bench. You have them all at your fingers' ends, you may elect one — I have scant others, they are well-nigh all nicknames, with the which people, so to speke, chuck me under the chin: that comes from my good sound German popularity. A man is gratified by popularity, I trow, even when he has not sought it out and at bottom is convinced that it rests on false understanding. It is always flattering, always does a bodye good. Choose one yourself, if you would call me by name, although you commonly do not call people by name at all; for lack of interest you do not know what they hight. But choose any one you list among the pet names the peasants give me. Only one I cannot and will not abide because it is distinctly a malicious slander and fits me not a whit. Whosoever calls me *Dicis et non facis* is in the wrong box. It too may even be a finger chucking my chin, but it is a calumny. I do ywisse what I say, keep my promise to a tittle; that is precisely my business principle, more or less as the Jews are the most reliable dealers, and when it comes to deceit, well, it is a common saying that it was always I, who believe in good faith and rightwiseness, who am beguiled."

I: "*Dicis et non es.* Ye would forsoothe sit there against me on the sofa and speak outwardly to me in good Kumpfish, in old-German snatches? Ye would visit me deliberately here in Italy of all places, where you are entirely out of your sphere and not on the peasant tongue at all? What an absurd want of style! In Kaisersaschern I could have suffered it. At Wittenberg or on the Wartburg, even in Leipzig you would have been credible to me. But not here under this pagan and Catholic sky!"

He (shaking his head and pained clucking with his tongue): "Tch, tch, tch! always this same distrust, this same lack of self-confidence! If you had the courage to say unto yourself: 'Where I am, there is Kaisersaschern' — well and good, the thing would be in frame, the Herr æstheticus would needs make moan no more over lack of style. Cocksblood! You would have the right to speak like that, yet you just haven't the courage or you act as though you lacked it. Self-belittlement, my friend — and you underestimate me too, if you limit me thuswise and try to make a German provincial of me. I am in fact German, German to the core, yet even so in an older, better way, to wit cosmopolitan from my heart. Wouldst deny me away, wouldst refuse to consider the old German romantic wander-urge and yearning after the fair land of Italy! German I am, but that I should once in good Düreresque style freeze and shiver after the sun, that Your Excellency will not grant me — not even when quite aside from the sun, I have delicate and urgent business here, with a fine, well-created human being. . . ."

Here an unspeakable disgust came over me, so that I shuddered violently. But there was no real difference between the grounds of my shudder; it might be at one and the same time for cold, too; the draught from him had got abruptly stronger, so that it went through my overcoat and pierced me to my marrow. Angrily I ask:

"Cannot you away with this nuisance, this icy draught?"

He: "Alas, no, I regret not to be able to gratify you. But the fact is, I *am* cold. How otherwise could I hold out and find it possible to dwell where I dwell?"

I (involuntarily): "You mean in the brenning pit of fier?"

He (laughs as though tickled): "Capital! Said in the good robust and merry German way. It has indeed many other pretty names, scholarly, pathetical, the Herr Doctor ex-Theologus knows them all, as carcer, exitium, confutatio, pernicies, condemnatio, and so on. But there is no remedy, the familiar German, the comic ones are still my favourites. However, let us for the nonce leave that place and the nature of it. I see by your face, you are at the point of asking about it; but that is far off, not in the least a brenning question — you will forgive me the bourd, that it is not brenning! There is time for it, plenteous, boundless time — time is the actual thing, the best we give, and our gift the houre-glasse — it is so fine, the little neck, through which the red sand runs, a threadlike trickle, does not minish at all to the eye in the upper cavitie, save at the very end; then it does seem to speed and to have gone fast. But that is so far away, the narrow part, it is not worth talking or thinking about. Albeit inasmuch as the glass is set and the sand has begun to run; for this reason, my good man, I would fain come to an understanding with you."

I (full scornfully): "Extraordinarily Dürerish. You love it. First 'how will I shiver after the sun'; and then the houre-glasse of the *Melancolia*. Is the magic square coming too? I am prepared for everything, can get used to everything. Get used to your shamelessness, your thee-ing and thou-ing and trusty fere-ing, which soothly always go particularly against the wood. After all I say 'thou' only to myself, which of likelihood explains why you do. According to you I am speaking with black Kaspar, which is one of the names, and so Kaspar and Samiel are one and the same."

He: "Off you go again!"

I: "Samiel. It giveth a man to laugh. Where then is your C-minor fortissimo of stringed tremoli, wood and trombones, ingenious bug to fright children, the romantic public, coming out of the F-sharp minor of the Glen as you out of your abyss — I wonder I hear it not!"

He: "Let that be. We have many a lovelier instrument and you shall hear them. We shall play for you, when you be ripe to hear. Everything is a matter of ripeness and of dear time. Just that I would speak of with you. But Samiel — that's a folish form. I am all for that is of the folk; but Samiel, too foolish, Johann Ballhorn from Lübeck corrected it. Sammael it is. And what signifies Sammael?"

I (defiant, do not answer).

He: "What, ne'er a word but mum? I like the discreet way in which you leave me to put it in German. It means angel of death."

I (between my teeth, which will not stay properly closed): "Yes, distinctly, that is what you look like! Just like unto an angel, exactly. Do you know how you look? Common is not the word for it. Like some shameless scum, a lewd losel, a make-bate, that is how you look, how you have found good to visit me — and no angel!"

He (looking down at himself, with his arms stretched out): "How then, how then? How do I look? No, it is really good that you ask me if I wot how I look, for by my troth I wot not. Or wist not, you called it to my attention. Be sure, I reck nothing at all to my outward appearance, I leave it so to say to itself. It is sheer chance how I look, or rather, it comes out like that, it happeth like that according to the circumstances, without my taking heed. Adaptation, mimicry, you know it, of course. Mummery and jugglery of mother Nature, who always has her tongue in her cheek. But you won't, my good fere, refer the adaptation, about which I know just as much and as little as the leaf butterfly, to yourself, and take it ill of me. You must admit that from the other side it has something suitable about it — on that side where you got it from, and indeed forewarned, from the side of your pretty song with the letter symbol — oh, really ingeniously done, and almost as though by inspiration:

> When once thou gavest to me
> At night the cooling draught,
> With poison didst undo me
> ....
> Then on the wound the serpent
> Fastened and firmly sucked —

Really gifted. That is what we recognized betimes and why from early on we had an eye on you — we saw that your case was quite definitely worth the trouble, that it was a case of the most favourable situation, whereof with only a little of our fire lighted under it, only a little heating, elation, intoxication, something brilliant could be brought out. Did not Bismarck say something about the Germans needing half a bottle of champagne to arrive at their normal height? Meseems he said something of the sort.

And that of right. Gifted but halt is the German — gifted enough to be angry with his paralysis, and to overcome it by hand-over-head illumination. You, my good man, well knew what you needed, and took the right road when you made your journey and *salva venia* summoned your French beloved to you."

"Hold thy tongue!"

"Hold thy tongue? We are coming on. We wax warm. At last you drop the polite plural number and say 'thou,' as it should be between people who are in league and contract for time and eternity."

"Will ye hold your tongue still?"

"Still? But we have been still for nigh five years and must after all sometime hold parley and advise over the whole and over the interesting situation wherein you find yourself. This is naturally a thing to keep wry about, but after all not at the length — when the houre-glasse is set, the red sand has begun to run through the fine-fine neck — ah, but only just begun! It is still almost nothing, what lies underneath, by comparison with all there is on top; we give time, plenteous time, abundant time by the eye, the end whereof we do not need to consider, not for a long time yet, nor need to trouble yet awhile even of the point of time where you could begin to take heed to the ending, where it might come to 'Respice finem.' Sithence it is a variable point, left to caprice and temper, and nobody knows where it should begin, and how nigh to the end one should lay it out. This is a good bourd and capital arrangement: the uncertainty and the free choice of the moment when the time is come to heed the eynde, overcasts in mist and jest the view of the appointed limit."

"Fables, fantasies!"

"Get along, one cannot please you, even against my psychology you are harsh — albeit you yourself on your Mount Zion at home called psychology a nice, neutral middle point and psychologists the most truth-loving people. I fable not a whit when I speak of the given time and the appointed end; I speak entirely to the point. Wheresoever the houre-glasse is set up and time fixed, unthinkable yet measured time and a fixed end, there we are in the field, there we are in clover. Time we sell — let us say XXIV years — can we see to the end of that? Is it a good solid amount? Therewith a man can live at rack and manger like a lord and astonish the world as a great nigromancer with much divel's work; the lenger it goes on, the more forget all paralysis and in highly illuminated state rise out of himselfe, yet never transcend but remain the same, though raised to his proper stature by the half-

bottle of champagne. In drunken bliss he savours all the rapture
of an almost unbearable draught, till he may with more or less of
right be convinced that a like infusion has not been in a thousand
years and in certain abandoned moments may simply hold himself a god. How will such an one come to think about the point
of time when it is become time to give heed to the end! Only, the
end is ours, at the end he is ours, that has to be agreed on, and not
merely silently, how silent so ever it be else, but from man to
man and expressly."

I: "So you would sell me time?"

He: "Time? Simple time? No, my dear fere, that is not devyll's
ware. For that we should not earn the reward, namely that the end
belongs to us. What manner of time, that is the heart of the
matter! Great time, mad time, quite bedivelled time, in which the
fun waxes fast and furious, with heaven-high leaping and springing — and again, of course, a bit miserable, very miserable indeed,
I not only admit that, I even emphasize it, with pride, for it is
sitting and fit, such is artist-way and artist-nature. That, as is well
knowen, is given at all times to excess on both sides and is in
quite normal way a bit excessive. Alway the pendulum swings
very wide to and fro between high spirits and melancholia, that
is usual, is so to speak still according to moderate bourgeois Nuer-
remberg way, in comparison with that which we purvey. For we
purvey the uttermost in this direction; we purvey towering flights
and illuminations, experiences of upliftings and unfetterings, of
freedom, certainty, facility, feeling of power and triumph, that
our man does not trust his wits — counting in besides the colossal
admiration for the made thing, which could soon bring him to
renounce every outside, foreign admiration — the thrills of self-
veneration, yes, of exquisite horror of himself, in which he appears to himself like an inspired mouthpiece, as a godlike monster. And correspondingly deep, honourably deep, doth he sink
in between-time, not only into void and desolation and unfruitful
melancholy but also into pains and sicknesse — familiar inciden-
tally, which had alway been there, which belong to his character,
yet which are only most honorably enhanced by the illumination
and the well-knowen 'sack of heyre.' Those are pains which a
man gladly pays, with pleasure and pride, for what he has so much
enjoyed, pains which he knows from the fairy-tale, the pains
which the little sea-maid, as from sharp knives, had in her beautiful human legs she got herself instead of her tail. You know
Andersen's Little Sea-maid? She would be a sweetheart for you!
Just say the word and I will bring her to your couch."

I: "If you could just keep quiet, prating jackanapes that you are!"

He: "How now! Need you always make a rude answer? Always you expect me to be still. But silence is not my motto, I do not belong to the Schweigestill family. And Mother Else, anyhow, has prattled in all proper discretion no end to you about her odd occasional guests. Neither am I come hither for the sake of silence to a pagan foreign land; but rather for express confirmation between us two and a firm contract upon payment against completion. I tell you, we have been silent more than four years — and now everything is taking the finest, most exquisite, most promising course, and the bell is now half cast. Shall I tell you how it stands and what is afoot?"

I: "It well appeareth I must listen."

He: "Wouldst like to besides, and art well content that thou canst hear. I trow forsooth you are on edge to hear and would grumble and growl an I kept it back, and that of right too. It is such a snug, familiar world wherein we are together, thou and I — we are right at home therein, pure Kaisersaschern, good old German air, from anno MD or thereabouts, shortly before Dr. Martinus came, who stood on such stout and sturdy footing with me and threw the roll, no, I mean the ink-pot at me, long before the thirty years' frolic. Bethink thee what lively movement of the people was with you in Germany's midst, on the Rhine and all over, how full of agitation and unrest, anxiety, presentiments; what press of pilgrims to the Sacred Blood at Niklashausen in the Tauberthal, what children's crusades, bleeding of the Host, famine, Peasants' League, war, the pest at Cologne, meteors, comets, and great omens, nuns with the stigmata, miraculous crosses on men's garments, and that amazing standard of the maiden's shift with the Cross, whereunder to march against the Turk! Good time, divellishly German time! Don't you feel all warm and snug at the memory? There the right planets come together in the sign of the Scorpion, as Master Dürer has eruditely drawn in the medical broadsheet, there came the tender little ones, the swarms of animated corkscrews, the loving guests from the West Indies into the German lands, the flagellants — ah, now you listen! As though I spake of the marching guild of penitents, the Flagellants, who flailed for their own and all other sins. But I mean those flagellates, the invisible tiny ones, the kind that have scourges, like our pale Venus, the spirochæta pallida, that is the true sort. But th'art right, it sounds so comfortingly like the depths of Middle Ages and the *flagellum hæreticorum fascinariorum*. Yea, verily, as fascinarii they may well shew themselves, our devotees, in the better cases, as in yours. They are moreover quite civilized and domesticated long since, and in old countries where they have been so many hundred years at home, they do not play such merry pranks and coarse preposterous jokes as erstwhile, with running sore and plague and worm-eaten nose. Baptist Spengler the painter does not look as though he, his body wrapped up in hair, would have to shake the warning rattle withersoever he went."

I: "Is he like that — Spengler?"

He: "Why not? I suppose you think you are the only one in like case? I know thou haddest thine liefer quite by thyself and art vexed at any comparison. My dear fellow, a man always has a great many companions. Spengler, of course, is an Esmeraldus. It is not without reason that he blinks, so sly and shamefast, and not for nothing does Inez Rodde call him a sneak. So it is: Leo Zink, the *Faunus ficarius*, has always heretofore escaped; but it got the clean, clever Spengler early on. Yet be calm, withhold your jealousy. It is a banal, tedious case, productive of nothing at all. He is no python, in whom we bring sensational deeds to pass. A little brighter, more given to the intellectual he may be become since the reception and would peradventure list not so much on reading the Goncourt journals or Abbé Galiani if he had not the relation with the higher world, nor had the privy memorandum. Psychology, my dear friend. Disease, indeed I mean repulsive, individual, private disease, makes a certain critical contrast to the world, to life's mean, puts a man in a mood rebellious and ironic against the bourgeois order, makes its man take refuge with the free spirit, with books, in cogitation. But more it is not with Spengler. The space that is still allotted him for reading, quoting, drinking red wine, and idling about, it isn't we who have sold it to him, it is anything rather than genialized time. A man of the world, just singed by our flame, weary, mildly interesting, no more. He rots away, liver, kidneys, stomach, heart, bowels; some day his voice will be a croak, or he will be deaf, after a few years he will ingloriously shuffle off this coyle, with a cynical quip on his lips — what then? It forceth but little, there was never any illumination, enhancing or enthusiasm, for it was not of the brain, not cerebral, you understand — our little ones in that case made no force of the upper and noble, it had obviously no fascination for them, it did not come to a metastasis into the metaphysical, metavenereal, meta-infectivus. . . ."

I (with venom): "How long must I needs sit and freeze and listen to your intolerable gibberish?"

He: "Gibberish? Have to listen? That's a funny chord to strike. In mine opinion you listen very attentively and are but impatient to know more, yea and all. You have just asked eagerly after your friend Spengler in Munich, and if I had not cut you off, you would avidly have asked me all this whole time about hell's fiery pit. Don't, I beg of you, pretend you're put on. I also have my self-respect, and know that I am no unbidden guest. To be short, the meta-spirochætose, that is the meningeal process, and I assure you, it is just as though certain of the little ones had a passion for the upper storey, a special preference for the head region, the meninges, the dura mater, the tentorium, and the pia, which protect the tender parenchyma inside and from the moment of the first general contagion swarmed passionately hither."

I: "It is with you as you say. The rampallion seems to have studied *medicinam*."

He: "No more than you theology, that is in bits and as a specialist. Will you gainsay that you studied the best of the arts and sciences also only as specialist and amateur? Your interest had to do with — me. I am obliged to you. But wherefore should I, Esmeralda's friend and cohabitant, in which quality you behold me before you, not have a special interest in the medical field concerned, which borders on it, and be at home in it as a specialist? Indeed, I constantly and with the greatest attention follow the latest results of research in this field. Item, some doctores assert and swear by Peter and Paul there must be brain specialists among the little ones, amateurs in the cerebral sphere, in short a *virus nerveux*. But these experts are in the aforementioned box. It is arsie-versie in the matter, for 'tis the brain which gapes at their visitation and looks forward expectantly, as you to mine, that it invites them to itself, draws them unto it, as though it could not bear at all to wait for them. Do you still remember? The philosopher, *De anima*: 'the acts of the person acting are performed on him the previously disposed to suffer it.' There you have it: on the disposition, the readiness, the invitation, all depends. That some men be more qualified to the practising of witch-craft, then other, and we know well how to discern them, of that already are aware the worthy authors of the *Malleus*."

I: "Slanderer, I have no connection with you. I did not invite you."

He: "La, la, sweet innocence! The far-travelled client of my little ones was I suppose not forewarned? And your doctors too you chose with sure instinct."

I: "I looked them out in the directory. Whom should I have

asked? And who could have told me that they would leave me in the lash? What did you do with my two physicians?"

He: "Put them away, put them away. Oh, of course we put the blunderers away in your interest. And at the right moment iwis, not too soon and not too late, when they had got the thing in train with their quackery and quicksilvery, and if we had left them they might have botched the beautiful case. We allowed them the provocation, then *basta* and away with them! So soon as they with their specific treatment had properly limited the first, cutaneously emphasized general infiltration, and thus given a powerful impetus to the metastasis upwards, their business was accomplished, they had to be removed. The fools, to wit, do not know, and if they know they cannot change it, that by the general treatment the upper, the meta-venereal processes are powerfully accelerated. Indeed, by not treating the fresh stages it is often enough forwarded; in short, the way they do it is wrong. In no case could we let the provocation by quackery and quickery go on. The regression of the general penetration was to be left to itself, that the progression up there should go on pretty slowly, in order that years, decades, of nigromantic time should be saved for you, a whole houre-glasseful of divel-time, genius-time. Narrow and small and finely circumscribed it is today, four years after you got it, the place up there in you; but it is there, the hearth, the workroom of the little ones, who on the liquor way, the water way as it were, got there, the place of incipient illumination."

I: "Do I trap you, blockhead? Do you betray yourself and name to me yourself the place in my brain, the fever hearth, that makes me imagine you, and without which you were not? Betrayest to me that in excited state I see and hear you, yet you are but a bauling before my eyes!"

He: "The Great God Logick! Little fool, it is topside the other waie: I am not the product of your pia hearth up there, rather the hearth enables you to perceive me, understand, and without it, indeed, you would not see me. Is therefore my existence dependent on your incipient drunkenness? Do I belong in your subjective? I ask you! Only patience, what goes on and progresses there will give you the capacity for a great deal more, will conquer quite other impediments and make you to soar over lameness and halting. Wait till Good Friday, and 'twill soon be Easter! Wait one, ten, twelve years, until the illumination, the dazzling radiance as all lame scruples and doubts fall away and you will know for what you pay, why you make over body and

DR. FAUSTUS 235

soul to us. Then shall osmotic growths *sine pudore* sprout out of the apothecary's sowing. . . ."

I (start up): "Hold thy foul mouth! I forbid thee to speak of my father!"

He: "Oh, thy father is not so ill placed in my mouth. He was a shrewd one, always wanting to speculate the elements. The mygrim, the point of attack for the knife-pains of the little sea-maid — after all, you have them from him. . . . Moreover, I have spoken quite correctly: osmosis, fluid diffusion, the proliferation process — the whole magic intreats of these. You have there the spinal sac with the pulsating column of fluid therein, reaching to the cerebrum, to the meninges, in whose tissues the furtive venereal meningitis is at its soundless stealthy work. But our little ones could not reach into the inside, into the parenchyma, however much they are drawn, however much they longingly draw thither — without fluid diffusion, osmosis, with the cell-fluid of the pia watering it, dissolving the tissue, and paving a way inside for the scourges. Everything comes from osmosis, my friend, in whose teasing manifestations you so early diverted yourself."

I: "Your baseness makes me to laugh. I wish Schildknapp would come back that I might laugh with him. I would tell him father-stories, I too. Of the tears in my father's eyes, when he said: 'And yet they are dead!' "

He: "Cock's body! You were right to laugh at his ruthful tears — aside from the fact that whoever has, by nature, dealings with the tempter is always at variance with the feelings of people, always tempted to laugh when they weep, and weep when they laugh. What then does 'dead' mean, when the flora grows so rankly, in such diverse colours and shapes? And when they are even heliotropic? What does 'dead' mean when the drop displays such a healthy appetite? What is sick, what well, my friend, about that we must not let the philistine have the last word. Whether he does understand life so well remains a question. What has come about by the way of death, of sickness, at that life has many a time clutched with joy and let itself be led by it higher and further. Have you forgotten what you learned in the schools, that God can bring good out of evil and that the occasion to it shall not be marred? Item, a man must have been always ill and mad in order that others no longer need be so. And where madness begins to be malady, there is nobody knows at all. If a man taken up in a rapture write in a margent note: 'Am blissful! Am beside myself! That I call new and great! Seething bliss of inspiration! My cheeks glow like molten iron! I am raging, you will all be raging, when this comes to you! Then God succour your poor sely souls!' Is that still mad healthiness, normal madness, or has he got it in the *meninges*? The bourgeois is the last to diagnose; for long in any case nothing further about it strikes him as strange, because forsooth artists are queer birds anyhow. If next day on a rebound he cry: 'Oh, flat and stale! Oh, a dog's life, when a man can do nothing! Were there but a war, so that somewhat would happen! If I could croak in good style! May hell pity me, for I am a son of hell!' Does he really mean that? Is it the literal truth that he says there of hell, or is it only metaphor for a little normal Dürer melancolia? In summa, we simply give you that for which the classic poet, the lofty and stately genius, so beautifully thanked his gods:

> All do the gods give, the Eternal,
> To their favourites, wholly:
> All the joys, the eternal,
> All the pangs, the eternal,
> Wholly."

I: "Mocker and liar! *Si diabolus non esset mendax et homicida!* If I must listen, at least speak to me not of sane and sound greatness and native gold! I know that gold made with fire instead of by the sun is not genuine."

He: "Who says so? Has the sun better fire then the kitchen? And sane and sound greatness! Whenever I hear of such, I laugh! Do you believe in anything like an *ingenium* that has nothing to do with hell? *Non datur!* The artist is the brother of the criminal and the madman. Do you ween that any important work was ever wrought except its maker learned to understand the way of the criminal and madman? Morbid and healthy! Without the morbid would life all its whole life never have survived. Genuine and false! Are we land-loping knaves? Do we draw the good things out of the nose of nothing? Where nothing is, there the Devil too has lost his right and no pallid Venus produces anything worth while! We make naught new — that is other people's matter. We only release, only set free. We let the lameness and self-consciousness, the chaste scruples and doubts go to the Devil. We physic away fatigue merely by a little charm-hyperæmia, the great and the small, of the person and of the time. That is it, you do not think of the passage of time, you do not think historically, when you complain that such and such a one could have it 'wholly,' joys and pains endlessly, without the hour-glass being set for him, the reckoning finally made. What he in his classical decades could have without us, certainly, that, nowadaies, we alone have to offer. And we offer better, we offer only the right and true — that is no lenger the classical, my friend, what we give to experience, it is the archaic, the primeval, that which long since has not been tried. Who knows today, who even knew in classical times, what inspiration is, what genuine, old, primeval enthusiasm, insicklied critique, unparalysed by thought or by the mortal domination of reason — who knows the divine raptus? I believe, indeed, the devil passes for a man of destructive criticism? Slander and again slander, my friend! Gog's sacrament! If there is anything he cannot abide, if there's one thing in the whole world he cannot stomach, it is destructive criticism. What he wants and gives is triumph over it, is shining, sparkling, vainglorious unreflectiveness!"

I: "Charlatan!"

He: "Yea, of a truth. When you set right the grossest false understandings about yourself, more out of love of truth than of self, then you are a cheap jack. I will not let my mouth be stopped by your shamefast ungraciousness; I know that you are but suppressing your emotions, you are listening to me with as much pleasure as the maid to the whisperer in church. . . . Let us just for an instance take the 'idea' — what you call that, what for a hundred years or so you have been calling it, sithence earlier there was no such category, as little as musical copyright and all that. The idea, then, a matter of three, four bars, no more, isn't it? All the residue is elaboration, sticking at it. Or isn't it? Good. But now we are all experts, all critics: we note that the idea is nothing new, that it all too much reminds us of something in Rimsky-Korsakov or Brahms. What is to be done? You just change it. But a changed idea, is that still an idea? Take Beethoven's notebooks. There is no thematic conception there as God gave it. He remoulds it and adds 'Meilleur.' Scant confidence in God's prompting, scant respect for it is expressed in that 'Meilleur' — itself not so very enthusiastic either. A genuine inspiration, immediate, absolute, unquestioned, ravishing, where there is no choice, no tinkering, no possible improvement; where all is as a sacred mandate, a visitation received by the possessed one with faltering and stumbling step, with shudders of awe from head to foot, with tears of joy blinding his eyes: no, that is not possible with God, who leaves the understanding too much to do. It comes but from the divel, the true master and giver of such rapture."

Even as he spake, and easily, a change came over the fellow: as I looked straight at him meseemed he was different, sat there no longer a rowdy losel, but changed for the better, I give my word. He now had on a white collar and a bow tie, horn-rimmed spectacles on his hooked nose. Behind them the dark, rather reddened eyes gleamed moistly. A mixture of sharpness and softness was on the visage; nose sharp, lips sharp, yet soft the chin with a dimple, a dimple in the cheek too — pale and vaulted the brow, out of which the hair retreats toward the top, yet from there to the sides thick, standing up black and woolly: a member of the intelligentsia, writer on art, on music for the ordinary press, a theoretician and critic, who himself composes, so far as thinking allows him. Soft, thin hands as well, which accompany his talk with gestures of refined awkwardness, sometimes delicately stroking his thick hair at temples and back. This was now the picture of the visitor in the sofa-corner. Taller he had not grown, and above all the voice, nasal, distinct, cultivated, pleasing, had remained the same; it kept the identity in all the fluidity of appearance. Then I hear him speak and see his wide lips, pinched in at the corners under the badly shaved upper one, protrude as he articulates.

"What is art today? A pilgrimage on peas. There's more to dancing in these times then a pair of red shoon, and you are not the only one the devil depresses. Look at them, your colleagues — I know, of course, that you do not look at them, you don't look in their direction, you cherish the illusion that you are alone and want everything for yourself, all the whole curse of the time. But do look at them for your consolation, your fellow-inaugurators of the new music, I mean the honest, serious ones, who see the consequences of the situation. I speak not of the folklorists and neo-classic asylists whose modernness consists in their forbidding themselves a musical outbreak and in wearing with more or less dignity the style-garment of a pre-individualistic period. Persuade themselves and others that the tedious has become interesting, because the interesting has begun to grow tedious."

I had to laugh, for although the cold continued to pursue me, I must confess that since his alteration I felt more comfortable in his presence. He smiled as well: that is, the corners of his mouth tensed a little and he slightly narrowed his eyes.

"They are powerless too," he went on, "but I believe we, thou and I, lever prefer the decent impotence of those who scorn to cloak the general sickness under colour of a dignified mummery. But the sickness is general, and the straightforward ones shew the symptoms just as well as the producers of back-formations. Does not production threaten to come to an end? And whatever of serious stuff gets on to paper betrays effort and distaste. Extrane-

ous, social grounds? Lack of demand? And as in the pre-liberal
period the possibility of production depends largely on the chance
of a Mæcenas? Right, but as explanation doesn't go far enough.
Composing itself has got too hard, devilishly hard. Where work
does not go any longer with sincerity how is one to work? But
so it stands, my friend, the masterpiece, the self-sufficient form,
belongs to traditional art, emancipated art rejects it. The thing
begins with this: that the right of command over all the tone-
combinations ever applied by no means belongs to you. Impossible the diminished seventh, impossible certain chromatic passing notes. Every composer of the better sort carries within
himself a canon of the forbidden, the self-forbidding, which by
degrees includes all the possibilities of tonality, in other words
all traditional music. What has become false, worn-out cliché, the
canon decides. Tonal sounds, chords in a composition with the
technical horizon of today, outbid every dissonance. As such
they are to be used, but cautiously and only *in extremis*, for the
shock is worse than the harshest discord of old. Everything depends on the technical horizon. The diminished seventh is right
and full of expression at the beginning of Op. 111. It corresponds
to Beethoven's whole technical niveau, doesn't it? — the tension
between consonance and the harshest dissonance known to him.
The principle of tonality and its dynamics lend to the chord its
specific weight. It has lost it — by a historical process which nobody reverses. Listen to the obsolete chord; even by itself alone
it stands for a technical general position which contradicts the
actual. Every sound carries the whole, carries the whole story in
itself. But therefore the judgment of the ear, what is right and
what wrong, is indisputably and directly related to it, to this one
chord, in itself not false, entirely without abstract reference to
the general technical niveau: we have there a claim on rightness
which the sound image makes upon the artist — a little severe,
don't you think? Then does not his activity exhaust itself in the
execution of the thing contained within the objective conditions of
production? In every bar that one dares to think, the situation as
regards technique presents itself to him as a problem. Technique
in all its aspects demands of him every moment that he do justice
to it, and give the only right answer which it at any moment permits. It comes down to this, that his compositions are nothing
more than solutions of that kind; nothing but the solving of technical puzzles. Art becomes critique. That is something quite honourable, who denies it? Much rebellion in strict obedience is
needed, much independence, much courage. But the danger of

being uncreative — what do you think? Is it perhaps still only a danger, or is it already a fixed and settled fact?"

He paused. He looked at me through his glasses with his humid reddened eyes, raised his hand in a fastidious gesture, and stroked his hair with his two middle fingers. I said:

"What are you waiting for? Should I admire your mockery? I have never doubted ye would know how to say to me what I know. Your way of producing it is very purposeful. What you mean by it all is to shew me that I could avail myself of, nor have, no one otherwise then the divel to kindle me to my work. And ye could at the same time not exclude the theoretic possibility of spontaneous harmony between a man's own needs and the moment, the possibility of 'rightness,' of a natural harmony, out of which one might create without a thought or any compulsion."

He (laughing): "A very theoretic possibility, in fact. My dear fellow, the situation is too critical to be dealt with without critique. Moreover I reject the reproach of a tendentious illumination of things. We do not need to involve ourselves further in dialectic extravagances on your account. What I do not deny is a certain general satisfaction which the state of the 'work' generally vouchsafes me. I am against 'works,' by and large. Why should I not find some pleasure in the sickness which has attacked the idea of the musical work? Don't blame it on social conditions. I am aware you tend to do so, and are in the habit of saying that these conditions produce nothing fixed and stable enough to guarantee the harmony of the self-sufficient work. True, but unimportant. The prohibitive difficulties of the work lie deep in the work itself. The historical movement of the musical material has turned against the self-contained work. It shrinks in time, it scorns extension in time, which is the dimensions of a musical work, and lets it stand empty. Not out of impotence, not out of incapacity to give form. Rather from a ruthless demand for compression, which taboos the superfluous, negates the phrase, shatters the ornament, stands opposed to any extension of time, which is the life-form of the work. Work, time, and pretence, they are one, and together they fall victim to critique. It no longer tolerates pretence and play, the fiction, the self-glorification of form, which censors the passions and human suffering, divides out the parts, translates into pictures. Only the non-fictional is still permissible, the unplayed, the undisguised and untransfigured expression of suffering in its actual moment. Its impotence and extremity are so ingrained that no seeming play with them is any lenger allowed."

I (very ironically): "Touching, touching! The devil waxes pathetic. The poor devil moralizes. Human suffering goes to his heart. How high-mindedly he shits on art! You would have done better not to mention your antipathy to the work if you did not want me to realize that your animadversions are naught but divel-farting."

He (unperturbed): "So far, so good. But at bottom you do agree that to face the facts of the time is neither sentimental nor malicious. Certain things are no longer possible. The pretence of feeling as a compositional work of art, the self-satisfied pretence of music itself, has become impossible and no longer to be pre-served — I mean the perennial notion that prescribed and formal-ized elements shall be introduced as though they were the in-violable necessity of the single case. Or put it the other way round: the special case behaving as though it were identical with the prescribed and familiar formula. For four hundred years all great music has found its satisfaction in pretending that this unity has been accomplished without a break — it has pleased itself with confusing the conventional universal law to which it is subject with its own peculiar concern. My friend, it cannot go on. The criticism of ornament, convention, and the abstract generality are all the same one. What it demolishes is the pretence in the bourgeois work of art; music, although she makes no picture, is also subject to it. Certainly, this 'not making a picture' gives her an advantage over the other arts. But music too by untiringly con-forming her specific concerns to the ruling conventions has as far as she could played a role in the highbrow swindle. The inclu-sion of expression in the general appeasement is the innermost principle of musical pretence. It is all up with it. The claim to consider the general harmonically contained in the particular contradicts itself. It is all up with the once bindingly valid con-ventions, which guaranteed the freedom of play."

I: "A man could know that and recognize freedom above and beyond all critique. He could heighten the play, by playing with forms out of which, as he well knew, life has disappeared."

He: "I know, I know. Parody. It might be fun, if it were not so melancholy in its aristocratic nihilism. Would you promise yourself much pleasure and profit from such tricks?"

I (retort angrily): "No."

He: "Terse and testy. But why so testy? Because I put to you friendly questions of conscience, just between ourselves? Because I shewed you your despairing heart and set before your eyes with the expert's insight the difficulties absolutely inseparable from

composition today? You might even so value me as an expert. The
Devil ought to know something about music. If I mistake not,
you were reading just now in a book by the Christian in love with
æsthetics. He knew and understood my particular relation to this
beautiful art — the most Christian of all arts, he finds — but Christian in reverse, as it were: introduced and developed by Christianity indeed, but then rejected and banned as the Divel's Kingdom.— so there you are. A highly theological business, music —
the way sin is, the way I am. The passion of that Christian for
music is true passion, and as such knowledge and corruption in
one. For there is true passion only in the ambiguous and ironic.
The highest passion concerns the absolutely questionable. . . .
No, musical I am indeed, don't worry about that. I have sung you
the role of poor Judas because of the difficulties into which music
like everything else has got today. Should I not have done so?
But I did it only to point out to you that you should break
through them, that you should lift yourself above them to giddy
heights of self-admiration, and do such things that you will behold them only with shudders of awe."

I: "An annunciation, in fact. I am to grow osmotic growths."

He: "It comes to the same thing. Ice crystals, or the same made
of starch, sugar, and cellulose, both are nature; we ask, for which
shall we praise Nature more. Your tendency, my friend, to inquire after the objective, the so-called truth, to question as worth-
less the subjective, pure experience: that is truly petty bourgeois,
you ought to overcome it. As you see me, so I exist to you. What
serves it to ask whether I really am? Is not 'really' what works,
is not truth experience and feeling? What uplifts you, what in-
creases your feeling of power and might and domination, damn
it, that is the truth — and whether ten times a lie when looked at
from the moral angle. This is what I think: that an untruth of a
kind that enhances power holds its own against any ineffectively
virtuous truth. And I mean too that creative, genius-giving disease,
disease that rides on high horse over all hindrances, and springs
with drunken daring from peak to peak, is a thousand times
dearer to life than plodding healthiness. I have never heard anything stupider then that from disease only disease can come. Life
is not scrupulous — by morals it sets not a fart. It takes the reckless product of disease, feeds on and digests it, and as soon as it
takes it to itself it is health. Before the fact of fitness for life, my
good man, all distinction of disease and health falls away. A whole
host and generation of youth, receptive, sound to the core, flings
itself on the work of the morbid genius, made genius by disease:

admires it, praises it, exalts it, carries it away, assimilates it unto
itself and makes it over to culture, which lives not on home-made
bread alone, but as well on provender and poison from the apothecary's shop at the sign of the Blessed Messengers. Thus saith to you
the unbowdlerized Sammael. He guarantees not only that toward
the end of your houre-glasse years your sense of your power and
splendour will more and more outweigh the pangs of the little
sea-maid and finally mount to most triumphant well-being, to a
sense of bursting health, to the walk and way of a god. That is
only the subjective side of the thing, I know; it would not suffice,
it would seem to you unsubstantial. Know, then, we pledge you
the success of that which with our help you will accomplish. You
will lead the way, you will strike up the march of the future, the
lads will swear by your name, who thanks to your madness will
no longer need to be mad. On your madness they will feed in
health, and in them you will become healthy. Do you understand? Not only will you break through the paralysing difficulties
of the time — you will break through time itself, by which I
mean the cultural epoch and its cult, and dare to be barbaric,
twice barbaric indeed, because of coming after the humane, after
all possible root-treatment and bourgeois raffinement. Believe me,
barbarism even has more grasp of theology then has a culture fallen away from cult, which even in the religious has seen only culture, only the humane, never excess, paradox, the mystic passion,
the utterly unbourgeois ordeal. But I hope you do not marvel
that 'the Great Adversary' speaks to you of religion. Gog's nails!
Who else, I should like to know, is to speak of it today? Surely
not the liberal theologian! After all I am by now its sole custodian!
In whom will you recognize theological existence if not in me?
And who can lead a theological existence without me? The religious is certainly my line: as certainly as it is not the line of
bourgeois culture. Since culture fell away from the cult and made
a cult of itself, it has become nothing else then a falling away;
and all the world after a mere five hundred years is as sick and
tired of it as though, *salva venia*, they had ladled it in with cook-
ing-spoons."

    It was now, it was even a little before this, when he was utter-
ing his taunts and mockage about the theological existence of the
Devil and being the guardian of the religious life, speaking in
flowing language like a lectour, that I noticed the merchaunte before me on the sofa had changed again; he seemed no longer to
be the spectacled intellectual and amateur of music who had
awhile been speaking. And he was no lenger just sitting in his

corner, he was riding légèrement, half-sitting, on the curved arm
of the sofa, his fingertips crossed in his lap and both thumbs
spread out. A little parted beard on his chin wagged up and down
as he talked, and above his open lips with the sharp teeth behind
them was the little moustache with stiff twisted points. I had to
laugh, in all my frozenness, at his metamorphosis into the old
familiar.

"Obedient servant," I say. "I ought to know you; and I find it
most civil of you to give me a privatissimum here in our hall. As
ye now are, my Protean friend, I look to find you ready to
quench my thirst for knowledge and conclusively demonstrate
your independent presence by telling me not only things I know
but also of some I would like to know. You have lectured me a
good deal about the houre-glasse time you purvey; also about the
payment in pains to be made now and again for the higher life;
but not about the end, about what comes afterwards, the eternal
obliteration. That is what excites curiosity, and you have not,
long as you have been squatting there, given space to the question in all your talk. Shall I not know the price in cross and
kreuzer? Answer me: what is life like in the Dragon's Den? What
have they to expect, who have listened to you, in the *spelunca*?"

He (laughs a falsetto laugh): "Of the *pernicies*, the *confutatio*
you want to have knowledge? Call that prying, I do, the ex-
uberance of the youthful scholar. There is time enough, so much
that you can't see to the end of it, and so much excitement coming first — you will have a plenty to do besides taking heed to the
end, or even noticing the moment when it might be time to take
heed to the ending. But I'll not deny you the information and do
not need to palliate, for what can seriously trouble you, that is
so far off? Only it is not easy actually to speak thereof — that is,
one can really not speak of it at all, because the actual is beyond
what by word can be declared; many words may be used and
fashioned, but all together they are but tokens, standing for names
which do not and cannot make claim to describe what is never
to be described and denounced in words. That is the secret delight and security of hell, that it is not to be informed on, that it
is protected from speech, that it just is, but cannot be public in
the newspaper, be brought by any word to critical knowledge,
wherefor precisely the words 'subterranean,' 'cellar,' 'thick walls,'
'soundlessness,' 'forgottenness,' 'hopelessness,' are the poor, weak
symbols. One must just be satisfied with symbolism, my good
man, when one is speaking of hell, for there everything ends —
not only the word that describes, but everything altogether. This

is indeed the chiefest characteristic and what in most general terms is to be uttered about it: both that which the newcomer thither first experiences, and what at first with his as it were sound senses he cannot grasp, and will not understand, because his reason or what limitation soever of his understanding prevents him, in short because it is quite unbelievable enough to make him turn white as a sheet, although it is opened to him at once on greeting, in the most emphatic and concise words, that *'here everything leaves off.'* Every compassion, every grace, every sparing, every last trace of consideration for the incredulous, imploring objection 'that you verily cannot do so unto a soul': it is done, it happens, and indeed without being called to any reckoning in words; in soundless cellar, far down beneath God's hearing, and happens to all eternity. No, it is bad to speak of it, it lies aside from and outside of speech, language has naught to do with and no connection with it, wherefore she knows not rightly what time-form to apply to it and helps herself perforce with the future tense, even as it is written: 'There shall be wailing and gnashing of teeth.' Good; these are a few word-sounds, chosen out of a rather extreme sphere of language, yet but weak symbols and without proper reference to what 'shall be' there, unrecorded, unreckoned, between thick walls. True it is that inside these echoless walls it gets right loud, measureless loud, and by much overfilling the ear with screeching and beseeching, gurgling and groaning, with yauling and bauling and caterwauling, with horrid winding and grinding and racking ecstasies of anguish no man can hear his own tune, for that it smothers in the general, in the thick-clotted diapason of trills and chirps lured from this everlasting dispensation of the unbelievable combined with the irresponsible. Nothing forgetting the dismal groans of lust mixted therewith; since endless torment, with no possible collapse, no swoon to put a period thereto, degenerates into shameful pleasure, wherefore such as have some intuitive knowledge speak indeed of the 'lusts of hell.' And therewith mockage and the extreme of ignominy such as belongs with martyrdom; for this bliss of hell is like a deep-voiced pitifull jeering and scorne of all the immeasureable anguish; it is accompanied by whinnying laughter and the pointing finger; whence the doctrine that the damned have not only torment but also mockery and shame to bear; yea, that hell is to be defined as a monstrous combination of suffering and derision, unendurable yet to be endured world without end. There will they devour their proper tongues for greatness of the agony, yet make no common cause on that account, for rather they are full of hatred and scorn against each other, and in the midst of their trills and quavers hurl at one another the foulest oaths. Yea, the finest and proudest, who never let a lewd word pass their lips, are forced to use the filthiest of all. A part of their torment and lust of shame standeth therein that they must cogitate the extremity of filthiness."

I: "Allow me, this is the first word you have said to me about what manner of suffering the damned have to bear. Pray note that you have only lectured to me on the affects of hell, but not about what objectively and in fact must await the damned."

He: "Your curiosity is childish and indiscreet. I put that in the foreground; but I am very well aware indeed, my good soul, what hides behind it. You assaye to question me in order to be feared, to be afraid of the pangs of hell. For the thought of backward turning and rescue, of your so-called soul-heal, of withdrawing from the promise lurks in the back of your mind and you are acting to summon up the *attritio cordis*, the heartfelt anguish and dread of what is to come, of which you may well have heard, that by it man can arrive at the so-called blessedness. Let me tell you, that is an entirely exploded theology. The attrition-theory has been scientifically superseded. It is shown that *contritio* is necessary, the real and true protestant remorse for sin, which means not merely fear repentance by churchly regulation but inner, religious conversion; ask yourself whether you are capable of that; ask yourself, your pride will not fail of an answer. The longer the less will you be able and willing to let yourself in for *contritio*, sithence the extravagant life you will lead is a great indulgence, out of the which a man does not so simply find the way back into the good safe average. Therefore, to your reassurance be it said, even hell will not afford you aught essentially new, only the more or less accustomed, and proudly so. It is at bottom only a continuation of the extravagant existence. To knit up in two words its quintessence, or if you like its chief matter, is that it leaves its denizens only the choice between extreme cold and an extreme heat which can melt granite. Between these two states they flee roaring to and fro, for in the one the other always seems heavenly refreshment but is at once and in the most hellish meaning of the word intolerable. The extreme in this must please you."

I: "It liketh me. Meanwhile I would warn you lest you feel all too certain of me. A certain shallowness in your theology might tempt you thereto. You rely on my pride preventing me from the *contritio* necessary to salvacion, and do not bethink yourself that there is a prideful *contritio*. The remorse of Cain, for instance, who was of the firm persuasion that his sin was greater than could ever be forgiven him. The *contritio* without hope, as complete disbelief in the possibility of mercy and forgiveness, the rocklike firm conviction of the sinner that he has done too grossly for even the Everlasting Goodness to be able to forgive his sin — only that is the true *contritio*. I call your attention to the fact that it is the nighest to redemption, for Goodness the most irresistible of all. You will admit that the everyday sinner can be but very moderately interesting to Mercy. In his case the act of grace has but little impetus, it is but a feeble motion. Mediocrity, in fact, has no theological status. A capacity for sin so healless that it makes its man despair from his heart of redemption — that is the true theological way to salvation."

He: "You are a sly dog! And where will the likes of you get the single-mindedness, the naïve recklessness of despair, which would be the premise for this sinfull waye to salvacion? Is it not playne to you that the conscious speculation on the charm which great guilt exercises on Goodness makes the act of mercy to the uttermost unpossible to it?"

I: "And yet only through this *non plus ultra* can the high prick of the dramatic-theological existence be arrived at; I mean the most abandoned guilt and the last and most irresistible challenge to the Everlasting Goodness."

He: "Not bad. Of a truth ingenious. And now I will tell you that precisely heads of your sort comprise the population of hell. It is not so easy to get into hell, we should long have been suffering for lack of space if we let Philip and Cheyney in. But your theologian in grain, your arrant wily-pie who speculates on speculation because he has speculation in his blood already from the father's side — there must be foul work an he did not belong to the divel."

As he said that, or even somewhat afore, the fellow changed again, the way clouds do, without knowing it, apparently; is no longer sitting on the arm of the couch before me in the room; there back in the sofa-corner is the unspeakable losel, the cheesy rapscallion in the cap, with the red eyes. And says to me in his slow, nasal, actor's voice:

"To make an end and a conclusion will be agreeable to you. I have devoted much time and tarried long to entreat of this matter with you — I hope and trust you realize. But also you are an attractive case, that I freely admit. From early on we had an eye on you, on your quick, arrogant head, your mighty *ingenium* and *memoriam.* They have made you study theology, as your conceit devised it, but you would soon name yourself no lenger of theologians, but put the Good Boke under the bench and from then on stuck to the figures, characters, and incantations of music, which pleased us not a little. For your vaine glory aspired to the elemental, and you thought to gain it in the form most mete for you, where algebraic magic is married with corresponding cleverness and calculation and yet at the same time it always boldly warres against reason and sobriety. But did we then not know that you were too clever and cold and chaste for the element; and did we not know that you were sore vexed thereat and piteously bored with your shamefast cleverness? Thus it was our busily prepensed plan that you should run into our arms, that is, of my little one, Esmeralda, and that you got it, the illumination, the aphrodisiacum of the brain, after which with body and soul and mind you so desperately longed. To be short, between us there needs no crosse way in the Spesser's Wood and no cercles. We are in league and business — with your blood you have affirmed it and promised yourself to us, and are baptized ours. This my visit concerns only the confirmation thereof. Time you have taken from us, a genius's time, high-flying time, full XXIV years *ab dato recessi*, which we set to you as the limit. When they are finished and fully expired, which is not to be foreseen, and such a time is also an eternity — then you shalbe fetched. Against this meanwhile shall we be in all things subject and obedient, and hell shall profit you, if you renay all living creature, all the Heavenly Host and all men, for that must be."

I (in an exceeding cold draught): "What? That is new. What signifies the *clausula*?"

He: "Renounce, it means. What otherwise? Do you think that jealousy dwells in the height and not also in the depths? To us you are, fine, well-create creature, promised and espoused. Thou maist not love."

I (really have to laugh): "Not love! Poor divel! Will you substantiate the report of your stupidity and wear a bell even as a cat, that you will base business and promise on so elastic, so ensnaring a concept as love? Will the Devil prohibit lust? If it be not so, then he must endure sympathy, yea, even *caritas*, else he is betrayed just as it is written in the books. What I have invited, and wherefore you allege that I have promised you — what is then the source of it, prithee, but love, even if that poisoned by you with God's sanction? The bond in which you assert we stand has itself to do with love, you doating fool. You allege that I wanted it and repaired to the wood, the crosse-waye, for the sake of the work. But they say that work itself has to do with love."

He (laughing through his nose): "Do, re, mi! Be assured that thy psychological feints do not trap me, any better then do the theological. Psychology — God warrant us, do you still hold with it? That is bad, bourgeois nineteenth century. The epoch is heartily sick of it, it will soon be a red rag to her, and he will simply get a crack on the pate, who disturbs life by psychology. We are entering into times, my friend, which will not be hood-winked by psychology. . . . This *en passant*. My condition was clear and direct, determined by the legitimate jealousy of hell. Love is forbidden you, in so far as it warms. Thy life shall be cold, therefore thou shalt love no human being. What are you thinking, then? The illumination leaves your mental powers to the last unimpaired, yes, heightens them to an ecstatie of delirium — what shall it then go short of save the dear soul and the price-less life of feeling? A general chilling of your life and your re-lations to men lies in the nature of things — rather it lies already in your nature; in feith we lay upon you nothing new, the little ones make nothing new and strange out of you, they only ingeni-ously strengthen and exaggerate all that you already are. The cold-ness in you is perhaps not prefigured, as well as the paternal head paynes out of which the pangs of the little sea-maid are to come? Cold we want you to be, that the fires of creation shall be hot enough to warm yourself in. Into them you will flee out of the cold of your life. . . ."

I: "And from the burning back to the ice. It seems to be hell in advance, which is already offered me on earth."

He: "It is that extravagant living, the only one that suffices a proud soul. Your arrogance will probably never want to exchange with a lukewarm one. Do you strike with me? A work-filled eternity of human life shall you enjoy. When the houre-glasse runs out, then I shall have good power to deal and dole with, to move and manage the fine-created Creature after my way and my pleasure, be it in life, soul, flesh, blood or goods — to all eternity!"

There it was again, the uncontrollable disgust that had already seized me once before and shaken me, together with the glacial wave of cold which came over me again from the tight-trousered *strizzi* there. I forgot myself in a fury of disgust, it was like a faint-ing-fit. And then I heard Schildknapp's easy, everyday voice, he sat there in the sofa-corner, saying to me:

"Of course you didn't miss anything. Newspapers and two

games of billiards, a round of Marsala and the good souls calling the *governo* over the coals."

I was sitting in my summer suit, by my lamp, the Christian's book on my knee. Can't be anything else: in my excitement I must have chased the losel out and carried my coat and rug back before Schildknapp returned.

CHAPTER XXVI

It consoles me to be able to tell myself that the reader cannot lay to my charge the extraordinary size of the last chapter, which considerably exceeds the disquieting number of pages in the one on Kretschmar's lectures. The unreasonable demand made upon the reader does not lie at my door and need not trouble me. To mitigate Adrian's account by subjecting it to any kind of editing; to dismiss the "dialogue" in a few numbered paragraphs (will the reader please note the protesting quotation-marks I have given the word, without concealing from myself that they can remove from it only part of its indwelling horror); to do this no regard for the possible failure of the reader's capacity could possibly move me. With rueful loyalty I had to reproduce a given thing; to transfer it from Adrian's music-paper to my manuscript; and that I have done, not only word for word, but also, I may say, letter for letter — often laying down the pen to recover myself, to measure my study floor with heavy, pensive tread or to throw myself on my sofa with my hands clasped upon my brow. So that, however strange it may seem, this chapter, which I had only to copy down, actually did not leave my sometimes trembling hand any faster than the earlier ones which I composed myself.

To copy, understandingly and critically, is in fact — at least for me, and Monsignor Hinterpförtner agrees with me — an occupation as intensive and time-consuming as putting down one's own thoughts. It is likely that the reader may before now have underestimated the number of days and weeks that I had spent upon the life-story of my departed friend. It is even more probable that his imagination will have fallen behind the point of time at which I am composing the present lines. He may laugh at my pedantry, but I consider it right to let him know that since I began writing almost a year has passed; and that whilst I have been composing the last chapters, April 1944 has arrived.

That date, of course, is the point where I now stand in my actual writing and not the one up to which my narrative has progressed. That has only reached the autumn of 1912, twenty months before the outbreak of the last war, when Adrian and Rüdiger Schildknapp came back from Palestrina to Munich and he lodged at first in Pension Gisela in Schwabing. I do not know why this double time-reckoning arrests my attention or why I am at pains to point out both the personal and the objective, the time in which the narrator moves and that in which the narrative does so. This is a quite extraordinary interweaving of time-units, destined, moreover, to include even a third: namely, the time which one day the courteous reader will take for the reading of what has been written; at which point he will be dealing with a threefold ordering of time: his own, that of the chronicler, and historic time.

I will not lose myself further in these speculations, to my mind as idle as they are agitating. I will only add that the word "historic" fits with a far more sinister emphasis the time in which, than about which, I write. In these last days the battle for Odessa has been raging, with heavy losses, ending in the recapture by the Russians of the famous city on the Black Sea — though the enemy was not able to disorganize our retreat. The case will be the same with Sebastopol, another of our pledges unto death, which the obviously superior antagonist appears to mean to wrest from us. Meanwhile the terrors of almost daily air raids upon our beleaguered Fortress Europa grows into incredible dimensions. What does it avail that many of these monsters, raining down ever more powerful, more horrible explosives, fall victim to our heroic defence? Thousands darken the skies of our fiercely united continent, and ever more of our cities fall in ruins. Leipzig, which played so significant a part in Leverkühn's development and tragedy, has lately been struck with might and main; its famous publishing quarter is, I hear, a heap of rubble, with immeasurable destruction of educational and literary property: a very heavy loss not only for us Germans but altogether for the world which makes culture its concern, but which in blindness or in even-handedness, I will not venture to say which, appears to pocket up the loss.

Yes, I fear it will prove our destruction that a fatally inspired policy has brought us into conflict with two powers at once: one of them richest in man-power and revolutionary élan; the other mightiest in productive capacity. It seems, indeed, that this American production-machine did not even need to run to capacity to throw out an absolutely crushing abundance of war material. That the flabby democracies did know after all how to use these frightful tools is a staggering revelation, weaning us daily from the mistaken idea that war is a German prerogative, and that all other peoples must prove to be bunglers and amateurs in the art. We have begun — Monsignor Hinterpförtner and I are no longer exceptions — to expect anything and everything from the war technique of the Anglo-Saxons. The fear of invasion grows: we await the attack, from all sides, with preponderance of material and millions of soldiers, on our European fortress — or shall I say our prison, our madhouse? It is expected, and only the most impressive accounts of our measures against enemy landings, measures that really do seem tremendous, and are, indeed, designed to protect us and our hemisphere from the loss of our present leaders, only these accounts can preserve our mental balance and prevent our yielding to the general horror of the future.

Certainly the time in which I write has vastly greater historical momentum than the time of which I write, Adrian's time, which brought him only to the threshold of our incredible epoch. I feel as though one should call out to him, as to all those who are no longer with us and were not with us when it began: "Lucky you!" and a fervent "Rest in peace!" Adrian is safe from the days we dwell in. The thought is dear to me, I prize it, and in exchange for that certainty I accept the terrors of the time in which I myself continue to live on. It is to me as though I stood here and lived for him, lived instead of him; as though I bore the burden his shoulders were spared, as though I showed my love by taking upon me living for him, living in his stead. The fancy, however illusory, however foolish, does me good, it flatters the always cherished desire to serve, to help, to protect him — this desire which during the lifetime of my friend found so very little satisfaction.

*

* *

It is worthy of remark that Adrian's stay in the Schwabing pension lasted only a few days and that he made no effort to find a suitable permanent dwelling in the city. Schildknapp had already written from Italy to his former abode in the Amalienstrasse and arranged to be received there. But Adrian was not thinking either of returning to his old place at Frau Senator Rodde's or even of remaining in Munich. His resolve seemed to have been taken long since and silently; he did not even go out to Pfeiffering near Waldshut to look over the ground again and close the bargain, but did it all by one telephone conversation and that a brief one. He called up the Schweigestills from Pension Gisela — it was

Mother Else herself who answered the call — introduced himself as one of the two bicyclists who had been privileged to inspect the house and farm, and asked whether and at what price they could let him have a sleeping-chamber in the upper storey and in the day-time the Abbot's room on the ground floor. Frau Schweigestill let the price rest for the moment — it proved to be very modest — but was concerned to find out which of the two earlier visitors it was, the writer or the musician. She obviously laboured to bring back her impressions of the visit and realize which was the musician; then she expressed some misgiving, though only in his own interest and from his own point of view. Even this she put only in the form that she thought he must know best what suited him. They, the Schweigestills, she said, did not set up to be pension-keepers as a business, they only took in occasionally, so to speak from case to case, lodgers and mealers; that the gentlemen had been able to gather the other time from what she said, and whether he, the speaker, represented such an occasion and such a case, that she must leave him to judge, he would have it pretty quiet and dull with them, and primitive as far as conveniences went, no bathroom, no W.C., just a peasant make-shift outside the house, and she did wonder that a gentleman of — if she had heard aright — not yet thirty, given to one of the fine arts, wanted to take quarters in the country, so far away from the centres of culture, but wonder was maybe not the right word, it was not hers and her husband's way to wonder, and if maybe it was just that he was looking for, because really most folks did wonder too much, then he might come, but it better be thought about, especially since Maxl, her husband, and she set store by an arrangement not made just out of some quirk and giving notice after they tried it a bit, but meaning from the first to bide, you understand, *net wahr, gellen's ja?* and so on.

He was coming for good, answered Adrian, and he had considered a long time. The kind of life that awaited him he had tried within himself, found it good and espoused it. On the price, a hundred and twenty marks a month, he was agreed. The choice of bedroom he left to her, and was looking forward with pleasure to the Abbot's room. In three days he would move in.

And so it was. Adrian employed his brief stay in the city in making arrangements with a copyist recommended to him (I think by Kretschmar), first bassoon in the Zapfenstösser orchestra, a man named Griepenkerl, who earned a bit of money in this way. He left in his hands a part of the partitur of *Love's Labour's Lost*. He had not quite finished with the work in Palestrina, was still orchestrating the last two acts, and was not yet quite clear in his mind about the sonata-form overture, the original conception of which had changed very much by the introduction of that striking second theme, itself quite foreign to the opera, playing so spirited a part in the recapitulation and closing allegro. He had besides much trouble with the time-markings and so on, which for extended stretches he had during composition neglected to put in. Moreover it was clear to me that not by chance had the end of his Italian sojourn and the end of the work failed to coincide. Even if he had consciously striven for such a coincidence, an unconscious intuition had prevented it. He was far too much the man of the *semper idem*, of self-assertion against circumstances, to regard it as desirable to come to the end of a task pursued in a former scene at the actual moment when he changed it for a new one. For the sake of the inner continuity it would be better, so he said to himself, to bring with him into the new situation a remnant of the old occupation, and only to fix the inward eye on something new when the outward new should have become routine.

With his never heavy luggage, to which belonged a brief-case with his scores and the rubber tub which in Italy too had furnished his bath, he travelled to his goal from the Starnberger station on one of the local trains, which stopped not only in Waldshut but ten minutes later in Pfeiffering. Two boxes of books and some oddments had been left to follow by freight train. It was near the end of October, the weather, still dry, was already raw and gloomy. The leaves were falling. The son of the house of Schweigestill, Gereon, the same who had introduced the new manure-spreader, a young farmer rather disobliging and curt but obviously knowing his business, awaited the guest at the little station, on the box of a trap with a high frame and stiff springs. While the luggage was put in, he let the thong of his whip play across the backs of the team of sturdy brown horses. Not many words were exchanged on the drive. Adrian had seen from the train the Rohmbühel with its crown of trees, the grey mirror of the Klammer; now his eyes rested on these sights from close at hand. Soon the cloister-baroque of the Schweigestill house came in sight; in the open square of the courtyard the vehicle rounded the old elm in the middle, whose leaves were now mostly lying on the bench beneath.

Frau Schweigestill stood under the gateway with the ecclesiastical coat of arms; beside her was her daughter Clementine, a brown-eyed country girl in modest peasant dress. Their words of greeting were drowned in the yapping of the yard dog, who in great excitement stepped into his food basin and almost dragged his straw-strewn kennel from its moorings. It was no use for mother and daughter, and even the stable-girl, Waltpurgis, helping to hand down the luggage, her bare feet caked with dung, to shout at him: "Kaschperl, hush your noise, be quiet!" The dog raved on and Adrian, after he had watched awhile smiling, went up to him. "Suso, Suso!" said he, not raising his voice, in a certain surprised and admonishing tone, and behold, probably from the influence of the soothing monotone, the animal became almost immediately quiet and allowed the magician to put out a hand and stroke his head, scarred with old bites, while the creature looked up at him with deeply serious yellow eyes.

"Courage you've got! My respects," said Frau Else when Adrian came back to the gate. "Most folks are feart of the beast and when he takes on, like now, one don't blame them, the young schoolmaster from the village who used to come to the children, oh, my, he was a poor body, he said every time: 'That dog, Frau Schweigestill, I'm just feart of him.' "

"Yes, yes," laughed Adrian, nodding, and they went into the house, into the pipe-tobacco air, and up to the upper storey, along the white, damp-smelling walls, where the goodwife showed him his bedroom with the gay clothes-press and the high-piled white bed. They had added something extra, a green reclining-chair with a knitted rug for the feet on the pine floor. Gereon and Waltpurgis brought up the bags.

Here and on the way downstairs they talked about arrangements for the guest's comfort, continuing in the Abbot's room, that characteristically patriarchal chamber, of which Adrian had long since mentally taken possession: about the large jug of hot water in the morning, the strong early-morning coffee, the times for meals; Adrian was not to take them with the family, they had not expected that, their hours being too early for him. At half past one and at eight he was to be served, preferably in the big front room (the peasant salon with the Nike and the square piano), Frau Schweigestill thought. It was always at his disposal. And she promised him light diet, milk, eggs, toast, vegetable soup, a good red beefsteak with spinach at midday, and afterwards a medium-sized omelet, with apple sauce — in short, things that were nourishing and agreeable to a delicate stomach like his.

"The stummick, my lord, it ain't mostly the stummick at all, eh, it's the head, the pernickety, overstrained head, it works on the stummick, even when 't ain't nothing wrong with it, like the way it is with seasickness and sick headache aha, he sometimes has it pretty bad?" She thought so already, from his looking so hard at the blinds and curtains in the bedroom; darkness, lying in the dark, night, black, especially no light in the eyes, that was the right thing, as long as the misery went on, and very strong tea, real sour with lemon. Frau Schweigestill was not unacquainted with migraine — that is, she had never had it herself but her Maxl had suffered from it periodically when he was younger, in time it had gone away. She would hear no apologies from the guest on the score of his infirmity, or his having smuggled a chronic patient into the house, so to speak; she said only: "Oh, get along with you!" Something of the sort, she thought, one would have guessed, for when anyone like him from over there where culture is going on came out to Pfeiffering like that, he would have his reasons for it, and obviously it was a case that had a claim on the understanding, Herr Leverkühn! But he'd come to the right address for understanding, if not for culture, eh? — and so on and so on, good woman that she was.

Between her and Adrian, as they stood or walked about, arrangements were made, which, surprisingly perhaps to both of them, were to regulate his outward existence for nineteen years. The village carpenter was called in to measure the space beside the doors in the Abbot's room for shelves to hold Adrian's books, not higher than the old panelling under the leather hangings; also the chandelier with the stumps of wax candles was wired for electricity. Various other changes came about through time, in the room that was destined to see the birth of so many masterpieces to this day largely withheld from public knowledge and admiration. A carpet almost covering the floor, only too necessary in winter, soon hid the worn boards; and to the corner bench, the only seat in the room besides the Savonarola chair in front of the work-table, there was added after a few days without any fastidious regard for style, which was not in Adrian's line, a very deep reading- and easy-chair covered with grey velvet, from Bernheimer's in Munich, a commendable piece, which together with its separate stool, a tabouret with a cushion, deserved the name of chaise-longue; it took the place of a divan, and did its owner almost two decades of service.

The purchases — the carpet and chair from the furnishing shop in the Maximiliansplatz — I mention partly with the aim of making it clear that there was convenient opportunity for communication with the city by numerous trains, some of them fast ones which took less than an hour. So that Adrian did not, as Frau

Schweigestill's way of talking would lead one to think, bury himself in solitude by settling in Pfeiffering, cut off from "culture." Even when he visited an evening entertainment, an academy concert or the Zapfenstösser orchestra, an opera performance or an evening company — and that too did happen — there was an eleven-o'clock train for him to travel home in. Of course he could not then count on being fetched from the station with the Schweigestill cart; in such cases he arranged beforehand with a Waldshut livery, or even, to his great satisfaction, returned on foot, on clear winter nights, by the road along the pond to the sleeping courtyard of the Schweigestill house. On these occasions he gave a sign to Kaschperl-Suso, at this hour free of his chain, that he might not rouse the house. He did this with a little metal pipe tuned by means of a screw, whose higher notes were of such an extreme vibration that the human ear could scarcely hear them from close by. On the other hand they had a very strong effect and at a surprising distance on the quite differently constituted ear-drum of the dog, and Kaschperl kept mum as a mouse when the mysterious sound, heard by no one else, came to him through the night.

It was curiosity, but it was also a power exerted by my friend, whose cool, reserved person, shy despite his haughtiness, was far from unattractive, that brought people out to visit him in his retreat. I will give Schildknapp the precedence which he did actually possess: of course he was the first to come, to see how Adrian did in the place they had found out together. After that, especially in the summer-time, he often spent the week-end in Pfeiffering. Zink and Spengler came on their bicycles, for Adrian, on his shopping tours in town, had paid his respects to the Roddes in Rambergstrasse and the two painters had heard from the daughters of Adrian's return and his present address. Probably Spengler's was the initiative in the visit, for Zink, more gifted and active as a painter than the other, but much less fine as a human being, had no instinctive sympathy for Adrian and was certainly only present as Spengler's inseparable: flattering, in the Austrian manner, with kiss-the-hand and disingenuous "Marvellous, marvellous!" at everything he saw, while at bottom unfriendly. His clownishness, the farcical effects he could produce with his long nose and the close-lying eyes which had such an absurdly hypnotic effect on women, made no play with Adrian, however grateful the latter always was for being amused. Vanity detracts from wit; the knavish Zink had a tiresome mania of attending to every word, to see whether he could not get a *double entendre* out of it, and this, as he probably saw, did not precisely enchant Adrian.

Spengler, blinking, a dimple in his cheek, laughed, or bleated, heartily at such little contretemps. The sexual interested him in a literary sense, sex and esprit lying with him very close together — which in itself is not so far wrong. His culture — we know indeed, his feeling for what was subtle, witty, discriminating — was founded on his accidental and unhappy relation to the sphere of sex, the physical fixation on it, which was sheer bad luck, and not further characteristic of his temperament or his sexuality. He smiled and prattled, in the language of that now vanished cultural and æsthetic epoch, about events in the world of artists and bibliophiles; retailed Munich gossip and dwelt very drolly on a story of how the Grand Duke of Weimar and the dramatic poet Richard Voss, travelling together in the Abruzzi, were set upon by genuine bandits — of course engaged by Voss. To Adrian, Spengler made clever politenesses about the Brentano song cycle, which he had bought and studied at the piano. He delivered himself at that time of the remark that occupation with these songs ended by spoiling one, quite definitely and almost dangerously. Afterwards one could hardly find pleasure in anything in that field. Said other quite good things about being spoiled, of which the needy artist himself was in the greatest danger, it seemed: it might be disastrous for him. For with every finished work he made life harder for himself, and in the end impossible. Spoilt by the extraordinary, his taste ruined for anything else, he must at last deteriorate through despair of executing the impossible. The problem for the highly gifted artist was how, despite his always increasing fastidiousness, his spreading disgust, he could still keep within the limits of the possible.

Thus the witty Spengler — solely on the basis of his specific fixation, as his blinking and bleating showed. The next guests were Jeanette Scheurl and Rudi Schwerdtfeger, who came to tea to see how Adrian did.

Jeanette and Schwerdtfeger sometimes played together, for the guests of old Mme Scheurl as well as privately, and they had planned the trip to Pfeiffering, and Rudi had done the telephoning. Whether he proposed it or whether it was Jeanette I do not know. They argued over it in Adrian's presence and each put on the other the merit of the attention they paid him. Jeanette's droll impulsiveness speaks for her initiative; on the other hand, it was very consistent with Rudi's amazing familiarity. He seemed to be of opinion that two years ago he had been *per du* with Adrian, whereas after all that had only been in carnival time, and even then entirely on Rudi's side. Now he blithely took it up again and desisted, with entire unconcern, only when Adrian for the second or third time refused to respond. The unconcealed merriment of Fräulein Scheurl at this repulse of his devotion moved him not at all. No trace of confusion showed in his blue eyes, which could burrow with such penetrating naïveté into the eyes of anyone who was making clever, learned, or cultured remarks. Even today I think of Schwerdtfeger and ask myself whether he actually understood how solitary Adrian was, thus how needy and exposed to temptation; whether he wanted to try his charms — to put it crudely, to get round him. Beyond a doubt he was born for conquest; but I should be afraid of doing him wrong were I to see him from this side alone. He was also a good fellow and an artist, and the fact that Adrian and he were later actually *per du* and called each other by their first names I should like not to regard as a cheap triumph of Schwerdtfeger's mania for pleasing people, but rather to refer it to his honestly recognizing the value of this extraordinary human being. I should like to think he was truly drawn to Adrian, and that his own feeling was the source of the unerring and staggering self-confidence which finally made conquest of coldness and melancholy. A fatal triumph! But I have fallen into my old, bad habit and got ahead of my story.

In her broad-brimmed hat, with a thin veil stretched across her nose, Jeanette Scheurl played Mozart on the square piano in the Schweigestills' peasant "big room," and Rudi Schwerdtfeger whistled with such artistry that one laughed for sheer pleasure. I heard him later at the Roddes' and Schlaginhaufens', and got him to tell me how, as quite a little lad, before he had violin lessons, he had begun to develop this technique and never stopped whistling the music he heard, or practising what he learned. His performance was brilliant, professional, fit for any cabaret, almost more impressive than his violin-playing; he must have been organically just right for it. The cantilena was wonderfully pleasing, more like a violin than a flute, the phrasing masterly, the little notes, staccato or legato, coming out with delicious precision, never or almost never faltering. In short, it was really capital, and not the least diverting thing about it was the combination of whistling 'prentice and serious artist which it presented. One involuntarily smiled as one applauded; Schwerdtfeger himself laughed like a boy, wriggling his shoulder in his jacket and making his little grimace with the corner of his mouth.

These, then, were Adrian's first guests in Pfeiffering. And soon
I came myself and on fine Sundays strolled at his side round the
pond and up the Rohmbühel. Only that one winter, after his return from Italy, did I live at any distance from him, for at Easter
1913 I had got my position at the Freising academy, our family's
Catholic connection being useful in this respect. I left Kaisersaschern and settled with wife and child at the edge of the Isar,
in this dignified city, seat of a bishopric for hundreds of years,
where with the exception of some months during the war I have
passed my own life in convenient touch with the capital and also
with my friend, and shared, in love and solicitude, the stresses and
the tragedy of his.

CHAPTER XXVII

BASSOONIST Griepenkerl had done a good and grateful piece of work on the score of *Love's Labour's Lost*. Just about the first words Adrian said to me when we met concerned the all but flawless copy and his joy over it. He also showed me a letter that the man had written to him in the midst of his exacting labours, wherein he expressed with intelligence a sort of anxious enthusiasm for the object of his pains. He could not, so he told its author, express how it took his breath away with its boldness, the novelty of its ideas. Not enough could he admire the fine subtlety of the workmanship, the versatile rhythms, the technique of instrumentation, by which an often considerable complication of parts was made perfectly clear; above all, the rich fantasy of the composition, showing itself in the manifold variations of a given theme. He instanced the beautiful and withal half-humorous music that belongs to the figure of Rosaline, or rather expresses Biron's desperate feeling for her, in the middle part of the tripartite bourrée in the last act, this witty revival of the old French dance; it must, he said, be characterized as brilliant and deft in the highest sense of the words. He added that this bourrée was not a little characteristic of the démodé archaic element of social conventionality which so charmingly but also so challengingly contrasted with the "modern," the free and more than free, the rebel parts, disdaining tonal connection, of the work. He feared indeed that these parts of the score, in all their unfamiliarity and rebellious heresy, would be better received than the strict and traditional. Here it often amounted to a rigidity, a more academic than artistic speculation in notes, a mosaic scarcely any longer effective musically, seeming rather more to be read than to be heard — and so on.

We laughed.

"When I hear of hearing!" said Adrian. "In my view it is quite enough if something has been heard *once;* I mean when the artist thought it out."

After a while he added: "As though people ever heard what had been heard then! Composing means to commission the Za-

pfenstösser orchestra to execute an angelic chorus. And anyhow
I consider angelic choruses to be highly speculative."
   For my part I thought Griepenkerl was wrong in his sharp distinction between archaic and modern elements in the work. "They
blend into and interpenetrate," I said, and he accepted the statement but showed little inclination to go into what was fixed and
finished; preferring apparently to put it behind him as not further interesting. Speculations about what to do with it, where to
send it, to whom to show it, he left to me. That Wendell Kretschmar should have it to read was the important thing to him. He
sent it to Lübeck, where the stutterer still was, and the latter actually produced it there, in a German version, a year later, after
war had broken out — I was not present — with the result that
during the performance two thirds of the audience left the theatre. Just as it is supposed to have happened six years before at
the Munich première of Debussy's *Pelléas et Mélisande*. There
were only two more performances of Adrian's opera, and it was
not, for the time, to penetrate beyond the Hansa city on the
Trave. The local critics agreed to a man with the judgment of
the lay audience and jeered at the "decimating" music which Herr
Kretschmar had taken up with. Only in the *Lübeck Börsenkurier*
an old music-professor named Immerthal — doubtless dead long
since — spoke of an error of justice which time would put right,
and declared in crabbed, old-fashioned language that the opera
was a work of the future, full of profound music, that the writer
was of course a mocker but a "god-witted man." This striking expression, which I had never before heard or read, nor ever since,
made a peculiar impression on me. And as I have never forgotten
it or the knowledgeable old codger who coined it, I think it must
be counted to his honour by the posterity he invoked as witness
against his spineless and torpid fellow-critics.
   At the time when I moved to Freising, Adrian was busy with
the composition of some songs and lieder, German and foreign,
or rather, English. In the first place he had gone back to William
Blake and set to music a very strange poem of this favourite author of his. "Silent, Silent Night," in four stanzas of three lines
each, the last stanza of which dismayingly enough runs:

> But an honest joy
> Does itself destroy
> For a harlot coy.

   These darkly shocking verses the composer had set to very
simple harmonies, which in relation to the tone-language of the

whole had a "falser," more heart-rent, uncanny effect than the most daring harmonic tensions, and made one actually experience the common chord growing monstrous. "Silent, Silent Night" is arranged for piano and voice. He set two poems by Keats, "Ode to a Nightingale" and the shorter "Ode on Melancholy" with a string-quartet accompaniment, which indeed left far behind and below it the traditional conception of an accompaniment. For in fact it was an extremely artificial form of variation in which no note of the singing voice and the four instruments was unthematic. There reigns here without interruption the closest relation between the parts so that the relation is not that of melody and accompaniment, but in all strictness that of constantly alternating primary and secondary parts.

They are glorious pieces — and almost unsung up till today, owing to the language they are in. Odd enough to make me smile was the expressiveness with which the composer enlarges in the "Nightingale" on the demand for southern sweetness of life which the song of the "immortal Bird" rouses in the soul of the poet. For, after all, Adrian in Italy had never displayed much gratitude or enthusiasm about the consolations of a sunny world, which make one forget "the weariness, the fever, and the fret Here, where men sit and hear each other groan." Musically the most priceless, the most perfect, beyond doubt, is the resolution and dissipation of the vision at the end, the

> Adieu! the fancy cannot cheat so well
> As she is famed to do, deceiving elf.
> Adieu! adieu! thy plaintive anthem fades
> ....
> Fled is that music: — do I wake or sleep?

I can well understand how the beauty of the poems, like that of an antique vase, challenged the music to crown them; not to make them completer, for they are complete, but to articulate more strongly and to throw into relief their proud and melancholy charm; to lend more lastingness to the priceless moment of their every detail than is granted to the breathed-out words; to such moments of condensed imagery as in the third stanza of the "Ode on Melancholy," the image of the "sovran shrine" which veiled Melancholy has in the temple of delight, though seen of none save him whose strenuous tongue can burst Joy's grape against his palate fine — all that is so brilliant that it scarcely leaves the music anything to say. It may be that it can only injure it, unless by simply speaking with it, and so lingering it out. I have often heard say that a poem must not be too good to furnish a good lied. Music is at home in the task of gilding the mediocre. Just as real virtuosity in an actor shows up more brilliantly in a poor piece. But Adrian's relation to art was too proud and critical for him to wish to let his light shine in darkness. He had to look very high, intellectually, where he was to feel himself called as musician, and so the German poem to which he gave himself productively is also of the highest rank if without the intellectual distinction of the Keats lyrics. In place of literary exquisiteness we have something more monumental, the high-pitched, sounding pathos of the religious hymn, which with its invocations and depictions of majesty and mildness yields even more to the music, is more faithfully compliant with it than are those British images with their Greek nobility.

It was Klopstock's *Spring Festival*, the famous song of the "Drop to the Bucket," which Leverkühn, with but few textual abbreviations, had composed for baritone, organ, and string orchestra — a thrilling piece of work, which was performed, through the efforts of some courageous conductors friendly to the new music, during the first World War and some years after it in several German music-centres and also in Switzerland. It received the enthusiastic approval of a minority and of course some spiteful and stupid opposition too. These performances contributed very much to the fact that at latest in the twenties an aura of esoteric fame began to unfold about the name of my friend. But this much I will say: deeply as I was moved — yet not really surprised — by this outburst of religious feeling, which was the purer and more pious for the restraint and absence of cheap effects, no harp-twanging (though the text is actually a challenge to it), no drum to give back the thunder of the Lord; however much went to my heart certain beauties not at all achieved by hackneyed tone-painting: the magnificent truths of the pæan; the oppressively slow movement of the black cloud; the twice-repeated thundering "Jehovah!" when "the shattered wood steams" (a powerful passage); the so new and enlightened concord of the high register of the organ with the strings at the end, when the Deity comes, no longer in storm, but in hushed murmurings and beneath it "arches the bow of peace"; yet despite all these I have never understood the work in its real spiritual sense, its inward necessity, its purpose, informed by fear, of seeking grace in praise. Did I at that time know the document, which my readers now know too, the record of the "dialogue" in the stone-floored sala? Only conditionally could I have named myself before that "a partner in your sorrow's mysteries," as it says in the "Ode on Melancholy"; only with the right of a general concern since our boyhood days for his soul's health; but not through actual knowledge, as it then stood. Only later did I learn to understand the composition of the *Spring Festival* as what it was: a plea to God, an atonement for sin, a work of *attritio cordis*, composed, as I realized with shudders, under the threat of that visitor insisting that he was really visible.

But in still another sense did I fail to understand the personal and intellectual background of this production based on Klopstock's poem. For I did not, as I should have done, connect it with conversations I had with him at this time, or rather he had with me, when he gave me, quite circumstantially, with great animation, accounts of studies and researches in fields very remote from my curiosity or my scientific comprehension: thrilling enrichments, that is, of his knowledge of nature and the cosmos. And now he strongly reminded me of the elder Leverkühn's musing mania for "speculating the elements."

Indeed, the composer of this setting for the *Spring Festival* did not conform to the poet's words that he "would not fling himself in the ocean of the worlds"; that only about the drop in the bucket, about the earth, would he hover and adore. For Adrian did fling himself into the immense, which astro-physical science seeks to measure, only to arrive at measures, figures, orders of greatness with which the human spirit has no longer any relation, and which lose themselves in the theoretic and abstract, in the entirely non-sensory, not to say non-sensical. Moreover I will not forget that it all began with a dwelling on the "drop," which does not ill deserve this name, as it consists mainly of water, the water of the oceans, which on the occasion of the creation "also ran out from the hand of the Almighty." On it, at first, we dwelt, and its dark secrets; for the wonders of the depths of the sea, the extravagant living things down there where no sun's ray penetrates, were the first matters of which Adrian told me, and indeed in such a strange and startling way that I was both entertained and bewildered, for he spoke as though he had personally seen and experienced it all.

Of course he had only read of these things, had got books about them and fed his fancy. But whether he had so concentrated on them, had so mastered these pictures mentally, or out of whatever whim it was, he pretended that in the region of the Bermudas, some nautical miles east of St. George, he had himself gone down into the sea and been shown by his companion the natural phenomena of the deeps. He spoke of this companion as an American scholar named Akercocke, in company with whom he was supposed to have set up a new deep-sea record.

I remember this conversation most vividly. It occurred at a week-end I was spending in Pfeiffering, after the simple meal served us in the big piano-room, when the primly clad young Clementine had kindly brought us each our half-litre mug of beer, and we sat smoking Zechbauer cigars, light and good. It was about the hour when Suso, the yard dog, in other words Kaschperl, was loosed from his chain and allowed to range the court-yard.

Then Adrian embarked with gusto on his jest, which he related to me in the most circumstantial manner: how he and Professor Akercocke climbed into a bullet-shaped diving-bell of only one point two metres inside diameter, equipped somewhat like a stratosphere balloon, and were dropped by a crane from the companion ship into the sea, at this point very deep. It had been more than exciting — at least for him, if not for his mentor or cicerone, from whom he had procured this experience and who took the thing more coolly as it was not his first descent. Their situation inside the two-ton hollow ball was anything but comfortable, but was compensated for by the knowledge of their perfect safety, absolutely watertight as it was, capable of withstanding immense pressure. It was provided with a supply of oxygen, a telephone, high-voltage searchlights, and quartz windows all round. Somewhat longer than three hours in all they spent beneath the surface of the ocean; it had passed like a dream, thanks to the sights they were vouchsafed, the glimpses into a world whose soundless, frantic foreignness was explained and even justified by its utter lack of contact with our own.

Even so it had been a strange moment, and his heart had missed a beat, when one morning at nine o'clock the four-hundred-pound armoured door had closed behind them and they swayed away from the ship and plunged into the water, crystal-clear at first, lighted by the sun. But this illumination of the inside of our "drop in the bucket" reached down only some fifty-seven metres. For at that depth light has come to an end; or rather, a new, unknown, irrelevant world here begins, into which Adrian with his guide went down to nearly fourteen times that depth, some thirty-six hundred feet, and there remained for half an hour, almost every moment painfully aware that a pressure of five hundred thousand tons rested upon their shelter.

Gradually, on the way down, the water had taken on a grey

colour, that of a darkness mixed with some still undaunted rays of light. Not easily did these become discouraged; it was the will and way of them to make light and they did so to their uttermost, so that the next stage of light's exhaustion and retreat actually had more colour than the previous one. Through the quartz windows the travellers looked into a blue-blackness hard to describe; perhaps best compared to the dull colour of the horizon on a clear thawing day. After that, indeed long before the hand of the indicator stood at seven hundred and fifty to seven hundred and sixty-five metres, came solid blackness all round, the blackness of interstellar space whither for eternities no weakest sun-ray had penetrated, the eternally still and virgin night, which now had to put up with a powerful artificial light from the upper world, not of cosmic origin, in order to be looked at and looked through.

Adrian spoke of the itch one felt to expose the unexposed, to look at the unlooked-at, the not-to-be and not-expecting-to-be looked-at. There was a feeling of indiscretion, even of guilt, bound up with it, not quite allayed by the feeling that science must be allowed to press just as far forwards as it is given the intelligence of scientists to go. The incredible eccentricities, some grisly, some comic, which nature here achieved, forms and features which seemed to have scarcely any connection with the upper world but rather to belong to another planet: these were the product of seclusion, sequestration, of reliance on being wrapped in eternal darkness. The arrival upon Mars of a human conveyance travelling through space — or rather, let us say, upon that half of Mercury which is eternally turned away from the sun — could excite no greater sensation in the inhabitants — if any — of that "near" planet, than the appearance of the Akercocke diving-bell down here. The mass curiosity with which these inconceivable creatures of the depths had crowded round the cabin had been indescribable — and quite indescribable too was everything that went whisking past the windows in a blur of motion: frantic caricatures of organic life; predatory mouths opening and shutting; obscene jaws, telescope eyes; the paper nautilus; silver- and gold-fish with goggling eyes on top of their heads; heteropods and pteropods, up to two or three yards long. Even those that floated passively in the flood, monsters compact of slime, yet with arms to catch their prey, polyps, acalephs, skyphomedusas — they all seemed to have been seized by spasms of twitching excitement.

It might well be that all these natives of the deep regarded this light-radiating guest as an outsize variation of themselves, for most of them could do what it could; that is to say, give out light by their own power. The visitors, Adrian said, had only to put out their own searchlight, when an extraordinary spectacle unfolded outside. Far and wide the darkness of the sea was illuminated by shooting and circling will-o'-the-wisps, caused by the light with which many of the creatures were equipped, so that in some cases the entire body was phosphorescent, while others had a searchlight, an electric lantern, with which presumably they not only lighted the darkness of their path, but also attracted their prey. They also probably used it in courtship. The ray from some of the larger ones cast such an intense white light that the observers' eyes were blinded. Others had eyeballs projecting on stalks; probably in order to perceive at the greatest possible distance the faintest gleam of light meant to lure or warn.

The narrator regretted that it was not possible to catch any of these monsters of the deep, at least some of the utterly unknown ones, and bring them to the surface. In order to do so, however, one would have to preserve for them while ascending the same tremendous atmospheric pressure they were used to and adapted to in their environment — the same that rested on our diving-bell — a disturbing thought. In their habitat the creatures counteracted it by an equal pressure of their tissues and cavities; so that if the outside pressure were decreased, they would inevitably burst. Some of them, alas, burst now, on coming into contact with the diving-bell: the watchers saw an unusually large, flesh-coloured wight, rather finely formed, just touch the vessel and fly into a thousand pieces.

Thus Adrian told his tale, as we smoked our cigars; quite as though he had himself been present and had all these things shown to him. He carried out the jest so well, with only half a smile, that I could but stare amazed even while I laughed and marvelled at his tale. His smile also probably expressed a teasing amusement at a certain resistance on my side, which must have been obvious to him, for he well knew my lack of interest, even amounting to distaste, for the tricks and mysteries of the natural, for "nature" altogether, and my allegiance to the sphere of the human and articulate. Obviously this knowledge of his was in large part what led him to go on with his reports or, as he put it, his experiences of the monstrously extra-human; plunging, carrying me along with him, "in den Ozean der Welten alle."

The transition was made easy for him by his previous descriptions. The alien, fantastic nature of the deep-sea life, which seemed no longer to belong to the same planet with us, was a point of departure. Another was the Klopstock phrase "The Drop to the

Bucket": how well its admiring humility described our own quite secondary position in the cosmos! This on account of our utter insignificance to any larger view; the almost undiscoverable situation not only of the earth but of our whole planetary system, the sun with its seven satellites, within the vortex of the Milky Way, to which it belongs — "*our*" Milky Way, to say nothing of the millions of other ones. The word "our" lends a certain intimacy to the vastness to which it refers; it takes the feeling of "home" and almost comically magnifies it into breath-takingly extended space, wherein then we are to consider ourselves as established if humble citizens. And here the tendency of nature to the spherical seems to be carried through: this was a third point to which Adrian linked his discourse on the cosmos; arriving at it partly through the strange experience of the sojourn in the hollow ball, the Akercocke diving-bell in which he purported to have spent some hours. In a hollow ball, so he was instructed, we all and sundry passed our days; for in the galactic system wherein we occupied an infinitesimal point somewhere at one side, the situation was as follows:

It was shaped more or less like a flat watch; round, and much less thick than its circumferance: an aggregation not literally immeasurable but still truly vast, a whirling disk of concentrated hosts of stars and star systems, star clusters, double stars, which described elliptical orbits about each other; of gas clouds, nebulæ, planetary nebulæ, stellar nebulæ, and so on. But this disk was only comparable to the flat round surface which results when one cuts an orange in half; for it was enclosed all round by a vapour of other stars, which again could not strictly speaking be called immeasurable, but as raised to a very high power of vastness and in whose spaces, mostly empty spaces, the given objects were so distributed that the whole structure formed a ball. Somewhere deep within this absurdly sparsely settled ball, belonging, in a very minor category, scarcely worth mention and not even easy to find, to the disk or condensed swarm of worlds, was the fixed star about which, along with its greater and smaller companions, sported the earth and its little moon. "The sun" — a body little deserving of the definite article — a gas ball registering six thousand degrees of heat on its surface, and a mere million and a half kilometres in diameter, was as far distant from the centre of the galactic inner plane as that was thick through — in other words thirty thousand light-years.

My general information permitted me to associate a concept, however imprecise, with the words "light-year." It was, of course,

a spatial concept and the word meant the span that light puts behind it in the course of a whole earth-year, at a speed peculiar
to it, of which I had a vague idea but Adrian had in his head the
exact figure of 186,000 miles per second. So a light-year amounted
to a round and net figure of six trillion miles, and the eccentricity
of our solar system amounted to thirty thousand times as much,
while the whole diameter of the galactic hollow ball came to two
hundred thousand light-years.

No, it was not immeasurable, but it was in this way that it was
to be measured. What is one to say to such an assault upon the
human understanding? I confess to being so made that nothing
but a resigned if also somewhat contemptuous shoulder-shrug remains to me in face of such ungraspable, such stunning statistics.
Enthusiasm for size, being overwhelmed by size — that is no doubt
a mental pleasure; but it is only possible in connections which a
human being can grasp. The Pyramids are large, Mont Blanc and
the inside of the dome of St. Peter's are large, unless one prefer to
reserve this attribute of largeness to the mental and moral world,
the nobility of the heart and of thought. The data of the cosmic
creation are nothing but a deafening bombardment of our intelligence with figures furnished with a comet's tail of a couple of
dozen ciphers, and comporting themselves as though they still had
something, anything, to do with measurement and understanding.
There is in all this monstrousness nothing that could appeal to the
likes of me as goodness, beauty, greatness; and I shall never understand the glory-to-God mental attitude which certain tem-
peraments assume when they contemplate the "works of God,"
meaning by the phrase the physics of the universe. And is a construction to be hailed as "the works of God" when one may just
as reasonably say: "Well, what then?" instead of "Glory to the
Lord"? The first rather than the second seems to me the right answer to two dozen ciphers after a one or even after a seven, which
really adds nothing to it; and I can see no sort of reason to fall in
the dust and adore the fifth power of a million.

It was also a telling fact that Klopstock in his soaring poesy expressing and arousing a fervid reverence confines himself to the
earth — the drop in the bucket — and leaves the quintillions alone.
My friend Adrian, the composer of Klopstock's hymns, does, as
I say, dwell on this aspect; but I should do wrong to arouse the
impression that he does so with any sort of emotion or emphasis.
Adrian's way of dealing with these insanities was cold, indifferent,
coloured by amusement at my unconcealed distaste. But also it
displayed a certain initiated familiarity, a persistence, I mean, in

the fiction that he had derived his knowledge not simply through reading, but rather by personal transmission, instruction, demonstration, experience, perhaps from his above-mentioned mentor, Professor Akercocke, who it appeared had been with him not only down in the darkness of the ocean deeps, but also up among the stars. . . . He behaved in a way as though he had got it from his mentor, and indeed more or less through actual observation, that the physical universe — this word in its widest and furthest connotation — should be called neither finite nor infinite, because both words described something somehow static, whereas the true situation was through and through dynamic in its nature, and the cosmos, at least for a long time, more precisely for nineteen hundred million years, has been in a state of furious expansion — that is, of explosion. Of this we were left in no doubt, due to the red-shift of the light which reaches us from numerous milky-way systems at a known distance from us: the stronger alteration of colour of this light toward the red end of the spectrum is in proportion to the greater distance from us of these nebulæ. Obviously they were moving away from us; and with the farthest ones, complexes one hundred and fifty million light-years away, the speed with which they moved was like that which the alpha particles of radioactive substance developed, amounting to twenty-five thousand kilometres a second, a rate of speed compared with which the splintering of a bursting shell was at a snail's pace. If then all the galaxies were to rush away from each other in the most exaggerated space of time, then the word "explosion" would just be — or rather had not for a long time been — adequate to describe the state of the world-pattern and its way of expansion. It might once have been static, earlier, and been simply a milliard light-years in diameter. As things were now, one could speak indeed of expansion, but not of any constant expansion, "finite" or "infinite." It seemed that his guide had been able to assure the questioner only of the fact that the sum of the collective existing galaxies was in the order of size of a hundred milliards, of which only a modest million were accessible to our telescopes.

Thus Adrian, smoking and smiling. I appealed to his conscience and demanded from him an admission that this spooking about with statistics forever escaping into the void could not possibly stir one to a feeling of the majesty of God or give rise to any moral elevation. It all looked very much more like devil's juggling.

"Admit," said I to him, "that the horrendous physical creation is in no way religiously productive. What reverence and what civilizing process born of reverence can come from the picture of a vast impropriety like this of the exploding universe? Absolutely none. Piety, reverence, intellectual decency, religious feeling, are only possible about men and through men, and by limitation to the earthly and human. Their fruit should, can, and will be a religiously tinged humanism, conditioned by feeling for the transcendental mystery of man, by the proud consciousness that he is no mere biological being, but with a decisive part of him belongs to an intellectual and spiritual world, that to him the Absolute is given, the ideas of truth, of freedom, of justice; that upon him the duty is laid to approach the consummate. In this pathos, this obligation, this reverence of man for himself, is God; in a hundred milliards of Milky Ways I cannot find him."

"So you are against the works," he answered, "and against physical nature, from which man comes and with him his incorporeal part, which in the end does occur in other places in the cosmos. Physical creation, this monstrosity of a world set-up, so annoying to you, is incontestably the premise for the moral, without which it would have no soil, and perhaps one must call the good the flower of evil — *une fleur du mal*. But your *homo Dei* is after all — or not after all, I beg pardon, I mean before all — a part of this abominable nature — with a not very generous quantum of potential spirituality. Moreover it is amusing to see how much your humanism, and probably all humanism, inclines to the mediæval geocentric — as it obviously must. In the popular belief, humanism is friendly to science; but it cannot be, for one cannot consider the subjects of science to be devil's work without seeing the same in science itself. That is Middle Ages. The Middle Ages were geocentric and anthropocentric. The Church, in which they survived, has set itself to oppose astronomical knowledge in the humanistic spirit; bedevilled and forbidden it to the honour of the human being; out of humanity has insisted on ignorance. You see, your humanism is pure Middle Ages. Its concern is a cosmology proper to Kaisersaschern and its towers: it leads to astrology, to observation of the position of the planets, the constellation and its favourable or unfavourable indications — quite naturally and rightly, for nothing is clearer than the intimate interdependence of the bodies of a cosmic little group so closely bound together as our solar system, and their near neighbourly mutual reference."

"We have already talked about astrological conjuncture," I broke in. "It was long ago, we were walking round the Cow Pond, and it was a musical conversation. At that time you defended the constellation."

"I still defend it today," he answered. "Astrological times knew

a lot. They knew, or divined, things which science in its broadest
scope is coming back to. That diseases, plagues, epidemics have
to do with the position of the stars was to those times an intuitive
certainty. Today we have got so far as to debate whether germs,
bacteria, organisms which, we say, can produce an influenza epidemic on earth come from other planets — Mars, Jupiter, or
Venus."

Contagious diseases, plague, black death, were probably not of
this planet; as, almost certainly indeed, life itself has not its origin
on our globe, but came hither from outside. He, Adrian, had it on
the best authority that it came from neighbouring stars which are
enveloped in an atmosphere more favourable to it, containing
much methane and ammonia, like Jupiter, Mars, and Venus. From
them, or from one of them — he left me the choice — life had
once, borne by cosmic projectiles or simply by radiation pressure,
arrived upon our formerly sterile and innocent planet. My humanistic *homo Dei*, that crowning achievement of life, was together with his obligations to the spiritual in all probability the
product of the marsh-gas fertility of a neighbouring star.

"The flower of evil," I repeated, nodding.

"And blooming mostly in mischief," he added.

Thus he taunted me, not only with my kindly view of the
world, but also by persisting in the whimsical pretence of a personal, direct, and special knowledge about the affairs of heaven
and earth. I did not know, but I might have been able to tell myself, that all this meant something, meant a new work: namely,
the cosmic music which he had in his mind, after the episode
of the new songs. It was the amazing symphony in one movement,
the orchestral fantasy that he was working out during the last
months of 1913 and the first of 1914, and which very much
against my expressed wish bore the title *Marvels of the Universe*.
I was mistrustful of the flippancy of that name and suggested the
title *Symphonia cosmologica*. But Adrian insisted, laughing, on
the other, mock-pathetic, ironic name, which certainly better prepared the knowing for the out-and-out bizarre and unpleasant
character of the work, even though often these images of the
monstrous and uncanny were grotesque in a solemn, formal,
mathematical way. This music has simply nothing in common
with the spirit of the *Spring Celebration*, which after all was in a
certain way the preparation for it: I mean with the spirit of humble glorification. If certain musical features of the writing peculiar
to Adrian had not indicated the author, one could scarcely believe that the same mind brought forth both. Nature and essence

of that nearly thirty-minutes-long orchestral world-portrait is mockery, a mockery which all too well confirms my opinion expressed in conversation, that preoccupation with the immeasurable extra-human affords nothing for piety to feed on: a luciferian sardonic mood, a sneering travesty of praise which seems to apply not only to the frightful clockwork of the world-structure but also to the medium used to describe it: yes, repeatedly with music itself, the cosmos of sound. The piece has contributed not a little to the reproach levelled at the art of my friend, as a virtuosity antipathetic to the artist mind, a blasphemy, a nihilistic sacrilege.

But enough on this theme. The next two chapters I mean to devote to some social experiences which I shared with Adrian Leverkühn at the turn of the year 1913–14, during the last Munich carnival before the outbreak of the war.

CHAPTER XXVIII

I HAVE already said that the lodger at the Schweigestills' did not quite bury himself in his cloistral solitude, guarded by Kaschperl-Suso. Though sporadically and with reserve, he cultivated a certain social life. Even so, he seemed to cling to the soothing necessity of an early leave-taking and fixed departure by the eleven-o'clock train. We met at the Roddes' in Rambergstrasse, with whose circle — Schwerdtfeger the fiddler and whistler, the Knöterichs, Dr. Kranich, Zink and Spengler — I had got on a friendly footing; further at the Schlaginhaufens', also at the home of Radbruch, Schildknapp's publisher, in Fürstenstrasse, and in the elegant *bel étage* of the Rhineland paper-manufacturer Bullinger, where also Rüdiger introduced us.

At the Roddes', as well as in the pillared Schlaginhaufen salon, they enjoyed my viola d'amore, and in any case it was the only contribution that I, a scholar and schoolmaster, never very lively in conversation, could make to this society. In the Rambergstrasse it was particularly the asthmatic Dr. Kranich and Baptist Spengler who kept me to it: the one out of his antiquarian interests (he liked to talk with me, in his clearly articulated, well-arranged sentences about numismatics and about the historical development of the viola family), the other out of a general taste for the out-of-the-way and even the decadent. Still I had in that house to have regard for Konrad Knöterich's craving to make himself heard playing cello and snorting the while. And the little audience had a justified preference for Schwerdtfeger's captivating violin-playing. So much the more did it flatter my vanity (I deny it not) that there was a lively demand from the much larger and more elevated public which the ambition of Frau Dr. Schlaginhaufen, née von Plausig, knew how to gather round her and her hard-of-hearing, Suabian-speaking husband. I had always cultivated my music merely as an amateur; but I was almost always obliged to bring my instrument with me to the Briennerstrasse, to regale the company with a chaconne or sarabande from the seventeenth century, a *"plaisir d'amour"* from the eighteenth, or to perform a sonata by Ariosti, the friend of Handel, or one of Haydn's written for the viola di bordone but quite possible for the viola d'amore as well.

Not only from Jeanette Scheurl did suggestions like the last proceed, but also from the General-Intendant, Excellency von Riedesel, whose patronage of the old instrument and old music did not indeed, as with Kranich, stem from scholarly or antiquarian interest, but was purely conservative in its origin, a great difference of course. This courtier, a former cavalry colonel, who had been appointed to his present post simply and solely because it had been well known that he played piano a little (how many centuries ago it seems, that one could become a General-Intendant solely because one was "noble" and played the piano a little!), Baron Riedesel, then, saw in everything old and historic a bulwark against the new and subversive, a sort of feudal argument against it, and supported it in this sense, without in fact understanding anything about it. For just as little as one understands the new and the young, without being at home in the traditional, just so must love for the old remain ungenuine and sterile if one shut oneself away from the new, which with historical inevitability grows out of it. Thus Riedesel esteemed and protected the ballet, and forsooth because it was "graceful." The word meant to him a shibboleth, a conservative arguing-point against the modern and insurrectionary. Of the traditional world of the Russian and French ballets, represented by a Tchaikovsky, a Ravel, a Stravinsky, he had no notion; ideas about the classical ballet such as those which the last-named Russian master later enunciated were remote from his mind: ballet as a triumph of plan and measure over unstable feeling, of order over chance, as a pattern of conscious, apolline activity, a paradigm for art. What hovered before his mind's eye were simply gauze petticoats, toe-pointing, tripping, and arms bent "gracefully" over heads, under the eyes of a court society asserting the "ideal," reprobating the hateful problematical, these sitting in their loges, while a well-trained bourgeoisie filled the parterre.

Well, there was much Wagner played at the Schlaginhaufens', since the dramatic soprano Tania Orlanda, tremendous woman, and the heroic Harald Kioeiclund, a man already stout, with a pince-nez and brazen voice, were frequent guests. But without Wagner's work, loud and violent as it was, Herr Riedesel and his Hoftheater could not have existed, so it was received, more or less, into the kingdom of the feudal and "graceful" and respect was paid it, the more readily because there were already newer works

which went still further, so that one could reject them, and play
off Wagner against them as a conservative. Thus His Excellence
himself could flatter the singers by playing their accompaniments
on the piano, although his pianistic virtuosity was scarcely equal
to the task and more than once compromised the effect. I did not
care for it when Kammersänger Kioeielund brayed out Sieg-
fried's pretty dull and long-winded smith's songs so that all the
vases and glass-ware in the salon rattled and rang in sympathy.
But I confess that I am not proof against such a heroic female
voice as the Orlanda's was at that time. The weight of her personality, the power of her organ, her practised technique produced the convincing illusion of a regal female soul possessed by
lofty emotion. When she sang Isolde's *"Frau Minne kenntest du
nicht,'* and marked by an energetic downward thrust of her arms
the ecstatic *"Die Fackel, wär's meines Lebens Licht lachend sie
zu löschen zagt' ich nicht,"* it did not lack much for me, with
tears in my eyes, to have knelt before the singer as she stood triumphantly smiling, overwhelmed with applause. Moreover it was
Adrian who had accompanied her, and he too smiled when he
rose from the piano-stool and his eyes dwelt on my face, moved
as it was almost to weeping.

It does one good, among such impressive performances, to contribute something oneself to the artistic entertainment, and I was
gratified when Excellence von Riedesel, seconded at once by our
long-legged elegant hostess, urged me in his south-German pronunciation, and voice made more strident by his officer's training,
to repeat the andante and minuet of Milandre (1770) which I
had once before played on my seven strings. How weak is man!
I was grateful to him, I utterly forgot my dislike of his smooth
and empty aristocrat's face, which out of sheer imperturbable
insolence positively shone; with the twisted blond moustaches,
the smooth-shaven cheeks, and the gleaming monocle in the eye
under the bleached brows. To Adrian, as well I knew, this titled
gentleman was a figure beyond judgment or sentence, beyond
hatred or scorn, yes, beyond laughter; he was not worth a shoulder-shrug — and just so, actually, I felt myself. But at such a moment, when he challenged me to contribute something "graceful,"
that the company might recover from the attack of the revolutionary arriviste, I could not help acceding to his request.

It was very strange, partly painful and partly comic, to observe
Riedesel's conservatism in contact with another brand of the same
thing. Here it was a matter not so much of "still" as "again"; for
this was an after- and anti-revolutionary conservatism, a revolt

against bourgeois liberal standards from the other end, not from rear but from the front; not from the old but from the new. Such a contact was encouraging as well as bewildering to the simple old conservatism; and occasion for it was afforded in our day, even in the Schlaginhaufen salon, where the social ambitions of the hostess brought people of every stripe together. For example, one of the guests was the private scholar Dr. Chaim Breisacher, a racial and intellectual type in high, one might almost say reckless development and of a fascinating ugliness. Here, obviously with a certain malicious pleasure, he played the role of ferment and foreigner. The hostess approved his dialectic readiness, produced with a decided Palatinate accent; also his turn for paradox, which made the ladies clap their hands over their heads in demure jubilation. As for himself, it was probably snobbishness that made him take pleasure in this society, as well as the need of astonishing elegant simplicity with ideas which, in a literary circle, would have made less of a sensation. I did not like him in the least, always saw in him an intellectual intrigant, and was convinced that he was repugnant to Adrian as well, although, on grounds to me unclear, we never came to any detailed conversation about Breisacher. But the man's scent for the intellectual weather of the time, his nose for the newest views, I have never denied, and some of all that I met for the first time in his person and his conversation in society.

He was a polyhistor, who knew how to talk about anything and everything; he was concerned with the philosophy of culture, but his views were anti-cultural, in so far as he gave out to see in the whole history of culture nothing but a process of decline. The most contemptuous word on his lips was the word "progress"; he had an annihilating way of pronouncing it; and one felt that the conservative scorn which he devoted to the idea was regarded by himself as the true legitimation of his presence in this society, the mark of his fitness for it. He had wit, but of no very sympathetic kind; as when he poured scorn on the development of painting from the primitive flat to the presentation of perspective. To condemn as incapacity or ignorance, even as clumsy primitivism, the rejection of perspective eye-deception by pre-perspective art; even pityingly to shrug the shoulder over it: this he declared to be the peak of silly modern arrogance. Rejection, renunciation, disdain were not incapacity, nor uninstructedness, nor evidence of poverty. As though illusion were not the cheapest principle in art, the most suited to the mob; as though it were not simply a sign of elevated taste to wish to know nothing of it! The

gift of wanting to know nothing of certain things was very close
to wisdom, was even a part of it; but it had unfortunately been
lost, and ordinary, impudent know-nothings called themselves
progressive.

The guests of Frau Schlaginhaufen née von Plausig somehow
found themselves very much at home listening to these remarks.
They may have felt that Breisacher was not quite the right person
to make them, but scarcely that they might not be the right people to applaud them.

It was the same thing, he said, with the change-over of music
from monody to part-music, to harmony, which people liked to
think of as cultural progress, when actually it had been just an
acquisition of barbarism.

"That is . . . pardon, barbarism?" croaked Herr von Riedesel,
who was of course accustomed to see in the barbaric a form, if a
slightly compromising one, of the conservative.

"Yes indeed, Excellence. The origins of polyphonic music —
that is, of singing simultaneously in fifths and fourths — lie remote
from the centre of musical civilization, far from Rome, where the
beautiful voice and the cult of it were at home. They lie in the
raw-throated north and seem to have been a sort of compensation for the rawness. They lie in England and France, particularly in savage Britain, which was the first to accept the third into
harmony. The so-called higher development, the complication,
the progress are thus sometimes the achievement of barbarism. I
leave it to you whether this is to be praised or not. . . ."

It was clear and plain that he was making fun of His Excellence
and the whole company, at the same time as he was ingratiating
himself with them as a conservative. Obviously he did not feel
comfortable so long as any of his audience knew what they were
to think. Of course polyphonic vocal music, this invention of progressivist barbarism, became the object of his conservative protection so soon as the historical transition from it to the harmonic-
chordal principle and therewith to instrumental music of the last
two centuries was complete. This, then, was the decline, namely
the deterioration of the great and only true art of counterpoint,
the cool and sacred play of numbers, which, thank God, had had
nothing to do with prostitution of feeling or blasphemous dynamic; and in this decline, right in the middle of it, belonged the
great Bach from Eisenach, whom Goethe quite rightly called a
harmonist. A man was not the inventor of the well-tempered
clavichord, accordingly of the possibility of understanding every
note ambiguously and exchanging them enharmonically, and thus

of the newer harmonic romanticism of modulation, without deserving the hard name which the wise one of Weimar gave him. Harmonic counterpoint? There was not such a thing. It was neither fish nor flesh. The softening, the effeminizing and falsification, the new interpretation put on the old and genuine polyphony understood as a combined sounding of various voices into the harmonic-chordal, had already begun in the sixteenth century, and people like Palestrina, the two Gabrielis, and our good Orlando di Lasso here on the spot had already played their shameful part in it. These gentlemen brought us the conception of the vocal polyphonic art, "humanly" at first, oh yes, and seemed to us therefore the greatest masters of this style. But that was simply because for the most part they delighted in a purely chordal texture of phrase, and their way of treating the polyphonic style had been miserably weakened by their regard for the harmonic factor, for the relation of consonance and dissonance.

While everybody marvelled and laughed and clapped his knees at these irritating remarks, I sought Adrian's eye, but he would not look at me. As for von Riedesel, he was a prey to sheer confusion.

"Pardon me," he said, "permit me . . . Bach, Palestrina . . . "

These names wore for him the nimbus of conservative authority, and here they were being assigned to the realm of modernistic disintegration. He sympathized — and at the same time found it all so unnatural that he even took his monocle out of his eye, thus robbing his face of every gleam of intelligence. He fared no better when Breisacher's cultural harangue shifted its theme to the field of Old Testament criticism, thus turning to his own personal sphere of origin, the Jewish race or people and its intellectual history. Even here he adhered to a double-faced, a crass and malicious conservatism. According to him, decline, besottedness, loss of every contact with the old and genuine, had set in earlier and in a more respectable place than anyone could have dreamed. I can only say that it was on the whole frantically funny. Biblical personages — revered by every Christian child — King David, King Solomon, and the prophets drivelling about dear God in heaven, these were the already debased representatives of an exploded late theology, which no longer had any idea of the old and genuine Hebraic actuality of Jahve, the Elohim of the people; and in the rites with which at the time of genuine folkishness they served this national god or rather forced him to physical presence, saw only "riddles of primeval time." He was particularly cutting about Solomon "the wise," and treated him with so little cere-

mony that the gentlemen whistled through their teeth and the
ladies cheered as well as they could for amazement.

"Pardon," said von Riedesel. "I am, to put it mildly . . . King
Solomon in all his glory. . . . Should you not — "

"No, Excellence, I should not," answered Breisacher. "The man
was an æsthete unnerved by erotic excesses and in a religious sense
a progressivist blockhead, typical of the back-formation of the
cult of the effectively present national god, the general concept
of the metaphysical power of the folk, into the preaching of an
abstract and generally human god in heaven; in other words, from
the religion of the people to the religion of the world. To prove
it we only need to read the scandalous speech which he made
after the first temple was finished, where he asks: 'But will God
indeed dwell on the earth?' as though Israel's whole and unique
task had not consisted therein, that it should build God a dwelling,
a tent, and provide all means for His constant presence. But Solomon was so bold as to declaim: 'Behold, the heaven and heaven
of heavens cannot contain Thee; how much less this house that
I have builded!' That is just twaddle and the beginning of the
end, that is the degenerate conception of the poets of the Psalms;
with whom God is already entirely exiled into the sky, and who
constantly sing of God in heaven, whereas the Pentateuch does
not even know it as the seat of the Godhead. There the Elohim
goes on ahead of the people in a pillar of fire, there He will dwell
among the people, go about among the people and have His sham-
bles — to avoid the thin word 'altar' substituted by a later humanity. Is it conceivable for a psalmist to make God ask: 'Do I then
eat the flesh of bulls and drink the blood of goats?' To put such
words in God's mouth is already simply unheard of, a slap of
impertinent enlightenment in the face of the Pentateuch, which
expressly describes the sacrifice as 'the bread' — that is, as the actual nourishment of Jahve. It is only a step from this question, as
also from the phrases of Solomon the 'wise,' to Maimonides, supposedly the greatest rabbinical scholar of the Middle Ages, actually
an assimilator of Aristotle, who manages to 'explain' the sacrifice
as a concession by God to the heathen instincts of the people —
ha, ha! Good, the sacrifice of blood and fat, which once, salted
and seasoned with savoury smells, fed God, made Him a body,
held Him to the present, is for the psalmist only a 'symbol' " (I
can still hear the accents of ineffable contempt in which Dr.
Breisacher uttered the word); "one no longer slaughters the
beast, but, incredibly enough, gratitude and humility. 'Whoso
offereth praise,' is the word now, 'glorifieth me'! And another

time: 'The sacrifices of God are a broken spirit.' In short, all that
ceased, long ago, to be folk and blood and religious reality; it is
nothing any more but weak water-gruel."

So much as a taste of Breisacher's highly conservative exegesis.
It was as amusing as it was repulsive. He could not say enough to
display the genuine cult of the real and by no means abstractly
universal, hence also not "almighty" and "all-present" God of the
people as a magic technique, a manipulation of dynamic forces,
physically not without its risks, in which mishaps might easily occur, catastrophic short circuits due to mistakes and failures. The
sons of Aaron had died because they had brought on "strange
fire." That was an instance of a technical mischance, the consequence of an error. Somebody named Uzza had laid hands on the
chest, the so-called ark of the covenant, as it threatened to slip
when it was being transported by wagon, and he fell dead on the
spot. That too was a transcendental dynamic discharge, occurring
through negligence — the negligence, indeed, of King David, who
was too fond of playing the harp, and had no real understanding
of things any more; for he had the ark conveyed as the Philistines
did, by wagon instead of on bearing-poles according to the well-
founded prescript of the Pentateuch. David, indeed, was quite as
ignorant of origins and quite as besotted, not to say brutalized,
as Solomon his son. He was too ignorant, for instance, to realize
the dynamic dangers of a general census of the population; and
by instituting one had brought about a serious biological misfortune, an epidemic with high mortality; a reaction of the metaphysical powers of the people, which might have been foreseen.
For a genuine folk simply could not stand such a mechanizing
registration, the dissolution by enumeration of the dynamic whole
into similar individuals. . . .

It merely gratified Breisacher when a lady interposed and said
she had not known that a census was such a sin.

"Sin?" he responded, in an exaggeratedly questioning tone. No,
in the genuine religion of a genuine folk such colourless theological conceptions as sin and punishment never occurred, in their
merely ethical causal connection. What we had here was the
causality of error, a working accident. Religion and ethics represented the decline of religion. All morality was "a purely intellectual" misunderstanding of the ritual. Was there anything more
god-forsaken than the "purely intellectual"? It had remained for
the characterless world-religion, out of "prayer" — *sit venia verbo*
— to make a begging appeal for mercy, an "O Lord," "God have
mercy," a "Help" and "Give" and "Be so good." Our so-called

prayer . . . "Pardon!" said von Riedesel, this time with real emphasis. "Quite right, of course, but 'Head bare at prayer was always my — "

"Prayer," finished Dr. Breisacher relentlessly, "is the vulgarized and rationalistically watered-down late form of something very vital, active and strong: the magic invocation, the coercion of God."

I really felt sorry for the Baron. Here was his aristocratic conservatism outbid by the frightfully clever playing of atavistic cards; by a radical conservatism that no longer had anything aristocratic about it, but rather something revolutionary; something more disrupting than any liberalism, and yet, as though in mockery, possessing a laudable conservative appeal. All that must bewilder the very depths of his soul. I imagined it giving him a sleepless night, but my sympathy may have been exaggerated. Certainly not everything that Breisacher said was correct. One could easily have disputed him and pointed out that the spirited condemnation of the sacrifice is not found first of all in the prophets but in the Pentateuch itself; for it is Moses who bluntly declares that the sacrifice is secondary and lays all the emphasis on obedience to God and the keeping of His commandments. But a sensitive man does not like to disturb another; it is unpleasant to break in on a train of thought with logical or historical objections; even in the anti-intellectual such a man respects and spares the intellectual. Today we see, of course, that it was the mistake of our civilization to have practised all too magnanimously this respect and forbearance. For we found after all that the opposite side met us with sheer impudence and the most determined intolerance.

I was already thinking of all these things when at the beginning of this work I made an exception to my general profession of friendliness towards the Jewish people, confessing that I had run across some pretty annoying specimens, and the name of the scholar Breisacher slipped prematurely from my pen. Yet can one quarrel with the Jewish spirit when its quick hearing and receptivity for the coming thing, the new, persists also in the most extraordinary situations, where the avant-garde coincides with the reactionary? In any case, it was at the Schlaginhaufens', and through this very Breisacher, that I first came in touch with the new world of anti-humanity, of which my easy-going soul till then had known nothing at all.

CHAPTER XXIX

The Munich carnival season, that period between Epiphany and Ash Wednesday, was celebrated by common consent with dance and mirth, with flaming cheeks and flashing eyes, and with all sorts of public and private entertainments. The carnival of 1914, in which I, the still youthful academy professor from Freising, alone or in company with Adrian, took part, has remained in my memory, a vivid or rather a portentous image. It was indeed the last carnival before the beginning of the four-year war which has now been telescoped with the horrors of today into one historical epoch; the last one before the so-called "first World War," which put an end for ever to the idyl of æsthetic guilelessness in the city on the Isar and its dionysiac easy-goingness — if I may put it like that. And it was also the time in which certain individual destinies in our circle of acquaintance unfolded before my eyes, and, almost unheeded outside our circle, led up to naked catastrophe. I go into it in these pages because what happened did to some extent touch the life and destiny of my hero, Adrian Leverkühn; yes, in one of them, to my actual knowledge, he was involved and active in an obscure and fatal way.

I am not referring to the case of Clarissa Rodde, the proud and flippant blonde who toyed with the macabre. She still lived among us, in her mother's house, and shared in the carnival gaieties. Soon afterwards, however, she prepared to leave town and fill an engagement as *jeune première* in the provinces, which her teacher, who played father parts at the Hoftheater, had got for her. The engagement proved a failure; and her teacher, a man of experience named Seiler, must be absolved from all responsibility for it. He had written a letter one day to the Frau Senator saying that his pupil was extraordinarily intelligent and full of enthusiasm, but that she had not enough natural gift for a successful career on the stage. She lacked, he said, the first requisite of all dramatic art, the instinct of the play-actor — what one calls theatre blood; and in all conscience he felt constrained to advise against her continuing. This had led to a *crise de nerves*, an outburst of despair on Clarissa's part, which went to the mother's heart, and Seiler had been asked to terminate the training and use his connections to get her a start as a beginner.

It is now twenty-four years since Clarissa's lamentable destiny fulfilled itself, as I shall relate in its proper place in my story. Here I have in mind what happened to her delicate and suffering sister Inez, who cultivated the past and its regrets — and to poor Rudi Schwerdtfeger, of whom I thought with horror when I mentioned just now, almost involuntarily, the share of the recluse Adrian Leverkühn in these events. The reader is already used to my anticipations and will not interpret them as muddle-headedness and disregard of literary conventions. The truth is simply that I fix my eye in advance with fear and dread, yes, with horror on certain things which I shall sooner or later have to tell; they stand before me and weigh me down, and I try to distribute their weight by referring to them beforehand, of course not comprehensibly to anybody but myself. I let them a little way out of the bag and hope by this means to make the telling more tolerable to myself, to take out the sting and mitigate the distress. So much in excuse of a "faulty" technique of narration and in explanation of my difficulties. I scarcely need to say that Adrian was remote from the beginnings of the events I shall speak of here, being aware of them only to a certain extent and that only through me, who had much more social curiosity or shall I say human sympathy.

As I mentioned earlier, neither of the two Rodde sisters, Clarissa and Inez, got on particularly well with their mother, the Frau Senator, and they not seldom betrayed that the informal, slightly lax and bohemian air of her salon, the uprooted existence, upholstered though it was with the remnants of upper-middle-class elegance, got on their nerves. They strained away from the hybrid milieu, but in different directions. The proud Clarissa reached outwards towards a definite career as an actress, for which, as her master had finally been forced to say, she lacked a real calling. While, on the other hand, the refined and pensive Inez, who was at bottom afraid of life, yearned back to the refuge, the psychological security of an assured bourgeois position, the route to which was marriage, for love if possible, but in God's name even without love. Inez walked this road, of course with the cordial approval of her mother, and came to grief, as her sister did on hers. It turned out tragically enough that this solution was not the right one: that neither for Inez personally, nor for her circum-

stances in view of the times she lived in, this upsetting and undermining social epoch, did it hold out any hope of satisfaction.

At this time there approached her a certain Dr. Helmut Institoris, instructor in æsthetics and the history of art at the Technical Institute in Munich, where he lectured on æsthetic theory and
the history of Renaissance architecture and handed round photographs in class. He had good prospects of being called one day
to the university, of becoming professor, member of the Academy
and so on; especially when he, a bachelor from a solid Würzburg
family, in expectancy of a good inheritance, should have enhanced
his dignity by setting up a household of his own where he could
gather society about him. He went courting, and he did not
worry about the financial situation of the girl he courted. On the
contrary, he belonged to those men who prefer in marriage to
have all the economic power in their hands and to have their wives
dependent on them.

Such an attitude does not speak for conscious strength. And
Institoris was in fact not a strong man; one realized it in the æsthetic admiration he showed for everything bursting with exuberant vitality. He was blond and dolichocephalic, rather small
and very good form, with smooth hair, parted and slightly oiled.
A blond moustache drooped over his mouth, and behind the gold-
rimmed glasses the blue eyes wore a gentle, high-minded expression, which made it hard to understand — or perhaps precisely
did make one understand — that he respected and revered brute
force, but of course only when it was beautiful. He belonged to
a type bred in those decades — the kind of man who, as Baptist
Spengler once aptly put it, "when consumption glows in his
cheeks, keeps on shrieking: 'How stark and beautiful is life!' "

Well, Institoris did not shriek, on the contrary he spoke rather
softly, with a lisp, even when he celebrated the Italian Renaissance
as a time that "reeked of blood and beauty." He was not consump-
tive, had at most, like nearly everybody, been slightly tubercular
in his youth. But he was delicate and nervous, suffered from his
sympathetic nerve, in his solar plexus, from which so many anx-
ieties and early fears of death proceed, and was an habitué of a
sanatorium for the wealthy in Meran. Surely he promised himself — and his doctors promised him — an improvement in his
health resulting from the regularity of a comfortable married life.

In the winter of 1913–14 he approached our Inez Rodde in a
way that made one guess it would end in an engagement. However, the affair dragged on for some time, into the early years of
the war: doubt and conscience-searching on both sides probably

induced a long and careful testing, to see whether they were truly born for each other. But when one saw the "pair" together in the Frau Senator's salon, to which Institoris had correctly sought an introduction, or in public places, often sitting apart and talking, it was just this question which seemed to be at issue between them, whether directly or not, and the friendly observer, seeing something like a trial engagement in the offing, involuntarily discussed the subject too within himself.

That it was Inez upon whom Helmut had cast his eye might surprise one at first, but one understood it better in the end. She was no Renaissance female — anything but that, in her temperamental sensitiveness, with her veiled glance, full of melancholy and distinction; her head drooping on the slender, extended stalk and the little pursed-up mouth that seemed to indicate a feeble and fluctuating love of mischief. But on the other hand, the wooer would not have known how to cope with his own ideal either; his masculine superiority would have been found sorely wanting — one only needed to imagine him paired with a full and rounded nature like the Orlanda's to smile and be convinced. And Inez was by no means without feminine charm; it was understandable that a man on the look-out might have fallen in love with her heavy hair, her little dimpling hands, her aristocratic air of setting store by herself. She might be what he needed. Her circumstances attracted him: namely, her patrician origin, on which she laid stress, though it was slightly breathed upon by her present transplanted state; the faint suggestion that she had come down in the world, and thus threatened no superiority. Indeed, he might cherish the thought that in making her his he would be raising and rehabilitating her. A widowed mother, half-impoverished, a little pleasure-seeking; a sister who was going on the stage; a circle more or less bohemian: these were connections which did not, in combination with his own dignity, displease him, especially since socially he lost nothing by them, did not endanger his career, and might be sure that Inez, correctly and amply supplied by the Frau Senator with a dowry of linen, perhaps even silver, would make a model housewife and hostess.

Thus things looked to me, as seen from Dr. Institoris's side. If I tried to look at him with the girl's eyes, the thing ceased to be plausible. I could not, even using all my imagination, ascribe to the man, unimpressive as he was, absorbed in himself, refined indeed, with an excellent education, but physically anything but commanding (he even had a tripping gait), any appeal for the other sex; whereas I felt that Inez, with all her maiden reserve and aus-

terity, needed such an appeal. Added to this was the contrast between the philosophical views, the theoretic posture towards life,
assumed by the two — which might be considered diametrical and
exemplary. It was, to put it briefly, the antithesis between æsthetics and ethics, which in fact largely dominated the cultural
dialectics of the time and was to some extent embodied in these
two young people: the conflict between a doctrinaire glorification of "life" in its splendid unthinkingness, and the pessimistic
reverence for suffering, with its depth and wisdom. One may say
that at its creative source this contrast had formed a personal
unity and only through time fell out and strove against itself. Dr.
Institoris was in the very marrow of his bones a man of the
Renaissance — one feels like commenting "Good God!" — and
Inez Rodde quite explicitly a child of pessimistic moralism. For
a world that "reeked of blood and beauty" she had no use at all,
and as for "life" she was seeking shelter from it in a strictly orthodox, modish, economically well-upholstered marriage, which
should protect her from all possible blows of fate. It was ironic
that the man — the manikin — who seemed desirous to offer her
this shelter raved about beautiful ruthlessness and Italian poisoners.

I doubt that they, when they were alone, discussed any con-
troversies of world-wide bearing. They talked of things nearer at
hand and simply tried to see how it would be to be engaged.
Philosophical discussion as a social diversion belonged more to
the larger group; and I do remember several occasions when we
were all sitting together, perhaps round an alcove table in a ball-
room, and the views of the two clashed in conversation. Institoris
might assert that only human beings with strong and brutal instincts could create great works; and Inez would protest, con-
tending that it had often been highly Christian characters, bowed
down by conscience, refined by suffering, their view of life
marked by melancholy, from whom had come great things in art.
Such antitheses I found idle and ephemeral; they seemed to do no
justice to actual fact, the seldom happy and certainly always precarious balance of vitality and infirmity which genius obviously
is. But in this discussion one side represented that which it was,
namely sickliness, the other that which it worshipped, namely
strength; and both must be allowed to have their voice.

Once, I recall, as we sat together (the Knöterichs, Zink and
Spengler, Schildknapp and his publisher Radbruch were also of
the party) the friendly difference arose not between the lovers,
as one tended to call them, but amusingly enough between Institoris and Rudi Schwerdtfeger, who was sitting with us, very

charming in his huntsman's costume. I no longer clearly remember the discussion; anyhow the disagreement arose from a quite innocent remark of Schwerdtfeger's, about which he had surely thought little or nothing. It was about "merit," so much I know; something fought for, achieved, accomplished by will-power and self-conquest, and Rudolf, who praised the occurrence warmly, and called it deserving, could not in the least understand what Institoris meant by denying any value to it and refusing to recognize any virtue that had to sweat for it to that extent. From the point of view of beauty, he said, it was not the will but the gift that was to be praised; it alone could be called meritorious. Effort was plebeian; aristocratic and therefore alone meritorious was solely what happened out of instinct, involuntarily and with ease. Now, the good Rudi was no hero or conqueror, and had never in his life done anything that did not come easy to him, as for instance his capital violin-playing. But what the other said did go against the grain with him, and although he dimly felt that the subject had something "higher" about it, out of his own reach, he would not let himself be talked down. He looked Institoris in the face, his lip curled angrily, and his blue eyes bored into the other's, first the right and then the left, by turns.

"After all, that is just nonsense," he said, but in a contained, rather subdued voice, betraying that he did not feel so sure of his argument. "Merit is merit, and a gift isn't a merit. You are always talking about beauty, doctor; but after all it is beautiful when somebody triumphs over himself and does something better than nature gave him to do. What do you say, Inez?" he turned appealingly to her with his question, in perfect innocence, for he had no idea of the fundamentally opposed nature of her views and Helmut's.

"You are right," she answered, a faint glow rising in her cheeks. "At least I think so. A gift is pleasing; but the word 'merit' implies admiration of a different kind, not applicable to a gift nor to the instinctive at all."

"There you have it!" cried Schwerdtfeger triumphantly, and Institoris laughed back:

"By all means. You went to the right shop."

There was something strange here; nobody could help feeling it, at least for the moment; nor did the flush in Inez's cheek immediately subside. It was just in her line to disagree with her lover in all such questions. But it was not in her line to agree with the boy Rudolf. He was utterly unaware that there was such a thing as immoralism, and one cannot well agree with a thesis while not understanding its opposite — at least not before it has been explained to him. In Inez's verdict, although it was logically quite natural and justified, there was after all something that put one off, and that something was underlined for me by the burst of laughter with which her sister Clarissa greeted Schwerdtfeger's undeserved triumph. It surely did not escape this haughty person with the too short chin when superiority, on grounds which have nothing to do with superiority, gave something away and was just as certainly of the opinion that it gave nothing away. "There!" she cried. "Jump up, Rudolf, say thank you, hop up, laddy, and bow! Fetch your rescuer an ice and engage her for the next waltz!"

That was always her way. She always stood up for her sister and said "Up with you!" whenever it was a matter of Inez's dignity. She said it to Institoris, too, the suitor, when he behaved with something less than alacrity in his gallantries, or was slow in the uptake. Altogether, out of pride she held with superiority, looked out for it, and showed herself highly surprised when she thought it did not get its due. If *he* wants something of *you*, she seemed to say, you have to hop up. I well remember how she once said: "Hop up!" to Schwerdtfeger on Adrian's behalf, he having expressed a wish — I think it was a ticket for Jeanette Scheurl to the Zapfenstösser orchestra — and Schwerdtfeger made some objection. "Yes, Rudolf, you just hop along and get it," said she. "For heaven's sake, have you lost your legs?"

"No, no," said he, "I only, certainly, of course I — but — "

"But me no buts," she cut him short, condescendingly, half farcically but also half reproachfully. And Adrian as well as Schwerdtfeger laughed; the latter, making his usual boyish grimace with the corner of his mouth and shrugging his shoulder inside his jacket, promised that he should be served.

It was as though Clarissa saw in Rudolf the sort of suitor who had to "hop"; and in fact he constantly, in the most naïve way, confidingly and unabashedly sued for Adrian's favour. About the real suitor who was courting her sister she often tried to worm an opinion out of me — and Inez herself did the same, in a shyer, more refined way, drawing back almost at once, as though she wanted to hear, and yet wanted to hear and know nothing. Both sisters had confidence in me; that is, they seemed to consider me capable of just evaluations of others, a capacity, of course, which, if it is to inspire full confidence, must stand outside any situation and view it with unclouded eye. The role of confidant is always at once gratifying and painful, for one always plays it with the premise that one does not come into consideration oneself. But how much better it is, I have often told myself, to inspire the world with confidence than to rouse its passion! How much better to seem to it "good" than "beautiful!"

A "good" man, that was in Inez Rodde's eyes probably one to whom the world stands in a purely ethical relation, not an æsthetically stimulated one; hence her confidence in me. But I must say that I served the sisters somewhat unequally and expressed my opinions about Institoris in a form proper to the person who asked for them. In conversation with Clarissa I spoke far more as I really felt; expressed myself as a psychologist about the motives of his choice and his hesitations (anyhow the hesitation was not all on one side), and did not scruple to poke a little fun at his "Miss Nancy" ways and worship of "brute instinct." She seemed to concur. When Inez herself talked to me, it was not the same. I deferred to feelings which *pro forma* I assumed in her, without actually believing in them; deferred to the reasonable grounds on which in all probability she would marry the man, and spoke with sober regard of his solid qualities, his knowledge, his human decency, his capital prospects. To give my words adequate warmth and yet not too much was a delicate task; for it seemed to me equally a responsibility whether I strengthened the girl in her doubts and depreciated the security for which she yearned, or on the other hand encouraged her to give herself while cherishing such doubts. I even had some ground for feeling, now and then, that I ran more of a risk by encouraging than by dissuading.

The truth was that she soon had enough of my opinions about Helmut Institoris and went on with her confidences in a general way, asking my opinion about certain other persons in the circle, for instance Zink and Spengler, or, for another example, Schwerdtfeger. What did I think about his violin-playing, she asked; about his character, whether and how much I respected him, what shade of seriousness or humour my regard showed. I answered as best I could, with all possible justice, quite as I have spoken of Rudolf in these pages, and she listened attentively, enlarging on my friendly commendation with some remarks of her own, to which again I could only agree, though I was rather struck by her insistence. Considering the girl's character, her confirmed and mistrustful view of life, her ideas were not surprising, but applied to this particular subject I must say they rather put me off.

Yet after all it was no wonder that she, knowing the attractive young man so much longer than I, and like Clarissa in a brother-and-sister relation with him, had observed him more closely and had more matter for a confidential conversation. He was a man without vice, she said (she used a milder word, yet it was clear that was what she meant); a clean man, hence his confidingness, for cleanness was confiding (a touching word in her mouth, since she herself was not confiding at all, save by exception to me). He did not drink, taking nothing but slightly sugared tea without cream, three times a day; he did not smoke, or at most only occasionally, he did not make a habit of it. For all such masculine pacifiers (I think I remember the word) — in short, for narcotics — flirtation was his substitute; he was utterly given to flirtation, he was a born flirt. She did not mean love or friendship; both of these by his very nature and, so to speak, under his hands became flirtation. A poseur? Yes and no. Certainly not in the ordinary vulgar sense. One need only see him with Bullinger, the manufacturer, who plumed himself so enormously on his money, and liked to sing:

> A happy heart and healthy blood
> Are better than much gold and goods

just to make people envious of his money. Rudolf was not like that at all. But he made it hard for one to feel sure of him all the time. His coquetry, his nice manners, his social coxcombry, his love of society altogether were really something frightful. Did I not find, she asked, that this whole free-and-easy, æsthetic life here in this place, for instance the smart Biedermeier celebration which we had lately attended in the Cococello Club, was in torturing contrast to the sadness and disillusionments of life? Did I not know, like her, that shudder at the spiritual vacuity which reigned in the average gathering, in glaring contrast to the feverish excitement induced by the wine, the music, and the undercurrents of human relations? Sometimes one could see how somebody talked with somebody else, preserving all the social forms, while his mind was entirely absent, fixed on another person at whom he was looking. . . . And then the disorder of the scene afterwards, the rubbish strewn about, the desolation of an empty salon at the end of an entertainment! She confessed that sometimes after she got home she wept for an hour before falling asleep. . . .

So she went on, expressing a general criticism and disapproval, and seeming to have forgotten Rudolf. But when she came back to him one had little doubt that he had been in her mind all the time. When she called him a coxcomb, she said, she meant something very harmless, almost laughable; yet it often made one feel

sad. For instance, he was always the last comer at a party, he had
to feel himself waited for, other people must always wait for him.
Then he set store by rivalry and social jealousy: would tell how
he had been at such and such houses, yesterday at the Langewiesches', or whoever his friends were; or at the Rollwagens',
who had the two thoroughbred daughters ("it always upsets me
just to hear that word"). But he always spoke apologetically, as
though he really meant: "I have to appear there now and again,
after all." Though one could be sure that he said the same thing
in the other place and tried to create the illusion that he liked
them best — just as though everybody set great store by that. Yet
he was so sure he was bringing joy to everybody that there was
something contagious about it. He came to tea at five o'clock
and said he had promised to be somewhere else between half past
five and six, at the Langewiesches' or Rollwagens' — probably it
was not true at all. Then he stopped on until half past six, to
show that he would rather be here, that he was so entertained
where he was that the others would have to wait. And was so
certain that one would be pleased that one actually was pleased.

We laughed, but I did so with reserve, for I saw distress written on her face. She spoke as though she thought it necessary —
did she really think it necessary? — to warn me not to put too
much confidence in Schwerdtfeger's amiable attentions. There
was nothing to them. She had once happened to hear, from a little
distance, word for word, how he implored somebody, to whom
she knew him to be profoundly indifferent, to remain at a gathering, not to go away; spoke in a low voice, with charming, intimate inflections: "Ah, do, come on, be sweet, stay with me." So
now, when he spoke to her in the same way, or to me, it might
be, the words would mean nothing at all.

In short, she confessed to a painful distrust of his seriousness, or
any display he made of attention and sympathy — for instance, if
one was not well and he came to see one. All that happened, as I
myself would learn, only to be "nice" and because it was proper
and socially the done thing, not from any inner feeling, one must
not imagine it. One might even expect actual bad taste. Somebody once warned him in jest not to make some girl — or it might
perhaps have been a married woman — unhappy, and he had actually answered, arrogantly: "Oh, there are so many unhappy!" She
had heard it with her own ears. One could only think: "God save
me from the humiliation of belonging to a man like that!"

But she did not want to be hard — perhaps the word "humiliation" was too strong. I must not misunderstand her, she did not

doubt that there was a certain fund of nobility in Rudolf's character. Sometimes even in company one could alter his loud and common mood to a gentler, more serious one, simply by a quiet word or surprised glance. It had really happened like that more than once, for Rudolf was extraordinarily susceptible; and then the Langewiesches and Rollwagens and whatever their names were became for the time mere shadows and phantoms for him. Yet it was enough for him to breathe other air, be exposed to other influences, to bring about a complete estrangement, a hopeless aloofness in the place of confidence and mutual understanding. Then he would feel it, for he really had fine feelings, and would try remorsefully to put things right. It was funny, and touching, but to restore good relations he might repeat some more or less apt phrase you had used, or a quotation you had once made from a book, to show that he had not forgotten, that he was at home among the higher things. Really it was enough to make one weep. And when he took leave for the evening, he showed his readiness to be sorry and do better: he came and said good-bye and made little jokes in dialect, at which one rather winced, for perhaps one was suffering from fatigue. But then when he had shaken hands all round he came back and said good-bye again, quite simply, so that one was able to respond. And that meant a good exit for him, which he simply had to have. At the two other houses he was going to he probably did the same thing. . . .

Have I said enough? This is no novel, in whose composition the author reveals the hearts of his characters indirectly, by the action he portrays. In a biography, of course, I must introduce things directly, by name, and simply state such psychological factors as have a bearing on the life I am describing. But after the singular expressions which my memory leads me to write down, expressions of what I might call a specific intensity, there can be no doubt as to the fact to be communicated. Inez Rodde was in love with young Schwerdtfeger. There were only two questions to be asked: first, did she know it, and second, when, at what point had her original brother-sister relation with him assumed this ardent and distressful colour?

The first question I answer with a yes. So well-read a girl, one might say psychologically trained, keeping watch with a poet's eye upon her own experiences must certainly have had an insight into the growth of her own feeling — however surprising, yes, unbelievable the development might have seemed to her at first. The apparent naïveté with which she bared her heart to me was no

evidence of ignorance; for what looked like simplicity was partly
a compulsive desire to communicate and partly a motion of confidence in me, a strangely disguised confidence, for to some extent
she was pretending that she thought me simple enough not to understand; and that was in itself a sort of confidence. But actually
she knew and was glad to know that the truth was not escaping
me since, to my honour be it spoken, she trusted her secret with
me. She might do so, of course, might be certain of my discretion
and my human sympathy, however hard it naturally is for a man
to enter into the feelings of a woman on fire with love for somebody of his own sex. It is much easier for us to follow the feelings
of a man for a woman — even though he be entirely indifferent to
her himself — than to put himself in the place of a woman in love
with another man. One does not at bottom "understand" that, one
just accepts it as a well-bred man should, in objective respect for
a law of nature — and indeed the attitude of a man is usually more
tolerant and benevolent than that of a woman, who mostly casts
a jealous eye on a friend who tells her a man is in love with her,
even though she cares nothing at all for the man.

I did not fail, then, in friendly good will, even though I was
prevented by nature from understanding in the sense of fellow-
feeling. My God, little Schwerdtfeger! His facial structure had
something of the pug about it, his voice was guttural, he was
more like a boy than a man, the lovely blue of his eyes, his good
straight growth and captivating violin-playing and whistling, his
general niceness admitted and agreed. Well, then, Inez Rodde
loved him. Not blindly, but for that reason suffering the more;
and my inward attitude was that of her mocking sister Clarissa,
who looked down her nose at the other sex: I should have liked
to say to him: "Hop, man! Hop up and do your duty — what do
you think of yourself?"

But hopping was not so simple, even if Rudolf had acknowledged the obligation. For there was Helmut Institoris, the bridegroom, or bridegroom *in spe*, Institoris the suitor. And here I
come back to the question: since when had Inez's sisterly relations with Rudolf turned into passionate love? My human powers
of intuition told me: it had happened when Dr. Helmut approached her, as man to woman, and began to woo her. I was and
remain convinced that Inez would never have fallen in love with
Schwerdtfeger without the entry of Institoris into her life. He
wooed her, but in a sense for another. A man not passionate himself could by his courtship and the trains of thought connected
with it arouse the woman in her: it might go that far. But he

could not arouse it for himself, though on grounds of good sense she was ready to accept him — that far it did not go. Instead her awakened femininity turned straightway to another man, towards whom thus far she had consciously felt only tranquil sisterly feelings — and now others had been released in her. It was not that she found him "the right one" or worthy of her love. No, it was her melancholy nature, seeking unhappiness, which fixed upon him as its object; upon him from whom she had heard with disgust the words: "There are so many unhappy ones!"

And stranger still: her inadequate suitor's predilection for soullessness and the beauty of instinct, so repugnant to her own views — had she not fallen victim to it herself, in her love for Rudolf? She was, in a way, betraying Institoris with his own convictions; for did not Rudolf represent to her wise and disillusioned gaze something like sweet unthinking life itself?

Compared with Institoris, who was a mere instructor in the beautiful, Rudolf had on his side the advantage of art at first hand: art, nourisher of the passions, transcender of the human. For by his art the person of the beloved is elevated, from art the emotions ever draw fresh food, when the artist's own individuality is associated with the joys his art purveys. Inez at bottom despised the æsthetic traffic of the sense-loving city into which she had been transplanted by her mother's craving for a less straitlaced life. But for the sake of her bourgeois security she took part in the festivities of a community which was just one great artsociety, and this it was emperilled the security she sought. My memory preserves pregnant and disquieting images of this time: I see us, the Roddes, the Knöterichs perhaps, and myself, after a particularly brilliant performance of a Tchaikovsky symphony in the Zapfenstösser concert hall, standing in the crowd in one of the front rows and applauding. The conductor had motioned the orchestra to stand up to receive the thanks of the audience for its beautiful work. Schwerdtfeger, a little to the left of the first violin, whose place he was soon to take, stood with his instrument under his arm, warm and beaming, face towards the hall and nodding to us with not quite permissible familiarity, while Inez, at whom I could not resist stealing a glance, with her head thrust out, her mouth mischievously pursed, kept her eyes obstinately directed at some other point on the stage, perhaps on the leader, or no, farther along, on the harps. Or another time I see Rudolf himself, all on fire over a classic performance by a guest colleague, standing in the front of an almost emptied hall, applauding up at the stage where the soloist stood bowing for the tenth time. Two

steps away, among the disarray of chairs, stands Inez, who sees
him and waits for him to stop clapping, turn round and speak to
her. He does not turn, he continues to applaud. But out of the
corner of his eye he looks — or perhaps not quite looks, perhaps
his blue eyes are only the slightest shade turned from a direct
gaze up at the platform and towards the corner where she stands
and waits. He does not pause in his enthusiastic activity. Another
few seconds and she turns away, pale with anger, lines between
her brows, and moves towards the door. At once he stops clapping
and follows her. At the door he overtakes her; she puts on an air
of chilling surprise to find him here, to find that he exists at all.
Refuses to speak, refuses her hand, her eyes, and hastens out.

I see that it was ill-judged of me to try to set down all the
trifling minutiæ which were the harvest of my observant eye.
They are not worth printing, the reader may easily find them
puerile or be annoyed by what seems like idle and boring speculation. But he must consider that I am suppressing a hundred others
that got caught as it were in the net of my perceptions, the perceptions of a sympathetic and benevolent friend; thanks to the
calamity they added up to, I cannot so easily dismiss them from
my mind. For years I watched the oncoming of a catastrophe, insignificant, it is true, in the light of world events; and I held
my peace about what I saw and feared. Only to Adrian did I
once speak, at the beginning, in Pfeiffering, although I had on the
whole small inclination, always feeling a certain reluctance to discuss the love-affairs of our circle with him, who lived in monkish
detachment from everything of the sort. Yet I did so: I told him
in confidence that Inez Rodde, although about to engage herself
to Institoris, was, so far as my observation went, hopelessly and
fatally in love with Rudi Schwerdtfeger. We were sitting in the
Abbot's room, playing chess.

"That's news!" he said. "You probably want me to miss my
move and lose my castle."

He smiled, shook his head, and added: "Poor soul!"

Then, as he considered his next play, with a pause between the
sentences: "But that's no joke for him. — He must see to it that he
gets out of it whole."

CHAPTER XXX

THE first glowing August days of 1914 found me changing from one crowded train to another, waiting in stations swarming with people, their platforms piled with left-behind luggage, on a headlong journey from Freising to Naumburg in Thuringia, where as reserve vice-sergeant-major I was joining my regiment.

War had broken out. The fate that so long had brooded over Europe was upon us, it raged. In the guise of a disciplined execution of all the plans previously made and rehearsed, it raged through our cities and towns, as terror and exaltation, as the inevitable, as "destiny"; as awareness of power and readiness for sacrifice, in the heads and hearts of men. It may well be, I like to think so, that elsewhere, in both enemy and allied countries, this short cut of fate was felt more as a catastrophe and "*grand malheur.*" We in the field heard these words so often from the lips of Frenchwomen, who did have the war on their soil, in their homes and on their hearths: "*Ah, monsieur, la guerre, quel grand malheur!*" But in our Germany its effect was undeniably and preeminently enthusiasm, historic ardour, joy at being released from dull everyday, and from a world-stagnation that could go on no longer; as hope for the future, an appeal to duty and manhood, in short as a holiday for heroes. My Freising top-formers had hot heads and glowing eyes. Youthful thirst for adventure, impatience to be off, were naïvely mingled with satisfaction at an early release from school. They stormed the recruiting stations, and I was glad that they need not look down on me for a stay-at-home.

I would by no means deny that I fully shared in the popular exultation which I just sought to characterize, though its more extravagant ebullitions were foreign to my nature. My conscience, speaking generally, was not perfectly clear. Such a "mobilization" for war, however stern and grim a face it wears, must always have something about it like an unlicensed holiday; however unreservedly one's duty, it seems a little like playing truant, like running away, like yielding to unbridled instinct. A settled man like me scarcely felt at ease in it all; and aside from personal and temperamental discomfort, I dimly felt a moral doubt: had we as a nation been so well-behaved up to now that this abandon, these transports, were legitimate? But now the moment had come for readiness to sacrifice and die; that carries one along over everything, it is so to speak the last word, after it there is no more to be said. If the war is felt more or less clearly as a general visitation, in which the individual, as well as the individual people, is ready to stand his man and atone with his blood for the weaknesses and sins of the time, including his own; if he thinks of himself as a sacrifice by which the old Adam is put away and from which in unity a new and higher life will be wrested, then our everyday morals are outbid by the abnormal and must be silent. Neither would I forget that then we went with relatively pure hearts and clean hands to war and did not think we had so behaved at home that a general and catastrophic blood-letting must needs be regarded as the inevitable logical consequence of our domestic doings. Thus it was five years ago, God help us, but not thirty! Justice and law, the habeas corpus, freedom and human dignity had been tolerably honoured in the land. Of course the sword-waving of that fundamentally unsoldierly play-actor, made for anything but war, who sat on the imperial throne was painful to the man of culture; moreover his attitude to the things of the mind was that of a retarded mentality. But his influence on them had exhausted itself in empty gestures of regulation. Culture had been free, she had stood at a respectable height; and though she had long been used to a complete absence of relations with the governing power, her younger representatives might see in a great national war, such as now broke out, a means of achieving a form of life in which state and culture might become one. In this we displayed the preoccupation with self which is peculiar to us: our naïve egoism finds it unimportant, yes, takes it entirely for granted, that for the sake of our development (and we are always developing) the rest of the world, further on than ourselves and not at all possessed by the dynamic of catastrophe, must shed its blood. They take that ill of us, not quite unfairly; for ethically speaking, the only way a people can achieve a higher form of communal life is not by a foreign war, but by a civil one — even with bloodshed. The idea is repugnant to us; yet we thought nothing at all, on the contrary we found it glorious, that our national unification — and even so a partial, a compromise unification — cost three serious wars. We were already long since a great power, we were quite used to it, and it did not make us as happy as we had expected. The feeling that it had not made us more winning, that our relation to the world had rather worsened than improved, lay, unconfessed, deep in our hearts. A new break-through seemed due: we would become a dominating world power — but such a position was not to be achieved by means of mere moral "home-work." War, then, and if needs must, war against everybody, to convince everybody and to win; that was our lot, our "sending" (the very word we use is Germanic, the idea pre-Christian, the whole concept a tragically mythological, musical-dramatic motif); that was what fate had willed, and we — only we! — enthusiastically responded and set forth. We were bursting with the consciousness that this was Germany's century, that history was holding her hand out over us; that after Spain, France, England, it was our turn to put our stamp on the world and be its leader; that the twentieth century was ours; that now, at the end of the bourgeois epoch begun some hundred and twenty years before, the world was to renew itself in our sign, in the sign of a never up to the end quite defined military socialism.

This picture, not to call it an idea, possessed all our heads, companionably side by side with another: the belief that we were forced into war, that sacred necessity called us to take our weapons — those well-polished weapons whose readiness and excellence always induced a secret temptation to test them. Then there was the fear of being overrun from all sides, from which fate only our enormous strength protected us, our power of carrying the war straightway into other lands. Attack and defence were the same, in our case: together they made up the feeling of a providence, a calling, a great hour, a sacred necessity. The peoples beyond our borders might consider us disturbers of the peace if they chose, enemies of life and not to be borne with; but we had the means to knock the world on the head until it changed its mind and came not only to admire but to love us.

Let nobody think I am being jocose. There is no occasion for that, first of all because I can by no means pretend to have excluded myself from the general emotion. I genuinely shared it, even though my normal staid professorial attitude would have held me aloof from any loud manifestation, or even have caused in me some slight protest, a subconscious misgiving at thinking and feeling what everybody else thought and felt. People of my sort have doubts whether every man's thoughts are the right ones. And still, it is a great pleasure to the superior individual, just once — and where should one find this once, if not here and now? — to lose himself altogether in the general.

I stopped two days in Munich to make my farewells in various quarters and supply some details of my equipment. The city was seething. There was a religious solemnity in the air, as well as cases of panic, rage, and dread; as for instance when the wild rumour sprang up that the water supply was poisoned, or a Serbian spy was supposed to have been discovered in the crowd. In order not to be taken for one and cut down by mistake, Dr. Breisacher, whom I met on the Ludwigstrasse, had decorated his coat with numerous little red, white, and black rosettes and flags. The state of war, the passing of the supreme authority from the civil to the military, and to a General Staff issuing proclamations, was accepted with mingled confidence and apprehension. It was soothing to know that the members of the royal family, who as commanders had left for headquarters, would have competent chiefs of staff at their side and could commit no royal ineptnesses. Under those circumstances they were loudly cheered on their way. I saw regiments, with nosegays tied to their rifle-barrels, marching out of barrack gates, accompanied by women with handkerchiefs to their faces, while civilian crowds quickly gathered and shouted godspeed, and the peasant lads promoted to heroship smiled back, proud, stupid, and shy. I saw a very young officer, in marching kit, standing on the back platform of a tram, faced to the rear, staring before him and into himself, obviously busy with thoughts of his own young life; then he pulled himself together and with a hasty smile looked round to see if anyone had noticed.

Again I was glad to feel that my situation was the same as his and that I need not remain behind those who were marching to protect their land. At least in the beginning I was the only one of our circle to go. The country was strong enough in man-power to afford to be particular, to consider cultural interests, to admit to much unfitness and to hurl to the front only the perfectly sound of our youth and manhood. In nearly all the men of our group there turned out to be some kind of weakness, something we had scarcely known, but it now procured their exemption. Knöterich, the Sugambian, was slightly tubercular. Zink, the artist, suffered from asthmatic attacks like whooping-cough and used to withdraw from society to get rid of them; his friend Baptist Spengler was ailing, as we know, everywhere by turns. Bullinger the business man was still young, but it appeared that as an industrialist he was indispensable. The Zapfenstösser orchestra was too important a feature of the city's artistic life for its members, among them Rudi Schwerdtfeger, not to be exempted from the service. Anyhow the occasion served to inform us, to our momentary surprise, that Rudi, in his earlier life, had had an operation that cost him one of his kidneys. He lived, we suddenly heard, with only one. That was quite enough, it appeared, and the ladies soon forgot all about it.

I could go on to mention many a case of reluctance, protection, favoritism, in the circles that frequented the Schlaginhaufens and the ladies Scheurl near the Botanical Gardens: circles where there was a fundamental objection to this war, as there had been to the last one: memories of the Rhenish alliance, Francophile sentiments, Catholic dislike of Prussia, and so on. Jeanette Scheurl was unhappy to tears. She was in despair over the savage flaring-up of the antagonism between the two countries to which she belonged, and which in her opinion ought to complement each other, instead of fighting. *"J'en ai assez jusqu'à la fin de mes jours,"* she said with angry sobs. Despite my dissimilar feelings I could but grant her a cultural sympathy.

To say good-bye to Adrian, whose personal detachment from the whole scene was the most understandable thing in the world to me, I went out to Pfeiffering, whence the son of the house, Gereon, had already departed with several horses for his base. I found Rüdiger Schildknapp there, for the present still free, spending a week-end with our friend. He had served in the marines and would be taken later, but after some months he was again released. It was not very different in my own case: let me say at once that I remained in the field a bare year, till the Argonne battles of 1915, and was shipped home, with the Cross I had earned only by putting up with discomforts and by catching a typhus infection.

So much by way of preface. Rüdiger's judgment of the war was conditioned by his admiration for the English, as was Jeanette Scheurl's by her French blood. The British declaration of war had gone home to him, his mood was unusually sombre. We should never in his opinion have challenged England by the treaty-breaking march into Belgium. France and Russia—well and good, one might take them on. But England? It was frightful folly. So then, inclined to an irritated realism, he saw in the war only filth, stench, horrible amputations, sexual licence, and lice and jeered his fill at the ideological journalism that turned an utter nuisance into a glorious event. Adrian did not gainsay him, and I, despite my deeper feelings, yet willingly conceded that there was some truth in what he said.

The three of us ate in the great Nike room that evening, and as Clementina Schweigestill moved to and fro quietly serving us,

I asked news of how Adrian's sister Ursula fared in Langensalza. Her marriage was of the happiest, it seemed; she had recovered very well from a weakness of the lungs, a slight apical catarrh, which she had got after three childbeds in quick succession, in 1911, 1912, and 1913. It was the Schneidewein offspring Rosa, Ezekiel, and Raimund who then saw the light. The period between these three and the next was a full decade; it would be ten years before the enchanting Nepomuk made his appearance.

During the meal and afterwards in the Abbot's room there was much talk on political and moral subjects. We spoke of the legendary manifestation of the German national character, which was supposed to reveal itself at moments of historical crisis like this — I referred to it with a certain emotion, in order to offset a little the drastically empirical interpretation that Schildknapp considered the only possible one: Germany's traditional role, the trespass against Belgium, which was so reminiscent of Frederick the Great's attack upon formally neutral Saxony; the yell of outrage that went up from the world, and the speech of our philosophical Chancellor, with its ingeniously presented admission of guilt, its folk-proverb: "Necessity knows no law," its plea to God in contempt of an old legal paper, in face of living necessity. It was due to Rüdiger that we ended by laughing; for he accepted my somewhat emotional representations and then turned into irresistible absurdity all this dignified regret, noble brutality, and respectable mischief-making by parodying the tall philosopher who had dressed up in poetic moralizations a strategic plan long since determined on. We might laugh, but there was no amusement in the virtuous roar that went up from a stunned world at this execution of a cut-and-dried plan of campaign, knowledge of which had long been public property. However, I saw that our host liked this line much better and was glad of the chance to laugh; so I willingly joined in, not without recalling what Plato had said of comedy and tragedy: how they grow on the same tree and a change of lighting suffices to make one into the other.

All together I did not allow my sympathy for Germany's necessity, her moral isolation and public proscription, which, so it seemed to me, was only the expression of the general fear of her strength and advantage in preparedness (I did admit that we reckoned the strength and the advantage as a harsh consolation in our outlawed state) — all together, I say, I did not allow my patriotic emotion, which was so much harder to explain than that of the others, to be dampened by the cold water thrown on our national traits. Indeed, I gave it words, walking up and down the room, while Schildknapp in the deep easy-chair smoked his shag pipe, and Adrian stood, the most of the time, in front of his old-German work-table with the sunken centre and the reading- and writing-desk set on it. For oddly enough he wrote on a slanting surface, like Erasmus in Holbein's portrait. A few books lay on the table: a little volume of Kleist, with the book-mark at the essay on marionettes; the indispensable volume of Shakespeare sonnets and another book with some of the plays — *Twelfth Night* I think, *Much Ado about Nothing,* and I believe *Two Gentlemen of Verona.* His work in hand lay there too: sheets, drafts, beginnings, notes, sketches in various stages of incompletion; often only the top line of the violin part or the wood-wind was filled out and quite below the progression of the bass, but between them simply white space, elsewhere the harmonic connection and the instrumental grouping were already made clear by the jotting down of the other orchestral parts. With his cigarette between his lips he would step up to the desk to look at his work, just as a chess-player measures on the chequered field the progress of a game, to which musical composition bears so suggestive a resemblance. We were all so comfortable together that he might even take a pencil and enter a clarinet or horn figure somewhere if he thought well of it.

We knew nothing precise about what was occupying him, now that that music of the cosmos had appeared in print from Schott's Sons in Mainz, under the same arrangements as the Brentano songs. Actually it was the suite of dramatic grotesques, whose themes, so we heard, he had taken from the old history and anecdote book, the *Gesta Romanorum.* He was trying these, without yet knowing whether anything would come of it or if he would continue. In any case, the characters were not to be men but puppets (hence the Kleist). As for the *Marvels of the Universe,* there was to have been a foreign performance of that solemn and arrogant work had not the war brought the plan to nothing We had spoken of it at table. The Lübeck performances of *Love's Labour's Lost,* even unsuccessful as they had proved, together with the mere existence of the Brentano cycle, had made some impression, and Adrian's name had begun in the inner circles of the art to have a certain esoteric and tentative fame — even this hardly at all in Germany and decidedly not in Munich. But there were other, more perceptive regions. A few weeks earlier he had had a letter from a Monsieur Monteux, director of the Russian

ballet in Paris, former member of the Colonne orchestra, wherein
this experimentally-minded director had announced his intention
of producing the *Marvels of the Universe,* together with some orchestral parts of *Love's Labour's Lost* as a concert pure and simple. He had in mind the Théâtre des Champs-Élysées for the performance, and invited Adrian to come to Paris, probably in order
to rehearse and conduct his own works. We had not asked our
friend whether he would, under favourable conditions, accept. In
any case, the circumstances were now such that there could be no
further talk of it.

I still see myself walking up and down the carpet and boards
of the old wainscoted room, with its overpowering chandelier, its
wall cupboards with their wrought-iron hinges, the flat leather
cushions on the corner bench, and the deep embrasures of the
windows; walking up and down and holding forth at large about
Germany; more for myself and certainly more for Schildknapp
than for Adrian, from whom I expected no interest. Used to
teaching and to talking, and, when I get warmed up, no bad
talker, I do not dislike listening to myself and take a certain pleasure in my command over words. Not without lively gesture I
challenged Rüdiger to set down what I said to the wartime journalism which so annoyed him. Surely one might be permitted a
little psychological participation in the national and even touching traits which our otherwise multiform German character was
evincing in this historic hour. In the last analysis, what we were
dealing with was the psychology of the break-through.

"In a nation like ours," I set forth, "the psychological is always
the primary and actually motivating; the political action is of the
second order of importance: reflex, expression, instrument. What
the break-through to world power, to which fate summons us,
means at bottom, is the break-through to the world — out of an
isolation of which we are painfully conscious, and which no vig-
orous reticulation into world economy has been able to break
down since the founding of the Reich. The bitter thing is that the
practical manifestation is an outbreak of war, though its true interpretation is longing, a thirst for unification."

"God bless your studies," I heard Adrian say here in a low
voice, with a half-laugh. He had not even glanced up from his
notes as he quoted the old student tag.

I remained standing and looked at him; he paid no heed. "You
mean," I retorted, "that I am talking nonsense?"

"Pardon," he hastily returned. "I lapsed into student lingo, because your *oratio* reminded me so much of our straw-threshing

disputes of anno so-and-so — what were the fellows' names? I notice I begin to forget them" (he was twenty-nine at the time). "Deutschmeyer? Dungersleben?"

"You mean the redoubtable Deutschlin," I said; "and there was one called Dungersheim. A Hubmeyer and Teutleben there were too. You have never had a memory for names. They were good, serious chaps."

"Certainly, of course. And look here, there was a Schappeler, and a socialist named Arzt. What do you say now? You did not even belong to their faculty. But today I seem to hear them when I hear you. Straw-threshing — by which I only mean once a student, always a student. Academic life keeps one young and critical."

"You did belong to their faculty," said I, "and yet you were at bottom more a guest than I. Of course, Adri. I was only a student, and you may well be right, I am one still. But so much the better if the academic keeps one young, if it preserves loyalty to the spirit, to free thought, to the higher interpretation of the crude event — "

"Are we talking about loyalty?" he asked. "I understood that Kaisersaschern would like to become a world capital. That is not very loyal."

"Get along with you," I cried, "you understood nothing of the sort and you understand very well what I meant about the German break-through to the world."

"It would not help much if I did understand, for at present, anyhow, the crude event will just make our shut-inness and shut-offness more complete, however far your military swarm into Europe. You see: I cannot go to Paris, you go there instead of me. Good too! Between ourselves, I would not have gone anyhow. You help me out of an embarrassment — "

"The war will be short," I said in a suppressed voice, for his words affected me painfully. "It cannot last long. We pay for the swift break-through with a wrong, an acknowledged one, which we declare ourselves ready to make good. We must take it on ourselves. . . ."

"And will know how to carry it with dignity," he broke in. "Germany has broad shoulders. And who denies that a real break-through is worth what the tame world calls a crime? I hope you don't suppose that I think small of the idea which it pleases you to chew over, in your straw. There is at bottom only one problem in the world, and this is its name. How does one break through? How does one get into the open? How does one burst the cocoon and become a butterfly? The whole situation is dominated by the question. Here too," said he, and twitched the little red marker in the volume of Kleist on the table — "here too it treats of the break-through, in the capital essay on marionettes, and it is called straight out 'the last chapter of the history of the world.' But it is talking only about the æsthetic, charm, free grace, which actually is reserved to the automaton and the god; that is, to the unconscious or an endless consciousness, whereas every reflection lying between nothing and infinity kills grace. The consciousness must, this writer thinks, have gone through an infinity in order that grace find itself again therein; and Adam must eat a second time from the tree of knowledge in order to fall back into the state of innocence."

"How glad I am," I put in, "that you have just read that! It is gloriously thought, and you are quite right to bring it into connection with the break-through. But do not say that it is speaking only of æsthetics, do not say *only*! One does wrong to see in æsthetics a separate and narrow field of the humane. It is much more than that, it is at bottom everything, it attracts or repels, the poet attaches to the word 'grace' the very widest possible meaning. Æsthetic release or the lack of it is a matter of one's fate, dealing out happiness or unhappiness, companionship or hopeless if proud isolation on earth. And one does not need to be a philologian to know that what is odious is also what is hated. Craving to break through from bondage, to cease being sealed up in the odious — tell me that I am straw-threshing again; but I feel, I have always felt and will assert against strongly held opposition, that this German is *kat exochen*, profoundly German, the very definition of Germanism, of a psychology threatened with envelopment, the poison of isolation, provincial boorishness, neurosis, implicit Satanism. . . ."

I broke off. He eyed me, and I believe the colour left his cheeks. The look he cast on me was the look, the familiar one that made me almost equally unhappy, no matter whether myself or another was its object: wordless, veiled, coldly remote to the point of offensiveness, followed by the smile with closed lips and sneeringly dilating nostrils — and then the turning away. He moved away from the table, not toward Schildknapp, but to the window niche, where he had hung a saint's picture on the panelling. Rüdiger talked away. In his opinion, he said, I was to be congratulated on going straight into the field, and actually on horseback. One should ride into the field or else not go at all. And he patted the neck of an imaginary nag. We laughed, and our parting when I left for the train was easy and cheerful. Good that it was not sentimental, it would have seemed tasteless. But Adrian's look I carried with me to war — perhaps it was that, and not the typhus infection from lice, which brought me home so soon, back to his side.

CHAPTER XXXI

"You go there instead of me," Adrian had said. And we did not get to Paris. Shall I confess that, privately and apart from the historical point of view, I felt a deep, intimately personal shame? Weeks long we had sent home terse, affectedly laconic dispatches, dressing our triumphs in cold matter-of-fact. Liége had long since fallen, we had won the battle for Lorraine. In accordance with the fixed master-plan we had swung with five armies across the Meuse, had taken Brussels, Namur, carried the day at Charleroi and Longwy, won a second series of battles at Sedan, Rethel, Saint-Quentin, and occupied Reims. We advanced as though on wings. It was just as we had dreamed: by the favour of the god of war, at destiny's nod, we were borne as on pinions. To gaze without flinching at the flames we kindled, could not help kindling, was incumbent upon our manhood, it was the supreme challenge to our heroic courage. I can still see vividly the picture of a gaunt Gaulish wife, standing on a height round which our battery was moving; at its foot a village lay shattered and smoking. "I am the last!" she cried, with a gesture of tragic power, such as is given to no German woman to make. "*Je suis la dernière!*" Raising her fists, she hurled her curses down on our heads, repeating three times: "*Méchants! Méchants! Méchants!*"

We looked the other way. We had to win, and ours was the hard trade of triumph. That I felt wretched enough myself sitting my horse, plagued with coughing and the racking pain in my limbs due to wet nights under canvas, actually afforded me a certain consolation.

Yet many more villages we shot up, still borne on victory's pinions. Then came the incomprehensible, the apparently senseless thing: the order to retreat. How should we have understood it? We belonged to the army group Hausen, south of Châlons-sur-Marne, streaming on to Paris, as the von Kluck group were doing at other points. We were ignorant that somewhere, after a five-day battle, the French had crushed von Bülow's right wing

— reason enough for the anxious cautiousness of a supreme commander who had been elevated to his rank on account of his uncle, to order a general withdrawal. We passed some of the villages that we had left smoking in our rear, and the hill where the tragic woman had stood. She was not there.

The wings were trustless. It should not have been. It had not been a war to be won in one swift onslaught. But as little as those at home did we understand what that meant. We did not understand the frantic jubilation of the world over the result of the battle of the Marne; over the fact that the short war on which our salvation hung had turned into a long one, which we could not stand. Our defeat was now only a matter of time, and of cost to the foe. We could have laid our weapons down and forced our leaders to an immediate peace, if only we had understood. But even among them probably only one here and there dared to think of it. After all, they had scarcely realized that the age of localized war had gone by and that every campaign to which we felt ourselves driven must end in a world conflagration. In such a one the advantage of the inner line, the fanatical devotion of the troops, the high state of preparedness, and a firmly based, strong authoritarian state had held out the chance of a lightning triumph. If this failed — and it stood written that it must fail — then, whatever we might still for years accomplish, we were lost in principle and before we began: this time, next time, always.

We did not know. Slowly the truth tortured its way into us; while the war, a rotting, decaying, misery-creating war, though from time to time flaring up in flattering, deceiving successes, this war, of which I too had said it *must* not last long, lasted four years. Shall I here and now go into details of that long-drawn-out giving way and giving up, the wearing out of our powers and our equipment, the shabbiness and shortages of life, the undernourishment, the loss of morale from the deprivations, the lapses into dishonesty and the gross luxury of the profiteer? I might well be censured for recklessly overstepping the limits of my purpose, which is personal and biographical. I lived through it all from the beginning to the bitter end in the hinterland, as a man on furlough and at length mustered out, given back to his teaching profession at Freising. For before Arras, during the second period of struggle for that fortified place, which lasted from the beginning of May until far on in July of 1915, the delousing measures were obviously inadequate; an infection took me for weeks to the isolation barracks, then for another month to a convalescent home for the sick and wounded in Taunus. At last I no longer resisted

the idea that I had fufilled my duty to my fatherland and would
do better to serve in my old place the cause of education.

That I did, and might once more be husband and father in the
frugal home, whose walls aud their too familiar contents, spared
perhaps for destruction by future bombing, today still form the
frame of my retired and impoverished life. It should be said once
more, certainly not in any boastful sense, but as a mere statement,
that I led my own life, without precisely neglecting it, only as it
were as an aside, with half my attention, with my left hand; that
my real concern and anxiety were centered upon the existence
of my childhood friend, to be back in whose nearness made me
so rejoice — if the word I use can describe the slight chill, the
shiver of dread, the painful lack of response which were my portion from him in the increasingly productive isolation of his life.
"To have an eye on him," to watch over his extraordinary and
puzzling course, always seemed to mine its real and pressing task.
It made up its true content, and thus it is I speak of the emptiness
of my present days.

The place he had elected as his home — "home" in that sense
I have spoken of, assimilative and not altogether acceptable —
was a relatively fortunate choice. During the years of approaching defeat and ever more gnawing stringency, he was, thank God,
on the Schweigestill farm as tolerably cared for as one could wish,
without knowledge or appreciation of the state of things, almost
unaffected by the slowly corroding changes under which our
blockaded and invested country suffered, even while militarily
still on the offensive. He took everything as a matter of course,
without any words, as something that proceeded from him and
lay in his nature, whose power of inertia and fixation on the
semper idem persisted in the face of outward circumstance. His
simple dietary needs the Schweigestill household could always
satisfy. More than that, and soon after my return from the field,
he came under the care of two females who had approached him
quite independently of each other and appointed themselves his
devotees. These were the damsels Meta Nackedey and Kunigunde
Rosenstiel: one a piano-teacher, the other an active partner in a
factory for the production of sausages-cases. It is certainly remarkable: a budding reputation such as had begun to attach itself to Leverkühn's name is unknown to the general, having its
seat in the initiate sphere, on the heights of connoisseurship;
from those heights the invitation to Paris had come. But at the
same time it may also be reflected in humbler, lowlier regions, in
the needy souls of poor creatures who stand out from the masses

through some sensibility of loneliness and suffering dressed up as "higher aspirations"; and these may find their happiness in a worship still fittingly paid to the rarest values. That it is women, and unmarried ones, need not surprise us; for human resignation is certainly the source of a prophetic intuition, which is not the less estimable because its origins are humble. There was not the least question that the immediately personal here played a considerable role; indeed, it predominated over the intellectual values; which even so, in both cases, could only be grasped and estimated in vague outline, as a matter of feeling and intuition. I myself, speaking as one who early submitted his own head and heart to the phenomenon of Adrian's cool and bafflingly self-contained existence, have I the smallest right to mock at the fascination which his aloneness, the nonconformity of his life, exerted upon these women? The Nackedey was a scurrying, deprecating creature, some thirty years old, forever dissolving in blushes and modesty, who speaking or listening blinked spasmodically and appealingly behind the pince-nez she wore, nodding her head and wrinkling up her nose. She, one day, when Adrian was in the city, had found herself beside him on the front platform of a tram, and when she discovered it, had rushed in headless flight through the crowd to the rear platform. Then, having collected herself for a few minutes, she had gone back, to speak to him by name, to tell him, blushing and paling by turns, her own, to add something of her circumstances and to say that she held his music sacred — to all which he had listened and then thanked her. Upon this followed their acquaintance, which Meta had certainly not brought about in order to let it drop. She paid a visit of homage to Pfeiffering, with a bouquet; and cultivated it from then on, in free competition with the Rosenstiel, both sides spurred on by jealousy. The Rosenstiel had begun it differently.

She was a raw-boned Jewess, of about the same age as Nackedey, with thick, unmanageable woolly hair and brown eyes where timeless grief stood written for the daughter of Zion despoiled and her people as a forsaken hearth. A capable business woman in a not very refined line (for the manufacture of sausage-cases has something gross about it, certainly), she had the elegiac habit of beginning all her sentences with "ah." Ah, yes! Ah, no! Ah, believe me! Ah, why not? Ah, I will go to Nuremburg tomorrow: she would say these things in a deep, harsh, desolate, complaining voice, and even when asked How are you? she would reply: "Ah, very well." But it was not the same when she wrote, which she uncommonly liked to do. For not only was Kunigunde, as

almost all Jews are, very musical, but also she had, though without any extensive reading, much purer and more fastidious relations with the German language than the national average, yes,
than most of the learned. She had set in train the acquaintance
with Adrian, which of her own motion she always called a
friendship (indeed, in time it did become something like that),
with an excellent letter, a long, well-turned protestation of devotion, in content not really extraordinary, but stylistically
formed on the best models of an older, humanistic Germany. The
recipient read it with a certain surprise, and on account of its
literary quality it could not possibly be passed over in silence.
She kept on writing to him at Pfeiffering, quite aside from her
frequent visits: explicitly, not very objectively, in matter not
further exciting, but in language very meticulous, clear and read-
able; not hand-written, moreover, but done on her business typewriter, with an ampersand for "and," expressing a reverence
which more nearly to define or justify she was either too shy or
else incapable. It was just reverence, an instinctive reverence
and devotion preserved loyally throughout many years; you
simply had to respect such a capital person, quite aside from any
other capacities she might have. I at least did so, and took pains
to pay the same silent respect to the elusive Nackedey; whereas
Adrian simply accepted the tributes and devotion of these followers of his with the utter heedlessness of his nature. And was
my lot then so different from theirs? I can count it to my credit
that I took pains to be benevolent towards them, while they,
quite primitively, could not endure each other and when they
met measured each other with narrowed eyes. In a certain sense
I was of their guild and might have been justified in feeling irritation over this reduced and spinsterish reproduction of my own
relation to Adrian.

These two, then, coming always with full hands during the
hunger-years, when he was already well taken care of so far as
the essentials were concerned, brought him everything imaginable that could be got hold of in underhand ways: sugar, tea,
coffee, chocolate, cakes, preserves, tobacco for cigarettes. He
could make presents to me, to Schildknapp, and to Rudi
Schwerdtfeger, whose assumption of intimacy never wavered;
and the names of those devoted women were often called blessed
among us! As for the cigarettes, Adrian never gave up smoking
except when forced to on the days when the migraine, with its
violent attacks like seasickness fell on him, and he kept his bed in
a darkened room, as happened two or three times in the month.

Otherwise he could not do without the stimulant and diversion; it had become a habit rather late, during his Leipzig time, and now, at least during his work, he must, so he said, have the interlude of rolling and inhaling else he could not hold out so long. At the time when I returned to civil life he was greatly given to the habit; and my impression was that he practised it not so much for the sake of the *Gesta*, though this was ostensibly the case, as it was because he was trying to put the *Gesta* behind him and be ready for new demands upon his genius. On his horizon, I am sure of it, there was already rising — probably since the outbreak of war, for a power of divination like his must have recognized therein a deep cleft and discontinuity, the opening of a new period of history, crowded with tumult and disruptions, agonies and wild vicissitudes — on the horizon of his creative life, I say, there was already rising the "*Apocalypsis cum figuris*," the work which was to give this life such a dizzying upward surge. Until then, so at least I see the process, he was employing the waiting-time with the brilliant marionette fantasies.

Adrian had learned through Schildknapp of the old book that passes for the source of most of the romantic myths of the Middle Ages. It is a translation from the Latin of the oldest Christian collection of fairy-tales and legends. I am quite willing to give Adrian's favourite with the like-coloured eyes due credit for the suggestion. They had read it together in the evenings and it appealed to Adrian's sense of the ridiculous, his craving to laugh, yes, to laugh until he cried. That was a craving which my less suggestible nature never knew how to feed, being hampered as well by an anxious feeling that all this dissolving in mirth had about it something unsuited to a nature I loved even while I feared it. Rüdiger, the like-eyed, shared my apprehensions not a whit. Indeed, I concealed them; they never hindered me from joining sincerely in such moods of abandon when they came about. But in the Silesian one marked a distinct satisfaction, as though he had performed a task, a mission, when he had managed to reduce Adrian to tears of laughter; and certainly he succeeded in a most fruitful and acceptable way with the old book of fables and jests.

I am of opinion that the *Gesta* — in their historical uninstructedness, pious Christian didacticism, and moral naïveté, with their eccentric casuistry of parricide, adultery, and complicated incest; their undocumented Roman emperors, with daughters whom they fantastically guarded and then offered for sale under the most hair-splitting conditions — it is not to be denied, I say, that all these fables, presented in a solemn Latinizing and indescribably

naïve style of translation, concerning knights in pilgrimage to the
Promised Land, wanton wives, artful procuresses, clerics given
to the black arts, do have an extraordinarily diverting effect. They
were in the highest degree calculated to stimulate Adrian's
penchant for parody, and the thought of dramatizing them musically in condensed form for the puppet theatre occupied him
from the day he made their acquaintance. There is for instance
the fundamentally unmoral fable, anticipating the *Decameron*,
"of the godless guile of old women," wherein an accomplice of
guilty passion, under a mask of sanctity succeeds in persuading a
noble and even exceptionally decent and honourable wife, while
her confiding husband is gone on a journey, that she is sinfully
minded to a youth who is consumed with desire for her. The
witch makes her little bitch fast for two days, and then gives it
bread spread with mustard to eat, which causes the little animal
to shed copious tears. Then she takes it to the virtuous lady, who
receives her respectfully, since everybody supposes she is a saint.
But when the lady looks at the weeping little bitch and asks in
surprise what causes its tears, the old woman behaves as though
she would rather not answer. When pressed to speak, she con-
fesses that this little dog is actually her own all-too-chaste
daughter, who by reason of the unbending denial of her favour
to a young man on fire for her had driven him to his death; and
now, in punishment therefor, she has been turned into this shape
and of course constantly weeps tears of despair over her doggish
estate. Telling these deliberate lies, the procuress weeps too, but
the lady is horrified at the thought of the similarity of her own
case with that of the little dog and tells the old woman of the
youth who suffers for her. Thereupon the woman puts it seriously
before her what an irretrievable pity it would be if she too were
to be turned into a little dog; and is then commissioned to fetch
the groaning suitor that in God's name he may cool his lust, so
that the two at the instance of a godless trick celebrate the sweetest adultery.

I still envy Rüdiger for having been the first to read aloud this
tale to our friend, in the Abbot's room; although I confess that
if it had been myself the effect might not have been the same.
Moreover his contribution to the future work was limited to this
first stimulation. When the point was reached of preparing the
fables for the puppet stage, the casting of them in dialogue form,
he refused his offices, for lack of time, or out of his well-known
refractory sense of freedom. Adrian did not take it ill of him, but
did what he could by himself for as long as I was away, sketch-

ing in the scenarios freely and more or less the dialogue, after which it was I who in my spare time quickly gave them their final form in mixed prose and rhymed lines.

The singers who according to Adrian's plan lend their voices to the acting puppets had to be given their places among the instruments in the orchestra, a very small one, composed of violin and double-bass, clarinet, bassoon, trumpet, and trombone, with percussion for one man, and a set of bells. With them is a speaker who, like the *testis* in the oratorio, condenses the plot in narration and recitative.

This loose treatment is most successful in the fifth, the real kernel of the suite, the tale "Of the Birth of the Holy Pope Gregory," a birth whose sinful singularity is by no means the end of the story; and all the shocking circumstances accompanying the hero's life not only are no hindrance to his final elevation to be the Vice-Gerent of Christ on earth, but make him, by God's peculiar favour, called and destined to that seat. The chain of complications is long, and I may as well relate in this place the history of the royal and orphaned brother-sister pair: the brother who loved the sister more than he should, so that he loses his head and puts her into a more than interesting condition, for he makes her the mother of a boy of extraordinary beauty. It is this boy, a brother-sister child in all the ill meaning of the word, about whom everything turns. The father seeks to do penance by a crusade to the Holy Land, and there finds his death; the child presses on toward uncertain destinies. For the Queen, resolved not to have the infant so monstrously begot baptized on her own responsibility, puts him and his princely cradle into a cask and entrusts him, not without a tablet of instructions and gold and silver for his upbringing, to the waves of the sea, which bring him "on the sixth feast-day" to the neighbourhood of a cloister presided over by a pious Abbot. The Abbot finds him, baptizes him with his own name, Gregory, and gives him an education perfectly suited to the lad's unusual physical and mental endowments. Meanwhile the sinful mother, to the regret of her whole realm, makes a vow not to marry, quite obviously not only because she regards herself as unconsecrate and unworthy of a Christian marriage but because she still cherishes a shameful loyalty to the departed brother. A powerful Duke of a foreign land seeks her hand, which she refuses; he is so wroth that he lays siege to her kingdom, overruns and conquers it, all but a single fortified city into which she retires. Now the youth Gregory, having learned of his origins, thinks to make a pilgrimage to the Holy Sepulchre;

but instead arrives by chance in his mother's city, where he learns of the misfortune of the head of the kingdom, has himself brought before her, and offers her, who as the story says "looks at him sharply" but does not know him, his services. He conquers the cruel Duke, frees the country, and is proposed by her retainers to the liberated Queen as her husband. She is indeed somewhat coy and asks for a day — only one — to think it over; and then against her oath she consents, so that, with the greatest approval and jubilation of the whole country, the marriage takes place and frightful is unsuspectingly heaped upon frightful, when the son of sin mounts the marriage bed with his own mother. I will not go further into all that; all I want is to describe the heavily emotional climax of the plot, which in the puppet theatre comes into its own in so surprising and admirable a way. At the very beginning the brother asks the sister why she looks so pale and "why the upper part of thine eyelids darken"; and she answers him: "It is no wonder, for I am with child and indeed full of remorse." When the news comes that her sinful brother-husband is dead she breaks out in the remarkable lament: "Gone is my hope, gone is my strength, my only brother, my second I!" and then covers the corpse with kisses from the soles of his feet to the crown of his head, so that her knights, unpleasantly impressed with such exaggerated grief, see themselves constrained to tear their sovereign lady away from the dead. Or when she becomes aware with whom she lives in tender wedded love, and says to him: "O my sweet son, thou art my only child, thou art my spouse and lord, thou art mine and my brother's son, O my sweet child, and O thou my God, why hast thou let me be born!" For so it is: by means of the tablet she had once written with her own hand, which she finds in the private chamber of her husband, she learns with whom she shares her couch, thank God without having borne him another brother and grandson of her brother. And now it is his turn to think of a penitential pilgrimage, which he straightway barefoot undertakes. He comes to a fisherman who, "by the fineness of his limbs," recognizes that he has no ordinary traveller before him, and the two agree that the utmost isolation is the only fitting thing. He rows him out sixteen miles into the ocean, to a rock where great seas surge, and there, chains being laid to his feet and the key thereof flung into the waves, Gregory spends seventeen years doing penance. At the end of this period there comes overwhelming, but to himself, it seems, scarce surprising favour and exaltation. For the Pope dies in Rome, and hardly is he dead when there comes down a voice from heaven: "Seek out Gregory the man of God

and set him up as My vicar on earth!" Then messengers haste in
all directions and arrive at the place of that fisherman, who be-
thinks himself. Then he catches a fish, in whose belly he finds the
key once sunk in the depths of the sea. He rows the messengers
to the stone of penance and they cry up to it: "O Gregory, thou
man of God, come down to us from the stone, for God wills for
thee to be set up for His vicar upon earth!" And what does he answer them? "If that please God," he says calmly, "may His will
be done!" But as he comes to Rome and when the bells are to be
rung, they do not wait but ring of themselves, all the bells ring of
their own accord, in witness to the fact that so pious and edify-
ing a pope had never been before. And the holy man's fame
reaches his mother, and she rightly decides that her life can be
better entrusted to no one else than to this chosen one; so she de-
parts for Rome to confess to the Holy Father, who, as he receives
her confession, recognizes her and says: "O my sweet mother,
sister, and wife, O my friend! The Devil thought to lead us to
hell, but the greater power of God has prevented him." And he
builds her a cloister where she rules as Abbess, but only for a short
time. For it is soon vouchsafed to them both to render up their
souls to God.

Upon this extravagantly sinful, simple, and appealing tale
then, did Adrian concentrate all the possible wit and terror, all
the childlike fervour, fantasy, and solemnity of musical presentation, and probably one may apply to the whole production, but
above all to this particular tale, the singular invention of the old
Lübeck professor, the word "God-witted." The memory comes
back to me, because the *Gesta* actually show something like a return to the musical style of *Love's Labour's Lost*, while the tone
language of the *Marvels of the Universe* leans more to that of the
Apocalypse or even the *Faust*. Such anticipations and overlappings
often occur in creative life; but I can explain to myself the artistic
attraction which this material had for my friend: it was an intellectual charm, not without a trace of malice and solvent travesty,
springing as it did from a critical rebound after the swollen pom-
posity of an art epoch nearing its end. The musical drama had
taken its materials from the romantic sagas, the myth-world of
the Middle Ages, and thus suggested that only such subjects were
worthy of music, or suited to its nature. Here the conclusion
seemed to be drawn; in a right destructive way, indeed, in that
the bizarre, and particularly the farcically erotic, takes the place
of the moralizing and priestly, all inflated pomp of production is
rejected and the action transferred to the puppet theatre, in it-

self already burlesque. Adrian was at pains when he was at work
on the *Gesta* to study the specific possibilities of the puppet play;
and the Catholic-baroque popular fondness for the theatre, which
was rife in the region where he led his hermit life, afforded him
opportunity. Close by, in Waldshut, lived a druggist who carved
and dressed marionettes, and Adrian repeatedly visited the man.
He also travelled to Mittenwald, the fiddle village in the valley of
the upper Isar, where the apothecary was an amateur of the same
art and with the help of his wife and his clever sons produced
puppet plays after Pocci and Christian Winter in the town, at-
tracting large audiences of townsfolk and strangers. Leverkühn
saw and studied these too; also, as I noticed, the very ingenious
hand puppets and shadow-plays of the Javanese.

Those were enjoyable and stimulating evenings when he played
for us — that is, to me, Schildknapp, and very likely Rudi
Schwerdtfeger, who persisted in being present now and then —
on the old square piano in the deep-windowed room with the
Nike, the latest-written parts of his amazing scores, in which the
harmonically most dominating, the rhythmically labyrinthine
was applied to the simplest material, and again a sort of musical
children's trumpet style to the most extraordinary. The meeting
of the Queen with the holy man whom she had borne to her
brother, and whom she had embraced as spouse, charmed tears
from us such as had never filled our eyes, uniquely mingled of
laughter and fantastic sensibility. Schwerdtfeger, in abandoned
familiarity, availed himself of the licence of the moment: with a
"You've done it magnificently!" embraced Adrian and pressed
him to his heart. I saw Rüdiger's mouth, always a bitter one, give
a wry twist and could not myself resist murmuring: "Enough!"
and putting out my hand to quench the unquenchable and restrain the unrestrained.

Rudolf may have had some trouble in following the conversation that ensued after the private performance in the Abbot's
room. We spoke of the union of the advanced with the popular,
the closing of the gulf between art and accessibility, high and low,
as once in a certain sense it had been brought about by the romantic movement, literary and musical. But after that had followed a
new and deeper cleavage and alienation between the good and the
easy, the worth-while and the entertaining, the advanced and the
generally enjoyable, which has become the destiny of art. Was
it sentimentality to say that music — and she stood for them all —
demanded with growing consciousness to step out of her dignified isolation, to find common ground without becoming com-

mon, and to speak a language which even the musically untaught
could understand, as it understood the Wolf's Glen and the Jung-
fernkranz and Wagner? Anyhow, sentimentality was not the
means to this end, but instead and much sooner irony, mockery;
which, clearing the air, made an opposing party against the romantic, against pathos and prophecy, sound-intoxication and literature and a bond with the objective and elemental — that is,
with the rediscovery of music itself as an organization of time.
A most precarious start. For how near did not lie the false primitive, and thus the romantic again! To remain on the height of intellect; to resolve into the matter-of-course the most exclusive
productions of European musical development, so that everybody
could grasp the new; to make themselves its master, applying it
unconcernedly as free building material and making tradition felt,
recoined into the opposite of the epigonal; to make technique,
however high it had climbed, entirely unimportant, and all the
arts of counterpoint and instrumentation to disappear and melt
together to an effect of simplicity very far from simplicity, an
intellectually winged simplicity — that seemed to be the object
and the craving of art.

It was mostly Adrian who talked, only slightly seconded by us.
Excited by the playing, he spoke with flushed cheeks and hot
eyes, slightly feverish; not in a steady stream but more as just
throwing out remarks, yet with so much animation that I felt
I had never seen him, either in mine or in Rüdiger's presence, so
eloquently taken out of himself. Schildknapp had given expression to his disbelief in the deromanticizing of music. Music was
after all too deeply and essentially bound up with the romantic
ever to reject it without serious natural damage to itself. To
which Adrian:

"I will gladly agree with you, if you mean by the romantic a
warmth of feeling which music in the service of technical intellectuality today rejects. It is probably self-denial. But what we
called the purification of the complicated into the simple is at bottom the same as the winning back of the vital and the power of
feeling. If it were possible — whoever succeeded in — how would
you say it?" he turned to me and then answered himself: " — the
break-through, you would say; whoever succeeded in the break-
through from intellectual coldness into a touch-and-go world of
new feeling, him one should call the saviour of art. Redemption,"
he went on, with a nervous shoulder-shrug, "a romantic word,
and a harmonic writer's word, shop talk for the cadence-blissful-
ness of harmonic music. Isn't it amusing that music for a long

time considered herself a means of release, whereas she herself, like all the arts, needed to be redeemed from a pompous isolation, which was the fruit of the culture-emancipation, the elevation of culture as a substitute for religion — from being alone with an élite of culture, called the public, which soon will no longer be, which even now no longer is, so that soon art will be entirely alone, alone to die, unless she were to find her way to the folk, that is, to say it unromantically, to human beings?"

He said and asked that all in one breath in a lowered, conversational tone, but with a concealed tremor which one understood only when he finished:

"The whole temper of art, believe me, will change, and withal into the blither and more modest; it is inevitable, and it is a good thing. Much melancholy ambition will fall away from her, and a new innocence, yes, harmlessness will be hers. The future will see in her, she herself will once more see in herself, the servant of a community which will comprise far more than 'education' and will not have culture but will perhaps be a culture. We can only with difficulty imagine such a thing; and yet it will be, and be the natural thing: an art without anguish, psychologically healthy, not solemn, unsadly confiding, an art *per du* with humanity. . . ."

He broke off, and we all three sat silent and shaken. It is painful and heart-stirring at once to hear talk of isolation from the community, remoteness from trust. With all my emotion I was yet in my deepest soul unsatisfied with his utterance, directly dissatisfied with him. What he had said did not fit with him, his pride, his arrogance if you like, which I loved, and to which art has a right. Art is mind, and mind does not at all need to feel itself obligated to the community, to society — it may not, in my view, for the sake of its freedom, its nobility. An art that "goes in unto" the folk, which makes her own the needs of the crowd, of the little man, of small minds, arrives at wretchedness, and to make it her duty *is* the worst small-mindedness, and the murder of mind and spirit. And it is my conviction that mind, in its most audacious, unrestrained advance and researches, can, however unsuited to the masses, be certain in some indirect way to serve man — in the long run men.

Doubtless that was also the natural opinion of Adrian. But it pleased him to deny it, and I was very much mistaken if I looked at that as a contradiction of his arrogance. More likely it was an effort to condescend, springing from the same arrogance. If only there had not been that trembling in his voice when he spoke of the need of art to be redeemed, of art being *per du* with humanity! That was feeling: despite everything it tempted me to give his hand a stolen pressure. But I did not do so; instead I kept an eye on Rudi Schwerdtfeger lest he again be moved to embrace him.

CHAPTER XXXII

INEZ RODDE's marriage to Professor Dr. Helmut Institoris took place at the beginning of the war, when the country was still in good condition and strong in hope, and I myself still in the field, in the spring of 1915. It went off with all the proper bourgeois flourishes: ceremonies civil and religious and a wedding dinner in the Hotel Vier Jahreszeiten, after which the young pair left for Dresden and the Saxon Switzerland. Such was the outcome of a long probation on both sides, which had evidently led to the conclusion that they were suited to each other. The reader will note the irony which I, truly without malice, express in the word "evidently," for such a condition either did not exist or else had existed from the beginning, and no development had occurred in the relations between the two since Helmut had first approached the daughter of the deceased Senator. What on both sides spoke for the union did so at the moment of betrothal and marriage no more and no less than it had in the beginning, and nothing new had been added. But the classic adage: "Look before you leap" had been formally complied with, and the very length of the test, added to the pressure due to the war, seemed finally to demand a positive solution. Indeed, it had ripened in haste several other unsettled affairs. Inez's consent, however, which she — on psychological or shall I say material grounds, that is to say for common-sense reasons — had always been more or less ready to give, had been the readier because Clarissa, toward the end of the previous year, had left Munich and entered on her first engagement in Celle on the Aller, so that her sister was left alone with a mother of whose bohemian leanings, tame as they were, she disapproved.

The Frau Senator, of course, felt a joyous satisfaction with the good bourgeois settlement her child was making, to which she had materially contributed by the entertaining she did and the social activities of her home. At her own expense she had thereby served the easy-going "south-German" love of life, which was her way of making up for what she had lost, and had her fading charms paid court to by the men she invited, Knöterich, Kranich,

Zink and Spengler, the young dramatic students, and so on. Yes, I
do not go too far, perhaps in the end only just far enough, when
I say that even with Rudi Schwerdtfeger she was on a jesting,
teasing travesty of a mother-and-son footing. Uncommonly often
when she talked with him her familiar affected cooing laugh
could be heard. But after all I have intimated or rather expressed
about Inez's inner life, I can leave it to the reader to imagine the
mingled distaste and embarrassment that she felt at the sight of
her mother's philandering. It has happened in my presence that
during such a scene she left the drawing-room with flushed cheeks
and shut herself in her room, at whose door after a quarter of an
hour, as she had probably hoped and expected, Rudolf knocked
to ask why she had gone away. Surely he knew the answer to his
question; as surely it could not be put in words. He would tell
her how much her presence was missed and coax her in all the
tender notes in his voice, including of course the brotherly ones,
to come back. He would not rest until she promised — perhaps
not with him, she would not quite do that, but a little while after
him — to return to the company.

I may be pardoned for adding this supplement, which impressed
itself on my memory, though it had been comfortably dropped
out of Frau Senator Rodde's now that Inez's betrothal and marriage were accomplished fact. She had provided the wedding with
due pomp and circumstance, and in the absence of any considerable dowry had not failed to supply a proper equipment of linen
and silver. She even parted with various pieces of furniture from
former days, such as carved chests and this or that gilt "occasional chair," to contribute to the furnishings of the imposing new
home which the young pair had rented in Prinzregentenstrasse,
two flights up, looking out on the English Garden. Yes, as though
to prove to herself and others that her social undertakings and all
the lively evenings in her drawing-room had really only served
to further her daughters' prospects of happiness and settlement in
life, she now expressed a distinct wish to retire, an inclination to
withdraw from the world. She no longer entertained, and a year
after Inez's marriage she gave up her apartment in the Rambergstrasse and put her widowed existence upon an altered footing.
She moved out to Pfeiffering, where almost without Adrian being
aware of it she took up her residence in the low building on the
square opposite the Schweigestill courtyard, with the chestnuts
in front of it, where formerly the painter of the melancholy landscapes of the Waldshut moors had had his quarters.

It is remarkable what charm this modest yet picturesque corner

of the earth possessed for every sort of distinguished resignation
or bruised humanity. Perhaps the explanation lay in the character
of the proprietors and especially in that of the stout-hearted landlady Frau Else Schweigestill and her power of "understanding."
She was amazingly clear-sighted, and she displayed her gift in occasional talk with Adrian, as when she told him that the Frau
Senator was moving in across the road. "It's pretty plain to see,"
she said in her peasant singsong, "easy as an'thing, I see it with
half an eye, Herr Leverkühn, eh! — she got out of conceit with
city folk's doings and lady and gentleman manners and ways, because she feels her age and she's singin' small, it takes different
people different ways, I mean, eh, some don't care a hoot, they
brazen it out and they look good too, they just get more restless
and roguish, eh, and put on false fronts and make ringlets of their
white hairs maybe and so on and so forth, real peart, and don't do
any more like they used to, and act audacious and it often takes
the men more than you'd think, eh, but with some that don't go,
and don't do, so when their cheeks fall in and their necks get
scrawny like a hen and nothin' to do for the teeth when you
laugh, so they can't hold out, and grieve at their looks in the glass
and act like a sick cat and hide away, and when 'taint the neck
and the teeth, then it's the hair, eh, and with this one it's the hair's
the worst, I could tell right off, otherways it's not so bad, none
of it, but the hair, it's goin' on top, eh, so the part's gone to rack
and ruin and she can't do an'thin' any more with the tongs, and
so she's struck all of a heap, for it's a great pain, believe me, and
so she just gives up the ghost eh, and moves out in the country,
to Schweigestills', and that's all 'tis."

Thus the mother, with her smoothly drawn hair, just lightly
silvered, with the parting in the middle showing the white skin.
Adrian, as I said, was little affected by the advent of the lodger
over the way, who, when she first visited the house, was brought
by their landlady to greet him. Then out of respect for his work
she matched his reserve with her own and only once just at first
had him for tea with her, in the two simple whitewashed low-
ceiled rooms on the ground floor, behind the chestnut trees, furnished quaintly enough with the elegant bourgeois relics of her
former household, the candelabra, the stuffed easy-chairs, the
Golden Horn in its heavy frame, the grand piano with the bro-
caded scarf. From then on, meeting in the village or on their
walks, they simply exchanged friendly greetings or stopped a few
minutes to chat about the sad state of the country and the growing food shortages in the cities. Out here one suffered much less,

so that the retirement of the Frau Senator had a practical justification and even became a genuine interest, for it enabled her to provide her daughters and also former friends of the house, like the Knöterichs, with supplies from Pfeiffering: eggs, butter, flour, sausages, and so on. During the worst years she made quite a business out of packing and posting provisions. The Knöterichs had taken over Inez Rodde, now rich and settled and well wadded against life, into their own social circle from the little group who had attended her mother's evenings. They also invited the numismatist Dr. Kranich, Schildknapp, Rudi Schwerdtfeger, and myself; but not Zink and Spengler, nor the little theatre people who had been Clarissa's colleagues. Instead their other guests were from university circles, or older and younger teachers of the two academies and their wives. With the Spanish exotic Frau Knöterich, Natalie, Inez was on friendly or even intimate terms, this although the really attractive woman had the reputation, pretty well confirmed, of being a morphine addict; a rumour that was justified by my observation of the speaking brilliance of her eyes at the beginning of an evening and her occasional disappearance in order to refresh her gradually waning spirits. I saw that Inez, who set such store by patrician dignity and conservative propriety, who indeed had only married to gratify those tastes, chose to go about with Natalie rather than with the staid spouses of her husband's colleagues, the typical German professors' wives. She even visited and received Natalie alone. And thus was revealed to me anew the split in her nature; the fact that despite her nostalgia for it, the bourgeois life had no real viability for her.

That she did not love her husband, that rather limited teacher of æsthetics, wrapped in his dreams of beauty and brutality, I could not doubt. It was a conscious love of respectability that she devoted to him, and so much is true, that she upheld with consummate distinction, refined yet more by her expression of delicate and fastidious roguishness, her husband's station in life. Her meticulous conduct of his household and his social activities might even be called pedantic; and she achieved it under economic conditions which year by year made it harder and harder to sustain the standards of bourgeois correctness. To aid her in the care of the handsome and expensive apartment with its Persian rugs and shining parquetry floors she had two well-trained maidservants, dressed very *comme il faut* in little caps and starched apronstrings. One of them served her as lady's maid. To ring for this Sophie was her passion. She did it all the time, to enjoy the aristocratic service and assure herself of the protection and care she

had bought with her marriage. It was Sophie who had to pack the
numberless trunks and boxes she took with her when she went to
the country with Institoris, to Tegernsee or Berchtesgaden, if
only for a few days. These mountains of luggage with which she
weighed herself down at every smallest excursion out of her nest
were to me likewise symbolic of her need of protection and her
fear of life.

I must describe a little more particularly the immaculate eight-
roomed apartment in the Prinzregentenstrasse. It had two drawing-rooms, one of which, more intimately furnished, served as
family living-room; a spacious dining-room in carved oak, and a
gentlemen's den and smoking-room supplied with leather-uphol-
stered comfort. The sleeping-room of the married pair had twin
beds with a semblance of a tester in polished yellow pear-wood
above them. On the toilette-table the glittering bottles, the silver
tools were ranged in rows according to size. All this was a pattern, one which still survived for some years into the period of
disintegration: a pattern establishment of German bourgeois culture, not least by virtue of the "good books" you found everywhere in living- and reception-rooms. The collection, on grounds
partly representative, partly psychological, avoided the exciting
and disturbing. It was dignified and cultured, with the histories of
Leopold von Ranke, the works of Gregorovius, art histories, German and French classics — in short, the solid and conservative —
as its foundation. With the years the apartment grew more beautiful, or at least fuller and more elaborate; for Dr. Institoris knew
this or that Munich artist of the more conservative Glaspalast
school. His taste in art, despite all his theoretic espousal of the
gorgeous and barbaric, was decidedly tame. In particular there
was a certain Nottebohm, a native of Hamburg, married, hollow-
cheeked, with a pointed beard; a droll man, clever at frightfully
funny imitations of actors, animals, musical instruments, and professors, a patron of the now declining carnival festival, as a portraitist clever at the social technique of catching subjects and as
an artist, I may say, possessing a glossy and inferior painting style.
Institoris, accustomed to professional familiarity with masterpieces, either did not distinguish between them and deft mediocrity, or else he thought his commissions were a due of friendship,
or else he asked nothing better than the refined and inoffensive
for the adornment of his walls. Therein doubtless he was supported by his wife, if not on grounds of taste, then as a matter of
feeling. So they both had themselves done for good money by
Nottebohm, very like and not at all speaking portraits, each alone

and both together; and later, when children came, the funny man
made a life-size family group of all the Institorises, a collection of
wooden dolls, on the respectable canvas of which a great deal of
highly varnished oil paint had been expended. All these adorned
the reception-rooms, in rich frames, provided with their own individual electric lighting above and below.

When children came, I said. For children did come; and with
what address, what persistent, one might almost say heroic ignoring of circumstances less and less favourable to the patrician and
bourgeois were they cared for and brought up — for a world, one
might say, as it had been and not as it was to become. At the end
of 1915 Inez presented her husband with a small daughter, named
Lucrezia, begot in the polished yellow bedstead with the tester,
next to the symmetrically ranged silver implements on the toilette-
table. Inez declared at once that she intended to make of her a
perfectly brought-up young girl, *une jeune fille accomplie*, she
said in her Karlsruhe French. Two years later came twins, also
female; they were christened Aennchen and Riekchen, with the
same correct pomp and ceremony, at home, with chocolate, port
wine, and dragées. The christening basin was silver, with a gar-
land of flowers. All three were fair, charmingly pampered, lisping
little beings, concerned about their frocks and sashes, obviously
under pressure from the mother's perfection-compulsion. They
were sensitive-plants grown in the shade, pathetically taken up
with themselves. They spent their early days in costly bassinets
with silk curtains, and were taken out to drive in little go-carts
of the most elegant construction, with rubber wheels, under the
lime trees of the Prinzregentenstrasse. They had a wet-nurse from
"the people," decked out in the traditional costume and ribbons
like a lamb for the sacrifice. Inez did not nurse her children herself, the family doctor having advised against it. Later a Fräulein,
a trained kindergarten teacher, took charge of them. The light,
bright room where they grew up, where their little beds stood,
where Inez visited them whenever the claims of the household
and her own person permitted, had a frieze of fairy-stories round
the walls, fabulous dwarf furniture, a gay linoleum-covered floor,
and a world of well-ordered toys, teddy-bears, lambs on wheels,
jumping-jacks, Käthe Kruse dolls, railway trains, on shelves along
the walls — in short, it was the very pattern of a children's paradise, correct in every detail.

Must I say now, or repeat, that with all this correctness things
were by no means correct, that they rested on self-will, not to
say on a lie, and were not only more and more challenged from

without, but for the sharper eye, the eye sharpened by sympathy, were crumbling within, they gave no happiness, neither were they truly believed in or willed? All this good fortune and good taste always seemed to me a conscious denial and whitewashing of the problem. It was in strange contradiction to Inez's cult of suffering, and in my opinion the woman was too shrewd not to see that the ideal little bourgeois brood which she had wilfully made of her children was the expression and over-all correction of the fact that she did not love them, but saw in them the fruits of a connection she had entered into with a bad conscience as a woman and in which she lived with physical repulsion.

Good God, it was certainly no intoxicating bliss for a woman to go to bed with Helmut Institoris! So much I understand of feminine dreams and demands; and I always had to imagine that Inez had merely tolerated receiving her children from him, out of a sense of duty and so to speak with her head turned away. For they were his, the looks of all three left no doubt of that, the likeness with him being much stronger than that with the mother, possibly because her psychological participation when she conceived them had been so slight. And I would in no way impugn the masculine honour of the little man. He was certainly a whole man, even in a manikin edition, and through him Inez learned desire — a hapless desire, a shallow soil whereon her passion was to spring up and grow rank.

I have said that Institoris, when he began to woo the maiden Inez, had actually done so for another. And so it was now too: as a husband he was only the awakener of errant longings, of a half-experience of joy at bottom only frustrating, which demanded fulfilment, confirmation, satisfaction, and made the pain she suffered on Rudi Schwerdtfeger's account, which she had so strangely revealed to me, flare up into passion. It is quite clear: when she was the object of courtship she began distressfully to think of him; as disillusioned wife she fell in love with him, in full consciousness and with utter abandonment to feeling and desire. And there can be no doubt that the young man could not avoid responding to this feeling towards him, coming as it did from a suffering and spiritually superior being. I had almost said it would have been "still finer" if he had *not* listened to it — and I could hear her sister's "Hop, man, hop, what's the matter with you — jump up!" Again, I am not writing a novel, and I do not claim the writer's omniscient eye, penetrating into the dramatic development of an affair hidden from all the rest of the world. But so much is certain: that Rudolf, driven into a corner, quite involuntarily and with a "What shall I do?" obeyed that haughty command, and I can very well imagine how his passion for flirtation, in the beginning a harmless amusement, betrayed him into situations more and more exciting and enflaming, ending in a liaison, which without this tendency of his to play with fire, he could have avoided.

In other words, under cover of the bourgeois propriety she had so nostalgically longed for as a refuge, Inez Institoris lived in adultery with a man in years, a youth in mental constitution and behaviour, a ladies' pet who made her suffer and doubt, just as a frivolous woman will cause anguish to a serious and loving man. In his arms then, her senses, aroused by an unloving marriage, found satisfaction. She lived thus for years, from a time which if I am right was not long after her marriage up to the end of the decade; and when she no longer so lived, it was because he whom she sought with all her strength to hold escaped her. It was she who, while playing the part of exemplary housewife and mother, managed the affair, manipulated and concealed the daily artifices and the double life, which naturally gnawed at her nerves and terrified her by threatening the precarious loveliness of her looks: for instance, it deepened the two furrows between her blond brows until she looked almost maniacal. And then, despite all the caution, cunning, and self-control used to hide such devious ways from society's eyes, the will to do so is never, on either side, quite clear or consistent. As for the man, of course it must flatter him if his good fortune is at least suspected; while for the woman it is a point of secret sexual pride to have it guessed that she need not content herself with the caresses, by nobody very highly rated, of her husband. So I scarcely deceive myself when I assume that knowledge of Inez Institoris's side-slip was fairly widespread in her Munich circle, although I have never, except with Adrian Leverkühn, exchanged a word with anybody on the subject. Yes, I would go so far as to reckon with the possibility that Helmut himself knew the truth: a certain admixture of cultured decency, deprecating and regretful toleration, and — love of peace, speaks for the supposition, and it does happen far from seldom that society takes the spouse for the only blind one, while he thinks that except for himself no one knows anything. This is the comment of an elderly man who has observed life.

I had not the impression that Inez troubled herself overmuch about what people knew. She did her best to prevent their knowing, but that was more to preserve the convenances; whoever actually must know, let them, so long as they left her alone. Passion is too much taken up with itself to be able to conceive that anyone would be seriously against it. At least, it is so in matters of love, where feeling claims for itself every right in the world and, however forbidden and scandalous, quite involuntarily reckons on understanding. How could Inez, if she considered herself otherwise quite unperceived, have taken my own knowledge so completely for granted? But she did so, as good as regardless, except that no name was mentioned, in an evening conversation which we had — it would be in the autumn of 1916 — and which obviously was of moment to her. At that time, unlike Adrian, who when he had spent the evening in Munich used to stick to his eleven-o'clock train back to Pfeiffering, I had rented a room in Schwabing, Hohenzollernstrasse, not far behind the Siegesthor, in order to be independent and on occasion to have a roof over my head in the city. So when as a near friend I was asked to the Institorises' for the evening meal, I could readily accept the invitation given by Inez at table and seconded by her husband to keep her company after supper, when Helmut, who was to play cards at the Allotria Club, should have left the house. He went out shortly after nine, wishing us a pleasant evening. Then the mistress of the house and her guest sat alone in the family livingroom. It was furnished with cushioned wicker chairs, and a bust of Inez, in alabaster, made by an artist friend, stood on a pedestal: very like, very piquant, considerably under life-size, but an uncommonly speaking likeness, with the heavy hair, the veiled glance, the delicate, outstretched neck, the mouth pursed in a disdainful sort of mischief.

And again I was the confidant, the "good" man, rousing no emotion, in contrast to the world of the irresistible, which was incorporated for Inez in the youth about whom she longed to talk to me. She said it herself: the things happening and having happened, the joy, the love and suffering, did not come into their own if they remained wordless, were only enjoyed and suffered. They were not satisfied in night and silence. The more secret they were, the more they required a third party, the intimate friend, the good man, to whom and with whom one could talk about them — and that was I. I saw it and took my role upon myself.

For a while after Helmut left, as it were while he was within hearing, we spoke of indifferent things. Then suddenly, almost abruptly, she said:

"Serenus, do you blame me, do you despise and condemn me?"

It would have been silly to pretend I did not understand.

"By no means, Inez," I replied. "God forbid! I have always been

told: 'Vengeance is mine, I will repay.' I know He includes the
punishment in the sin and saturates it therewith so that one cannot be distinguished from the other and happiness and punishment are the same. You must suffer very much. Would I sit here
if I were constituted a moral judge over you? That I fear for
you I do not deny. But I would have kept that to myself if not
for your question whether I blame you."

"What is suffering, what fear and humiliating danger," said
she, "in comparison with the one sweet, indispensable triumph,
without which one would not live: to hold to its better self that
frivolous, evasive, worldly, torturing, irresponsible charmingness,
which yet has true human value; to drive its flippancy to serious
feeling, to possess the elusive, and at last, at last, not only once
but for confirmation and reassurance never often enough, to see
it in the state that suits its worth, the state of devotion, of deep
suspiring passion!"

I do not say the woman used exactly these words, but she expressed herself in very like ones. She was well read, accustomed to
articulate her inner life in speech; as a girl she had even attempted
verse. What she said had a cultured precision and something of
the boldness that always arises when language tries seriously to
achieve feeling and life, to make them first truly live, to exhaust
them in it. This is no everyday effort, but a product of emotion,
and in so far feeling and mind are related, but also in so far mind
gets its thrilling effect. As she went on speaking, seldom listening, with half an ear, to what I threw in, her words, I must
frankly say, were soaked in a sensual bliss that makes me scruple
to report them directly. Sympathy, discretion, human reverence
prevent me, and also, maybe, a philistine reluctance to impose
anything so painful upon the reader. She repeated herself often
in a compulsive effort to express in better terms what she had already said without in her opinion doing it justice. And always
there was this curious equation of worthiness with sensual passion,
this fixed and strangely drunken idea that inward worthiness
could only fulfil itself, realize itself, in fleshly desire, which obviously was something of like value with "worth"; that it was at
once the highest and the most indispensable happiness to keep
them together. I cannot describe the glowing, albeit melancholy
and insecure, unsatisfied notes in her voice as she spoke of this
mixture of the two conceptions *worth* and *desire;* how much desire appeared as the profoundly serious element, sternly opposed
to the hated "society" one, "society" where true worth in play
and coquetry betrayed itself; which was the inhuman, treacherous

element of its exterior surface amiability; and which one must take from it, tear from it, to have it alone, utterly alone, alone in the most final sense of the word. The disciplining of lovableness till it became love: that was what it amounted to; but at the same time there was more abstruse matter, about something wherein thought and sense mystically melted into one; the idea that the contradiction between the frivolity of society and the melancholy untrustworthiness of life in general was resolved in his embrace, the suffering it caused most sweetly avenged.

Of what I said myself I scarcely know by now any details, except one question intended of course to point out her erotic over-estimation of the object of her love and to inquire how it was possible: I remember I delicately hinted that the being to whom she devoted it was not after all actually so vital, glorious, or consummately desirable; that the military examination had showed a physiological functional defect and the removal of an organ. The answer was in the sense that this defect only brought the lovable closer to the suffering soul; that without it there would have been no hope at all, it was just that which had made the fickle one accessible to the cry of pain; more still, and revealing enough: that the shortening of life which might result from it was more of a consolation and assurance to her who demanded possession than it was a moderation of her love. For the rest, all the strangely embarrassing details from that first talk were repeated now, only resolved in almost spiteful satisfaction: he might now make the same deprecating remark that he would have to show himself at the Langewiesches' or the Rollwagens' (people whom one did not know oneself) and thus betray that he said the same thing to them; but now there was triumph in the thought. The "raciness" of the Rollwagen girls was no longer worrying or distressing: mouth to mouth with him, the sting was drawn from those too ingratiating requests to indifferent people that they really must stop on longer with him. As for that frightful "There are so many unhappy ones already": there was a kind of sigh on which the ignominy of the words was blown away. This woman was plainly filled with the thought that while she did indeed belong to the world of enlightenment and suffering, yet at the same time she was a woman and in her femininity possessed a means of snatching life and happiness for herself, of bringing arrogance to her feet and her heart. Earlier, indeed, by a look, a serious word, one could put light-headedness a moment in a thoughtful mood, temporarily win it; one could oblige it, after a flippant farewell, to turn back and correct it by a silent and serious one. But now these temporary gains had been confirmed in possession, in union; in so far as possession and union were possible in duality, in so far as a brooding femininity could secure them. It was this which Inez mistrusted, betraying her lack of faith in the loyalty of the beloved. "Serenus," said she, "it is inevitable, I know it, he will leave me." And I saw the folds between her brows deepen and her face take on a half-mad expression. "But then woe to him! And woe to me!" she added tonelessly, and I could not help recalling Adrian's words when I first told him about the affair: "He must see that he gets out of it whole."

For me the talk was a real sacrifice. It lasted two hours, and much self-denial, human sympathy, friendly goodwill were needed to hold out. Inez seemed conscious of that too, but I must say that her gratitude for the patience, time, and nervous strain one devoted to her was, oddly enough, unmistakably mixed with a sort of malicious satisfaction, a dog-in-the-manger attitude expressing itself in an occasional enigmatic smile. I cannot think of it today without wondering how I bore it so long. In fact we sat on until Institoris got back from the Allotria, where he had been playing tarok with some gentlemen. An expression of embarrassed conjecture crossed his face when he saw us still there. He thanked me for so kindly taking his place and I did not sit down again after greeting him. I kissed the hand of the mistress of the house and left, really unnerved, half angry, half sorry, and went through the silent empty streets to my quarters.

CHAPTER XXXIII

THE time of which I write was for us Germans an era of national collapse, of capitulation, of uprisings due to exhaustion, of helpless surrender into the hands of strangers. The time *in* which I write, which must serve me to set down these recollections here in my silence and solitude, this time has a horribly swollen belly, it carries in its womb a national catastrophe compared with which the defeat of those earlier days seems a moderate misfortune, the sensible liquidation of an unsuccessful enterprise. Even an ignominious issue remains something other and more normal than the judgment that now hangs over us, such as once fell on Sodom and Gomorrah; such as the first time we had not after all invoked.

That it approaches, that it long since became inevitable: of that I cannot believe anybody still cherishes the smallest doubt. Monsignor Hinterpförtner and I are certainly no longer alone in the trembling — and at the same time, God help us, secretly sustaining — realization. That it remains shrouded in silence is uncanny enough. It is already uncanny when among a great host of the blind some few who have the use of their eyes must live with sealed lips. But it becomes sheer horror, so it seems to me, when everybody knows and everybody is bound to silence, while we read the truth from each other in eyes that stare or else shun a meeting.

I have sought faithfully, from day to day, to be justified of my biographical task. In a permanent state of excitement I have tried to give worthy shape to the personal and intimate; and I have let go by what has gone by in the outer world during the time in which I write. The invasion of France, long recognized as a possibility, has come, a technical and military feat of the first, or rather of an altogether unique order, prepared with the fullest deliberation, in which we could the less prevent the enemy since we did not dare concentrate our defence at the single point of landing, being uncertain whether or not to regard it as one among many further attacks at points we could not guess. Vain and fatal both were our hesitations. This was the one. And soon troops, tanks, weapons, and every sort of equipment were brought on shore, more than we could throw back into the sea. The port of Cherbourg, we could confidently trust, had been put out of commission by the skill of German engineers; but it surrendered after a heroic radiogram to the Führer from the Commandant as well as the Admiral. And for days now a battle has been raging for the Norman city of Caen — a struggle which probably, if our fears see truly, is already the opening of the way to the French capital, that Paris to which in the New Order the role of European Luna Park and house of mirth was assigned, and where now, scarcely held in check by the combined strength of the German and French police, resistance is boldly raising its head.

Yes, how much has happened that had its effect on my own solitary activities, while yet I refused to look without-doors! It was not many days after the amazing landing in Normandy that our new reprisal weapon, already many times mentioned with heartfelt joy by our Führer, appeared on the scene of the western theatre of war: the robot bomb, a most admirable means of offence, which only sacred necessity could inspire in the mind of inventive genius; these flying messengers of destruction, sent off in numbers without a crew from the French coast, which explode over southern England and, unless all signs fail, have become a real calamity to the foe. Are they capable of averting actual catastrophe from us? Fate did not will that the installations should be ready in time to prevent or disturb the invasion. Meantime we read that Perugia is taken. It lies, though we do not say so, between Rome and Florence. We already hear whispers of a strategic plan to abandon the whole peninsula, perhaps to free more troops for the faltering defence in the east, whither our soldiers want at no price at all to be sent. A Russian wave is rolling up; it has taken Vitebsk and now threatens Minsk, the capital of White Russia, after whose fall, so our whispering news service tells us, there will be no longer any stopping them in the east either.

No stopping them! My soul, think not on it! Do not venture to measure what it would mean if in this our uniquely frightful extremity the dam should break, as it is on the point of doing, and there were no more hold against the boundless hatred that we have fanned to flame among the peoples round us! True, by the destruction of our cities from the air, Germany has long since become a theatre of war; but it still remains for it to become so in the most actual sense, a sense that we cannot and may not conceive. Our propaganda even has a strange way of warning the foe against the wounding of our soil, the sacred German soil, as against a horrible crime. . . . The sacred German soil! As though there were anything still sacred about it, as though it were not long since deconsecrate over and over again, through uncounted crimes against law and justice and both morally and *de facto* laid open to judgment and enforcement! Let it come! Nothing more remains to hope, to wish, to will. The cry for peace with the Anglo-Saxon, the offer to continue alone the war against the Sarmatic flood, the demand that some part of the condition of unconditional surrender be remitted, in other words that they treat with us — but with whom? All that is nothing but eye-wash: the demand of a regime which will not understand, even today seems not to understand, that its staff is broken, that it must disappear, laden with the curse of having made itself, us, Germany, the Reich, I go further and say all that is German, intolerable to the world.

Such at the moment is the background of my biographical activity. It seemed to me I owed a sketch of it to the reader. As for the background of my actual narrative, up to the point whither I have brought it, I have characterized it at the beginning of this chapter in the phrase "into the hands of strangers." "It is frightful to fall into the hands of strangers": this sentence and the bitter truth of it I thought through and suffered through, often, in those days of collapse and surrender. For as a German, despite a universalistic shading which my relation to the world takes on through my Catholic tradition, I cherish a lively feeling for the national type, the characteristic life-idiom of my country, so to speak, its idea, the way it asserts itself as a facet of the human, against other no doubt equally justifiable variations of the same, and can so assert itself only by a certain outward manifestation, sustained by a nation standing erect on its feet. The unexampled horror of a decisive military defeat overwhelms this idea, physically refutes it, by imposing an ideology foreign to it — and in the first instance bound up with words, with the way we express ourselves. Handed over utterly into the power of this foreign ideology, one feels with all one's being that just because it is foreign it bodes no good. The beaten French tasted this awful experience in 1870, when their negotiators, seeking to soften the conditions of the victors, priced very high the renown, "*la gloire*," ensuing from the entry of our troops into Paris. But the German statesmen answered them that the word *gloire* or any equivalent for it did not occur in our vocabulary. They talked about it in hushed voices, in the French Chamber. Anxiously they tried to comprehend what it meant to surrender at discretion to a foe whose conceptions did not embrace the idea of *gloire*.

Often and often I thought of it, when the Jacobin-Puritan virtue jargon, which four years long had disputed the war propaganda of the "agreed peace," became the current language of victory. I saw it confirmed that it is only a step from capitulation to pure abdication and the suggestion to the conqueror that he would please take over the conduct of the defeated country according to his own ideas, since for its own part it did not know what to do. Such impulses France knew, forty-seven years before, and they were not strange to us now. Still they are rejected. The defeated must continue somehow to be responsible for themselves; outside leading-strings are there only for the purpose of preventing the Revolution which fills the vacuum after the departure of the old authority from going to extremes and endangering the bourgeois order of things for the victors. Thus in 1918 the continuation of the blockade after we laid down our arms in the west served to control the German Revolution, to keep it on bourgeois-democratic rails and prevent it from degenerating into the Russian proletarian. Thus bourgeois imperialism, crowned with the laurels of victory, could not do enough to warn against "anarchy"; not firmly enough reject all dealing with workmen's and soldiers' councils and bodies of that kind, not clearly enough protest that only with a settled Germany could peace be signed and only such would get enough to eat. What we had for a government followed this paternal lead, held with the National Assembly against the dictatorship of the proletariat and meekly waved away the advances of the Soviets, even when they concerned grain-deliveries. Not to my entire satisfaction, I may add. As a moderate man and son of culture I have indeed a natural horror of radical revolution and the dictatorship of the lower classes, which I find it hard, owing to my tradition, to envisage otherwise than in the image of anarchy and mob rule — in short, of the destruction of culture. But when I recall the grotesque anecdote about the two saviours of European civilization, the German and the Italian, both of them in the pay of finance capital, walking together through the Uffizi Gallery in Florence, where they certainly did not belong, and one of them saying to the other that all these "glorious art treasures" would have been destroyed by Bolshevism if heaven had not prevented it by raising them up — when I recall all this, then my notions about classes and masses take on another colour, and the dictatorship of the proletariat begins to seem to me, a German burgher, an ideal situ-

ation compared with the now possible one of the dictatorship of
the scum of the earth. Bolshevism to my knowledge has never destroyed any works of art. That was far more within the sphere
of activity of those who assert that they are protecting us from it.
There did not lack much for their zeal in destroying the things of
the spirit — a zeal that is entirely foreign to the masses — to have
made sacrifice of the works of the hero of these pages, Adrian
Leverkühn. For there is no doubt that their triumph and the historical sanction to regulate this world according to their beastly
will would have destroyed his life-work and his immortality.

Twenty-six years ago it was revulsion against the self-righteous
blandishments of the rhetorical burgher and "son of the revolution," which proved stronger in my heart than the fear of disorder, and made me want just what he did not: that my conquered country should turn towards its brother in tribulation,
towards Russia. I was ready to put up with the social revolution —
yes, to agree to it — which would arise from such comradery. The
Russian Revolution shook me. There was no doubt in my mind of
the historical superiority of its principles over those of the powers which set their foot on our necks.

Since then history has taught me to regard with other eyes our
conquerors of that day, who will shortly conquer us again in alliance with the revolution of the East. It is true that certain strata
of bourgeois democracy seemed and seem today ripe for what I
termed the dictatorship of the scum: willing to make common
cause with it to linger out their privileges. Still, leaders have
arisen, who like myself, who am a son of humanism, saw in this
dictatorship the ultimate that can or may be laid upon humanity
and moved their world to a life-and-death struggle against it. Not
enough can these men be thanked, and it shows that the democracy of the western lands, in all the anachronistic state of their institutions through the passage of time, all the rigidity of their conceptions of freeodm in resisting the new and inevitable, is after all
essentially in the line of human progress, of goodwill to the improvement of society and its renewal, alteration, rejuvenation; it
shows that western democracy is after all capable, by its own nature, of a transition into conditions more justified of life.

All this by the way. What I want to recall here in this biography is the loss of authority of the monarchic military state, so
long the form and habit of our life; it was far advanced as defeat
approached and now with defeat it is complete. Its collapse and
abdication result in a situation of permanent hunger and want,
progressive depreciation of the currency, progressive laxity and

loose speculation, a certain regrettable and unearned dispensing of civilian freedom from all restraint, the degeneration of a national structure so long held together by discipline into debating groups of masterless citizens. Such a very gratifying sight that is not, and no deduction can be made from the word "painful" when I use it here to characterize the impressions I got as a purely passive observer from the gatherings of certain "Councils of Intellectual Workers" then springing up in Munich hotels. If I were a novel-writer, I could make out of my tortured recollections a most lively picture of such a futile and flagitious assemblage. There was a writer of belles-lettres, who spoke, not without charm, even with a sybaritic and dimpling relish, on the theme of "Revolution and Love of Humanity," and unloosed a free discussion – all too free, diffuse, and confused – by such misbegotten types as only see the light at moments like this: lunatics, dreamers, clowns, flibbertigibbets and fly-by-nights, plotters and small-time philosophers. There were speeches for and against love of human kind, for and against the authorities, for and against the people. A little girl spoke a piece, a common soldier was with difficulty prevented from reading to the end a manuscript that began "Dear citizens and citizenesses!" and would doubtless have gone on the whole night; an angry student launched an embittered invective against all the previous speakers, without vouchsafing to the assemblage a single positive expression of opinion – and so on. The audience revelled in rude interruptions; it was turbulent, childish, and uncivilized, the leadership was incapable, the air frightful, and the result less than nothing. I kept looking round and asking myself whether I was the only sufferer; and I was grateful at last to be out of doors, where the tram service had stopped hours before and the sound of some probably entirely aimless shots echoed through the winter night.

Leverkühn, to whom I conveyed these impressions of mine, was unusually ailing at this time, in a way that had something humiliating in its torments. It was as though he were pinched and plagued with hot pincers, without being in immediate danger of his life. That, however, seemed to have arrived at its nadir, so that he was just prolonging it by dragging on from one day to the next. He had been attacked by a stomach ailment, not yielding to any dietary measures, beginning with violent headache, lasting several days and recurring in a few more; with hours, yes, whole days of retching from an empty stomach, sheer misery, undignified, niggling, humiliating, ending in utter exhaustion and persistent sensitivity to light after the attack had passed. There was no thought that the condition might be due to psychological causes, the tribulations of the time, the national defeat with its desolating consequences. In his rustic, not to say cloistered retreat, far from the city, these things scarcely touched him, though he was kept posted on them, not through the newspapers, which he never read, but by his so sympathetic and yet so unruffled housekeeper, Frau Else Schweigestill. The events, which certainly for a man of insight were not a sudden shock but the coming to pass of the long expected, could produce in him scarcely a shoulder-shrug, and he found my efforts to see in the evil the good which it might conceal, to be in the same vein as the comment which I had made at the war's beginning — and that makes me think of that cold, incredulous "God bless your studies!" with which he then answered me.

And still! Little as it was possible to connect his worsening health in any temperamental way with the national misfortune, yet my tendency to see the one in the light of the other and find symbolic parallels in them, this inclination, which after all might be due simply to the fact that they were happening at the same time, was not diminished by his remoteness from outward things, however much I might conceal the thought and refrain from bringing it up even indirectly.

Adrian had not asked for a physician, because he wanted to interpret his sufferings as familiar and hereditary, as merely an acute intensification of his father's migraine. It was Frau Schweigestill who at last insisted on calling in Dr. Kürbis, the Waldshut district physician, the same who had once delivered the Fräulein from Bayreuth. The good man would not hear of migraine, since the often excessive pains were not one-sided as is the case with migraine but consisted in a raging torment in and above both eyes, and moreover were considered by the physician to be a secondary symptom. His diagnosis, stated with all reserve, was of something like a stomach ulcer, and while he prepared the patient for a possible hæmorrhage, which did not occur, he prescribed a solution of nitrate of silver to be taken internally. When this did not answer he went over to strong doses of quinine, twice daily, and that did in fact give temporary relief. But at intervals of two weeks, and then for two whole days, the attacks, very like violent seasickness, came back; and Kürbis's diagnosis began to waver or rather he settled on a different one: he decided that my friend's sufferings were definitely to be ascribed to a chronic catarrh of the stomach with considerable dilatation on the right side, together with circulatory stoppages which decreased the flow of blood to the

brain. He now prescribed Karlsbad effervescent salts and a diet of
the smallest possible volume, so that the fare consisted of almost
nothing but tender meat. He prohibited liquids, soup and vege-
tables, flour and bread. This treatment was directed towards the
desperately violent acidity from which the patient suffered, and
which Kürbis was inclined to ascribe at least in part to nervous
causes — that is, to a central influence, the brain, which here for
the first time began to play a role in his diagnostic speculations.
More and more, after the dilatation of the stomach had been
cured without diminishing the headaches and nausea, he shifted
his explanation of the symptoms to the brain, confirmed therein
by the emphatic demand of the patient to be spared the light.
Even when he was out of bed he spent entire half-days in a
densely dark room. One sunny morning had been enough to fatigue his nerves so much that he thirsted after darkness and enjoyed it like a beneficent element. I myself have spent many
hours of the day talking with him in the Abbot's room, where it
was so dark that only after the eyes got used to it could one see
the outlines of the furniture and a pallid gleam upon the walls.

About this time ice-caps and morning cold showers for the
head were prescribed, and they did better than the other means,
though only as palliatives, whose ameliorating effects did not justify one in speaking of a cure. The unnatural condition was not
removed, the attacks recurred intermittently, and the afflicted one
declared he could stand them if it were not for the permanent and
constant pain in the head, above the eyes, and that indescribable,
paralysis-like feeling all over from the top of the head to the tips of
the toes, which seemed to affect the organs of speech as well. The
sufferer's words dragged, perhaps unconsciously, and he moved
his lips so idly that what he said was badly articulated. I think it
was rather that he did not care, for it did not prevent him from
talking; and I sometimes even got the impression that he exploited
the impediment and took pleasure in saying things in a not quite
articulate way, only half meant to be understood, speaking as
though out of a dream, for which he found this kind of communication suitable. He talked to me about the little sea-maid in
Andersen's fairy-tale, which he uncommonly loved and admired;
not least the really capital picture of the horrid kingdom of the
sea-witch, behind the raging whirlpools, in the wood of polyps,
whither the yearning child ventured in order to gain human legs
instead of her fish's tail; and through the love of the dark-eyed
prince (while she herself had eyes "blue as the depths of sea")
perhaps to win, like human beings, an immortal soul. He played

with the comparison between the knife-sharp pains which the beautiful dumb one found herself ready to bear every step she took on her lovely new white pins and what he himself had ceaselessly to endure. He called her his sister in affliction and made intimate, humorous, and objective comments on her behaviour, her wilfulness, and her sentimental infatuation for the two-legged world of men.

"It begins," he said, "with the cult of the marble statue that had got down to the bottom of the sea, the boy, who is obviously by Thorwaldsen, and her illegitimate taste for it. Her grandmother should have taken the thing away from her instead of letting her plant a rose-red mourning wreath in the blue sand. They had let her go through too much, too early, after that the yearning and the hysterical overestimation of the upper world and the immortal soul cannot be controlled. An immortal soul — but why? A perfectly absurd wish; it is much more soothing to know that after death one will be the foam on the sea, as Nature wills. A proper nixie would have taken this empty-headed prince, who did not know how to value her and who married someone else before her face and eyes, led him to the marble steps of his palace, drawn him into the water, and tenderly drowned him instead of making her fate depend as she did on his stupidity. Probably he would have loved her much more passionately with the fish-tail she was born with than with those extremely painful legs. . . ."

And with an objectivity that could only be in jest, but with drawn brows and reluctantly moving, half-articulating lips, he spoke of the æsthetic advantages of the nixie's shape over that of the forked human kind, of the charm of the lines with which the feminine form flowed from the hips into the smooth-scaled, strong, and supple fish-tail, so well adapted for steering and darting. He rejected all idea of a monstrosity, whatever attaches in the popular mind to mythological combinations of the human and the animal; and declared that he did not find admissible mythological fictions of that kind. The sea-wife had a perfectly complete and charming organic reality, beauty and inevitability; you saw that at once, when she became so pathetically déclassée after she had bought herself legs, which nobody thanked her for. Here we unquestionably had a perfectly natural phenomenon, nature herself was guilty of it, if she was guilty of it, which he did not believe, in fact he knew better — and so on.

I still hear him speaking, or murmuring, with a sinister humour which I answered as lightly; with some misgiving as usual in my heart, along with silent admiration for the whimsical relish he knew how to extract from the pressure obviously resting on him. It was this that made me agree to his rejecting the proposal which Dr. Kürbis at that time in duty bound put before him: he recommended or asked consideration for a consultation with a higher medical authority; but Adrian avoided it, would have none of it. He had, he said, in the first place full confidence in Kürbis; but also he was convinced that he, more or less alone, out of his own nature and powers, would have to get rid of the evil. This corresponded with my own feeling. I should have been more inclined to a change of air, a sojourn at a cure, which the doctor also suggested, without, as we might have expected, being able to persuade the patient. Much too much was he dependent on his elected and habitual frame of house and courtyard, church-tower, pond, and hill; too much on his ancient study, his velvet chair, to let himself in for exchanging all this, even for four weeks, for the abomination of a resort existence, with table d'hôte, promenade, and band. Above all, he pleaded for consideration for Frau Schweigestill, whom he would not wish to offend by preferring some outside, public care and service to hers. He felt, he said, far and away better provided for here, in her understanding, humanly wise and motherly care. Really one might ask where else he could have what he had here, with her who brought him according to the new regimen every four hours something to eat: at eight o'clock an egg, cocoa, and rusk, at twelve a little steak or cutlet, at four soup, meat, and vegetable, at eight o'clock cold joint and tea. This diet was beneficial. It guarded against the fever attending the digestion of hearty meals.

The Nackedey and Kunigunde Rosenstiel came by turns to Pfeiffering. They brought flowers, preserves, peppermint lozenges, and whatever else the market shortages allowed. Not always, in fact only seldom were they admitted, which put neither of them off. Kunigunde consoled herself with particularly well-turned letters in the purest, most stately German. This consolation, true, the Nackedey lacked.

I was always glad to see Rüdiger Schildknapp, with his Adrian-eyes, at my friend's retreat. His presence had a soothing and cheering effect; would it had oftener been vouchsafed! But Adrian's illness was just one of those serious cases which always seemed to paralyse Rüdiger's obligingness; we know how the feeling of being urgently desired made him jib and refuse. He did not lack excuses, I mean rationalizations of this odd psychological trait: wrapped up in his literary bread-winning, this confounded translation, he could really scarcely get away, and besides, his own health was suffering under the bad food conditions. He often had intestinal catarrh and when he appeared in Pfeiffering — for he did come now and again — he wore a flannel body-belt, also a damp bandage in a gutta-percha sheath, a source of bitter wit and Anglo-Saxon jokes for him and thus a diversion for Adrian, who could raise himself with no one so well as with Rüdiger above the torments of the body into the free air of jest and laughter.

Frau Senator Rodde came too, of course, from time to time, crossing the road from her over-furnished retreat to inquire of Frau Schweigestill about Adrian's health if she could not see him herself. If he could receive her, or if they met out of doors, she told him about her daughters, and when she smiled kept her lips closed over a gap in her front teeth, for here too, in addition to the hair, there were losses which made her shun society. Clarissa, she said, loved her profession and did not falter in pursuit of it, despite a certain coldness on the part of the public, carping critics, and the impertinent cruelty of this or that producer who tried to distract her by calling "Tempo, tempo!" from the wings when she was about to enjoy a solo scene. The first engagement in Celle had come to an end and the next one had not carried her much further: she was playing the juvenile lead in remote East Prussian Elbing. But she had prospects of an engagement in the west, in Pforzheim, whence it was but a step to the stage of Karlsruhe or Stuttgart. The main thing, in this profession, was not to get stuck in the provinces, but to be attached betimes to an important state theatre or a private one in a metropolis. Clarissa hoped to succeed. But from her letters, at least those to her sister, it appeared that her success was of a more personal, that is erotic, kind rather than an artistic one. Many were the snares to which she saw herself exposed; repulsing them took much of her energy and mocking coolness. To Inez, though not to her mother directly, she announced that a rich warehouse-owner, a well-preserved man with a white beard, wanted to make her his mistress and set her up extravagantly with an apartment, a car, and clothes — when she could silence the regisseur's impudent "Tempo!" and make the critics fall in line. But she was much too proud to establish her life on such foundations. It was her personality, not her person, that was important to her. The rich man was turned down and Clarissa went on fighting her way in Elbing.

About her daughter Institoris in Munich Frau Rodde talked in less detail: her life was not so lively or eventful, more normal and secure — regarded superficially, and Frau Rodde obviously wanted to regard it thus. I mean she represented Inez's marriage as happy,

which was certainly a large order of sentimental superficiality.
The twins had just been born, and the Frau Senator spoke with
simple feeling of the event, of the three spoilt little darlings, whom
she visited from time to time in their ideal nursery. Expressly and
with pride she praised her older daughter for the unbending will-
power with which she kept her housekeeping up to the mark
despite all contrary circumstances. You could not tell whether
the Frau Senator really did not know what the birds on the
house-tops talked about, the Schwerdtfeger affair, or whether she
only pretended. Adrian, as the reader knows, knew of it from me.
But one day he received Rudolf's confession — a singular business indeed.

The violinist was most sympathetic during the acute illness of
our friend, loyal and attached; yes, it seemed as though he wanted
to use the occasion to show how much store he set by Adrian's
favour and good will. It was even my impression that he believed
he could use the sufferer's reduced and as he probably thought
more or less helpless state to exert his quite imperturbable ingrati-
atingness, enforced by all his personal charm, to conquer a coolness, dryness, and ironic withdrawal which annoyed him, on
grounds more or less serious, or hurt him, or wounded his vanity,
or possibly some genuine feeling on his part — God knows what it
was. In speaking of Rudolf's inconstant nature — as one has to
speak of it — one runs a risk of saying too much. But also one
should not say too little, and for my part this nature and its manifestations appeared to me always in the light of an absolutely
naïve, childish, yes, puckish possession, whose reflection I sometimes saw laughing out of his so very pretty blue eyes.

Suffice it to say that Schwerdtfeger zealously concerned himself with Adrian's condition. He often rang up to inquire of Frau
Schweigestill and offered to come out whenever a visit might be
tolerable or welcome. Soon afterwards, on a day when there was
an improvement, he would appear; he displayed the most winning delight at the reunion, and twice at the beginning addressed
Adrian with *du*, only the third time, as Adrian did not respond,
to correct himself and be satisfied with the first name and *Sie*. As
a sort of consolation and by way of experiment Adrian sometimes
called him Rudolf, though never Rudi, as everybody else did,
and he dropped this too after a while. However, he congratulated the violinist on the great success he had recently had in a
Nuremberg concert, and particularly with his playing of Bach's
Partita in E major for violin alone, which had received the live-
liest commendation from public and press. The result was his ap-

pearance as soloist at one of the Munich Academy concerts in the Odeon, where his clean, sweet, technically perfect interpretation of Tartini pleased everybody extraordinarily. They put up with his "small tone." He had musical and also personal compensations to make up for it. His rise to the position of leader in the Zapfenstösser orchestra — the former holder having retired to devote himself to teaching — was by this time a settled thing, despite his youth, and he looked considerably younger than he was, yes, remarkably enough, younger than when I first met him.

But with all this, Rudi appeared depressed by certain circumstances of his private life; in short by his liaison with Inez Institoris, about which he relieved himself in private to Adrian. "In private" is even an understatement, for the conversation took place in a darkened room, each being aware of the other's presence only as a shadowy outline; and that was, no doubt, an encouragement and easement to Schwerdtfeger in his confidences. The day was an uncommonly brilliant one in January 1919, with sunshine, blue sky, and glittering snow, and Adrian, soon after Rudolf appeared and the first greetings took place, out of doors, was seized with such severe head pains that he asked his guest to share with him at least for a while the well-tried remedy of darkness. They had exchanged the Nike salon, where they had sat at first, for the Abbot's room, shutting out the light with blinds and hangings, so that it was as I had known it: at first complete night to the eyes, then they learned to distinguish more or less the position of the furniture and perceived the weakly trickling shimmer of the outer light, a pallid gleam on the walls. Adrian, in his velvet chair, excused himself many times into the darkness on account of the inconvenience, but Schwerdtfeger, who had taken the Savonarola chair at the writing-table, was entirely satisfied. If it did the other good — and he could well understand how it would do so — then he preferred it that way too. They talked with lowered voices, partly on account of Adrian's condition, partly because one tends to lower one's voice in the dark. It even produces a certain inclination to silence, to the extinction of speech; but Schwerdtfeger's Dresden upbringing did not tolerate any pauses. He chatted away over the bad patches, in defiance of the uncertainty one is in under such conditions about the other party's reactions. They skimmed over the desperate political situation, the fights in the capital, came to speak of the latest in the musical world, and Rudolf, in the purest tone, whistled something from Falla's *Nights in the Gardens of Spain* and Debussy's Sonata for flute, viola, and harp. He whistled the bourrée from *Love's Labour's Lost* too, precisely in the right pitch, and then the comic theme of the weeping little dog from the puppet play *Of the Godless Guile*, without being able to judge whether Adrian cared for it or not. At length he sighed and said he did not feel like whistling, but on the contrary was heavy-hearted, or perhaps not that so much as angry, vexed, impatient, also worried and not knowing what to do, and so, after all, heavy-hearted. Why? To answer that was not so easy and not even permissible, or at most among friends, where you were not obliged to be so careful about this man-of-honour attitude that you must keep your affairs with women to yourself. He was accustomed to observe it, he was no chatterbox. But he was not merely a man of honour either, people mistook him when they thought so, a shallow amoroso and man of pleasure: that was loathsome. He was a man and an artist; he had no use for this man-of-honour attitude; and certainly Adrian knew, for everybody did, what he meant. In short, it was about Inez Rodde, or rather Institoris, and his relations with her, which he could not help. "I can't help it, Adrian, believe me! I never seduced her, but she me, and the horns of little Institoris, to use that silly expression, are altogether her work, not mine. What do you do when a woman clings to you like a drowning person and simply will have you for her lover? Do you leave your garment in her hands and flee? No, people do not do that now, there are other man-of-honour rules, you are not to say no, especially if the woman is pretty, though in rather a fatal and suffering way." But he was fatal and suffering too, a nervous and often afflicted artist, he wasn't a young light-head or sonny-boy, whatever people thought. Inez imagined all sorts of things about him, quite falsely, and that resulted in a crooked sort of relationship, as though such a relation in and for itself were not crooked enough, with the silly situations it was always bringing about and the need for caution every minute. Inez got round all that better than he did, for the simple reason that she was so passionately in love; he could say that because she was so on the basis of her false imaginings. He was at a disadvantage because he was not in love: "I never have loved her, I admit it openly, I always just had friendly and brotherly feelings for her, and that I let myself in with her like this and the stupid thing drags on because she clings to it, that is just a matter of duty and decency on my side." But he must in confidence say this: that it was awkward, yes, degrading, when the passion, a really desperate passion, was on the woman's side while the man was just doing his knightly duty. It reversed the possessive relation somehow and led to an uncomfortable preponderance on the part of the woman so that he must say that Inez behaved with his person and his body as actually and rightly a man behaves with a woman, added to which her morbid and feverish jealousy, quite unjustified anyhow, had to do with the undivided possession of his person; unjustified, as he said, for he had enough with her, in fact enough *of* her and her clinging, and his invisible auditor could scarcely conceive what a refreshment for him, under these circumstances, was the society of a man so highly placed and by him very highly esteemed, the sphere of such a one and conversation with him. People mostly judged him falsely; he much preferred having a serious, elevating, and worth-while talk with such a man to going to bed with women; yes, if he were to characterize himself, he thought, after detailed self-examination, it would be as a platonic nature.

And suddenly, as it were in illustration of what he had just said, Rudi came to speak of the violin concerto which he so greatly wished to have Adrian write for him, if possible with all rights of performance reserved. That was his dream. "I need you, Adrian, for my advancement, my development, my purification, in a way, from all those other affairs. On my word, that is the way I feel, I've never been more in earnest about anything, about what I need. And the concerto I want from you, that is just the most concrete, I mean the most symbolic expression for this need. And you would do it wonderfully, much better than Delius or Prokofiev — with an unheard-of simple and singable first theme in the main movement that comes in again after the cadenza. That is always the best moment in the classic violin concerto, when after the solo acrobatics the first theme comes in again. But you don't need to do it like that, you don't need to have a cadenza at all, that is just a convention. You can throw them all overboard, even the arrangement of the movements, it doesn't need to have any movements, for my part you can have the allegro molto in the middle, a real 'Devil's trill,' and you can juggle with the rhythm, as only you can do, and the adagio can come at the end, as transfiguration — it couldn't be too unconventional, and anyhow I want to put that down, that it will make people cry. I want to get it into myself so I could play it in my sleep, and brood over it and love every note like a mother, and you would be the father — it would be between us like a child, a platonic child — yes, *our* concerto, that would be so exactly the fulfilment of everything that I understand by platonic."

Thus Schwerdtfeger. I have in these pages spoken many times

in his favour, and today too, when I go over it all again I feel mildly towards him, to a considerable extent touched by his tragic end. But the reader will now understand better certain expressions which I applied to him, that "impish naïveté" or childish devilry in his nature. In Adrian's place — but there is really no sense in putting myself in his place; I would not have tolerated some of the things Rudi said. It was distinctly an abuse of the darkness. Not only that he repeatedly went too far in his frankness about his relations with Inez — but also he went too far in another direction, culpably and impishly too far, betrayed by the darkness, I might say, if the notion of any betrayal is in place and one ought not to speak instead of an impudent intrusion of familiarity upon solitude.

That is in fact the right description of Rudi Schwerdtfeger's relation to Adrian Leverkühn. The plan took years to carry out, and a certain sad success cannot be denied to it. In the long run the defencelessness of solitude against such a wooing was proved, certainly to the destruction of the wooer.

CHAPTER XXXIV

Not only with the little sea-maid's knifelike pains did Leverkühn at the time of his worst state of health compare his own torments. In conversation he had another parallel, which he visualized with remarkable clarity. I called it to mind when some months later, in the spring of 1919, the illness lifted like a miracle from off him, and his spirit, phœnixlike, rose to its fullest freedom and most amazing power, in an unchecked, not to say unbridled, anyhow an unintermitted flow of almost breathless productivity. But just that very thing betrayed to me that the two states, the depressive and the exalted, were not inwardly sharply distinguished from each other. They were not separate and without all connection, for the present state had been preparing in the former one and to some extent had already been contained in it — just as indeed, on the other hand, the outbreak of the healthy and creative epoch was by no means a time of enjoyment, but rather in its own way one of affliction, of painful urgency and compulsion. . . . Ah, I write badly! My eagerness to say everything at once makes my sentences run over, hurries them away from the thought they began by intending to express, and makes them seem to rush on and lose it from sight. I shall do well to take the reproof from the reader's mouth. The way my ideas tumble over themselves and get lost is a result of the excitement generated by my memory of this time, the time after the collapse of the authoritarian German state, with its far-reaching accompanying laxity, which affected me as well, laying siege to my settled view of the world with new conceptions hard for it to digest. I felt that an epoch was ending, which had not only included the nineteenth century, but gone far back to the end of the Middle Ages, to the loosening of scholastic ties, the emancipation of the individual, the birth of freedom. This was the epoch which I had in very truth regarded as that of my more extended spiritual home, in short the epoch of bourgeois humanism. And I felt as I say that its hour had come; that a mutation of life would be consummated; the world would enter into a new, still nameless constellation. And moreover this feeling of mine, riveting my attention, was a product not only of the end of the war but already the product of its beginning, fourteen years after the turn of the century. It had lain at the bottom of the panic, the awful sense of destiny which people like me felt at that time. No wonder the disintegration of defeat increased this feeling to its highest pitch, no wonder either that in a defeated country like Germany it occupied the mind far more than among the victorious nations, whose average mental state, precisely on account of victory, was much more conservative. They by no means felt the war as the massive and decisive historical break which it seemed to us. They saw in it a disturbance, now happily past, after which life could return to the path out of which it had been thrust. I envied them. I envied in particular France, for the sanction which, at least apparently, had been vouchsafed by the victory to its conservative bourgeois intellectual constitution; for the sense of security in the classic and rational, which it might draw from its triumph. Certainly, I should at that time have felt better and more at home the other side of the Rhine than here, where, as I said, much that was new, alarming, and destructive, which none the less my conscience obliged me to take stock of, urged itself upon my world-picture. And here I think of the distracting discussion evenings in the Schwabing apartment of a certain Sixtus Kridwiss, whose acquaintance I made at the Schlaginhaufens'. I will come back to those evenings presently, only saying for the moment that the gatherings and intellectual conferences, in which I often out of pure conscientiousness took part, set about me shrewdly. And at this same time with my whole deeply stirred and often dismayed soul I was sharing intimately in the birth of a work which did not fail of certain bold and prophetic associations with those same conferences; which confirmed and realized them on a higher, more creative plane. . . . When I add that besides all this I had my teaching work to perform and might not neglect my duties as head of a family, it will be understood that I was subject to a strain which together with a diet low in calories reduced me physically not a little.

This too I say only to characterize the fleeting, insecure times we lived in; certainly not to direct the reader's attention upon my inconsiderable person, to which only a place in the background of these memoirs is fitting. I have already given expression to my regret that my zeal to communicate must here and there give an impression of flightiness. It is however a wrong impression, for I stick very well by my trains of thought, and have not forgotten that I intended to introduce a second striking and pregnant comparison, in addition to that with the little sea-maid, which Adrian made at the time of his utmost and torturing sufferings.

"How do I feel?" he said to me. "Quite a lot like Johannes Martyr in the cauldron of oil. You must imagine it pretty much like that. I squat there, a pious sufferer, in the tub, with a lively wood fire crackling underneath, faithfully fanned up by a bravo with a hand-bellows, and in the presence of Imperial Majesty who looks on from close by. It is the Emperor Nero, you must know, a magnificent big Turk with Italian brocade on his back. The hangman's helper in a flowing jacket and a codpiece pours the boiling oil over the back of my neck from a long-handled ladle, as I duly and devoutly squat. I am basted properly, like a roast, a hell-roast; it is worth seeing, and you are invited to mingle with the deeply interested persons behind the barrier, the magistrates, the invited public, partly in turbans and partly in good old-German caps with hats on top of them. Respectable townsfolk — and their pensive mood rejoices in the protection of halberdiers. One points out to the other what happens to a hell-roast. They have two fingers on the cheek and two under the nose. A fat man is raising his hand, as though to say: 'God save us all!' On the women's faces, simple edification. Do you see it? We are all close together, the scene is faithfully filled with figures. Nero's little dog has come too, so there shan't be even a tiny empty space. He has a cross little fox-terrier face. In the background you see the towers and gables and pointed oriels of Kaisersaschern. . . ."

Of course he should have said Nuremberg. For what he described — described with the same intimate confidence as he had the tapering of the nixie's body into the fish-tail, so that I recognized it long before he got to the end — was the first sheet of Dürer's series of woodcuts of the Apocalypse. How could I not have recalled the comparison, when later Adrian's purpose slowly revealed itself, though at the time it seemed far-fetched to me, while immediately suggesting certain vague divinations. This was the work which he was mastering, the while it mastered him; for which his powers were slowly gathering head while they lay stretched in torments. Was I not right to say that the depressive and the exalted states of the artist, illness and health, are by no means sharply divided from each other? That rather in illness, as it were under the lee of it, elements of health are at work, and elements of illness, working geniuslike, are carried over into health? It is not otherwise, I thank the insight given me by a friendship which caused me much distress and alarm, but always filled me too with pride: genius is a form of vital power deeply experienced in illness, creating out of illness, through illness creative.

The conception of the apocalyptic oratorio, the secret preoccupation with it, then, went far back into a time of apparently complete exhaustion, and the vehemence and rapidity with which afterwards, in a few months, it was put on paper always gave me the idea that that period of prostration had been a sort of refuge and retreat, into which his nature withdrew, in order that, unspied on, unsuspected, in some hidden sanctuary, shut away by suffering from our healthy life, he might preserve and develop conceptions for which ordinary well-being would never summon the reckless courage. Indeed, they seemed to be as it were robbed from the depths, fetched up from there and brought to the light of day. That his purpose only revealed itself to me by degrees from visit to visit, I have already said. He wrote, sketched, collected, studied, combined; that could not be hidden from me, with inward satisfaction I realized it. Anticipatory announcements came out, from week to week, in a half-joking half-silence; in a repulse that out of fear or annoyance protected a not quite canny secret; in a laugh, with drawn brows; in phrases like "Stop prying, keep your little soul pure!" or "You always hear about it soon enough!" or, more frankly, somewhat readier to confess: "Yes, there are holy horrors brewing; the theological virus, it seems, does not get out of one's blood so easily. Without your knowing it, it leaves a strong precipitate."

The hint confirmed suspicions that had arisen in my mind on seeing what he read. On his work-table I discovered an extraordinary old volume: a thirteenth-century French metrical translation of the *Vision of St. Paul,* the Greek text of which dates back to the fourth century. To my question about where it came from he answered:

"The Rosenstiel got it. Not the first curiosity she has dug up for me. An enterprising female, that. It has not escaped her that I have a weakness for people who have been 'down below.' By below I mean in hell. That makes a bond between people as far apart as Paul and Virgil's Æneas. Remember how Dante refers to them as brothers, as two who have been down below?"

I remembered. "Unfortunately," I said, "your *filia hospitalis* can't read that to you."

"No," he laughed, "for the old French I have to use my own eyes."

At the time, that is, when he could not have used them, as the pain above and in their depths made reading impossible, Clementine Schweigestill often had to read aloud to him: matter indeed that came oddly enough but after all not so unsuitably from the lips of the kindly peasant girl. I myself had seen the good child with Adrian in the Abbot's room: he reclined in the Bernheim chaise-longue while she sat very stiff-backed in the Savonarola chair at the table and in touchingly plaintive, painfully high-German schoolgirl accents read aloud out of a discoloured old cardboard volume. It too had probably come into the house through the offices of the keen-nosed Rosenstiel: it was the ecstatic narrative of Mechthild of Magdeburg. I sat down noiselessly in a corner and for some time listened with astonishment to this quaint, devout, and blundering performance.

So then I learned that it was often thus. The brown-eyed maiden sat by the sufferer, in her modest Bavarian peasant costume, which betrayed the influence of the parish priest: a frock of olive-green wool, high-necked, with a thick row of tiny metal buttons, the bodice that flattened the youthful bosom ending in a point over the wide gathered skirt that fell to her feet. As sole adornment she wore below the neck ruche a chain made of old silver coins. So she sat and read or intoned, in her naïve accents, from writings to which surely the parish priest could have had no objection: the early Christian and mediæval accounts of visions and speculations about the other world. Now and then Mother Schweigestill would put her head round the door to look for her daughter, whom she might have needed in the house; but she nodded approvingly at the pair and withdrew. Or perhaps she too sat down to listen for ten minutes on a chair near the door, then noiselessly disappeared. If it was not the transports of Mechthild that Clementine rehearsed, then it was those of Hildegarde of Bingen; if neither of these, then a German version of the *Historia ecclesiastica gentis anglorum* by the learned monk known as the Venerable Bede: a work in which is transmitted a good part of the Celtic fantasies about the beyond, the visionary experiences of early Irish and Anglo-Saxon times. This whole ecstatic literature from the pre-Christian and early Christian eschatologies forms a rich fabric of tradition, full of recurrent motifs. Into it Adrian spun himself round like a cocoon, to stimulate himself for a work which should gather up all their elements into one single focus, assemble them in one pregnant, portentous synthesis and in relentless transmission hold up to humanity the mirror of the revelation, that it might see therein what is oncoming and near at hand.

"And end is come, the end is come, it watcheth for thee, behold, it is come. The morning is come unto thee, O thou that dwellest in the land." These words Leverkühn makes his *testis*, the witness, the narrator, announce in a spectral melody, built up of perfect fourths and diminished fifths, and set above pedal harmonies alien to the key; they then form the text of that boldly archaic *responsorium*, which they unforgettably repeat by two four-part choruses in contrary motion. These words, indeed, do not belong to the Revelation of St. John, they originate in another layer, the prophecy of the Babylonian exile, the visions and lamentations of Ezekiel, to which, moreover, the mysterious epistle from Patmos, from the time of Nero, stands in a relation of the most singular dependence. Thus the "eating of the little book," which Albrecht Dürer also boldly made the subject of one of his woodcuts, is taken almost word for word from Ezekiel, down to the detail that it (or the "roll," therein "lamentations and mourning and woe") in the mouth of the obediently eating one was as honey for sweetness. So also the great whore, the woman on the beast, is quite extensively prefigured, with similar turns of phrase. In depicting her the Nuremberger amused himself by using the portrait study he had brought with him of a Venetian courtesan. In fact there is an apocalyptic tradition which hands down to these ecstatics visions and experiences to a certain extent already framed, however odd it may seem, psychologically, that a raving man should rave in the same pattern as another who came before him: that one is ecstatic not independently, so to speak, but by rote. Still it seems to be the case, and I point it out in connection with the statement that Leverkühn in the text for his incommensurable choral work by no means confined himself to the Revelation of St. John, but took in this whole prophetic tradition, so that his work amounts to the creation of a new and independent Apocalypse, a sort of résumé of the whole literature. The title, *Apocalypsis cum figuris*, is in homage to Dürer and is intended to emphasize the visual and actualizing, the graphic character, the minuteness, the saturation, in short, of space with fantastically exact detail: the feature is common to both works. But it is far from being the case that Adrian's mammoth fresco follows the Nuremberger's fifteen illustrations in any programmatic sense. True, many words of the same mysterious document which also inspired Dürer underlie this fright-

ful and consummate work of tonal art. But Adrian broadened the
scope both of choral recitative and of ariosa by including also
much from the Lamentations in the Psalter, for instance that piercing "For my soul is full of troubles and my life draweth nigh unto
the grave," as also the expressive denunciations and images of
terror from the Apocrypha; then certain fragments from the
Lamentations of Jeremiah, today unspeakably offensive in their
effect; and even remoter matter still, all of which must contribute
to produce the general impression of a view opening into the
other world and the final reckoning breaking in; of a journey
into hell, wherein are worked through the visional representations
of the hereafter, in the earlier, shamanistic stages, as well as those
developed from antiquity and Christianity, down to Dante. Leverkühn's tone-picture draws much from Dante's poem; and still
more from that crowded wall, swarming with bodies, where
here angels perform staccato on trumpets of destruction, there
Charon's bark unloads its freight, the dead rise, saints pray, dæmonic masks await the nod of the serpent-wreathed Minos, the
damned man, voluptuous in flesh, clung round, carried and drawn
by grinning sons of the pit, makes horrid descent, covering one
eye with his hand and with the other staring transfixed with horror into bottomless perdition; while not far off Grace draws up
two sinning souls from the snare into redemption — in short, from
the groups and the scenic structure of the Last Judgment.

A man of culture, such as I am, when he essays to talk about
a work with which he is in such painfully close touch may be
pardoned for comparing it with existing and familiar cultural
monuments. To do this gives me the needed reassurance, still
needed even as it was at the time when I was present with horror,
amaze, consternation, and pride, at its birth — an experience that
I suppose was due to my loving devotion to its author but actually went beyond my mental capacities, so that I trembled and
was carried away. For after that first period when he repulsed me
and hugged his secret, he then began to give the friend of his
childhood access to his doing and striving; so that at every visit to
Pfeiffering — and of course I went as often as I could, and almost
always over Saturday and Sunday — I was allowed to see new
parts as they developed, also accretions and drafts, of a scope at
times fairly incredible. Here were vastly complex problems, technical and intellectual, subjecting themselves to the strictest law.
Contemplating the mere manufacture of the work a steady-going
man used to a moderate bourgeois rate of accomplishment might
well go pale with terror. Yes, I confess that in my simple human

fear the largest factor was, I should say, the perfectly uncanny
rapidity with which the work came to be: the chief part of it in
four and a half months, a period which one would have allowed
for the mere mechanical task of putting it down.

Obviously and admittedly this man lived at the time in a state
of tension so high as to be anything but agreeable. It was more
like a constant tyranny: the flashing up and stating of a problem,
the task of composition (over which he had heretofore always
lingered), was one with its lightninglike solution. Scarcely did it
leave him time to follow with the pen the haunting and hunting
inspirations which gave him no rest, which made him their slave.
Still in the most fragile health, he worked ten hours a day and
more, broken only by a short pause at midday and now and then
a walk round the pond or up the hill, brief excursions more like
flight than recreation. One could see by his step, first hasty and
then halting, that they were merely another form of unrest.
Many a Sunday evening I spent with him and always remarked
how little he was his own master, how little he could stick to
the everyday, indifferent subjects which he deliberately chose,
by way of relaxation, to talk about with me. I see him suddenly
stiffen from a relaxed posture; see his gaze go staring and listening, his lips part and — unwelcome sight to me — the flickering
red rise in his cheeks. What was that? Was it one of those melodic illuminations to which he was, I might almost say, exposed
and with which powers whereof I refuse to know aught kept
their pact with him? Was it one of those so mightily plastic
themes in which the apocalyptic work abounds, rising to his
mind, there at once to be checked and chilled, to be bridled and
bitted and made to take its proper place in the whole structure?
I see him with a murmured "Go on, go on!" move to his table,
open the folder of orchestral drafts with such violence as sometimes to tear one, and with a grimace whose mingled meaning I
will not try to convey but which in my eyes distorted the lofty,
intelligent beauty his features wore by right, read to himself,
where perhaps was sketched that frightful chorus of humanity
fleeing before the four horsemen, stumbling, fallen, overridden;
or there was noted down the awful scream given to the mocking,
bleating bassoon, the "Wail of the Bird"; or perhaps that song
and answer, like an antiphony, which on first hearing so gripped
my heart — the harsh choral fugue to the words of Jeremiah:

Wherefore doth a living man complain,
A man for the punishment of his sins?

Let us search and try our ways,
And turn again to the Lord. . . .

We have transgressed and have rebelled:
Thou hast not pardoned.
Thou hast covered with anger
And persecuted us:
Thou hast slain, thou hast not pitied. . . .

Thou hast made us as the offscouring
And refuse in the midst of the people.

I call the piece a fugue, and it gives that impression, yet the
theme is not faithfully repeated, but rather develops with the development of the whole, so that a style is loosened and in a way
reduced *ad absurdum*, to which the artist seems to submit himself — which cannot occur without reference back to the archaic
fugal forms of certain canzoni and ricercari of the pre-Bach time,
in which the fugue theme is not always clearly defined and adhered to.

Here or there he might look, seize his pen, throw it down again,
murmur: "Good, till tomorrow," and turn back to me, the flush
still on his brow. But I knew or feared that the "till tomorrow"
would not be adhered to: that after I left he would sit down and
work out what had so unsummoned flashed into his mind as we
talked. Then he would take two luminol tablets to give his sleep
the soundness which must compensate for its briefness. For next
day he would begin again at daybreak. He quoted:

"Up, psalter and harp —
I will be early up."

He lived in fear that the state of illumination with which he was
blest — or with which he was afflicted — might be untimely withdrawn. And in fact he did suffer a relapse. It was shortly before
he got to the end, that frightful finis, which demanded all his
courage and which, so far from being a romantic music of redemption, relentlessly confirms the theologically negative and
pitiless character of the whole. It was, I say, just before he made
port with those roaring brass passages, heavily scored and widely
spaced out, which make one think of an open abyss wherein one
must hopelessly sink. The relapse lasted for three weeks with pain
and nausea, a condition in which, in his own words, he lost the
memory of what it meant to compose, or even how it was done.

It passed. At the beginning of August 1919 he was working again; and before this month, with its many hot, sunny days, was over, his task was finished. The four and a half months which I gave as the period of production are reckoned up to the beginning of the relapse. Including the final working period, the sketch of the *Apocalypse* had taken him, in all, amazingly enough, six months to put on paper.

CHAPTER XXXIV (continued)

AND now: is that all I have to say in his biography about this work of my departed friend: this work a thousandfold hated, thought of with shuddering and yet a hundredfold beloved and exalted? No, I still have much on my heart about it and about certain of its characteristics, which — of course with undeviating admiration — disturbed and depressed me, or, better put, absorbed my attention even while they disturbed my mind. But at the same time I had it in mind to connect those very qualities and characteristics with the abstract speculations to which I was exposed in the house of Herr Sextus Kridwiss and to which I referred on an earlier page. I am free to confess that the novel experiences of these Kridwiss evenings, combined with my participation in Adrian's solitary work, were responsible for the mental strain of my life at that time and in the end for the loss of a good twelve pounds' weight.

Kridwiss was an expert in the graphic arts and fine editions, collector of east-Asiatic coloured wood-carvings and ceramics, a field in which, invited by this or that cultural organization, he gave interesting and well-informed lectures in various cities of the Reich and even abroad. He was an ageless, rather dainty little gentleman, with a strong Rhenish-Hessian accent and uncommon intellectual liveliness. He seemed not to have connections of any opinion-forming kind so far as one could tell, but out of pure curiosity "listened in" at all the events of the day; and when this or that came to his ears he would describe it as "*scho' enorm wischtich.*" The reception-room of his house in Martiusstrasse, Schwabing, was decorated with charming Chinese paintings in India ink and colour (from the Sung period!) and he made it a meeting-place for the leading or rather the initiate members of the intellectual life of Munich, as many of them as the good city harboured in her walls. Kridwiss arranged informal discussion evenings for gentlemen, intimate round-table sittings of not more than eight or ten personalities; one put in an appearance at about nine o'clock and with no great entertainment on the part of the host proceeded to free association and the exchange of ideas. Of course intellectual high tension was not unintermittedly sustained; the talk often slipped into comfortable everyday channels, since thanks to Kridwiss's social tastes and obligations the level was rather uneven. For instance there took part in the sessions two members of the grand-ducal house of Hesse-Nassau, then studying in Munich, friendly young folk whom the host with a certain *empressement* called the beautiful princes. In their presence, if only because they were so much younger than the rest of us, we practised a certain reserve. I cannot say however that they disturbed us much. Often a more highbrow conversation went painlessly over their heads, while they smiled in modest silence or made suitably serious faces. More annoying for me personally was the presence of Dr. Chaim Breisacher, the lover of paradox, already known to the reader. I long ago admitted that I could not endure the man; but his penetration and keen scent appeared to be indispensable on these occasions. I was also irritated by the presence of Bullinger, the manufacturer; he was legitimated only by his high income tax, but he talked dogmatically on the loftiest cultural themes.

I must confess further that really I could feel no proper liking to any of the table round, nor extend to any one of them a feeling of genuine confidence. Helmut Institoris was also a guest, and him I except, since I had friendly relations with him through his wife; yet even here the associations evoked were painful ones, though on other grounds. But one might ask what I could have against Dr. Unruhe, Egon Unruhe, a philosophic palæozoologist who in his writings brilliantly combined a profound knowledge of geological periods and fossilization with the interpretation and scientific verification of our store of primitive sagas. In this theory, a sublimated Darwinism if you like, everything there became true and real, though a sophisticated humanity had long since ceased to believe it. Yes, whence my distrust of this learned and conscientiously intellectual man? Whence the same distrust of Professor Georg Vogler, the literary historian, who had written a much esteemed history of German literature from the point of view of racial origins, wherein an author is discussed and evaluated not as writer and comprehensively trained mind, but as the genuine blood-and-soil product of his real, concrete, specific corner of the Reich, engendering him and by him engendered. All that was very worthy, strong-minded, fit and proper, and critically worth thinking about. The art-critic and Dürer scholar Professor Gilgen Holzschuher, another guest, was not acceptable to me either, on grounds similarly hard to justify; and the same was true without reservation of the poet Daniel zur Höhe who was often present. He was a lean man of thirty in a black clericlike habit closed to the throat, with a profile like a bird of prey and a hammering delivery, as for instance: "Yes, yes, yes, yes, not so bad, oh certainly, one may say so!" nervously and continuously tapping the floor the while with the balls of his feet. He loved to cross his arms on his chest or thrust one hand Napoleonlike in his coat, and his poet dreams dealt with a world subjected by sanguinary campaigns to the pure spirit, by it held in terror and high discipline, as he had described it in his work, I believe his only one, the *Proclamations*. It had appeared before the war, printed on hand-made paper, a lyrical and rhetorical outburst of riotous terrorism, to which one had to concede considerable verbal power. The signatory to these proclamations was an entity named *Christus Imperator Maximus*, a commanding energumen who levied troops prepared to die for the subjection of the globe. He promulgated messages like Orders of the Day, stipulated abandonedly ruthless conditions, proclaimed poverty and chastity, and could not do enough in the hammering, fist-pounding line to exact unquestioned and unlimited obedience. "Soldiers!" the poem ended, "I deliver to you to plunder — *the World!*"

All this was "beautiful" and mightily acclaimed as such; "beautiful" in a cruelly and absolutely beauty-ous way, in the impudently detached, flippant, and irresponsible style poets permit themselves: it was, in fact, the tallest æsthetic misdemeanour I have ever come across. Helmut Institoris, of course, was sympathetic; but indeed both author and work had enjoyed a measure of serious respect from the public, and my antipathy was not quite so sure of itself, because I was conscious of my general irritation with the whole Kridwiss circle and the pretensions of its cultural position, of which my intellectual conscience forced me to take account.

I will try, in as small space as possible, to sketch the essential of these experiences, which our host rightly found "enormously important" and which Daniel zur Höhe accompanied with his stereotyped "Oh yes, yes, yes, not so bad, yes, certainly, one may say so," even when it did not exactly go so far as the plundering of the world by the tough and dedicated soldiery of *Christus Imperator Maximus*. That was, of course, only symbolic poesy, whereas the interest of the conferences lay in surveys of sociological actualities, analyses of the present and the future, which even so had something in common with the ascetic and "beautiful" nightmares of Daniel's fantasy. I have called attention above, quite apart from these evenings, to the disturbance and destruction of apparently fixed values of life brought about by the war, especially in the conquered countries, which were thus in a psychological sense further on than the others. Very strongly felt and objectively confirmed was the enormous loss of value which the individual had sustained, the ruthlessness which made life today stride away over the single person and precipitate itself as a general indifference to the sufferings and destruction of human beings. This carelessness, this indifference to the individual fate, might appear to be the result of the four years' carnival of blood just behind us; but appearances were deceptive. As in many another respect here too the war only completed, defined, and drastically put in practice a process that had been on the way long before and had made itself the basis of a new feeling about life. This was not a matter for praise or blame, rather of objective perception and statement. However, the least passionate recognition of the actual, just out of sheer pleasure in recognition, always contains some shade of approbation; so why should one not accompany such objective perceptions of the time with a many-sided, yes, all-embracing critique of the bourgeois tradition? By the bourgeois tradition I mean the values of culture, enlightenment, humanity, in short of such dreams as the uplifting of the people through scientific civilization. They who practised this critique were men of education, culture, science. They did it, indeed, smiling; with a blitheness and intellectual complacency which lent the thing a special, pungent, disquieting, or even slightly perverse charm. It is probably superfluous to state that not for a moment did they recognize the form of government which we got as a result of defeat, the freedom that fell in our laps, in a word the democratic republic, as anything to be taken seriously as the legitimized frame of the new situation. With one accord they treated it as ephemeral, as meaningless from the start, yes, as a bad joke to be dismissed with a shrug.

They cited de Tocqueville, who had said that out of revolution as out of a common source two streams issued, the one leading men to free arrangements, the other to absolute power. In the free arrangements none of the gentlemen conversationalists at Kridwiss's any longer believed, since the very concept was self-contradictory: freedom by the act of assertion being driven to limit the freedom of its antagonist and thus to stultify itself and its own principles. Such was in fact its ultimate fate, though oftener the prepossession about "human rights" was thrown overboard at the start. And this was far more likely than that we would let ourselves in today for the dialectic process which turned freedom into the dictatorship of its party. In the end it all came down to dictatorship, to force, for with the demolition of the traditional national and social forms through the French Revolution an epoch had dawned which, consciously or not, confessedly or not, steered its course toward despotic tyranny over the masses; and they, reduced to one uniform level, atomized, out of touch, were as powerless as the single individual.

"Quite right, quite right. Oh, indeed yes, one may say so!" zur Höhe assured us, and pounded with his feet. Of course one may say so; only one might, for my taste, dealing with this description of a mounting barbarism, have said so with rather more fear and trembling and rather less blithe satisfaction. One was left with the hope that the complacency of these gentlemen had to do with their recognition of the state of things and not with the state of things in itself. Let me set down as clearly as I can a picture of this distressing good humour of theirs. No one will be surprised that, in the conversations of this avant-garde of culture and critique, a book which had appeared seven years before the war, "*Réflexions sur la violence*" by Sorel, played an important part. The author's relentless prognostication of war and anarchy, his characterization of Europe as the war-breeding soil, his theory that the peoples of our continent can unite only in the one idea, that of making war — all justified its public in calling it the book of the day. But even more trenchant and telling was its perception and statement of the fact that in this age of the masses parliamentary discussion must prove entirely inadequate for the shaping of political decisions; that in its stead the masses would have in the future to be provided with mythical fictions, devised like primitive battle-cries, to release and activate political energies. This was in fact the crass and inflaming prophecy of the book: that popular myths or rather those proper for the masses would become the vehicle of political action; fables, insane visions, chimæras, which needed to have nothing to do with truth or reason or science in order to be creative, to determine the course of life and history, and thus to prove themselves dynamic realities. Not for nothing, of course, did the book bear its alarming title; for it dealt with violence as the triumphant antithesis of truth. It made plain that the fate of truth was bound up with the fate of the individual, yes, identical with it: being for both truth and the individual a cheapening, a devaluation. It opened a mocking abyss between truth and power, truth and life, truth and the community. It showed by implication that precedence belonged far more to the community; that truth had the community as its goal, and that whoever would share in the community must be prepared to scrap considerable elements of truth and science and line up for the *sacrificium intellectus*.

And now imagine (here is the "clear picture" I promised to give) how these gentlemen, scientists themselves, scholars and teachers — Vogler, Unruhe, Holzschuher, Institoris, and Breisacher as well — revelled in a situation which for me had about it so much that was terrifying, and which they regarded as either already in full swing or inevitably on the way. They amused themselves by imagining a legal process in which one of these mass myths was up for discussion in the service of the political drive for the undermining of the bourgeois social order. Its protagonists had to defend themselves against the charge of lying and falsification; but plaintiff and defendant did not so much attack each other as in the most laughable way miss each other's points. The fantastic thing was the mighty apparatus of scientific witness which was invoked — quite futilely — to prove that humbug was humbug and a scandalous affront to truth. For the dynamic, historically creative fiction, the so-called lie and falsification, in other words the community-forming belief, was simply inaccessible to this line of attack. Science strove, on the plane of decent, objective truth, to confute the dynamic lie; but arguments on that plane could only seem irrelevant to the champions of the dynamic, who merely smiled a superior smile. Science, truth — good God! The dramatic expositions of the group were possessed by the spirit and the accent of that ejaculation. They could scarcely contain their mirth at the desperate campaign waged by reason and criticism against wholly untouchable, wholly invulnerable belief. And with their united powers they knew how to set science in a light of such comic impotence that even the "beautiful princes," in their childlike way, were brilliantly entertained. The happy board did not hesitate to prescribe to justice, which had to say the last word and pronounce the judgment, the same self-abnegation which they themselves practised. A jurisprudence that wished to rest on popular feeling and not to isolate itself from the community could not venture to espouse the point of view of theoretic, anti-communal, so-called truth; it had to prove itself modern as well as patriotic, patriotic in the most modern sense, by respecting the fruitful *falsum*, acquitting its apostles, and dismissing science with a flea in its ear.

"Oh yes, yes, yes, certainly, one may say so" — thump, thump.

Although I felt sick at my stomach, I would not play the spoil-
sport; I showed no repugnance, but rather joined as well as I
could in the general mirth; particularly since this did not necessarily mean agreement but only, at least provisionally, a smiling,
gratified intellectual recognition of what was or was to be. I did
once suggest that "if we wanted to be serious for a moment," we
might consider whether a thinking man, to whom the extremity
of our situation lay very much at heart, would not perhaps do
better to make truth and not the community his goal, since the
latter would indirectly and in the long run be better served by
truth, even the bitter truth, than by a train of thought which
proposed to serve it at the expense of truth, but actually, by such
denial, destroyed from within in the most unnatural way the basis
of genuine community. Never in my life have I made a remark
that fell more utterly and completely flat than this one. I admit
that it was a tactless remark, unsuited to the prevailing intellectual
climate, and permeated with an idealism of course well known,
only too well known, well known to the point of being bad taste,
and merely embarrassing to the new ideas. Much better was it for
me to chime in with the others; to look at the new, to explore it,
and instead of offering it futile and certainly boring opposition, to
adapt my conceptions to the course of the discussion and in the
frame of them to make myself a picture of the future and of a
world even now, if unawares, in the throes of birth — and this no
matter how I might be feeling in the pit of my stomach.

It was an old-new world of revolutionary reaction, in which
the values bound up with the idea of the individual — shall we say
truth, freedom, law, reason? — were entirely rejected and shorn
of power, or else had taken on a meaning quite different from that
given them for centuries. Wrenched away from the washed-out
theoretic, based on the relative and pumped full of fresh blood,
they were referred to the far higher court of violence, authority,
the dictatorship of belief — not, let me say, in a reactionary, anachronistic way as of yesterday or the day before, but so that it was
like the most novel setting back of humanity into mediævally
theocratic conditions and situations. That was as little reactionary
as though one were to describe as regression the track round a
sphere, which of course leads back to where it started. There it
was: progress and reaction, the old and the new, the past and the
future became one; the political Right more and more coincided
with the Left. That thought was free, that research worked without assumptions: these were conceptions which, far from representing progress, belonged to a superseded and uninteresting

world. Freedom was given to thought that it might justify force; just as seven hundred years ago reason had been free to discuss faith and demonstrate dogma; for that she was there, and for that today thinking was there, or would be there tomorrow. Research *certainly* had assumptions — of course it had! They were force, the authority of the community; and indeed they were so taken for granted as such that science never came upon the thought that perhaps it was not free. Subjectively, indeed, it was free, entirely so, within an objective restraint so native and incorporate that it was in no way felt as a fetter. To make oneself clear as to what was coming and to get rid of the silly fear of it one need only remind oneself that the absoluteness of definite premises and sacrosanct conditions had never been a hindrance to fancy and individual boldness of thought. On the contrary, precisely because from the very first mediæval man had received a closed intellectual frame from the Church as something absolute and taken for granted, he had been far more imaginative than the burgher of the individualist age; he had been able to surrender himself far more freely and sure-footedly to his personal fantasy.

Oh, yes, force created a firm ground under the feet; it was antiabstract, and I did very well to conceive to myself, working together with Kridwiss's friends, how the old-new would in this and that field systematically transform life. The pedagogue, for instance, knew that in elementary instruction even today the tendency was to depart from the primary learning of letters and sounds and to adopt the method of word-learning; to link writing with concrete looking at things. This meant in a way a departure from the abstract universal letter-script, not bound up with speech; in a way a return to the word-writing of earlier peoples. I thought privately: why words anyhow, why writing, why speech? Radical objectivity must stick to things and to them only. And I recalled a satire of Swift's in which some learned scholars with reform gone to their heads decided, in order to save their lungs and avoid empty phrases, to do away altogether with words and speech and to converse by pointing to the things themselves, which in the interest of understanding were to be carried about on the back in as large numbers as possible. It is a very witty piece of writing: for the women, the masses, and the analphabetic, they it is who rebel against the innovation and insist on talking in words. Well, my interlocutors did not go so far with their proposals as Swift's scholars. They wore the air of disinterested observers, and as "*enorm wischtisch*" they fixed their eyes on the general readiness, already far advanced, to drop out of hand our so-called cultural conquests for the sake of a simplification regarded as inevitable and timely. One might, if one chose, describe it as deliberate rebarbarization. Was I to trust my ears? But now I had to laugh, yet at the same time was amazed when the gentlemen at this point came upon the subject of dental medicine and quite objectively began to talk about Adrian's and my symbolic musical critique of the dead tooth. I am sure I went the colour of a turkey-cock for laughing, while listening to a discussion, pursued with the same intellectual satisfaction as before, about the growing tendency of dentists to pull out forthwith all teeth with dead nerves; since it had been concluded — after a long, painstaking, and refined development in the nineteenth-century technique of root treatment — that they were to be regarded as infectious foreign bodies. Observe — it was Dr. Breisacher who acutely pointed this out, and met with general agreement — that the hygienic point of view therein represented must be considered, in a way, as a rationalization of the fundamental tendency to let things drop, to give up, to get away, to simplify. For in a matter of hygiene it was quite in place to suspect an ideological basis. There was no doubt that in the future, after we had begun to practise a large-scale elimination of the unfit, the diseased and weak-minded, we would justify the policy by similar hygienic arguments for the purification of society and the race. Whereas in reality — none of those present denied, but on the contrary rather emphasized the fact — that the real reason lay far deeper down, in the renunciation of all the humane softness of the bourgeois epoch; in an instinctive self-preparation of humanity for harsh and sinister times which mocked our humans ideals; for an age of over-all wars and revolutions which would probably take us back far behind the Christian civilization of the Middle Ages; in a return to the dark era before it arose after the collapse of the classic culture. . . .

CHAPTER XXXIV (conclusion)

IT will perhaps be granted that a man labouring to digest such novelties as these might lose twelve pounds' weight. Certainly I should not have lost them if I had not taken seriously my experiences at the Kridwiss sessions, but had stood firm in the conviction that these gentlemen were talking nonsense. However, that was not in the least the way I felt. I did not for a moment conceal from myself that with an acuity worthy of note they had laid their fingers on the pulse of the time and were prognosticating accordingly. But I must repeat that I should have been so endlessly grateful, and perhaps should have lost only six pounds instead of twelve, if they themselves had been more alarmed over their findings or had opposed to them a little ethical criticism. They might have said: Unhappily it looks as though things would follow this and this course. Consequently one must take steps to warn people of what is coming and do one's best to prevent it. But what in a way they were saying was: It is coming, it is coming, and when it is here it will find us on the crest of the moment. It is interesting, it is even good, simply by virtue of being what is inevitably going to be, and to recognize it is sufficient of an achievement and satisfaction. It is not our affair to go on to do anything against it. — Thus these learned gentlemen, in private. But that about the satisfaction of recognizing it was a fraud. They sympathized with what they recognized; without this sympathy they could not have recognized it. That was the whole point, and because of it, in my irritation and nervous excitement, I lost weight.

No, all that is not quite right. Merely through my conscientious visits to the Kridwiss group and the ideas to which I deliberately exposed myself, I should not have got thinner by twelve pounds or even half as much. I should never have taken all that speechifying to heart if it had not constituted a cold-blooded intellectual commentary upon a fervid experience of art and friendship: I mean the birth of a work of art very near to me, near through its creator, not through itself, that I may not say, for too much belonged to it that was alien and frightful to my mind. In that all too homelike rural retreat there was being built up with feverish speed a work which had a peculiar kinship with, was in spirit a parallel to, the things I had heard at Kridwiss's table-round.

At that table had been set up as the order of the day a critique of tradition which was the result of the destruction of living values long regarded as inviolable. The comment had been explicitly made — I do not recall by whom, Breisacher, Unruhe, Holzschuher? — that such criticism must of necessity turn against traditional art-forms and species, for instance against the æsthetic theatre, which had lain within the bourgeois circle of life and was a concern of culture. Yes. And right there before my very eyes was taking place the passing of the dramatic form into the epic, the music drama was changing to oratorio, the operatic drama to operatic cantata — and indeed in a spirit, a fundamental state of mind, which agreed very precisely with the derogatory judgments of my fellow-talkers in the Martiusstrasse about the position of the individual and all individualism in the world. It was, I will say, a state of mind which, no longer interested in the psychological, pressed for the objective, for a language that expressed the absolute, the binding and compulsory, and in consequence by choice laid on itself the pious fetters of pre-classically strict form. How often in my strained observation of Adrian's activity I was forced to remember the early impressions we boys had got from that voluble stutterer, his teacher, with his antithesis of "harmonic subjectivity" and "polyphonic objectivity"! The track round the sphere, of which there had been talk in those torturingly clever conversations at Kridwiss's, this track, on which regress and progress, the old and the new, past and future, became one — I saw it all realized here, in a regression full of modern novelty, going back beyond Bach's and Handel's harmonic art to the remoter past of true polyphony.

I have preserved a letter which Adrian sent to me at that time to Freising from Pfeiffering, where he was at work on the hymn of "a great multitude, which no man could number, of all nations, and kindreds, and people, and tongues, standing before the throne and before the Lamb" (see Dürer's seventh sheet). The letter asked me to visit him, and it was signed Perotinus Magnus; a suggestive joke and playful identification full of self-mockery, for this Perotinus was in charge of church music at Notre Dame in the twelfth century, a composer whose directions contributed to the development of the young art of polyphony. The jesting signature vividly reminded me of a similar one of Richard Wagner, who at the time of *Parsifal* added to his name signed to a letter the title "Member of the High Consistory." For a man who is not an artist the question is intriguing: how serious is the artist in what ought to be, and seems, his most pressing and earnest concern; how seriously does he take himself in it, and how much tired disillusionment, affectation, flippant sense of the ridiculous is at work? If the query were unjustified, how then could that great master of the musical theatre, at work on this his most consecrated task, have mocked himself with such a title? I felt much the same at sight of Adrian's signature. Yes, my questioning, my concern and anxiety went further and in the silence of my heart dealt with the legitimacy of his activity, his claim in time to the sphere into which he had plunged, the re-creation of which he pursued at all costs and with the most developed means. In short, I was consumed with loving and anxious suspicion of an æstheticism which my friend's saying: "the antithesis of bourgeois culture is not barbarism, but collectivism," abandoned to the most tormenting doubts.

Here no one can follow me who has not as I have experienced in his very soul how near æstheticism and barbarism are to each other: æstheticism as the herald of barbarism. I experienced this distress certainly not for myself but in the light of my friendship for a beloved and emperilled artist soul. The revival of ritual music from a profane epoch has its dangers. It served indeed the ends of the Church, did it not? But before that it had served less civilized ones, the ends of the medicine-man, magic ends. That was in times when all celestial affairs were in the hands of the priest-medicine-man, the priest-wizard. Can it be denied that this was a pre-cultural, a barbaric condition of cult art; and is it comprehensible or not that the late and cultural revival of the cult in art, which aims by atomization to arrive at collectivism, seizes upon means that belong to a stage of civilization not only priestly but primitive? The enormous difficulties which every rehearsal and performance of Leverkühn's *Apocalypse* presents, have directly to do with all that. You have there ensembles which begin as "speaking" choruses and only by stages, by the way of the most extraordinary transitions, turn into the richest vocal music; then choruses which pass through all the stages from graded whisperings, antiphonal speech, and humming up to the most polyphonic song — accompanied by sounds which begin as mere noise, like tom-toms and thundering gongs, savage, fanatical, ritual, and end by arriving at the purest music. How often has this intimidating work, in its urge to reveal in the language of music the most hidden things, the beast in man as well as his sublimest stirrings, incurred the reproach both of blood-boltered barbarism and of bloodless intellectuality! I say incurred; for its idea, in a way, is to take in the life-history of music, from its pre-musical, magic, rhythmical, elementary stage to its most complex consummation; and thus it does perhaps expose itself to such reproaches not only in part but as a whole.

Let me give an illustration that has always been the target of scorn and hatred, and hence the special object of my painful human feeling. But first I must go back a little. We all know that it was the earliest concern, the first conquest of the musician to rid sound of its raw and primitive features, to fix to one single note the singing which in primeval times must have been a howling glissando over several notes, and to win from chaos a musical system. Certainly and of course: ordering and normalizing the notes was the condition and first self-manifestation of what we understand by music. Stuck there, so to speak, a naturalistic atavism, a barbaric rudiment from pre-musical days, is the gliding voice, the glissando, a device to be used with the greatest restraint on profoundly cultural grounds; I have always been inclined to sense in it an anti-cultural, anti-human appeal. What I have in mind is Leverkühn's preference for the glissando. Of course "preference" is not the right word; I only mean that at least in this work, the *Apocalypse*, he makes exceptionally frequent use of it, and certainly these images of terror offer a most tempting and at the same time most legitimate occasion for the employment of that savage device. In the place where the four voices of the altar order the letting loose of the four avenging angels, who mow down rider and steed, Emperor and Pope, and a third of mankind, how terrifying is the effect of the trombone glissandos which here represent the theme! This destructive sliding through the seven positions of the instrument! The theme represented by howling — what horror! And what acoustic panic results from the repeated drum-glissandos, an effect made possible on the chromatic or machine drum by changing the tuning to various pitches during the drum-roll. The effect is extremely uncanny. But most shattering of all is the application of the glissando to the human voice, which after all was the first target in organizing the tonic material and ridding song of its primitive howling over several notes: the return, in short, to this primitive stage, as the chorus of the *Apocalypse* does it in the form of frightfully shrieking human voices at the opening of the seventh seal, when the sun became black and the moon became as blood and the ships are overturned.

I may be allowed here to say a word on the treatment of the chorus in my friend's work: this never before attempted breaking-up of the choral voices into groups both interweaving with and singing against each other; into a sort of dramatic dialogue and into single cries which, to be sure, have their distant classic model in the crashing answer "Barrabam!" of the *St. Matthew Passion*. The *Apocalypse* has no orchestral interludes; but instead the chorus more than once achieves a marked and astonishing orchestral effect: thus in the choral variations which represent the pæan of the hundred and forty-four thousand redeemed, filling the heavens with their voices, here the four choral parts simply sing in the same rhythm, while the orchestra adds to and sets against them the richest, most varied and contrasting ones. The extremely harsh clashes produced by the part-writing in this piece (and not here alone) have offered much occasion for spiteful jeers. But so it is: so must one accept it; and I at least do so, consenting if amazed. The whole work is dominated by the paradox (if it is a paradox) that in it dissonance stands for the expression of everything lofty, solemn, pious, everything of the spirit; while consonance and firm tonality are reserved for the world of hell, in this context a world of banality and commonplace.

But I wanted to say something else: I wanted to point out the singular interchange which often takes place between the voices and the orchestra. Chorus and orchestra are here not clearly separated from each other as symbols of the human and the material world; they merge into each other, the chorus is "instrumentalized," the orchestra as it were "vocalized," to that degree and to that end that the boundary between man and thing seems shifted: an advantage, surely, to artistic unity, yet — at least for my feeling — there is about it something oppressive, dangerous, malignant. A few details: the part of the "Whore of Babylon, the Woman on the Beast, with whom the kings of the earth have committed fornication," is, surprisingly enough, a most graceful coloratura of great virtuosity; its brilliant runs blend at times with the orchestra exactly like a flute. On the other hand, the muted trumpet suggests a grotesque vox humana, as does also the saxophone, which plays a conspicuous part in several of the small chamber orchestras which accompany the singing of the devils, the shameful round of song by the sons of the Pit. Adrian's capacity for mocking imitation, which was rooted deep in the melancholy of his being, became creative here in the parody of the

different musical styles in which the insipid wantonness of hell
indulges: French impressionism is burlesqued, along with bourgeois drawing-room music, Tchaikovsky, music-hall, the synco-
pations and rhythmic somersaults of jazz — like a tilting-ring it
goes round and round, gaily glittering, above the fundamental utterance of the main orchestra, which, grave, sombre, and complex,
asserts with radical severity the intellectual level of the work as
a whole.

Forward! I have still so much on my heart about this scarcely
opened testament of my friend; it seems to me I shall do best to
go on, stating my opinions in the light of that reproach whose
plausibility I admit though I would bite my tongue out sooner
than recognize its justice: the reproach of barbarism. It has been
levelled at the characteristic feature of the work, its combination
of very new and very old; but surely this is by no means an arbitrary combination; rather it lies in the nature of things: it rests,
I might say, on the curvature of the world, which makes the last
return unto the first. Thus the elder art did not know rhythm as
music later understood it. Song was set according to the metrical
laws of speech, it did not run articulated by bars and musical periods; rather it obeyed the spirit of free recitation. And how is it
with the rhythm of our, the latest, music? Has it too not moved
nearer to a verbal accent? Has it not been relaxed by an excessive
flexibility? In Beethoven there are already movements of a rhythmic freedom foreshadowing things to come — a freedom which in
Leverkühn is complete but for his bar-lines, which, as an ironically conservative conventional feature, he still retained. But without regard to symmetry, and fitted exclusively to the verbal accent, the rhythm actually changes from bar to bar. I spoke of
impressions. There are impressions which, unimportant as they
seem to the reason, work on in the subconscious mind and there
exercise a decisive influence. So it was now: the figure of that
queer fish across the ocean and his arbitrary, ingenuous musical
activity, of whom another queer fish, Adrian's teacher, had told
us in our youth, and about whom my companion expressed himself with such spirited approval as we walked home that night:
the figure and the history of Johann Conrad Beissel was such an
impression. Why should I behave as though I had not already,
long ago and repeatedly thought of that strict schoolmaster and
beginner in the art of song, at Ephrata across the sea? A whole
world lies between his naïve unabashed theory and the work of
Leverkühn, pushed to the very limits of musical erudition, technique, intellectuality. And yet for me, the understanding friend,

the spirit of the inventor of the "master" and "servant" notes and of musical hymn-recitation moves ghostlike in it.

Do I, with these personal interpolations, contribute anything which will explain that reproach which hurts me so, which I seek to interpret without making the smallest concession to it: the reproach of barbarism? It has probably more to do with a certain touch, like an icy finger, of mass-modernity in this work of religious vision, which knows the theological almost exclusively as judgment and terror: a touch of "streamline," to venture the insulting word. Take the *testis*, the witness and narrator of the horrid happenings: the "I, Johannes," the describer of the beasts of the abyss, with the heads of lions, calves, men, and eagles — this part, by tradition assigned to a tenor, is here given to a tenor indeed but one of almost castrato-like high register, whose chilly crow, objective, reporterlike, stands in terrifying contrast to the content of his catastrophic announcements. When in 1926 at the festival of the International Society for New Music at Frankfurt the *Apocalypse* had its first and so far its last performance (under Klemperer) this extremely difficult part was taken and sung in masterly fashion by a tenor with the voice of a eunuch, named Erbe, whose piercing communications did actually sound like "Latest News of World Destruction." That was altogether in the spirit of the work, the singer had with the greatest intelligence grasped the idea. — Or take as another example of easy technical facility in horror, the effect of being at home in it: I mean the loud-speaker effects (in an oratorio!) which the composer has indicated in various places and which achieve an otherwise never realized gradation in the volume and distance of the musical sound: of such a kind that by means of the loud-speaker some parts are brought into prominence, while others recede as distant choruses and orchestras. Again think of the jazz — certainly very incidental — used to suggest the purely infernal element: one will bear with me for making bitter application of the expression "streamlined" for a work which, judged by its intellectual and psychological basic mood, has more to do with Kaisersaschern than with modern slickness and which I am fain to characterize as a dynamic archaism.

Soullessness! I well know this is at bottom what they mean who apply the word "barbaric" to Adrian's creation. Have they ever, even if only with the reading eye, heard certain lyrical parts — or may I only say moments? — of the *Apocalypse:* song passages accompanied by a chamber orchestra, which could bring tears to the eyes of a man more callous than I am, since they are like a fervid prayer for a soul. I shall be forgiven for an argument more or less into the blue; but to call soullessness the yearning for a soul — the yearning of the little sea-maid — that is what I would characterize as barbarism, as inhumanity!

I write it down in a mood of self-defence; and another emotion seizes me: the memory of that pandemonium of laughter, of hellish merriment which, brief but horrible, forms the end of the first part of the *Apocalypse*. I hate, love, and fear it; for — may I be pardoned for this all too personal excuse? — I have always feared Adrian's proneness to laughter, never been able, like Rüdiger Schildknapp, to play a good second to it; and the same fear, the same shrinking and misgiving awkwardness I feel at this gehennan gaudium, sweeping through fifty bars, beginning with the chuckle of a single voice and rapidly gaining ground, embracing choir and orchestra, frightfully swelling in rhythmic upheavals and contrary motions to a fortissimo tutti, an overwhelming, sardonically yelling, screeching, bawling, bleating, howling, piping, whinnying salvo, the mocking, exulting laughter of the Pit. So much do I shudder at this episode in and for itself, and the way it stands out by reason of its position in the whole, this hurricane of hellish merriment, that I could hardly have brought myself to speak of it if it were not that here, precisely here, is revealed to me, in a way to make my heart stop beating, the profoundest mystery of this music, which is a mystery of identity.

For this hellish laughter at the end of the first part has its pendant in the truly extraordinary chorus of children which, accompanied by a chamber orchestra, opens the second part: a piece of cosmic music of the spheres, icily clear, glassily transparent, of brittle dissonances indeed, but withal of an — I would like to say — inaccessibly unearthly and alien beauty of sound, filling the heart with longing without hope. And this piece, which has won, touched, and ravished even the reluctant, is in its musical essence, for him who has ears to hear and eyes to see, the devil's laughter all over again. Everywhere is Adrian Leverkühn great in making unlike the like. One knows his way of modifying rhythmically a fugal subject already in its first answer, in such a way that despite a strict preservation of its thematic essence it is as repetition no longer recognizable. So here — but nowhere else as here is the effect so profound, mysterious and great. Every word that turns into sound the idea of Beyond, of transformation in the mystical sense, and thus of change, transformation, transfiguration, is here exactly reproduced. The passages of horror just before heard are given, indeed, to the indescribable children's chorus at quite a different pitch, and in changed orchestration and rhythms; but in the searing, susurrant tones of spheres and angels there is not one note which does not occur, with rigid correspondence, in the hellish laughter.

That is Adrian Leverkühn. Utterly. That is the music he represents; and that correspondence is its profound significance, calculation raised to mystery. Thus love with painful discrimination has taught me to see this music, though in accordance with my own simple nature I would perhaps have been glad to see it otherwise.

CHAPTER XXXV

THE new numeral stands at the head of a chapter that will report a death, a human catastrophe in the circle round my friend. And yet, my God, what chapter, what sentence, what word that I have written has not been pervaded by the catastrophic, when that has become the air we breathe! What word did not shake, as only too often the hand that wrote it, with the vibrations not alone of the catastrophe towards which my story strives but simultaneously of that cataclysm in whose sign the world — at least the bourgeois, the human world — stands today?

Here we shall be dealing with a private, human disaster, scarcely noted by the public. To it many factors contributed: masculine rascality, feminine frailty, feminine pride and professional unsuccess. It is twenty-two years since, almost before my eyes, Clarissa Rodde the actress, sister of the just as obviously doomed Inez, went to her death: at the end of the winter season of 1921-2, in the month of May, at Pfeiffering in her mother's house and with scant consideration for that mother's feelings, with rash and resolute hand she took her life, using the poison that she had long kept in readiness for the moment when her pride could no longer endure to live.

I will relate in few words the events which led to the frightful deed, so shattering to us all though at bottom we could hardly condemn it, together with the circumstances under which it was committed. I have already mentioned that her Munich teacher's warnings had proved all too well founded: Clarissa's artistic career had not in the course of years risen from lowly provincial beginnings to more respectable and dignified heights. From Elbing in East Prussia she went to Pforzheim in Baden — in other words she advanced not at all or very little, the larger theatres of the Reich gave her not a thought. She was a failure or at least lacking any genuine success, for the simple reason, so hard for the person concerned to grasp, that her natural talent was not equal to her ambition. No genuine theatre blood gave body to her knowledge or her hopes or won for her the minds and hearts of the contrarious public. She lacked the primitive basis, that which in all art is the decisive thing but most of all in the art of the actor — whether that be to the honour or the dishonour of art and in particular the art of the stage.

There was another factor which added to Clarissa's emotional confusion. As I had long before observed with regret, she did not make a clear distinction between her stage life and her real one. Possibly just because she was no true actress, she played actress even outside the theatre. The personal and physical nature of stage art led her to make up in private life with rouge and cosmetics, exaggerated hairdressing and extravagant hats: an entirely unnecessary and mistaken self-dramatization which affected her friends painfully, invited criticism from the conventional, and encouraged the licentious. All this without wish or intention on her part, for Clarissa was the most mockingly aloof, chaste, and high-minded creature imaginable, though her armour of arrogance may well have been a defence mechanism against the demands of her own femininity. If so, she was the blood sister of Inez Institoris, the beloved — or *ci-devant* beloved — of Rudi Schwerdtfeger.

In any case, to that well-preserved sixty-year-old man who wanted to make her his mistress, there succeeded this or that unchronicled trifler with less solid prospects, or one or another favourable critic who might have been useful to her but being repulsed revenged himself by pouring public scorn on her performance. And finally fate overtook her and put to shame her contemptuous way of looking down her nose. It was a defeat the more lamentable in that the conqueror of her maidenhood was not at all worthy of his triumph and was not even so deemed by Clarissa herself. He was a pseudo-Mephistopheles, a Pforzheim petticoat-chaser, back-stage hanger-on and provincial roué, by profession a criminal lawyer. He was equipped for conquest with nothing but a cheap and cynical eloquence, fine linen, and much black hair on his hands. One evening after the play, probably a little the worse for wine, the prickly but at bottom shy, inexperienced, and defenceless creature yielded to his practised technique of seduction and afterwards was prey to the most scathing self-contempt. For the betrayer had indeed been able to capture her senses for the moment but she actually felt for him only the hatred his triumph aroused, together with a certain astonishment that she, Clarissa Rodde, could have been thus betrayed. She scornfully rejected his further addresses; but she was frightened lest he might betray their relation — in fact he was already threatening to do so as a means of bringing pressure.

Meanwhile decent human prospects had opened to the girl in her disillusioned and nervous state. Among her social connections she had made the acquaintance of a young Alsatian business man who sometimes came over from Strasbourg to Pforzheim and had fallen desperately in love with the proud and stately blonde. Clarissa was not at this time entirely without an engagement; having remained for another season at the Pforzheim theatre, though only in secondary and unrewarding parts. Even so, the re-engagement was due to the sympathy and mediation of an elderly dramatist, who while sceptical as to her acting abilities esteemed her general intellectual and human worth, which was so greatly, even disadvantageously superior to the average among the little stage folk. Perhaps, who knows, this man even loved her, but was too much resigned to the disappointments and disillusionments of life to summon up courage to declare his inclination.

At the beginning of the new season, then, Clarissa met the young man who promised to rescue her from her unsuccessful career and to offer her as his wife a peaceful and secure, yes, well-furnished existence in a sphere strange to her, indeed, but socially not alien to her own origins. With unmistakable joy and hope, with gratitude, yes, with a tenderness rooted in her gratitude, she wrote to her sister and even to her mother of Henri's wooing and also about the disapproval of his family. He was about the same age as Clarissa, his mother's darling, his father's business partner, and altogether the light of his family's eyes. He put his case to them with ardour and strength of purpose; but it would have taken more than that to overcome all at once the prejudice of his bourgeois clan against an itinerant actress and a *boche* into the bargain. Henri understood his family's concern for refinement and good taste, their fear that he might be getting entangled. It was not so easy to convince them that he would by no means be doing so in bringing Clarissa home; the best way would be for him to present her personally to his loving parents, jealous brothers and sisters, and prejudiced aunts, and towards this goal he had been working for weeks, that they might consent and arrange an interview. In regular letters and repeated trips to Pforzheim he reported progress to his betrothed.

Clarissa was confident of success. Her social equality, only clouded by the profession she was ready to renounce, must become plain to Henri's anxious clan at a personal meeting. In her letters and during a visit she made to Munich she took for granted her coming official betrothal and the future she anticipated. That future, to be sure, looked quite different from the earlier dreams of this uprooted child of patrician stock, striving towards intellectual and artistic goals. But now it was her haven, her happiness: a bourgeois happiness, which obviously looked more acceptable because it possessed the charm of novelty; the foreign nationality was a new frame into which she would be transplanted. In fancy she heard her future children prattling in French.

Then the spectre of her past rose up to blast her hopes. It was a stupid, cynical, ignoble spectre but bold and ruthless; and it put her to shame, it drove the poor soul into a corner and brought her to her death. That villain learned in the law, to whom in a weak moment she had surrendered, used his single conquest to enforce her. Henri's family, Henri himself should learn of their relation if she did not yield to him again. From all that we later learned, there must have been desperate scenes between the murderer and his victim. In vain the girl implored him — on her knees at last — to spare her, to release her, not to make her pay for her peace with the betrayal of the man who loved her, whose love she returned. Precisely this confession roused the wretch to cruelty. He made no bones of saying that in giving herself to him now, she was buying peace only for the moment, buying the trip to Strasbourg, the betrothal. He would never release her: to pay himself for his present silence he would compel her to his will whenever he chose. He would speak out as soon as she denied her debt. She would be forced to live in adultery: a just punishment for her philistinism, for what the wretch called her cowardly retreat into bourgeois society. If all that went wrong, if even without his treachery her little bridegroom learned the truth, then there still remained the last resort, the out-crowing drug which for so long she had kept in that objet d'art, the book with the death's-head on the lid. Not for nothing had she felt superior to life and made macabre mock of it by her possession of the Hippocratic drug — a mock that was more in character than the bourgeois peace treaty with life for which she had been preparing.

In my opinion the wretch, aside from satisfying his lust, had aimed at her death. His abnormal vanity demanded a female corpse on his path, he itched to have a human being die and perish, if not precisely for him, yet on his account. Alas, that Clarissa had to gratify him! She saw the situation clearly, just as I see it, as we all had to see it. Once again she yielded, to gain a present peace, and was thereby more than ever in his power. She probably thought that once accepted by the family, once married to Henri and safe in another country, she would find ways and means to defy her oppressor. It was not to be. Obviously her tormentor had made up his mind not to let matters go as far as marriage. An anonymous letter referring in the third person to Clarissa's lover did its work with Henri and his Strasbourg family. He sent it to her that she might, if possible, deny it. His accompanying letter did not precisely display an unshakable faith and love.

Clarissa received the registered letter in Pfeiffering, where after the close of the Pforzheim theatre season she was spending a few weeks with her mother in the cottage under the chestnut trees. It was early afternoon. The Frau Senator saw her daughter hurrying back from a walk she had taken alone, after the midday meal. They met on the little open place in front of the house and Clarissa brushed past her mother with a blank, dazed look and fugitive smile, into her own room, where with a swift and violent movement she turned the key in the door. Next door the old lady presently heard her daughter at the wash-hand-stand, gargling her throat — we know now that it was to cool the fearful corrosive action of the acid. Then there was a silence — long and uncanny. After twenty minutes the Frau Senator knocked and called Clarissa's name. Repeatedly and urgently she called but no answer came. The frightened woman, with her scanty hair awry over her brow, her partly toothless gums, ran across to the main building and in half-choked words told Frau Schweigestill; that experienced soul followed her with a manservant. After repeated knocking and calling they forced the door. Clarissa lay with open eyes on the sofa at the foot of the bed, a piece from the seventies or eighties of the last century, with a back and side arm; I knew it from the Rambergstrasse. She had retreated there when death came upon her while she gargled her throat.

"Not anythin' to do, dear Frau Senator," said Frau Schweigestill, one finger on her cheek, shaking her head, at sight of the halfsitting, half-lying figure. The same only too convincing sight met my eyes when I hurried over from Freising, having been informed by our landlady on the telephone. I took the wailing mother in my arms, a distressed and consolatory family friend; we stood beside the body together with Frau Schweigestill and Adrian. Dark blue spots of congested blood on Clarissa's lovely hands and on her face indicated death by quick suffocation, the abrupt paralysis of the organs of breathing by a dose of cyanide large enough to kill a regiment. On the table, empty, the screws taken out of the bottom, was that bronze container, the book with the name Hippocrates in Greek letters, and the skull upon it.

There was a hasty pencilled note to her betrothed, with the words: "*Je t'aime. Une fois je t'ai trompé, mais je t'aime.*"

The young man came to the funeral, the arrangements for which fell to my lot. He was heart-broken — or rather he was *désolé*, which of course quite wrongly does not sound quite so serious, somehow a little more like a phrase. I would not cast doubt on the pain with which he cried out: "Ah, monsieur, I loved her enough to pardon her. Everything might have been well — and now — *comme ça!*"

Yes, "*comme ça!*" It really might all have been otherwise if he had not been such a son of his family and if Clarissa had had in him a more responsible support.

That night we wrote, Adrian, Frau Schweigestill, and I, while the Frau Senator in the deepest grief sat by the rigid husk of her child, the public announcement of the death. It had to be signed by Clarissa's nearest relatives, and we were to give it an unmistakably palliating tone. We agreed on a formula which said that the deceased had died after grave and incurable affliction. This was read by the Munich dean on whom I called to get consent for the church service so intensely desired by the Frau Senator. I did not begin too diplomatically, for I naïvely admitted in confidence that Clarissa had preferred death to a life of dishonour. The man of God, a sturdy cleric of true Lutheran type, would not listen to me. Frankly, it took me some time to understand that on the one hand, indeed, the Church did not wish to see herself put on one side; but on the other she was not ready to give her parting blessing to a declared suicide, however honourable a one. In short, the sturdy cleric wanted nothing else than that I should tell him a lie. So then I came round with almost ridiculous promptness, described the event as incomprehensible; allowed that a mistake, a wrong bottle was quite possible, yes, probable. Whereupon the fat-head showed himself flattered by the weight we attached to the services of his firm and declared himself ready to conduct the funeral.

It took place in the Munich Waldfried cemetery, attended by the whole circle of friends of the Rodde family. Rudi Schwerdtfeger, Zink and Spengler, even Schildknapp, they were all there. The mourning was sincere, for everybody had been fond of poor, proud, pert Clarissa. Inez Institoris, in deepest black, represented her mother, who did not appear. The daughter received the condolences with dignity, her delicate neck stretched out. In this tragic outcome of her sister's struggle I could not help seeing an ill omen for her own fate. And in speaking with her I got the impression that she rather envied than mourned for her sister. Her husband's income was more and more reduced by the fall of the exchange, in some circles so desired and promoted. The bulwark of luxury, her protection against life, threatened to fail the frightened woman; it was already doubtful whether they could keep the expensive home on the English Garden. As for Rudi Schwerdtfeger, he had indeed paid Clarissa the last honours; but he left the cemetery as soon as he could after his condolences to the relatives. Adrian commented on their briefness and formality.

This was probably the first time Inez had seen her lover since he broke off their affair — I fear rather brutally, for to do it "nicely" was hardly possible in view of the desperation with which she clung to him. As she stood there beside her slender husband, at her sister's grave, she was a forsaken woman, and in all likelihood desperately unhappy. But she had gathered round her a little group of women as a consolation and substitute, and they now stood with her, more for her sake than in Clarissa's honour. To this close little circle, partnership, corporation, club, or what you will, belonged Natalie Knöterich as Inez's nearest friend; also a divorced woman writer, a Rumanian-Siebenbürgerin, author of various farces and mistress of a bohemian salon in Schwabing; the actress Rosa Zwitscher, a performer who frequently displayed great nervous intensity; and one or two other females whom it is unnecessary to describe, especially since I am not certain of their active membership in the group.

The cement that bound them together was — as the reader is already prepared to hear — morphine. It was an extremely strong bond; for the confraternity not only helped each other out with their unhealthy partnership in the drug that was their bliss and bane; but also on the moral side there exists a sad yet tender mutual respect and solidarity among the slaves of the craving. In this case the sinners were also held together by a definite philosophy or motto originating with Inez Institoris and subscribed to by all the five or six friends. Inez, that is, espoused the view — I have on occasion heard it from her lips — that pain is an indignity, that it is shameful to suffer. But quite aside from that concrete and particular humiliation from physical or emotional suffering, life in and for itself, mere existence, animal existence, was an ignoble fetter and unworthy burden, and it was nothing less than noble and high-minded, it was an exercise of a human right, it was intellectually justifiable to slough off the burden, so to speak, to win freedom, ease, an as it were bodiless well-being by providing the physical with the blessed stuff which purveyed such emancipation from suffering.

That such a philosophy took in its stride the physically ruinous consequences of the self-indulgent habit, belonged obviously to its nobility, and probably it was the consciousness of their common early ruin that stimulated the companions to such tenderness, yes, to being tenderly in love with each other. Not without repulsion did I observe their raptures, the lighting up of their glances, their gushing embraces and kisses when they met in society. Yet I confess my private impatience with this dispensation — confess it with a certain surprise, since I do not at all care for myself in the role of carping pharisee. It may be the sentimental disingenuousness to which the vice leads, or is always immanent in it, that causes my unconquerable distaste. Moreover I took amiss the reckless indifference to her children which Inez displayed as this evil habit grew on her; it stamped as false all her pretended devotion to her coddled little white-skinned darlings. In short, the woman had become deeply offensive to me after I knew and saw what she let herself in for. She perfectly saw that I had given her up, and repaid the perception with a smile which in its hysterical malice reminded me of that other smile on her face when for two hours on end she had assumed my human sympathy with her love and her lust.

Indeed, she had small ground to be cheerful; for the way she debased herself was a sorry sight. Probably she took over-doses, which did not increase her animation but reduced her to a state in which she could not appear in public. Mme Zwitscher acted more brilliantly by the help of the drug, and it actually heightened Natalie Knöterich's charm. But it happened repeatedly to poor Inez that she came half-dazed to the table and sat with glazed eyes and nodding head with her eldest daughter and her worried and petty little husband, at the still well-kept-up board sparkling with silver and glass. But one admission I will make: Inez, as we know, committed a few years later a capital crime, which aroused general horror and put an end to her bourgeois existence. I shuddered at the awful deed; at the same time, in memory of my old friendship, I felt almost, nay, I felt definitely proud that in all her sunken state she found the strength, the furious energy to commit it.

CHAPTER XXXVI

O GERMANY, thou art undone! And I am mindful of thy hopes. Those hopes, I mean, which you aroused (it may even be that you did not share them) after your former relatively mild collapse and the abdication of the Empire. The world then placed on you certain hopes; and you seemed — aside from that reckless, utterly crazy, desperate, and hysterical "inflation" of your own misery, the giddy heavenward climb of the exchange — that aside, you seemed for some years to be about to justify, to some extent, those hopes.

True, the fantastic improprieties of that period, a deliberate attempt to make faces at the rest of the world, were really not unlike what we have seen since 1933 and of course since 1939. On a smaller scale they too were monstrously incredible and exaggerated; the scene displayed the same vicious san-culottism. But the debauch on 'change, the bombast of despair did one day come to an end; the face of our economic life lost its distorted, insane grimace and assumed a look of returning sanity. An epoch of psychological convalescence seemed to be dawning. There was some hope for Germany of social progress in peace and freedom; of adult and forward-looking effort; of a voluntary adaptation of our thoughts and feelings to those of the normal world. Despite all her inherent weakness and self-hatred, this was beyond a doubt the meaning and the hope of the German republic — again, the hope I mean is the one she awakened in the world outside. It was an attempt, a not utterly and entirely hopeless attempt (the second since the failure of Bismarck and his unification performance) to normalize Germany in the sense of Europeanizing or "democratizing" it, of making it part of the social life of peoples. Who will deny that much honest belief in the possibility of this process was alive in the other countries? Who will dispute the existence of a hopeful movement, plain to see on every hand among us Germans, save in this or that unregenerate spot — for instance typically in our good city of Munich?

I am speaking of the twenties of the twentieth century, in particular of course of their second half, which quite seriously witnessed nothing less than a shift of the cultural centre from France to Germany. It is a telling fact that, as I mentioned earlier, the first performance of Adrian Leverkühn's apocalyptic oratorio took place in Germany — or more precisely its first complete performance. The scene was Frankfurt, always one of the most friendly and free-minded cities in the Reich. Even so, it did not come about without angry opposition, bitter reproaches and outcries against the piece as a mockery of art, an expression of nihilism, a crime against music, in short, to use the current and fashionable condemnation, as a specimen of cultural Bolshevism. But the work, and the audacity which presented it, found intelligent and eloquent defenders: about the year 1927 courageous friendliness to the outer world and the cause of freedom was at its height, as an offset to the nationalistic-Wagnerian-romantic forces of reaction, at home particularly in Munich. It was certainly an element of our public life in the first half of the decade. I am thinking of cultural events like the Music Festival in Weimar in 1920 and the first one at Donaueschingen in the following year. On both occasions, unfortunately in the absence of the composer, some works of Leverkühn were given, together with those of other artists representative of the new intellectual and musical attitude. The audience was by no means unreceptive; I might say that they were, in the field of art, republican-minded. In Weimar the Cosmic Symphony was conducted by Bruno Walter with a particularly sure rhythmical sense. At the festival in Baden, in co-operation with Hans Platner's famous marionette theatre, they gave all five pieces of the *Gesta Romanorum* — an experience ravishing the feelings to and fro between pious emotion and laughter as never before.

But I would also recall the share which German artists and friends of art had in the founding of the International Society for Contemporary Music, in 1922, and the performances by the society two years later in Prague, when choral and instrumental portions of Adrian's *Apocalypsis cum figuris* were given before a public including famous guests from all the lands of music. The composition had already appeared in print, not, like Leverkühn's earlier work, published by Schott in Mainz but by the "Universal Editions" in Vienna, whose youthful editor Dr. Edelmann was scarcely thirty years old but already played an influential part in the musical life of central Europe. One day Edelmann bobbed up unexpectedly in Pfeiffering, in fact even before the *Apocalypse* was finished (it was in the weeks of interruption through the attack of illness) to offer the guest of the Schweigestills his service as editor and publisher. The visit was supposed to be in connection with an article on Adrian's work, which had recently appeared in the advanced radical Vienna musical magazine *Anbruch*, from the pen of the Hungarian musicologist and culture-philosopher Desiderius Fehér. Fehér had expressed himself with great warmth about the high intellectual level and religious content of the music; its pride and despair, its diabolic cleverness, amounting to afflatus; he invoked the attention of the world of culture, with ardour increased by the writer's confessed chagrin at not having himself discovered this most interesting and thrilling phenomenon. He had, as he put it, needed to be guided from outside, from above, from a sphere higher than all learning, the sphere of love and faith, in a word the eternal feminine. In short the article, which mingled the analytical with the lyrical in a way congenial to its theme, gave one a glimpse, even though in very vague outline, of a female figure who was its real inspirer: a sensitive woman, wise and well-informed, actively at work for her faith. But as Dr. Edelmann's visit had turned out to be prompted by the Vienna publication, one might say that indirectly it too was an effect of that fine and scrupulous love and energy in the background.

Only indirectly? I am not quite sure. I think it possible that the young musician and man of business may have received direct stimulation, suggestion, and instruction from that sphere, and I am strengthened in my guess by the fact that he knew more than the rather mystery-making article had allowed itself to tell. He knew the name and mentioned it — not at once, not as accepted fact, but in the course of the conversation, towards the end. In the beginning he had almost been refused admission; then, when he had managed to get himself received, he had asked Leverkühn to tell him about his present work and he heard about the oratorio. Was that for the first time? I doubt it. Adrian was suffering almost to the point of collapse; but in the end was prevailed upon to play, in the Nike room, considerable portions from the manuscript, whereupon Dr. Edelmann secured it on the spot for the "Editions." The contract came from the Bayerischer Hof in Munich next day. But before he left he had asked Adrian, using the Viennese mode of address modelled on the French: "Meister, do you know" (I think he even said "Does Meister know") "Frau von Tolna?"

I am about to do something that would, in a novel, break all the canons: I mean to introduce into the narrative an invisible character. This invisible figure is Frau von Tolna and I cannot set her before the reader's eye or give the smallest idea of her outward appearance, for I have not seen her and never had a description of her, since no one I know ever saw her either. I leave it an open question whether Dr. Edelmann himself, or only that associate editor of the *Anbruch* who was a countryman of hers, could boast of her acquaintance. As for Adrian, he answered in the negative the question put by the Viennese. He did not know the lady, he said; but he did not, in his turn, ask who she was, nor did Edelmann give any explanation of his question, other than merely by saying: "At all events, you have" (or "Meister has") "no warmer admirer than she."

Obviously he regarded the negative reply as the conditioned and guarded truth that it was. Adrian could answer as he did because his relation to the Hungarian noblewoman lacked any personal contact; I may add that by mutual consent it was always to lack it, to the end. It is another matter that for a long time they had carried on a correspondence, in which she showed herself the shrewdest and most initiate connoisseur of his work, the most devoted friend, confidante, and counsellor, unconditionally and unfailingly at his service; while on his side he went to the furthest limits of communicativeness and confidingness of which a solitary soul like his is capable. We know of those other needy, yearning female beings who by selfless devotion won a modest niche in the life-history of this certainly immortal genius. Here now is a third, of quite different mould, not only equalling in disinterestedness those other simpler souls, but even excelling them in the ascetic renunciation of any direct approach, the inviolable observance of his privacy, the aloofness, the restraint, the persistent invisibility. None of this, of course, was due to shyness or awkwardness, for this was a woman of the world, who to the hermit of Pfeiffering did really represent the world: the world as he loved it, needed it, and so far as he could stand it; the world at a distance, keeping itself removed out of tact and good sense.

I set down here what I know of this extraordinary being. Mme de Tolna was the wealthy widow of a dissipated nobleman, who however had not died of his excesses but in a racing accident. She was left childless, the owner of a palace in Budapest, a vast estate a few hours south of the capital, near Stuhlweissenburg, between the Plattensee and the Danube, and besides these a castellated villa on the same lake, Balaton. The estate, with its splendid, comfortably modernized eighteenth-century manor-house, comprised enormous wheat-growing tracts and extensive sugar-beet plantations, the harvests being manufactured in refining works on the property itself. None of these residences — palatial town house, manorial estate, or summer villa — did the owner occupy for long at a time. Mostly, one may say almost always, she was travelling, leaving her homes, to which she obviously did not cling, from which restlessness or painful memories drove her away, to the care of managers and major-domos. She lived in Paris, Naples, Egypt, the Engadine, attended from place to place by a lady's maid, a male official something like a courier and quartermaster, and a body-physician for her sole service, which made one suspect that she was in delicate health.

Her mobility however seemed not to suffer; and combined with an enthusiasm resting on instinct, intuition, knowledge, sensibility — God knows what! — mysterious perception, soul-affinity, she commanded most unusual resources. It turned out that this woman had been present, mingling unobtrusively in the audience wherever people had been bold enough to perform any of Adrian's music: in Lübeck, at the much-ridiculed première of his opera; in Zürich, in Weimar, in Prague. How often she had been near him in Munich and so near to his lodging, without revealing herself, I would not know. But she also — it came out by accident — knew Pfeiffering; had secretly made acquaintance with the setting of Adrian's activity, his immediate surroundings; had, if I am not mistaken, stood under the window of the Abbot's chamber and gone away unseen. All that is thrilling enough; but even stranger, summoning up the image of the devout pilgrim is a fact which I learned long afterwards and also more or less by chance: she had actually gone to Kaisersaschern, was acquainted with Oberweiler and the Buchel farm itself, and thus was aware of the parallel — to me always faintly depressing — between Adrian's childhood setting and the frame of his later life.

I forgot to say that she had not omitted Palestrina, the village in the Sabine Hills. She spent some weeks in the Manardi house and, it appeared, made quick and close friends with Signora Manardi. When in her half-German, half-French letters she mentioned the Signora, she called her Mère Manardi. She gave the same title to Frau Schweigestill, whom, according to her own evidence, she had seen without being seen or noticed. And herself? Was it her idea to attach herself to all these maternal figures and call them sisters? What name fitted her in relation to Adrian Leverkühn? Which did she want or claim? A protecting deity, an Egeria, a soul-mate? The first letter she wrote, from Brussels, was accompanied by a gift sent to him in homage: a ring the like

of which I have never seen — though in all conscience that does
not mean much, since the present writer is little versed in the
precious material things of this world. It was a jewel of great
beauty and — to me — incalculable value. The engraved hoop itself
was old Renaissance work; the stone a splendid specimen of clear
pale-green emerald from the Urals, cut with large facets, a glorious sight. One could imagine that it had once adorned the hand of
a prince of the Church — the pagan inscription it bore was
scarcely evidence to the contrary. On the hard upper facet of
the precious beryl two lines were graven in the tiniest Greek
characters. Translated they ran somewhat like this:

> What a trembling seized on the laurel-bush of Apollo!
> Trembles the entire frame! Flee, profane one! Depart!

It was not hard for me to place the lines as the beginning of
a hymn to Apollo, by Callimachus. They describe with unearthly
terror the sign of an epiphany of the god at his shrine. The writing, with all its tininess, was clear and sharp. Rather more blurred
was the sign carved beneath, like a vignette. Under a glass it revealed itself as a winged snakelike monster whose tongue was
clearly arrow-shaped. The mythological fantasy made me think
of the sting or shot-wound of the Chrysæan Philoctetes and the
epithet Æschylus has for the arrow: "hissing winged snake"; I
recalled too the connection between the arrow of Phœbus and
the ray of the sun.

I can testify that Adrian was childishly delighted with this considerable gift, speaking of a sympathetic someone in the background. He accepted it without a thought, though he never, in
fact, showed himself to others wearing it, but instead made a
practice — or shall I say a ritual? — of putting it on for his working hours. I know that during the writing of the whole of the
Apocalypse he wore the jewel on his left hand.

Did he think that a ring is the symbol of a bond, a fetter, yes,
of possession? Obviously he thought no such thing; seeing in that
precious link of an invisible chain, which he stuck on his finger
while he composed, nothing more than a sort of bridge between
his hermit state and the outside world; as a mere cloudy symbol
of a personality, about whose features or individual traits he evidently inquired far less than I did. Was there, I asked myself,
something in the woman's outward appearance that might explain
the fundamental condition of her relations with Adrian, the invisibility, the avoidance, the rule that they should never set eyes
on each other? She might be ugly, lame, crippled, disfigured by

a skin ailment. I do not so interpret it; but rather think that if some blemish existed it lay in the realm of the spirit and taught her to understand every sort of need for consideration and scrupulous tact. Adrian never once sought to break that law; he silently acquiesced in the bounds set to the relationship within the realms of intellect and spirit.

I use unwillingly this banal phrase. There is something colourless and weak about it, not consistent with the practical energy characteristic of this care, concern, and devotion, remote and shrouded though it was. During the composition of the *Apocalypse* the two carried on an exchange of letters altogether objective in their content, hers evincing a serious and solid European culture, both musically and generally speaking. My friend's correspondent knew how to give him suggestions for the textual structure of the work, from material not easily accessible. It turned out, for instance, that that old-French metrical version of the vision of St. Paul had come to him from the "outer world." The same outer world was constantly, if by round-about ways and through intermediaries, active on his behalf. It was "the world" which instigated that stimulating article in the *Anbruch*, certainly the only publication where enthusiasm for Leverkühn's music could get a hearing. It was "the world" which saw to it that the "Universal Editions" had secured the oratorio while it was still being written. In 1921 it put at the disposal of the Platner marionette theatre, privately, so that the source of the gift was left vague, considerable sums for the expensive and musically adequate production of the *Gesta* in Domaueschingen.

I must dwell a little on this point, and the sweeping gesture accompanying it, this "putting at the disposal of." Adrian could have no shadow of doubt that he might command any and every resource of this woman of the world who had become the recluse's devotee. Her wealth was obviously a burden on her conscience, although she had never known life without it and probably would not have known how to live. To lay on the altar of genius as much of it as possible, as much as she ever dared to offer, was her confessed desire; and if Adrian had wished, his whole manner of life might have changed from one day to the next on the costly scale of that gem, adorned with which only the four walls of the Abbot's chamber ever saw him. He knew it as well as I did. I need not say that he never for a moment seriously considered it. Differently constituted from me, for whom some intoxication had always lain in the thought of vast wealth lying at his feet, which he need only grasp to secure himself a princely existence, he had certainly never actually come to grips with such an idea. But once, when by exception he had left his Pfeiffering nest on a journey, he had had a fleeting glimpse, tasted an experimental sip, of the almost regal form of life which privately I could not help wishing might be permanently his.

That is twenty years since, and came about when he accepted the standing invitation of Mme de Tolna to live for as long as he chose in one of her residences — that is, of course, when she was not there. He was then, in the spring of 1924, in Vienna, where in the Ehrbar Hall and in the setting of one of the so-called *Anbruch* evenings Rudi Schwerdtfeger at last and finally played the violin concerto written for him. It was a great success, not least for Rudi himself. I say not least, and mean above all; for a certain concentration of interest on the art of the interpreter is inherent in the intention of the work, which, though the hand of the musician is unmistakable, is not one of Leverkühn's highest and proudest effects, but at least in part has something complimentary and condescending, I might better say affable about it which reminded me of an early prophecy from lips now forever mute. — Adrian declined to appear before the applauding audience at the end of the piece and left the house while we were looking for him. We found him later, the producer, the beaming Rudi, and I, in the restaurant of the little hotel in the Herrengasse where he stopped alone, Schwerdtfeger having thought it due to himself to go to a hotel in the Ring.

The celebration was brief — Adrian had headache. But it seems the temporary relaxation of his plan of life led him to decide next day not to return at once to the Schweigestills' but to please his friend of the outer world by visiting her Hungarian estate. The condition that she should be absent was complied with, for she was at the time in Vienna, though invisible. He sent a wire to the estate making announcement of his visit, and hasty arrangements were made by messages to and fro. He set off, not accompanied by me, for much to my regret I could scarcely spare time even for the concert. This time it was not Rüdiger Schildknapp either. The like-eyed one did not exert himself to go to Vienna — probably he did not have the money. No, quite naturally it was Rudi Schwerdtfeger, who was already on the spot and free. Moreover, he had just collaborated successfully with Adrian in their common enterprise, and his indefatigable self-confidence had been crowned with success — a success heavy with fate.

In this company, then, Adrian was received on the estate as though he were the lord of the manor come home from abroad.

The two spent twelve days in stately domesticity in the dix-huitième salons and apartments of Castle Tolna, in drives through the princely estate and along the gay shores of the Plattensee, attended by an obsequious retinue, some of whom were Turks. They might use and enjoy a library in five languages; two glorious grand pianos stood on the platform of the music-room; there was a house organ and every conceivable luxury. Adrian said that in the village belonging to the property the deepest poverty prevailed and an entirely archaic, pre-revolutionary stage of development. Their guide, the manager of the estate, himself told them, with compassionate head-shakings, as a fact worth mention, that the villagers only had meat one day in the year, at Christmas, and had not even tallow candles, but literally went to bed with the chickens. To alter these shocking conditions, to which habit and ignorance had rendered those who saw them callous — for instance the indescribable filth of the village street, the utter lack of sanitation in the dwelling-hovels — would have amounted to a revolutionary deed, to which no single individual, certainly not a woman, could bring herself. But one may suspect that the sight of the village was among the things which prevented Adrian's invisible friend from spending much time upon her own property.

But I am not the man to give more than a bare sketch of this slightly fantastic episode in my friend's austere life. I was not at his side and could not have been, even had he asked me. It was Schwerdtfeger, he could describe it. But he is dead.

CHAPTER XXXVII

I SHOULD do better to deal with this section as I did with some
earlier ones: not giving it a number of its own, but treating it
simply as a continuation. To go on without any marked cæsura
would be correct, for the subject of the narrative is the same:
"the outer world," and the history of my departed friend's connection or lack of connection with it. At this point, however, all
mystery, all delicacy, all discretion are abandoned. No longer is
"the world" embodied in the figure of a shrouded tutelary god-
dess showering priceless symbolic gifts. In her place we have the
international business man and concert agent, naïvely persistent,
profuse of promises, rebuffed by no reserve, certainly superficial,
yet for all that to me even an engaging type. We met him in the
person of Herr Saul Fitelberg, who appeared in Pfeiffering one
lovely day in late summer when I happened to be there. It was a
Saturday afternoon, and Sunday morning early I was returning
home as it was my wife's birthday. For at least an hour he amused
Adrian and me and made us laugh; and then, with his business
unaccomplished — in so far as there had been anything so concrete as business about it — he departed with complete equanimity.

It was the year 1923; one cannot say that the man had waked
up very early. However, he had not waited for the Prague and
Frankfurt concerts; they belonged to a future by then not very
distant. But there had been Weimar, and Donaueschingen, aside
from the Swiss performances of Leverkühn's youthful works: it
took no extraordinary intuition to guess that here was something
to prize and to promote. And the *Apocalypse* had appeared in
print, and I think it quite possible that Monsieur Saul was in a
position to study that work. In short, the man had picked up the
scent, he wanted to make a kill, to build up a reputation, discover
a genius and as his manager introduce him to a social world always and above all avid for new things. Such were the motives
that led him to force his way so blandly into the retreat where
genius created and suffered.

Here is how it happened: I had reached Pfeiffering early in the afternoon; Adrian and I returned soon after four from a walk in the meadows after tea and saw to our surprise an automobile standing in the courtyard, by the elm tree. It was not an ordinary taxi, but more like a private car, the kind one sees, with chauffeur, out in front of an automobile business, for hire by the hour or the day. The driver, whose uniform was designed to carry the same idea, stood beside the car smoking, and as we passed him he lifted his peaked cap with a broad grin, probably thinking of the jokes his amazing passenger had made on the way. Frau Schweigestill came towards us from the house, a visiting-card in her hand, and spoke in subdued and startled voice. A man was there, she told us, a "man of the world" — the phrase, as she whispered it, and as a rapid summing-up of a guest she had that moment clapped eyes on, had something uncannily perceptive about it, almost sibylline. Perhaps the euphemism is more understandable coupled with the other which Frau Else supplied on top of it: she called the man a crazy loon. "*Scher Madame,*" was what he had called her, and after that "*petite maman,*" and he had pinched Clementine's cheek. Frau Else had shut the girl into her room until the "man of the world" should be gone. But she couldn't send him off with a flea in his ear, eh, him coming like that from Munich in a car? So there he was, waiting in the big room. With misgiving we examined the card, which gave us all the information we needed; it read: "Saul Fitelberg. *Arrangements musicaux. Représentant de nombreux artistes prominents.*" I rejoiced that I was on the spot to protect Adrian; I should not have liked him to be delivered over alone to this "*représentant.*" We betook ourselves to the Nike room.

Fitelberg was already standing at the door, and although Adrian let me go in first, the man's whole attention was at once addressed to him. After one cursory glance at me through his horn-rimmed glasses he swung his whole plump body round to look beyond me at the man on whose account he had let himself in for the expense of a two hours' auto journey. Of course it is no great feat to distinguish between a simple high-school teacher and a man set apart by genius. But the visitor's swift orientation, his glib recognition of my unimportance despite my walking in ahead, his pounce on his proper prey — all in all, it was an impressive performance.

"Cher maître," he began, with a smile, rattling off his speech with a harsh accent but uncommon fluency: "Comme je suis heureux, comme je suis ému de vous trouver! Même pour un homme gâté, endurci comme moi, c'est toujours une expérience touchante de rencontrer un grand homme. — Enchanté, monsieur le professeur," he added in passing as Adrian presented me, and put out his hand carelessly, turning again at once to the right address.

"Vous maudirez l'intrus, cher Monsieur Leverkühn," said he, accenting the name on the last syllable as though it were spelt Le Vercune. "Mais pour moi, étant une fois à Munich, c'était tout à fait impossible de manquer — oh, yes, I speak German," he interrupted himself, with the same not unpleasant hard quality in his voice: "Not well, not perfectly, but I can make myself understood. Du reste, je suis convaincu that you know French perfectly. Your settings to the Verlaine poems are the best evidence in the world. Mais après tout, we are on German soil — how German, how homely, how full of character! I am enchanted with the idyllic setting in which you, Maître, have been so wise as to settle down. . . . Mais oui, certainement, let us sit down, many thanks, a thousand thanks!"

He was a man of perhaps forty, fat, not pot-bellied but fleshy and soft in his limbs and his thick white hands; smooth-shaven, full-faced, with a double chin, strongly marked arched brows, and lively almond-shaped eyes full of southern meltingness behind the horn-rimmed glasses. His hair was thinning, but he had sound white teeth which were always visible, for he smiled all the time. He was dressed in elegant summer clothes, a waisted striped blue flannel suit and canvas shoes with yellow leather bands. Mother Schweigestill's description of him was amusingly justified by his easy manner and refreshing lightness of touch. Like his rapid-fire, slightly indistinct, always rather high-pitched voice, sometimes breaking into a treble, his airiness was peculiar to his whole bearing, counteracting the plumpness of his person, while actually, in a way, in harmony with it. I found this lightness of touch refreshing; it had become part of him, and it did actually inspire the absurdly soothing conviction that we all take life unconscionably hard. It seemed always to be saying: "Why not? So what? Means nothing. Let's be happy!" And involuntarily one strove to chime in.

That he was anything but stupid will be evident when I repeat his conversation, which is still fresh in my mind. I shall do well to leave the word entirely to him, since whatever Adrian or I interpolated or replied played scarcely any role. We sat down at one end of the massive long table which was the chief furnishing of the peasant room: Adrian and I next to each other, our

guest opposite. He did not beat about the bush very long; his
hopes and intents came out quite soon.

"Maître," said he, "I quite understood how you must cling to
the distinguished retirement of the abode you have chosen — oh,
yes, I have seen it all, the hill, the pond, the village, and church,
et puis cette maison pleine de dignité avec son hôtesse maternelle
et vigoureuse. Madame Schweige-still! Ça veut dire: 'Je sais me
taire. Silence, silence!' Comme c'est charmant! How long have
you lived here? Ten years? Without a break — or nearly so? C'est
étonnant! But oh, how easy to understand! And still, figurez-
vous, I have come to tempt you away, to betray you to a temporary unfaithfulness, to bear you on my mantle through the air
and show you the kingdoms of the earth and the glory of them
— or even more, to lay them at your feet. . . . Forgive my pompous way of talking. It is really ridiculously exaggéré, especially
as far as the 'glories' go. It is not so grand as that, nothing so very
thrilling about those glories; I am saying that who after all am the
son of little people, living in very humble circumstances, really
miese, you know, from Lublin in the middle of Poland; of really
quite little Jewish parents — I am a Jew, you must know, and
Fitelberg is a very ordinary, low-class, Polish-German-Jewish
name; only I have made it the name of a respected protagonist
of avant-garde culture, whom great artists call their friend. C'est
la verité pure, simple et irréfutable. The reason is that from my
youth up I have aspired to higher things, more intellectual and interesting — above all to whatever is a novelty and sensation — the
scandalous today which tomorrow will be the fashion, the dernier
cri, the best-seller'— in short, art. A qui le dis-je? Au commence-
ment était le scandale.

"Thank God, that lousy Lublin lies far behind me. More than
twenty years I have been living in Paris — will you believe it, for
a whole year I attended philosophy lectures at the Sorbonne!
But à la longue they bored me. Not that philosophy couldn't be
a best-seller too. It could. But for me it is too abstract. And I
have a vague feeling that it is in Germany one should study metaphysics — perhaps the Herr Professor, my honoured vis-à-vis,
will agree with me. . . . After that I had a little boulevard
theatre, small, exclusive, un creux, une petite caverne for a hundred people, nommé 'Théâtre des fourberies gracieuses.' Isn't that
a peach of a name? But what would you, the thing wasn't finan-
cially possible. So few seats, they had to be so high-priced, we
had to make presents of them. We were lewd enough, I do assure
you; but too high-brow too, as they say in English. James Joyce,

Picasso, Ezra Pound, the Duchesse de Clermont-Tonnère — it wasn't enough of an audience. En un mot, the fourberies gracieuses had to fold up after a short season. But the experiment was not entirely without fruit, for it had put me in touch with the leaders of the artistic life of Paris, painters, musicians, writers. In Paris today — even here I may say it — beats the pulse of the living world; and in my position as director, it opened to me the doors of several aristocratic salons where all these artists gathered. . . .

"Perhaps that surprises you? Perhaps you will say 'How did he do it? How did the little Jewish boy from the Polish provinces manage to move in on these fastidious circles, all among the *crême de la crême?*' Ah, gentlemen, nothing easier. How quickly one learns to tie a white tie, to enter a salon with complete nonchalance, even if it goes a few steps down, and to forget the sensation that you don't know what to do with your hands! After that you just keep on saying 'madame'; 'Ah, madame, O madame, que pensez-vous, madame; on me dit, madame, que vous êtes fanatique de musique?' That is as good as all there is to it. Believe me, from the outside these things are exaggéré.

"Enfin, I cashed in on the connections I owed to the Fourberies, and they multiplied when I opened my agency for the presentation of contemporary music. Best of all, I had found myself, for as I stand here, I am a born impresario; I can't help it, it is my joy and pride, I find my satisfaction et mes délices in discovering talent, genius, interesting personalities, beating the drum, making society mad with enthusiasm or at least with excitement, for that is all they ask, et nous nous rencontrons dans ce désir. Society demands to be excited, challenged, torn in sunder for and against; it is grateful for that as for nothing else, for the diversion and the turmoil qui fournit le sujet for caricatures in the papers and endless, endless chatter. The way to fame, in Paris, leads through notoriety — at a proper première people jump up several times during the evening and yell 'Insulte! Impudence! Bouffonerie ignominieuse!' while six or seven initiates, Erik Satie, a few surréalistes, Virgil Thomson, shout from the loges: 'Quelle précision! Quel esprit! C'est divin! C'est suprême! Bravo! Bravo!'

"I fear I shock you, messieurs — if not Monsieur Le Vercune, then perhaps the Herr Professor. But in the first place I hasten to add that a concert evening never yet broke down in the middle; that is not what even the most outraged want at bottom; on the contrary they want to go on being outraged, that is what makes them enjoy the evening, and besides, remarkable as it is, the informed minority always command the heavier guns. Of course I

do not mean that every performance of outstanding character
must go as I have described it. With proper publicity, adequate
intimidation beforehand, one can guarantee an entirely dignified
result; and in particular if one were to present today a citizen of
a former enemy nation, a German, one could count on an entirely
courteous reception from the public.

"That is indeed the sound speculation upon which my propo-
sition, my invitation is based. A German, un boche qui par son
génie appartient au monde et qui marche à la tête du progrès musical! That is today a most piquant challenge to the curiosity, the
broad-mindedness, the snobisme, the good breeding of the public
— the more piquant, the less this artist disguises his national traits,
his Germanisme, the more he gives occasion for the cry: 'Ah, ça
c'est bien allemand, par exemple!' For that you do, cher Maître,
why not say so? You give this occasion everywhere — not so
much in your beginnings, the time of the *Phosphorescence de la
mer* and your comic opera, but later and more and more from
work to work. Naturellement, you think I have in mind your
ferocious discipline, and que vous enchaînez votre art dans un
système de regles inexorables et néo-classiques, forcing it to move
in these iron bands — if not with grace, yet with boldness and
esprit. But if it is that that I mean, I mean at the same time more
than that when I speak of your qualité d'Allemand; I mean — how
shall I put it? — a certain four-squareness, rhythmical heaviness,
immobility, grossièreté, which are old-German — en effet, entre
nous, one finds them in Bach too. Will you take offence at my
criticism? Non, j'en suis sûr — you are too great. Your themes —
they consist almost throughout of even note values, minims,
crotchets, quavers; true enough, they are syncopated and tied but
for all that they remain clumsy and unwieldy, often with a hammering, machinelike effect. C'est 'boche' dans un degré fascinant.
Don't think I am finding fault, it is simply énormement charac-
teristique, and in the series of concerts of international music
which I am arranging, this note is quite indispensable. . . .

"You see, I am spreading out my magic cloak. I will take you
to Paris, to Brussels, Antwerp, Venice, Copenhagen. You will be
received with the intensest interest. I will put the best orchestras
and soloists at your service. You shall direct the *Phosphorescence*,
portions of *Love's Labour's Lost*, your Cosmologic Symphony.
You will accompany on the piano your songs by French and
English poets and the whole world will be enchanted that a German, yesterday's foe, displays this broad-mindedness in the choice
of his texts — ce cosmopolitisme génereux et versatile! My friend

Madame Maia de Strozzi-Pečič, a Croatian, today perhaps the most beautiful soprano voice in the two hemispheres, will consider it an honour to sing your songs. For the instrumental part of Keats's hymns I will engage the Flonzaley Quartet from Geneva or the Pro Arte from Brussels. The very best of the best — are you satisfied?

"What do I hear — you do not conduct? You don't? And you would not play piano? You decline to accompany your own songs? I understand. Cher Maître, je vous comprends à demi-mot! It is not your way to linger with the finished work. For you the doing of a work is its performance, it is done when it is written down. You do not play it, you do not conduct it, for you would straightway change it, resolve it in variations and variants, develop it further and perhaps spoil it. How well I understand! Mais c'est dommage, pourtant. The concerts will suffer a decided loss of personal appeal. Ah, bah, we must see what we can do. We must look about among the world-famous conductors to interpret — we shall not need to look long. The permanent accompanist of Madame de Strozzi-Pečič will take over for the songs, and if only you, Maître, are simply present and show yourself to the public, nothing will be lost, everything will be gained.

"But that is the condition — ah, non! You cannot inflict upon me the performance of your works in absentia. Your personal appearance is indispensable, particulièrement à Paris, where musical renown is made in three or four salons. What does it cost you to say a few times: 'Tout le monde sait, madame, que votre jugement musical est infaillible?' It costs you nothing and you will have a lot of satisfaction from it. As social events my productions rank next after the premières of Diaghilev's Ballet Russe — if they do rank after them. You would be invited out every evening. Nothing harder, generally speaking, than getting into real Paris society. But for an artist nothing is easier, even if he is only standing in the vestibule to fame, I mean the sensational appeal. Curiosity levels every barrier, it knocks the exclusive right out of the field. . . .

"But why do I talk so much about elegant society and its itches? I can see that I am not succeeding in kindling your curiosity, cher Maître. How could I? I have not seriously been trying to. What do you care about elegant society? Entre nous, what do I care about it? For business reasons — this and that. But personally? Not that much. This milieu, this Pfeiffering and your presence, Maître, do not a little to make me realize my indifference, my contempt, for that world of frivolity and superficiality.

Dites-moi donc: don't you come from Kaisersaschern on the
Saale? What a serious, dignified place of origin! Well, for me, I
call Lublin my birthplace — likewise a dignified spot and grey
with age, from which one carries into life a fund of sévérité, un
état d'âme solennel et un peu gauche. . . . Ah, I am the last person to want to glorify elegant society to you. But Paris will give
you the chance to make the most interesting and stimulating contacts among your brothers in Apollo, among the sons of the
Muses, your aspiring colleagues and peers, painters, writers, stars
of the ballet, above all musicians. The summits of European tradition and experiment, they are all my friends, and they are ready
to be yours. Jean Cocteau the poet, Massine the ballet-master,
Manuel de Falla the composer, Les Six, the six great ones of the
new music — this whole elevated, audacious, amusing, aggressive
sphere, it waits only for you, you belong to it, as soon as ever
you will. . . .

"Is it possible that I read in your manner a certain resistance
even to that? But here, cher Maître, every shyness, every embarras is really quite out of place — whatever may be the ground
for such habits of seclusion. I am far from searching for grounds;
that they exist is quite enough for my cultivated and I may say
respectful perceptions. This Pfeiffering, ce refuge étrange et éré-
mitique — there must be some peculiar and interesting psychological association: I do not ask, I consider all possibilities, I
frankly bring them all up, even the most fantastic. Eh bien, what
then? Is that a reason for embarras, in a sphere where there reigns
unlimited freedom from prejudice? A freedom from prejudice
which for its part has its own good reasons too? Oh, la, la! Such
a circle of arbiters elegantiarum and society cheer-leaders is usually an assortment of demi-fous excentriques, expended souls and
elderly crapules — un impresario, c'est un espèce d'infirmier, voilà!

"And now you see how badly I conduct my affair, in what
utterly-maladroit fashion! That I point it out is all that speaks in
my favour. With the idea of encouraging you I anger your pride
and work with my eyes open against my interests. For I tell myself, of course, that people like you — though I should speak not
of people like you, but only of yourself — you regard your existence, your *destin* as something unique and consider it too sacred to lump it in with anyone else's. You do not want to hear
about other *destinées*, only about your own, as something quite
unique — I know, I understand. You abhor all generalizing, classi-
fying, subsuming, as a derogation of your dignity. You insist on
the incomparableness of the personal case. You pay tribute to an

arrogant personal uniqueness — maybe you have to do that. 'Does
one live when others live?' I have read that question somewhere,
I am not sure precisely where, but in some very prominent place.
Privately or publicly you all ask it; only out of good manners
and for appearance' sake do you take notice of each other — if you
do take notice of each other. Wolf, Brahms, and Bruckner lived
for years in the same town — Vienna, that is — but avoided each
other the whole time and none of them, so far as I know, ever
met the others. It would have been penible too, considering their
opinions of each other. They did not judge or criticize like colleagues; their comments were meant to annihilate, to leave their
author alone in the field. Brahms thought as little as possible of
Bruckner's symphonies, he called them huge shapeless serpents.
And Bruckner's opinion of Brahms was very low. He found the
first theme of the D-minor Concerto very good, but asserted that
Brahms never came near inventing anything so good a second
time. You don't want to know anything of each other. For Wolf
Brahms meant le dernier ennui. And have you ever read his critique of Bruckner's Seventh in the Vienna *Salonblatt*? There you
have his opinion of the man's importance. He charged him with
'lack of intelligence' — avec quelque raison, for Bruckner was of
course what one calls a simple, childlike soul, wholly given to his
majestic figured-bass music and a complete idiot in all matters of
European culture. But if one happens on certain utterances of
Wolf about Dostoyevsky, in his letters, qui sont simplement stu-
péfiant, one is driven to ask what kind of mind he had himself.
The text of his unfinished opera *Manuel Venegas*, which a certain
Dr. Hörnes has restored, he called a wonder, Shakespearian, the
height of poetic creation, and became offensive when friends expressed their doubts. Moreover, not satisfied with composing a
hymn for male voices, *To the Fatherland*, he wanted to dedicate
it to the German Kaiser. What do you say to that? The memorial
was rejected. Tout cela est un peu embarrassant, n'est-ce pas?
Une confusion tragique.

"Tragique, messieurs. I call it that, because in my opinion the
unhappiness of the world rests on the disunity of the intellect, the
stupidity, the lack of comprehension, which separates its spheres
from each other. Wagner poured scorn on the picturesque impressionism of his time, calling it all 'daubs' — he was sternly conservative in that field. But his own harmonic productions have
a lot to do with impressionism, they lead up to it and as dissonances often go beyond the impressionistic. Against the Paris
daubers he set up Titian as the true and the good. A la bonne

heure! But actually his taste in art was more likely somewhere between Piloty and Makart, the inventor of the decorative bouquet; while Titian was more in Lenbach's line, and Lenbach had an understanding of Wagner that made him call *Parsifal* music-hall stuff — to the Master's very face. Ah, ah, comme c'est mélancholique, tout ça!

"Gentlemen, I have been rambling frightfully. I mean I have wandered from my subject and my purpose. Take my garrulity as an expression of the fact that I have given up the idea that brought me here. I have convinced myself that it is not possible. You will not set foot on my magic cloak. I am not to introduce you to the world as your entrepreneur. You decline, and that ought to be a bigger disappointment to me than it actually is. Sincèrement, I ask myself whether it really is one at all. One may come to Pfeiffering with a practical purpose in mind — but that must always take second place. One comes, even if one is an impresario, first of all to salute a great man. No failure on the practical side can decrease this pleasure, especially when a good part of it consists in the disappointment. So it is, cher Maître: your inaccessibility gives me among other things satisfaction as well; that is due to the understanding, the sympathy which I involuntarily feel towards it. I do so against my own interests, but I do it — as a human being, I might say, if that were not too large a category; perhaps I ought to express myself more specifically.

"You probably do not realize, cher Maître, how German is your répugnance, which, if you will permit me to speak en psychologue, I find characteristically made up of arrogance and a sense of inferiority, of scorn and fear. I might call it the ressentiment of the serious-minded against the salon world. Well, I am a Jew, you know, Fitelberg is undeniably a Jewish name. I have the Old Testament in my bones, a thing no less serious-minded than being German is, and not conducive to a taste for the sphere of the valse brillante. In Germany the superstition prevails that there is nothing but valse brillante outside its borders and nothing but serious-mindedness inside them. And still, as a Jew one feels sceptical towards the world, and leans to German serious-mindedness — at the risk, of course, of getting kicked in the pants for one's pains. To be German, that means above all to be national — and who expects a Jew to be nationalistic? Not only that nobody would believe him, but everybody would bash his head in for having the impudence to try it on. We Jews have everything to fear from the German character, qui est essentiellement antisémitique; and that is reason enough, of course, for us to plump for the worldly side and arrange sensational entertainments. It does not follow that we are windbags, or that we have fallen on our heads. We perfectly well know the difference between Gounod's *Faust* and Goethe's, even when we speak French, then too. . . .

"Gentlemen, I say all that only out of pure resignation. On the business side we have said everything. I am as good as gone; I have the door-handle in my hand, we have got up, I am still running on just pour prendre congé. Gounod's *Faust*, gentlemen — who turns up his nose at it? Not I, and not you, I am glad to know. A pearl — a marguérite, full of the most ravishing musical inventions. Laisse-moi, laisse-moi contempler — enchanting! Massenet is enchanting, he too. He must have been particularly charming as a teacher — as professor at the Conservatoire, there are little stories about it. From the beginning his pupils in composition were urged to produce, no matter whether or not they were technically able to write a movement free from flaws. Humane, n'est-ce pas? Not German, it isn't, but humane. A lad came to him with a song just composed — fresh, showing some talent. 'Tiens,' says Massenet, 'that is really quite nice. Listen, of course you must have a little friend; play it to her, she will certainly love it and the rest will happen of itself.' It is not certain what he meant by 'the rest,' probably various things, both love and art. Have you pupils, Master? They wouldn't be so fortunate. But you have none. Bruckner had some. He had from the first wrestled with music and its sacred difficulties, like Jacob with the angel, and he demanded the same from his pupils. Years on end they had to practise the sacred craft, the fundamentals of harmony and the strict style before they were allowed to make a song, and this music-teaching had not the faintest connection with any little friend. A man may have a simple, childlike temperament; but music is the mysterious revelation of the highest wisdom, a divine service, and the profession of music-teacher a priestly office. . . .

"Comme c'est respectable! Pas précisément humain mais extrèmement respectable. Why should we Jews, who are a priestly people, even when we are minaudering about in Parisian salons, not feel drawn to the Germans and let ourselves lean to the German side and an ironic view, as against the world, against art for the little friend? In us nationalism would be impertinent enough to provoke a pogrom. We are international — but we are pro-German, like nobody else in the world, simply because we can't help perceiving the role of Germany and Judaism on earth. Une analogie frappante! In just the same way they are both hated,

despised, feared, envied, in the same measure they alienate and are
alienated. People talk about the age of nationalism. But actually
there are only two nationalisms, the German and the Jewish, and
all the rest is child's play. — Is not the downright Frenchness of
an Anatole France the purest cosmopolitanism alongside German
isolation in the subjective and the Jewish conceit of the chosen
race. . . . France — a nationalistic pseudonym. A German writer
could not well call himself Germany, such a name one gives to a
battleship. He has to content himself with German — and that is
a Jewish name, oh la, la.

"Gentlemen, this is now really the door-knob. I am already outside. I must just say one more thing. The Germans should leave
it to the Jews to be pro-German. With their nationalism, their
pride, their foible of 'differentness,' their hatred of being put in
order and equalized, their refusal to let themselves be introduced
into the world and adopted socially, they will get into trouble,
real Jewish trouble, je vous le jure. The Germans should let the
Jew be the médiateur between them and society, be the manager,
the impresario. He is altogether the right man for it, one should
not turn him out, he is international, and he is pro-German. Mais
c'est en vain. Et c'est très dommage! Am I still talking? No, I left
long ago. Cher Maître, j'étais enchanté. J'ai manqué ma mission
but I am delighted. Mes respects, monsieur le professeur. Vous
m'avez assisté trop peu, mais je ne vous en veux pas. Mille choses
à Madame Schwei-ge-still. Adieu, adieu. . . ."

CHAPTER XXXVIII

My readers are aware that Adrian in the end complied with Rudi Schwerdtfeger's long-cherished and expressed desire, and wrote for him a violin concerto of his own. He dedicated to Rudi personally the brilliant composition, so extraordinarily suited to a violin technique, and even accompanied him to Vienna for the first performance. In its place I shall speak about the circumstance that some months later, towards the end of 1924, he was present at the later performances in Berne and Zürich. But first I should like to discuss with its very serious implications my earlier, perhaps premature — perhaps, coming from me, unfitting — critique of the concerto. I said that it falls somewhat out of the frame of Leverkühn's ruthlessly radical and uncompromising work as a whole. And I suggested that this was due to a kind of concession to concert virtuosity as shown in the musical attitude of the piece. I cannot help thinking that posterity will agree with my "judgment" — my God, how I hate the word! — and what I am doing here is simply giving the psychological explanation of a phenomenon to which the key would otherwise be lacking.

There is one strange thing about the piece: cast in three movements, it has no key-signature, but, if I may so express myself, three *tonalities* are built into it: B-flat major, C major, and D major, of which, as a musician can see, the D major forms a sort of secondary dominant, the B-flat major a subdominant, while the C major keeps the strict middle. Now between these keys the work plays most ingeniously, so that for most of the time none of them clearly comes into force but is only indicated by its proportional share in the general sound-complex. Throughout long and complicated sections all three are superimposed one above the other, until at last, in a way electrifying to any concert audience, C major openly and triumphantly declares itself. There, in the first movement, inscribed "*andante amoroso*," of a dulcet tenderness bordering on mockery, there is a leading chord which to my ear has something French about it: c, g, e, b-flat, d, f-sharp, a, a harmony which, with the high f of the violin above it, contains,

as one sees, the tonic chords of those three main keys. Here one
has, so to speak, the soul of the work, also one has in it the soul
of the main theme of this movement, which is taken up again in
the third, a gay series of variations. In its way it is a wonderful
stroke of melodic invention, a rich, intoxicating cantilena of great
breadth, which decidedly has something showy about it, and also
a melancholy that does not lack in grace if the performer so interpret it. The characteristically delightful thing about the invention is the unexpected and subtly accentuated rise of the melodic
line after reaching a certain high climax, by a further step, from
which then, treated in the most perfect, perhaps all too perfect
taste, it flutes and sings itself away. It is one of those physically
effective manifestations capturing head and shoulders, bordering
on the "heavenly," of which only music and no other art is capable. And the tutti-glorification of just this theme in the last part
of the variation movement brings the bursting out into the open
C major. But just before it comes a bold flourish — a plain remi-
niscence of the first violin part leading to the finale of Beethoven's A-minor Quartet; only that here the magnificent phrase
is followed by something different, a feast of melody in which the
parody of being carried away becomes a passion which is seriously meant and therefore creates a somewhat embarrassing effect.

I know that Leverkühn, before composing the piece, studied
very carefully the management of the violin in Bériot, Vieuxtemps, and Wieniawski and then applied his knowledge in a way
half-respectful, half caricature and moreover with such a challenge to the technique of the player — especially in the extremely
abandoned and virtuoso middle movement, a scherzo, wherein
there is a quotation from Tartini's Devil's Trill Sonata — that the
good Rudi had his work cut out to be equal to the demands upon
him. Beads of sweat stood out beneath his blond locks every time
he performed it, and the whites of his pretty azure eyes were
bloodshot. But how much he got out of it, how much opportunity for "flirtation" in a heightened sense of the word, lay in a
work which I to the Master's very face called "the apotheosis of
salon music"! I was, of course, certain beforehand that he would
not take the description amiss, but accept it with a smile.

I cannot think of that hybrid production without recalling a
conversation which took place one evening at the home of Bullinger, the Munich manufacturer. Bullinger, as we know, occupied the *bel étage* of an elegant apartment-house he had built in
Wiedemayerstrasse; beneath its windows the Isar, that uncor-
rupted glacial stream, purled past in its well-regulated bed. The

Crœsus entertained some fifteen guests at seven-o'clock dinner; he kept open house, with a trained staff, and a lady housekeeper who presided with affectedly elegant manners and obviously would have liked to marry. The guests were mostly people in the financial and business world. But it was known that Bullinger loved to air his views at large in intellectual circles; and on occasion he would gather a selection of artistic and academic elements for an evening in his agreeable quarters. No one, myself included, I confess, saw any reason to despise his cuisine or the spacious amenities of his drawing-rooms as a setting for stimulating discussion.

This time the group consisted of Jeanette Scheurl, Herr and Frau Knöterich, Schildknapp, Rudi Schwerdtfeger, Zink and Spengler, Kranich the numismatist, Radbruch the publisher and his wife, the actress Zwitscher, the farce-writer from Bukovina, whose name was Binder-Majoresku, myself and my dear wife. Adrian, urged by me and also by Schildknapp and Schwerdtfeger, was there too. I do not inquire whose plea had been decisive, nor do I flatter myself in the least that it was mine. At table he sat next Jeanette, whose society was always a comfort to him, and he saw other familiar faces about him as well; so he seemed not to regret having yielded but rather to have enjoyed the three hours of his stay. I remarked again with unspoken amusement the involuntary attention and more or less timid reverence paid to him. After all, he was only thirty-nine years old, and besides, but few of the guests present possessed enough musical knowledge for such an attitude on any rational grounds. It amused me, I say; yet gave me a pang at my heart as well. For the behaviour of these people was really due to the indescribable atmosphere of aloofness which he carried about wherever he went. In increasing degree, more and more perceptible and baffling as the years went by, it wrapped him round and gave one the feeling that he came from a country where nobody else lived.

This evening, as I said, he seemed quite comfortable; he was even conversational, which I ascribed in some degree to the effect of Bullinger's champagne-and-bitters cocktail and his wonderful Pfalz wine. Adrian talked with Spengler, who was already in wretched health, his disease having attacked his heart, and laughed with the rest of us at the clowneries of Leo Zink, who leaned back at table and covered himself with his huge damask serviette like a sheet up to his fantastic nose and folded his hands peacefully atop. Adrian was even more amused by the jester's adroitness when we were called on to look at a well-intentioned still-life by Bullinger, who dabbled in oils. To save the company the embarrassment of criticizing it, Zink examined the painting with a thousand acclamations and Good-graciouses which might mean anything and nothing; looked at it from every point of view and even turned it over and looked at the back. This gush of ecstatic yet wholly meaningless verbiage was Zink's social technique; at bottom he was not a pleasant man, and this was his way of taking part in conversations that went over his head as dilettante painter and enthusiast of carnival balls. He even practised it in the conversation I have in mind, touching the fields of æsthetics and ethics.

It developed as a sequel to some gramophone music with which the host regaled us after the coffee, as we smoked and drank liqueurs. Very good gramophone records had begun to be produced, and Bullinger played several enjoyable ones for us from his valuable cabinet: the well-recorded waltzes from Gounod's *Faust* came first, I remember. Baptist Spengler could only criticize them on the ground that they were drawing-room music, much too elegant for folk-dances on the meadow. It was agreed that their style was more suitable in the case of the charming ball-music in Berlioz's *Symphonie fantastique* and we asked to hear a record of the latter. It was not there; but Rudi Schferdtfeger whistled the air faultlessly, in violin timbre, pure and perfect, and laughed at the applause, shrugging his shoulder inside his coat, in the way he had, and drawing down one corner of his mouth in a grimace. By way of comparison with the French somebody now demanded something Viennese: Lanner, Johann Strauss the younger. Our host gave us willingly from his store, until a lady — it was Frau Radbruch, the publisher's wife — suggested that with all this frivolous stuff we might be boring the great composer who was present. Everybody, in concern, agreed with her; Adrian, who had not understood, asked what she had said. When it was repeated he made lively protest. In God's name no, that was all a mistake. No one could take more pleasure than he in these things — in their way they were masterly.

"You underestimate my musical education," said he. "In my early days I had a teacher" (he looked across at me with his deep, subtle, lovely smile) "crammed full of the whole world of sound; a bubbling enthusiast, too much in love with every, I really mean every, organized noise, for me to have learned any contempt from him. There was no such thing as being 'too good' for any sort of music. A man who knew the best, the highest and austerest; but for him music was music — if it just was music. He objected to Goethe's saying that art is concerned with the good

and difficult; he held that 'light' music is difficult too, if it is
good, which it can be, just as well as 'heavy' music. Some of that
stuck by me, I got it from him. Of course I have always grasped
the idea that one must be very well anchored in the good and
'heavy' to take up with the 'light.' "

There was silence in the room. What he had said, at bottom,
was that he alone had the right to enjoy the pleasant things we had
been regaled with. They tried not to understand it thus, but they
suspected that was what he meant. Schildknapp and I exchanged
looks. Dr. Kranich went "H'm, h'm." Jeanette Scheurl whispered
"Magnifique!" Leo Zink's fatuous "Jesus, Jesus!" rose above the
rest, in pretended acclamation, but really out of spite. "Genuine
Adrian Leverkühn!" cried Schwerdtfeger, red in the face from
one Vieille Cure after another, but also, I felt sure, out of private
chagrin.

"You haven't by chance," Adrian went on, "Delilah's D-sharp
major aria from *Samson* by Saint-Saëns?" The question was addressed to Bullinger, who found great satisfaction in replying:

"Not have it? My dear sir, what do you think of me? Here it
is — not at all 'by chance,' I assure you!"

Adrian answered: "Oh, good! It came into my head, because
Kretschmar, my teacher, he was an organist, a fugue-man, you
must know, had a peculiarly passionate feeling for the piece, a
real *faible*. He could laugh at it too, but that did not lessen his
admiration, which may have concerned only the consummate-
ness of the thing in its own genre. Listen."

The needle touched the plate. Bullinger put down the heavy
lid. Through the loud-speaker poured a proud mezzo-soprano
voice, which did not much trouble about clear enunciation: you
understood: *"Mon cœur s'ouvre à ta voix"* and not a great deal
else. But the singing, unfortunately accompanied by a rather
whining orchestra, was wonderful in its warmth, tenderness, sombre lament for happiness, like the melody, which indeed in both
of the structurally similar strophes of the aria reaches its full
beauty only in the middle and finishes in a way to overpower the
senses, especially the second time, when the violin, now quite
sonorous, emphasizes with pleasing effect the voluptuous vocal line and repeats the closing figure in delicate and melancholy
postlude.

They were moved. One lady wiped an eye with her embroidered party handkerchief. "Crazy beautiful!" said Bullinger, using
a phrase now in favour among stricter connoisseurs, who rejected
the sentimental "lovely." It might be said to be used here exactly

in its right and proper place, and perhaps that was what amused Adrian.

"Well, there!" he said, laughing. "You understand now how a serious man can be capable of adoring the thing. Intellectual beauty it has not, of course, it is typically sensual. But after all one must not blush for the sensual, nor be afraid of it."

"And yet, perhaps," Dr. Kranich was heard to say. He spoke, as always, very clearly, with distinct articulation, though wheezing with asthma. "Perhaps, after all, in art. In this realm in fact one may, or one should, be afraid of the nothing-but-sensual; one should be ashamed of it, for, as the poet said, it is the common, the vulgar: 'Vulgar is everything that does not speak to the mind and spirit and arouses nothing but a sensual interest.'"

"A noble saying," Adrian responded. "We shall do well to let it echo for a bit in our minds before we think of anything to dispute it."

"And what would you think of then?" the scholar wanted to know.

Adrian had made a grimace, shrugged a shoulder, as much as to say: "I can't help the facts." Then he replied:

"Idealism leaves out of count that the mind and spirit are by no means addressed by the spiritual alone; they can be most deeply moved by the animal sadness of sensual beauty. They have even paid homage to frivolity. Philine, after all, is nothing but a little strumpet, but Wilhelm Meister, who is not so very different from his creator, pays her a respect in which the vulgarity of innocent sensuality is openly denied."

"His complaisance, his toleration of the questionable," returned the numismatist, "have never been looked on as the most exemplary traits of our Olympian's character. And one may see a danger to culture when the spirit closes its eyes to the vulgar and sensual, or even winks at them."

"Obviously we have different opinions as to the danger."

"You might as well say I am a coward, at once!"

"God forbid! A knightly defender of fear and censure is no coward, he is simply knightly. For myself, I would only like to break a lance for a certain breadth of view in matters of artistic morality. One grants it, or allows it, it seems to me, more readily in other arts than in music. That may be very honourable but it does seriously narrow its field. What becomes of the whole jingle-jangle if you apply the most rigorously intellectual standards? A few 'pure spectra' of Bach. Perhaps nothing else audible would survive at all."

A servant came round with whisky, beer, and soda-water on a huge tray.

"Who would want to be a spoil-sport?" said Kranich, and got a "Bravo!" and a clap on the shoulder from Bullinger. To me, and very likely to some of the other guests, the exchange was a duel suddenly struck up between uncompromising mediocrity and painful depth of experience. But I have interpolated this scene, not only because I feel the close connection between it and the concerto upon which Adrian was then at work, but also because even then both concerto and conversation directed my attention to the person of the young man upon whose obstinate insistence the piece had been written and for whom it represented a conquest in more than one sense of the word. Probably it is my fate to be able to speak only stiffly, dryly, and analytically about the phenomenon of love: of that which Adrian had one day characterized to me as an amazing and always somewhat unnatural alteration in the relation between the I and the not-I. Reverence for the mystery in general, and personal reverence as well, combine to close my lips or make me chary of words when I come to speak of the transformation, always in the sign of the dæmonic, the phenomenon in and for itself half miraculous which negatives the singleness of the individual soul. Even so, I will show that it was a specific sharpening of my wits through my classical scholarship, an acquirement which otherwise tends rather to take the edge off one's reactions towards life, which put me in a position to see or understand as much as I did.

There remains no doubt — I say it in all calmness — that tireless, self-confident perseverance, put off by nothing, had won the day over aloofness and reserve. Such a conquest, considering the polarity — I emphasize the word — the polarity of the partners, the intellectual antithesis between them, could have only one definite character, and that, in a freakish sort of way, was what had always been sought and striven after. It is perfectly clear to me that a man of Schwerdtfeger's make-up had always, whether consciously or not, given this particular meaning and coloration to his wooing of Adrian — though of course I do not mean that it lacked nobler motives. On the contrary, the suitor was perfectly serious when he said how necessary Adrian's friendship was to the fulfilment of his nature, how it would develop, elevate, improve it. But he was illogical enough to use his native gift of coquetry — and then to feel put off when the melancholy preference he aroused did not lack the signs of ironic eroticism.

To me the most remarkable and thrilling thing about all this

was to see how the victim did not see that he had been bewitched. He gave himself credit for an initiative that belonged
entirely to the other party, and was full of fantastic astonishment
at frankly reckless and regardless advances that might better be
called seduction. Yes, Adrian talked about the *miracle* of that undaunted single-mindedness, undistracted by melancholy or emotion; I have little doubt that his astonishment went back to that
distant evening when Schwerdtfeger appeared in his room to beg
him to come back because the party was so dull without him.
And yet in these so-called miracles you could always see poor
Rudi's "higher," his free and decent characteristics as an artist,
which I have repeatedly celebrated. There is a letter which Adrian
at about the time of the Bullinger dinner wrote to Schwerdtfeger,
who should of course have destroyed it but which, partly out of
sentiment, partly as a trophy he did in fact preserve. I refrain
from quoting it, merely characterizing it as a human document
which affects the reader like the baring of a wound and whose
painful lack of reserve the writer probably considered an uttermost hazard. It was not. And the way it proved not to be was
really beautiful. At once, with all expedition, with no torturing
delay, Rudi's visit to Pfeiffering followed. There were explanations, there was assurance of the profoundest gratitude: the revelation of a simple, bold, and utterly sincere bearing, zealously
concerned to obviate all humiliation. . . . That I must commend,
I cannot help it. And I suspect — and in a way approve — that on
this occasion the composition and dedication of the violin concerto were decided on.

It took Adrian to Vienna. It took him, with Rudi Schwerdtfeger, to the estate in Hungary. When they returned, Rudolf rejoiced in the prerogative that up to then, from our childhood on,
had been mine alone: he and Adrian were *per du*.

CHAPTER XXXIX

Poor Rudi! Brief was the triumph of your childish dæmony. It had entered into a field of power far more charged with fate, far more dæmonic than its own, which speedily shattered, consumed, and extinguished it. Unhappy "*Du*"! It was inappropriate to the blue-eyed mediocrity that had achieved it; nor could he who so far condescended refrain from avenging the humiliation inseparable from the condescension, pleasurable though that may have been. The revenge was automatic, cold-eyed, secret. But let me tell my tale.

In the last days of 1924 the successful violin concerto was repeated in Berne and Zürich, as part of two performances of the Swiss Chamber Orchestra, whose director, Herr Paul Sacher, had invited Schferdtfeger, on very flattering terms and with the express wish that the composer might honour the occasion with his presence. Adrian demurred, but Rudolf knew how to plead and the recent "*Du*" was strong enough to open the way for what was to come.

The concerto occupied a place in the middle of a program including German classics and contemporary Russian music. It was performed twice: in the Hall of the Conservatorium at Berne and also in Zürich, in the Tonhalle. Thanks to the exertions of the soloist, who gave all that he had to its execution, the piece fully asserted both its fascination and its intellectual appeal. True, the critics remarked a certain lack of unity in the style, even in the level of the composition, and the public too was slightly more reserved than in Vienna. However, it not only gave the performers a lively ovation but on both evenings insisted on the appearance of the composer, who gratified his interpreter by appearing repeatedly hand in hand with him to acknowledge the applause. I was not present at this twice repeated unique event, the exposure of the recluse in person to the gaze of the crowd. I was out of it. I heard about it, however, from Jeanette Scheurl, who was in Zürich for the second performance and also met Adrian in the private house where he and Schwerdtfeger lodged.

It was in the Mythenstrasse, near the lake, the home of Herr and Frau Reiff, an elderly, wealthy, childless pair. They were friends of art, who had always enjoyed extending hospitality to prominent artists on tour and entertaining them socially. The husband was a retired silk-manufacturer, a Swiss of the old democratic mould. He had a glass eye, which imparted a rather stony expression to his bearded face and belied his character, for he was of a lively and liberal frame and loved nothing better than playing the gallant with prima donnas and soubrettes in his drawing-room. Sometimes he entertained the company, not too badly, with his cello, accompanied by his wife, who came from Germany and had once been a singer. She lacked his sense of humour, but was the energetic, hospitable housewife personified, warmly seconding her husband's pleasure at entertaining celebrities and giving their drawing-rooms an atmosphere of unforced virtuosity. She had in her boudoir a whole tableful of photographs of European celebrities, gratefully dedicated to the Reiff hospitality.

Even before Schwerdtfeger's name had appeared in the papers the couple had invited him, for as an open-handed Mæcenas the old industrialist heard sooner than ordinary people about coming musical events. They had promptly extended the invitation to Adrian so soon as they knew he was coming too. Their apartment was spacious, there was plenty of room for guests; in fact on their arrival from Berne the two musicians found Jeanette Scheurl already installed, for she came every year for a few weeks on a visit. But it was not Jeanette Scheurl next whom Adrian was placed at the supper the Reiffs gave for a small circle of friends after the concert.

The master of the house sat at the head of the table, drinking orange-juice out of wonderful engraved crystal, and despite his staring gaze exchanging free and easy repartée with the dramatic soprano of the municipal theatre, a powerful female who in the course of the evening thumped herself repeatedly on the breast with her fist. There was another opera singer there, the heroic baritone, a Balt by birth, a tall man with a booming voice, who, however, talked with intelligence. Then of course Kapellmeister Sacher, who had arranged the concert, Dr. Andreæ, the regular conductor of the Tonhalle, and Dr. Schuh, the excellent music-critic of the *Neue Züricher Zeitung* — all these were present with their wives. At the other end of the table Frau Reiff energetically presided between Adrian and Schwerdtfeger, next to whom sat, respectively, a young, or still young professional woman, Mlle Godeau, a French Swiss, and her aunt, a thoroughly good-natured, almost Russian-looking old dame with a little moustache. Marie (in other words Mlle Godeau) addressed her as *"ma tante"* or Tante Isabeau; she apparently lived with her niece as companion and housekeeper.

It is undoubtedly incumbent on me to give a picture of the niece, since a little later, for excellent reasons, my eyes dwelt long upon her in anxious scrutiny. If ever the word "sympathetic" was indispensable to the description of a person, it is so in the present case, when I seek to convey the picture of this woman: from head to foot, in every feature, with every word, every smile, every expression of her being, she corresponded to the tranquil, temperate, æsthetic, and moral climate purveyed by this word. She had the loveliest black eyes in the world. I will begin with them: black as jet they were, as tar, as ripe blackberries; eyes not large indeed, but with a clear and open shine from their dark depths, under brows whose fine, even line had as little to do with cosmetics as had the the temperate native red of the gentle lips. There was nothing artificial, no make-up about her, no accentuation by borrowed colour. Her native genuine sweetness — the way, for instance, in which the dark-brown hair was drawn back from her brow and sensitive temples, leaving the ears free and lying heavy at the back of her neck — set its stamp on the hands as well. They were sensible and beautiful, by no means small, but slender and small-boned, the wrists encircled by the cuffs of a white silk blouse. And just so too the throat rose out of a flat white collar, slender and round like a column, crowned by the piquantly pointed oval of the ivory-tinted face. The shapely little nose was remarkable for the animation of the open nostrils. Her not precisely frequent smile, her still less frequent laugh, which always caused a certain appealing look of strain round the almost translucent region of the temples, revealed the enamel of her even, close-set teeth.

It will be seen that I seek to summon up in a spirit of painstaking love the figure of this woman whom Adrian for a short time thought to marry. It was in that white silk evening blouse which so enhanced — perhaps with intention — her brunette type that I too saw Marie for the first time. Afterwards I saw her chiefly in one of her still more becoming simple everyday and travelling costumes of dark tartan with patent-leather belt and mother-of-pearl buttons; or else in the knee-length smock which she put on over it when she worked with lead-pencils and coloured crayons at her drawing-board. She was a designer, so Adrian had been told by Frau Reiff; an artist who sketched and worked out for the smaller Paris opera and vaudeville stages, the Gaieté Lyrique, the old Théâtre du Trianon, the figurines, costumes, and settings which then served as models for costumiers and decorators. The artist, a native of Nyon on Lake Geneva, lived and worked in the tiny rooms of a flat on the Ile de Paris, companioned by Tante Isabeau. Her reputation for inventiveness and industry was on the increase, as were her professional grasp of costume history and her fastidious taste. Her present visit in Zürich was a business one; and she told her neighbour on the right that in a few weeks she would be coming to Munich, where she was to create the settings for a modern comedy of manners at the Schauspielhaus.

Adrian divided his attention between her and the hostess, while opposite him the tired but happy Rudi joked with *"ma tante."* She laughed till the tears ran down; often she leaned over with wet face and shaking voice to repeat something her neighbour had just said and her niece absolutely must hear. Marie would nod and smile, obviously pleased to see her aunt so well amused; her eyes rested gratefully on the source of the old lady's enjoyment, while he in his turn did his utmost to provoke her to yet another repetition of what he had said. Mlle Godeau talked with Adrian, answering his questions about her work in Paris, about recent productions of the French ballet and opera which were only partly known to him, works by Poulenc, Auric, Rieti. They exchanged animated views on Ravel's *Daphnis et Chloé* and the *Jeux* of Debussy, Scarlatti's music to the *Donne di buon umore* by Goldoni, Cimarosa's *Il Matrimonio segreto,* and *L'Éducation manquée* by Chabrier. For some of these Marie had designed new settings, and she made sketches on her place-card to illustrate solutions for various scenic problems. Saul Fitelberg she knew — oh, of course! It was then she showed the gleaming enamel of her teeth, her voice rang out in a hearty laugh, and her temples got that lovely look of strain. Her German was effortless, with a slight, delightful foreign accent; her voice had a warm, appealing quality, it was a singing voice, a "material" beyond a doubt. To be specific, not only was it like Elsbeth Leverkühn's in colour and register but sometimes one really might think, as one listened, that one heard the voice of Adrian's mother.

But a company of fifteen people, like this one, usually breaks up on rising from table into groups and makes fresh contacts. Adrian scarcely exchanged a word after supper with Marie Godeau. Sacher, Andreæ, and Schuh, with Jeanette Scheurl, engaged him in a long conversation about Zürich and Munich musical

events, while the Paris ladies, with the opera singers, the host and
hostess, and Schwerdtfeger, sat at the table with the priceless
Sèvres service and with amazement watched the elderly Herr
Reiff empty one cup of strong coffee after another. He declared
in his impressive Swiss German that he did it by his doctor's advice, to strengthen his heart and make him fall asleep more easily.
The three house guests retired soon after the departure of the
rest of the company. Mlle Godeau was staying for several days
with her aunt at Hotel Eden au Lac. When Schwerdtfeger, who
was to accompany Adrian the next morning to Munich, bade them
good-bye, he expressed a lively hope of seeing them there later.
Marie waited a moment, until Adrian echoed the wish, and then
pleasantly reciprocated.

✻

✻   ✻

The first weeks of June 1925 had gone by when I read in the
paper that my friend's attractive Zürich table partner had arrived
in our capital and with her aunt was staying in Pension Gisela in
Schwabing; not by chance, for Adrian told me he had recommended it to her. He had stopped there for a few days on his return from Italy. The Schauspielhaus, in order to arouse interest
in the coming première, had given publicity to the news of her
arrival; it was at once confirmed to us by an invitation from the
Schlaginhaufens to spend the next Saturday evening with them
to meet the well-known stage designer.

I cannot describe the suspense with which I looked forward to
this meeting. Curiosity, pleasurable expectation, apprehension,
mingled in my mind and resulted in profound excitement. Why?
Not — or not only — because Adrian on his return from Switzerland had told me among other things of his meeting with Marie
and had given me a description of her which, as a simple statement, included the likeness of her voice to his mother's and in
other ways besides had made me prick up my ears. Certainly it
was no enthusiastic portrayal, on the contrary his words were
quiet and casual, his manner unembarrassed, he talked looking off
into the room. But that the meeting had made an impression on
him was clear, if only because he knew Marie's first and her last
name. And we know that in society he seldom knew the name of
the person he spoke with. Of course he did much more than
merely mention her, besides.

But that was not all that caused my heart to beat so strangely
in joy and fear. On my next visit to Pfeiffering, Adrian let fall

remarks to the effect that he had now lived here a very long time. He might possibly make changes in his outward life; at least he might soon put an end to his hermit state: he was considering matters, and so on. In short you could interpret his remarks only as an intention to marry. I had the courage to ask whether his hints were connected with a certain social event in Zürich; to that he replied:

"Who can prevent you from making guesses? Anyhow this cabined, cribbed, confined space is not at all the right theatre. If I mistake not, it was on Mount Zion, back home, that you once made me similar revelations. We ought to climb up to the Rohm-bühel for this conversation."

Imagine my astonishment!

"My dear friend," said I, "this is a sensation, it is thrilling."

He advised me to moderate my transports. He would soon be forty; that he thought was warning enough not to put off the step. I was not to ask any more questions. I would see in good time. I did not conceal from myself my joy that this new idea meant the severance of the impish and anomalous bond with Schwerdtfeger; I rejoiced to interpret it as a conscious means to that end. How the fiddler and whistler would take it was a minor matter, which did not unduly upset me since Schwerdtfeger had already, with the concert, arrived at the goal of his childish ambition. After that triumph, I thought, he would be ready to take a more reasonable place in Adrian Leverkühn's life. But what I was revolving in my mind was my friend's singular way of speaking of his intention as though its realization depended on himself alone; as though he did not need to give a thought to the girl's consent. I was more than ready to approve a self-confidence so strong as to assume that it needed only to choose, only to make known its choice. And yet I did feel some trepidation at this naïveté, it seemed to me like another manifestation of that remoteness and other-worldness he carried about like an aura. Against my will, I doubted whether this man was made to win the love of women. If I were quite candid with myself, I even doubted that he believed it himself. I thought perhaps he struggled against the feeling and purposely so put it as though his success were a matter of course. Whether the woman of his choice had so far any inkling of his feelings and plans remained obscure.

It remained obscure so far as I was concerned even after the evening party in the Briennerstrasse where I first met Marie Godeau. How much I liked her will be clear from the description I gave above. Not only the mild dark depth of her eyes — and I

knew what an appeal that must make to Adrian's sensibilities —
her delightful smile, her musical voice; not only these won me to
her, but also the friendly and intelligent seriousness of her character, the directness so far above all cooing femininity, the decision, even the bluntness of the independent, capable woman. It rejoiced me to think of her as Adrian Leverkühn's life-partner; I
could well understand the feeling she gave him. Did not "the
world" come near to him in her, the world from which he shrank
— and, in an artistic and musical sense, that part of the world
which was outside Germany? And it came in the most serious,
friendly guise, awakening confidence, promising fulfilment, encouraging him to abandon his recluse state. Did he not love her
out of his own world of musical theology, oratorio, mathematical
number-magic? It gave me hope, it excited me, to see these two
human beings together in one room, although in fact they were
not together for long at a time. Once a shift in the grouping
brought Marie, Adrian, myself, and another person together,
when I removed myself almost at once in the hope that the other
person would take the hint and move off too.

The affair at the Schlaginhaufens' was not a dinner but a nine-
o'clock evening company with a buffet in the dining-room next
the salon. The picture had changed considerably since the war.
There was no Baron Riedesel to represent the claims of the
"graceful" in art: that piano-playing cavalry officer had disappeared through history's trapdoor. Herr von Gleichen-Russwurm,
the descendant of the poet Schiller, was not there either. He had
been convicted of attempted conspiracy to defraud and been retired from the world to a sort of voluntary arrest on his Bavarian
estate. His scheme had been consummately ingenious, as well as
sheerly crazy and incredible besides. The Baron had insured a
piece of jewellery for a sum higher than its value, and had then
ostensibly sent it, carefully packed, to be reset by a jeweller in
another city. When the packet arrived, there was nothing found
in it but a dead mouse. This mouse had most incompetently failed
to perform the task expected of it by the sender. Obviously the
idea had been to have it gnaw through the wrappings and get
away, leaving the conclusion to be drawn that the parcel had
somehow got a hole in it through which the valuable piece had
fallen out and got lost. The insurance would then have been due.
But the wretched little animal had died without making the hole
that was to have explained the absence of the jewel. And the inventor of this ingenious knavery was most comically exposed.
Possibly he had got the idea from some book on the history of

culture and fallen victim to his own erudition. Or again, the confusion in moral standards prevailing at the time may have been responsible for his freakish inspiration.

Our hostess, née von Plausig, had had by now to resign herself to the loss of many things, among them the idea of bringing art and aristocracy together in her salon. The presence of some former ladies of the court, talking French with Jeanette Scheurl, reminded one of old times. Otherwise, mingling among the stars of the theatre one saw this or that deputy of the Catholic People's party and a few higher and not so high functionaries of the new state. Some of these were people of family, such as a certain Herr von Stengel, indefatigably jolly and ready for anything. But there were other elements, anathema in word and deed to the "liberalistic" republic, whose intention to avenge the German "shame," their conviction that they represented a coming world, was written large on their brows.

Well, it is always like that: an observer might have found that I spent more time with Marie Godeau and her good Tantchen than Adrian did, who doubtless was there on her account. He had greeted her at once with obvious pleasure, but after that spent most of his time with his dear Jeanette and the Social-Democratic member, a serious and knowledgeable admirer of Bach. My own conduct was natural after all that Adrian had confided to me, quite aside from the attractiveness of the object. Rudi Schwerdtfeger was there too; Tante Isabeau was enchanted to see him again. He made her laugh — and Marie smile — as he had in Zürich, but did not interrupt a sedate conversation we had about Paris and Munich events in the world of art, also political and European ones, relations between France and Germany; just at the end for a few minutes Adrian joined our group, standing. He always had to catch the eleven-o'clock train to Waldshut, and his stay that evening had lasted scarcely an hour and a half. The rest of us remained a little longer.

This was, as I said, on Saturday evening. Some days later, on a Thursday, I heard from him by telephone.

CHAPTER XL

HE called me up in Freising and said he wanted to ask a favour
of me. His voice was level and subdued, indicating headache. He
had the feeling, he said, that one should do the honours of Munich a bit for the ladies in Pension Gisela. The idea was to offer
them an excursion into the country, just now at its best in this
beautiful winter weather. He made no claim to have originated
the plan, it had come from Rudi Schwerdtfeger. But he had taken
it up and thought it over. They had been considering Füssen and
Neu-Schwanstein. But perhaps Oberammergau would be even
better, with a sledge from there to Ettal; he personally was fond
of the cloister, and they might drive by way of Linderhof, also
a curiosity worth seeing. What did I think?

I said I thought the idea and also the choice of Ettal were
excellent.

"Of course you must both come with us," he said, "you and
your wife. We'll make it a Saturday — so far as I know you have
no classes on Saturday this semester. Let us say a week from the
day after tomorrow unless there is too big a thaw. I have told
Schildknapp already; he is mad about that sort of thing and wants
to go on skis and be drawn by the sledge."

I said I thought all that was capital.

He wanted to make this much clear, he went on. The plan, as
he had said, was originally Schwerdtfeger's, but I would probably
understand his, Adrian's, wish that they should not get that impression in Pension Gisela. He would not like to have Rudolf invite them, but rather laid stress on doing it himself, though even
so not too directly. Would I be so good as to wangle the thing
for him in such a way that before my next visit to Pfeiffering, in
other words the next day but one, I called upon the ladies in their
pension and in a sense as his messenger, if only by inference,
brought them the invitation?

"You would be obliging me very much by this friendly service," he ended, with a curious formality.

I began to put some questions in my turn, but then suppressed them and simply promised him to carry out his wish, assuring him that I was very much pleased with the enterprise, for him and for all of us. So I was. I had already seriously asked myself how the intentions he had confided to me were to be furthered and things set going. It did not seem advisable just to leave to chance further occasions for meeting with the woman of his choice. The situation did not afford a very wide margin, it had to be helped out, there was need of initiative — and here it was. Was the idea really Schwerdtfeger's, or had Adrian merely put it off on him out of shyness at assuming quite contrary to his nature the role of a lover, and suddenly taking thought for social affairs and sleighing-parties? All this seemed to me so much beneath his dignity that I wished he had told the truth rather than made the fiddler responsible for the idea; yet I could not quite suppress the question whether our pixy platonist might not have had a hand in the enterprise.

But as for questions, after all I had but one: why did Adrian — if he wanted to let Marie know that he was making plans in order to see her — not address himself to her direct, ring her up, even go to Munich, call on the ladies and put his plans before them? I did not know then that what was involved was a tendency, an idea, in a way a sort of rehearsal for something to come later; a pattern, I mean, of sending to the beloved — for that is what I must call her — and leaving it to someone else to speak to her.

The first time it was I to whom he entrusted the message, and I readily performed my office. Then it was that I saw Marie in the white smock she wore over the collarless plaid blouse, and very well it became her. I found her at her drawing-board, a flat, heavy piece of wood set up at a slant, with an electric light fastened to it. She rose to greet me. We sat perhaps twenty minutes in the little sitting-room. Both ladies proved receptive to the attention shown them, and welcomed with enthusiasm the plan for an excursion, of which I only said that I had not originated it — after dropping the remark that I was on the way to my friend Leverkühn. They said that without such gallant escorts they might probably never have seen anything of the famous environment of Munich or the Bavarian Alps. The day was fixed on, the time of meeting. I was able to bring Adrian a gratifying report; I made it quite circumstantial, weaving into it praises of Marie's appearance in her working smock. He thanked me in the words, spoken so far as I could hear without humour:

"Well, you see, it is a good thing after all to have reliable friends."

The railway line to the village of the Passion Play is for most of the distance the same as the Garmisch-Partenkirchen line, only branching off at the end. It goes through Waldshut and Pfeiffering. Adrian lived half-way to our goal, so it was only the rest of us, Schwerdtfeger, Schildknapp, the guests from Paris, and my wife and myself who forgathered at about ten in the morning at the station in Munich. Without Adrian we covered the first hour through the flat and frozen countryside, beguiling the time with sandwiches and red wine brought by my wife. Schildknapp made us all laugh by his exaggerated eagerness to get as much as the rest: "Don't make the long fellow come short," he clamoured in English, using a nickname he went by among us. His natural, unconcealed, and amusingly parodied fear of not getting enough to eat was irresistibly comic; with goggling eyes he chewed a tongue sandwich in imitation of a starving man. All these jests were unmistakably for Mlle Godeau's benefit; he liked her, of course, as much as the rest of us did. She was wearing a most becoming olive-green winter costume, trimmed with bands of brown fur. A sort of suggestibility in my nature, simply because I knew what was toward, tempted me to revel again and again in the sight of her eyes, the pitch-black, coal-black, merry gleam between the darkness of her lashes.

When Adrian joined us, greeted with shouts by our high-spirited group, I got a sudden start — if that is the right word for my feelings, and truly there was something startling about them. We were sitting at close quarters, not in a compartment but in an open section of a second-class coach of a through train. Thus Adrian had under his own eyes the whole range of blue and black and like-coloured ones: attraction and indifference, stimulation and equability, there they all were and would remain for the whole day, which thus stood in a way in the sign of this constellation, perhaps ought to stand in it, that the initiated might recognize therein the real idea of the excursion.

There was a natural fitness in the fact that after Adrian joined us the landscape began to rise and the mountain scenery under snow, though still at some distance, to come into view. Schildknapp distinguished himself by knowing the names of this or that ridge or wall. The Bavarian Alps boast no august or awe-inspiring giants. Yet in their pure white dress they afforded a scene of glorious winter splendour, mounting bold and austere between wooded gorge and wide expanse as we wound among them. The day, however, was cloudy, inclined to frost and snow, and was to clear only towards evening. Our attention even in the midst of

conversation was mostly given to the view. Marie led the talk
to their common experience in Zürich, the evening in the Tonhalle and the violin concerto. I looked at Adrian talking with her.
He had sat down on the opposite bench; she was between Schildknapp and Schwerdtfeger, while Tantchen chattered good-
naturedly with Helene and me. I could see that he had to guard
himself as he gazed at her face, her black eyes. With his blue
ones Rudolf looked on, watched Adrian's absorption, and then
saw how he checked himself and turned away. Did he feel rec-
ompensed by the praises that Adrian was singing in his behalf?
Marie had modestly refrained from any expression of opinion
about the music; so they spoke only of the performance, and
Adrian emphatically declared that even with the soloist himself
sitting opposite, he could not refrain from calling his playing
masterly, consummate, simply incomparable. He added a few cordial, even glowing words about Rudi's artistic development in
general and his undoubtedly great future.

The man thus spoken of seemed to disclaim the praise; he said:
"Now, now!" and "*Tu' di fei halten,*" and protested that the Master was exaggerating frightfully; but he was red with pleasure.
Not a doubt but he was overjoyed to have himself praised to the
skies in Marie's hearing; but his delight in the fact that it was
Adrian who extolled him was just as manifest, and his gratitude
expressed itself in admiration of Adrian's way of speaking. Marie
had heard and read about the part performance of the *Apocalypse* in Prague, and she asked about the work. Adrian put her off.
"Let us," he said, "not speak of these pious peccadilloes!" Rudi
was enchanted.

"Pious peccadilloes!" he repeated, in ecstasy. "Did you hear
that? The way he talks! How he knows how to use words! He is
masterly, our Master!"

And he pressed Adrian's knee. He was one of those people who
always have to touch and feel — the arm, the shoulder, the elbow.
He did it even to me, and also to women, most of whom did not
dislike it.

In Oberammergau our little party walked about through the
spick and span village, admiring the quaint peasant houses with
their rich ornament of carven balconies and ridge-poles; distin-
guishing those of the Apostles, the Saviour, and the Mother of
God. While they climbed the near-by Calvarienberg I left them
for a little while to find a livery stable I knew and engage a
sledge. I joined them for dinner at an inn that had a glass dance-
floor lighted from beneath and surrounded by little tables. Dur-

ing the theatre season it was doubtless crowded with foreigners;
now, to our satisfaction, it was almost empty. There were only
two groups of other guests: at one table an invalidish gentleman
with a nursing sister in attendance, at the other a party of young
folk come out for the winter sports. From a platform an orchestra of five instruments dispensed light music; they displeased no
one by the long intervals they made between the pieces. What they
played was trivial and they played even that badly and haltingly.
After our roast fowl Rudi Schwerdtfeger could stand it no longer
and made up his mind to let his light shine, as it says in the Good
Book. He took the violinist's fiddle away from him, and after
turning it round in his hands and seeing where it came from, he
improvised magnificently on it, weaving in, to the amusement of
our party, some snatches from the cadenza of "his" concerto. The
orchestra stood open-mouthed. Then he asked the pianist, a
weary-eyed youth who had certainly dreamed of something
higher than his present occupation, if he could accompany Dvořák's *Humoresque*, and on the mediocre fiddle played the popular
piece, with its many grace notes, charming glides, and pretty
double stopping; so pertly and brilliantly that he won loud applause from everybody in the place, ourselves and the neighbouring tables, the amazed musicians, and the two waiters as well.
    It was after all a stereotyped pleasantry, as Schildknapp jeal-
ously muttered in my ear; but charming and dramatic too, in
short "nice," in perfect Rudi Schwerdtfeger style. We stayed
longer than we meant, the other guests having left, over our coffee
and gentian brandy. We even had a little dance ourselves, on the
glass floor: Schildknapp and Schwerdtfeger dancing by turns with
Mlle Godeau and my good Helene, God knows what sort of
dance, under the benevolent eye of the three who refrained. The
sledge was waiting outside, a roomy one with a pair of horses and
well provided with fur rugs. I took the place next the coachman
and Schildknapp made good his threat of being dragged on skis
behind us — the driver had brought a pair. The other five found
comfortable quarters in the body of the vehicle. It was the most
happily planned part of the program, aside from the fact that
Rüdiger's virile enterprise miscarried. Standing in the icy wind,
dragged over all the bumps in the road, showered with snow, he
caught cold in his most sensitive place and fell victim to one of
his intestinal catarrhs, which kept him in bed for days. Of course
this misfortune was only revealed afterwards. I, for my part, love
to be borne along snugly wrapped and warm, to the subdued
chiming of the bells, through the pure, sharp, frosty air; so it

seemed to me that everybody else felt the same. To know that
behind me Adrian and Marie were sitting looking into each other's eyes made my heart beat with a mixture of curiosity, joy,
concern, and fervent hope.

Linderhof, the small rococo castle of Ludwig II, lies among
woods and mountains in a remote solitude of splendid beauty.
Never was there a more fairy-tale retreat for a misanthropic monarch. But despite all the enthusiasm induced by the magic of the
locality, we felt put off by the taste which that prince displayed
in his ceaseless itch to build, in reality an expression of the compulsion to glorify his regal estate. We stopped at Linderhof and
guided by the castellan went through the sumptuous overladen
little rooms which formed the "living-apartments" of the fantastic abode. There the mad monarch spent his days, consumed with
the idea of his own majesty; von Bülow played to him, and he
listened to the beguiling voice of Kainz. In the castles of princes
the largest room is usually the throne-room. Here there is none.
Instead there is the bedchamber, of a size very striking compared
with the smallness of the living-rooms. The state bed, raised solemnly on a dais and looking rather short on account of its exaggerated width, is flanked like a bier with gold candelabra.

With due and proper interest, if with some private head-
shaking, we took it all in and then under a brightening sky continued on our way to Kloster Ettal, which has a solid architectural reputation on account of its Benedictine Abbey and baroque
church. I recall that as we drove and later while we took our
evening meal in the cleanly hotel opposite the cloister we talked
at length about the "unhappy" King (why, really, unhappy?)
into whose eccentric sphere we had penetrated. The discussion
was intermitted only by a visit to the church; it was in the main
a controversy between Rudi Schwerdtfeger and me over the so-
called madness, the incapacity for reigning, the dethronement and
legal restraint of Ludwig. To Rudi's great astonishment I pronounced all that unjustifiable, a brutal piece of philistinism, and
in addition a political move in the interest of the succession.

Rudi took his stand on the interpretation, not so much popular
as bourgeois and official, that the King was "completely crackers"
as he put it. It had been absolutely necessary for the sake of the
country to turn him over to psychiatrists and keepers and set up
a mentally sound regency. He, Rudolf, did not understand why
there should be any question about it. In the way he had when
some point of view was completely new to him, he bored his blue
eyes into my right and my left in turn as I spoke and his lip

curled angrily. I must say that I surprised even myself by the eloquence which the subject aroused in me, although before that day
I had scarcely given it a thought. I found that unconsciously I
had formed quite decided opinions. Insanity, I explained, was an
ambiguous conception, used quite arbitrarily by the average man,
on the basis of criteria very much open to question. Very early,
and in close correspondence with his own averageness, the philistine established his personal standards of "reasonable" behaviour.
What went beyond those norms was insanity. But a sovereign
King, surrounded by devotion, dispensed from criticism and responsibility, licensed, in support of his dignity, to live in a style
forbidden to the wealthiest private man, could give way to such
fantastic tastes and tendencies; to the gratification of such baffling
passions and desires, such nervous attractions and repulsions, that
a haughty and consummate exploitation of them might very easily look like madness. To what mortal below this regal elevation
would it be given to create for himself, as Ludwig had done,
gilded solitudes in chosen sites of glorious natural beauty! These
castles, certainly, were monuments of royal misanthropy. But if
we are hardly justified in considering it a symptom of mental
aberration when a man of average equipment avoids his fellows,
why then should it be allowable to do so when the same taste is
able to gratify itself on a regal scale?

But six learned professional alienists had established the insanity
of the King and declared the necessity for his internment.

Those compliant alienists had done what they did because they
were called on to do it. Without ever seeing Ludwig, without
having examined him even according to their own methods, without ever having spoken a word to him. A conversation with him
about music and poetry would just as well have convinced those
idiots of his madness. On the basis of their verdict this man was
deprived of the right to dispose of his own person, which doubtless departed from the normal, though it by no means followed
that he was mad. They degraded him to the status of a patient,
shut him up in his castle by the lake, unscrewed the door-knobs
and barred the windows. He had not put up with it, he had
sought freedom or death and in death had taken his doctor-jailer
with him: that was evidence of his sense of dignity, but no convincing proof of the diagnosis of madness. Nor did the bearing
of his entourage speak for it, they having been ready to fight on
his behalf; nor the fanatical love of the peasants, eager to die for
their "Kini." When they had seen him driving through his mountains, at night, alone, wrapped in furs, in a golden sledge with

outriders, in the gleam of torches, they had seen no madman, but a King after their own rude romantic hearts. And if he had succeeded in swimming across the lake, as he had obviously meant to do, they would have come to his rescue on the other side with pitchforks and flails against all the medicos and politicians in the world.

But his frantic extravagance was a definite sign of an unbalanced mind; it had become intolerable; and his powerlessness to govern had followed upon his unwillingness to govern: he had merely dreamed his kingship, refusing to exercise it in any normal form. In such a way no state can survive.

"Oh, nonsense, Rudolf. A normally constructed minister-president can govern a modern federated state even if the king is too sensitive to stand the sight of his and his colleagues' faces. Bavaria would not have been ruined even if they had gone on letting Ludwig indulge his solitary hobbies, and the extravagance of a king meant nothing, it was just words, a pretext and swindle. The money stayed in the country and stonemasons and gold-beaters got rich on his fairy palaces. More than that, the estates had paid for themselves over and over, with the entrance fees drawn from the romantic curiosity of two hemispheres. We ourselves had to-day contributed to turn the madness into good business. . . . Why, I don't understand you, Rudolf," I cried. "You open your mouth in astonishment at my apologia, but I am the one who has the right to be surprised at you and not to understand how you, precisely you — I mean as an artist, and anyhow, just you . . ."

I sought for words to explain why I was surprised, and found none. My eloquence faltered; and all the time I had the feeling that it was an impropriety for me to hold forth like that in Adrian's presence. He should have spoken. And yet perhaps it was better that I did it; for my mind misgave me lest he be capable of agreeing with Schwerdtfeger. I had to prevent that by speaking myself, in his proper spirit. I thought Marie Godeau also was taking my action in that sense, regarding me, whom he had sent to her about the day's excursion, as his mouthpiece. For she looked at him while I was working myself up, as though she were listening to him and not to me. For his part, indeed, he had an enigmatic smile on his lips, a smile that was far from confirming me as his representative.

"What is truth?" he said at last. And Rüdiger Schildknapp chimed in at once, asserting that truth had various aspects, of which in the present case the medical and practical were perhaps not the highest ones, yet even so could not quite be brushed aside.

In the naturalistic view of truth, he added, the dull and the melancholy were remarkably enough united. That was not to be taken as an attack on "our Rudolf," who certainly was not melancholic; but it might pass as a characterization of a whole epoch, the nineteenth century, which had exhibited a distinct tendency to both dullness and gloom. Adrian laughed — not, of course, out of surprise. In his presence one had always the feeling that all the ideas and points of view made vocal round about him were present in himself; that he, ironically listening, left it to the individual human constitutions to express and represent them. The hope was expressed that the young twentieth century might develop a more elevated and intellectually a more cheerful temper. Then the conversation split up and exhausted itself in disjointed speculation on the signs, if any, that this might come to pass. Fatigue began to set in, following on all our activity in the wintry mountain air. The time-table too put in its word, we summoned our driver, and under a brilliantly starry sky drove to the little station and waited on the platform for the Munich train.

The homeward journey was a quiet one, if only out of respect for the slumbering Tantchen. Schildknapp now and then made a low-voiced remark to Mlle Godeau. I reassured myself, in conversation with Schwerdtfeger, that he had taken nothing amiss. Adrian talked commonplaces with Helene. Against all expectation and to my unspoken gratification and amusement, he did not leave us in Waldshut, but insisted on accompanying our Paris guests back to Munich and their pension. The rest of us said good-bye at the station and went our ways, while he escorted aunt and niece in a taxi to their pension — a chivalrous act which in my eyes had the meaning that he spent the last moments of the declining day only in the company of the black eyes.

The usual eleven-o'clock train bore him back to his modest retreat, where from afar off he announced his coming by the high notes of his pipe to the watchful and prowling Kaschperl-Suso.

CHAPTER XLI

My sympathetic readers and friends: let me go on with my tale. Over Germany destruction thickens. Rats grown fat on corpses house in the rubble of our cities; the thunder of the Russian cannon rolls on towards Berlin; the crossing of the Rhine was child's play to the Anglo-Saxons; our own will seems to have united with the enemy's to make it that. "An end is come, the end is come, it watcheth for thee, behold it is come. The morning is come unto thee, O thou that dwellest in the land." But let me go on. What happened between Adrian and Rudi Schwerdtfeger only two days after that so memorable excursion, what happened and how it happened — I know, let the objection be ten times raised that I could not know it because I was not there. No, I was not there. But today it is psychological fact that I was there, for whoever has lived a story like this, lived it through, as I have lived this one, that frightful intimacy makes him an eye- and ear-witness even to its hidden phases.

Adrian phoned and asked the companion of his Hungarian journey to come to him at Pfeiffering. He must come as soon as possible, for the matter was pressing. Rudolf was always compliant. He received the summons at ten in the morning — during Adrian's working hours, in itself an unusual event — and by four in the afternoon the violinist was on the spot. He was to play that evening at a subscription concert by the Zapfenstösser orchestra — Adrian had never once thought of it.

"You ordered me," Rudolf said, "what's up?"

"I'll tell you at once," answered Adrian. "But the great thing is that you are here. I am glad to see you, even more than usual. Remember that!"

"A golden frame for whatever you have to say," responded Rudi, with a wonderfully flowery turn of phrase.

Adrian suggested that they should take a walk, one talked better walking. Schwerdtfeger agreed with pleasure, only regretting that he had not much time, he had to be at the station for the six-o'clock train, so as not to be late for his concert. Adrian struck his forehead and begged pardon for his forgetfulness. Perhaps Rudi would find it more understandable when he heard what he had to say.

It was thawing. The snow where it had been shovelled was melting and settling; the paths were beginning to be slushy; the friends wore their overshoes. Rudolf had not even taken off his short fur jacket, and Adrian had put on his camel's-hair ulster. They walked towards the Klammerweiher and round its banks. Adrian asked what the evening program was to be. "Again Brahms's First as pièce de résistance — again the 'Tenth Symphony'? Well, you should be pleased: you have some good things in the adagio." Then he related that as a lad beginning piano, long before he knew anything about Brahms, he had invented a motif almost identical with the highly romantic horn theme in the last movement, though without the rhythmical trick of the dotted quaver following the semiquaver, but melodically in the same spirit.

"Interesting," said Schwerdtfeger.

"Well, and our Saturday excursion?" Had he enjoyed himself? Did he think the others had?

"Could not have gone off better," declared Rudolf. He was sure that everybody remembered the day with pleasure, except probably Schildknapp, who had overdone himself and was now ill in bed. "He is always too ambitious when ladies are present." Anyhow, he, Rudolf, had no reason to be sympathetic, for Rüdiger had been rather rude to him.

"He knows you can take a joke."

"So I can. But he did not need to rub it in like that, after Serenus had borne down so hard with his loyalist propaganda."

"He is a schoolmaster. We have to let him instruct and correct."

"With red ink, yes. At the moment I feel quite indifferent to both of them — now I am here and you have something to tell me."

"Quite right. And when we talk about the excursion we are actually on the subject — a subject about which you could oblige me very much."

"Oblige you?"

"Tell me, what do you think of Marie Godeau?"

"The Godeau? Everybody must like her — surely you do too?"

"Like is not quite the right word. I will confess to you that ever since Zürich she has been very much in my mind, quite seriously, so that it is hard to bear the thought of the meeting as a mere episode, after which she will go away and I may never see her again. I feel as though I should like — as though I must — always see her and have her about me."

Schwerdtfeger stood still and looked at the speaker, first in the one eye and then in the other.

"Really?" said he, going on again, with bent head.

"It is true," Adrian assured him. "I am sure you won't take it ill of me for confiding in you. It is precisely because I feel I can rely on you."

"You may rely on me," Rudolf murmured.

Adrian went on:

"Look at it humanly speaking. I am getting on in years — I am by now forty. Would you, as my friend, want me to spend the rest of my life in this cloister? Consider me, I say, as a human being who suddenly realizes, with a sort of pang at the lateness of the hour, that he would like a real home, a companion congenial in the fullest sense of the word; in short, a warmer and more human atmosphere round him. Not only for the sake of comfort, to be better bedded down; but most of all because he hopes to get from it good and fine things for his working energy and enthusiasm, for the human content of his future work."

Schwerdtfeger was silent for a few paces. Then he said in a depressed tone:

"You've said human and human being four times. I've counted. Frankness for frankness: something shrinks together inside me, it makes me squirm when you use the word as you do use it in reference to yourself. It sounds so incredibly unsuitable — yes, humiliating, in your mouth. Excuse me saying so. Has your music been inhuman up till now? Then it owes its greatness to its inhumanity. Forgive the simplicity of the remark, but I would not want to hear any humanly inspired work from you."

"No? You really mean that? And yet you have already three times played one before the public? And had it dedicated to you? I know you are not saying cruel things to me on purpose. But don't you think it's cruel to let me know that only out of inhumanity I am what I am and that humanity is not becoming to me? Cruel, and thoughtless — anyhow cruelty always comes of thoughtlessness. That I have nothing to do with humanity, may have nothing to do with it, that is said to me by the very person who had the amazing patience to win me over for the human and persuaded me to say *du*; the person in whom for the first time in my life I found human warmth."

"It seems to have been a temporary makeshift."

"And suppose it were? Suppose it were a matter of getting into practice, a preliminary stage, and none the less worth while for all that? A man came into my life; by his heartfelt holding out he overcame death — you might really put it like that. He released the human in me, taught me happiness. It may never be known or be put in any biography. But will that diminish its importance, or dim the glory which in private belongs to it?"

"You know how to turn things very flatteringly for me."

"I don't turn them, I just state them as they are."

"Anyhow, we are not speaking of me but of Marie Godeau. In order always to see her and have her about you, as you say, you must take her for your wife."

"That is my wish and hope."

"Oh! Does she know?"

"I am afraid not. I am afraid I do not command the means of expression to bring my feelings and desires home to her. It embarrasses me to play the languishing swain in the company of others."

"Why don't you go to see her?"

"Because I shrink from the idea of coming down on her with confessions and offers when on account of my awkwardness she has probably not the faintest idea of my feelings. In her eyes I am still the interesting recluse. I dread her failure to understand and the hasty repulse that might be the result."

"Why don't you write her?"

"Because it might embarrass her even more. She would have to answer, and I don't know if she is good at writing. What pains she would have to take to spare me if she had to say no! And how it would hurt me! I dread the abstractness of an exchange like that — it strikes me it could be a danger to my happiness. I don't like to think of Marie, alone, by herself, uninfluenced by any personal contact — I might almost say personal pressure — having to write an answer to a written proposal. You see, I am afraid of both ways: the direct attack and the approach by letter."

"Then what way do you see?"

"I told you that in this difficult situation you could be a great help to me. I would send you to her."

"Me?"

"You, Rudi. Would it seem so absurd to you if you were to consummate your service to me — I am tempted to say to my salvation — by being my mediator, my agent, my interpreter between me and life, my advocate for happiness? Posterity might not hear of it — again, perhaps it might. It is an idea of mine, an inspiration, the way something comes when you compose. You must always assume beforehand that the inspiration is not altogether new. What is there in notes themselves, that is altogether new? But the way it looks just here, in this light, in this connection, something that has always been there may be new, new-alive, one might say; original and unique."

"The newness is my least concern. What you are saying is new enough to stagger me. If I understand you, I am to pay your addresses to Marie for you, ask for her hand for you?"

"You do understand me — you could scarcely mistake. The ease with which you do so speaks for the naturalness of the thing."

"Do you think so? Why don't you send your Serenus?"

"You are probably making fun of my Serenus. Obviously it amuses you to picture my Serenus as love's messenger. We just spoke of personal impressions which the girl should not be quite without in making her decision. Don't be surprised that I imagine she would incline her ear to your words more than to anything such a sober-sides as my Serenus could say."

"I do not feel in the least like joking, Adri — because in the first place it goes to my heart and makes me feel solemn, the role you assign to me in your life, and even before posterity. I asked about Zeitblom because he has been your friend so much longer — "

"Yes, longer."

"Good, then only longer. But don't you think this only would make his task easier and himself better at it?"

"Listen, how would it be if we just dropped him out of our minds? In my eyes he has nothing to do with love-affairs and that sort of thing. It is you, not he, in whom I have confided, you know the whole story, I have opened to you the most secret pages in the book of my heart, as they used to say. If you now open them to her and let her read; if you talk to her of me, speak well of me, by degrees betray my feelings, and the life-wishes bound up with them! Try her, gently, appealingly — 'nicely,' the way you have — try if she, well, yes, if she could love me! Will you? You don't have to bring me her final consent — God forbid! A little encouragement is quite enough as a conclusion to your mission. If you bring me that much back, that the thought of sharing my life with me is not utterly repugnant to her, not exactly monstrous — then my turn will come and I will speak with her and her aunt myself."

They had left the Rohmbühel on their left and walked through the little pine wood behind it, where the water was dripping from the boughs. Now they struck into the path at the edge of the village, which brought them back home. Here and there a cottager or peasant saluted by name the long-standing lodger of the Schweigestills. Rudolf, after a little while, began again:

"You may be sure that it will be easy for me to speak well of you. So much the more, Adri, because you praised me so to her. But I will be quite open with you — as open as you have been with me. When you asked me what I thought of Marie Godeau, I had the answer ready that everybody must like her. I will confess that there was more in that answer than there seemed. I should never have admitted it to you if you had not, as you put it with such old-world poetry, let me read in the book of your heart."

"You see me truly impatient for your confession."

"You've really heard it already. The girl — you don't like the word — the woman, then, Marie — I am not indifferent to her either; and when I say not indifferent, even that is not quite the right way to put it. She is the nicest, loveliest feminine creature, I think, that has come my way. Even in Zürich — after I had played, I had played *you* and was feeling warm and susceptible, she already charmed me. And here — you know it was I suggested the excursion, and in the interval, as you do not know, I had seen her: I had tea in Pension Gisela, with her and Tante Isabeau, we had such a nice time. . . . I repeat, Adri, that I only come to speak of it on account of our present talk and our mutual frankness."

Leverkühn was silent a little. Then he said, in an oddly faltering and neutral voice:

"No, I did not know that — about your feelings nor about the tea. I seem to have been so ridiculous as to forget that you are flesh and blood too and not wrapped up in asbestos against the attraction of the lovely and precious. So you love her, or let us say, you are in love with her. But now let me ask you one thing: does it stand so that our intentions cut across each other, so that you want to ask her to be your wife?"

Schwerdtfeger seemed to consider. He said:

"No, I hadn't thought of that yet."

"No? Did you think you would simply seduce her?"

"How you talk, Adrian! Don't say such things! No, I hadn't thought of that either."

"Well, then, let me tell you that your confession, your open and gratifying confession, is much more likely to make me stick to my request than to put me off it."

"What do you mean?"

"I mean it in more than one sense. I thought of you for this service of love because you would be much more in your element than, let us say, Serenus Zeitblom. You give out something he has not got to give, which seems to be favourable to my wishes and hopes. But aside from this: it seems now that you even to a certain extent share my feelings, though not, as you assure me, my hopes. You will speak out of your own feelings, for me and my hopes. I cannot possibly think of a more ordained or desirable wooer."

"If you look at it like that—"

"Do not think I see it only in that light. I see it also in the light of a sacrifice, and you can certainly demand that I should look at it like that. Demand it then, with all the emphasis you can summon! For that means that you, the sacrifice recognized as sacrifice, still want to make it. You make it in the spirit of the role that you play in my life, as a final contribution to the merit you have acquired for the sake of my humanity; the service which perhaps may remain hidden, or perhaps be revealed. Do you consent?"

Rudolf answered:

"Yes, I will go and do your errand to the best of my powers."

"We will shake hands on it," said Adrian, "when you leave."

They had got back to the house, and Schwerdtfeger had still time to have a bite with his friend in the Nike-saal. Gereon Schweigestill had put the horse in for him: despite Rudolf's plea not to trouble himself, Adrian accompanied him to the station, bouncing on the seat of the little cart.

"No, it is the right thing to do, this time quite particularly," he declared.

The accommodating local train drew up at the little Pfeiffering halt. The two clasped hands through the open window.

"Not another word," said Adrian: "Only 'nicely'!"

He raised his arm as he turned to go. He never again saw the traveller whom the train bore away. He only received a letter from him — a letter to which he denied all answer.

CHAPTER XLII

THE next time I was with him, ten or eleven days later, the letter was already in his hands and he announced to me his definite decision not to answer it. He looked pale and made the impression of a man who has had a heavy blow. A tendency, which indeed I had noticed in him some time back, to walk with his head and torso slightly bent to one side was now more marked. Still he was, or purported to be, perfectly calm, even cool, and seemed almost to need to excuse himself for his shoulder-shrugging composure over the treachery he had been the victim of.

"I hardly think," he said, "you expected any outburst of moral indignation. A disloyal friend. Well, what of it? I cannot feel greatly outraged at the way of the world. It is bitter, of course; you ask yourself whom you can trust, when your own right hand strikes you in the breast. But what will you have? Friends are like that today. What remains with me is chagrin — and the knowledge that I deserve to be whipped."

I asked what he had to be ashamed of.

"Of behaviour," he answered, "so silly that it reminds me of a schoolboy who finds a bird's nest and out of sheer joy shows it to another boy who then goes and steals it."

What could I say except:

"It is no sin or shame to be trusting, surely; they are the portion of the thief."

If only I could have met his self-reproaches with a little more conviction! But the truth was that I agreed with him. His whole attitude, the whole set-up with the second-hand wooing, and Rudolf of all people as go-between: I found it forced, devious, unseemly. I needed only to imagine that instead of speaking myself to my Helene, instead of using my own tongue, I had sent some attractive friend of mine to tell her my love, to see the whole equivocal absurdity of what he had done. But why then object to his remorse — if remorse it was that spoke in his words and manner? He had lost friend and beloved at one blow. And by his own fault, one must admit. If only one could have been quite certain

— if only I myself had been certain — that we were dealing with a fault, an unconscious false step, a fatal lack of judgment! If only the suspicion had not stolen into my brooding mind that he had to some extent foreseen what would happen and that it had come about as he wanted it to! Could he have seriously conceived the idea that what Rudolf "gave out" — in other words the young man's undeniable sexual appeal — could be made to work and woo for him, Adrian? Was it credible that he had counted on it? Sometimes the speculation arose in my mind that while putting it as though urging the other to a sacrifice, he had elected himself as the actual victim; that he deliberately brought together what really did belong together, in an affinity of "niceness" and charm in order to abdicate and retreat again into his fastness. But such an idea was more like me than it was like him. Such a motive, so soft and sacrificial, such abnegation might have sprung from my reverence for him and lain at the bottom of an apparent gaucherie, a so-called stupidity that he was supposed to have committed. But events were to bring me face to face with a reality harsher, colder, crueller than my good nature would have been capable of without stiffening in icy horror. That was a reality without witness or proof; I recognized it only by its staring gaze; and for all of me it shall remain dumb, for I am not the man to give it words.

I am certain that Schwerdtfeger, so far as he knew himself, went to Marie Godeau with the best and most correct intentions. But it is no less certain that these intentions had never from the first been very firm on their feet. They were endangered from within, prone to relax, to melt, to change their character. His vanity had been flattered by what Adrian had been at pains to impress upon him about his personal significance for the life and humanity of his great friend; he had accepted the interpretation, so skilfully instilled, that his present mission arose out of this significance. But jealousy worked against those first feelings. He resented the fact that Adrian, after the conquest he had made of him, had changed his mind; that he, Rudolf, now counted for nothing except as a tool and instrument. I believe that in his secret heart he now felt free, in other words not bound to repay with good faith the other's disloyalty and egotism. This is fairly clear to me. And it is clear, too, that to go wooing for another man is an intriguing enterprise, particularly for a fanatical male coquette, whose morale must have been prone to relax in the anticipation of a flirtation even if only a vicarious one.

Does anyone doubt that I could tell what happened between Rudolf and Marie Godeau, just as I knew the whole course of the

dialogue between him and Adrian in Pfeiffering? Does anyone
doubt that I was "there"? I think not. But I also think that a precise account is no longer useful or desirable. Its issue, heavy with
fate, however delightful it looked at first to others if not to me,
was not, we must assume, the fruit of only one interview. A second was necessary and inevitable after the way in which Marie
dismissed him the first time. It was Tante Isabeau whom Rudolf met when he entered the little vestibule of the pension. He
inquired after her niece and asked if he might have a few words
of private conversation with her, in the interest of a third party.
The old lady directed him to the living- and working-room with
a mischievous smile which betrayed her disbelief in the existence
of the third party. He entered and was greeted by Marie with
surprise and pleasure; she was about to inform her aunt when he
told her, to her increasing if obviously not unpleasant astonishment, that her aunt knew he was here and would come in after
he had spoken with herself on a weighty and wonderful theme.
What did she reply? Something jesting and commonplace, of
course. "I am certainly most curious," or the like. And asked the
gentleman to sit down comfortably for his recital.

He seated himself in an easy-chair beside her drawing-board.
Nobody could say he broke his word. He kept it, honourably. He
spoke to her of Adrian, of his importance and greatness, of which
the public would only slowly become aware; of his, Rudolf's admiration, his devotion to the extraordinary man. He talked of Zürich, and of the meeting at the Schlaginhaufens', of the day in the
mountains. He revealed to her that his friend loved her — but how
does one reveal to a woman that another man loves her? Do you
bend over her, gaze into her eyes, take in an appealing grasp the
hand that you profess to hope you may lay in another's? I do not
know. I had had to convey only an invitation to an excursion, not
an offer of marriage. All I know is that she hastily drew back her
hand, either from his or only from her lap, where it had been
lying; that a blush overspread the southern paleness of her face and
the laughter disappeared from her eyes. She did not understand,
she was really not sure she understood. She inquired if she had
understood aright: was Rudolf proposing to her for Dr. Leverkühn? Yes, he said, he was; actuated by friendship and a sense of
duty. Adrian, in his scrupulous delicacy, had asked him to represent him and he felt he could not refuse. Her distinctly cool,
distinctly mocking comment, that it was certainly very kind of
him, was not calculated to relieve his embarrassment. The extraordinary nature of his situation and role only now struck him,

mingled with the thought that something not very complimentary to her was involved in it. Her manner expressed sheer surprise and umbrage — and that both startled and secretly pleased him. He struggled for a while, stammering, to justify himself. She did not know, he said, how hard it was to refuse a man like that. And he had felt to some extent responsible for the turn Adrian's life had taken, because it had been he who had moved him to the Swiss journey and thus brought about the meeting with Marie. Yes, it was strange: the violin concerto was dedicated to him, but in the end it had been the medium of the composer's meeting with her. He begged her to understand that his sense of responsibility had largely contributed to his readiness to perform this service for Adrian.

Here there was another quick withdrawal of the hand which he had tried to take as he pleaded with her. She answered that he need not trouble himself further, it was not important that she should understand the role he had assumed, She regretted to be obliged to shatter his friendly hopes, but though she was of course not unimpressed by the personality of his principal, the reverence she felt for the great man had nothing to do with any feelings that could form the basis of a union for which he had argued with so much eloquence. The acquaintance with Dr. Leverkühn had been a source of pleasure and an honour as well; but unfortunately the answer that she must now give would probably make further meetings too painful. She sincerely regretted being obliged to take the view that Dr. Leverkühn's messenger and representative was also necessarily affected by this change in the situation. Certainly after what had happened it would be better and less embarrassing if they did not meet again. And now she must bid him a friendly farewell: "Adieu, monsieur!"

He implored her: "Marie!" But she merely expressed her amazement at his use of her first name and repeated her farewell — the sound of her voice rings clearly in my ears: "Adieu, monsieur!"

He went, his tail between his legs — to all appearance, that is. Inwardly he was blissful. Adrian's plan of marrying had turned out to be the nonsensical idea it had been from the first, and she had taken it very ill indeed that he had been willing to espouse it. She had been enchantingly angry. He did not hasten to let Adrian know the result of his visit, overjoyed as he was to have saved his own face by the honest admission that he was not himself indifferent to her. What he did now was to sit down and compose a letter to Mlle Godeau. He said that he could not submit to her "Adieu, monsieur"; for the sake of his life and reason he must see

her again, and put to her in person the question which he here
wrote down with his whole heart and soul: did she not understand that a man, out of veneration for another man, could sacrifice his own feelings and act regardless of them, making himself
a selfless advocate of the other's desire? And could she not further
understand that the suppressed, the loyally controlled feelings
must burst forth, freely, exultantly, so soon as the other man
proved to have no prospects of success? He begged her pardon
for the treason, which he had committed against nobody but
himself. He could not regret it, but he was overjoyed that there
was no longer any disloyalty involved if he told her that — he
loved her.

In that style. Not unclever. Winged by his genius for flirtation,
and, as I fully believe, all unconscious that in substituting his own
wooing for Adrian's, his declaration of love remained bound up
with an offer of marriage which of his own motion, considering
his nature, would never have entered his flirtatious head. Tante
Isabeau read the letter aloud to Marie, who had been unwilling to
accept it. Rudolf received no reply. But two days later he had
himself announced to Tante by the housemaid at Pension Gisela
and was not refused entrance. Marie was out. After his first visit,
as the old lady with sly reproof betrayed to him, she had wept a
few tears on her Tante's breast. Which in my view was an invention of Tante's. She emphasized her niece's pride. Marie's was a
proud nature but full of deep feeling, she said. Definite hope of
another meeting she could not give him. But she would say this
much, that she herself would spare no pains to represent to her
niece the uprightness of his conduct.

In another two days he was there again. Mme Ferblantier —
this was Tante's name, she was a widow — went in to her niece.
She remained some time; at last she came out and with an encouraging twinkle ushered him in. Of course he had brought flowers.

What else is there to say? I am too old and sad to relish describing a scene whose details can be of moment to no one. Rudolf repeated his wooing, only this time not for Adrian but himself. Of course the feather-headed youth was as suited to the
married state as I am to the role of Don Juan. But it is idle to
speculate on the chances for future happiness of a union doomed
to no future at all, destined to be brought to naught by a violent
blow from the hand of fate. Marie had dared to love the breaker
of hearts, the fiddler with the "little tone," whose artistic gifts
and certain success had been vouched for to her by so weighty
an authority. She confided in herself to hold and bind him, in her

power to domesticate the wild-fowl she had caught. She gave him her hands, received his kiss, and it was not four-and-twenty hours before the glad news had gone the rounds of our circle that Rudi was caught, that Konzertmeister Schwerdtfeger and Marie Godeau were an engaged pair. We also heard that he would not renew his contract with the Zapfenstösser orchestra but marry in Paris and there devote his services to a new musical group just being organized, called the Orchestre Symphonique.

No doubt he was very welcome there, and just as certainly the arrangements to release him went forward slowly in Munich, where there was reluctance to let him go. However, his presence at the next concert — it was the first after that one to which he had come back at the last minute from Pfeiffering — was interpreted as a sort of farewell performance. The conductor, Dr. Edschmidt, had chosen for the evening an especially house-filling program, Berlioz and Wagner, and as they say, all Munich was there. Familiar faces looked from the rows of seats, and when I stood up I had to bow repeatedly: there were the Schlaginhaufens and their social circle, the Radbruchs with Schildknapp, Jeanette Scheurl, Mmes Zwitscher and Binder-Majurescu, and the rest, all of whom had certainly come with the thought uppermost in their minds of seeing Benedict the married man, in other words Rudi Schwerdtfeger, up there, left front, at his music-stand. His betrothed was not present; we heard that she had returned to Paris. I bowed to Inez Institoris. She was alone, or rather with the Knöterichs and without her husband, who was unmusical and would be spending the evening at the Allotria. She sat rather far back, in a frock so simple as to look almost poverty-stricken; her head thrust forward on its slanting stalk, her eyebrows raised, the mouth pursed in that look of not quite innocent mischief. As she returned my greeting I could not help the irritating impression that she was forever smiling in malicious triumph over that evening in her living-room and her exploitation of my long-suffering sympathy.

As for Schwerdtfeger, well knowing how many curious eyes he would meet, he scarcely during the whole evening looked down into the parterre. At the times when he might have done so, he listened to his instrument or turned over the score.

The last number was the overture to the *Meistersinger*, played with breadth and élan. The crashing applause, loud enough anyhow, rose still higher as Ferdinand Edschmidt motioned to the orchestra to stand up, and put out his hand gratefully to his Konzertmeister. By then I was already in the aisle, intent on my over-

coat, which was handed out before there was a crowd round the
garde-robe. I intended to walk for at least a part of my way
home; that is, to my stop in Schwabing. But in front of the building I met a gentleman of the Kridwiss group, the Dürer expert,
Professor Gilgen Holzschuher, who had also been at the concert.
He involved me in a conversation which began with a criticism of
the evening's program: this combination of Berlioz and Wagner,
of foreign virtuosity and German mastery, was tasteless, and also
it only ill concealed a political tendency. All too much it looked
like pacifism and German-French rapprochement; this Edschmidt
was known to be a republican and nationally unreliable. The
thought had spoilt his whole evening. Unfortunately, everything
today was politics, there was no longer any intellectual clarity.
To restore it we must above all have at the head of our great orchestras men of unquestionably German views.

I did not tell him that it was he himself who was making politics of everything, and that the word "German" is today by no
means synonymous with intellectual clarity, being, as it is, a party
cry. I only suggested that a great deal of virtuosity, foreign or
not, was after all a component of Wagner's internationally so
well-tolerated art — and then charitably distracted his mind by
speaking of an article on problems of proportion in Gothic architecture, which he had recently written for the periodical Art and
Artists. The politenesses I expressed about it rendered him quite
happy, pliable and unpolitical; I utilized this bettered mood to bid
him good-bye and turn right as he turned left in front of the hall.

I went by way of the upper Türkenstrasse, reached the Ludwigstrasse, and walked along the silent Monumental-Chaussée
(asphalted now, years ago), on the left side, in the direction of
the Siegestor. The evening was cloudy and very mild, and my
overcoat began to feel oppressive, so I stopped at the Theresien-
strasse halt to pick up a tram to Schwabing. I don't know why
it took so long for one to come, but there are always many blocks
in the traffic. At last number ten appeared, quite conveniently for
me; I can still see and hear it approaching from the Feldherrnhalle. These Munich trams, painted in the Bavarian light-blue, are
heavily built and either for that reason or some characteristic of
the subsoil make considerable noise. Electric sparks flashed under
the wheels of the vehicle and even more on top of the contact
with the pole, where they sent out hissing showers of cold flame.

The car stopped, I got on in front and went inside. Close to
the sliding door was an empty seat, obviously just vacated. The
tram was full, two gentlemen stood clinging to straps at the rear

door. Most of the passengers were home-goers from the concert.
Among them, in the middle of the opposite bench, sat Schwerdtfeger, with his violin-case between his knees. Under his overcoat
he wore a white cache-nez over his dress tie, but as usual was
bareheaded. Of course he had seen me come in, but he avoided my
eye. He looked young and charming, with his unruly waving blond
locks, his colour heightened by his recent honourable exertions; by
contrast the blue eyes seemed a little swollen. But even that became him, as did the curling lips that could whistle in so masterly a
fashion. I am not a quick observer, only by degrees was I aware
of other people I knew. I exchanged a greeting with Dr. Kranich,
who sat on Schwerdtfeger's side of the tram, at some distance
from him, near the rear door. Bending forward by chance, I was
aware to my surprise of Inez Institoris, on the same bench with
myself, several seats away, towards the middle of the tram, diagonally opposite to Rudi Schwerdtfeger. I say to my surprise, for
certainly this was not her way home. But a few seats farther on I
saw her friend Frau Binder-Majurescu, who lived far out in Schwabing, beyond the "Grossen Wirt," so I assumed that Inez was going to drink tea with her.

But now I could see why Schwerdtfeger kept his head mostly
turned to the right so that I saw only his rather too blunt profile.
I was not the only person he wanted to ignore: the man whom
he must regard as Adrian's alter ego. I reproached him mentally:
why did he have to take just this particular tram? It was probably an unjust reproach, for he had not necessarily got in at the
same time with Inez. She might have got in later, as I had, or if it
had been the other way he could hardly have rushed out again at
sight of her.

We were passing the university, and the conductor, in his felt
boots, was standing in front of me to take my ten pfennige and
give me my ticket, when the incredible thing happened — at first,
like everything entirely unexpected, quite incomprehensible. There
was a burst of shooting: sharp, abrupt, shattering detonations, one
after the other, three, four, five, with furious, deafening rapidity.
Over there Schwerdtfeger, his violin-case still in his hands, sank
first against the shoulder and then into the lap of the lady next to
him on his right, who for her part, the one on his left as well,
leaned away from him in horror, while a general commotion ensued in the vehicle, more like flight and shrieking panic than any
activity showing presence of mind. Out in front the driver, God
knows why, kept up a ceaseless clamour like mad on the bell, perhaps to summon the police. Of course there were none within hear-

ing. There was an almost dangerous surging to and fro inside the tram, which had come to a stop. Many passengers were pushing to get out, while others, curious or anxious to do something, squeezed in from the platforms. The two gentlemen who had been standing in the gangway had like me flung themselves on Inez — of course far too late. We did not need to "wrest" the revolver from her, she had let it fall, or rather cast it from her in the direction of her victim. Her face was white as paper, with sharply defined, bright-red spots on the cheekbones. She had her eyes shut and an insane smile was on her pursed-up mouth.

They held her by the arms, and I rushed over to Rudolf, who had been stretched out on the now empty bench. On the other side, bleeding, in a fainting-fit, lay the lady upon whom he had fallen. She had received a glancing wound in the arm, which turned out not to be serious.

Several people were standing by Rudolf, among them Dr. Kranich, holding his hand.

"What a horrible, senseless, irrational deed!" said he, pale in the face, but in his clear, scholarly, well-articulated, short-winded way of speaking. He said "hor-r-r-ible," as actors often pronounce it. He added that he had never more regretted not being a doctor instead of only a numismatist, and actually at that moment the knowledge of coins did seem to me the most futile of the branches of science, more futile even than philology, a position by no means easy to sustain. In fact there was no doctor present, not among all those concert-goers, though doctors are usually music-lovers, so many of them being Jews. I bent over Rudolf. He gave signs of life, but was frightfully injured. There was a bleeding wound under one eye. Other bullets had, it turned out, gone into the throat, the lungs, and the coronary arteries. He lifted his head and tried to say something; but bubbles of blood welled out between his lips, whose gentle fullness seemed all at once so touching to me; his eyes rolled and his head fell back with a thud on the bench.

I cannot express the mournful pity which almost overcame me. I felt that in a way I had always loved him and I must confess that my sympathy for him was far stronger than for her, the unhappy creature who by suffering and by pain-deadening, demoralizing vice had been worked up to the revolting deed. I made myself known as a close friend of both parties and advised that the wounded man be carried over into the university, where the janitor could telephone for the police and an ambulance, and where, to my knowledge, there was a small first-aid station. I ar-

ranged that they should bring the author of the crime thither
as well.

All this was done. A studious, spectacled young man had with
my help lifted poor Rudolf from the tram, behind which, by now,
two or three more had come to a stop. Out of one of these hurried up a doctor with an instrument-case and directed, rather su-
perfluously, the work of carrying Rudolf in. A reporter came too,
asking questions. The memory still tortures me of the trouble we
had to rouse the janitor from his basement quarters. The doctor,
a youngish man, who introduced himself to everybody, tried to
administer first aid to the now unconscious victim after we had
laid him on a sofa. The ambulance came with surprising quick-
ness. Rudolf died, as the doctor after examination indicated to me
was unfortunately probable, on the way to the hospital.

As for me I attached myself to the later arriving police and
their now convulsively sobbing charge, to make known her connections and bespeak her admission into the psychiatric clinic.
But this, for the present night, was not permitted.

It struck midnight from the church when I left the office and,
looking about for an auto, set out to perform the painful duty
that still remained to me. I felt bound to go to Prinzregentenstrasse, to inform the little husband, as gently as might be, of what
had happened. I got a chance of a car just when it was no longer
worth while. I found the house-door barred, but the light went
on when I rang and Institoris himself came down — to find me instead of his wife at the door. He had a way of snapping his mouth
open for air and drawing his lower lip across his teeth.

"Oh, what is it?" he said. "It is you? How is she coming? . . .
Has something — ?"

I said almost nothing on the stairs. Above in the living-room,
where I had heard Inez's distressing confessions, I told him, after
a few words of preparation, what had happened and what I had
been witness to. He had been standing, and after I had done he sat
down suddenly in one of the basket-chairs. But after that he displayed the self-control of a man who has lived a long time in an
oppressive and threatening atmosphere.

"So then," said he, "it came like that." And it was clear that his
dread had concerned chiefly the manner in which the inevitable
tragedy would be consummated.

"I will go to her," he declared, and stood up again. "I hope they
will let me speak to her there" (he meant in the police cells).

I could not give him much hope for tonight. But he said in a shaken voice that he thought it was his duty to try; flung on his coat and hastened off.

Alone in the room, with Inez's bust, distinguished and sinister, looking down from its pedestal, my thoughts went thither where it will be believed they had in the last hour often and constantly gone. One more painful announcement it seemed to me had to be made. But a strange rigidity that seized on my limbs and even the muscles of my face prevented me from lifting the receiver and asking to be connected with Pfeiffering. No, that is not quite true, I did lift it, I held it dangling in my hand and heard the muffled voice, as from the depths of the sea, of the Fräulein at the other end. But a realization born of my already morbid exhaustion that I was about to disturb quite uselessly the nocturnal peace of the Schweigestill household, that it was not necessary to tell Adrian now, that I should only in a way be making myself ridiculous, checked my intention and I put the receiver down.

CHAPTER XLIII

My tale is hastening to its end — like all else today. Everything rushes and presses on, the world stands in the sign of the end — at least it does for us Germans. Our "thousand-year" history, refuted, reduced *ad absurdum*, weighed in the balance and found unblest, turns out to be a road leading nowhere, or rather into despair, an unexampled bankruptcy, a *descensus Averno* lighted by the dance of roaring flames. If it be true, as we say in Germany, that every way to the right goal must also be right in each of its parts, then it will be agreed that the way that led to this sinful issue — I use the word in its strictest, most religious sense — was everywhere wrong and fatal, at every single one of its turns, however bitter it may be for love to consent to such logic. To recognize because we must our infamy is not the same thing as to deny our love. I, a simple German man and scholar, have loved much that is German. My life, insignificant but capable of fascination and devotion, has been dedicated to my love for a great German man and artist. It was always a love full of fear and dread, yet eternally faithful to this German whose inscrutable guiltiness and awful end had no power to affect my feeling for him — such love it may be as is only a reflection of the everlasting mercy.

Awaiting the final collapse, beyond which the mind refuses its office, I have withdrawn within my Freising hermitage and shun the sight of our horribly punished Munich: the fallen statues, the gaping eyeholes in the façades, which both disguise the yawning void behind them and advertise it by the growing piles of rubble on the pavements. My heart contracts in pity for the reckless folly of my own sons, who, like the masses of the people, trusted, exulted, struggled, and sacrificed and now long since are reduced, with millions of their like, to staring at the bitter fruit of disillusion as it mellows into decay and final utter despair. To me, who could not believe in their belief or share their hopes, they will be brought no nearer by the present agony of their souls. They will still lay it to my charge — as though things would have turned out differently had I dreamed with them their insane dream. God help them! I am alone with my old Helene, who cares for my physical part, and to whom sometimes I read aloud from my pages such portions as suit her simplicity. In the midst of ruin all my thoughts are addressed to the completion of this work.

The *Apocalypsis cum figuris*, that great and piercing prophecy of the end, was performed at Frankfurt on the Main in February 1926, about a year after the frightful events that I chronicled in my last chapter. It may have been due in part to the disheartenment they left in their wake that Adrian could not bring himself to break through his usual retirement and be present at the performance, a highly sensational event, also one accompanied by much malicious abuse and shallow ridicule. He never heard the work, one of the two chief monuments of his proud and austere life; but after all he used to say about "hearing" I do not feel entitled to lament the fact. Besides myself, who took care to be free for the occasion, from our circle of acquaintances there was present only our dear Jeanette Scheurl, who despite her narrow means made the journey to Frankfurt and reported on the performance to her friend at Pfeiffering, in her very individual mixed French and Bavarian dialect. Adrian especially prized this peasant-aristocrat, her presence had a beneficial and soothing effect on him, like a sort of guardian spirit. Actually I have seen him sitting hand in hand with her in a corner of the Abbot's room, silent and as it were in safe-keeping. This hand-in-hand was not like him, it was a change which I saw with emotion, even with pleasure, but yet not quite without anxiety.

More than ever too, at that time, he liked to have Rüdiger Schildknapp with him. True, the like-eyed one was chary as ever of his presence, but when our shabby gentleman did appear he was ready for one of those long walks across country which Adrian loved, especially when he was unable to work; for Rüdiger seasoned his idleness with bitter and grotesque humour. Poor as a church-mouse, he had at that time much trouble with his neglected and decayed teeth and talked about nothing but dishonest dentists who pretended to treat him out of friendship but then suddenly presented impossible bills. He railed about conditions of payment, which he had neglected to observe, and then had been compelled to find another man, well knowing that he never could or would satisfy him — and more of the same. They had tortured him by pressing a considerable bridge on roots which had been left in and shortly began to loosen under the weight, so that the grisly prospect, the removal of the artificial structure, was imminent, and the consequence would be more bills which he could not pay. "It is all going to pieces," he announced in hollow tones; but had no objection when Adrian laughed till he cried at all this misery. Indeed it seemed Rüdiger could look down on it himself and bent double with schoolboy laughter.

This gallows humour of his made his company just the right thing for our recluse. I am unfortunately without talent in that line, but I did what I could to encourage the mostly recalcitrant Rüdiger to visit Pfeiffering. Adrian's life during this whole year was idle and void. He fell victim to a dearth of ideas, his mental stagnation tormented, depressed, and alarmed him, as his letters showed; indeed he put forward his condition as the chief ground for his refusal to go to Frankfurt. It was impossible for him to think about things he had already done while in a state of incapacity to do better. The past was only tolerable if one felt above it, instead of having to stare stupidly at it aware of one's present impotence. Fallow and hollow, he called his state: a dog's life, a *vie végétale*, without past or future, root or fruit, an idyll too idle for words. The one saving grace was that he could rail at it. Actually he could pray for a war, a revolution, any external convulsion just to shock him out of his torpor. Of composition he had literally not the smallest conception, not the faintest memory of how it was done; he confidently believed that he would never write another note. "May hell have pity on me!" "Pray for my poor soul!" such expressions repeated themselves in the letters. They filled me with gloom, yet on the other hand could even raise my spirits, as I reflected that after all only the youthful playmate and nobody else in the world could be the recipient of such confidences.

In my replies I tried to console him by pointing out how hard it is for human beings to think beyond their immediate situation. It is a matter of feeling and not of reason: prone to consider the present their abiding lot, they are incapable, so to speak, of seeing round the corner — and that probably applies more to bad situations than to good ones. Adrian's low morale was easily explainable by the cruel disappointments he had lately suffered. And I was weak and "poetical" enough to compare the fallow ground of his mind with the "winter-resting earth," in whose womb life, preparing new shoots, worked secretly on. I felt myself that the image was inapplicable to the extremes of Adrian's nature, his swing between penitential paralysis and compensating creative release. The stagnation of his impulse to create was accompanied though not caused by a new low-water mark in his physical state:

severe attacks of migraine confined him to darkness; catarrh of
the stomach, bronchial tubes, and throat attacked him by turns,
particularly during the winter of 1926, and would of itself have
been enough to prevent the trip to Frankfurt. It did in fact prevent another journey which humanly speaking was still more immediate and urgent, but categorically forbidden by his doctor.

At the end of the year, at the same age, seventy-five years and
strange to say almost on the same day, Max Schweigestill and
Jonathan Leverkühn departed this life: the father and proprietor
of Adrian's Bavarian asylum and home, and his own father up in
Buchel. The mother's telegram announcing the peaceful passing
of Jonathan Leverkühn, the speculator of the elements, found his
son standing at the bier of that equally quiet and thoughtful
smoker with the other dialect. "Maxl" had gradually handed over
the business to Gereon, his heir, just as Jonathan had done to
George; now he had stepped aside for ever. Adrian might be certain that Elsbeth Leverkühn bore this loss with the same quiet
resignation, the same understanding acceptance of the human lot,
as Mother Schweigestill showed. A journey to Saxon Thuringia
to the burial was out of the question in Adrian's present condition. But despite fever and weakness he insisted, against his doctor's advice, on taking part the following Sunday in the funeral
of his old friend, in the village church at Pfeiffering. It was attended by hosts of people from the region round about. I too paid
last honours to the departed, with the feeling that I was doing
honour to Jonathan as well. We went back on foot to the Schweigestill house, oddly and rather irrationally moved as we noted that
the odour of the old man's pipe tobacco, though he himself was
gone, still hung on the air of living-room and passage just as it
always had.

"That lasts," Adrian said, "a long time, maybe as long as the
house. In Buchel too. The time we last, a little shorter, a little
longer, we call immortality."

That was after Christmas; the two fathers, their faces already
half-turned away, half-estranged from earthly things, had still been
present at the Christmas feast. Now, as the light waxed, in the beginning of the new year, Adrian's health markedly improved, the
succession of harassing attacks came to an end. He seemed psychologically to have overcome the shipwreck of his life-plans and
all the damage bound up with it, his mind rose up, a giant re-
freshed — indeed, his trouble might now be to keep his poise in
the storm of ideas rushing upon him. This (1927) was the year of
the high and miraculous harvest of chamber music: first the en-

semble for three strings, three wood-wind instruments, and piano, a discursive piece, I might say, with very long themes, in the character of an improvisation, worked out in many ways without ever recurring undisguised. How I love the yearning, the urgent longing, which characterizes it; the romantic note — since after all it is treated with the strictest of modern devices — thematic, indeed, but with such considerable variation that actually there are no "reprises." The first movement is expressly called "fantasia," the second is an adagio surging up in a powerful crescendo, the third the finale, which begins lightly enough, almost playfully, becomes increasingly contrapuntal and at the same time takes on more and more a character of tragic gravity, until it ends in a sombre epilogue like a funeral march. The piano is never used for harmonic fillings, its part is soloistic as in a piano concerto — probably a survival from the violin concerto. What I perhaps most profoundly admire is the mastery with which the problem of sound-combination is solved. Nowhere do the wind instruments cover up the strings, but always allow them to have their own say and alternate with them; only in a very few places are strings and wind instruments combined in a tutti. If I am to sum up the whole impression: it is as though one were lured from a firm and familiar setting-out into ever remoter regions — everything comes contrary to expectation. "I have," Adrian said to me, "not wanted to write a sonata but a novel."

This tendency to musical prose comes to its height in the string quartet, Leverkühn's most esoteric work, perhaps, which followed on the heels of the ensemble piece. Where, otherwise, chamber music forms the playground for thematic work, here it is almost provocatively avoided. There are altogether no thematic connections, developments, variations, and no repetitions; unbroken, in an apparently entirely free way, the new follows, held together by similarity of tone or colour, or, almost more, by contrast. Of traditional forms not a trace. It is as though the Master, in this apparently anarchic piece, was taking a deep breath for the *Faust* cantata, the most coherent of his works. In the quartet he only followed his ear, the inner logic of the idea. At the same time polyphony predominates in the extreme, and every part is quite independent at every moment. The whole is articulated by very clearly contrasted tempi, although the parts are to be played without interruption. The first part, inscribed *moderato*, is like a profoundly reflective, tensely intellectual conversation, like four instruments taking counsel among themselves, an exchange serious

and quiet in its course, almost without dynamic variety. There
follows a presto part as though whispered in delirium, played
muted by all four instruments, then a slow movement, kept
shorter, in which the viola leads throughout, accompanied by in-
terjections from the other instruments, so that one is reminded
of a song-scene. In the *"Allegro con fuoco"* the polyphony is
given free rein in long lines. I know nothing more stirring than
the end, where it is as though there were tongues of flame from
all four sides, a combination of runs and trills which gives the impression of a whole orchestra. Really, by resetting the widely
spaced chords and using the best registers of every instrument, a
sonority is achieved which goes beyond the usual boundaries of
chamber music; and I do not doubt that the critics will hold it
against the quartet altogether that it is an orchestral piece in disguise. They will be wrong. Study of the score shows that the
most subtle knowledge of the string-quartet medium is involved.
Indeed, Adrian had repeatedly expressed to me the view that the
old distinctions between chamber music and orchestral music are
not tenable, and that since the emancipation of colour they merge
into one another. The tendency to the hybrid, to mixing and exchanging, as it showed itself already in the treatment of the vocal
and instrumental elements in the *Apocalypse*, was growing on
him. "I have learned in my philosophy courses, that to set limits
already means to have passed them. I have always stuck to that."
What he meant was the Hegel-Kant critique, and the saying
shows how profoundly his creative power sprang from the intellect — and from early impressions.

This is entirely true of the *Trio* for violin, viola, and cello:
scarcely playable, in fact to be mastered technically only by three
virtuosos and astonishing as much by its fanatical emphasis on
construction, the intellectual achievement it exhibits, as by the unsuspected combinations of sound, by which an ear coveting the
unknown has won from the three instruments a combinational
fantasy unparalleled. "Impossible, but refreshing," so Adrian in a
good mood characterized the work, which he had begun to write
down even during the composition of the ensemble piece, carried
in his mind and developed, burdened as it was with the work on
the quartet, of which one would have thought that it alone must
have consumed a man's organizing powers for long and to the
utmost. It was an exuberant interweaving of inspirations, challenges, realizations, and resummonings to the mastery of new
tasks, a tumult of problems which broke in together with their

solutions — "a night," Adrian said, "where it doesn't get dark for the lightnings."

"A rather sharp and spasmodic sort of illumination," he would add. "What then — I am spasmodic myself, it gets me by the hair like the devil and goes along me so that my whole carcass quivers. Ideas, my friend, are a bad lot, they have hot cheeks, they make your own burn too, in none too lovesome a way. When one has a humanist for a bosom friend, one ought to be able to make a clear distinction between bliss and martyrdom. . . ." He added that sometimes he did not know whether the peaceful incapacity of his former state were not preferable in comparison with his present sufferings.

I reproached him with ingratitude. With amazement, with tears of joy in my eyes, yet secret and loving concern, I read and heard, from week to week, what he put on paper: in the neatest, most precise, yes, even elegant notation, betraying not a trace of "spasms." This was what, as he fancifully put it, his familiar friend Mr. Akercocke told him to do and demanded of him. In one breath, or rather in one breathlessness, he wrote down the three pieces, any one of which would have been enough to make memorable the year of its production; actually he began with the draft of the trio on the very day on which he finished the "lento" of the quartet, which he composed last. "It goes," he once wrote to me, when I had been unable to visit him for two weeks, "as though I had studied in Cracow." I did not understand the allusion until I recalled that at Cracow, in the sixteenth century, courses were publicly given in magic.

I can assure my readers that I paid great attention to his archaic style and allusions, which he had always been given to but now even more frequently, or should I say "ofttimes," came into his letters and even his speech. The reason was soon to be made clear. The first hint came when I saw among his papers a note that he had written with a broad pen-nib: "This sadnesse moved Dr. Faustum that he made note of his lamentacyon."

He saw what I was looking at and took away the slip of paper with "Fie on a gentleman and brother! What concerns you not, meddle not with!" What he was planning and thought to carry out, no man aiding, he still kept from me. But from that moment on I knew what I knew. It is beyond all doubt that the year of the chamber music, 1927, was also the year when the *Lamentation of Dr. Faustus* was conceived. Incredible as it sounds, while his mind was wrestling with problems so highly complicated that one can imagine their being mastered only by dint of the sheerest, most exclusive concentration, he was already looking ahead, reaching out, casting forward, with the second oratorio in view: the crushing *Lamentation*. From his serious preoccupation with that work he was at first distracted by another interest, both priceless and heart-piercing.

CHAPTER XLIV

URSULA SCHNEIDEWEIN, Adrian's sister in Langensalza, gave birth to her first three children, one after the other, in 1911, 1912, and 1913. After that she had lung trouble and spent some months in a sanatorium in the Harz Mountains. The trouble, a catarrh of the apex of the lung, then seemed to have been cured, and throughout the ten years that passed before the birth of her youngest, little Nepomuk, Ursula had been a capable wife and mother to her family, although the years of privation during and after the war took the bloom off her health. She was subject to colds, beginning in the head and going to the bronchial cords; her looks, belied by her sweet-tempered and active ways, were if not precisely ailing, yet delicate and pale.

The pregnancy of 1923 seemed rather to increase than to lower her vitality. True, she got round from it rather slowly, and the feverish affection which ten years before had brought her to the sanatorium flickered up afresh. There had been some talk of interrupting her housewifely duties a second time for special treatment. But the symptoms died away — under the influence as I strongly suspect of psychological well-being, maternal happiness, and joy in her little son, who was the most placid, friendly, affectionate, easy-to-tend baby in the world. For some years the brave woman kept sturdy and strong; until May of 1928, when the five-year-old Nepomuk got a severe attack of measles, and the anxious day-and-night nursing of the exceptionally beloved child became a heavy drain upon the mother's strength. She herself had an attack of illness, after which the cough and the fluctuations of temperature did not subside; and now the doctor insisted on a sojourn at a cure, which, without undue optimism, he reckoned at half a year.

This was what brought Nepomuk Schneidewein to Pfeiffering. His sister Rosa, seventeen years old, and her brother Ezekiel, a year younger, were employed in the shop; while the fifteen-year-old Raimund was still at school. Rosa had of course the natural duty of keeping house for her father in her mother's absence and was likely to be too busy to take over the care of her little brother. Ursula had thought of Adrian. She wrote that the doctor would consider it a happy solution if the little convalescent could spend some time in the country air of Upper Bavaria. She asked her brother to sound his landlady, whether or not Frau Else would be willing to play the part of mother or grandmother to the little one for a time. Else Schweigestill, and even more enthusiastically Clementine, readily consented; and in the middle of June of that year Johannes Schneidewein took his wife to the same sanatorium, near Suderode in the Harz, where she had been benefited before; while Rosa and her little brother travelled south, bringing him to the bosom of her uncle's second home.

I was not present when the brother and sister arrived in the courtyard. Adrian described the scene to me: the whole house, mother, daughter, Gereon, maidservants and menservants, in sheer delight, laughing for pure pleasure, stood about the little man and could not gaze enough at so much loveliness. Especially the womenfolk of course were quite beside themselves, and of the women in particular the servants. They bent over the little one in a circle, convulsed with rapture; squatted down beside him and called on Jesus, Mary, and Joseph at sight of the beautiful little lad. His sister stood looking on indulgently: clearly she had expected nothing different, being used to see everyone fall in love with the youngest of the family.

Nepomuk — Nepo as his family called him, or "Echo" as ever since he began to prattle he had called himself, quaintly missing out the first consonant — was dressed with warm-weather rustic simplicity in a sleeveless white cotton shirt, linen shorts, and worn leather shoes on his stockingless feet. But it always seemed as though one were looking at a fairy princeling. The graceful perfection of the small figure with the slender, shapely legs, the indescribable comeliness of the little head, long in shape, covered with an innocent tumble of light hair; the features despite their childishness with something finished and well-modelled about them; even the upward glance of the long-lashed clear blue eyes, ineffably pure and sweet, at once full of depth and sparkling with mischief — no, it was not even all these together that gave such an impression of faerie, of a guest from some finer, tinier sphere. For there was besides the stance and bearing of the child as he stood the centre of the circle of "big people" all exclaiming, laughing, even sighing with emotion. There was his smile, of course not quite free from coquetry and consciousness of the charm he wielded; his words and gestures, sweetly instructive, benignly condescending, as though he were a friendly ambassador from that other, better clime. There was the silvery small voice and what it uttered, still with baby blunders, in the father's slightly drawling, weighty Swiss speech, which the mother had early taken over. The little man rounded his *r's* on his tongue; he paused between syllables; he accompanied his words, in a way I have never seen before in a child, with vague but expressive explanatory gestures of arms and hands, often quite unconnected with what he said, and rather puzzling while at the same time wholly delicious.

So much for the moment as a description of Nepo Schneidewein, or Echo as everybody, following his example, straightway called him. It is written by one not present when he came, and only as clumsy words can approximate the scene. How many writers before me have bemoaned the inadequacy of language to arrive at visualization or to produce an exact portrait of an individual! The word is made for praise and homage; to the word it is given to astonish, to admire, and to bless; it may characterize a phenomenon through the emotion it arouses; but it cannot conjure up or reproduce. Instead of attempting the impossible I shall probably do more for my adorable little subject by confessing that today, after fully seventeen years, tears come in my eyes when I think of him, while at the same time the thought of him fills me with an odd, ethereal, not quite sublunary lifting of the heart.

The replies he made, with that bewitching play of gesture, to questions about his mother, his journey, his stay in the great city of Munich, had as I said a pronounced Swiss accent and much dialect, rendered in the silvery timbre of his voice: "*huesli*" for house, "*a bitzli*" for a little bit. He liked to say "well": "Well, it was lovely." Fragments of grown-up language came too: if he had not remembered something, he said it had "slipped his mind." And finally he said: "Well, nothing more of news" — obviously because he wanted to break up the group; for the words fell from his honey-sweet lips: "Echo thinks best to not be outdoors any more. Better go in the huesli and see the uncle." And he put out his hand to his sister to take him in. But just then Adrian, who had been resting and putting himself to rights, came out to welcome his niece.

"And so this," said he, after he had greeted the young girl and exclaimed over her likeness to her mother, "is the new member of the family?"

He held Nepomuk's hand, gazed into the starry eyes, and soon was lost in the sweet depths of that azure upturned smile.

"Well, well!" was all he said, nodding slowly at the girl and then turning back to gaze again. His emotion could escape nobody, certainly not the child. So when Echo addressed his uncle for the first time, his words, instead of sounding forward, seemed to be placating and making light of something, loyally reducing it to simple and friendly terms: "Well, you are glad I did come, yes?" Everyone laughed, Adrian too.

"I should say so," he answered. "And I hope you are glad too, to make our acquaintance."

"It is most pleasant meeting all," the child said quaintly.

The others would have burst out laughing again, but Adrian shook his head at them with his finger on his lips.

"The child," he said softly, "must not be bewildered by our laughter. And there is no ground for laughter, do you think, Mother Schweigestill?" turning to her.

"Not a speck," said she in an exaggeratedly firm voice, and put the corner of her apron to her eye.

"So let us go in," he decided, and took Nepomuk's hand again to lead him. "Of course you have a little refreshment for our guests."

Accordingly, in the Nike salon, Rosa Schneidewein was served with coffee and the little one with milk and cake. His uncle sat with him at the table and watched him as he ate, daintily. Adrian talked with his niece the while, but did not hear much that she said, so taken up he was with looking at the elf and just as much with controlling his feelings, not to betray them and make them a burden. His concern was unnecessary, for Echo seemed no longer to mark mere silent admiration or enraptured looks; while it would have been a sin to miss that sweet lifting of the eyes in thanks for handing the jam or a piece of cake.

At length the little man uttered the single word: " 'Nuff." It was, his sister explained, what he had always said from a tiny child, when he had done; it meant "Echo has had enough." When Mother Schweigestill would have pressed him to take something more, he said with a certain superior reasonableness:

"Echo would be best without it."

He rubbed his eyes with his little fists, a sign that he was sleepy. They put him to bed, and while he slept Adrian talked with Sister Rosa in his workroom. She was to stay only till the third day, her duties in Langensalza summoned her home. When she left, Nepomuk wept a little, but then promised to be "good" until she came to fetch him. My God, how he kept his word! How incapable he was of not keeping it! He brought something like a state of bliss, a constant heart-warming gaiety and tenderness not only to the farm but to the village as well, and even as far as Waldshut. For the Schweigestills, mother and daughter, eager to be seen with him, confident of the same rapturous reception everywhere, took him with them to the apothecary, the shoemaker, the general store, in order that everybody might hear him "speak his piece," with bewitching play of gesture and impressive, deliberate enunciation: about Pauline who was bur-r-nt up, out of Slovenly Peter, or Jochen, who did come home from play so dir-rty that Mrs. Duck and Mr. Drake were amazed and even Mr. Pig was per-rfectly dazed. The Pfeiffering pastor heard him recite his prayer, with folded hands held out before his face — a strange old prayer it was, beginning "Naught availeth for timely Death." And the pastor, in his emotion, could only say: "Ah, thou dear child of God, thou little blessed one!" stroking his hair with a white priestly hand and presenting him with a coloured picture of the Lamb of God. The schoolmaster felt "a new man" after talking with him. At market and in the street every third person asked Fräul'n Clementine or Mother Schweigestill what was this had dropped down from heaven. People stared and nudged each other: "Just look, just look!" or else, not very differently from the pastor: "Ah, dear little one, little blessed one!" Women, in most cases, showed a tendency to kneel down in front of Nepomuk.

When I was next at the farm, two weeks had already passed since he came; he had settled in and was well known to the neighbourhood. I saw him first at a distance: Adrian showed him to me round the corner of the house, sitting on the ground in the kitchen garden at the back, between a strawberry and a vegetable bed, one little leg stretched out, the other half drawn up, his hair falling in strands on his forehead. He was looking, it seemed with somewhat detached approval, at a picture-book his uncle had given him, holding it on his knee, with the right hand at the margin. But the little left hand and arm, with which he turned the page, unconsciously continuing the turning motion remained in the air in an incredibly graceful posture beside the book, the small hand open. To me it seemed I had never seen a child so ravishingly posed. I could not even in fancy conceive my own affording such a sight; to myself I thought that thus must the little angels up above turn the pages of their heavenly choirbooks.

We went up to him, that I might make the acquaintance of the wonder-child. I did so with pedagogic restraint, with a view to reducing the situation to the everyday, and determined not to be sentimental. I put on a strict face, frowned, pitched my voice low, and spoke to him in the proper brisk and patronizing way: "Well, my son? Being a good lad, eh? And what are we up to here?" But even as I spoke I seemed to myself unspeakably fatuous; and even worse, he saw it too, apparently shared my view, and felt ashamed on my account. He hung his head, drawing down his mouth as one does to keep from laughing; it so upset me that I said nothing more for some time. He was not yet of an age when a lad is expected to stand up and be respectful to his elders; he deserved, if any creature ever did, the tender consideration and indulgence we grant to those not long on this earth, unpractised and strange to its ways. He said we should "sitty down" and so we did, with the manikin between us in the grass, and looked at his picture-book with him. It was probably among the most acceptable of the children's books in the shop, with pictures in English taste, a sort of Kate Greenaway style and not at all bad rhymes. Nepomuk (I called him that, not Echo; the latter I was idiot enough to find "sentimental") knew almost all of them by heart, and "read" them to us, following the lines with his finger, of course always in the wrong place.

The strange thing is that today I know those verses by heart myself, only because I heard them once — or it may have been more than once — recited in that little voice of his, with its enchanting intonation. How well I still know the one about the organ-grinders who met at a street corner, one of whom had a grudge against the other so that neither would budge from the spot. I could recite to any child — though not nearly so well as Echo did — what the neighbours had to bear from the hullabaloo those hurdy-gurdies kept up. The mice did keep a fasting feast, the rats they ran away. It ends:

> And only one, a puppy-dog,
> Listened till silence fell;
> And when he got back to his home
> That dog felt far from well.

You would have to see the little lad's troubled head-shake and hear his voice fall as he recounted the indisposition of the little dog. You would have to see the minuscule grandezza of his bearing as he imitated the two quaint little gentlemen meeting each other on the beach:

Good morning, m'sieur!
No bathing, I fear!

This for several reasons: first because the water is so wet and only forty-three degrees, but also "three guests from Sweden" are there:

A swordfish, a sawfish and shark
Swimming close in you can mark.

He uttered so drolly this confidential warning, had such a large-eyed way of enumerating the three undesirable guests, and fell into a key so mingled of horror and satisfaction at the news that they were swimming close in, that we both burst out laughing. He looked into our faces, observing our merriment with roguish curiosity, mine in particular, I thought — probably he wanted to see whether my uncalled-for schoolmaster solemnity was being thawed out.

Good heavens, it certainly was! After my first foolish attempts I did not return to it, except that I always addressed this little ambassador from childhood and fairyland as Nepomuk, speaking in a firm voice and only calling him Echo when I mentioned him to his uncle, who like the women had taken up the name. The reader will understand that the pedagogue in me felt somewhat disturbed or even embarrassed at this incontestably adorable love-liness, which yet was a prey to time, destined to mature and par-take of the earthly lot. In no long space the smiling azure of these eyes would lose their other-world purity. This face, this angelic air, as it were an explicit aura of childlikeness; the lightly cleft chin, the charming mouth, which when he smiled showed the gleaming milk teeth; the lips that then became somewhat fuller than in repose, and at their corners showed two softly curving lines coming from the fine little nose and setting off his mouth and chin from his cheeks: this face, I say, would become the face of a more or less ordinary boy, whom one would have to treat practically and prosaically and who would have no rea-son to greet a pedagogic approach with any of the ironic under-standing betrayed by Nepomuk. And yet there was something here — that elfin mockery seemed to express a consciousness of it — which put it out of one's power to believe in time and time's common work, or its action upon this pure and precious being. Such was the impression it gave of its extraordinary completeness in itself; the conviction it inspired that this was a manifestation of "the child" on earth; the feeling that it had "come down to us" as, I say it again, an envoy and message-bearer; all this lulled the reason in dreams beyond the claims of logic and tinged with the hues of our Christian theology. It could not deny inevitable growth; but it took refuge in the sphere of the mythical and timeless, the simultaneous and abiding, wherein the Saviour's form as a grown man is no contradiction to the Babe in the Mother's arms which He also is; which He always is, always before His worshipping saints lifting His little hand in the sign of the Cross.

What extravagance, what fanaticism, it will be said! But I can do no more than give account of my own experience, and I must confess that the slightly other-worldly existence of this child always produced in me a sense of my own clumsiness. But I should have patterned myself — and tried to do so — on Adrian, who was no schoolman but an artist and took things as they came, apparently without thought of their proneness to change. In other words, he gave to impermanent becoming the character of being; he believed in the image: a tranquillizing belief, so at least it seemed to me, which, adjusted to the image, would not let its composure be disturbed no matter how unearthly that image might be. Echo, the fairy princeling, had come; very well, one must treat him according to his kind, and that was all. Such seemed to be Adrian's position. Of course he was far removed from the frowning brow or any avuncular "That's a good lad." But on the other hand, he left the "little angel" ecstasies to simpler folk. He behaved to the little one with a delicacy and warmth, smiling or serious as occasion called it out; without flattery or fawning, even without tenderness. It is a fact that I never saw him caress the child, scarcely even smooth his hair. Only he liked to walk with him in the fields, hand in hand.

But however he behaved, he could not deceive me: I saw that his little nephew's appearance had made a bright spot in his life, that he loved him from the first day on. No mistaking the fact that the sweet, light, elfin charm, working as it were without a trace despite the child's serious, old-fashioned language, occupied and filled his days, although he had the boy with him only at certain times. The child's care of course fell on the women; and as mother and daughter had much else to do, he often played by himself in some safe spot. Owing to the measles he still needed as much sleep as quite small children do, and slept during the day in addition to the usual afternoon nap, dropping off wherever he happened to be. "Night!" he would say, just as when he went to bed. It fact "Night!" was his good-bye on all occasions, when he or anyone else went away. It was the companion-piece to the

" 'Nuff" he always said when he had had enough. He would offer his little hand, too, when he said "Night" before he fell asleep in the grass or as he sat in his chair. I once found Adrian in the back garden sitting on a very narrow bench made of three boards nailed together, watching Echo asleep at his feet. "He gave me his hand first," he announced when he looked up and saw me. He had not heard me approach.

Else and Clementine Schweigestill told me that Nepomuk was the best, most biddable, untroublesome child they had ever seen — which agreed with the stories of his earliest days. Actually I have known him to weep when he hurt himself, but never howl or roar or blubber as unruly children do. It would have been unthinkable. If he were forbidden, as for instance at an inconvenient time, to go with the stable-boy to the horses, or with Waltpurgis into the cow-stalls, he would assent to the verdict quite readily and even say: "In a little while, maybe tomorrow or next day," in a tone meant to console the grown-ups who, certainly against their will, had denied the request. Yes, he would even pat the disappointed one as though to say: "Don't take it to heart! Next time you won't have to refuse, maybe you can let me."

It was the same when he could not go to Adrian in the Abbot's room. He was much drawn to his uncle, even in the first two weeks; by the time I got there it was plain that he clung especially to Adrian and wanted to be with him. Of course this was partly because it was the unusual, a treat, while the society of the women was a commonplace. Yet how could it have escaped him that this man, his mother's brother, occupied among the rustics of Pfeiffering a unique, honoured, even rather intimidating place? And their respectful bearing must also make the boy eager to be with his uncle. But one cannot say that Adrian met the little boy half-way. Whole days might go by and he would not see him, would deny himself the undoubtedly beloved sight. Then again they would spend long hours together; taking walks hand in hand as far as the little one could go, strolling in friendly silence or chatting in Echo's little language, through the countryside lush with the season in which he had come and sweet with scents of lilac, alder-bush, and jasmine. The light-footed lad would be before him in the narrow lanes between walls of corn already ripening yellow for the harvest, their blades, with nodding ears as high as himself, mounting out of the mould.

Out of the earth, I might better say, for the little one said it, expressing his joy that heaven gave the "firsty earff" a drink last night.

"A drink, Echo?" asked his uncle, letting pass the rest of the child's metaphorical language. "You mean the rain?"

"Yes, the rain," his little companion agreed more explicitly; but he would not go further into the matter.

"Imagine, he talks about the earth being thirsty, and uses a figure of speech like that," Adrian related to me next time, in wonder. "Isn't that a bit strange? Yes," he nodded, with a certain amazed recognition, "he is pretty far along."

When he was obliged to go into the city, Adrian brought the boy all sorts of presents: various animals, a jack-in-the-box, a toy railway with lights that switched on and off as it roared round the curves; a magic casket in which the greatest treasure was a glass filled with red wine which did not run out when the glass was turned upside down. Echo liked these things, of course, but when he had played with them he soon said: " 'Nuff," and much preferred to have his uncle show and explain some object of grown-up use — always the same and always new, for a child's persistence and appetite for repetition are great in matters of entertainment. The carved ivory paper-knife; the globe turning on its axis, with broken land-masses, deep bays, strange-shaped inland seas, and vast blue-dyed oceans; the clock on the chimney-piece that struck the hours, whose weights one could wind up with a crank out of the well into which they had sunk; those were some of the wonders which the little boy coveted to examine, when the slender figure stood at the door and the little voice inquired:

"Are you look cross because I do come?"

"No, Echo, not very cross. But the weights are only half-way down."

In this case it might be the music-box he asked for. It was my contribution, I had brought it to him: a small brown box to be wound up underneath. The roller, provided with metal tongues, turned along the tuned teeth of a comb and played, at first briskly and daintily, then slowly running down, three well-harmonized, demure little tinkling melodies, to which Echo listened always with the same rapt attention, the same unforgettable mixture of delight, surprise, and dreamy musing.

His uncle's manuscripts too, those runes strewn over the staves, adorned with little stems and tails, connected by slurs and strokes, some blank, some filled in with black; he liked to look at them too and have it explained what all those marks were about — just between ourselves, they were about him, and I should like to know whether he divined that, whether it could be read in his eyes that he gathered it from the master's explanations. This child, sooner than any of us, was privileged to get an "insight" into the drafts of the score of Ariel's songs, on which Adrian was privately at work. He had combined the first, full of ghostly "dispersèd" voices of nature, the "Come unto these yellow sands," with the second, pure loveliness: "Where the bee sucks, there suck I," into a single song for soprano, celeste, muted violin, an oboe, a bass clarinet, and the flageolet notes of the harp. And truly he who hears these "gently spiriting" sounds or even hears them by reading alone, with his spirit's ear, may well ask with Ferdinand: "Where should this music be? I' th' air or th' earth?" For he who made it has caught in its gossamer, whispering web not only the hovering childlike-pure, bewildering light swiftness of "my dainty Ariel," but the whole elfin world from the hills, brooks, and groves which in Prospero's description as weak masters and demi-puppets by moonshine for their pastime midnight mushrooms make and the green sour ringlets whereof the ewe not bites. Echo always asked to see once more the place in the notes where the dog says "Bow-wow" and chanticleer cries "Cock-a-diddle-dow." And Adrian told him about the wicked witch Sycorax and her little slave, whom she, because he was a spirit too delicate to obey her earthy and abhorred commands, confined in a cloven pine, in which plight he spent a dozen painful years, until the good master of spells came and freed him. Nepomuk wanted to know how old the little spirit was when he was imprisoned and then how old when he was freed, after twelve years. But his uncle said that the spirit had no age, that he was the same after as before imprisonment, the same child of air — with which Echo seemed content.

The Master of the Abbot's room told him other stories, as well as he could remember them: Rumpelstiltskin, Falada and Rapunzel and the Singing, Soaring Lark; for the stories the little one had to sit on his uncle's knee, sidewise, sometimes putting one arm round his neck. "Well, that does sound most nice," he would say when a tale was done; but often he went to sleep with his head on the story-teller's breast. Then his uncle sat without moving, his chin resting lightly on the hair of the sleeping child, until one of the women came and fetched him away.

As I said, for days they might keep the child from him, because he was busy, or perhaps a headache shut him away in silence and darkness.

But after such a day, when he had not seen Echo, he liked to go when the child was put to bed, softly, hardly seen, to his room to hear the evening prayer, The child said his prayers lying on his back, his hands folded on his chest, one or both of the women being present. They were very singular things he recited, the heavenly blue of his eyes cast up to the ceiling, and he had a whole range of them so that he hardly ever said the same ones two evenings running.

> Whoso hedeth Goddes stevene
> In hym is God and he in hevene.
> The same commaunde myselfe would keepe,
> And me insure my seemely slepe.
>   Amen.

Or:

> A mannes misdeede, however grete,
> On Goddes merci he may wait,
> My sinne to Him a lytyl thynge is,
> God doth but smile and pardon bringes.
>   Amen.

Or:

> Whoso for this brief cesoun
> Barters hevens blysse
> Hath betrayed his resoun
> His house the rainbow is;
> Give me to build on the firme grounde
> And Thy eternal joys to sound.
>   Amen.

Or, remarkable for its unmistakable coloration by the Protestant doctrine of predestination:

> Through sin no let has been,
> Save when some goode be seen.
> Mannes good deede shall serve him wel,
> Save that he were born for hell.
> O that I may and mine I love
> Be borne for blessedness above!
>   Amen.

Or sometimes:

> The sun up-hon the divell shines
> And parts as pure away
> Keep me safe in the vale of earthe,
> Till that I pay the debt of deathe.
>   Amen.

And lastly:

> Mark, whoso for other pray
> Himself he saves that waye.
> Echo prayes for all gainst harms,
> May God hold him too in His armes.
>
>   Amen.

This verse I myself heard him say, and was greatly touched; I think he did not know I was there.

Outside the door Adrian asked: "What do you say to this theological speculation? He prays for all creation, expressly in order that he himself may be included. Should a pious child know that he serves himself in that he prays for others? Surely the unselfishness is gone so soon as one sees that it is of use."

"You are right that far," I replied. "But he turns the thing into unselfishness so soon as he may not pray only for himself but does so for us all."

"Yes, for us all," Adrian said softly.

"Anyhow we are talking as though he had thought these things up himself. Have you ever asked him where he learned them, from his father or from whom?"

The answer was: "Oh, no, I would rather let the question rest and assume that he would not know."

It seemed that the Schweigestills felt the same. So far as I know they never asked the child the source of his little evening prayers. From them I heard the ones which I had not listened to from outside. I had them recited to me at a time when Nepomuk Schneidewein was no longer with us.

CHAPTER XLV

HE was taken from us, that strangely seraphic little being was
taken from this earth — oh, my God, why should I seek soft
words for the harshest, most incomprehensible cruelty I have
ever witnessed? Even yet it tempts my heart to bitter murmur,
yes, to rebellion. He was set on with frightful, savage fury and
in a few days snatched away by an illness of which there had been
for a long time no case in the vicinity. Our good Dr. Kürbis was
greatly surprised by the violence of its recurrence; but he told us
that children convalescing from measles or whooping-cough were
susceptible to it.

The whole thing lasted scarcely two weeks, including the earliest signs that all was not quite well with the child; from those beginnings no one — I believe no one at all — even dreamed of the
horror to come. It was the middle of August; the harvest was in
full swing, with a considerable increase in the number of hands.
For two months Nepomuk had been the joy of the house. Now
a slight cold glazed the sweet clarity of his eyes; it was surely
only this annoying affection that took away his appetite, made
him fretful, and increased the drowsiness to which he had been
subject ever since we knew him. He said " 'Nuff" to all that was
offered him: food, play, picture-books, fairy-tales. " 'Nuff," he
said, his little face painfully drawn, and turned away. Soon there
appeared an intolerance of light and sound, more disquieting still.
He seemed to feel that the wagons driving into the yard made
more noise than usual, that voices were louder. "Speak more
low," he begged, whispering to show them how. Not even the
delicate tinkling of the music-box would he hear; at once uttered
his tortured " 'Nuff, 'nuff!" stopped the works himself, and then
wept bitterly. He fled from the high-summer sunshine of yard
and garden, went indoors and crouched there, rubbing his eyes.
It was hard to watch him seeking comfort, going from one to another of his loving ones, putting his arms about their necks, only
after a little to turn disconsolate away. Thus he clung to Mother
Schweigestill, to Clementine, to Waltpurgis. The same impulse

brought him to his uncle, to press himself against his breast, to look up at him, even to smile faintly and listen to his gentle words. But then the little head would droop lower and lower; he would murmur: "Night!" slip to his feet, and go away with unsteady tread.

The doctor came. He gave him some drops for his nose and prescribed a tonic, but did not conceal his fear that a more serious illness was setting in. In the Abbot's room he expressed this concern to his patient of many years.

"You think so?" asked Adrian, going pale.

"The thing doesn't look quite right to me," the doctor said.

"Right?"

The words had been repeated in such a startled, almost startling tone that Kürbis asked himself if he had not gone too far.

"Well, in the sense I mentioned," he answered. "You yourself might look better too, sir. Your heart is set on the little lad?"

"Oh, yes," was the reply. "It is a responsibility, doctor. The child was given in our charge here in the country to strengthen his health. . . ."

"The clinical picture, in so far as one can speak of such a thing," responded the doctor, "gives no warrant for a discouraging diagnosis. I will come again tomorrow."

He did so, and now he could diagnose the case with all too much certainty. Nepomuk had had an abrupt vomiting-spell, like the outbreak of an illness; head pains set in accompanied by moderate fever and within a few hours had obviously become all but intolerable. When the doctor came the child had already been put to bed and was holding his head with both hands, uttering shrieks which went on as long as his breath held out, a martyrdom to all who heard them, and they could be heard throughout the house. At intervals he put out his little hands to those about him, crying: "Echo's head, Echo's head!" Then another violent spell of vomiting would fetch him upright, to sink back again in convulsions.

Kürbis tested the child's eyes, the pupils of which were tiny and showed a tendency to squint. The pulse raced. Muscular contractions developed, and an incipient rigidity of the neck. It was cerebro-spinal meningitis, inflammation of the meninges. The good man pronounced the name with a deprecating movement of the head shoulderwards, probably in the hope that they might not know the almost complete powerlessness of medical science in the face of this fatal onslaught. A hint lay in his suggestion that they might telegraph and let the parents know. The presence of the mother, at least, would probably have a soothing effect on the little patient. He also asked for a consultation with a physician from the capital, as he wanted to share the responsibility of a case which was unfortunately not at all light. "I am a simple man," he said. "This is a case for a higher authority." A gloomy irony lay, I believe, in his words. In any case, he was quite competent to undertake the spinal puncture necessary to confirm the diagnosis as well as to afford the only possible relief from the pains. Frau Schweigestill, pale but capable, as ever loyal to the "human," held the moaning child in bed, chin and knees almost touching, and between the separated vertebræ Kürbis drove his needle into the spinal canal and drew out the fluid drop by drop. Almost at once the frantic headache yielded. If it returned, the doctor said — he knew that after a couple of hours it must return, for the relief from pressure given by drawing off the fluid from the brain cavity lasted only that long — then they must use, besides the indispensable ice-bag, the chloral which he prescribed and ordered from the county town.

After the puncture Nepomuk fell into a sleep of exhaustion. But then he was roused by fresh vomiting, skull-splitting headache, and convulsions that shook his small frame. The heart-rending moans and yelling screams began again: the typical "hydrocephalic shriek," against which only the physician, precisely because he knows it is typical, is tolerably armed. The typical leaves one calm, only what we think of as individual puts us beside ourselves. Science is calm. Science did not, however, prevent our good country doctor from going over quite soon from the bromide and chloral preparations to morphine, which was more efficacious. He may have decided as much for the sake of the family — I have in mind particularly one of its members — as out of pity for the martyred child. Only once in twenty-four hours might the fluid be drawn off, and for only two of these did the relief last. Twenty-two hours of shrieking, writhing torture, of a child, of this child, who folded his twitching little hands and stammered: "Echo will be good, Echo will be good!" Let me add that for those who saw him a minor symptom was perhaps the most dreadful of all: the squinting of the heaven's-blue eyes, caused by the paralysis of the eye-muscles accompanying the rigidity of the neck. It changed the sweet face almost beyond recognition, horribly; and in combination with the gnashing of the teeth, which presently began, gave it a look as though he were possessed.

Next afternoon, fetched from Waldshut by Gereon Schweigestill, the consulting authority arrived from Munich. He was a Professor von Rothenbuch; Kürbis had suggested him among others and Adrian had chosen him on account of his great reputation. He was a tall man, with one eye half-closed as though from constant examination. He had a social presence and had been ennobled personally by the late King; was much sought after and high-priced. He vetoed the morphine, as its effect might obscure the appearance of a coma, "which has not yet supervened." He permitted only codeine. Obviously he was primarily concerned with the typical progress of the case and a clear clinical picture in all its stages. After the examination he confirmed the dispositions of his obsequious rural colleague: avoidance of light, head kept cool and bedded high, very gentle handling, alcohol rubs, concentrated nourishment; it would probably become necessary to give it by a tube through the nose. Very likely because he was not in the home of the child's parents his sympathy was candid and unequivocal. A clouding of the consciousness, legitimate and not prematurely induced by morphine, would not be long in appearing, and would grow progressively worse. The child would suffer less, and finally not at all. Even more unsightly symptoms, therefore, must not be taken too seriously. After he had had the goodness to carry out the second puncture with his own hands, he took a dignified leave and did not return.

For my part, I was kept posted daily on the dreadful situation by Mother Schweigestill on the telephone. Only on Saturday, the fourth day after the onslaught of the disease, could I get to Pfeiffering. By then, after furious spasms which seemed to stretch the little body on the rack and made his eyeballs roll up in his head, the coma had set in. The shrieking stopped; there remained only the gnashing of the teeth. Frau Schweigestill, worn with lack of sleep, her eyes swollen with weeping, met me at the door and urged me to go at once to Adrian. There was time enough to see the poor baby, whose parents had been with him since the night before. I would see soon enough. But the Herr Doctor, he needed me to talk to him, just between ourselves things weren't right with him, sometimes it seemed to her he was talking crazy like.

In distress of mind I went to him. He sat at his desk and as I entered glanced up, almost with contempt. Shockingly pale, he had the same red eyes as the rest of the household; with his mouth firmly shut, he kept mechanically moving his tongue to and fro inside his lower lip.

"Is that you, good soul?" he said as I went to him and laid my hand on his shoulder. "What are you doing here? This is no place for you. Cross yourself, like this, forehead to shoulders, the way you learned as a child. That will keep you safe."

And when I spoke a few words of consolation and hope:

"Spare yourself," he roughly interrupted; "spare yourself the humanistic quibbles. He is taking him. Just let him make it short. Perhaps he can't make it any shorter, with his miserable means."

And he sprang up, stood against the wall, and leaned the back of his head against the panelling.

"Take him, monster!" he cried, in a voice that pierced me to the marrow. "Take him, hell-hound, but make all the haste you can, if you won't tolerate any of this either, cur, swine, viper! I thought," he said in a low, confidential voice, and turned to me suddenly, taking a step forwards and looking at me with a lost, forlorn gaze I shall never forget, "I thought he would concede this much, after all, maybe just this; but no, where should he learn mercy, who is without any bowels of compassion? Probably it was just exactly this he had to crush in his beastly fury. Take him, scum, filth, excrement!" he shrieked, and stepped away from me again as though back to the Cross. "Take his body, you have power over that. But you'll have to put up with leaving me his soul, his sweet and precious soul, that is where you lose out and make yourself a laughing-stock — and for that I will laugh you to scorn, æons on end. Let there be eternities rolled between my place and his, yet I shall know that he is there whence you were thrown out, orts and draff that you are! The thought will be moisture on my tongue and a hosannah to mock you in my foulest cursings!"

He covered his face with his hands, turned round and leaned his forehead against the wall.

What could I say? Or do? How could I meet such words? "But my dear fellow, for heaven's sake be calm! You are beside yourself, your sufferings make you imagine preposterous things." That is the sort of thing one says, and out of reverence for the psyche, especially in the case of such a man, one does not think of the physical remedies, sedatives, bromide, and so on, even though we had them in the house.

To my imploring efforts at consolation he only responded:

"Save yourself the trouble, just cross yourself, that's what's going on up there. Do it not only for yourself, but at the same time for me and my guilty soul. What a sin, what a crime" — he was sitting now at his desk, his temples between his fists — "that we

let him come, that I let him be near me, that I feasted my eyes on
him! You must know that children are tender stuff, they are receptive for poisonous influences — "

Now it was I, in very truth, who cried out and indignantly
repudiated his words.

"Adrian, no!" I cried. "What are you doing, torturing yourself
with absurd accusations, blaming yourself for a blind dispensation
that could snatch away the dear child, perhaps too dear for this
earth, wherever he chanced to be! It may rend our hearts but
must not rob us of our reason. You have done nothing but loving-
kindness to him. . . ."

He only waved me aside. I sat perhaps an hour with him, speaking softly now and then, and he muttered answers that I scarcely
understood. Then I said I would visit the patient.

"Yes, do that," he retorted and added, hardly:

"But don't talk the way you did at first: 'Well, my lad, that's a
good boy,' and so on. In the first place he won't hear you, and
then it would most likely offend your humanistic taste."

I was leaving when he stopped me, calling my name, my last
name, Zeitblom, which sounded hard too. And when I turned
round:

"I find," he said, "that it is not to be."

"What, Adrian, is not to be?"

"The good and noble," he answered me; "what we call the human, although it is good, and noble. What human beings have
fought for and stormed citadels, what the ecstatics exultantly announced — that is not to be. It will be taken back. I will take
it back."

"I don't quite understand, dear man. What will you take back?"

"The Ninth Symphony," he replied. And then no more came,
though I waited for it.

Dazed and grievously afflicted I went up into the fatal room.
The atmosphere of the sick-chamber reigned there, clean and
bare, heavy with the odours of drugs, though the windows were
wide open. But the blinds were almost shut, only a crack showed.
Several people were standing round Nepomuk's bed. I put out my
hand to them, my eyes already on the dying child. He lay on his
side, his legs drawn up, elbows and knees together. The cheeks
were very flushed; he drew a breath, then one waited long for
the next. His eyes were not quite closed, but between the lashes
no iris showed, only blackness, for the pupils had grown unevenly
larger; they had almost swallowed up the colour. Yet it was good
when one saw the mirroring black. For sometimes it was white in

the crack, and then the little arms pressed closer to the sides, the grinding spasm, cruel to see but perhaps no longer felt, twisted the little limbs.

The mother was sobbing. I had squeezed her hand, I did so again. Yes, she was there, Ursel, the brown-eyed daughter of the Buchel farm, Adrian's sister; and the woebegone face of the now thirty-nine-year-old woman moved me as I saw, stronger than ever, the paternal, the old-German features of Jonathan Leverkühn. With her was her husband, to whom the wire had been sent and he had fetched her from Suderode: Johannes Schneidewein, a tall, fine-looking, simple man with a blond beard, with Nepomuk's blue eyes, with the honest and sober speech that Ursula had early caught from him, whose rhythm we had known in the timbre of Echo, our sprite.

With the others in the room, aside from Frau Schweigestill, who was moving to and fro, was the woolly-haired Kunigunde Rosenstiel. On a visit she had been allowed to make she had learned to know the little lad and treasured him passionately in her melancholy heart. She had at that time, on her typewriter with the ampersand and on the letter-paper of her inelegant firm, written a long letter to Adrian in model German describing her feelings. Now, driving Meta Nackedey from the field, she had succeeded in relieving the Schweigestills and then Ursel Schneidewein in the care of the child; changed his ice-bag, rubbed him with spirit, tried to give him food and medicine, and at night unwillingly and seldom yielded to another her place by his bed.

The Schweigestills, Adrian, his family, Kunigunde, and I ate an almost silent meal in the Nike-saal together, one of the women rising very often to look to the patient. On Sunday morning I should have, hard as it was, to leave Pfeiffering. I still had a whole stack of Latin unseens to correct for Monday. I parted from Adrian with soothing hopes on my lips, and the way he left me was better than the way he had received me the day before. With a sort of smile he spoke, in English, the words:

" 'Then to the elements. Be free, and fare thou well!' "

He turned quickly away.

Nepomuk Schneidewein, Echo, the child, Adrian's last love, fell on sleep twelve hours later. His parents took the little coffin with them, back to their home.

CHAPTER XLVI

For nearly four weeks now I have entered nothing in these records; deterred in the first place by a sort of mental exhaustion caused by reliving the scenes described in the last chapter, and secondly by the events of today, now rushing headlong on each other's heels. Foreseen as a logical sequence, and in a way longed for, they now after all excite an incredulous horror. Our unhappy nation, undermined by fear and dread, incapable of understanding, in dazed fatalism lets them pass over its head, and my spirit too, worn with old sorrow, weary with old wrong, is helplessly exposed to them as well.

Since the end of March — it is now the 25th of April in this year of destiny 1945 — our resistance in the west has been visibly disintegrating. The papers, already half-unmuzzled, register the truth. Rumour, fed by enemy announcements on the radio and stories told by fugitives, knows no censorship, but carries the individual details of swiftly spreading catastrophe about the land, into regions not yet swallowed, not yet liberated by it, and even hither into my retreat. No hold any more: everybody surrenders, everybody runs away. Our shattered, battered cities fall like ripe plums. Darmstadt, Würzburg, Frankfurt are gone; Mannheim and Cassell, even Münster and Leipzig are in foreign hands. One day the English reached Bremen, the Americans were at the gates of Upper Franconia; Nuremberg, city of the national celebrations so uplifting to unenlightened hearts, Nuremberg surrendered. The great ones of the regime, who wallowed in power, riches, and wrong, now rage and kill themselves: justice is done.

Russian corps after taking Königsberg and Vienna were free to force the Oder; they moved a million strong against the capital, lying in its rubble, already abandoned by all the government officials. Russian troops carried out with their heavy artillery the sentence long since inflicted from the air. They are now approaching the centre of Berlin. Last year the horrible man escaped with his life — by now surely only an insanely flaring and flickering existence — from the plot of desperate patriots trying to salvage the future of Germany and the last remnant of her material goods. Now he has commanded his soldiery to drown in a sea of blood the attack on Berlin and to shoot every officer who speaks of surrender. And the order has been in considerable measure obeyed. At the same time strange radio messages in German, no longer quite sane, rove the upper air; some of them commend the population to the benevolence of the conquerors, even including the secret police, who they say have been much slandered. Others are transmitted by a "freedom movement" christened Werwolf: a band of raving-mad lads who hide in the woods and break out nightly; they have already deserved well of the Fatherland by many a gallant murder of the invaders. The fantastic mingles with the horrible: up to the very end the crudely legendary, the grim deposit of saga in the soul of the nation, is invoked, with all its familiar echoes and reverberations.

A transatlantic general has forced the population of Weimar to file past the crematories of the neighbouring concentration-camp. He declared that these citizens — who had gone in apparent righteousness about their daily concerns and sought to know nothing, although the wind brought to their noses the stench of burning human flesh — he declared that they too were guilty of the abominations on which he forced them now to turn their eyes. Was that unjust? Let them look, I look with them. In spirit I let myself be shouldered in their dazed or shuddering ranks. Germany had become a thick-walled underground torture-chamber, converted into one by a profligate dictatorship vowed to nihilism from its beginnings on. Now the torture-chamber has been broken open, open lies our shame before the eyes of the world. Foreign commissions inspect those incredible photographs everywhere displayed, and tell their countrymen that what they have seen surpasses in horribleness anything the human imagination can conceive. I say our shame. For is it mere hypochondria to say to oneself that everything German, even the German mind and spirit, German thought, the German Word, is involved in this scandalous exposure and made subject to the same distrust? Is the sense of guilt quite morbid which makes one ask oneself the question how Germany, whatever her future manifestations, can ever presume to open her mouth in human affairs?

Let us call them the sinister possibilities of human nature in general that here come to light. German human beings, tens of thousands, hundreds of thousands of them it is, who have perpetrated what humanity shudders at; and all that is German now stands forth as an abomination and a warning. How will it be to belong to a land whose history witnesses this hideous default; a land self-maddened, psychologically burnt-out, which quite understandably despairs of governing itself and thinks it for the best that it become a colony of foreign powers; a nation that will have to live shut in like the ghetto Jews, because a frightfully swollen hatred round all its borders will not permit it to emerge; a nation that cannot show its face outside?

Curses, curses on the corrupters of an originally decent species of human being, law-abiding, only too docile, only all too willingly living on theory, who thus went to school to Evil! How good it is to curse — or rather how good it would be, if only the cursing came from a free and unobstructed heart! We are present at the last gasp of a blood state which, as Luther put it, "took on its shoulders" immeasurable crimes; which roared and bellowed to the ravished and reeling masses proclamations cancelling all human rights; which set up its gaudy banners for youth to march under, and they marched, with proud tread and flashing eyes, in pure and ardent faith. But a patriotism which would assert that a blood state like that was so forced, so foreign to our national character that it could not take root among us: such a patriotism would seem to me more high-minded than realistic. For was this government, in word and deed, anything but the distorted, vulgarized, besmirched symbol of a state of mind, a notion of world affairs which we must recognize as both genuine and characteristic? Indeed, must not the Christian and humane man shrink as he sees it stamped upon the features of our greatest, the mightiest embodiments of our essential Germanness? I ask — and should I not? Ah, it is no longer in question that this beaten people now standing wild-eyed in face of the void stand there just because they have failed, failed horribly in their last and uttermost attempt to find the political form suited to their particular needs.

*

*   *

Yet how strangely the times, these very times in which I write, are linked with the period that forms the frame of this biography! For the last years of my hero's rational existence, the two years 1929 and 1930, after the shipwreck of his marriage plans, the loss of his friend, the snatching away of the marvellous child — those years were part and parcel of the mounting and spreading harms which then overwhelmed the country and now are being blotted out in blood and flames.

And for Adrian Leverkühn they were years of immense and highly stimulated, one is tempted to say monstrous creative activity, which made even the sympathetic onlooker giddy. One could not help feeling that it was by way of being a compensation and atonement for the loss of human happiness and mutual love which had befallen him. I spoke of two years, but that is incorrect, since only a part of each, the second half of one and some months of the other, sufficed to produce the whole composition, his last and in a somewhat historical sense his utmost work: the symphonic cantata *The Lamentation of Dr. Faustus*, the plan of which, as I have already explained, goes back to before the advent of little Nepomuk Schneidewein in Pfeiffering. To it I will now devote my poor powers.

But first I must not fail to shed some light upon the personal condition of its creator, a man now forty-four years old; to speak of his appearance and way of life as they then seemed to my always anxious and observant eye. What I should first set down is the fact — I have mentioned it earlier in these pages — that his looks, which, so long as he was smooth-shaven, had shown such a likeness to his mother, had of late considerably altered. The change was due to a dark growth of beard, mixed with grey, a sort of chin-beard, with the addition of a drooping little strip of moustache. Though much heavier on the chin, it did not leave the cheeks free; but even on the chin it was heavier at the sides than in the middle, and thus was not like an imperial. One bore with the unfamiliarity resulting from the partial covering of the features, because it was this beard — and perhaps a growing tendency he had to carry his head on one side — that gave his countenance something spiritualized and suffering, even Christlike. I could not help loving this expression, and felt that my sympathy with it was justified in that obviously it did not indicate weakness but went with an almost excessive energy and an unexceptionable state of health, which my friend could not enough celebrate. He dwelt on it in the somewhat retarded, sometimes hesitant, sometimes slightly monotonous manner of speech which I had lately noted in him and which I liked to explain as a sign of productive absorption, of self-control and poise in the midst of a distracting whirl of ideas. The irksome physical conditions that had victimized him so long, the catarrh of the stomach, the throat trouble, the tormenting attacks of headache were all gone, his day was his own, and freedom to work in it. He himself declared his health to be perfect, magnificent; and one could read in his eyes the creative energy with which he daily arose to his task. It filled me

with pride, yet again it made me fearful of relapses. His eyes, in
his former state half overhung by the drooping lids, were now
almost exaggeratedly wide open, and above the iris one saw a
strip of white. That might perhaps alarm me, the more because
there was about the widened gaze a fixity — or shall I say it was
a stare? — the nature of which I puzzled over until it occurred to
me that it depended on the unvarying size of the not quite round,
rather irregularly lengthened pupils, as though they remained unaffected by any alteration in the lighting.

I am talking about a rigidness to some extent internal, one
needed to be a very much concerned observer to perceive it.
There was another, more obvious and striking manifestation of
an opposite kind, noticed by our dear Jeanette Scheurl, who mentioned it to me after a visit. She need not have, of course. This
was the recent habit, for instance when he was thinking, of moving his eyeballs rapidly to and fro rather far, from one side to the
other, rolling them, as we say. Some people might be startled by
it. If I myself found it easy — and it seems to me I did find it so
— to lay such habits, eccentric enough if you like, to the enormous strain he was under; yet privately I was relieved to think
that except for myself scarcely anyone saw him, and that precisely because I feared outsiders might be alarmed. In practice,
any sort of social intercourse with the city was now excluded. Invitations were declined by the faithful landlady on the telephone,
or even remained unanswered. Short trips on errands were given
up, the last one having been made to buy toys for the dead child.
Clothes that had been worn to evening parties and on public occasions hung unused in his wardrobe, his dress was the simplest
everyday. Not a dressing-gown, for he never used one, even in
the mornings, only when he got up in the night and sat an hour
or two in his chair. But a loose coat like a pea-jacket, closed to
the throat so that he needed no tie, worn with some odd pair of
checked trousers, loose and unpressed: such was at this time his
habitual garb. He wore it out of doors too, for the regular, indispensable long walks he took to get the air into his lungs. One
might have spoken of an unkemptness in his appearance if his
natural distinction had not, on intellectual grounds, belied the
statement.

For whom, indeed, should he have taken pains? He saw Jeanette
Scheurl, with whom he went through certain seventeenth-century
music she had brought with her (I remember a chaconne of Ja-
copo Melani which literally anticipates a passage in *Tristan*).
From time to time he saw Rüdiger Schildknapp, the like-eyed,

with whom he laughed. I could not refrain from thinking deso-
lately that only the like eyes were left, the black and the blue
ones having disappeared. . . . He saw, lastly, me, when I went
to spend the week-end. And that was all. Moreover, there were
few hours in which he could wish for society, for not excepting
Sunday (which he had never "kept holy") he worked eight hours
a day, with an intermission for an afternoon rest in a darkened
room. So that on my visits to Pfeiffering I was left very much to
myself. As though I regretted it! I was near him, near the source
of the beloved work, beloved through all my sufferings and shud-
derings. For a decade and a half now it has been a buried, forbidden treasure, whose resurrection may come about through the destructive liberation we now endure. There were years in which
we children of the dungeon dreamed of a hymn of exultation, a
Fidelio, a Ninth Symphony, to celebrate the dawn of a freed Germany — freed by herself. Now only this can avail us, only this
will be sung from our very souls: the Lamentation of the son of
hell, the lament of men and God, issuing from the subjective, but
always broadening out and as it were laying hold on the Cosmos; the most frightful lament ever set up on this earth.

Woe, woe! A De Profundis, which in my zeal and love I am
bound to call matchless. Yet has it not — from the point of view
of creative art and musical history as well as that of individual
fulfilment — a jubilant, a highly triumphant bearing upon this
awe-inspiring faculty of compensation and redress? Does it not
mean the "break-through," of which we so often talked when we
were considering the destiny of art, its state and hour? We spoke
of it as a problem, a paradoxical possibility: the recovery, I would
not say the reconstitution — and yet for the sake of exactness I
will say it — of expressivism, of the highest and profoundest claim
of feeling to a stage of intellectuality and formal strictness, which
must be arrived at in order that we may experience a reversal of
this calculated coldness and its conversion into a voice expressive
of the soul and a warmth and sincerity of creature confidence. Is
that not the "break-through"?

I put in the form of a question what is nothing more than the
description of a condition that has its explanation in the thing itself as well as in its artistic and formal aspect. The Lamentation,
that is — and what we have here is an abiding, inexhaustibly accentuated lament of the most painfully Ecce-homo kind — the
Lamentation is expression itself; one may state boldly that all expressivism is really lament; just as music, so soon as it is conscious
of itself as expression at the beginning of its modern history, be-

comes lament and "*lasciatemi morire*," the lament of Ariadne, to the softly echoing plaintive song of nymphs. It does not lack significance that the *Faust* cantata is stylistically so strongly and unmistakably linked with the seventeenth century and Monteverdi, whose music — again not without significance — favoured the echo-effect, sometimes to the point of being a mannerism. The echo, the giving back of the human voice as nature-sound, and the revelation of it *as* nature-sound, is essentially a lament: Nature's melancholy "Alas!" in view of man, her effort to utter his solitary state. Conversely, the lament of the nymphs on its side is related to the echo. In Leverkühn's last and loftiest creation, echo, favourite device of the baroque, is employed with unspeakably mournful effect.

A lament of such gigantic dimensions is, I say, of necessity an expressive work, a work of expression, and therewith it is a work of liberation; just as the earlier music, to which it links itself across the centuries, sought to be a liberation of expression. Only that the dialectic process — by which, at the stage of development that this work occupies, is consummated by the change from the strictest constraint to the free language of feeling, the birth of freedom from bondage — the dialectic process appears as endlessly more complicated in its logic, endlessly more miraculous and amazing than at the time of the madrigalists. Here I will remind the reader of a conversation I had with Adrian on a long-ago day, the day of his sister's wedding at Buchel, as we walked round the Cow Trough. He developed for me — under pressure of a headache — his idea of the "strict style," derived from the way in which, as in the lied "*O lieb Mädel, wie schlecht bist du,*" melody and harmony are determined by the permutation of a fundamental five-note motif, the symbolic letters h, e, a, e, e-flat. He showed me the "magic square" of a style of technique which yet developed the extreme of variety out of identical material and in which there is no longer anything unthematic, anything that could not prove itself to be a variation of an ever constant element. This style, this technique, he said, admitted no note, not one, which did not fulfil its thematic function in the whole structure — there was no longer any free note.

Now, have I not, when I attempted to give some idea of Leverkühn's apocalyptic oratorio, referred to the substantial identity of the most blest with the most accurst, the inner unity of the chorus of child angels and the hellish laughter of the damned? There, to the mystic horror of one sensitive to it, is realized a Utopia in form, of terrifying ingenuity, which in the *Faust* cantata becomes universal, seizes upon the whole work and, if I may so put it, causes it to be completely swallowed up by thematic thinking. This giant "lamento" (it lasts an hour and a quarter) is very certainly non-dynamic, lacking in development, without drama, in the same way that concentric rings made by a stone thrown into water spread ever farther, without drama and always the same. A mammoth variation-piece of lamentation — as such negatively related to the finale of the Ninth Symphony with its variations of exultation — broadens out in circles, each of which draws the other resistlessly after it: movements, large-scale variations, which correspond to the textual units of chapters of a book and in themselves are nothing else than series of variations. But all of them go back for the theme to a highly plastic fundamental figure of notes, which is inspired by a certain passage of the text.

We recall that in the old chap-book which tells the story of the arch-magician's life and death, sections of which Leverkühn with a few bold adaptations put together as the basis of his movements, Dr. Faustus, as his hour-glass is running out, invites his friends and familiars, "magistros, Baccalaureos and other students," to the village of Rimlich near Wittenberg, entertains them there hospitably all day long, at night takes one more drink of "Johann's wine" with them, and then in an address both dignified and penitential announces and gives them to know his fate and that its fulfilment is now at hand. In this "Oratio Fausti ad Studiosos" he asks them, when they find him strangled and dead, charitably to convey his body into the earth; for he dies, he says, as a bad and as a good Christian: a good one by the power of his repentance, and because in his heart he always hopes for mercy on his soul; a bad one in so far as he knows that he is now facing a horrible end and the Devil will and must have his body. These words: "For I die as a good and as a bad Christian," form the general theme of the variations. If you count the syllables, there are twelve, and all twelve notes of the chromatic scale are set to it, with all the thinkable intervals therein. It already occurs and makes itself felt long before it is reintroduced with the text, in its place as a choral group — there is no true solo in the Faustus — rising up until the middle, then descending, in the spirit and inflexion of the Monteverdi Lamento. It is the basis of all the music — or rather, it lies almost as key behind everything and is responsible for the identity of the most varied forms — that identity which exists between the crystalline angelic choir and the hellish yelling in the Apocalypse and which has now become all-embracing: a formal treatment strict to the last degree, which no longer knows anything unthematic, in which the order of the basic material becomes total, and within which the idea of a fugue rather declines into an absurdity, just because there is no longer any free note. But it serves now a higher purpose; for — oh, marvel, oh, deep diabolic jest! — just by virtue of the absoluteness of the form the music is, as language, freed. In a more concrete and physical sense the work is done, indeed, before the composition even begins, and this can now go on wholly unrestrained; that is, it can give itself over to expression, which, thus lifted beyond the structural element, or within its uttermost severity, is won back again. The creator of *"Fausti Wehe-klage"* can, in the previously organized material, unhampered, untroubled by the already given structure, yield himself to subjectivity; and so this, his technically most rigid work, a work of extreme calculation, is at the same time purely expressive. The return to Monteverdi and the style of his time is what I meant by "the reconstruction of expressiveness," of expressiveness in its first and original manifestation, expressiveness as lament.

Here marshalled and employed are all the means of expression of that emancipatory epoch of which I have already mentioned the echo-effect — especially suitable for a work wholly based on the variation-principle, and thus to some extent static, in which every transformation is itself already the echo of the previous one. It does not lack echo-like continuations, the further repetition of the closing phrase of a theme in higher pitch. There are faint reminiscences of Orphic lamentation, which make Orpheus and Faust brothers as invokers of the world of shades: as in that episode where Faust summons Helen, who is to bear him a son. There are a hundred references to the tone and spirit of the madrigal, and a whole movement, the exhortation to his friends at the meal on the last night, is written in strict madrigal form.

But precisely in the sense of résumé there are offered musical moments of the greatest conceivable possibility of expression: not as mechanical imitation or regression, of course; no, it is like a perfectly conscious control over all the "characters" of expressiveness which have ever been precipitated in the history of music, and which here, in a sort of alchemical process of distillation, have been refined to fundamental types of emotional significance, and crystallized. Here is the deep-drawn sigh at such words as: "Ah, Faustus, thou senceles, wilfull, desperate herte! Ah, ah, reason, mischief, presumption, and free will . . ." the recurrent suspensions, even though only as a rhythmical device, the chromatic melody, the awful collective silence before the beginning

of a phrase, repetitions such as in that *"Lasciatemi,"* the linger-
ing-out of syllables, falling intervals, dying-away declamations —
against immense contrast like the entry of the tragic chorus, *a
capella* and in full force, after Faust's descent into hell, an orchestral piece in the form of grand ballet-music and galop of fantastic rhythmic variety — an overwhelming outburst of lamentation
after an orgy of infernal jollity.

This wild conception of the carrying-off of Faust as a dance-
furioso recalls most of all the spirit of the *Apocalypsis cum
figuris;* next to it, perhaps, the horrible — I do not hesitate to say
cynical — choral scherzo, wherein "the evil spirit sets to at the
gloomy Faustus with strange mocking jests and sayings" — that
frightful "then silence, suffer, keepe faith, abstain; of thy ill lot
to none complayne; it is too late, of Gode dispair, thy ill luck
runneth everywhere." But for the rest, Leverkühn's late work has
little in common with that of his thirties. It is stylistically purer,
darker in tone as a whole and without parody, not more conservative in its facing towards the past, but mellower, more melodious;
more counterpoint than polyphony — by which I mean the lesser
parts for all their independence pay more heed to the main part,
which often dies away in long melodic curves, and the kernel of
which, out of which everything develops, is just that twelve-note
idea: "For I die as a bad and as a good Christian." Long ago I
said in these pages that in *Faustus* too that letter symbol, the
Hetæra-Esmeralda figure, first perceived by me, very often gov-
erns melody and harmony. that is to say, everywhere where
there is reference to the bond and the vow, the promise and the
blood pact.

Above all the *Faust* cantata is distinguished from the *Apocalypse* by its great orchestral interludes, which sometimes only
express in general the attitude of the work to its subject, a statement, a "Thus it is." But sometimes, like the awful ballet-music
of the descent to hell, they also stand for parts of the plot. The
orchestration of this horror-dance consists of nothing but wind
instruments and a continuous accompaniment, which, composed
of two harps, harpsichord, piano, celeste, glockenspiel, and percussion, pervades the work throughout as a sort of "continuo,"
appearing again and again. Some choral pieces are accompanied
only by it. To others, wind instruments, to still others strings are
added; others again have a full orchestral accompaniment. Purely
orchestral is the end: a symphonic adagio, into which the chorus
of lament, opening powerfully after the inferno-galop, gradually
passes over — it is, as it were, the reverse of the "Ode to Joy," the

negative, equally a work of genius, of that transition of the symphony into vocal jubilation. It is the revocation.

My poor, great friend! How often, reading in this achievement of his decline, his posthumous work, which prophetically anticipates so much destruction, have I recalled the distressful words he uttered at the death of the child. It is not to be, goodness, joy, hope, that was not to be, it would be taken back, it must be taken back! "Alas, it is not to be!" How the words stand, almost like a musical direction, above the choral and orchestral movements of "*Dr. Fausti Wehe-klag*"; how they speak in every note and accent of this "Ode to Sorrow"! He wrote it, no doubt, with his eye on Beethoven's Ninth, as its counterpart in a most melancholy sense of the word. But it is not only that it more than once formally negates the symphony, reverses it into the negative; no, for even in the religious it is negative — by which I do not at all mean it denies the religious. A work that deals with the Tempter, with apostasy, with damnation, what else could it be but a religious work? What I mean is a conversion, a proud and bitter change of heart, as I, at least, read it in the "friendly plea" of Dr. Faustus to the companions of his last hour, that they should betake themselves to bed, *sleep in peace*, and let naught trouble them. In the frame of the cantata one can scarcely help recognizing this instruction as the conscious and deliberate reversal of the "Watch with me" of Gethsemane. And again the Johann's wine, the draught drunk by the parting soul with his friends, has an altogether ritual stamp, it is conceived as another Last Supper. But linked with it is an inversion of the temptation idea, in such a way that Faust rejects as temptation the thought of being saved: not only out of formal loyalty to the pact and because it is "too late," but because with his whole soul he despises the positivism of the world for which one would save him, the lie of its godliness. This becomes clearer still and is worked out even more powerfully in the scene with the good old doctor and neighbour who invites Faust to come to see him, in order to make a pious effort to convert him. In the cantata he is clearly drawn in the character of a tempter; and the tempting of Jesus by Satan is unmistakably suggested; as unmistakably also is the "*Apage!*" by the proudly despairing "No!" uttered to false and flabby middle-class piety.

But another and last, truly the last change of mind must be thought on, and that profoundly. At the end of this work of endless lamentation, softly, above the reason and with the speaking unspokenness given to music alone, it touches the feelings. I mean the closing movement of the piece, where the choir loses itself and which sounds like the lament of God over the lost state of His world, like the Creator's rueful "I have not willed it." Here, towards the end, I find that the uttermost accents of mourning are reached, the final despair achieves a voice, and — I will not say it, it would mean to disparage the uncompromising character of the work, its irremediable anguish to say that it affords, down to its very last note, any other consolation than what lies in voicing it, in simply giving sorrow words; in the fact, that is, that a voice is given the creature for its woe. No, this dark tone-poem permits up to the very end no consolation, appeasement, transfiguration. But take our artist paradox: grant that expressiveness — expression as lament — is the issue of the whole construction: then may we not parallel with it another, a religious one, and say too (though only in the lowest whisper) that out of the sheerly irremediable hope might germinate? It would be but a hope beyond hopelessness, the transcendence of despair — not betrayal to her, but the miracle that passes belief. For listen to the end, listen with me: one group of instruments after another retires, and what remains, as the work fades on the air, is the high G of a cello, the last word, the last fainting sound, slowly dying in a pianissimo-fermata. Then nothing more: silence, and night. But that tone which vibrates in the silence, which is no longer there, to which only the spirit hearkens, and which was the voice of mourning, is so no more. It changes its meaning; it abides as a light in the night

CHAPTER XLVII

"Watch with me!" In his cantata Adrian might if he chose transform that cry of human and divine agony into the masculine pride and self-confidence of his Faust's "Sleep quietly and fear nothing!" But the human remains, after all: the instinctive longing, if not for aid, then certainly for the presence of human sympathy, the plea: "Forsake me not! Be about me at my hour!"

And so, when the year 1930 was almost half gone, in the month of May, Leverkühn, by various means, invited a company to Pfeiffering, all his friends and acquaintances, even some whom he knew but little or not at all, a good many people, as many as thirty: partly by written cards, partly through me, and again by some of those invited passing on the invitation to others. Some, again, out of sheer curiosity invited themselves, in other words begged an invitation from me or some other member of the more intimate circle. On his cards Adrian had let it be known that he wished to give to a favourably disposed group of friends some idea of his just finished choral symphonic work, by playing some of its characteristic parts on the piano. He thus aroused the interest of certain people whom he had not thought of inviting, as for instance the dramatic soprano Tanya Orlanda and Herr Kioeielund, who had themselves bidden through the Schlaginhaufens; and the publisher Radbruch and his wife, who attached themselves to Schildknapp. Adrian had also sent a written card to Baptist Spengler, though he certainly must have known that Spengler had not been for a month and more among the living. That intellectual and wit, only in the middle of his forties, had most regrettably succumbed to his heart trouble.

As for me, I admit I was not at ease about the whole affair. Why it is hard to say. This summons to a large number of people most of whom were both inwardly and outwardly very remote from him to come to his most intimate retreat, to the end that they should be initiated into his most intimate work: it was not like Adrian; it made me uneasy, not so much in itself as because it seemed a strange thing for him to do. Though in and for itself it went against me too. On whatever grounds — and I do think I have indicated the grounds — in my heart I liked better to feel he was alone in his refugium, seen only by his humanly minded, respectful, and devoted hosts and by us few, Schild-knapp, our dear Jeanette, the adoring Rosenstiel and Nackedey and myself, than to have the eyes of a mixed gathering, not used to him, focused on him who in his turn was not used to the world. But what was there for me to do but put my hand to the enterprise which he himself had already gone so far in, to carry out his instructions and do my telephoning? There were no re-grets; on the contrary, as I said, only additional requests for an invitation.

Not only did I look with disfavour on the whole affair. I will go further in my confession and set down that I was tempted to remain away myself. Yet against that course was my anxious sense of duty, the feeling that I must, willy-nilly, be present and watch over everything. And so on that Saturday afternoon I betook my-self with Helene to Munich, where we caught the local train for Waldshut-Garmisch. We shared the compartment with Schild-knapp, Jeanette Scheurl, and Kunigunde Rosenstiel. The rest of the guests were scattered in different coaches, with exception of the Schlaginhaufen pair, the Suabian-speaking old rentier and the former von Plausig, who together with their friends from the op-era made the trip by car. They arrived before we did, and the car did good service in Pfeiffering, going to and fro several times between the little station and Hof Schweigestill and conveying the guests by groups, such of them, that is, as did not prefer to walk. The weather held, though a storm rumbled faintly on the horizon. No arrangements had been made to fetch the guests; and Frau Schweigestill, whom Helene and I sought out in the kitchen, explained to us in no small consternation that Adrian had not said a word to prepare her for the invasion. Now in all haste, with Clementine's help, she was making sandwiches for these people, to be served with coffee and sweet cider.

Meanwhile the baying of old Suso or Kaschperl, jumping about and rattling his chain in front of his kennel, seemed never to stop; he became quiet only when no more guests came and the company had gathered in the Nike salon, whither the servants hastily fetched chairs from the family quarters and even from the sleeping-chambers above. In addition to the guests already named, I mention a few more of those present, at random and from mem-ory: the wealthy Bullinger, Leo Zink, the painter, whom neither

Adrian nor I really liked and whom he had presumably invited
along with the departed Spengler; Helmut Institoris, now a sort
of widower; the clearly articulating Dr. Kranich; Frau Binder-
Majorescu, the Knöterichs, the hollow-cheeked jester and academy portrait-painter Nottebohm and his wife, brought by Institoris. Also there were Sixtus Kridwiss and the members of his
discussion group: Dr. Unruhe, the researcher into the strata of
the earth, Professors Vogler and Holzschuher, Daniel zur Höhe,
the poet, in a black buttoned-up frock coat; and to my great annoyance even that quibbling sophist Chaim Breisacher. The professional musical element was represented, in addition to the opera
singers, by Dr. Edschmid, the director of the Zapfenstösser orchestra. To my utter astonishment—and probably not only to
mine—who should have found his way hither but Baron Gleichen-Russwurm, who, so far as I know, was making his first social appearance since that affair with the mouse, and had brought
his wife with him, a full-bosomed, elegant Austrian dame. It appeared that Adrian, eight days beforehand, had sent an invitation
to his estate, and most likely the so fantastically compromised descendant of the poet Schiller had joyfully seized upon the unique
opportunity to reinstate himself in society.

Well, so all these people, some thirty, as I said, at first stood
about expectantly in the salon, greeted each other, exchanged
their feelings of anticipation. Rüdiger Schildknapp, in his everlasting shabby sports clothes, was surrounded by females. Women,
in fact, formed the majority of the guests. I heard the voices of
the dramatic singers rising euphoniously above all the rest; the
clear, asthmatic articulation of Dr. Kranich; Bullinger's swagger-
ing tones, the assurances of Kridwiss that this gathering and what
it promised was "*scho'enorm wichtich*," and zur Höhe's concur-
rence: "*Ja wohl, man kann es sagen*," as he pounded with the balls
of his feet. The Baroness Gleichen moved about, seeking sympathy for the obscure fatality that had befallen her and her husband: "You know about this *ennui* we have had," she was saying
to all and sundry. From the beginning I had observed that many
of the guests did not notice Adrian's presence and spoke as though
we were still waiting for him, simply because they did not recognize him. He was sitting at the heavy oval table in the centre
of the room, where we had once talked with Saul Fitelberg; he
had his back to the light, and was dressed in his everyday clothes.
But several guests asked me who the gentleman was, and when,
at first in some surprise, I set them right they hastened with an
"Oh, really!" of sudden enlightenment to greet their host. How

he must have changed, under my very eyes, for that to be possible! Of course, the beard made a great difference, and I said so to those who could not feel convinced that it was he. Near his chair the woolly-headed Rosenstiel stood erect for a long time, like a sentinel; this was why Meta Nackedey kept as far off as possible, in a remote corner of the room. However, Kunigunde had the decency to leave her post after a while, whereon the other adoring soul occupied it straightway. Open on the rack of the square piano against the wall stood the score of *The Lamentation of Dr. Faustus*.

I kept my eyes on my friend, and while talking with one and another of the guests did not miss the sign which he gave me with his head and eyebrows, to the effect that I should have people take their seats. I did so at once, inviting those nearest me, making signs to those farther off, and even bringing myself to clap my hands for silence, that the announcement might be made that Dr. Leverkühn would now begin his lecture. A man knows by a certain numbness of the features that he has gone pale; the drops of perspiration which may come out on his brow are deathly cold as well. My hands, when I very feebly clapped them, shook as they shake now when I set myself to write down the horrible memory.

The audience obeyed with fair alacrity. Silence and order were quickly established. It happened that at the table with Adrian sat the old Schlaginhaufens, Jeanette Scheurl, Schildknapp, my wife and myself. The other guests were irregularly bestowed at both sides of the room, on various kinds of seats, the sofa, painted wooden chairs, horsehair arm-chairs; some of the men leaned against the walls. Adrian showed no sign of gratifying the general expectation, mine included, by going to the piano. He sat with his hands folded, his head drooped to one side, looking straight in front of him, yet hardly with an outward gaze. He began in the now complete hush to address the assembly, in the slightly monotonous, rather faltering voice I was familiar with; in the sense of a greeting, it seemed to me at first, and at first it really was that. I must bring myself to add that he often mis-spoke — and in my agony I dug my nails into my palms — and in correcting one mistake made another, so that after a while he paid no further attention, but simply passed them over. Anyhow, I need not have been so agonized over his various irregularities of pronunciation, for he used in part, as he had always enjoyed doing in writing, a sort of elder German, with its defects and open sentence-structure, always with something doubtful and unregulated about it;

how long ago is it, indeed, that our tongue outgrew the barbaric and got tolerably regulated as to grammar and spelling!

He began in a low murmur, so that very few understood his opening sentence or made anything out of it. Perhaps they took it as a whim, a rhetorical flourish; it went something like this:

"Esteemed, in especial dear and beloved brethren and sisters."

After that he was silent for a little, as though considering, his cheek resting against one hand that was supported by the elbow on the table. What followed was also taken as a whimsical introductory, intended to be humorous; and although the immobility of his features, the weariness of his looks, his pallor contradicted the idea, yet a responsive laugh ran through the room, a slight sniff, a titter from the ladies.

"Firstly," said he, "I will exhibit to you my thankfulness for the courtesy and the friendship, both undeserved by me, ye have vouchsafed in that ye are come hither into this place, afoot and by wagon, since out of the desolation of this retreat I have written to and called you, likewise had you written to and called by my leal famulus and special friend, which yet knoweth how to put me in remembrance of our school-days from youth up, since we did study together at Halla; but thereof, and of how high-mindedness and abominacyon did in that study already begin, more hereafter in my Sermoni."

Some of them looked over at me and smirked, who out of emotion was unable to smile, feeling that our dear man did not look as though he thought of me with any such particular tenderness. But just the fact that they saw tears in my eyes diverted most of them; and I remember with disgust that at this point Leo Zink loudly blew his big nose, the butt of most of his own jokes, to caricature my perceptible emotion. His performance elicited more titters. Adrian seemed not to notice.

"Before aught else," he went on, "must I pray" (he said "play," corrected it, and then went back again to his mistake) "and beg you not to take it amiss or crosswise that our hound Praestigiar, he is called Suso but of a truth is named Praestigiar, did demean himself so ill and make so hellish a yauling and bauling that you have for my sake undergone stress and strain. It were better we had handed each of you a whistle we have pitched so high that only the hound can hear it and understand from afar off that good and bidden friends are coming, coveting to hear in what manner of life under his guard I have lived these many years."

There was another polite laugh at his words about the whistle, but it sounded strained. He continued, and said:

"Now have I a friendly Christian request to you, that ye may not take and receive in evil part my homily, but that ye would rather construe it all to the best, inasmuch as I verily crave to make unto you, good and sely ones, which if not without sin are yet but ordinarily and tolerably sinful, wherefore I cordially despise yet fervidly envy you, a full confession from one human being to another, for now the houre-glasse standeth before my eyes, the finishing whereof I must carefully expect: when the last grain runs through the narrow neck and he will fetch me, to whom I have given myselfe so dearly with my proper blood that I shall both body and soul everlastingly be his and fall in his hands and his power when the glass is run and the time, which is his ware, be fully expired."

Again here and there somebody tittered or sniffed; but others shook their heads and made disapproving noises as though the words had been in bad taste. Some of the guests put on a look of dark foreboding.

"Know, then," said he, at the table, "ye good and godly folk" (he said "god and goodly"), "with your modest sins and resting in Goodes godness, for I have suppressed it so long in me but will no longer hide it, that already since my twenty-first year I am wedded to Satan and with due knowing of peril, out of well-considered courage, pride, and presumption because I would win glory in this world, I made with him a bond and vow, so that all which during the term of four-and-twenty years I brought forth, and which mankind justly regarded with mistrust, is only with his help come to pass and is divel's work, infused by the angel of death. For I well thought that he that will eat the kernel must crack the nut, and one must today take the divel to favour, because to great enterprise and devises one can use and have none other save him."

A strained and painful stillness now reigned in the room. Only a few listened unperturbed; there were many raised eyebrows, and faces wherein one read: "What is all this and what is it leading up to?" If he had but once smiled or put on a face to explain his words as a mystification got up by the artist, matters would have been half-way made good. But he did not, he sat there in dead earnest. Some of the guests looked inquiringly at me, as if to ask what it all meant and how I would account for it. Perhaps I ought to have intervened and broken up the meeting. But on what pretext? The only explanations were humiliating and extreme; I felt that I must let things take their course, in the hope that he would soon begin to play and give us notes instead of words.

Never had I felt more strongly the advantage that music, which says nothing and everything, has over the unequivocal word; yes, the saving irresponsibility of all art, compared with the bareness and baldness of unmediated revelation. But to interrupt not only went against my sense of reverence, but also my very soul cried out to hear, even though among those who listened with me only very few were worthy. Only hold out and listen, I said in my heart to the others, since after all he did invite you as his fellow human beings!

After a reflective pause my friend went on:

"Believe not, dear brothers and sisters, that for the promission and conclusion of the pact a crosse way in the wood, many circles and impure conjuration were needed, since already St. Thomas teacheth that for falling away there needs not words with which invocation takes place, rather any act be enough, even without express allegiance. For it was but a butterfly, a bright cream-licker, Hetæra Esmeralda, she charmed me with her touch, the milk-witch, and I followed after her into the twilit shadowy foliage that her transparent nakedness loveth, and where I caught her, who in flight is like a wind-blown petal, caught her and caressed with her, defying her warning, so did it befall. For as she charmed me, so she bewitched me and forgave me in love — so I was initiate, and the promise confirmed."

I started, for now came a voice from the audience: it came from Daniel zur Höhe the poet, in his priestly garment, pounding with his feet and hammering out his words:

"It is beautiful. It has beauty. Very good, oh, very good, one may say so!"

Some people hissed. I too turned disapprovingly towards the speaker, though privately I was grateful for what he said. His words were silly enough; but they classified what we were hearing, put it under a soothing and recognized rubric, namely the æsthetic, which, inapplicable as that was and however much it angered me, did make me feel easier. For it seemed to me that a sort of relieved "Ah-h!" went through the audience, and one lady, Radbruch the publisher's wife, was encouraged by zur Höhe's words to say:

"One thinks one is hearing poetry."

Alas, one did not think so for long! This æsthetic interpretation, however conveniently offered, was not tenable. What we heard had nothing at all in common with zur Höhe the poet's tall tomfooleries about obedience, violence, blood, and world-plunder. This was dead sober earnest, a confession, the truth, to

listen to which a man in extreme agony of soul had called together his fellow-men — an act of fantastic good faith, moreover,
for one's fellow-men are not meant or made to face such truth
otherwise than with cold shivers and with the conclusion that,
when it was no longer possible to regard it as poetry, they very
soon unanimously and audibly came to about it.

It did not look as though those interpolations had reached our
host at all. His thoughts, whenever he paused in his address, obviously made him inaccessible to them.

"But only mark," he resumed, "heartily respected loving
friends, that you have to do with a god-forsaken and despairing
man, whose carcass belongeth not in consecrate earth, among
Christians dead in the faith, but on the horse-dung with the
cadavers of dead animals. On the bier, I say to you beforehand,
you will always find it lying on its face, and though you turn it
five times you will ever find it on its face. For long before I dal-
lied with the poison butterfly, my froward soul in high mind and
arrogance was on the way to Satan though my goal stood in
doubt; and from youth up I worked towards him, as you must
know, indeed, that man is made for hell or blessedness, made and
foredestined, and I was born for hell. So did I feed my arrogance
with sugar, studying divinity at Halla Academie, yet not for the
service of God but the other, and my study of divinity was secretly already the beginning of the bond and the disguised move
not Biblewards, but to him, to him the great religiosus. For who
can hold that will away, and 'twas but a short step from the divinity school over to Leipzig and to music, that I solely and entirely then busied myself with figuris, characteribus, formis con-
jurationum, and what other so ever are the names of invocations
and magic.

"So my desperate heart hath trifled all away. I had I suppose a
good toward wit and gifts gratiously given me from above which
I could have used in all honour and modesty, but felt all-too well:
it is the time when uprightly and in pious sober wise, naught of
work is to be wrought and art grown unpossible without the
divel's help and fires of hell under the cauldron. . . '. Yea verily,
dear mates, that art is stuck and grown too heavy and scorneth
itselfe and God's poor man knoweth no longer where to turn in
his sore plight, that is belike the fault in the times. But an one invite the divel as guest, to pass beyond all this and get to the break-
through, he chargeth his soul and taketh the guilt of the time
upon his own shoulders, so that he is damned. For it hath been
said 'Be sober, and watch!' But that is not the affair of some;

rather, instead of shrewdly concerning themselves with what
is needful upon earth that it may be better there, and discreetly
doing it, that among men such order shall be stablished that
again for the beautiful work living soil and true harmony be
prepared, man playeth the truant and breaketh out in hellish
drunkenness; so giveth he his soul thereto and cometh among the
carrion.

"So, courteous and beloved brothers and sisters, have I borne
me, and let nigromantia, carmina, incantatio, veneficium, and what
names so ever be all my aim and striving. And I soon came to the
speech of that one, the make-bate, the losel, in the Italian room,
have held much parley with him, and he had much to tell me of
the quality, fundament, and substance of hell. Sold me time too,
four and twenty years, boundless to the eye, and promised too
great things and much fire under the cauldron, to the end that not
withstanding I should be capable of the work although it were
too hard and my head too shrewd and mocking thereto. Only
certes I should suffer the knives of pain therefor, even in the
time, as the little sea-maid suffered them in her legs, which was
my sister and sweet bride, and named Hyphialta. For he brought
her me to my bed as my bed-sister that I gan woo her and loved
her ever more, whether she came to me with the fishes tail or
with legs. Oftentimes indeed she came with the tail, for the pains
she suffered as with knives in the legs outweighed her lust, and I
had much feeling for the wise wherein her tender body went over
so sweetly into the scaly tail. But higher was my delight even so
in the pure human form and so for my part I had greater lust
when she came to me in legs."

There was a stir in the room. Somebody was leaving, the old
Schlaginhaufen pair it was: they got up from our table and looking neither right nor left, on tiptoe, the husband guiding his
spouse by the elbow passed through the seated groups and out at
the door. Not two minutes went by before the noise and the
throbbing of their engine were heard, starting up in the yard.
They were driving away.

Many of the audience were upset by this, for now they had lost
their means of conveyance to the station. But there was no perceptible inclination among the guests to follow the Schlaginhaufens' example. They all sat spellbound, and when quiet was
restored outside, zur Höhe raised his voice again in his dogmatic
"Beautiful! Ah, indeed yes, it is beautiful."

I too was just on the point of opening my mouth, to beg our
friend to make an end of the introduction and play to us from the

work itself, when he, unaffected by the incident, continued his address:

"Thereupon did Hyphialta get with child and accounted me a little son, to whom with my whole soul I clung, a hallowed little lad, lovelier than is ever born, and as though come hither from afar and of old stamp. But since the child was flesh and blood and it was ordained that I might love no human being, he slew it, merciless, and used thereto mine own proper eyes. For you must know that when a soul is drawn violently to evil, its gaze is venomous and like to a basilisk, and chiefly for children. So this little son full of sweet sayings went from me hence, in Augst-month, though I had thought anon such tenderness might be let. I had well thought before that I, as devil's disciple, might love in flesh and blood what was not female, but he wooed me for my thou in boundless confidence, until I graunted it. Hence I must slay him too, and sent him to his death by force and order. For the magisterulus had marked that I was minded to marry me and was exceeding wroth, sith in the wedded state he saw apostasy from him, and a trick for atonement. So he forced me to use precisely this intent, that I coldly murdered the trusting one and will have confessed it today and here before you all, that I sit before you also as murtherer."

Another group of guests left the room at this point: little Helmut Institoris got up in silent protest, white, his underlip drawn across his teeth. So did his friends the academy portraitist Nottebohm, and his markedly bourgeois high-chested wife, whom we used to call "the maternal bosom." They all went out in silence. But outside they had probably not held their tongues; for shortly afterwards Frau Schweigestill came quietly in, in her apron, with her smooth grey head, and stood near the door, with folded hands. She listened as Adrian said:

"But whatever sinner was I, ye friends, a murtherer, enemy to man, given to divelish concubinage, yet aside from all that I have ever busied myself as a worker and did never arrest" (again he seemed to bethink and correct himself, but went back to "arrest" again), "arrest nor rist, but toiled and moiled and produced hard things, according to the word of the apostle: 'Who seeks hard things, to him it is hard.' For as God doth nothing great through us, without our unction, so neither the other. Only the shame and the intellectual mockery and what in the time was against the work, that he kept aside, the residue I had to do myself, even also after strange infusions. For there was oftentimes heard by me all manner of instrument: an organ or positive, more delectable then harpes, lutes, fiddles, trombones, clarigolds, citerns, waights, anomes, cornets, and hornpipes, four of each, that I had thought myself in heaven had I not known differently. Much of it I wrote down. Often too, certain children were with me in the room, boys and girls who sang to me a motet from sheets of notes, smiled a funny little knowing smile, and exchanged their glances. They were most pretty children. Sometimes their hair was lifted as though from hot air and they smoothed it again with their pretty hands, that were dimpled and had little rubies on them. Out of their nostrils curled sometimes little yellow worms, crawled down to their breasts and disappeared — "

These words were the signal for another group of listeners to leave the room: the scholars Unruhe, Vogler, and Holzschuher, one of whom I saw press the base of his palms to his temples as he went out. But Sixtus Kridwiss, at whose house they held their discussions, kept his place, looking much excited. Even after these had gone, there remained some twenty persons, though many of them had risen and seemed ready to flee. Leo Zink had his eyebrows raised in malicious anticipation, saying "Jessas, na!" just as he did when he was pronouncing on somebody's painting. A little troop of women had gathered round Leverkühn as though to protect him: Kunigunde Rosenstiel, Meta Nackedey, Jeanette Scheurl — these three. Else Schweigestill held aloof.

And we heard:

"So the Evil One hath strengthened his words in good faith through four-and-twenty years and all is finished up till the last, with murther and lechery have I brought it to fullness and perhaps through Grace good can come of what was create in evil, I know not. Mayhap to God it seemeth I sought the hard and laboured might and main, perhaps, perhaps it will be to my credit that I applied myself and obstinately finished all — but I cannot say and have not courage to hope for it. My sin is greater than that it can be forgiven me, and I have raised it to its height, for my head speculated that the contrite unbelief in the possibility of Grace and pardon might be the most intriguing of all for the Everlasting Goodness, where yet I see that such impudent calculation makes compassion unpossible. Yet basing upon that I went further in speculation and reckoned that this last depravity must be the uttermost spur for Goodness to display its everlastingness. And so then, that I carried on an atrocious competition with the Goodness above, which were more inexhaustible, it or my speculation — so ye see that I am damned, and there is no pity for me for that I destroy all and every beforehand by speculation.

"But since my time is at an end, which aforetime I bought with my soul, I have summoned you to me before my end, courteous and loving brethren and sisters, to the end that my ghostly departure may not be hidden from you. I beseech you hereupon, ye would hold me in kindly remembrance, also others whom perchance to invite I forgat, with friendly commendations to salute and not to misdeam anything done by me. All this bespoke and beknown, will I now to take leave to play you a little out of the construction which I heard from the lovely instrument of Satan and which in part the knowing children sang to me."

He stood up, pale as death.

"This man," in the stillness one heard the voice of Dr. Kranich, wheezing yet clearly articulate: "This man is mad. There has been for a long time no doubt of it, and it is most regrettable that in our circle the profession of alienist is not represented. I, as a numismatist, feel myself entirely incompetent in this situation."

With that he too went away.

Leverkühn, surrounded by the women, Schildknapp, Helene, and myself, had sat down at the brown square piano and flattened the pages of the score with his right hand. We saw tears run down his cheeks and fall on the keyboard, wetting it, as he attacked the keys in a strongly dissonant chord. At the same time he opened his mouth as though to sing, but only a wail which will ring for ever in my ears broke from his lips. He spread out his arms, bending over the instrument and seeming about to embrace it, when suddenly, as though smitten by a blow, he fell sidewise from his seat and to the floor.

Frau Schweigestill, though she had stood farther off, was by him sooner than the rest of us, who, I know not why, wavered a second before we moved. She lifted the head of the unconscious man and holding him in her motherly arms she cried to those still in the room, standing anigh and gaping: "Let me see the backs of ye, all and sundry! City folk all, with not a smitch of understanding, and there's need of that here! Talked about th'everlasting mercy, poor soul, I don't know if it goes 's far's that, but human understanding, believe me, that doos!"

EPILOGUE

IT is finished. An old man, bent, well-nigh broken by the horrors of the times in which he wrote and those which were the burden of his writing, looks with dubious satisfaction on the high stack of teeming paper which is the work of his industry, the product of these years filled to running over with past memories and present events. A task has been mastered, for which by nature I was not the man, to which I was not born, but rather called by love and loyalty — and by my status as eyewitness. What these can accomplish, what devotion can do, that has been done — I must needs be content.

When I began writing down these memories, the biography of Adrian Leverkühn, there existed with reference to its author as much as to the art of its subject not the faintest prospect of its publication. But now that the monstrous national perversion which then held the Continent, and more than the Continent, in its grip, has celebrated its orgies down to the bitter end; now that its prime movers have had themselves poisoned by their physicians, drenched with petrol and set on fire, that nothing of them might remain — now, I say, it might be possible to think of the publication of my labour of love. But those evil men willed that Germany be destroyed down to the ground; and one dares not hope it could very soon be capable of any sort of cultural activity, even the printing of a book. In actual fact I have sometimes pondered ways and means of sending these pages to America, in order that they might first be laid before the public in an English translation. To me it seems as though this might not run quite counter to the wishes of my departed friend. True, there comes the thought of the essentially foreign impression my book must make in that cultural climate and coupled with it the dismaying prospect that its translation into English must turn out, at least in some all too radically German parts, to be an impossibility.

What I further foresee is the feeling of emptiness which will be my lot when after a brief report on the closing scenes of the great composer's life I shall have rendered my account and drawn it to a close. The work on it, harrowing and consuming as it has been, I shall miss. As the regular performance of a task it kept me busy and filled the years which would have been still harder to bear in idleness. I now look about me for an activity which could in future replace it. And at first I look in vain. It is true, the barriers that eleven years ago kept me from practising my profession have now fallen to the guns of history. Germany is free, in so far as one may apply the word to a land prostrate and proscribed. It may be that soon nothing will stand in the way of my return to my teaching. Monsignor Hinterpförtner has already taken occasion to refer to the possibility. Shall I once more impress upon the hearts of my top-form pupils in the humanities the cultural ideas in which reverence for the deities of the depths blends with the civilized cult of Olympic reason and clarity, to make for a unity in uprightness? But ah, I fear that in this savage decade a generation of youth has grown up which understands my language as little as I theirs. I fear the youth of my land has become too strange to me for me to be their teacher still. And more: Germany herself, the unhappy nation, is strange to me, utterly strange and that because, convinced of her awful end, I drew back from her sins and hid from them in my seclusion. Must I not ask myself whether or not I did right? And again: did I actually do it? I have clung to one man, one suffering, significant human being, clung unto death; and I have depicted his life, which never ceased to fill me with love and grief. To me it seems as though this loyalty might atone for my having fled in horror from my country's guilt.

*

*   *

Reverence forbids me to describe Adrian's condition when he came to himself after the twelve hours' unconsciousness into which the paralytic stroke at the piano had plunged him. No, not to himself did he come; rather he found himself as a stranger, who was only the burnt-out husk of his personality, having at bottom nothing to do with him who had been called Adrian Leverkühn. After all, the word "dementia" originally meant nothing else than this aberration from self, self-alienation.

I will say this much: that he did not remain in Pfeiffering. Rüdiger Schildknapp and I assumed the hard duty of conveying the patient, treated by Dr. Kürbis with sedatives for the journey, to Munich and a private hospital for nervous diseases, in Nymphenburg, directed by Dr. von Hösslin. There Adrian remained for three months. The prognosis of the specialist stated without reservation that this was a disease of the brain which could only run its course. But in the measure that it did so, it would pass through the present crass manifestations and with suitable treatment arrive at quieter, though unfortunately not more hopeful phases. This information it was which after some consultation determined Schildknapp and myself to delay our announcement of the catastrophe to Adrian's mother, Elsbeth Leverkühn at Buchel. It was certain that on the receipt of such news she would hasten to him; and if more calmness might be hoped for, it seemed no more than human to spare her the intolerable, shattering spectacle of her child before that was in any measure improved by institutional treatment.

Her child! For that and nothing more was Adrian Leverkühn again. She came one day, the old mother, when the year was passing into autumn. She came to Pfeiffering, to take him back to his Thuringian home, the scene of his childhood, to which his outward frame of life had so long stood in such singular correspondence. She came to a helpless infant, who had no longer any memory of his manhood's proud flight, or at most some very dark and obscure vision buried in his depths; who clung to her skirts as of yore, and whom as in early days she must — or might — tend and coax and reprove for being "naughty." Anything more fearfully touching or lamentable cannot be imagined than to see a free spirit, once bold and defiant, once soaring in a giddy arc above an astonished world, now creeping broken back to his mother's arms. But my conviction, resting on unequivocal evidence, is that the maternal experiences from so tragic and wretched a return, in all its grief, some appeasement as well. The Icarus-flight of the hero son, the steep ascent of the male escaped from her outgrown care, is to a mother an error both sinful and incomprehensible: in her heart, with secret anger she hears the austere, estranging words: "Woman, what have I to do with thee?" And when he falls and is shattered she takes him back, the "poor, dear child," to her bosom, thinking nothing else than that he would have done better never to have gone away.

I have reason to believe that within the blackness of his spirit's night Adrian felt a horror of this soft humiliation; that an instinctive repulsion, a remnant of his pride was still alive, before he surrendered with gloomy relish to the comfort which an exhausted spirit must after all find in complete mental abdication. Evidence of this compulsive rebellion and of urge to flight from the maternal is supplied, at least in part, by the attempt at suicide

which he made when we had succeeded in making him understand that Elsbeth Leverkühn had been told of his illness and was
on her way to him. What happened was this:

After three months' treatment in the von Hösslin establishment,
where I was allowed to see my friend only seldom and always
only for a few minutes, he achieved a degree of composure — I
do not say improvement — which enabled the physician to consent to private care in quiet Pfeiffering. Financial reasons too
spoke for this course. And so once more the patient's familiar surroundings received him. At first he continued under the supervision of the attendant who had brought him back. But his behaviour seemed to warrant the removal of this precaution, and
for the time being he was attended by the family, particularly by
Frau Schweigestill. Gereon had brought a capable daughter-in-
law into the house (Clementine had become the wife of the
Waldshut station-master) and the mother was now retired, with
leisure to devote her human feeling to her lodger, who after all
these years had become, though so much above her, something
like her son. He trusted her as he did no one else. To sit hand in
hand with her in the Abbot's room or in the garden behind the
house was obviously most soothing to him. I found him thus when
I went for the first time to Pfeiffering. The look he directed upon
me as I approached had something violent and unbalanced about
it, quickly resolved, to my great grief, in gloomy repugnance.
Perhaps he recognized in me the companion of his sane existence,
all memory of which he rejected. On a cautious hint from Frau
Else that he should speak "nicely" to me, his face only darkened
still more, its expression was even menacing. There was nothing
for me to do save in sadness to withdraw.

The moment had now come to compose the letter which should
as gently as possible inform his mother of the facts. To delay
longer would have been unfair to her, and the answering telegram
announcing her arrival followed without a day's delay. As I said,
Adrian had been told; but it was hard to know if he had grasped
the news. An hour later, however, when he was supposed to be
asleep, he escaped unnoticed from the house. Gereon and a farm-
hand came up with him by the Klammerweiher; he had removed
his outer clothing and was standing up to his neck where the water deepened so abruptly from the bank. He was just disappearing when the man plunged after him and brought him out. As
they were bringing him back to the house he spoke repeatedly of
the coldness of the water and added that it was very hard to
drown oneself in a pond one had bathed and swum in often as a

boy. But that he had never done in the Klammer pool, only in its counterpart at Buchel, the Cow Trough.

My guess, which amounts almost to certainty, is that a mystic idea of salvation was behind his frustrated attempt to escape. The idea is familiar to the older theology and in particular to early Protestantism: namely, that those who had invoked the Devil could save their souls by "yielding their bodies." Very likely Adrian acted in this sense, among others, and God alone knows whether we did right in not letting him so act up to the end. Not all that happens in madness is therefore simply to be prevented, and the obligation to preserve life was in this case obeyed in scarcely anyone's interest save the mother's — for undoubtedly the maternal would prefer an irresponsible son to a dead one.

She came, Jonathan Leverkühn's brown-eyed widow with the smooth white head, bent on taking her lost and erring son back into childhood. When they met, Adrian trembled for a long time, resting his head on the breast of the woman he called *Mutter* and *Du*. Frau Schweigestill, who kept out of the way, he called *Mutter* and *Sie*. Elsbeth spoke to her son, in the still melodious voice which all her life long she had refrained from song. But during the journey north into central Germany, accompanied fortunately by the attendant familiar to Adrian, there came without warning or occasion an outburst of rage against his mother, an unexpected seizure, which obliged Frau Leverkühn to retire to another compartment for the remainder, almost half of the journey, leaving the patient alone with his attendant.

It was an isolated occurrence. Nothing of the sort happened again. When she approached him as they arrived in Weissenfels he joined her with demonstrations of love and pleasure, followed her at her heels to Buchel, and was the most docile of children to her who expended herself on his care with a fullness of devotion which only a mother can give. At Buchel, where likewise for years a daughter-in-law had presided and two grandchildren were growing up, he occupied the upstairs room he had once shared with his elder brother, and once more it was the old linden, instead of the elm, whose boughs stirred in the breeze beneath his window and whose marvellous scent he seemed to enjoy. They could confidently leave him free to sit and dream the hours away on the round bench where once the loud-voiced stable-girl had taught us children how to sing canons. His mother took care that he got exercise: arm in arm they often walked through the quiet countryside. When they met someone he would put out his hand; she did not restrain him, and they would all exchange greetings in turn while standing.

As for me, I saw our dear man again in 1935, being by then *emeritus*. I found myself at Buchel, a sorrowful gratulant on the occasion of his fiftieth birthday. The linden was in bloom, he sat beneath it, his mother beside him. I confess my knees trembled as I approached him with flowers in my hand. He seemed grown smaller, which might be due to the bent and drooping posture, from which he lifted to me a narrow face, an Ecce-homo countenance, despite the healthy country colour, with woeful open mouth and vacant eyes. In Pfeiffering he had wished not to recognize me. Now there was no doubt at all that, despite reminders from his mother, he connected with my appearance no memories whatever. Of what I said to him about his birthday, the meaning of my visit, he obviously understood nothing. Only the flowers seemed to arouse his interest for a moment, then they lay forgotten.

I saw him once more in 1939, after the conquest of Poland, a year before his death, which his mother, at eighty, still survived. She led me up the stair to his room, entering it with the encouraging words: "Just come in, he will not notice you!" while I stood profoundly moved at the door. At the back of the room, on a sofa the foot end of which was towards me, so that I could look into his face, there lay under a light woollen coverlet he that was once Adrian Leverkühn, whose immortal part is now so called. The colourless hands, whose sensitive shape I had always loved, lay crossed on his breast, like a saint's on a mediæval tomb. The beard, grown greyer, still lengthened more the hollow face, so that it was now strikingly like an El Greco nobleman's. What a mocking game Nature here played, one might say: presenting a picture of the utmost spirituality, just there whence the spirit had fled! The eyes lay deep in their sockets, the brows were bushier; from under them the apparition directed upon me an unspeakably earnest look, so searching as to be almost threatening. It made me quail; but even in a second it had as it were collapsed, the eyeballs rolled upwards, half disappearing under the lids and ceaselessly moving from side to side. I refused the mother's repeated invitation to come closer, and turned weeping away.

On the 25th of August 1940 the news reached me in Freising that that remnant of a life had been quenched: a life which had given to my own, in love and effort, pride and pain, its essential content. At the open grave in the little Oberweiler churchyard stood with me, besides the relatives, Jeanette Scheurl, Rüdiger Schildknapp, Kunigunde Rosenstiel, and Meta Nackedey; also a stranger, a veiled unknown, who disappeared as the first clods fell on the coffin.

Germany, the hectic on her cheek, was reeling then at the height of her dissolute triumphs, about to gain the whole world by virtue of the one pact she was minded to keep, which she had signed with her blood. Today, clung round by demons, a hand over one eye, with the other staring into horrors, down she flings from despair to despair. When will she reach the bottom of the abyss? When, out of uttermost hopelessness — a miracle beyond the power of belief — will the light of hope dawn? A lonely man folds his hands and speaks: "God be merciful to thy poor soul, my friend, my Fatherland!"

AUTHOR'S NOTE

It does not seem supererogatory to inform the reader that the form of musical composition delineated in Chapter XXII, known as the twelve-tone or row system, is in truth the intellectual property of a contemporary composer and theoretician, Arnold Schönberg. I have transferred this technique in a certain ideational context to the fictitious figure of a musician, the tragic hero of my novel. In fact, the passages of this book that deal with musical theory are indebted in numerous details to Schönberg's *Harmonielehre*.

LONDON FIELDS
by Martin Amis

Two murders in the making: the first, of a femme fatale intent on goading one of her lovers into killing her, and the other, that of the Earth itself.

"An uninhibited high-energy performance...[Amis] is one of the most gifted novelists of his generation."

—Time

0-679-73034-6/$11.00

. . . .

A HISTORY OF THE WORLD IN 10½ CHAPTERS
by Julian Barnes

A hilariously revisionist account of the voyage of Noah's ark—with a sneak preview of heaven—that is "by turns funny, harrowing, satirical, consolatory, absurd" *(Washington Post Book World)*.

0-679-73137-7/$9.95

. . . .

THE SHELTERING SKY
by Paul Bowles

The story of three American travelers adrift in the cities and deserts of North Africa after the Second World War.

"His art far exceeds that of...the great American writers of our day."

—Gore Vidal

0-679-72979-8/$9.95

. . . .

THE STRANGER
by Albert Camus

Through the story of an ordinary man who unwittingly gets drawn into a senseless murder, Camus explores what he termed "the nakedness of man faced with the absurd."

0-679-72020-0/$7.95

. . . .

THE REMAINS OF THE DAY
by Kazuo Ishiguro

A profoundly compelling portrait of the perfect English butler and of his
fading, insular world in postwar England.

"One of the best books of the year."

—*The New York Times Book Review*

0-679-73172-5/$9.95

. . . .

THE WOMAN WARRIOR
by Maxine Hong Kingston

"A remarkable book...As an account of growing up female and Chinese-
American in California, in a laundry of course, it is anti-nostalgic; it burns the
fat right out of the mind. As a dream—of the 'female avenger'—it is dizzying,
elemental, a poem turned into a sword."

—*The New York Times*

0-679-72188-6/$9.00

. . . .

LOLITA
by Vladimir Nabokov

The controversial novel that tells the story of the aging Humbert Humbert's
obsessive, devouring, and doomed passion for the nymphet Dolores Haze.

"The only convincing love story of our century."

—*Vanity Fair*

0-679-72316-1/$9.00

. . . .

THE PASSION
by Jeanette Winterson

Intertwining the destinies of two remarkable people—the soldier Henri, for
eight years Napoleon's faithful cook, and Villanelle, the red-haired daughter of
a Venetian boatman—*The Passion* is "a deeply imagined and beautiful book,
often arrestingly so" *(The New York Times Book Review)*.

0-679-72437-0/$9.00

. . . .

Available at your local bookstore, or call toll-free to order:
1-800-733-3000 (credit cards only). Prices subject to change.

___ The Ark Sakura by Kobo Abe	$8.95	0-679-72161-4
___ The Woman in the Dunes by Kobo Abe	$10.00	0-679-73378-7
___ Chromos by Felipe Alfau	$11.00	0-679-73443-0
___ Locos: A Comedy of Gestures by Felipe Alfau	$8.95	0-679-72846-5
___ Dead Babies by Martin Amis	$10.00	0-679-73449-X
___ Einstein's Monsters by Martin Amis	$8.95	0-679-72996-8
___ London Fields by Martin Amis	$11.00	0-679-73034-6
___ Success by Martin Amis	$10.00	0-679-73448-1
___ For Every Sin by Aharon Appelfeld	$9.95	0-679-72758-2
___ One Day of Life by Manlio Argueta	$10.00	0-679-73243-8
___ Collected Poems by W. H. Auden	$22.50	0-679-73197-0
___ The Dyer's Hand by W. H. Auden	$12.95	0-679-72484-2
___ Forewords and Afterwords by W. H. Auden	$12.95	0-679-72485-0
___ Selected Poems by W. H. Auden	$11.00	0-679-72483-4
___ Flaubert's Parrot by Julian Barnes	$8.95	0-679-73136-9
___ A History of the World in 10½ Chapters by Julian Barnes	$9.95	0-679-73137-7
___ The Tattered Cloak and Other Novels by Nina Berberova	$11.00	0-679-73366-3
___ About Looking by John Berger	$10.00	0-679-73655-7
___ And Our Faces, My Heart, Brief as Photos by John Berger	$9.00	0-679-73656-5
___ G. by John Berger	$11.00	0-679-73654-9
___ A Man for All Seasons by Robert Bolt	$7.95	0-679-72822-8
___ The Sheltering Sky by Paul Bowles	$9.95	0-679-72979-8
___ Possession by A. S. Byatt	$12.00	0-679-73590-9
___ The Virgin in the Garden by A. S. Byatt	$12.00	0-679-73829-0
___ Exile and the Kingdom by Albert Camus	$10.00	0-679-73385-X
___ The Fall by Albert Camus	$9.00	0-679-72022-7
___ The Myth of Sisyphus and Other Essays by Albert Camus	$9.00	0-679-73373-6
___ The Plague by Albert Camus	$10.00	0-679-72021-9
___ The Rebel by Albert Camus	$11.00	0-679-73384-1
___ The Stranger by Albert Camus	$7.95	0-679-72020-0
___ Bullet Park by John Cheever	$10.00	0-679-73787-1
___ Falconer by John Cheever	$10.00	0-679-73786-3
___ Oh What a Paradise It Seems by John Cheever	$8.00	0-679-73785-5
___ No Telephone to Heaven by Michelle Cliff	$11.00	0-670-73042-4
___ Age of Iron by J. M. Coetzee	$10.00	0-679-73292-6
___ Last Tales by Isak Dinesen	$12.00	0-679-73640-9
___ Out of Africa and Shadows on the Grass by Isak Dinesen	$12.00	0-679-72475-3
___ Seven Gothic Tales by Isak Dinesen	$12.00	0-679-73641-7
___ The Book of Daniel by E. L. Doctorow	$10.00	0-679-73657-3
___ Loon Lake by E. L. Doctorow	$10.00	0-679-73625-5
___ Ragtime by E. L. Doctorow	$10.00	0-679-73626-3
___ World's Fair by E. L. Doctorow	$11.00	0-679-73628-X
___ Love, Pain, and the Whole Damn Thing by Doris Dörrie	$9.00	0-679-72992-5
___ The Assignment by Friedrich Dürrenmatt	$7.95	0-679-72233-5

VINTAGE INTERNATIONAL

___ Invisible Man by Ralph Ellison	$10.00	0-679-72313-7
___ Scandal by Shusaku Endo	$8.95	0-679-72355-2
___ Absalom, Absalom! by William Faulkner	$9.95	0-679-73218-7
___ As I Lay Dying by William Faulkner	$8.95	0-679-73225-X
___ Go Down, Moses by William Faulkner	$9.95	0-679-73217-9
___ The Hamlet by William Faulkner	$10.00	0-679-73653-0
___ Intruder in the Dust by William Faulkner	$9.00	0-679-73651-4
___ Light in August by William Faulkner	$9.95	0-679-73226-8
___ The Sound and the Fury by William Faulkner	$8.95	0-679-73224-1
___ The Unvanquished by William Faulkner	$9.00	0-679-73652-2
___ The Good Soldier by Ford Madox Ford	$10.00	0-679-72218-1
___ Howards End by E. M. Forster	$8.95	0-679-72255-6
___ A Room With a View by E. M. Forster	$8.00	0-679-72476-1
___ Where Angels Fear to Tread by E. M. Forster	$9.00	0-679-73634-4
___ Christopher Unborn by Carlos Fuentes	$12.95	0-679-73222-5
___ The Story of My Wife by Milán Füst	$8.95	0-679-72217-3
___ The Story of a Shipwrecked Sailor by Gabriel García Márquez	$9.00	0-679-72205-X
___ The Tin Drum by Günter Grass	$15.00	0-679-72575-X
___ Claudius the God by Robert Graves	$14.00	0-679-72573-3
___ I, Claudius by Robert Graves	$11.00	0-679-72477-X
___ Aurora's Motive by Erich Hackl	$7.95	0-679-72435-4
___ Dispatches by Michael Herr	$10.00	0-679-73525-9
___ Walter Winchell by Michael Herr	$9.00	0-679-73393-0
___ The Swimming-Pool Library by Alan Hollinghurst	$12.00	0-679-72256-4
___ I Served the King of England by Bohumil Hrabal	$10.95	0-679-72786-8
___ An Artist of the Floating World by Kazuo Ishiguro	$9.00	0-679-72266-1
___ A Pale View of Hills by Kazuo Ishiguro	$9.00	0-679-72267-X
___ The Remains of the Day by Kazuo Ishiguro	$11.00	0-679-73172-5
___ Dubliners by James Joyce	$10.00	0-679-73990-4
___ A Portrait of the Artist as a Young Man by James Joyce	$9.00	0-679-73989-0
___ Ulysses by James Joyce	$14.95	0-679-72276-9
___ The Emperor by Ryszard Kapuściński	$9.00	0-679-72203-3
___ Shah of Shahs by Ryszard Kapuściński	$9.00	0-679-73801-0
___ The Soccer War by Ryszard Kapuściński	$10.00	0-679-73805-3
___ China Men by Maxine Hong Kingston	$9.95	0-679-72328-5
___ Tripmaster Monkey by Maxine Hong Kingston	$11.00	0-679-72789-2
___ The Woman Warrior by Maxine Hong Kingston	$10.00	0-679-72188-6
___ Barabbas by Pär Lagerkvist	$8.00	0-679-72544-X
___ The Plumed Serpent by D. H. Lawrence	$12.00	0-679-73493-7
___ The Virgin & the Gipsy by D. H. Lawrence	$10.00	0-679-74077-5
___ The Radiance of the King by Camara Laye	$9.95	0-679-72200-9
___ The Fifth Child by Doris Lessing	$8.00	0-679-72182-7
___ The Drowned and the Saved by Primo Levi	$10.00	0-679-72186-X
___ The Real Life of Alejandro Mayta by Mario Vargas Llosa	$11.00	0-679-72478-8
___ My Traitor's Heart by Rian Malan	$10.95	0-679-73215-2

VINTAGE INTERNATIONAL

___ Kiss of the Spider Woman by Manuel Puig	$10.00	0-679-72449-4
___ Grey Is the Color of Hope by Irina Ratushinskaya	$8.95	0-679-72447-8
___ Memoirs of an Anti-Semite	$10.95	0-679-73182-2
by Gregor von Rezzori		
___ The Snows of Yesteryear by Gregor von Rezzori	$10.95	0-679-73181-4
___ The Notebooks of Malte Laurids Brigge	$10.95	0-679-73245-4
by Rainer Maria Rilke		
___ Selected Poetry by Rainer Maria Rilke	$12.00	0-679-72201-7
___ The Age of Reason by Jean-Paul Sartre	$12.00	0-679-73895-9
___ No Exit and 3 Other Plays by Jean-Paul Sartre	$10.00	0-679-72516-4
___ The Reprieve by Jean-Paul Sartre	$12.00	0-679-74078-3
___ Troubled Sleep by Jean-Paul Sartre	$12.00	0-679-74079-1
___ All You Who Sleep Tonight by Vikram Seth	$7.00	0-679-73025-7
___ The Golden Gate by Vikram Seth	$11.00	0-679-73457-0
___ And Quiet Flows the Don by Mikhail Sholokhov	$12.95	0-679-72521-0
___ By Grand Central Station I Sat Down and Wept	$10.00	0-679-73804-5
by Elizabeth Smart		
___ Ake: The Years of Childhood by Wole Soyinka	$11.00	0-679-72540-7
___ Ìsarà: A Voyage Around "Essay"	$9.95	0-679-73246-2
by Wole Soyinka		
___ Children of Light by Robert Stone	$10.00	0-679-73593-3
___ A Flag for Sunrise by Robert Stone	$12.00	0-679-73762-6
___ Lie Down in Darkness by William Styron	$12.00	0-679-73597-6
___ Sophie's Choice by William Styron	$13.00	0-679-73637-9
___ Confessions of Zeno by Italo Svevo	$12.00	0-679-72234-3
___ Learning to Swim by Graham Swift	$9.00	0-679-73978-5
___ Shuttlecock by Graham Swift	$10.00	0-679-73933-5
___ Waterland by Graham Swift	$11.00	0-679-73979-3
___ The Beautiful Mrs. Seidenman	$9.95	0-679-73214-4
by Andrzej Szczypiorski		
___ Diary of a Mad Old Man by Junichiro Tanizaki	$10.00	0-679-73024-9
___ The Key by Junichiro Tanizaki	$10.00	0-679-73023-0
___ On the Golden Porch by Tatyana Tolstaya	$8.95	0-679-72843-0
___ The Eye of the Story by Eudora Welty	$8.95	0-679-73004-4
___ Losing Battles by Eudora Welty	$8.95	0-679-72882-1
___ The Optimist's Daughter by Eudora Welty	$9.00	0-679-72883-X
___ The Passion by Jeanette Winterson	$10.00	0-679-72437-0
___ Sexing the Cherry by Jeanette Winterson	$9.00	0-679-73316-7